Leap Second

More by Brooke Shaffer

The Timekeeper Chronicles

The Chivalrous Welshman
Time to Kill
Tick Tock
Windup
Stopwatch
Free Time
Leap Second
Imminence (Summer 2022)

The Hands of Time
In the Hands of the Enemy
The Hands Pulling the Strings (Winter 2021)

The Lone Wolf
Wolf Pack
Alpha Wolf (Spring 2022)

Singles
Of Saints and Sinners

Leap Second
Book Six of The Chivalrous Welshman
The Timekeeper Chronicles

Brooke Shaffer

Black Bear Publishing

ISBN:
Hardcover: 978-1-953113-10-8
Softcover: 978-1-953113-11-5
eBook: 978-1-953113-12-2

For Pastor Tim, a soft-spoken but mighty lion

"All right, Tommen, I'm going to lift the Suppression, and I want you to pay close attention to the changes," Walter instructed, putting his hand gently on his son's head and lifting the Suppression that had draped him for the last two years.

Hands be damned, Walter was going to instruct him in Time and Banding. Tommen had just been released from the hospital, and he still looked a wreck. Walter had Banded him a little bit in order to take the edge off the pain and swelling, but he couldn't go back to school with a sudden, miraculous healing. But even that was small potatoes compared to the beating that awaited him if he didn't learn to defend himself.

In a way, Walter almost hated having to instruct Tommen so early. He was every bit the sweet little boy his pa had described him to be. His English was still pretty crude, but he had a bigger heart than Walter had ever imagined and could express his feelings without having to say a word. To see him picked on and bullied and beaten put Walter in such a rage, he could feel the shadow of the monster of his past life begin to stir. *Is it time?* the shadow monster asked. *Can I come out now?*

No, Walter resolved. *I'm going to teach him how to defend himself.*

He still hated to do it. Humans weren't supposed to begin training until they were at least thirteen years old. Mostly it had to do with mental and psychological maturity, but there was an aspect of physical maturity that helped, too. Most of all, though, Walter just didn't want to subject Tommen to the rigors of Time and the Wheel so darn early. He was such a sweet boy; he should be more worried about staying away from girls and their cooties rather than running away from Tyler Freeman and his gangbangers. For God's sake, they weren't even teenagers yet.

"How do you feel, Tommen?" Walter asked once the Suppression had been lifted.

Tommen looked around, seemingly distracted. Then, "I feel different."

"Different how?"

It was tough to tell whether his lack of words came from his deficiency in English or because he honestly didn't know how to describe the changes. Finally he answered, "First it's like the clock goes too fast. Then it goes too slow. But it's all the same."

Walter looked at the clock on the wall. As a Timekeeper, he had a greater sensitivity to Time, able to perceive each millisecond as it passed, but still able to function in Base Time.

"You are feeling Time now," Walter explained. "Just like you see things with your eyes and hear things with your ears, you can also feel Time."

"With what?" Tommen wondered.

Good question. I'm not quite sure myself. "Your mind. You can feel it in your brain."

"Whoa..."

"But you can do more than that, too. You can manipulate Time."

"And I can hurt Tyler to get back at him?"

Walter shook his head and knelt down. "Believe me, Tommen, I know you want to hurt him back. It's not right what he did to you, but Time is a powerful thing. It can be used to heal or hurt. I don't want you to use it to hurt anyone, okay? Right now, all I want you to do is use it to run away from Tyler if you need to."

"But he'll chase me!"

"I know. But now I'm going to show you some things, how to manipulate Time. It's going to be strange at first, but once you start practicing and getting good, it'll just be second nature."

"Oh." He paused and looked thoughtful. Then, "I have a question."

"What's that?"

"What's ma-ni-pu-late?"

Walter smiled and nodded. "I'm going to show you."

Thursday

Chapter One
Invisible

Pain. Compression, constriction, like a boa constrictor tightening, clamping down with all its mighty strength. Searing agony, like a live wire being shoved through him, unable to feel anything else. Immersion, like being submerged in a pool of little plastic balls. No, not plastic balls, small water balloons, all squishy and sloshing around. Tightening again, like rubber pulling against skin. Knives, stabbing into him, Julius Caesar style.

Light. Gray and murky. Air, chilly compared to...some other time. Thin, not so humid, but damp. A breeze, promising rain. Bringing rain. Drip drop, raindrops falling and pointing out every little ache and pain. Tiny bullets tearing through him, lingering pain as they dribbled away.

Cold. Light mist was too cold. Made him shiver.

Hot. Just the energy needed to shiver was exhausting and he might as well have been out doing heavy labor all day.

Fatigue. Feeling in his body came back slowly, but only brought aches, pains, fatigue. More compression, tightening in his left arm, live wire shoved directly from his wrist all the way up his arm to his brain. Nothing else mattered. He knew he had some cuts, bumps, bruises, and scrapes, but they were nothing compared to the agony screaming through his arm.

He groaned, his first conscious use of breath as his chest expanded in order to make room for his lungs as they took in fresh air. He ached, in his chest and lungs, felt like he had a cold or something, all the crud built up in his lungs that he couldn't quite cough up. Even now he coughed, but it was weak, wheezy and unproductive.

The movement jolted his body, and there was more pain in his arm. Hot tears leaked from his eyes even as he shivered again. Couldn't stay warm, couldn't cool down. But he definitely couldn't just stay there on the ground. Had to get up. Had to get out of the dirt. Had to look around and see his surroundings.

Once he learned that even the tiniest movements, and sometimes even no movement at all, sent shockwaves of pain through his arm, he was able to mentally prepare himself for it, though his concentration was broken momentarily by a wave of dizziness and nausea. It certainly did nothing to make the pain go away or even lessen, but he was ready for it, able to file it away and think of other things.

He lay alone in the forest, a graveyard of burned out trees and charcoal remains. The fire had been put out, it seemed. He did not see smoke anywhere. Even the misting rain did not produce steam from small hotspots left in the coals.

The burned shells of the cabins were not far away, blackened husks standing there like wraiths in the rainy gloom. Some stuff had been pulled out of them and scattered, some items appeared to be partially submerged in muddy ash as the firefighters did their post-fire overhaul, looking for anything that could fuel a rekindle.

The mist let up for a moment, but a chill breeze promised more and worse to come. But even though the breeze was cold, he felt terribly warm, as if he'd been out in the sun for way too long and was burning. His left arm felt like melting rubber.

Looking at it, he understood why. His hand was white and blistered, everything from wrist to fingertip swollen grossly. When he tried to move just one finger, he may as well have cut it off with an ax, and he gasped in pain, fresh tears springing to his eyes. Everything hurt. Literally, everything. The skin hurt from moving, stretching, folding, rubbing. Every layer of skin hurt, from the top layer where his previous sunburn was peeling, all the way to the very roots of his knuckle hair. Even the deep muscle protested movement, like pulling internal stitches. The thought of it made his stomach twist, and he thought he was going to be sick. Taking a breath, he continued his initial examination.

As for his arm, it was hard to tell. His jacket had melted to the skin. Some places it looked like skin and synthetic fiber had bubbled up a little in some twisted blister, but mostly it looked like a sticky, melted, burned, blistery mess. And fucking hell, did it hurt. Mother of God Almighty in Heaven Above, Hail Mary and all that, it hurt. It hurt all the way up to his shoulder where the collar finally came loose, though only in bubbles here and there. His neck and ear felt hot and painful, face a little warm. His ribs and left side smarted, too, the jacket still haphazardly melted almost all the way to the zipper.

He didn't know a lot about burns, but he knew that what he had here was not good. He had to see a doctor about this.

Had to get up. Had to stand up and get moving. Had to get out of this place.

He'd no sooner stood than he was driven to his knees again, throwing up whatever was left in his stomach. His first instinct was to catch himself on his right arm and throw his left arm to his stomach to wretch. But this time around, his left arm was useless. His hand hit the ground first with an ungraceful thump and a scrape in the ash, sending pain shooting up his arm. It could take no weight, and he couldn't bring it tight to his stomach. He might have been able to force it if he really had to, but this was not a life and death situation, or he hoped it wasn't. So he just used his right arm for support and made a conscious effort to keep his left arm out of the way.

The whole time he was vomiting, and for several minutes afterwards, he alternated between shivering and sweating. He tried to clear his head, think logically, and figure out exactly what was going on, but he couldn't. He seemed to have no higher brain functions, only the bestial need to survive. He had to find a safe place, a warm, dry place where he could lick his wounds and get something to eat. Then maybe he could sleep a little more and give his body a better shot at healing.

He took several calm, even breaths, preparing himself for the searing pain in his arm, preparing himself for the nausea in his head and stomach. He'd been awake for a good five or ten minutes now, and he still hadn't even made it to his feet. But he couldn't stay like this forever; he had to get moving.

With a gasp and a grunt and a few determined snorts, he got to his feet, telling himself to ignore the nausea, file away the pain, and focus on taking steps. One at a time, he had to get moving. First he was going to go out there into the clearing in the camp, and he was going to orient himself with the landscape. Once he knew where he was and which way was up, he would make a decision, choose a direction, and keep going. One thing at a time.

Once he forced his limbs to work and carry him forward, he found all of the other stuff, the injuries which his pain receptors classified as comparatively minor. His right hand was burned also, but it felt no worse than an accidental touch on a hot stove. He was afraid to look, instead contenting himself with that minor assessment. His knees and back throbbed a bit, but were no worse for wear. His neck and shoulders ached, probably from hitting the ground.

As he moved, he began to recall bits and pieces of information. His campers had been the ones to start the fire. He'd helped to save Mr. Wilson before the garage burned down. Before he had been evacuated, Rifun had found him and taken him back to camp. He'd shown him the true nature of the Akari. It wasn't just about Time, but Matter and Energy also. He'd shown him how to feel Matter and separate it, how to stop the fire from burning.

But, fool that he was, he'd tried to go a step further on his own. Unsatisfied with all the information he'd been given, he'd gone ahead and bulled his way through, convinced of his own might and superiority and ability to put out the fire single-handedly after a single lesson. He'd felt the Matter, but touched the Energy. He touched the fire, the very balance of that Energy as wood and plastic and everything else burned, and it backfired. Literally. There had been some kind of explosion, that much he knew.

Now he stumbled into the clearing on wooden legs and looked

around. Everything was deserted. The cabins were technically still standing, blackened timbers praising old world building practices, though the front porches were completely gone, as were the roofs. The main hall was the only wooden building that still stood proudly, defiantly, looking only a bit inconvenienced. The main office was gone. The nurse's office and camp store were gone. The bathrooms, showers, and laundry still stood, only because that little piggy's house was made of brick instead of sticks.

Well, he figured he couldn't be in too bad a shape if his sense of humor was still there. At the same time, he'd been in a lot worse shape and still had a sense of humor, so it was hard to tell.

His whole body hurt, and what he really wanted was to lie down and take a nap. He knew that wasn't an option, for a variety of reasons, none of them good. He had to find someplace safe. He had to find people.

Another wave of pain lanced through his arm, and he cringed, which only made it hurt more. He had to do something about it. Burns were painful, but they were easy. He had to keep it cool and stop the burning. There was a creek that ran nearby. It was only seasonal, but maybe there was something there after all the rain.

It was a course of action, but general logic caught up to him halfway through the forest. In the time he'd been out, the burning process had probably already been stopped because it had already been cooled. That was why his hand was swollen so bad. There was nothing he could do that hadn't already been done, at least as far as emergency management was concerned.

The creek was dry when he finally stumbled across it, but he still sat down beside it, as much to rest his legs as give himself a break and wait for the nausea to pass. His body heaved, but he had nothing to give, and he sat there in the mud, shivering and sweating.

Can't stop now, especially not here. You have to get up, get back to camp, at least get on a road. If you can get on a road, then even if you collapse, someone might find you. But they won't find you out here in the middle of the woods. Now get up!

There was a disconnect between his motivation and his movements, but he was on his feet again in time, momentarily disoriented but moving in the right direction. If nothing else, if he just kept following the trails, eventually he would circle around to where he needed to be.

He made it back to camp and paused, staring up the hill. It was muddy, covered in ash and debris, and had never looked so steep and treacherous. Just staring at it made his knees wobble and his back ache. Why had he gone to visit the creek anyway? It had been useless. He should have used his energy to start making for safety instead of gallivanting through the forest on some ill-conceived medical rescue like he actually knew what the hell he was doing. He was more than injured, he was sick. His judgment was cloudy. The shockwave had probably concussed him, too.

As he thought about it, he realized that everything going through his mind was in Welsh. That wasn't a problem until he realized that he couldn't conjure up anything else. Not English, not Irish, nothing. It was a side effect of his concussion on the ski hill last year, and if he got too stressed out or bumped his head a little too hard, things got bad again. Case in point, only being able to think and speak in Welsh. It would also explain the nausea and dizziness.

He closed his eyes and took a breath, tried to calm down. He was not well. He had to find a doctor, an ambulance, even some hermit with a ham radio might work.

Reluctantly, he got his legs to move and started up the hill. It began to rain. Not just a light mist as earlier, but full rain pouring down from the sky, with wind and a little thunder and lightning in the distance. Because things really just couldn't get any worse. He slipped in the mud and instinctively reached out to catch himself. He cried out as his hand hit the ground. When he brought it up, he saw that the blister on his palm had broken and sticky fluid was leaking everywhere, knives stabbing the freshly exposed wound.

His first instinct was to peel away the blistered flesh, but his better judgment kicked in at the last second. He couldn't expose himself to infection like that. His body was already working overtime trying to heal itself of just the injury; he didn't need to add infection into that mix. As he shivered again then broke out in sweat, he figured he probably already had some kind of infection going on.

But he couldn't just leave his wound exposed, especially since it was already dirty. Cautiously, he turned his palm up to the misting rain and tried to brush away as much dirt as possible. With the fluid draining, it helped to ease the pain a little, enough that he got most of the wound clean. Now the problem was that the blister was open and he had nothing with which to wrap it and keep it clean.

He took a breath, knowing he couldn't just sit there in the dirt and debate the problem. Using his good arm, he got back on his feet and trudged the rest of the way up the hill. He slipped a couple more times, always being sure to throw his left arm out of the way, enduring the screaming pain for the sake of keeping everything clean. When he finally got to the parking lot and examined everything, he saw that while his arm had stayed clean, his wild movements had opened up several more blisters. Some of them were on his arm in his melted coat, so the leaking was slower. He couldn't determine if any of them had gotten any kind of debris in them, or whether the melted coat was having any positive effect as far as covering the wounds.

He sat down to rest a minute. It was still raining off and on, but he was sweating. Whether it was from the fever and chills or the exertion from the climb was impossible to tell. The only good news came from the fact that it was all downhill from here. Three and a half miles down the mountain, then another ten miles to town. In that stretch, he had to come across a vehicle at some point. If not a vehicle, then at least a house where he might be able to borrow a phone.

But that meant getting up. And moving. A lot of moving. Thirteen and a half miles. That was a half marathon or something. He could barely make the mile run in gym class. Competitive eating was more his sport; why couldn't rescue involve that in some way?

Compared to when he first woke up and looked around, he figured he was much more lucid and sane. He felt bits and pieces of himself coming back, his humor, his stubbornness, his determination, his personality overall. As much as he wanted to whine and cradle his arm which was still aching like a motherfucker, he had to get to safety of some form. He had to get out of the rain at least.

He also had to stop stopping because then when he wanted to get going, the nausea caught up to him. Nausea and dizziness on a mountain did not work well. He forced himself to stay focused and think of other things as he made his way across the parking lot. He paused when he got to the edge of the lot, where the drive started down the mountain. His body jerked like it wanted to vomit, but he refused to go through that again when he had nothing to give. Instead, he found a tree and tried to force himself to pee or do anything normal, something that might kick his brain back into gear.

What he got was a knife in the back, right in the kidneys. He managed to go, but it was almost as agonizing as any of the pain in his arm. Fuck, so there was every chance he had some kind of internal damage, too. He had to find help, and fast.

With that bit of bad news in mind, he started down the road, grateful for the reprieve as it wound down, down, and down some more. A few times he almost pitched forward. Once he actually did. He did everything in his power to keep his arm protected, but he still managed to break a few blisters. Carefully, he sat down on the side of the road.

He'd never make it to town at this rate. He had to do something to protect his arm. Carefully, he slipped his right arm through the sleeve. Maybe he could just carefully —

It was like trying to rip out porcupine quills, or maybe a fish hook. Or maybe part of his own flesh. Through blurry vision, he inspected where his chest, shoulder, shirt, and jacket all melted together. The shirt wasn't bad as it was eighty percent cotton, but that last twenty percent of polyester, plus the eighty percent polyester of his jacket, that was all gone, melted right into his flesh. A few places, like a small spot on his chest around the zipper, he managed to carefully peel away, but there was nothing he could do for the rest of the right side of his body.

He wiggled around and got his pocket knife. It was wet and dirty, but still flicked open. Wiping it clean on his pants, he started tearing into the jacket. It was a goner, anyway. Ignoring the pain, he cut and hacked away at the fabric, then did his best to break the zipper which was trapped in a melted mess of polyester and a little skin. Sheer hand strength couldn't tear the fabric, but he was able to use a rock and his knife to wrench it free.

As he looked at his coat, he began to regret his decision to cut it apart. If he had an infection with fever and chills, he needed to stay warm; there was no way he could hope to put it back on and keep himself warm now. Furthermore, any hope he'd had of using the jacket as a makeshift bandage died when he saw all the dirt and debris. Well, why not? He'd lain in the dirt, gone traipsing through the forest, and fallen in the mud several times. Of course it was going to be dirty.

Still, the pockets were full of his stuff.

Of course! His stuff! *Duh, idiot. You've only been camping like a mountain man, but you still have twenty-first century technology at your disposal. Like phones.*

But, in accordance with his luck so far, his phone was dead. No surprise, given the cold and however much time he'd been out. His phone didn't exactly have awesome battery life. Plus, who knew what sort of damage it may have sustained from the heat of the fire or any rain that had gotten to it?

At the very least, his hearing aid charger appeared to be in tact. Not that it was going to do him much good out here. But it was the small victories that counted, he supposed.

For a moment, he entertained the thought of using Matter, to see if he could separate flesh from fabric. On the one hand, it might be an easy, simple, slightly-less-than-pain-free way of fixing his arm. Maybe he could use Time to heal it up a little. On the other hand, he had no good experience using Matter so far, and he had no way of knowing just how far the damage extended. He might heal the blister but exacerbate the infection. And if he did have internal damage, he had no idea how to fix that either. Time was not medicine, and there was no way to know which way his body was going to go in its own healing. He could heal the damage or kill himself in record time.

He decided to leave it alone. He was on a road now, and as long as he followed the road and got somewhere near civilization, he had a chance of being rescued. Or he could be hit by a car again while stumbling around on a mountainside. Hey, it had worked as well as anything else the first time around. He smiled ruefully to himself.

Groaning, he stood, the remains of his jacket slung over one shoulder. His shivered. He sweat. He shivered again. The rain let up a little and blue skies appeared in the distant horizon.

Then there were voices. People. He realized that he was close to the bus garage. Maybe the firefighters were still there. Maybe it was someone looking to vandalize a burned out building. Who cared? People! People meant civilization and phones and help.

He rounded the corner to the bus garage drive, pleasantly surprised to find that it was full of firefighters, a few police, rescue dogs, DNR officers and their crews, the whole works.

He did a quick survey of the scene. True, he could probably walk up to anyone and ask a question, but it might be better to skip the searching and the questions and go straight to the command post. Talk to the man in charge who had the power to make decisions and make everyone's life easier.

He spotted what looked like the command center, a large fold-up table under a tent where half a dozen important-looking men and women huddled in light coats, hats, and peel-back gloves on their hands which held steaming cups of coffee. An officer with a dog approached the table and reported something. They conversed. One of the official people left with the officer to go do something or other. That was probably going to be his best bet, then.

No one paid him any mind as he walked into camp. One team of people headed out in one direction, into the woods, dog at the lead. Another team was just coming in beside him, comprised of mostly firefighters from the looks of things. A third team of firefighters, all of them with shiny badges, stood outside the burned garage, arms folded, speaking quietly, none of them looking pleased with the weather.

In the command tent, something came across the radio, which the commanders paid close attention to. One of them marked something on a sheet of paper, another marked up what appeared to be a very large map, and a third relayed something or other back to the radio team.

As he approached them, someone beat him to the table, and he waited patiently in line.

"Section four is clear," the person reported, some DNR personnel if his uniform was any indication. "No sign of him or anyone else for that matter."

Someone was missing? Had someone gone missing in the fire? Well, it was very possible that he was the one they were looking for. All he had to do was talk to them and wrap this whole thing up.

The person went away, and he stepped up to the table.

"Excuse me, hi," he began. "Am I the one you're looking for?"

"So, all we have left is section one and five," one of the commanders mused, looking at the map. "One is the largest, but it covers the most likely area, assuming he's thinking somewhat straight."

"Should we start packing things up, in case we have to move base?" another commander inquired.

He took a step closer and raised his voice a little. "Um, hello? Hi. Excuse me. I realize I'm not an official person or anything, but I think you might—"

"We'll wait until five gets back," the first commander said. "They're the farthest out, and we'll be moving in the other direction."

"Hey!" he shouted. "Hey, I'm right here! Listen to me!"

Before anyone could say more, another person approached the table. "Five is just returning. No dice." And he left.

The first commander grunted, then turned to the second. "All right, start getting things packed up and moved. I want a search grid established and teams ready to move out by the time team one returns."

"Yes sir."

The second commander left the safety of the tent and started barking orders to grab this, pack up that, and she wanted to see someone named Nelson immediately. The first commander marked something down on his papers. When he looked up, his expression was grim.

"How did it go, Walt?"

Tommen turned to see his dad ducking under the tent flap.

"Dad!"

"Not well," Walter replied, looking at the commander. "No sign of him or anyone. Honestly, I was kind of hoping to come back and find that someone else had found him while I was gone."

The commander shook his head. "No, but team one is still out there. Even if he isn't completely lucid, if he's thinking at all, that's where he'll be."

"I know."

The commander frowned as Walter sighed. "He's out there somewhere, Walt. There were no bodies in the wreckage, and the dogs came up dry. All right, cadavers don't go very far. He's on the move. If your boy is half as good at surviving as you say he is, he's probably back in Wellspring by now. If his phone is dead or damaged, he'll have to borrow someone else's. We'll get a call soon enough, I'm sure."

His optimism was cooler than it should have been, Tommen thought, and it did little to lift his dad's mood. But that still didn't explain why no one acknowledged him.

"Dad, I'm right here," Tommen said. "It's me. It's Tommen. I'm fine. Well, okay, I'm definitely not fine. My arm is burned, my kidneys hurt like shit—Hey!"

He followed his dad out of the tent toward another tent where water, coffee, and assorted snacks were set out. His dad grabbed a cup of coffee and a granola bar. Tommen waited until he turned so he could stand face-to-face with him.

"Dad. It's me. I'm right here. See? In front of you? Right here?

Getting in your face like you hate? Swearing like fucking shit because I know you fucking hate that shit, too? What the fuck? What's going on? Why won't you acknowledge me?"

Then something strange happened. His dad moved, but he moved right through Tommen. It was like the feeling he got going through portals to the Wheel, the air being sucked from his lungs and everything else. He was left coughing and gasping for air and completely confused.

What—the—fuck? What the fuck just happened? His dad had literally walked right through him. Okay, ignoring him, fine. A little weird since this whole operation seemed to be about him, but still, fine. Plausible. Walking through him? That was not even possible. That was physically impossible. He should not be able to do that. Neither of them should be able to do that.

Tommen turned and watched his dad walk away, shoulders hunched against the rain, steps slow. He had no idea his son was right there in the middle of camp. No one had any clue that the person they were searching for walked among them. They were about to pack up and move to another area without any idea that their subject had already returned.

The question then became not only why he was invisible, but how it had happened. More than that, how could he become visible again?

He took a few steps back, trying to sort this all out in his mind. Okay. So. He was invisible. Did that mean he was dead? Was he a ghost, doomed to limbo between life and the afterlife? Was there an afterlife? Had he been banned from it?

He felt another heatwave course through him followed by a chilly shiver. Well, he took that as a pretty good indication that he was still alive in some form. He'd never heard any ghost story where the ghost was injured and sick. Well, okay, so maybe he had. The ghost of someone who'd had some terrible bodily harm done to them. But none of those stories had ever included anything about those ethereal wounds getting infected. Infection took germs and microorganisms, which were living things.

Oh, for goodness' sake, he had to stop overanalyzing things. Until further notice, he was determined to say that he was merely invisible. Alive, dead, didn't matter. He was invisible. He was injured. So in order to get treatment, he had to become visible again. In order to become visible, he had to get some semblance of an idea of how he became invisible. How the hell did he do that?

Well, he could always try the easy way and consider all the things he'd done in the last—how long had it been? A day? Two days? More? Didn't matter.

The last thing he remembered doing was trying to put out the fire in one of the cabins. He'd tried to bypass manipulating the Matter because of all the complex chemical reactions of the materials melting together, instead trying to touch the fire, the Energy directly, cut the power at its source as it were.

Maybe this was an Imprint. Maybe the combination of Energy and a little bit of Time had thrown him out of sync with the universe. What if everything he was doing was merely an Imprint, and no one would see these movements here and now for a couple seconds, or minutes, or even days? It was certainly an interesting train of thought, but that still didn't explain how his dad had walked right through him. That couldn't be explained by a mere Imprint.

"Banding is Time," he said aloud. "Disguises are Matter. But portals...those are Energy."

Could he have inadvertently opened a portal when he touched the Energy? The amount of energy needed to open a portal to anywhere was a Herculean effort, demonstrated time and again by his dad and the twins. Touching raw Energy and having it backfire might prove to be enough for him to open a portal on his own

It was impossible to Band while unconscious. There was no reason not to think one also couldn't control Matter and Energy while unconscious. What if a portal had opened when he touched the Energy, but when he went unconscious, it closed? What if he'd fallen into the Land In Between, the dimension from which no one had ever returned?

Tommen mulled that over for a moment. That was an interesting theory, too. It was different than he expected, though, if that's really where he was. He was expecting to see more ghosts or other-worldly things or just...he wasn't even sure. He certainly didn't imagine such a feared dimension looking exactly like home and being exactly like home. But then, he wasn't sure what he'd thought it would look like in the first place. Why shouldn't it look like home?

But then, if that was the case, what were his limits here? Could he walk through walls? Could he manipulate doors and scare the shit out of people? Could he pick up a pen and start writing spooky messages? Could he find some group of idiot teenagers conducting a seance and speak through them, tell them to call for help and get the Ghostbusters on the case?

There were just too many unknowns. If this really was the Land In Between from which no one had ever returned, it wasn't like there was a vast wealth of knowledge of how to break out.

Everyone's attention was suddenly distracted by a van pulling into the command post, right in the center of operations. It was a news van, to no one's surprise. Why wouldn't a children's camp burning to the ground be news? Tommen did not recognize the reporter as she got out and approached the command post, camera guy in tow. As they spoke, Tommen got closer. Maybe he could do some kind of ghost photobomb on the news story. Hey, couldn't hurt to try.

"Good morning, Harold," the reporter greeted the lead commander. "Quite the operation you've got going on here."

"Indeed," Harold replied levelly. "So why'd you park in the middle of it?"

"You know, you weren't entirely honest with me last night during our live interview, when we were talking about the fire. I got a little tip that says not everyone made it out with some 'minor injuries' as you said. Word on the street is that you've got a missing boy."

After a moment, Harold relented. "We were hoping it would be an easy find. Maybe he'd just wandered off a short distance. No need for media hype."

"But if this little party is any indication, you might just need the media hype to keep everyone on the lookout for your missing person. How about letting us in on it a little? Don't let your pride jeopardize someone's life."

The commander raised a brow, but he did not dispute the validity of her claim. It was easy to get lost in the mountains, and unlike some places, there wasn't a town or a road behind every hill where someone might just happen upon help. After a moment of consideration, he nodded. "All right. We'll get it out there."

"Excellent."

Tommen wanted to folded his arms, but a sharp stab of pain in his arm told him otherwise. He was about to become a media sensation for the second time in a year. Now how many people could brag about that?

Harold called Walter over to the table. His dad seemed reluctant, but he understood the need for help and vigilance. Their crews might be completely ineffective, but some poor farmer living up in the sticks around these parts might just catch a glimpse of a wounded and confused seventeen year old young man.

"Do you have a recent picture of him that we can use?" the reporter, Jaylee, inquired. Tommen had a hard time deciding just how concerned she really was. She seemed more concerned about how to deliver the story in such a way so as to boost her own career.

"Yeah, I do," Walter answered, bringing out his phone. "Just give me a minute; I'm not very good on my phone."

Curious, Tommen looked over his shoulder. Well, the man was honest when he said he wasn't very good on his phone. More accurately, he wasn't very fast. He knew what to do, but he wasn't as quick as most teenagers. He chose a recent photo of Tommen and Becky in his room playing video games. It had been a prank photo, his dad trying to catch them doing something embarrassing but not getting anything.

"Will this work?" he asked, showing Jaylee the picture.

"Yeah, that's a great photo." She took out a business card. "Do you have Internet out here or no?"

"Not really. I'd have to go back to town for anything significant."

"Well, when we're done here, maybe you can come back with us to town, we can talk a bit, and then you can email the photo to the studio. How does that sound?"

"Sounds like I don't have a choice, but I'm meeting a couple friends in town in a little bit anyway. Maybe I'll just head back now."

"Excellent."

Tommen followed his dad out of the camp. "Dad, I'm right here. Please, look at me." He jumped in front of him, steeling himself for the strange walkthrough experience. When it was over, he continued following. "Tell me you felt something. A thought, a feeling, something, anything at all."

But then, even if he had felt something, his thoughts were probably so consumed with finding Tommen that no one thought stood out above any other.

The car was parked at the end of the drive, just off the road. Tommen stared at it for a second. Could he ride in the car? Would he just walk through it? Would he have to open the door? Would his dad notice anything strange? Could he pull off some kind of horror movie trope, appear in the mirror when his dad checked, but when he turned around, there was nothing there? Would it work? If it did, would it be enough?

His dad got in the driver's seat. Well, only one way to find out. Tommen's hand passed through the door, but when he ducked inside, he was able to sit on the seat with no problem. Now just what were the rules here? Were things solid only when he needed them to be? If he thought long enough and hard enough, would he just go flying out of the car when it started? Would a tree become ethereal? The ones in the forest around camp had seemed solid enough. But then, they'd all been burned of their leaves and small branches, and he'd avoided running into the trees; he did not habitually test their solidity, so why should he start now?

He looked out the window to the dirt drive. No footprints led up to the passenger door, yet the ground was solid beneath his feet. And he definitely remembered dirt and debris on his clothes and in his wounds. What were the rules here? Was there a way to bend and manipulate them?

Then they were pulling around in the drive, his dad looking both ways before rolling out into the road. He leaned back and relaxed in the same way he did when he was in his cruiser, but his gaze was blank. The man was preoccupied, and why not? If it wasn't Tommen, it was him. If it wasn't him, it was Tommen. Neither of them could catch a break, it seemed.

"I'm right here, Dad," Tommen said, willing himself to be heard even though his dad did not appear to hear any of it. "I'm here. I'm alive. And I'm going to find a way to break out of this invisibility or in-between dimension."

He sighed and leaned back in the seat, forcing his arm to go up and rest on his head in an effort to keep the swelling down. If no one could see him, that meant no one could help him. That mean that he was going to have to be his own doctor. He didn't know jack shit about wilderness first aid, not on this level. The last guy he'd tried to help had died. But then, Saul had had five arrows and a bullet in his back.

Tommen rubbed his face with his good hand. He had to get out of this. One way or another, he was going to make himself visible again. And after that, he was going to fucking kill Rifun.

They rode in silence all the way down the mountain into Wellspring.

Chapter Two
Missing Persons

Walter had woken up that morning praying it had all just been a bad dream. Maybe it had just been a dream that Tommen had called and said the camp was burning down. Maybe he'd just imagined going up there and being told that he was missing. Maybe his case at work had overwhelmed him and sent his imagination on a frenzied rollercoaster ride.

But as he got up and around, he knew he was only lying to himself. His first clue came from his phone; yes, Tommen had called him yesterday afternoon. His next clue came from the gas gauge in the car; yes, he had stopped to get gas coming back from Wellspring. His third clue came from walking in the door at work.

"So, is Tommen sleeping in this morning?" Standish wondered as he poured creamer in his coffee. "Or can you not get him to shut up about camp?"

Walter didn't even have the strength to sigh. "He didn't come home yesterday."

Standish regarded him with a wary eye. "What do you mean?"

"He's missing. He went missing trying to gather up the rest of the kids for evacuation. Nearest anyone can tell, they think he somehow injured himself and might be wandering around in the wilderness, lost and confused."

"Shit."

"Search and Rescue is out looking for him."

Standish turned to face him. "So what the hell are you doing here?"

Walter raised a brow. "Working. Same as you. We have a case, unless something's changed."

"Right." Standish patted him on the shoulder. "Well, give me five minutes to get my poop in a group, and then we'll get going."

Those five minutes were actually spent talking to Steggmann who confronted Walter in his cubicle and basically told him to get his ass back up to Wellspring to look for his son. Chief's orders, he was to spend the next two days looking for his boy somewhere in those hills. Standish would work with someone else on the case in the meantime.

So Walter had gone home to change out of his blues into something a little more appropriate for search and rescue in the mountains in the cold and wet. He Banded the whole way up there, at least when he got out of the city and could more easily weave through traffic, returning to Base Time only once he got almost into Wellspring. The diner wasn't open yet, but once he got up the mountain near the campsite, the firefighters' auxiliary force had come out with a grill and copious amounts of bacon, sausage, eggs, toast, and, of course, coffee.

"Didn't expect to see you up here," the fire chief commented as Walter parked and approached.

"I didn't expect so many to come out," Walter admitted, looking around. Aside from the fire department, the DNR had come out, as well as canine units from the local police department.

"It's a big mountain, and there's a kid missing. You bet your ass we're going to turn out. You eaten?"

"No, diner's closed."

"Well, help yourself. And don't say you're not hungry. No one's going out there without eating first. We don't need any more emergencies than we already have. And that's an order."

Walter nodded and grabbed a plate. "How long have you guys been out?"

"We had a few experienced crews out overnight, but we've been here since about four. Listen, have some food and coffee, and we're all going to meet up in about half an hour for assignments."

Half an hour turned into an hour, but that was to be expected. The team of leaders was re-introduced for all the new people coming in, and a large map of the area was set up on an easel. They went over the basic details of the case, the fire, last known location, all of that. They detailed the boundaries for the various search locations. There were five locations in this zone. If they couldn't find Tommen in any of the locations, they would move on to the next zone.

"We have every reason to believe that Tommen is alive at this point in time," the top commander, a DNR officer who knew the mountains like the back of his hand, said earnestly. "Fire crews found no evidence of any bodies in the fire zone, and the cadaver dogs have come up clean. According to familiars, Tommen is very well-versed in wilderness survival. However, he is not from the area. It may be a simple case of being lost. He may have also fallen and somehow injured himself so as to be mentally impaired in some way.

"He is sixteen years old, described as being roughly six-foot-one, very skinny, white with brown hair and brown eyes. He has difficulty hearing and wears hearing aids. At this time, it is possible the batteries may have died, so he may not hear you when you call out. This may be visual only. Last known clothing was brown cargo shorts, a blue T-shirt, tennis shoes, and a red jacket. Any questions?"

Someone in the back asked, "Was dispatch able to ping his phone at all, give even a rough estimate of location?"

The commander shook his head. "No, they weren't. That's another reason why we believe he may be injured, if his phone was damaged so it couldn't be tracked. Any more questions?"

"Do we have a photo to show homeowners in the area?" someone else asked.

"Not at this time, but we will."

When there were no further questions, everyone was divided into their teams and sent to their search locations. Walter was sent to section five. Each team had at least one medical person with them as well as a dog that went out just ahead of them. Unlike the movies, the dog wasn't given an article of clothing to sniff and then told to search for that scent. But, by sending the dog out ahead of the rest of the team into fresh ground, they might have a better chance of picking up human scent.

Walter had been on plenty of searches in his day, especially when he worked Missing Persons. Little kids, when they got scared, liked to hide in teeny tiny places that no one could get to. Teenagers usually liked to think they were all that, Mr. or Miss I-Can-Totally-Survive-Anything-and-Still-Look-Hot, which usually meant they left a lot of clues behind.

Tommen knew plenty about wilderness survival. If he was lucid, he'd probably already have a shelter, food, water, and a fire going. He'd be camping while they, the teams, were out stomping around in the cold and wet. But if he wasn't lucid, if he was injured, anything could happen.

The only things of interest they found were an abandoned moonshine still and a cranky bull elk. Otherwise, section five was devoid of all human life. They returned to camp to dry out and get some food before packing up and heading over to zone two, which was north of camp.

Walter, however, got distracted by a news reporter. She was friendly enough, but like most reporters, she was just in it for the story. At the same time, that kind of enthusiasm would get his son's picture out there in the event that one of the hermit neighbors out here came across him. Assuming they had cable in the first place.

So he returned to Wellspring, a long, slow drive. It wasn't a very big town, one road in, one road out, and very little to brag about in between, but the diner was decent. He'd only gotten a cup of coffee and a granola bar when he returned to the command site, but he knew he needed more. Well, he didn't really; thanks to Time, his metabolism was pretty damn slow. What he really needed was something to do, something to claim part of his attention for a short time.

He rubbed his eyes as the waitress poured him a cup of coffee and handed him a menu. Retirement was looking better and better every day. Except retirement wouldn't have changed anything about this. Nothing he could have done would have prevented this. Well, short of forbidding Tommen to work at the camp, but that was hardly plausible.

He jumped as his phone rang, and he answered without looking at the caller ID.

"Hello?" he asked.

"Walt, it's Laura. I just went to the precinct to see if you wanted to have lunch, but they said you'd be gone for the next couple days."

"Yeah, they told me to leave and get my butt up here to Wellspring to help look."

"And well they should. Listen, do you want me to come up there? I don't know how much help I'll be for looking, but I'll do what I can."

He hesitated. Micah and possibly Kayla were supposed to be coming up to meet him so they could do their own searching, Time-style, without interference.

"If you want to," he said finally. "It's a lot of cold and wet up here, though."

"Oh, please, do I strike you as the pretty princess type?"

"No, ma'am, you don't."

She laughed. "Good answer. All right, I'll see if I can't get some directions up that way. Where should I meet you?"

He let out a breath. "Well, it's a two-hour drive up here. Why don't you call when you think you're about half an hour out? Then I might have a better idea."

"Fair enough. Okay, I'll see you in a couple hours. Let me know if anything happens."

"I will."

He hung up and just picked up the menu when the waitress came back.

"Know about what you want?" she asked amiably.

"I haven't even given it a thought," he told her.

"Why don't you have the same thing you've had the last three times you were here? Two eggs, sunny side up; hashbrowns, nice and crispy with onions and peppers; bacon, extra crispy; maple sausage links; whole wheat toast, barely toast, I should say, more like warm bread; a glass of orange juice, and another refill on your coffee."

"Have I had that the last three times?" He thought a second. "Have I been here three times?"

The waitress grinned. "No. I just thought that it might be a good suggestion, especially if you're going back out to go searching anytime soon."

"Guess that's what I'll have, then."

She left, and Walter was left staring at the place mat which was a collage of advertisements for various businesses. Most of them were farming or agriculture related, butchering, logging, tilling, excavating, and one little advertisement for a quilt shop in the next town. His phone rang again, but he didn't recognize the number.

"Walter, it's Harold." The DNR officer and lead person for the search and rescue.

"Did you find him?" Walter asked.

"Sorry to say, we didn't. I'm just calling to let you know we're heading to zone two. Do you know where that is?"

"I heard the location, but can't say as I know how to get there."

So Harold gave him directions, a little pithy encouragement, and hung up. He'd no sooner done that than Walter's food arrived.

"Did I really order all of this?" he wondered, staring at the two plates required to hold it all. "What kind of eggs you got back there, ostrich eggs?"

The waitress shrugged and grinned coyly. "Close enough, I guess."

"I can feel the cholesterol already."

But there was no denying that it was good food. Maybe Walter really was hungry or maybe he just needed the mood lift, but the food was good. Had he been going home afterwards and could put it in the fridge or something, he would have saved some in a carryout box. But, with no fridge handy in the wilderness, he just took his time and ate slowly until both plates were clean and his orange juice was gone.

"How's that cholesterol feeling?" the waitress asked when she returned.

"Well, let me just say that it was worth every bite," Walter replied diplomatically.

"Awesome, glad to hear it. And how will you be splitting the bill?"

"Well, if anyone else wants to pay for it, I won't complain. Otherwise, I guess I'll take it."

She fished out her slim black book and set it down. "Whenever you're ready."

He was ready to get going, certainly, but no one he was supposed to meet with had shown up yet. Come on, people, his son was missing in the wilderness and he wanted to get out there to help search. Stop weighing him down with all this waiting and useless meetings and stuff.

The waitress had just returned to collect his bill when the door opened and Jaylee the news reporter walked in, her camera guy close behind. They helped themselves to seats across from Walter.

"Looks like you started without us," she observed, smiling hugely.

"I finished without you," Walter informed her even as he took the receipts and signed them, handing one back to the waitress and pocketing the other.

"Anything I can get for you?" she asked of the newcomers. "Are you here for a minute, or do you have time to look at the menu?"

"Oh, we can't stay too long," Jaylee said, cutting off whatever her camera guy had to say. "But I'll take a coffee. What about you, Jeff?"

"Orange juice would be great."

Jaylee didn't miss a beat once the waitress turned her back. "All right, so you have my business card, right? Well, if not, I have another one. Anyway, if you could email that picture to the studio, we can get it out there for the five o'clock news. Or, sometimes what they'll do, at least for Amber Alerts, they'll interrupt a broadcast, or, you know, slip in a commercial break, give a brief description and picture. That way we're not waiting hours for the five o'clock news. The sooner the better, right?"

Walter had largely tuned her out as he dug out the business card, then had to navigate back through his phone to find the picture. Then he had to figure out how to attach said picture to an email. He could do it on the computer easily enough, but his biggest problem with doing it on the phone was that his fingers were usually too big to tap the button he wanted when all the buttons were packed together. So it took him several tries before he actually got the picture attached. Then he mistyped the email, which bounced it back to him, but rather than just fix the email address, he had to delete the whole thing and go through the whole process again.

He sighed. He didn't care what the kids all said. Technology was not easy to use. It was made for little hands with little fingers and sharp eyes that could handle staring at the bright screen for more than five minutes. More than once, Walter had considered getting some reading glasses or something, but he always put it off, telling himself he was still youthful. After all, everyone he knew who got reading glasses like that never got one pair. They got one pair for the car, one pair for the kitchen, one for the living room, one for the bedroom, one as a spare, and women generally got one pair for their purse, or one for each purse as the situation demanded.

Walter did not want to be that guy. Bad enough he was getting old. But as he told himself, he couldn't retire until Tommen was out of high school. As an extension of that, he couldn't do any retirement things until that time either, which included getting half a dozen pairs of reading glasses. Besides, reading glasses wouldn't make his fingers smaller when it came to trying to poke tiny buttons on his phone. That was his excuse and he was sticking to it.

"All right, I think I got it sent now," he said, trying to sound at least modestly confident in his abilities, even though he wasn't.

Jaylee's phone jingled and she checked it, nodding and smiling. If she grinned any bigger, her lips were going to touch her ears. "Yep, there is it. All right, I will get that forwarded to our editors and they'll get it all doctored up and slip it in to the broadcast tonight."

"And what are you going to say about him?" Walter asked suspiciously.

"Well, I haven't reviewed the whole segment. It was probably on the noon news, but we were on our way here and didn't get to see it or anything."

"He's a good kid. Sixteen years old, almost seventeen, about six-one, skinny enough that you'd think he's starving even though he eats me out of house and home. White, Welsh, speaks with an accent. Brown hair, brown eyes. He is hard of hearing and wears hearing aids. Loves to laugh and crack jokes, play pranks. He's a science nerd who loves physics especially. He usually comes across as a bit of an outcast, but is actually very sweet and sensitive. How he puts up with his girlfriend, I will never know, but I've always admired his loyalty and determination to do the right thing.

"He is very conscious of his surroundings and knows a thing or five about wilderness survival. I'm half-expecting to find him out there camping leisurely with a shelter, food, water, the whole works. He's not an idiot when it comes to these mountains. He was born and raised in these mountains. A different part of them, maybe, but he knows them still. Even if he is injured, he will find a way to survive until help comes."

Walter couldn't decide if Jaylee was texting a friend or tapping out notes on her phone while he spoke, but if she couldn't be bothered to pay attention and get the information she needed for her story, then that was on her. At least her camera guy, Jeff, looked serious enough that he probably caught whatever she didn't. On the other hand, maybe Walter was stereotyping. Female reporters were expected to be young, slim, and pretty, but that didn't mean she wasn't smart or concerned. Maybe it was just the age difference. Walter's generation—or his perceived generation, anyway—expected conversation to be personal and intimate with no other distractions. Tommen's generation didn't know how to have a conversation without distractions.

Whatever the case, she finished poking away on her phone and accepted a refill on her coffee.

"How many people out here actually have TV?" Walter wondered.

"More than you might think," Jeff answered. "And people talk, too. So if one neighbor hears the story, you can bet that they're going to tell all their surrounding neighbors, whether or not they have TV. It's country gossip, true, but no one likes to hear about kids getting lost in the woods, especially under such tragic circumstances."

Walter nodded grimly. He wanted his boy found, and he wanted to go home. He didn't want his son turned into the poster child for Amber Alerts and Wilderness Safety. Just couldn't leave that boy alone for ten minutes and he was getting into trouble.

"How long are you out here for, Mr. Forbes?" Jaylee inquired. "I understand you're a cop down in Charleston."

"That's right. I have a couple days off," Walter answered evasively.

"You think they'll find your son in a couple days?"

"I expect so. If he's injured, I can't imagine he would get far. If he's not injured, he'll find a way to get back to civilization and contact someone."

"I like your optimism. Logic in the midst of crisis. Believe me, not all parents are so clear-headed."

Where she got the idea of him being clear-headed, he would never know. Maybe it was a way of complimenting him and trying to keep him calm, keep him from becoming depraved like most parents. Of the parents who didn't go insane, they fell into two categories: First, they didn't care because they didn't care about their child or they had been instrumental in their child's disappearance, or; second, they had the mental fortitude of some other experience, such as a job or previous similar experience, to know and understand what was going on and what had to be done. Walter liked to think he fell in that second category, but that certainly didn't mean he wasn't worried sick.

"What grade is Tommen going into?" Jaylee asked politely. "Seventeen, got to be a senior, right?"

"Junior. He'd like to be a senior, but not so fast."

"Ready for high school to be over and done with?"

"Absolutely. He seems to think he has other important things he'd like to do in life, like travel."

"Hey, travel can be a good thing. Refreshes the soul and whatnot. Good experience, meeting new people in new cultures, where they think everything you do is backwards. Ah, I remember when I went to Thailand. Right after my first year of college, I thought it was going to be awesome. Well, it was, but not in the way I imagined it. Where does he want to go?"

"Anywhere but here."

"Oh, so sweet." She straightened and finished off her coffee. "Well, if I can just get some contact information from you, I will be on my way. Get this to the studio and, like I said, five o'clock news. Assuming you haven't found him by then."

Walter appreciated her optimism, but he had a hard time sharing it. As much as he did want to believe that Tommen would be safe and sound, camping on the hillside while they all trudged about in the rain, his better judgment, combined with past experience, said that he was probably going to be cold, wet, sick, and injured.

Oh. Wait. No. It was him that usually ended up like that. Tommen was usually pretty okay. So he might be camping out there. He had to hang onto that hope until he was definitively proven otherwise.

He stood and shook Jaylee's and Jeff's hands as they took their bills to the counter and left the diner. Watching them walk by the windows, Walter could see that she was already going over the story and how awesome it was going to be, if her flagrant hand gestures were any indication. Well, nothing he could do about it now, and if it got his son's photo out there and helped to find him out there in the boonies, well, all the better, he supposed.

He sat down again and checked his watch. After a minute, the waitress approached.

"Get you a refill on your coffee? On the house as long as you promise to come back for supper."

"No, but a glass of water would do nicely, thank you."

She got it for him, and he got out his phone again. He'd no sooner dialed Micah's number than he heard Micah's phone go off as he entered the diner, followed by Kayla. He hung up as they sat down across from him. The waitress sighed but got them a couple menus and took drink orders.

"Took you long enough," Walter said. "I not only started and finished without you, but I had a whole meeting, too, before you got here."

"Hey, don't blame us," Micah told him. "Blame that thing you made us bring."

"So you did get it."

"Barely," Kayla growled. "Believe me, we've learned a lot about them since they all got rounded up and essentially decommissioned or reassigned. One of those things is that they are pack animals, or herd animals. You can't take just one."

"Wait, so you have two out there?"

"That's what I'm saying."

Walter folded his arms. "Well, double the tracking power, I guess."

"Walt, we don't even know if this is going to work," Micah said. "It's the first time in a very long time, like over a century, where this has been attempted. And if it does work, what are the implications for future use?"

"Means we might be able to track Rifun, too."

"Or that he can track us."

"He's demonstrated that he can do that anyway. He already has fire in his possession; why are we so afraid to pick up a torch, too?"

"Because dousing the flame would be easier?"

"If you have a plan, I'm all ears."

Before anyone could say more, the waitress returned and took Micah's and Kayla's orders. Then she looked at Walter and raised a brow. "So, got any other friends coming in today?"

"Well, let's just say I hope not, at least not at this time," Walter told her. "Thank you for being so understanding."

"Hey, doesn't bother me any, but this isn't an office."

Her tone was difficult to judge as she headed off to the kitchen to deliver the ticket.

"Okay," Micah said, getting down to business. "What's the plan for when we leave here?"

"Rephrase," Kayla cut in. "What's been done so far?"

Walter did his best to describe the search efforts so far, but without having a working knowledge of the area, he couldn't say with one hundred percent certainty where the zone boundaries were or the sections or the command posts or any of that. He only knew that zone one, which was south and sort of east of the camp, was complete with no evidence of Tommen, and crews were moving to zone two, which was north and east of the camp. Zone three was north and a little west, and zone four was west and south between the zones already covered. News crews were running the story and had Tommen's photo, along with information on who to contact if anyone spotted him wandering around in the forest.

"Sounds like a decent plan," Micah mused, throwing up a Band so they could speak without sounding like the lunatics they were. "What are we hoping to accomplish? And how are we going to accomplish it if they're going to be searching all around the area we're going to be searching? Trackers aren't exactly German Shepherds."

"No, but we're going to be using a Band to slip in and out," Walter explained.

"Trackers track Time," Kayla said. "How are we going—? Okay. I think I see what you're saying."

"They track Time, but they're blind to the Akari, are they not?"

She shrugged uncertainly. "Honestly, we don't know. Like I said, there is a lot about them that we don't understand. I mean, during Rifun's coup, they did attack those who used Time and not those who used the Akari. But that may have been on Rifun's orders so he didn't get attacked himself. Granted, he's not using the Akari like he thinks he is, but to someone who doesn't know the difference, well, there is no difference."

"We don't have much of a choice. We can only use the information we have. Right now, the information we have says they won't attack the Akari, but they will track Time."

Micah leaned back. "So, does that mean you're starting to come over to the Akarin side?"

"I haven't made a decision on that yet, but I can't deny that there does seem to be a difference between it and Time, and there does seem to be something to it. I'm just not sure what. But let me say it this way, it's not going to hurt my feelings if the Akari helps me find my boy and Time doesn't. I don't care. I just want my son back."

Micah dropped the Band. "I hear you. I understand. We want him back, too."

"Micaiah manning the store today?"

"He is. He's just irate that he can't be out here looking, but he's meeting with a lawyer today and—"

"About what?"

"About what has to be done to the shop when he leaves and I take over solo. It's only a short-term measure, and we're still hoping to find someone else to take it over before then, but we have to plan for everything."

"Plus he's not so confident about his leg, running around up and down these mountains," Kayla threw in.

Walter raised a brow as he put up his own Band. "He went into a Time Trial, started a coup, fought in a bona fide battle, killed the Bat, and he's worried about a little hiking?"

Kayla shrugged. "It's what he said."

The Band dissipated. Hardly five minutes later, the waitress returned with the food. She looked at Walter again. "You've been here long enough; can I get you something else to eat before you leave?"

Walter chuckled. "No, I'm fine, thanks."

"This is good food," Kayla murmured. "I'm impressed."

"Glad I could accommodate."

"Does that mean you're buying?"

"Of course not."

"What about you?" Kayla jabbed Micah in the ribs.

Micah raised a brow. "I don't know how my brother would feel about me taking his wife out to lunch like that."

"Oh, please. He'd probably be more offended that you didn't."

"Then he needs to give me a raise."

Walter wished he could fully enjoy their mirth, but while he allowed a smile and a chuckle here and there, he really just couldn't get into the spirit of things. He was tired of sitting here in this diner doing nothing. He wanted to be out there on the mountain doing whatever it took to find his son.

After another minute or two of anxious waiting, he stood. "I'm going to go up and check out the situation. Then I'll come back for the two of you."

For a moment, the two of them looked hurt. Still, they agreed and watched him go. He felt bad that he'd been so short with them, but he couldn't just do nothing. The first time, he'd been made to wait until Rifun called and made his demands. This time, there were no such demands. Instead, time was of the essence, especially if Tommen really was injured. If he had a concussion or other similar injury, he needed to get to a hospital as soon as possible.

The drive from Wellspring to the camp was atrociously long, and seemed to get longer every time he made the trip. That was the thing about these mountain roads; they turned every mile into ten miles. Once he was fairly confident that no one was around, he Banded. It wouldn't make him feel any better about the drive itself, but at least it might cut down on the time spent doing bullshit things.

He didn't drop the Band until he was just south of the drive leading to the burned out bus garage. From what Walter had heard, Tommen had helped save the life of the camp director when he'd gone missing. Fell down one of the mechanic holes trying to get a bus started. Tommen had found him and gotten him out, or so the general story went. There were a number of variations.

A new command post had been set up in the parking lot of the camp, a grim sight amid the ruins and burned out husks of buildings situated against a gray sky that was finally beginning to clear. He parked and went to meet the commander.

"Glad to have you back, Walter," Harold said. "I'm afraid all the teams have already gone out."

"Oh. Well, I had a couple meetings, so I wasn't sure if I would make it out in time, anyway," Walter replied honestly.

"The good news is that we're set up here for zone two and three command."

"But nobody is here now?"

"Only who you see here. We got a wilderness chopper going to come out in a bit, see if they can see something we can't, eyes in the sky sort of thing."

"All right. Well, I have a few guys coming to help — I think — so I guess I'll go meet them and direct them up here. We'll be back in time for zone three search."

"Very good. We'll put them to work, to be sure."

Walter thanked him and turned away, going back to his car and starting back down the mountain. He'd never thought that he would make it to the zone two search, but he needed to know where everyone was and where they were going to be, that way he had an idea of where and how he was going to smuggle in Micah, Kayla, and two Trackers.

He wasn't sure where the idea had come from, to use the Trackers. He knew only that it was a dangerous gamble. They were animals, by all accounts, but highly intelligent and highly trainable. Rifun had managed to tame them, but before that, they were virtually unknown, banned even, because of how ferocious they were said to be. On the one hand, the stories could be true, and the Trackers they brought out today were as likely to turn on them and eat them as help them find Tommen. On the other hand, the stories could be similar to the ones old pioneers once had about bears and wolves, that they were just mindless killers, without taking the time to study and understand how they lived and survived.

Well, today would be the test run, to see whether the Trackers could be used reliably or not. If they could, well, maybe there would be a future in store for them. But, first thing's first, they had to find Tommen.

He pulled into the diner parking lot just as Micah and Kayla were paying their bill and leaving. They had brought Kayla's little truck, the large shell topper on it keeping the Trackers in, the blacked out windows keeping them from being seen. There did not appear to be any movement inside the bed of the truck.

"Two Trackers, just as the commander ordered," Kayla said, patting the side of the truck. Inside, there was suddenly movement, like two large dogs standing and waiting for their master to open the door and let them run.

"All right," Walter said, nodding. "We'll take them up and see what we can find. In the event we get separated, the camp is ten miles east of here, three and a half miles up. Big sign, can't miss it. Once you're pretty sure you're alone, park and wait for me. Or I'll wait for you. Then we'll Band and go up together. Sound like a plan?"

"Only one we've got," Micah said.

As he turned to open the door, however, a large F-150 covered in bumper stickers and a paramedic decal pulled into the lot. A moment later, Laura stepped out. She was not working, so she wasn't in uniform, instead opting for heavy jeans, a rain jacket over heavy flannel, and hiking boots.

"Oh, good, I was hoping I would catch you before you left," she said.

"You're early," Walter commented. "I told you to call."

She shrugged. "Well, traffic was light, and I'm fast when I want to be. As for calling, I thought I'd get something to eat first before heading out. Then I'd call. Just luck that we ran into each other here."

"Yeah, we were about to head up, but by this time, zone two is already out searching. Zone three won't be ready for a little bit."

"Have you guys eaten?"

Micah and Kayla nodded. It was Kayla who answered, "Yeah. Food's great." She grinned and slapped Walter on the back. "Maybe you two ought to have lunch first, like she said. We'll go up ahead of you and see what's what. You two can catch up later."

Walter enjoyed spending time with Laura. He did. She was smart, funny, always ready with a witty comeback, but also compassionate in her own, unique, paramedic way. On a normal day, he would not have said no to having lunch with her. But he just wanted to get out there and search for his son. He was tired of this stalling. He almost felt guilty when Laura seemed to recognize this and said, "You look raring to go, I can tell. If you've eaten, then go ahead and go. I'll just grab something quick and meet you guys up there."

"Thank you." Walter said the words before his brain could tell him not to. "We'll see you up there later. I'll ride with them, and then back with you if that's all right."

"Of course."

He gave her directions to the camp and at least walked her to the door of the diner, apologizing the whole way. She shushed him and told him to get up there to look for Tommen. She'd be along.

When Walter returned to Kayla's truck, he found her and Micah laughing about something.

"I don't know what you're laughing about, but I'm pretty sure it has something to do with me and Laura," he said grudgingly as he got in the back seat.

It only made the two of them laugh harder. It was Micah who answered. "You and Laura are so much like Tommen and Becky. Like father, like son, huh?"

"Can we get going, please?"

"Oh, lighten up, Walter," Kayla told him. "It's almost a compliment."

"Almost?"

"Sure. You and Tommen are both kind, loyal, sweet, and very caring. The difference is, you're old enough to know to defer to Laura, while Tommen is still trying to work out reconciling his man card with Becky's personality. He can't beat her, and he knows it. All that's left is to join her."

"Yeah, that's the part I'm worried about."

Kayla made a face in the mirror. "That's not what I meant. What I mean is that they're both bulls locking horns, neither of them strong enough to outdo the other by sheer force. But they both enjoy the challenge. Same with you and Laura, just in a gentler, calmer —"

"Older?"

"More mature sense. You know when to put the fight aside."

Walter shook his head. "Now I'm getting dating advice."

"Hey, Micaiah and I have been married a long time. I think we're more than qualified to dispense some dating and marriage advice here and there."

"You and every one of my coworkers. Half of them seem to think we should be married by this time next year. And that would be great, except..."

"Except for the Timekeeper thing?" Micah finished.

"Yeah. The Timekeeper thing."

Kayla sighed. "Walt, I know that that seems like an insurmountable barrier, but I don't think it is. Not as much as you're fearing."

"I have decades left in me before I even begin to age again," Walter reminded her.

"And Laura only has a few decades left period. Why not spend that time to make her happy? 'Until death do we part' is getting shorter and shorter for her with each passing year and each passing romance."

"You want me to propose up there on the mountaintop?"

"Certainly not. But it's something to think about."

Well, easy for her to say, Mrs. I've-Been-Married-For-Fifty-Years. And Mr. I've-Been-Hiding-My-Wife-For-Ten-Years, can't forget him. They were both in Time. They were both in the Akari, whatever it was. Furthermore, they were both still in their physical prime. Walter was not. Walter was older, looking at retirement. Every woman he looked at would be facing the same thing. Old age, retirement, failing health. Young people could enjoy each other for a long time. With such a staggering difference between Time and non-Time, divorce was almost inevitable. But him...he would have to watch Laura die. There was no way he could give her up in old age just because it became inconvenient for him to care for her, or because she might start to notice how he didn't age. He wasn't sure he could take that kind of trauma.

"Walt, you're quiet back there," Kayla said after a minute or two. "I hope I didn't kill your mood."

"No mood to kill," he told her, probably a little more sharply than intended. "My son is still missing."

"And that's what we're here to rectify. Relax, Walter. We'll find him."

He turned and looked through the window into the bed. This window was only tinted, but darkly. In the gloom, it was impossible to tell the exact sizes and shapes of the Trackers, other than big size and definitely-not-a-dog shape. It was almost awful to think that these ugly things, which had been attacking Time Agents left and right earlier in the year, which had even attacked his boy, were now going to be used to help find his boy. The world was turning upside down, and he was left spinning on the hamster wheel.

Chapter Three
Search Party

It had been late the previous evening when Micah got woken up and told to get ready. After some fighting with the sheets and a lot of dodged questions from Micaiah, he finally got the story of what happened and what was going on. The summer camp where Tommen was working had burned down. While trying to rescue counselors, campers, or kittens—Micah couldn't recall which—Tommen had gone missing. The thought was that he'd somehow gotten injured, probably a head injury, and was wandering around the woods with no clue where he was or which way was up. Furthermore, his phone was broken and couldn't be pinged, or even roughly guessed at. They had only his last known location and a description to go on.

Walter was not convinced that everything was so innocent. There was a chance that Rifun was involved. Even if he wasn't involved, however unlikely, and Tommen was injured and wandering around on his own, he would probably use Time in some way. Maybe he'd used a Fast Band to heal a wound or get from one place to another. Maybe he was using a Slow Band to try and pass the time until a search and rescue team found him. Maybe something completely different had happened. Whatever the case, Time was probably in use.

Walter's brilliant plan—with heavy sarcasm from Micaiah—was to use a Tracker to find him. If they could smell a Band wake a week old from a hundred miles away, then they should be able to pinpoint right where Tommen was, regardless of any movement or injuries. Seeing how Walter had not called back to say that Tommen had been found otherwise, their options were quickly running out.

When it came to wilderness survival, every second counted; Saul had proven that much.

But the thing was, despite Rifun using them in the Wheel, Trackers were actually more widely used by the Akarin, or they had been. Way back in the day, Trackers were used for everything from training to, well, tracking. They were a powerful motivator for new recruits, to get them to use the Akari rather than Time. They were also adept at finding Whispers who had, essentially, turned Runner, turned traitor. And they were used to intimidate Time Agents, a rather forceful force field to keep arresting Timekeepers at bay. Their use had been discontinued in favor of a much gentler approach to recruiting and what amounted to public relations.

From what Micah understood, many of them had been butchered in order to keep them from turning on their masters or going on a wild killing spree. Some had been turned loose on uninhabited worlds. But there were a few kept in the kennels, too. Just in case. Documentation ended shortly after that and their existence kept secret, up until Rifun found them in the dark corners of the Wheel and the Akarin fortress—through Cassius—and then used them to wreak havoc on Time Agents hiding throughout the universe.

And now they were expected to use one to find one kid lost in the Appalachian Mountains. Well, that hadn't gone so well at first. There was still a lot that was unknown about the Trackers, despite the wealth of knowledge—again, with heavy sarcasm—about them in either the Akarin Archives or the Wheel Archives. So no one quite knew that Trackers were pack animals and required at least two of them in order to function at a base level, never mind do their job for more than two minutes. Kayla had been the one to suggest such a technique when their one Tracker had gone ballistic as soon as it lost sight of its friends. She also suggested that maybe that was why they had been so violent against their targets in the past when Rifun was using them, because he only sent them one at a time.

Their second problem was that their Trackers had been "rescued" from the Wheel and kept in the old kennels on the third sub-floor of the Akarin fortress. They were trained, but they were trained according to Rifun's wishes, which meant seek and destroy. Or at the very least, seek, subdue, and return to the Wheel. Supposedly, Rifun had also taught them to track the Akari, but not to engage so violently. Anyone who had used the Akari while around the Trackers had been growled at and, basically, cornered, but not touched. Likely they were told to tree the cat and wait for the hunter. The next problem stemming from this was that they weren't entirely sure how to re-train the Trackers, or what they would want to re-train them to do.

Finally, the third problem that arose from using the Trackers to find Tommen was getting them to the search site and using them in a Band of some form without being attacked themselves. It was like rubbing alcohol under someone's nose and then asking them to smell anything else.

The fourth problem didn't have much to do with the Tracker as it did Micaiah when he informed Micah—only after they'd gotten the two Trackers home and chained up in their makeshift garage which wasn't visible from the road—that he wouldn't be going to the search site. He had a meeting with the lawyer that day at the bakery that he couldn't miss or postpone. Kayla would be going in his stead. She'd gone with them and seemed to have a better understanding of the Trackers, a better animal sense as it were. Furthermore, Micaiah didn't trust his leg to go hiking and control a Tracker at the same time, and he would only slow them down.

Micah called bullshit on that second point. After all the griping, complaining, moaning, and groaning Micaiah had given him about his leg, plus going into battle, there was no way he shouldn't be able to do a little hiking with an untamed hound. But he wasn't going, and that was that.

So, early the next morning—or maybe it was the same morning—after Micaiah left for work, Micah and Kayla took the time to do a little research and observation of the Trackers. Micah observed that they were ugly fuckers. Both of them were vomit green in color. One of them looked like it was half-horse, half-goat, half-dog, half-snake, half-something he didn't have a name for. The other was like a pig and a goat combined with Medusa or something. Kayla, however, observed that the pig-goat appeared to be the dominant of the pair, despite being slightly smaller. It was more apt to stand its ground and appear to defend the other one. Meanwhile, the other one seemed to be more energetic—more playful or more of a hothead was impossible to tell. It would look like it was getting ready to charge or do something, but the pig-goat would step in front of it, like one person putting his arm out to hold another person back.

When they were loading them in Kayla's truck, they both came to the conclusion that the Trackers had to be loaded together. The ugly ass one wanted the pig-goat to go first, maybe as deference to the dominant one. The pig-goat wanted the ugly ass one to go first, maybe to ensure the safety of his pack or herd or whatever, defend it against the weird upwalkers who were doing strange things to them. And it was no easy feat to pick them up, either. The pig-goat was about the size of a small Labrador, but weighed about as much as a full-grown bull, or that's how it seemed to Micah. He couldn't speak for Kayla and the ugly ass one, but she didn't look like she was having such a great time of it either.

By the time they actually got on the road, it was later than either of them wanted. But, in the interest of not being attacked while driving, they both refrained from using either the Akari or Time. They would test that out once they were out in the open, not in an enclosed vehicle at seventy miles an hour.

For all intents and purposes, the Trackers were the perfect riding companions. They lay down and didn't cause trouble. They didn't wiggle around and throw off the balance of the bed, didn't bark...or...make whatever noise at passing vehicles, though that may have been from the black rubbed coating Kayla had put over the windows to keep people from looking in. At any rate, once they got going, it was easy to forget the Trackers were even there, but Micah was still uneasy about it.

"Do we really want to trust these things?" he asked as they

neared Wellspring.

"I don't know," Kayla admitted. "But they might be our best shot at finding Tommen. Search dogs don't distinguish scent, not like they do in the movies. But with Time thrown in the mix, Tommen might have a distinctive enough 'scent' to attract the attention of these Trackers."

"Yeah, but, why not let Search and Rescue do their jobs?"

Kayla hesitated for half a second. "I think Walter is tired of trying to do things 'the right way' and leaving everything in Earth-side hands while sinister Time forces are at work. I think he really just wants to get his son back and say fuck the rest of it."

Micah nodded. "Makes sense. Second time in a year that Tommen has gone missing. I can see where he might be a little frustrated."

"A little frustrated? That's putting it mildly."

Driving in Base Time with normal traffic and the mission ahead put them both on edge a little. They themselves got frustrated and a little snippy, especially when it came to looking for exits, roads, landmarks, and so forth. When they finally arrived in Wellspring and spotted Walter's car at the diner, Micah was too happy to get out, stretch his legs, and get a bite to eat.

Although, their stress level was not helped any by Walter's anxious waiting, and Micah was glad when he finally decided to go up and take a look around at the search site and scope some things out for them.

"At least it will give him something to do," he said when Kayla tried to talk him down from a growing surly attitude.

"Micah, everyone is doing. Everyone is going. Everyone is looking. No one is finding. That's what he's upset about."

"I know, but he doesn't have to take it out on everyone."

Probably the only thing that calmed his growing irritation was Laura's unexpected appearance. Watching Micaiah and Kayla get all cute was annoying for Micah, mostly because he knew them, lived with them, and sometimes had to listen to them, which made him both jealous and frustrated at himself. Watching Walter and Laura, though, that was funny. That was funny as hell, actually. They were both on the same page, but neither seemed to realize it, or if they did, neither seemed to want to admit to it. They were as clunky and awkward as a couple of teenagers, like Tommen and Becky, but with fewer raging hormones.

Naturally, when confronted about it, Walter got on the defensive side, citing Time and this and that. For as valid as his points were, and even as valid as Kayla's points were, the whole thing was still hilarious, even as Micah elected to keep his mouth shut for most of it, instead smiling like an idiot most of the way up the mountain.

"You can pull off here," Walter said, indicating a dirt drive. "It will be out of the way, and it's not far from the campsite."

Kayla did as directed, parking and turning off the truck. Then she glanced back and forth between him and Walter. "Ready for this?"

"Ready as we'll ever be."

"Here goes."

Encasing the truck in a Fast Band elicited an immediate reaction from the Trackers in the back as they scrambled to their paws, er, hooves? They put their ugly muzzles to the back window, breathing heavily and fogging it up, occasionally shifting and pawing at the window with a hoof.

"Well, we're not dead yet," Micah said after a few tense seconds. "Guess we better get out and let them out."

"I hope they didn't poop in the bed or anything," Kayla grumbled, opening her door, then getting in the backseat to grab both heavy duty leashes and Animal Control sticks.

"Where did you get those?" Micah asked as she handed him one.

"Oh, well...I kind of stole them. Borrowed. Only borrowed them." She headed to the tailgate. "I'll return them once we get back." She paused. "Here goes nothing."

She stood off to the side and reached around, while Micah and Walter stood at the ready. It was the moment of truth, when they discovered just how the Trackers would react.

Kayla wasn't even able to open the tailgate before the Trackers had scrambled out through the window opening and hit the ground. They immediately went to her, completely oblivious to Micah and Walter right there. They sniffed and licked and pawed at her like a couple of hound dogs, wanting to chew but doing nothing that would break the skin and damage the prize. No matter where Kayla went, they were sure to follow. After a minute, they got smart and managed to trip her up. Once she was on the ground, they were all over her.

Not wanting to see her carried off to the Wheel or God knew where, Micah approached and managed to hook the ugly ass one with the Animal Control stick. Only when the collar tightened did the thing react, jumping and writhing and contorting like a creature possessed. Walter jumped in with the other stick to control the pig-goat, leaping to the rescue of its friend. It did not appreciate the stick either and turned on Walter, snapping wildly and trying to get to him.

Kayla scrambled to her feet and grabbed the regular leashes. Without collars, she had to hook the leashes to themselves, but tied them in such a way that they wouldn't tighten down too far. With her pulling and the men pushing, she got them to a tree where she tied them off long enough to loosen the sticks and slip them off.

Once she did that, the Trackers became relatively calm. They did not appear to like the leashes much better, but they were not being strangled anyway.

"Okay," Micah sighed. "We're not dead. We got them out of the truck, now what do we do with them? Who wants to walk the dogs, er, goats?"

"I'll take one," Kayla said, untying the ugly ass Tracker. It was not as calm and friendly as before, if it could be described as such, but as long as she did not try to force it away from its pig-goat friend, it did not do anything treacherous.

"I'll take the other," Micah decided.

But when he approached the pig-goat, it charged him and tried to attack.

"Maybe I'll try," Walter suggested.

He was able to approach the pig-goat and untie the leash without being attacked.

"So why don't they like me?" Micah whined, even if he was secretly grateful. "Walter had a stick just as much as I did."

"But you had the first stick," Kayla mused thoughtfully. "Maybe they think you led the charge. Maybe they think you're the leader, and Walter was just following you."

"And why do they like you?"

"Because so far, I've been the one handling them the most, studying them the most, and calling most of the shots. I'm the leader; I am to be followed. You're the meanie who strangles them with sticks. Walter is the grunt who follows the lead of others; he's harmless."

"Basic animal psychology. I totally knew that."

"Right. Well, as you've said before, we're not dead yet. Time to walk these guys."

"I was told that Tommen's last known location was over there," Walter said, pointing. "I think we should start there."

It made sense. Micah would have gladly gotten out of their way and let the dogs lead, but the Trackers seemed to want to keep an eye on him and have him within sight at all times.

The five of them picked their way down an embankment on the other side of the road. It was slippery with wet leaves, and every one of them slid down at least once, even the Trackers.

"So, somewhere around here," Walter said, looking around as if looking for a sign telling them which way to go or where to start. He looked at the Trackers. "How do we get them to start searching, or do they just pick up the scent on their own?"

"Honestly, I don't know," Kayla answered. "I mean, these were Rifun's hounds once. Even if the Akarin used standard commands, he wouldn't have used the same ones. His hounds, his words."

Micah shifted his stance. "Well, maybe instead of batting this back and forth, we can start with something simple. Like Search!"

The Trackers looked at him.

"Rifun wouldn't use English," Walter said. "Too obvious, at least where we're concerned."

"He's Malagasy," Kayla agreed. "That's what he would be using, something near and dear to him that no one else would know."

"Well," Micah said, pulling out his phone, "I don't speak Malagasy, but Google does."

"How the hell do you have signal out here?"

"Because Search and Rescue command up there in their infinite wisdom set up a portable, temporary hotspot up there at the top of the mountain so everyone can stay in touch with good signal via radio or cell phone. I don't need to get into it, just leech a little off the fringes. And...here we are. Malagasy word for search. And...*Tadaso!*"

It was like firing a gun, and both Kayla and Walter got jolted forward, Kayla almost losing her grip on the leash. The Trackers were on the case, running around like a couple of mad dogs. They wound around trees and bushes, getting tangled and strangled and stopped and everything else until finally Kayla and Walter made the decision to just let them off their leashes and do their work. If they ran off and got scooped up by federal agents and carted away for testing, well, the three of them had no idea what happened, what they were, or anything at all.

They followed the Trackers back up the hill to the road. They did a few circles, but finally got going up the road toward the campsite. The Trackers would disappear from sight, then return to make sure they were still coming, hooves clicking wildly on the road. Once they saw their current masters were still alive and following, they would dart off again.

"Okay, so he finishes up whatever he's doing, rescuing campers or something, but then he returns to camp," Walter huffed as they trudged their way up the hill. "Question is, why? The firefighters said that everyone had made it out by that point and they were the last to evacuate. He said as much on the phone. What would bring him back?"

"Force, maybe," Kayla said. "If Rifun was involved in some way, he may have forced Tommen to come back."

"But to what end?" Micah wondered. "I mean, there's fire. Rifun is powerful, but he's just as human as me and you. He can burn just as easily as we can, and he's got a terrible fear of fire."

"How do you know that?" Walter asked.

"Maybe…" Kayla mused.

"Maybe what?"

She did not answer before they reached the crest of the hill and entered the parking lot. Search and Rescue command had set up their post, but with all the teams out, the area appeared largely deserted. The Trackers, however, were across the lot and going nuts, yelping and squealing and making all sorts of unearthly noises. The trio got there as fast as they could, hoping to find something, anything that would shed some light on things.

The Trackers were romping around in a small circle, as if chasing each other's tails. There was nothing around that Micah could see and say was significant. He glanced at Kayla who looked equally confused. Before anyone could say anything, however, the Trackers bounded off again, pushing and snapping at each other like a couple of puppies. Or maybe kids. The three humans simply watched them bound down the hillside until they came to a stop at one of the burned out cabins. There they began romping in circles again around what may have been a porch, this time yipping much louder, yipping until they were hoarse even.

When the three of them approached, the Trackers took off and did a huge loop around all the cabins, returning to the first one and running in circles, finally sitting down and panting heavily.

"Okay, so this place is significant," Walter said. "Why?"

"Maybe we should consider something else," Micah began slowly. "If the Trackers can smell Time a week old, I mean, the camp hasn't been burned down long. Tommen may have used Time all the time while at camp. If this was his cabin, it would make sense."

"How do we tell the difference?" Kayla wondered.

Micah only had one idea, but he wasn't sure how well it would go over. He told Kayla as much before facing the Trackers, praying they wouldn't maul him as soon as he said it. *"Akari tadaso!"*

The Trackers were decidedly less energetic this time around. Whether it was because they were tired or because they were confused from Kayla's Band was hard to tell. Maybe they didn't understand "Akari" and they were confused why they had been told to search for something they evidently thought they already found. Still, they did their job.

This time the search took them down the hillside into the forest. In his peripheral vision, Micah could see Walter getting excited. Maybe the Trackers really were going to take him to his son; maybe they really were the right tool for the job. Maybe there was a future with this.

They came to a place that, like everything else, was burned out. There were three large boulders situated around a common spot. Maybe some special log or tree had been there, Micah didn't know. Kayla examined the boulders with great interest as the Trackers did their little romp, then sat down.

"What is it?" Walter asked.

"These boulders are split," she stated. "They're completely bone dry."

"That's what rocks do when they go dry. And they go dry when they're exposed to fire," Micah stated.

"Yes, but that takes time. These are deciduous trees. Fire travels primarily through the canopy. All the brush and undergrowth that would have been here on the ground would have burned too fast for these boulders to split like this, and these are huge boulders. It would take a lot more than one fire to do this."

"What are you saying?" Walter inquired. "That Tommen could have done this?"

"Rifun more likely."

"Rifun isn't that strong."

"He doesn't have to be." She paused, looking for the right words. "The Akari is more than Time, Walter. It's also Matter and

Energy. He wouldn't have needed to split a rock by force when he could have just reached into it and forced it to break from the inside out. It's not much different from manipulating Time, really. Rather than feeling Time, you feel Matter. Once you feel it, you can manipulate it, to an extent."

"You're joking."

"No. It's how Disguises work. It's how Building worked before the art was almost lost."

"And Energy?"

"Energy is how you open portals to anywhere."

Walter pinched the bridge of his nose. Micah couldn't blame him. He'd felt the same way, once, like he was caught up in a bad science fiction novel. Oh, wait.

"What does this mean for Tommen?" Walter asked finally.

"It means Rifun is probably teaching him things. Maybe..." She hesitated again. "Maybe Rifun started the fire."

"No, Tommen said his campers did that."

"Okay, so his campers started the fire. Maybe Rifun saw the fire and took the opportunity to take Tommen aside and teach him a few lessons."

"Lessons in what? And why did he need fire?"

"For the Energy. It is very hard to give good lessons in Energy because Energy is so unstable. Fire would provide the perfect opportunity to a lesson. A fire this size means there could have been a lot of lessons."

"What would—you know what? Forget that. How does this help us find him? Is he still out there, under Rifun's thumb, being taught God knows what?"

"I don't know. Micah, what did you say that word was?"

Micah looked at the Trackers, and they looked at him. If he had to guess, he might even say they looked excited to be out doing something, out working. *"Akari tadaso!"*

They bolted off again, this time heading back for camp, both of them looking very intent on a trail. They made another loop of the campsite before settling on the same cabin as before. Micah and the others watched them sniff around, high and low, occasionally pawing at this or that. Then they moved off, away from the cabin, heading east. Walter was the first in line after them, his hopes up once again.

The Trackers paused once and looked around as if they'd lost the scent. One put its muzzle up, then went to a tree. It reached up as high as it could go on its hooves, sniffing and yipping. The second Tracker made a small circle, got up on its hind hooves an arm's length from the tree, sniffing and yipping also. They got down and did a meandering weave around the trees, moving back and forth, but always returning to the spot around that one tree. Kayla bade them sit while the three of them checked out the area.

"I don't see anything particularly interesting about this spot," Kayla said finally. "Nothing looks touched, not like the other place."

"What if he was injured," Walter stated slowly. "What if Rifun got him back here in the fire, tried to teach him some crazy lesson? What if Tommen tried to get away, used Time or the Akari or whatever to run from Rifun? Maybe this place or hereabouts is where he got injured. Being injured, he drops his Band and just keeps running. Wham, straight into the forest. Injured, confused, not sure why he's running, only that he has to."

"Sounds plausible," Micah said. "I mean, if you're running from fire and a crackpot like Rifun, that's a pretty good dose of fear and a powerful motivator to keep running, especially if you can't remember why."

"Why don't we do a quick check while we're here?" Walter suggested, moving off in the general direction that they were already going.

"Why don't we let Search and Rescue do the searching for us?" Kayla said, moving ahead to stop him. "They're already out searching this way. Meanwhile, we have two Trackers that we have to return somehow, plus several articles of stolen merchandise. You have to meet your girlfriend, anyway. Maybe you can both come this way and look together, hm?"

Micah could see the war in Walter's mind. He wanted to plow ahead, search and find with no one to stop him. Micah didn't blame him. He could understand how Walter might think Kayla was being unreasonable. But they were not enough of a Search and Rescue team to be effective, and they would more likely just get lost and injured themselves. They were out here, and they had accomplished their goal, that is, tracing the Time and Akari movements in the area, trying to determine where Tommen might have gone. So far, all evidence pointed to a location where teams were already searching.

Finally, Walter relented. "Okay. I could use a cup of coffee and a good sitdown anyway, rest my knees and my back."

"I'll agree to that," Micah said, trying to lighten the mood a little. "I don't know how Tommen did it, walking and running up and down that hill every day. Jeez."

They managed to get the leashes back on the Trackers and returned to the truck.

"Do Trackers get treats or something?" Micah wondered when they got them lifted back into the bed. Kayla closed the tailgate, but opened the window. "I mean, how do we reward them for a job well done? Or do you think they understand, or what? I mean, they did a good job, and we might use them in the future."

"I don't know," Kayla admitted. "Maybe we can find something for them later. Maybe pick up a package of hamburger at the store or something on the way out."

"Are you two taking off, then?" Walter asked.

"I expect so. We'll drop you off at the command post as if you just arrived, but otherwise, we have to get these guys back to the kennels. Maybe we'll head to the store here in town, pick up the hamburger, drop them off, then come back to 'help' with the search."

Walter nodded. "It would be much appreciated."

Kayla smiled and put a hand on his shoulder. "It'll be all right, Walt. We'll find Tommen. Like you said, he's probably camping out there on the hillside, warm and dry and well-fed while we're out here, cold, wet, and starving."

True to their word, Micah and Kayla dropped Walter off at the command post, promising to be back as quick as they could before the zone three teams could leave. Then they were heading back down the mountain.

"If Rifun is teaching Tommen about Matter and Energy, subjectually, then we need to intercept him," Kayla said.

"Subjectually?" Micah echoed. "Is that a word?"

"It means that Rifun is teaching Tommen Matter and Energy as the whole subject, versus teaching him about Disguise and Gravity, or portals or anything like that. By topic. Okay, that is dangerous stuff. It's like teaching him about explosives without educating him on volatile compounds, reactions, mixtures, any of that, just giving him a whole bunch of buckets of stuff and told to have fun mixing up whatever he wants. It's going to get him killed. I'm...almost surprised it didn't already, honestly, with that big of a fire, that much Energy to play with."

"Subjectually..." Micah whispered, shaking his head. "Wow."

"Micah..."

"I know, I know. And Tommen is young, dumb, and impressionable. He feels left out, left behind by the rest of us, which I totally get. Believe me, I totally understand how he's feeling. But that just makes it easier for Rifun to sink his claws into him, however much Tommen may protest and try to fight. He's playing the psychology of it."

"Exactly. We need to find him, and fast. Rifun's got the jump on us, and as long as he has better party tricks than we do, Tommen may still go after him, in spite of everything Rifun has done so far."

It was a morbid thought as they bounced along the mountain road for a while before finally tuning off on the slightly nicer road leading to Wellspring. They passed Laura on the way up, waving briefly, then pulled into a small deli and grocery store.

"You really think we should get them a package of hamburger?" Micah asked.

"Would you rather offer them a Caesar salad?" Kayla shot

back. "I don't know what they consider a treat. At any rate, they haven't eaten since we got them; they're probably starving." Well, there was that. "Stay here and make sure they don't run off. I'll go in and grab something."

So Micah sat in the truck. He leaned the seat back so he could peer through the rear window. As near as he could tell, they were still back there, sleeping or just pretending to, he couldn't tell. They were definitely ugly fuckers, no doubt about that. Micah certainly wouldn't want one lying on his rug in front of a roaring fire while it snowed outside. But they had their uses. If their little adventure today was any indication, they might prove very valuable going forward, especially if they managed to find a use for them in the war against the Borelians. He wasn't sure what use, but a use.

Kayla returned a few minutes later with a package of ground beef and a salad, saying, "One or the other, they better eat them."

Micah opened the back window, and Kayla tossed the food inside, jerking her hands out of the way as sharp teeth snapped greedily at the food. It was impossible to tell which one they preferred, because they ate everything, including the plastic packaging.

"I'd say it was a tie," Micah said after a minute of stunned silence. "Maybe add some dressing to the salad next time; it looked a little dry."

"Maybe," Kayla said blankly.

She put up another Akari Band, then she and Micah went around to get them out of the bed once more. They seemed thrilled to be out and about again, but it was only a trip to the fortress, which they did not seem to relish.

"How did they work for you?" the kennel keeper inquired. He'd thought the whole excursion a waste of time at best and a death wish at worst.

"Actually, they may have done exactly as we need them to," Kayla told him. "We may have found our missing man."

"Surprising. I will make a note of it."

"Good. And make sure they get fed well. They're starving."

The kennel keeper merely grunted and opened the kennel door so they could toss the Trackers inside. If he had to put any word to it, Micah might have said the things looked sad and rejected, like a couple of dogs being returned to the pound. Maybe it was him. Maybe he was getting sentimental. He needed to find a girlfriend.

He and Kayla returned to the truck where she dropped the Band, both of them no worse for wear.

"I'm going to call Cai and let him know what we found," she said, digging out her phone. "It'll keep him in the loop, and maybe he can do some digging of his own later on."

"Hello?" Micaiah answered after a couple rings.

Kayla turned the phone on speaker, and between the two of them, they got the story across. Micaiah did not interrupt, and was silent for a long moment after they were done.

"And you're sure about the rocks and the Matter and everything else?" he asked slowly.

"As sure as I can be," Kayla answered. "It's the only thing that makes sense, why Rifun would take Tommen back into that fire."

Micaiah grunted. "All right. I'll do some looking around. Are you guys on your way?"

"No, we promised we'd do some searching for a bit. We'll be home tonight."

"Okay. See you then."

Kayla put her phone away and turned on the truck. "All right, time to do some more running around in the cold and wet on the side of a mountain."

Micah grimaced. "I can't wait."

Chapter Four
Julianna

Tommen went with his dad back to Wellspring. He watched him have breakfast or lunch or whatever one wanted to call it. He watched his interview or meeting with the reporter. He had to admit he was a little moved by his dad's description of him. He watched his dad get frustrated that nothing was being done. Tommen figured he could relate. After all, he was only sitting *right fucking next to him!* Watching his dad eat. Very tasty-looking food. Discussing his disappearance right in front of him. It was like reading his obituary in the newspaper when he wasn't even dead yet. Seriously.

He had to say that he was surprised when Micah and Kayla walked in the door. But then, maybe he wasn't surprised. It was obvious his dad suspected Time was involved in some way, and he didn't blame him. Naturally, he was going to call in some specialized forces for that. But why call Micah and Kayla and not his Lieutenants? Well, obvious reason, because Rifun was involved. And if Rifun was involved, the Akari was probably involved in some way, too. Best to bring out the big guns right from the start.

He was still trying to figure out his relationship to Time, inasmuch as Banding was concerned. His dad had Banded the car on the way back, and Tommen had been cool with that. He did not appear to have suffered any side effects. And when Kayla or Micah Banded in the diner, so as not to sound like freaks when their conversation turned to Time and whatnot, Tommen was naturally not included in such Bands. That was fine with him; he expected it.

What was weird, though, was how the Bands themselves changed. His dad was still using Time; this much he knew. But his

Time Bands were invisible, the same way Akari Bands were normally invisible. Similarly, whenever Kayla or Micah used an Akari Band, it was like a visible, almost blinding, white, like angel from heaven here to deliver a message from God kind of white light.

Eventually, growing anxious, his dad left again, and Tommen rode along, back up to the command post, minor chitchat, and then back down to Wellspring. Not a lot had changed except his dad apparently felt a tiny bit better about doing something. Micah and Kayla were just walking out the door, ready to go, when Laura showed up.

Tommen thought back to when he had gone to lunch with his dad when he first met Laura. Actually, it was the only time he'd met Laura. But she seemed to be okay by him. Seeing her show up to this rescue operation, he had to concede a little more respect to her. Watching him and her talk and flirt a little, he came to the conclusion that dating was fundamentally the same, no matter how old the parties were. She was still in control, and he was still a doofus.

At the same time, though, she was a paramedic. Tommen didn't know a lot of paramedics when they were off the job, but his dad had mentioned on several occasions that most carried a small bag in their personal vehicles in the event that they came across an accident while off-duty, or for home emergencies. Maybe she would have something for his burns.

He'd quickly figured out how to maneuver the whole solid wall thing, that is, he just pushed right through it, like a bedsheet. He knew it was there, and then he was past it. How the whole thing about seats and everything worked, he still wasn't sure. But he found Laura's bag in the backseat easily enough, and the woman did not pack light. He'd seen smaller bags on ambulances. Hot damn, she even carried her own portable oxygen tank? How many accidents did she come across while off-duty?

Now came the question of, even if she did have some miracle burn ointment, how did he go about using it? He couldn't open up the bag; his fingers slipped right through the zipper pull. He could reach inside the bag through the fabric, and he could feel that she had a small field trauma bay in there, but he couldn't actually move anything.

Hm...maybe it was a matter of Matter, feeling the objects as he touched them, manipulating them that way. He pulled his hand out and tried it with the zipper; this would be a lot easier if he could see what he was touching and find what he needed.

Okay, Matter, feeling an object, knowing it from the inside-out, touching it at the molecular, no, the atomic level. Feeling the plastic and the metal and whatever else they make zippers out of. Feel the zipper, feel it in relation to the bag, feel the mechanism, the track, all of it...

It was like a bad trance, Tommen thought, and it got him no closer to actually opening the bag. In fact, it did nothing for him at all as he got out of Laura's truck and found his dad, Micah, and Kayla had already gone. Well, it wasn't hard to figure out where they went, but Tommen was in no mood to walk there.

Instead, he went into the diner and sat down across from Laura who was speaking to the waitress.

"Oh, that's cool," the waitress was saying. "Yeah, I imagine they'll need all the help they can get, especially medically."

"That's why I brought my own bag, just in case," Laura said. "If he's hurt, after all this time, he'll need some real emergency intervention before taking him in."

"You think he's injured?"

Laura nodded. "I do. His dad brags enough about his survival skills that there's no reason not to think he's hurt in some way. Head injury, broken bones, burns."

"Well, survival is one thing when everything is in tact. Does his dad ever brag about his knowledge of wilderness medicine?"

"He was mum on that one. I don't know if he knows anything. Honestly, I've only actually met him once, but sometimes it feels like he's at lunch or dinner with us, the way Walter talks about him."

"It's good his dad is so dedicated. I wish my dad had been half that interested in me."

"I hear you, believe me."

The waitress shifted her stance. "Well, I'll get that order in for you and have your food out fast. Sounds like you got places to be."

"Thank you."

Damn. So there went Tommen's hopes of eavesdropping on a very convenient and very practical discussion about what to do for severe burns. As it was, as long as he kept it elevated and kept it cool, he could at least manage the pain. It was always there at the forefront, if he let his mind go there, but he was finding ways to cope. The fever and chills still plagued him, but the nausea had subsided for the most part. Though looking around at all the good food in the diner was doing nothing for him.

Laura brought out her phone and started poking away. Suddenly it erupted with, "Welcome to eParamedic! Please enter—"

"Oh, shut up," Laura hissed, punching off the volume. "Why the hell did they put sound in this app anyway?"

To make it easy and convenient for me? Tommen thought, moving to stand behind her and look over her shoulder. She was smart, he would give her that. As she herself said, always brush up and don't try to memorize everything, because you can't. Her own words were proving true as she began looking through treatments and protocols.

It would have been nice if everything had pictures and easy step-by-step instructions, one, two, three. Instead, it looked more like a complicated flow chart. Is patient conscious? Yes, go to question two. No, go to question three. And so on. She perused the concussion instructions, broken bones, hypothermia, saving burns for the very last it seemed. And she was a fast reader, too. She was a skimmer. Of course, she already knew the stuff; she only had to brush up. He was an idiot who was trying to actually learn off of these.

" 'Characteristics of a second-degree partial-thickness burn,' " Tommen read aloud. " 'Skin may be pink, red, or white. Blisters are present and obvious and may be of varying sizes, and—' hey! No, go back. Dammit, you're reading too fast."

He figured he got about a fifth of the information, but it was enough, he supposed.

Rule one, don't lance the blisters. It can cause infection because the body is not prepared to heal itself and defend against infections as most of the body's defense mechanisms are destroyed. He looked at his arm, especially his hand. Well, rules were made to be broken, weren't they? Besides, he'd cleaned it out as best he could, and he did his best to not touch anything.

Rule two, keep the patient warm to ward off shock and maintain body temperature as the body may not be able to regulate itself, depending on the extent of the injuries. Tommen fingered his cut-up coat in his hand and ran his tongue over his teeth. Okay, so that hadn't been his smartest move, and he knew it. He would own that one. Good thing it was August, even if rainy.

Rule three, ensure sufficient fluid intake. As the fluid built up in his arm in the blisters and edema, it was not only drawing fluid away from the rest of his body—made worse by lancing the blisters—but it caused cell death which would put a strain on the kidneys with all the material needing to be filtered, and could cause kidney failure. Excellent. Because that was what he wanted to hear, that things could actually get worse. So he just had to drink a shit ton of water and start peeing like crazy to keep shit from building up in his kidneys. How did he go about doing this, anyway?

Rule four, don't use lotions, ointments, or creams, as it could cause infection or other contamination. Well, so much for the aloe vera.

Tommen rubbed his face. He was doing this all sorts of wrong. Where was the section on how to fix his screw ups so he didn't lose his hand or entire arm?

From what he could gather, the most he would be able to do outside of a hospital was wrap his entire arm in a sterile dressing, and use more sterile dressing to separate his fingers do they didn't stick together. Even as he thought about it, he gently pulled his fingers apart, noting the sticky mess that oozed out between them when he did. Then he had to keep it elevated. Anything more than that was on a doctor. Problem was, he had access to none of those things right now. Laura probably had exactly what he needed in her bag, but he couldn't get into it.

Laura ate quickly and tipped well, hurrying out to her truck with Tommen invisibly in tow. He looked longingly at the bag in the backseat. She had what he needed, but he couldn't get to it. This was more than frustrating; this was infuriating.

They passed Micah and Kayla on the way up, and Tommen had a sinking feeling that he should have gone with them. Reading Laura's little app to see what he needed to do for his wounds was great; what would be even better was getting out of wherever he was so he could get real, professional help.

They pulled into the parking lot of the camp. Command had been set up, and it looked like the first team was just getting back, no good news to report. His dad was sitting a short distance away from the command tent, coffee in hand. He did not look as strained and defeated as he had before, Tommen thought as he slipped out of the truck and approached. Walter stood and hugged Laura. Was it awkward, or did it just look that way to Tommen? To think of all the things they did when they thought he wasn't looking. How far did he want to go with this?

"Okay, what's the plan?" Laura asked.

"Well, if they don't find him, zone two teams are going to come back," Walter explained. "They're going to have a quick lunch, then move on to zone three. It was a little late for me to join anyway."

The way he spoke was less like a confused, anxious, grieving father, Tommen thought, and more like that of a man who knew the answer and just needed to be told go. Maybe the three of them had found something up here. Maybe they had an answer for what happened and they were just waiting for everyone to clear out so they could do it in private, whatever "it" was. Either way, Tommen was going to be sticking close to them.

Well, "close" was a relative term. The teams were slow to

return, which meant Walter and Laura stayed in the command camp. That was fine and dandy, but they were being cute again. She was trying to encourage him and take his mind off the situation at hand, and he was thanking her for being there, for being so helpful, she knew so much, he was sure that they would find him and she would make sure he got the care he needed and the tongue-lashing he deserved for going off on his own. It was cute. It was sickening. For fuck's sake, they were both around fifty years old. Did old people still flirt like a couple of teenagers?

So Tommen wandered off a short distance, looking at the papers and maps on the command tables, listening to this or that conversation, eavesdropping on the radios. After a while, though, his attention span craved something new, something to do. He glanced back at the two lovebirds. They'd moved position, but remained at the post. Seeing how only three of the six teams had returned, plus there was lunch yet, Tommen suspected they would be there for a while and wouldn't wander off too far.

He returned to the camp. It had been scoured over and over again by the various teams until there was nothing left but mud, burned out buildings, and blackened trees. As he approached Wolf Cabin, he saw that there were also hoofprints in the mud. It was way too soon for any deer to return here, to say nothing of all the human activity, so what had been here? He followed the tracks beyond the cabin into the woods, in the direction of his fall. The prints wove around a few trees, but largely stayed right around the area where he'd woken up.

"Now what came through here?" he wondered aloud.

"They used Trackers to try and find you," a female voice said behind him.

Tommen almost jumped out of his skin as he whirled around, swinging his arm wildly, sending shooting pain up and down his arm even as several more blisters tore open.

A woman stood about forty feet from him, dressed like she had just walked out of *Little House on the Prairie*, long, proper dress, proper shoes and stockings, dark hair pulled up in a proper bun. She had a high, narrow forehead and a hooked nose, small eyes and thin lips. He could almost imagine her at the front of a little one room schoolhouse, slapping rulers across the hands of disobedient children or just taking them out to the woodshed herself. But the one thing he didn't miss was the scars on her face, tiny one-inch squares, as if someone had taken a wire mesh and burned it into her skin.

"What? Wait. You...can see me?" Tommen asked.

"Did you think you were alone here?" she retorted.

"I don't know. I don't know where 'here' is. I mean, I have an idea, I think, but...I don't know. Am I dead?"

She grinned and shook her head, a grotesque thing to behold as the little squares twisted and contorted with the motion of her face. "You are in the in-between dimension. The Land In Between, from which no one has ever returned."

"How did I get here?"

"The way almost all creatures get here. They opened a portal, but it collapsed on them halfway through."

"But I didn't open a portal. I don't know how to open portals."

"Ah, but you did. And you do. Portals are a manipulation of Energy. You tried to put out the fire by manipulating the Energy rather than the Matter. I suppose I don't need to tell you now that Energy is very unstable and very finicky. When it backfired on you and caused the explosion, it was enough to tear open a portal. Likely you were subconsciously trying to save yourself, reaching for a place where you felt safe and wanted to go. Home, for instance. But the concussive force of the explosion knocked you out before you got all the way through the portal, and it sent you here instead."

Tommen looked around at the trees and the burned landscape, the at the woman who was now about fifteen feet from him. "Who are you?"

"Ah, of course. Introductions. I am Julianna Brown."

"Julianna Brown. I've heard that name before."

"I expect you have. Richard was my husband; he wrote the

Akari journal."

Tommen took a step back. "What did you say?"

She sighed. "Please, Tommen, let me explain—"

"How do you know my name?"

"I know quite a bit about you."

"And how do you know what I did here? The only other person here was Rifun."

"If you would rein in your paranoia for just a few minutes, I could explain a few things," Julianna said irritably. When Tommen calmed down, she began again, more slowly this time. "Yes, I know who you are. I was there the night you walked into the old salt cave."

Tommen felt a chill snake down his spine. "You were the screaming demon."

"Yes. Richard was my husband and a great Akari-bearer. He wrote down the words of the Author herself as a manual for mastering the Akari. For good. But there were those who would try to use it for evil. Cassius was one such man. He had my husband imprisoned, sentenced to die unless the journal was turned over to him. I searched for it and found it, but Cassius did not release Richard as promised. So I broke into the prison and stole it back.

"I fled to America, but Cassius was like a mad dog. Once he got his mind fixed on something..." She shook her head. "Anyway, I had heard stories of the Time Portal, and I hoped to use it to escape. Cassius followed me in, but he did not see me hide the journal in the old miner's bones. He attacked me and tried to kill me, but I managed to escape. I got out of the cave and did my best to hide in the chaos of World War II. That was where I Harvested an old friend of yours, Lily Guile."

"Hardly a friend," Tommen said. His first instinct was to fold his arms, but his left arm was decidedly against such a motion.

"Anyway, I Harvested her and trained her a bit. Then the Dispersal of '63 came around, and Cassius had returned, madder than ever. He pursued me again. I returned to the cave to look for the journal, but it was gone. Cassius followed me again. Cassius and

Rifun, actually. This time, they caught me and cut up my face as you see here. Before they could kill me, I opened a portal and tried to escape, but it closed on me. I've been stuck here ever since."

Tommen wished he was better at discerning liars. The obvious ones, like the campers he'd been watching over, those were easy to spot. It was much harder to tell a liar when she was so convincing. On the other hand, it could be the truth. Certainly no one cut up their own face and conjured up a story about being pursued by a sadistic murderer just for shits and giggles. Besides, who would she have to impress with it anymore?

"Once I was here and learned how to move around here, I eventually discovered the whereabouts of my husband's journal. You had found it, an innocent little boy who almost stumbled into the hands of a killer.

"When Cassius and Rifun turned up again and started going after Lily, I took an interest in things once more. I watched her, to be sure, to make sure nothing happened to her. But I also began to take an interest in you. You are an extraordinary young man with great talent, great potential."

"Rifun said something similar," Tommen said flatly.

Julianna frowned. "Tommen, you cannot base everything you encounter on the actions of a single person. Your encounter with Rifun cast a very long shadow over the Akari, true. But your encounter with Micaiah and the Akarin opened your mind to new possibilities."

"Yeah, like Matter and Energy and—no. Wait. Rifun did that." Tommen shifted his stance. "So you claim to be Akarin, then."

She shook her head. "No. Perhaps at one time, but when Richard began journaling and writing the words of the Author, I saw that the Akarin were flawed and greedy, self-serving in the most despicable ways. Not all of them, certainly. Some were very good. But as a whole, they had fallen, succumbed to the same lust that drives the Time industry through its constant cycles of war and peace."

He studied her for a moment, trying to judge her words. Whether or not they were true, she certainly believed them. That was the world according to Julianna, assuming that was even her real name. He had no reason to doubt her, but he had no reason to believe her, either. At the same time, what did it matter whether or not he believed her? It didn't change his predicament any.

"Okay, fine. Let's say for a minute that I believe you and everything you just told me is true," he said. "Playing hypotheticals here."

"All right," Julianna said, nodding.

"Why do I care about any of that?"

"You asked. You wanted to know. Your paranoia told you to get some kind of story out of me."

Well, there was that. "Fine, fair enough. I'll give you that. But, like I said, assuming it's all true, how does it help me out any? What does it change?"

"Nothing whatsoever, except now you have met another person and can actually talk to someone, versus everyone out there—" She gestured in the direction of the command post. "—who merely looks through you and continues their own conversations. It's a sanity thing."

"Are there others?"

"Of course there are. You don't create a dreaded dimension by having only one or two people disappear. But our population throughout the universe is fairly low, so unless you go to a big city and know what to look for, chances are, you won't run into anyone else. I'm here only because—well, it's not important."

"Yes, it is, especially if you say it isn't."

She hesitated. "I've learned to use this dimension, make it work for me. I'll show you a few tricks, too, about getting around. But overall, I keep...I keep an eye on things in certain places and certain people. I noticed when you and Rifun started dabbling in Matter and Energy, and I came to investigate."

Tommen grunted.

"Regardless, first we need to do something about your arm. The blisters have broken, and you're contracting infection. Your kidneys are also in overload because of cell death caused by the edema, and you've lost a lot of fluids, especially in your GI tract; your body is pulling blood from your intestines to try and compensate in your arm. No doubt you've been experiencing nausea, too."

She pushed past him and headed up toward the command post. After a minute, Tommen followed. "Great. I'd love to fix myself up. I even know where the supplies are. I don't know how to grab them, though."

"Have you ever set out fish traps? Not nets, but the traps where fish swim into, but they can't get back out?"

"I know what you're talking about, but I've never done it."

"This dimension is a lot like that. Easy to get in, impossible to get out. We can pull whatever we need."

They reached Laura's truck. Julianna turned around and looked at Tommen's arm. With the blisters broken, his skin looked like it was sloughing off like leprosy, this amid the melted fabric of his coat, the few blisters that remained in tact, and the uneven swelling throughout. It hurt like a bitch, but he kept it up as much as he could.

"So, wait, if we can just pull stuff like this, is there a way to send a message to my dad that I'm alive?" Tommen asked. "Can I tell him where I am?"

"Pulling things into this dimension is one of the most advanced things you can learn. It is difficult and dangerous in itself."

"But you can do it."

She ducked out of the truck with a handful of supplies, gloves, gauze, wrap, sterile water, the whole works. She gave Tommen an unreadable look. "Sure. It can be done. But if you can't get out, what would be the point?"

"To give him reassurance that I am alive, that I'm all right. Even if they have to call off the search, I'm still here. Help him not to worry so much."

"To what end? You would see him suffer knowing you are alive and separated forever, rather than see him grieve and eventually move on? Would you rather be lovers looking through a mirror, or a ghost in an old home?"

"I'd rather be alive and well and not here."

She barked a laugh. "Wouldn't we all?" She shook her head. "No. I won't do it. You are going to hate me, but you will see that it is for the best. And the good news is that your dad has good friends around him to support him. Even better that his girlfriend is so supportive as well. Think of how much better it will be for the two of them if he isn't distracted, knowing that you're alive but forever gone?"

"Who are you to say that that's the better road?" Tommen challenged. "At least then he would know. Versus having the search called off and he never knew what became of me."

Julianna just shook her head again and took him over to an empty table that would be used later for lunch. She made him sit and put his left arm on the table, as gently as he dared.

"I'm going to warn you now," she said. "This is going to hurt."

That was about like having the dentist say that "this might hurt a little" right before ripping out a perfectly healthy tooth with no anesthesia. Or an old war doctor taking the saw to a dead limb on the battlefield with only whiskey for comfort. Half the nerves in Tommen's arm were dead; the other half were as raw as an exposed wire. Not like a little light switch either, but the huge ass primary lines running directly from the power plant to everywhere else. Holy fuck, it hurt. He wiggled and fidgeted and yelled and groaned and beat his fist on the table. She soaked his whole arm, making sure to get part of his chest, ribs, and neck where he was also burned. When she was done with the water, she left him alone for a few minutes while she prepared the gauze.

He was exhausted from the pain and the yelling. His face was wet with tears, and he wanted nothing more than to curl up and go to sleep. As it was, the best he could do was rest his head on his good arm on the table.

"Your skin will heal in time," Julianna said as she gently placed thick gauze between his fingers. "As it does, the fabric pieces from your coat and the dead skin will fall off." She began wrapping his hand, keeping it secure without binding it. "You seem to have the right idea, trying to keep it clean and elevated, but you need to make a more conscious effort. The bandages will help, but they're only as good as you are."

"I know." Tommen rubbed his eyes.

She wrapped his hand, lower arm, and upper arm separately, but from a distance, it looked like one long bandage. She finished up the wrapping and pinned the gauze.

"How does that feel?" she asked.

"I don't even feel anything anymore," he told her.

"Does it feel better, worse, what?"

"I don't know. Better? It's not exposed to air or anything, and I guess it's comfortable. As comfortable as it can be. Can't you—well, maybe you can't. But can't I just use Time to heal it? Like, not now, but in a few days once it starts healing properly on its own?"

"I wouldn't recommend it. Cuts and bruises are one thing, but this is serious damage on a much deeper level. Unless you have a really good understanding of anatomy, I would just tell you to let it be. Your body is having a hard time as it is. Banding your arm would only throw off an already tenuous balance."

She had a point, he supposed. Even his dad only Pinpoint Banded in stages when it came to things like broken bones and busted knees. Part of it was to stave off suspicion of such a miracle healing, but the other part was to give his body a chance to rest and recover and figure out what the hell was going on. One minute it's calling in all the troops to get things repair, the next thing it knows, it's already done the repair work before the workers got there. Why shouldn't it be a similar story for him? And if his body really was pulling blood from his intestines and everywhere else, plus the fluid buildup, he could easily die from blood loss or something, he was sure.

"All right, now that that's taken care of, take off your shirt if you can," Julianna ordered.

He was able to, partly. It was probably just dumb luck that the melting had stopped around the zipper of his coat, which made snipping the rest of the fabric easier.

Not that he was an expert, but it appeared that the second-degree burn extended most of the way down his side under his arm, over his shoulder, partway across his chest, and partway up his neck. His ear and side of his face, as well as the rest of his chest was all first-degree. Red, painful, worse than a sunburn so there might be some scarring, but not as terrible as the rest. Julianna taped some gauze around his shoulder and under his arm to protect the second-degree burns there, then grabbed a cotton T-shirt that had been tossed in the backseat of Laura's pickup.

"The bandages will have to be changed daily for the first week or so," she said finally. "They're going to soak up a lot of fluid and, hopefully, a lot of the infection." She handed him a hypothermic blanket. "Here, put this around you; you're shaking like a leaf."

Back to the fever and chills then, Tommen mused as he wrapped the blanket around his shoulders. Well, that was probably the infection kicking in. He looked at her as she peeled off her gloves and tossed them away. No garbage cans or penalties for littering, then.

"What do we do now?" he asked.

"We?" She looked at him. "What is this 'we' you speak of?"

"I don't know. I mean, I'm new here. I don't understand the rules. Fine, what do I do now?"

"Anything you want. You can go anywhere, do anything you couldn't do before. You could walk right into the Oval Office or Buckingham Palace or the Kremlin, listen in on top-secret government meetings. You can visit any country in the world without worrying about passports, customs, or, really, anything at all. You can see all the sights, experience all the festivities and goings-on without needing to plan or pay for anything. If you figure out a few sneaky little tricks, you can go haunt an old house or an old enemy from school."

"Are there any rules, though? Like, can I fly or walk on the moon, breathe in space, things like that?"

"The only rules that I know of are these: One, portals don't work here. We're stuck between dimensions. It's like balancing the power switch between on and off; not enough power to quite do either or. So, basically, you are stuck here on Earth. Unless you did traveling the old-fashioned way and hitched a ride on the space shuttle. But I digress. And the second rule, Time abilities do not work here. In this dimension...this is Time. You are living in it. You do not control it. There are no Fast or Slow Bands. There is no Predict. There is no Harvesting. Time controls you."

"In Soviet Russia, right?"

Julianna's expression turned confused, but she brushed it off quickly, saying, "But, if you want, I'll show you one my tricks. It's a simple thing to make getting from here to there easier."

"Here to where?"

"Anywhere. It can turn a day of walking into a couple hours. If you're interested. At first, I mean, you probably want to go anywhere and everywhere. See the sights and so on, so—"

"Could I die here?" Tommen interrupted.

"Well, we're generally unaffected by things like cars and falling trees—"

"Could I die of old age? I'm barely an Apprentice, so it's not like I have a century left in me plus my natural lifespan."

Julianna was silent for a moment before saying quietly, "I don't know. Honestly, I don't talk to anyone that often or keep company for very long. But seeing how Time abilities don't work here to keep you young, it...is feasible, I suppose." She frowned. "I guess I've never really thought about it."

Tommen glanced at his dad and Laura. Micah and Kayla had returned, and the four of them stood around talking. It appeared to be moderately light-hearted, certainly not a huge dark cloud of doom and gloom, but Tommen could see the strain on his dad's face. He wanted to be out searching. More than that, he was probably torn over Laura's presence. On the one hand, he was probably grateful for her presence and support. On the other hand, had she not been there, they could be doing an investigation on their own. Strictly speaking, they still could, if they just Banded, but there was no telling what the search would entail. How strange it would look if the three of them were suddenly there, and then suddenly not there. Poor Laura.

"If everything you've just told me is true, then my dad is going to outlive me," he said.

"Just another reason not to tell him where you are," she said quietly.

The sky had cleared up to nothing more than wispy clouds and a lot of sunshine. It was early afternoon. One of the search teams still had not returned, but lunch was being set out for the other five. Walter and the others moved to get in line.

Is this what it was like to go dark? To turn your back on everyone you knew, who knew you, to plunge into the murky waters of anonymity? To create a whole new life and treat everyone as a stranger? After a moment, Tommen decided that no, this was much worse. At least in going dark, his dad and the twins still had a chance to meet up from time to time through the Wheel or the Akarin or whatever. They had the ability to keep tabs on each other and see what they were up to, like social media for Time Agents or whoever. Tommen couldn't even do that. He had no ability to communicate, and as far as anyone was concerned, he was gone. Disappeared. Burned alive or wandered off to be torn apart by wild animals. Who could know?

"It's hard," Julianna said. "But they're going to be here for a few days yet, I'm thinking. Why don't I show you a few things about moving around in this dimension? It will take your mind off it for a while. Then, if you still want to, you can come back and do whatever you want, like I said before."

He didn't want to. He didn't want to leave. It felt like giving up, like reading his own obituary and actually believing that he had died. He wanted to stay and help with the search somehow, as if he might be able to rig some tripwire that would alert them to his presence. Was there any way to do that? But then, if there was no way to escape, even if he could communicate, was it worth it?

Chapter Five
Two Panes of Glass

For reasons that I never figured out in the real world or in this dimension, you Timekeepers like to name things. Scouts call their work Scouting. We Harvesters call our work Harvesting. But you Timekeepers...you have to name all your fancy little tricks. Banding, Predict, Internal, External, I don't know. I never cared to learn all the nuances." Julianna shrugged casually. "So while I simply refer to this particular trick as Walking, because that really is all you're doing, some of the Timekeepers here have taken to calling it Traveling or Condensing, depending on who you ask. There's nothing particularly special about it; it simply shortens the time it takes to travel from one place to another. For example. Take my hand."

Tommen did so, unsure what to expect. She started walking, and he followed. They headed south, down the mountain. Suddenly they were at the bottom of the mountain. Then he blinked and they were somewhere on the highway. Hardly a minute later, they were standing on a hillside overlooking Charleston. He took a step away from her, releasing her hand.

"How did you do that?"

She raised a brow. "I simply thought of where I wanted to go, and I Walked there."

"But, I mean, did you condense the time, the distance, how did that happen?"

"Some speculate that it could be a residual Time effect, a shadow of your Banding that makes a long time seem like a short time."

"A Slow Band," Tommen mused.

"If you say so. It's only a theory. Frankly, it doesn't matter, and I don't care. I just know that it makes traveling a lot easier."

She held out her hand and he took it again. In a matter of two minutes, they'd made the two-hour journey back to the camp where everything was basically exactly as it had been. Lunch was being served to the grunts while the people in charge brooded over maps and argued over this and that.

"Does that work in the real world? Like, do regular Timekeepers know about that? Can they do it out there?"

Julianna shrugged once more. "How should I know? It would certainly explain how Rifun and Cassius were able to catch up to me so quickly."

"Wait. Does Rifun know I'm here?"

"You ask these things as if you expect me to know the answers. I don't know. This is only the in-between dimension. That doesn't make you God, all knowing and all powerful and whatnot. It just makes you invisible."

Tommen grunted. There had to be a way. He wasn't about to give up just because some random woman told him to. He looked around at all the people gathered. They were here to find him. Even if the regular people gave up, he had to get a message out somehow. Maybe if he did get a message out, his dad and the twins could do some research on how to rescue him. He didn't have access to the Archives, but they would.

"I know what you're thinking," Julianna said, interrupting his thoughts. "It's not going to work. Cleverer men than you have tried."

"Yeah? Well, no one denies that the ancient world had some pretty good thinkers and inventors, but electricity and indoor plumbing are pretty recent inventions. I'm still going to try," he retorted. Was that a good analogy? Would she understand it? Maybe he needed to start paying better attention in English class. "You said the Walking or Condensing or whatever is only one ability to be found in here. What are the others?"

She studied him for a long moment. Then, without breaking

her gaze, said, "Fine. I'll show you one more that can be combined with Walking. Use those two for a while, master them if you can. Then maybe we'll talk again. But in the end, you will see that I'm right. We're stuck here, between two panes of glass."

"Even bulletproof glass can be broken." Was that a good, snappy comeback, or did it just sound lame? He couldn't decide. "What's the other ability?"

"Time travel, to an extent."

As she spoke, it was like a cloud passed over the sun. The people around them in the command post faded away. Even the parking lot and the burned buildings faded away, replaced by trees. Tommen looked around to see a young Indian hunter stalking after a flock of turkeys, his gaze fixed firmly on a nice, plump tom. He found his shot, drew back his bow string, and released. The turkey flopped around a bit, but it was a goner.

"You're not actually traveling back in time," Julianna told him. "You can't influence anything, can't change anything. If you take a few steps, you'll find that you are still on pavement. You may still trip over rocks and whatnot. This is really for observation only, to study times gone by."

Then the image faded out, and modern life returned.

"How did you do that?" Tommen asked, awed. "How do you use it with Traveling or whatever?"

"Now if I told you that, it would take all the fun and mystery out of it. Besides, it's not like you've got anywhere to be immediately. I'm sure you can figure it out on your own if you tried."

She started walking away.

"Wait, you're just going to leave me here? What if I don't master it? What if I do something stupid and end up making my situation worse?"

She looked back. "Believe me, Tommen, there is only one possible way to make your situation worse, and it takes a lot of conscious effort to do so. You can't trip into that one. As for the mastery of these abilities, well, it really doesn't take much."

"What if I need more supplies, to dress my arm and stuff?"

That one she paused to consider. Finally she nodded and returned to Laura's truck to gather a few supplies for him.

"Are you, like, actually stealing stuff from her?" Tommen wondered. "Like, will she notice that stuff is gone?"

"Am I actually taking stuff? Yes, I am. Will she notice? Maybe. Depends on how meticulous she is in her inventory." She took a large plastic zipper bag from the lunch crew and stuffed the medical supplies in it before handing it to him.

He took the bag. "Why doesn't the trap go both ways?"

"Because that's what the Author has decreed. I don't know." She took a step back. "Those supplies should last you a couple days. I expect you will have at least a basic understanding on the Walking and the time travel by then, so we might see each other again soon. Otherwise, welcome to the Land In Between. Hope you enjoy your stay because you don't have much of a choice."

He glared at her back as she walked away, but his irritation was short-lived as she began to Walk away, disappearing in the blink of an eye. So Walking was like a Double-Band, then? Fast Band to move quickly, Slow Band to make it seem fast? Well, might as well try it out for himself, he supposed.

He looked back at his dad and the teams. No go on zone two either. They would do a search of zone three this evening, then move to zone four tomorrow if they had to. If there was no luck in zone four, they had a much larger zone five area they could cover, but the farther they got from the camp, the harder it was going to be to pick up clues. If he hadn't left any clues so far, well, it didn't bode well, say it that way.

Tommen sat down and pretended to be interested in the medical supplies. It wasn't anything too complicated, really. Sterile water, gauze, gloves. He leaned back as far as he dared. If there was a way to bring things in, there had to be a way to push things out, even if it was just a little thing. A note or message of some form, like Micaiah did when he was locked up in prison in the Wheel.

He didn't have time to hope to figure things out on his own eventually. Search and Rescue teams only did intensive searches for a couple of days before giving up; the mountains were just too vast with too many unknowns. It didn't help that he hadn't left any kind of clue when he returned to the fire with Rifun. That meant that he had only a couple days to master these new abilities and get Julianna to teach him more.

So, where did he want to go? Just because he was determined to master these abilities and get noticed and get help didn't mean there weren't places he didn't want to visit. If he could really condense a few days into a few hours and go wherever he wanted, he might as well do a little traveling while he was out and about.

Maybe he would head home first, just to pick an easy place to start. He turned in roughly the direction of home, starting out and trying to will himself to go faster. He tried to think of the Bands he might normally use, the Fast Band, the Slow Band, tying it all together and willing himself forward toward home. The good news was that there were a couple hundred miles between the camp and home, so he didn't need an immediate start. But any start would have been helpful. By the time he got halfway down the mountain, he wasn't sure he had any will left.

Maybe Julianna had been bullshitting him. Maybe it really was as simple as a Double Band. A Fast Band to condense the Time down, a Slow Band to make him perceive only a few seconds. And yet, no matter how hard he tried, he couldn't conjure up any Time Bands. He knew how to do it, and it didn't feel like he'd been hit with any kind of Suppression, he was just simply being told no. It was a strange feeling, actually.

Okay, so if Time didn't work, what about the Akari? Could he Band with that? His abilities there weren't quite as tight, but he had a pretty good idea of how to do it. Although, it would be his first time creating an Akari Band out of the blue; with Rifun, he'd always taken a Time Band and shaved it down. Now he was going to —

Suddenly, he was on the outskirts of Charleston, exactly where he wanted to go, and with almost no time and effort at all. Now how had he done that exactly?

He looked around, tried to get his bearings. He was on the outskirts around the northwestern corner, if it could be called that. He turned east and though about the bakery. Micah was out searching, which meant Micaiah had to be at the shop. Tommen tried to will himself to the bakery, but he still ended up walking three-quarters of the way anyway before the Condensing kicked in. There had to be an easier way to switch it on and off.

Jenna and Kyle were both working, Kyle in front, Jenna in the back. Micaiah was in the office meeting with an official-looking man in a dark suit. A lawyer?

Go anywhere and do anything, Tommen heard Julianna say. Sit in on high-profile meetings, travel anywhere without having to worry about anything. What would you do?

So he entered the office, unhindered and unnoticed. To his dismay, the meeting appeared to be just wrapping up.

"Give me a call when you and your brother decide what you are going to do," the lawyer was saying. "You have my card, and all the information and the forms will be in the folders I gave you. If you want this done before the end of the year, I would suggest getting it in as soon as possible, certainly no later than Thanksgiving."

"I don't think it will take us quite that long," Micaiah told him. "I would be more surprised if we didn't have it back by Halloween."

"Of course. You seem to have thought this out some already, which is good."

There was some more banal small talk before the lawyer finally left, grabbing a cup of coffee on his way out. Micaiah went through the folders for what seemed to be the billionth time. Tommen glanced over his shoulder. They appeared to be transfer of ownership papers, not that he was any expert. This was probably the paperwork for Micaiah to transfer his half of the business over to Micah and give him total control over the bakery. Although, looking at it, Micaiah seemed to hold a sixty-forty stake in the business rather than a fifty-fifty. Huh.

Well, details anyway, not that they mattered.

"Come on, Micaiah, turn around and say you see me," Tommen said. "Time doesn't seem to work, but what about the Akari? You're the most well-versed out of all of us. Tell me you see me. Or can at least hear me. Help me out here!"

But he got nothing. Micaiah pushed the folders aside and returned to his computer. Then he thought better of it and put the folders in his pack which he carried when he rode his motorcycle. When he returned to his computer, Tommen was standing right in front of him. But Micaiah obliviously reached through him to continue his work.

"Cai, please tell me you can see me or hear me or at least feel me as happy thoughts in the back of your mind. Don't leave me hanging, because you are my best source for — Hey!"

Micaiah printed something off, grabbed it from the printer, then left the office. It was some kind of special sales flyer. He paused long enough to inform Kyle and Jenna of the promotion, then taped it up on the window. Tommen followed closely, yelling the whole time but getting no response. And Micaiah was not known for his patience or his subtlety. If he could hear Tommen, there was no way he would have put up with it for so long without making some comment.

He returned to the office, but Tommen did not go with him. He stayed out in the dining room and looked around. Was there some way he could manipulate something to get someone's attention? He headed over to the community bulletin board. Mostly it was a bunch of business cards, but here and there were advertisements for fundraisers for various groups, sales at local stores, and so on.

He focused on one of the thumb tacks pinning a stack of business cards. Maybe if he could will it into the in-between dimension and cause the cards to fall, create enough mischief, then Micaiah would have to come and investigate. Maybe passive appearance was out of the question, but active searching might yield something.

But he neither grabbed the thumb tack, nor attracted anyone's attention. After probably half a hundred fruitless attempts, he left the store, willing himself back to the camp but getting nowhere until he finally tapped into the Akari Bands, or what he supposed were the Akari Bands. It could have been something entirely different; he didn't know. The most instruction he'd had in the Akari came from a mass murderer; who knew what kind of weird things he was shoving down his throat?

Well, the basics of Traveling he was beginning to understand, and he was sure to refine them. But what if he wanted to travel elsewhere? He turned east again and started walking. He headed for a land unknown, only spoken of in distant stories, separated by time, space, and a pretty large expanse of water.

He started Traveling before he knew quite what was going on, and the sheer distance meant that he had time to process his Traveling. He was doing great, or so he thought, until he hit water. He wasn't sure if he'd been swimming or if he was drowning or what as the water seemed to be moving through him and yet moving in him at the same time, drowning him and yet not drowning him, the pressure crushing him and yet completely invisible at the same time.

Panic rose in him and he turned around, hoping he was facing the right direction. He pulled at everything he'd been doing so far, hoping to invoke Travel again.

Then he was pulling himself onto a sandy beach, coughing and sputtering, yet completely dry. Fucking hell. Of all the stupid ideas he'd had so far today, that had to be one of them. *Yeah, sure, cross an ocean while you're neither solid nor perfectly invisible. Drown but don't drown. Then you'll never be able to get a message to your dad and all of this will be for naught.*

He got his legs around in front of him and he sat there in the sand. He had no idea where he was, but he figured that it wouldn't take a lot of effort to find out, if he cared to. For a few minutes, though, he was just going to relax and try to calm his wounded pride.

Once he did that, it was hardly five hundred feet to the nearest sign. Myrtle Beach. Well, there were worse places to be than South Carolina, he figured.

He looked out over the ocean. So much water. So vast. With no end in sight. Was this how the flatlanders from Kansas and Nebraska felt when they visited West Virginia and saw its mountains? So huge. So sprawling. With no end in sight. Just up and down forever. He'd always found it rather amusing. Now he thought he might understand how they felt.

He might have turned away and told himself it wasn't important, except it was important. For one, figuring out how to cross oceans would be a pretty impressive feat and might constitute mastery of the Traveling ability. For two, now that he'd had his ass kicked by it, he wanted revenge. And for three, he wanted to check out this whole time traveling thing, but not just anywhere. He wanted to do some research of his own.

Had Tommen been solid and in the real world, he would have paced a pretty good line in the sand, trying to figure out how to cross the ocean. He looked at his bandaged arm. It was still dry, which was weird, but he wasn't going to question it. It had hurt like a mother when he crawled out of the water, but it was dry. Furthermore, his hearing aids were dry, as was the charger and his phone. He hadn't gotten wet in the least. But he'd still been coughing up water, or his body had thought it was. Could it have all been psychological? No, couldn't have been, not entirely. He'd definitely spit up water, and he remembered washing off his arm when he fell on it walking up the hill. How did this work?

Maybe he should start with something a little smaller than an ocean. A lake would suffice, or even a swimming pool. The latter he found at a nearby hotel, but it was difficult to tell the effects of the Traveling when, by the time he stopped, he ended up an unknown distance away. How did he control this thing? How did he set a start and stop point so he didn't overshoot his destination or come up short and drown in the ocean?

Maybe it was just a matter of will. If the Akari was a living thing, tapping into some hidden power of the universe or something, maybe he just had to tell it where he wanted to go. Sounded dumb, but he wasn't about to discount anything yet.

But then, where to go? Eventually he just picked a direction, hesitated a moment, then said aloud, "Take me to the nearest lake."

He started walking, becoming more accustomed to the feel of the Traveling and trying to tap into it. A few steps in, it was like everything began to blur as he made the jump to hyperspace. Then it was over, and he looked out over a small forest lake. That had actually worked? Just, ask and ye shall receive? Or was it all psychological? He thought it made a difference, when it was more of a placebo effect. Well, only one way to find out.

"Okay..." He stared out over the lake. "Let's try this again. Take me to the other side of the lake."

He started walking. Suddenly, he was on the other side of the lake. He didn't remember walking on the water or across the lake bed. He didn't remember walking around the lake. But somehow, he made it to the other side.

How did that happen? Maybe he needed to find a lake that was a little bigger, something that couldn't be easily explained away. Well, the biggest lakes he knew of in North America were the Great Lakes; might as well try them first. He had no clue where he was presently, but, hey, ask and ye shall receive, right?

The basic Traveling over land he thought he was mastering pretty well, though he couldn't say where he'd ended up, or even if the lake he was looking at was one of the Great Lakes. He didn't see any signs saying, "Canada, That Way" or anything. But at the same time, he couldn't see the other side, which was what he wanted. Now it was time to put his money where his mouth was and cross the lake without drowning.

He sighed. "Round two. Let's see what the Akari can do. Get me across this lake."

His heart pounding in his chest, he started walking. Before he knew it, he was Traveling. His first sensation was that he was out on open water, and then he was on solid ground. He still didn't see any "Welcome to Canada" signs, but he'd made it across. He found a large boulder and crawled on top to sit on it and look out over the water.

He was in way over his head. He'd thought the Akari was just a different flavor of Time. Now he was seeing that it was so much more. There was easily ten times more power to be had. It was exhilarating and terrifying at the same time, the powers of the gods and the universe at his fingertips. And he'd thought a few new magic tricks was going to help him beat Rifun.

"Okay, back across the lake," he said, walking, and then Traveling. He paused at the far side of the lake only briefly before continuing Traveling. He knew where he wanted to go, and he was determined to get there in one shot. He didn't want to stop at the shoreline or any of that, just go straight through. He knew that if he made a stop beforehand, he'd never make it across. He couldn't say why the ocean intimidated him so much; it was only water. Lots and lots of it. With salt. And sharks.

For all his bravado, with the vastness of the ocean, he did perceive it in his Traveling. He saw it for a good ten minutes to a half hour as he crossed the open ocean. He still wasn't sure how he did it. He wasn't exactly walking on the waves doing a Jesus trick, but he wasn't swimming or walking on the sea bed either. It was like he was...part of the water? Maybe like it carried him? Or maybe it was the Akari carrying him like a life boat. He couldn't decide. He only knew that when he finally touched solid land, he dropped to his knees and could have cried if he thought it wouldn't make it look like a dolt from Hollywood. If he hadn't been stranded at sea for a month with no food, water or human contact, he wasn't going to pull that stunt.

He stood and looked around. Somehow, he couldn't quite wrap his mind around the fact that he'd literally just crossed the open ocean. More than that, he'd done it in no more than an hour. He hadn't packed a bag, hadn't boarded a plane, hadn't had to go through customs or any of that. One minute he'd been in Canada, and now he was...well, he didn't know where he was really, just on the far side of the Atlantic Ocean somewhere. Holy shit.

"Maybe there is an Author."

The words were out before he could call them back. It was a strange thing to consider, that maybe there was someone out there who could have simply written, "And then he lost concentration, tumbled beneath the waves, and drowned." But instead, there was a happy ending to his jaunt across the ocean. Of course, that remained to be seen, whether the ending was happy, but he'd made it to solid ground, anyway, and no hole had opened up to swallow him, either.

Did that make him agnostic, then? Did that mean he had to give up his staunch atheism? Well, maybe as far as the Great Big Something went, but he wasn't entirely convinced on the rest of it. As for the Author? Did that make God the Author, or the Author, God, or was that separate? Were there levels to this deism, or how did that all work? The more he thought about it, the more it started to sound like some New Age bullshit, the same kind Rifun was spouting at the camp. Okay. Great Big Something, check. The rest of it? Up for debate at least.

Tommen moved forward, unsure of where he wanted to go or how to figure out where he was. Well, it wasn't hard. At the top of the rise was a road. He just followed the road to the nearest town. That nearest town just so happened to be London. And ho — ly — shit. Was it ever big. Charleston had a city population of roughly sixty thousand, with a metro population of about five hundred thousand, and that was a pretty wide area, all things considering. To think that London had a population of one million was unfathomable.

Tommen was almost ready to move on, when he stopped to consider his location. Then all he needed was to figure out this time travel business. Was that another case of ask and ye shall receive? Why did he have to ask? At least Time he could manipulate at will. He couldn't see the Akari, didn't understand it, so why did he have to ask permission?

One million people, he thought, looking around. All of them moving to and fro, walking, biking, driving, riding the huge double-decker buses he'd only ever seen in movies. Imagine it a hundred and fifty years ago, people walking around, riding in carriages. Rich men dressed in proper top hats, ladies in pretty dresses.

As he thought it, modern London began to melt away, enormous skyscrapers replaced by modestly tall yet immodestly decorated stone buildings, pavement replaced by cobblestone, cars replaced by carriages. But the one thing he did notice was that the people didn't change, not really. The rich still strutted while the beggars still begged. Young women, and even old women still huddled together in groups, gossiping secretively while young men had their nineteenth century dick-measuring contests, just by a different name.

Tommen was almost afraid to move, as if by moving, the mirage would suddenly vanish. But it did not. And he walked harmlessly down the street.

He kept an ear out, acutely aware that his hearing aids could go out at any time. Then he heard it. He turned. There, a group of women in their late forties or early fifties, all of them looking very well to do.

"So, Elizabeth has a granddaughter now, you say?" one of the women was saying.

Another woman, looking to be the leader of this gossip ring, nodded. "That's what I said. Her daughter Paige just had the little babe three days ago. Victoria is her name."

"Well, a proper British name and a proper British family ought to do her some good," a third woman sniffed. "At least it might make up for her unfortunate parentage."

"Well, there is that. Elizabeth is saving her that embarrassment. She is to be known as the granddaughter of Mr. Balk. The only saving grace for Paige is that she is wed, though her choice of husband really could have been better."

"He can't be all bad," a fourth woman, this one seeming to be in her mid-thirties, said. "As long as he can look the part and knows enough to do what his wife and father-in-law tell him to do, he might just survive."

"He's a drunk," the first woman shot back.

"And so is your husband. You still run the household. Same

with her."

Tommen listened through probably fifteen more minutes of gossip and prattle before finally getting general directions as to where he might find the new child, her proud mother, and embarrassment of a father. Even then, it still took a good hour and a half to actually find the house. Nineteenth century London was smaller, but not by much, and its roads were just as twisted and confusing.

The house he found was beautiful, certainly befitting a wealthy British banker and his family. Tommen let himself in, past the butler, and roaming the corridors until he spotted a man who, at first, was unfamiliar. When he realized who it was, his jaw almost hit the floor.

Walter could generally get away with being in his mid-forties to his mid-fifties. He wasn't young, but he wasn't old, as much as he seemed to feel like it. And he went through what Tommen considered to be the normal cycles of gaining and losing weight. All of this did him many favors, actually, seeing as he could settle down in places longer than some Time Agents.

This man, however, was not only trim, but he was young. Tall and handsome, young Walter looked the epitome of power and success in London. His hair was styled, mustache as bushy as ever, but with snobbish style and elegance. The mustache was the only way Tommen even thought to give him a second look. The brown hair, blond mustache, and blue eyes settled his identity.

"Holy fuck," Tommen said, finding a chair and trying to sit down in an astonished heap, only to discover that the chair was an illusion, and he went to the floor in an astonished heap instead.

This was his dad as a very wealthy, very powerful young man. He stood over a cradle. After a minute, Tommen went over and peered in.

Well, she had a British name, but little Victoria was all Walter. High forehead, long nose, bright blue eyes, brown hair. Three days old and she was already her father's child. Maybe that was the reason for all the scorn. The upper crust could dress her up all they wanted, but she would always remind them of her father, a Welsh barbarian whom they despised.

"Walter!" a female voice hissed.

Both Walter and Tommen looked up to see a gorgeous young woman enter the room. At one time she may have been perfectly slender, but pregnancy and childbirth had done her no favors, and a tiny head sat on a too big body. Her jaw jutted forward and her nose was hooked beneath her beady little brown eyes which burned with rage and concern. Tommen could only conclude that this was Paige.

"Don't wake her up," she said, crossing the room as fast as she could. She sighed when she saw Victoria looking up at them and smiling, bubbles forming between little pink lips. "I just got her to sleep."

"I didn't wake her up," Walter told her. He kept his volume low, but the edge in his voice was enough to pop a balloon across the room. "I was just looking. She's mine, too, you know."

"I never forget," Paige growled. She rolled her eyes. "My father wants you. Go now. I'll have to get her back to sleep."

Tommen followed his dad out of the room, completely baffled by the exchange. That had been pure, unadulterated hostility. That had been the smoldering anger his dad talked about; the only thing he needed to set it off was a drink. Sometimes not even that.

When he exited the room, the time travel thing changed. He wasn't sure whether he went forward or back; he guessed forward since Paige still looked a little heavy with the post-childbirth weight. He wasn't even sure what she and his dad were arguing about; he just remembered being stunned when his dad hit her. It wasn't just a little push, it wasn't a finger in the face. It was an outright shove to the chest and a slap to the face. Looking at him, Tommen didn't even think his dad was drunk.

Almost out of sheer terror, he left the room, as if afraid the ghosts might spot him and come after him, too. He ended up in what looked like some kind of formal dining room. Six men sat around a large table. Tommen didn't recognize any of them, not that he expected to. They all wore the fine smoking jackets expected of wealthy men, with the cigars and fine brandy to match.

"So, we're just going to wrap this up very quickly," the man at the head of the table—whom Tommen could probably safely guess was Mr. Balk—said, tapping his cigar ash into an ashtray that probably cost more than Tommen's shoes. "The magistrate will hear only that Paige's dreadful former lover attempted to break in and rape her. He killed the child. You attempted to intervene. You chased him off, but in the struggle, Paige perished. I expect—"

He was cut off as the door opened and Walter walked in. No longer was he the fine young man of wealth and fortune. Rather, he was the street beggar, the man who'd had and squandered all. He was dirty, smelly, and all of his hair had grown out, from his head to his beard. But there was no mistaking the deep-set eyes and bushy mustache. And the strength in his arms. And the rage.

"My God, how did you get in here?" Mr. Balk said, visibly recoiling. "Brigsby! Remove this man! Leave now, murderer, or I will have the constable on you, and there will be nowhere in the civilized world you can run where I won't—"

Walter said nothing as, quick as a snake, he brandished a knife and ran it through Mr. Balk's throat. The wealthy man spit blood in Walter's face, then went down. The other men began to panic, but Walter was not only strong, he was fast. He caught another man by the collar and smashed his face into the table before cutting his throat. One man tried to go after him with his own knife, but Walter simply grabbed his arm, manipulated him to turn him around and stab another man in the chest before killing the knife-wielder. Of the two men left, one was cowering in a corner. Walter kicked him onto his back and cut his throat. Then he turned his eyes on the last man, the man who had killed Paige and Victoria.

Walter said nothing as he walked up to the man and plunged his knife deep into the man's chest. Then he removed it and cut the man's throat.

When all was said and done, Walter simply took one of the pristine white cloths and wiped his face. Then he grabbed the bottle of brandy, poured himself a glass, and sat down to drink.

Tommen slowly backed out of the room. He had little doubt that his dad was sometimes forced to shoot someone. Maybe the criminal was attacking him or someone else, maybe it was a hostage situation. But all this time, even after his dad had confessed to his former life and the things he'd done, Tommen never could have appreciated exactly what that previous life had been. If it had been difficult to reconcile the two different men before, it was even harder now.

He'd watched his dad as a young man, wealthy and rich, with a beautiful—well, homely anyway—wife and newborn daughter who looked just like him. He'd watched his dad hit his wife. He'd watched him murder six men in cold blood, stone cold sober. And he'd never shed a tear or questioned himself, just helped himself to the brandy.

Just earlier that morning, Tommen had watched his dad flirt and banter playfully with his girlfriend, with no harsh words, angry undertones or subtext, and certainly no violence. He'd watched him get emotional when trying to describe Tommen's disappearance and tell about what a great kid and great outdoorsman he was, how he would survive. If there had been any anger involved, it would probably be only at himself, maybe Rifun with his suspected involvement.

These were two different men. Tommen watched as he lost his grip on the time travel. The illusion faded and busy streets and modern life took over, people walking, talking on cell phones, having coffee.

He faced west. Before he knew what was happening, he was Traveling. More than that, he was time traveling, until he stood at the entrance of a very large, very imposing prison-like building. Well, of course it looked like a prison. It was a prison. Beaumaris Gaol. Where his dad had been locked up for a year and a half.

Tommen took three steps inside, then turned and ran. He'd seen the sights and heard the wails. Those he expected. They still scared the shit out of him, but they were expected. The thing that really got to him was the smells. It was death and rot and raw sewage. It was despair and suicide and unforgivable repentance. It was a living graveyard.

Now Tommen understood his dad's fear of the dark. He understood the nightmares that plagued him, that made him toss and turn at night, that haunted his nights and made him come awake like a raging grizzly, desperate to be free of his demons. He understood why his dad had been so terrified of going to the black cells of the Wheel. Tommen hadn't even gone in any of the cells, but he hadn't needed to. He understood. He knew he could never fully understand the whole experience, staying in that hellhole for eighteen months, but he figured he had a pretty good idea.

He also resolved to never speak of these things to his dad. In the event that he did find a way to escape this in-between dimension, he would never tell his dad of what he had seen. He might be a little more empathetic, a little more understanding, a little more patient, but he would never tell his dad that he had gone back in time and seen what he had.

As he walked away from the prison, a group of people were walking up the path. Tourists by the looks of them. Tommen turned around to see the time travel had faded and it was present day. Beaumaris Gaol had been turned into a museum, open to the public with tours and a little gift shop. At one time, he might have considered following them. Now, though, he was rooted to the ground. He couldn't go in there, not now, knowing what he knew.

He continued down the path, shoving one hand in a pocket, minding his left arm as much as he could. Had all of that really happened? There were no words to describe what Tommen was feeling, the disparity as he tried to tell himself both that his dad had once been that man, and that he wasn't that man. There was no reconciling it. He had no idea what to do with it. He paused and looked back up at the old prison. When he turned to continue, he startled as he saw Julianna blocking his path.

"Shit, don't scare me like that," Tommen said, putting a hand to his chest to calm his racing heart, as if it would do any good.

"It's hard, isn't it?" she said. "To watch and see the way things were, how different they are from the things you knew."

"I don't know what you mean."

She ignored his comment. "I saw your dad once, you know. In passing. I was on my way into the prison to deliver my husband's journal to Cassius. Your dad had faked his death and was being carted out. I didn't know it was him until I got stuck here and could review my life, see where I had gone and what I had done wrong."

"Fascinating bit of information. What does that have to do with you sneaking up on me?"

Now she grew serious. "I know why you're doing this, and don't tell me it has to do with a history lesson."

"I admit, I was curious."

"I don't doubt that, but it's not why you came here in the first place. You came here because you thought that crossing an ocean might prove your mastery of these abilities and that I would teach you more. You think that if you just learn enough, something amazing will come to your modern, invincible, teenage mind, and you might be able to break out of this dimension. Sorry to say, but you are very easy to predict. And also unoriginal. Do you know how many times people have tried to break out of here?"

"Do you know how many times Einstein failed to invent the light bulb?"

"Ten thousand and one, I'm sure. But sheer determination and mind-over-matter philosophies will not give men the ability to read minds or use telekinetic abilities. Positive thinking has never stopped the executioner's blade from swinging. Willing something to be true does not make it so. A child who innocently yet sincerely believes that he is a kangaroo will not miraculously grow a tail and a pouch."

"Maybe, but that doesn't mean that it can't happen, or that I won't be the one to accomplish this breakout. After all, men can't breathe underwater or in space, and yet we go there with the help of equipment. So it might not be mind-over-matter, only the sheer determination to build something to bust out first and drag me along with it."

He could feel her scrutiny as she studied him. If he had to guess, she almost seemed afraid of something. Was Rifun able to get to her even here? He couldn't see how, but that didn't mean there wasn't a way. Rifun could do some pretty scary shit.

"Fine," she said at last. "So, we're here. I can't stop you and you won't take no for an answer."

"What do you expect from me?" Tommen wondered. "That I'm just going to roll over and play dead because someone tells me to? No. I'm going to fight as long as I can. Since I seem to have a lot of time on my hands suddenly, well, that's a lot of time to fight for my freedom."

"Do you think this is prison?"

"Two panes of glass, like you said. Yeah, I can go anywhere, do anything, blah, blah, blah. But I can't talk to my dad or my friends or my girlfriend. I won't have any friends here if what you said is true and there aren't many people around here. If I can't fight to free myself, if I give up, I might as well save everyone the trouble and kill myself right now."

The severity of his words hit him suddenly and drove the breath from his lungs. What if she was right? What if there really was no way out? What if he would never be able to talk to his dad or anyone else ever again? What would be the point of living after that? It wasn't like this limbo dimension was a hopping place where he could make friends and start a new life; it was almost conspicuously empty, devoid of life. Maybe such was the fate of anyone who stayed too long, cut off from civilization, like being stranded on a desert island with only a coconut named Charlie for company.

Finally, Julianna nodded. "All right. Fine. Like I said, I can't stop you. The only way you're going to learn is to learn."

"So will you teach me?" Tommen asked, hoping he sounded polite and curious, and not totally desperate.

"I will teach you. But on one condition. If you find a way out, then take me with you."

"Deal. And, honestly, I think—what?"

"What's wrong?"

Tommen carefully removed his hearing aids. He flicked them on and off, but it was no use. He sighed and stuffed them in a pocket. "They're dead. Shit."

Julianna shook her head. "That's nothing. Maybe that's what I'll teach you next."

"Teach me what?"

"Just like slipping small items through the dimensions, there is a way to siphon electricity, too, if need be. It won't be a lot, but it'll get your hearing aids charged and ready."

"My phone, too?"

She shrugged. "I suppose, if you really want. There's no wi-fi in this dimension, as you might imagine."

"The games might prove useful entertainment."

"Your time, your problem. I assume your plug-ins are all American standard plug-ins, right? Yes, that's what I thought. Well, I'll meet you on the other side of the pond, then, I suppose. I'll show you how to charge your hearing aids—and your phone—and then I'll show you a few more things about this dimension."

"Wait, are you going to take me with you or what?"

"No. I want you to Walk over on your own."

"Where are we going to meet?"

But she was already gone, walking away down the hill, then Walking away, gone in less than a minute. As she walked, he could almost see what looked like the wake of a Band. Maybe it was similar to a wake. Either way, Tommen stepped into it and started walking. Then he, too, was Traveling.

Getting out of a Traveling Band, or whatever it could be called, was less like having the air sucked from his lungs, as in a Time Band, and more like tripping over a rock or a tree root. He landed hard on the ground, less than a foot from Julianna. She merely regarded him as he stood and brushed himself off.

"So, where are we?" he asked, looking around and trying to be casual about the whole thing.

"Some small town in Virginia, I believe. It's not important. Come on, let's get your ears back on you."

He followed her down the road about half a mile before coming to their first house. She explained things as they walked inside, completely unhindered.

"If you can plug it in, you can steal the electricity. The neat things about the dimensions is that the boundaries are almost exclusively in the realm of Energy. Well, what is electricity but Energy? The two play nice with each other, and the transfer is almost seamless. It takes longer to charge because of the barrier, and I don't know how long you intend to wait, but having some is better than having none, I figure. Go ahead and try it out."

They were in the kitchen of the house, everything quiet as the occupants were still at school or work or wherever. Tommen dug out his hearing aid charger and plugged it in. The light flickered a bit, but when he inserted his hearing aids, they began charging. Then he dug out his phone and its charger from another pocket in his ripped jacket and plugged that in, too. Like she said, it took a lot longer and seemed a bit sketchy at times, but otherwise, it did exactly what it was supposed to.

"So there you have it," Julianna said once his hearing aids were charged. Normally it only took about two to three hours, but with the discrepancy or whatever, it had taken five and a half, made bearable only by some special Condensing, which Tommen was becoming convinced was like some sort of Time. His phone was only seventy percent charged, or so it said. She stretched. "It takes a little longer, like I said, but there it is. Hearing aids and phone."

"Sweet." He slipped his hearing aids back in place. "Oh my gosh, I can hear again. Thank you."

"Oh, don't thank me just yet. We still have a lot of work to do."

"Okay. I'll catch up in a minute. I want to see if I can't get my phone to charge a little more."

She shrugged and headed outside. As soon as she was gone, Tommen turned on his phone. She was a liar. A bad one. Time may not work in the in-between dimension, but there was something else here. The Akari, something else, he didn't know, but he was determined to use it and find a way out of here. And if Energy was the connection between the two dimensions, then maybe he could use it to his advantage.

His phone turned on, everything exactly where it should be. The little icons across the top told him he had no cell or wi-fi signal. At the same time, as the son of a cop, he knew a few things, like how to tap into dispatch. All it took were three magic numbers.

Chapter Six
Signal

Zone two came up empty. Walter expected as much, but he still held out a little hope that Tommen might be found. He didn't know what to expect anymore, actually. Hope was a fickle thing. It might be hard to kill, but it seemed to have a mind of its own as it wandered here and there, in and out of his soul.

He was grateful for Laura coming out and doing what she could to help, and he told her as much. The search and rescue command post was thrilled to have a paramedic with them, especially when she brought all her own supplies. Micah and Kayla, well, all hands were good hands, but Laura was definitely the preferred company.

Lunch was meant to be quick, but it didn't turn out that way. It had been cold and rainy that morning, which put the rescuers in bad spirits, even more so when their intended target was still missing, but blue skies and warmer temperatures were very welcome. While chowing down on sandwiches, hot dogs, and pasta salad, the men and women chatted amiably about anything but the task at hand. Walter didn't blame them, really. For as hyperfocused as he was, he knew that not all conversation had to be business, not if they wanted to keep searching effectively and keep from killing each other.

Still, it was hard to engage in such light-hearted conversation, talking about work or the weather or anything else. Walter figured he must have done some conversing because no one gave him any funny looks or avoided him like he might be diseased.

Then, if that wasn't enough of a delay, there were always the technical difficulties as the commanders tried to figure out how to proceed. Walter had assumed that they already had everything planned out. In actuality, they'd had everything planned out inasmuch as they had expected to have already found Tommen. They'd had basic ideas and plans of plans for zones three and four, but hadn't quite gotten them perfected yet.

In a way, it angered Walter. Somehow it felt as though they had given up or were going at it half-ass, putting on a show so it looked like they were searching when they fully intended to pack up and leave, go home to a good dinner, and not think about it anymore. At the same time, he knew he was just being paranoid. Like father, like son, he supposed, just like everything else. No, the men and women here would do their best to find Tommen. He knew that. Just like he knew that logistical errors and everything else were bound to pop up and delay things for a short time here and there.

Soon enough, though, they were on their way again. He and Laura were sent out with a team in one particular section, and Micah and Kayla went with another group to a different section. Everyone was connected via radio, but yelling and shouting "Eureka" worked just as well in a pinch.

Zone three encompassed the north and western sections beyond the burn zone. Section one, where Walter and Laura were searching, was the northernmost section, extending down into the valley.

"You think Tommen came this way?" Laura wondered.

"There's a good bet," Walter answered, trying to remain optimistic. "It's easier to go downhill, versus trying to climb. If he's injured, it's a lot less expended energy. Fire travels uphill easier than downhill, if he was trying to outrun it. And water, obviously, flows downhill, so he might be following the dry stream bed to try and find a river or other water source."

It was a logical assumption, and Walter half-expected to walk around the next bend and find a little campsite with roasted rabbit and a teepee.

It was not to be. The only thing he saw were more trees, more mountains, and a dry stream bed. At some point, the stream bed was supposed to make a sharp right turn to the east, and that was the cutoff point for the section and the search zone. Walter found it easily enough, electing to search north to south. And yet, he found himself standing there at the bend in the river, looking at what lay beyond. Far enough north was Pennsylvania. Far enough east was Maryland and Virginia. In two days, it was unlikely that Tommen could have gotten that far, not if he was injured. But still, it left a lot to the imagination, and that was a lot of ground to cover.

The search crews were doing everything right and proper, by the book, the same way Walter had done it a hundred times in Missing Persons. He was not part of that crew this time. His job was to try to think like Tommen and figure out where he might go. So, yes, the search crews did a proper grid search, covering every square inch of ground. Walter followed the stream bed, tried to think of where Tommen might go, what he might look for if he was trying to escape fire or maybe survive the night in the wilderness.

Were he terribly injured, disoriented, confused, all that, the grid search would find him. But with all the searching they had been doing, it was looking more and more like, even if he was injured, his bigger problem was being lost. So, time to think like Tommen. Time to think like a woodsman. He would need shelter, a safe place to go to be protected from the elements and any predators. He would need water, both for basic hydration as well as to clean any wounds he may have sustained. He would need food, for obvious reasons. He wasn't much for foraging, but he knew how to rig a few basic traps. So even if they didn't find him, finding traps might give them an indication of his general location.

Walter didn't find any of it. He found no shelters, though he found several places that would be good for shelters. He found no water, only dry beds. He found no traps or any evidence of hunting of any kind. The forest and mountains beyond the burn zone were pristine and untouched, virgin ground that God probably still considered good as long as man didn't screw it up.

Even during the height of summer, evening came early in the mountains as the sun disappeared behind the tall peaks. Walter made his way back up the hill in the semi-dark, tripping over rocks and roots and everything else, grateful that no one was around to see his blunders. He'd already passed through the net of the search crews. By now he figured they'd be on their way back.

He made it back to the command post feeling rather dejected. He was the first one back of the search crews, but the parking lot was far from empty. The commanders were still looking, plotting, planning, and bickering. A few grunts set up some scene lights while another crew started on a light dinner to ease the hunger pangs the crews would be returning with, without spoiling the dinners they would be going home to.

Walter grabbed a few of the snacks already out as well as a cup of coffee. He sat down in a heap, unsure what to make of it all. Two search zones, complete, and completely empty. A third search zone looking just as bleak. His mood wasn't helped any when he saw Laura return with the same grim expression everyone else seemed to be wearing around the place. She grabbed snacks and a coffee for herself before sitting down next to him.

"We'll find him, Walt," Laura said gently. "With as dark as it's getting, he's probably hunkered down in whatever little shelter he's built for himself."

He nodded absently and took a drink of coffee. It was a nice sentiment, and he tried to hang onto it. The funny thing was, even when Tommen had been kidnapped by Rifun, at least there had been a logical end date to that standoff. This time around, there was no time limit. They weren't waiting for demands or an ultimatum or anything of that nature. This was all out in the open, left to chance and hope.

He took another drink of coffee and looked around, his attention briefly drawn to the commanders as someone's phone went off. With the scene lights on, it was almost possible to forget that the sun was going down except for how the lights gave way long shadows beyond.

"Wait, wait, wait," the command said, his voice getting louder. "What did you say? You got it?"

Walter stood abruptly, almost spilling his plate of snacks, absently setting them on his chair as he approached the command station, Laura close behind.

"What is it?" Walter demanded.

"Hang on, Richard, let me put you on speakerphone," the commander, Harold, said. He tapped a button on his phone and set it on the table.

"This is Richard Irving, Emergency Dispatcher in Northampton County, Virginia. We received the Amber Alert for Tommen Forbes earlier this morning, which included his phone number," the man on the other end, Richard, explained, his tone suggesting he'd given this speech several times already. "When we have that information, it's set on a loop in the national database, to scan for the phone automatically every, I don't know, half an hour I think it is. Well, that loop went off about five minutes ago, and we got a hit."

"I can't say that I know where Northampton County is, Mr. Irving," Walter said, eager to jump in his car and go.

"We're on the coast. But I will tell you that the signal is very sketchy. One second it's there, the next it's gone. It almost looked like he tried to call 9-1-1 but the call can't connect. If the battery is damaged or has only a tenuous charge, that could be the problem."

"But it's definitely there?" Laura asked.

"As near as we can tell. It's a private residence, average house out in the country. We've dispatched local law enforcement to the residence and they will contact you if they find anything."

"Where is the address?"

"I'm sorry, sir, but I can't give that information out. Law enforcement will be contacting you."

Harold picked up the phone and turned off speakerphone, making nice with the dispatcher for a few minutes before hanging up and looking at Walter.

"How in the hell did your boy get from here to the east coast in two days?"

Using Time, I imagine. "I don't know, but I'm going to head over there and find out."

"Walt, at least wait for the local officers to call," Laura said, stopping him. "You don't want to drive out there for nothing."

"What do you mean for nothing? They pinged his phone."

"They pinged something. Okay, I don't know how technology works in the techie world, but I know that hackers and telemarketers are very smart and sophisticated. They could be using Tommen's number as a telemarketing scam. My daughter said that something similar happened to her."

Walter moved out of the way and paced a few times. "I can't do nothing."

"Waiting isn't always the same as doing nothing. Sit down and take a breath."

He sat, but he only stayed sitting for about two minutes before he was up and pacing again. After about five minutes, he Banded and headed off into the woods, toward section four where Micah and Kayla were searching.

They weren't far from the burn zone, heading back to camp, expressions telling the whole story. Walter brought them into the Band.

"What's up?" Micah asked. "Find him?"

"Maybe," Walter said, choosing his words carefully. "Laura's not letting me go, though."

"Why? Where is he?" Kayla wondered.

"Northampton County, Virginia. It's on the coast. Said they finally pinged his phone, but it was sketchy. Private residence is all they told me. Right now, they're waiting for the local boys to search the place and call back."

"And if Laura's got you grounded, then that means you're asking us to go in your place," Micah concluded.

"I am. I'll call you if the officers call me with any information. Otherwise, go with all caution. We don't know if Rifun is involved.

This could be another hostage situation."

It sounded ridiculous, and yet so likely. Nevertheless, Micah and Kayla agreed. Walter let them out of the Band, then returned to the command post. He was excited and terrified. Tommen was alive. How he got to Virginia was another matter, but he was alive. Even if he was injured, he had the presence of mind to at least try and call for help, regardless if his phone was busted.

Micah and Kayla could have just Banded and gone on their merry way, but they still put on a show for the others, informing command that they were leaving, then facing Walter. At least they didn't have to give him heaps of fake sympathy. They hoped things turned out well and that Tommen would be able to come home soon. Then maybe they could hear the story of how he ended up on the east coast and all have a good laugh. Walter thanked them and saw them off.

Not two minutes after they left, Walter's phone rang. The area code was from Virginia.

"Walter Forbes," he answered formally.

"Captain Forbes," the officer greeted. "I'm Lieutenant Brigham of Northampton Police Department. We were dispatched to a residence because dispatched pinged your missing son's number from here."

"That's correct."

"I'm sorry to say, Mr. Forbes, but there's no one here. I called dispatch to confirm, but the response doesn't make sense. They say that the signal is still sketchy and still pinging from this location. I talked to the homeowner and he has no idea what could be going on."

"Have you checked the whole property? Neighboring properties? If the signal is sketchy, it could be within a mile of that location."

"We have a team out searching, but as of right now, it's a no go. I'm sorry."

Walter's heart sank. "Well, technology can do all sorts of things these days. Thank you for following up and giving it a shot."

"Of course. We take missing children with the utmost seriousness. I'm sorry we couldn't do more."

He hung up and sank back in his chair. Laura frowned and put a hand on his knee. "Nothing?"

He shook his head. "Dispatch says the signal is still there, still pinging, still sketchy, but boots on the ground say there's nothing there."

"I'm sorry. But, like you said, it could be within a mile radius, if the signal is that bad. He could still turn up."

She excused herself to go find a tree, leaving Walter alone with his thoughts. His only hope now rested with Micah and Kayla. With Time at their disposal, maybe they would find something the officers couldn't, like a trail of clues leading to Rifun, for instance. After a minute or two, he called them. No answer. If they were in a Band, they wouldn't get the call. That was fine. He could wait. Who knew, maybe they really would find something, and all his fretting would be for nothing.

Laura returned, handing him a fresh cup of coffee. As if he really needed any more of this stuff. He was getting old. He shouldn't be having caffeine past five o'clock, and here it was almost eight. The teams were returning, all of them with no good news, perking up at the news that Tommen's phone had been pinged, then being crushed again when it turned out to be a false alarm.

"We'll find him, Walter," Laura repeated. "Just not tonight."

He sighed and stood. "Yeah. Just not tonight. Let's go home. Maybe getting away from here will help clear my head."

"Sounds like a good idea. Do you want me to come by your place and cook? I don't think you're going to be making any gourmet meals tonight."

Walter was ready to refuse, but nodded at the last minute. "That would be nice, thank you."

He followed her back to her truck and got in, trying not to look like a sullen teenager who just got dumped by his girlfriend the night before prom. The ride back to Wellspring was quiet. One might have mistaken the town for being busy if one didn't know that ninety percent of the cars belonged to the search and rescue teams. The one dinky motel was packed; those left out in the cold either lived nearby or knew someone who lived nearby and elected to couch surf for the duration of the mission.

Walter's car was still in the diner's parking lot, the last one to leave.

"First one home gets to start dinner, I guess," he said, getting out of Laura's truck.

She grinned. "I'll be sure to go extra slow then."

He shook his head as he got in the car and started it. He followed her out of the parking lot, through the zigzag of streets until they found the highway. No sooner had they merged than Walter's phone rang. It was Micah.

"Talk to me, Micah, where is he?" Walter asked.

"I wish I had a straight answer for you, Walt, but I don't," Micah sighed.

"Entertain me. Start at the beginning."

"Okay, fair enough. So, we get out here to Virginia, find Northampton County, and then we spend probably an hour or more looking for the little country house with a whole bunch of cop cars hanging around. That was the easy part. The cops were just leaving, so we slipped out of the Band and made a few laps around the block until they all left before Banding again and going in to do our own investigation.

"Obviously, you've gathered that he wasn't there. We couldn't find him or any evidence that anything was noticeably disturbed, you know, a big 'Help me' written in blood or something. But, call it a hunch, but there was something not right about the place. I don't know, maybe it was a sixth Time sense or Akari sense or something. Kayla felt it, too. So we do another quick check, still nothing.

"Well, Kayla gets this idea to bring the Trackers back and see if maybe they can turn up something. Without going into detail, we got the Trackers again, same ones as before. We take them in the house—

in a Band, mind you, the homeowner was home by this time—"

"You realize that could be considered criminal trespassing, if not breaking and entering," Walter interrupted, searching for some kind of humor.

"Yeah, well, you're out of your jurisdiction anyway," Micah said smartly. "Anyway, so we take the Trackers in the house and they go absolutely nuts. Like, rabid, bloodhound, tear everything apart kind of nuts. Okay, they weren't just prancing around in circles, they were going after something. But, the weird thing was, it was only in the kitchen and only around this one spot on the counter."

"Was there anything obvious or significant on that part of the counter?"

"Not that we saw. It was clean, no dishes or anything. Plates in the cupboard, pots and pans in the cabinet, outlet on the wall."

"Was there anything unusual about the outlet? If Tommen had to charge his phone or do anything to it—"

"No. It was clean. Nothing plugged in. You remember the Trackers, Walter. With the two of them crashing around, well, let's just say we had to take some extra time to make sure everything was put back to rights as best we could. It was not a pleasant experience."

Walter nodded even though neither of his callers could see. "All right. Well, you know how to reach me if something does turn up. Where are you heading now?"

"We just returned the Trackers, so we'll be heading home. What about you?"

"Heading home. Laura's offered to cook for me, so I can't complain too bad."

"Just dinner, huh?"

"Micah..."

"I didn't say anything."

"You implied."

"Hey, Tommen is a stupid teenager who thinks with his dick more than his head. You are a mature, responsible adult, capable of rational thought and critical reasoning."

"Thanks for calling me old."

"I didn't say that."

"More implications."

Micah sighed. "Point is, I don't care if you fuck your girlfriend. Long as it's good. Ow!" Walter snickered as he imagined Kayla punching Micah in the arm. "All right, I guess if I want to survive this trip, I need to get off that topic."

"Why don't we all head home for the night, get something to eat, get some sleep, and reconvene in the morning?"

"Sounds like a plan. I'll make sure to pass everything on to Micaiah and let him know what's happening."

"Thanks, Micah."

He hung up, feeling more confused than anything. How did this all happen, and how did it fit into the bigger scheme of things? Why had Tommen's phone pinged in Virginia, and why had the Trackers gone crazy at the house where he was supposed to have been? Why wasn't he in that house? Why were there no clues?

Walter felt the dark cloud of brooding settle over him for the duration of the drive home. It let up only a little once he got back into familiar territory and pulled into the driveway. Laura was already there and had let herself in. She was just taking off her boots when Walter walked in the door.

"What sounds good for dinner?" Laura wondered.

He paused and let out a breath. "Uh...I don't know. I barely even know what I have in the cupboards."

"I'll find something. Why don't you go change your shirt and get washed up? You look terrible."

He raised a brow. "Yes, Mom."

He headed to his room to find a new shirt. Stripping off his old shirt, he momentarily reflected on how much he sweat when he was nervous. Was that just him, or did he need to find a new deodorant? Was he only just now concerned because Laura was in the house? He thought a minute, then realized he couldn't remember a time when he had been this concerned about how he looked and smelled. He might have likened it to being a middle school again, except he'd never been in middle school. It was like Tommen when he started middle school and started noticing girls. He couldn't hold half a conversation, but if and when he ever did, he was going to look and smell fabulous; of that he had been determined. His resolve only lasted through sixth and seventh grade. After that, he'd ditched the cologne and the body spray and everything else, instead settling on the usual daily showers and basic hygiene.

When he emerged from his bedroom, Laura was just setting the timer on the oven for just under an hour.

"Meatloaf," she said. "I wasn't sure what else to make; your cupboards are a little sparse."

Walter chuckled. "Of course they are; Tommen isn't here to consume every last scrap of stale bread and moldy cheese. Of course, bread and cheese never even have a chance to get stale or moldy when he's in the house."

She smiled. "Maybe, but that doesn't mean you have to starve."

"Believe me, I'm not starving." He patted his belly. He'd lost a good amount of weight since dating Laura, or he thought he had. His shirts were a little looser and he'd dropped a pant size. Although, this stress wasn't going to help him any. He'd probably gain it all back and then some.

Laura sat in the little chair at the puny kitchen table. "I have to be to work tomorrow evening, and I'm working a forty-eight hour shift, maybe more if Hank is still out sick; he's got something pretty bad going on."

"As long as he doesn't spread it around to you and then to me, and I take it to the precinct," Walter said.

"Actually, what I was getting at is, do you want me to come tomorrow? I will, but it won't be for very long. You'd either have to drive or get another ride home or come home early with me."

Walter shook his head. "No, that's all right. I want to say yes, and I appreciate your support and willingness to help, but it's probably better for you to just stay home. I don't think you or I will find him if the search crews can't. It'll save you gas and time and having to put up with my cheerful mood."

"If you're sure. Like I said, I'll come while I'm able to."

He put his hands on her shoulders. "I know. I appreciate it." He kissed her on the cheek. "Really, I do. You have no idea how grateful I am."

She patted his hand. "Okay."

They watched a little TV while they waited for the food to cook. Even once it was served and Walter was back in his recliner and Laura on the couch, the best they managed to do was an old movie from the fifties. Walter tried to get into it, but with limited success. His thoughts always wandered back to the campsite, the searching, and his missing son.

How in the hell had he ended up in Virginia? Had it just been the sketchy cell signal and the local boys not finding anything, well, he could dismiss it as a fluke. But when Micah and Kayla went out and said there was definitely something fishy about the place, he couldn't just dismiss that. They didn't know what was fishy, only that it was, and they had to figure out what.

"Walter!"

He jumped and looked up at Laura who stood over him. "What?"

"I asked if you wanted any more meatloaf. Otherwise, I'm going to start dishing it out."

"Oh, no, I'm fine. Thank you."

He handed her his dish and watched her head into the kitchen. After a minute or two, he stood and went out to the kitchen also, squeezing past her to the get to the sink and start the water. He and Tommen never really let the sink get full of dishes; there were so few of them that by the time the sink got even half-full they needed one of the dirty dishes in it. It was just easier to wash everything as it was dirtied. So even though there were only half a dozen dishes to wash, he stood at the soapy water while Laura manned the rinse water and drying rack.

"Are you staying for the rest of the movie?" he asked as he pulled the stopper on the sink.

She raised a brow. "So I can see if Charlotte and Ricky make up and fall in love, which they inevitably will, much to the dismay of frightful old Mrs. Whitson? Please."

"I didn't think it was that bad."

"You weren't even paying attention." She laughed as he blushed. "No, I think I'll head home. You need to get some sleep before getting up and going up early. Or at least try to get some sleep. Even just lying in bed resting is better than forcing yourself to stay up to watch a movie you don't care about."

"If you insist."

"Doctor's orders."

"You're not a doctor."

"No," Laura admitted, sitting down to pull her shoes on, "but if you ever need a ride in a bus, I'm the one who holds your life in my hands, so you better be nice to me and do as I say."

"Well, yes, ma'am."

"That's more like it."

She stood, took his hands in hers, and kissed him on the cheek, the same way he'd done to her. "You're a sweet, charming man, Walter. I hope Tommen comes home soon. And you can always call if you want me to come help or if you just want to talk. Okay?"

He walked her out to her truck and saw her off, watching her disappear over the rise. He wasn't a hormone-driven horny teenager anymore, true, but he wouldn't say he didn't kind of want to sleep with her. But his urges were decades dormant, so he wasn't sure just how well that would work out. At the very least, he thought it might be nice to have someone sleep beside him once. Although, given his propensity for nightmares and the demons that haunted him, maybe that wasn't such a good idea either. Grudgingly, he turned and went back inside the house.

He liked having dinner at her place better, he thought, running his hand along the back of the little chair at the tiny kitchen table. At least there they could have a proper sit-down dinner, where they could have a real conversation face-to-face conversation and not have to watch TV constantly for entertainment. He'd told her all of this before. Apparently, she preferred having dinner at his place for the sheer fact that it was a real house and not an apartment, where there was actually a little room between him and his neighbors. If she heard her neighbors, well, that was nothing new. If he heard his neighbors, there was probably something wrong, depending on the time of day.

Didn't matter, he supposed. Either place had its ups and downs. He might have considered moving except he'd just spent a lot of time and money working on the remodeling; he wanted to take a little time to enjoy it. Besides, it only had to last as long as he did in this life. Once he went dark, it wouldn't matter anymore. In his next life, he could have an apartment or a mansion, or anything in between. He could live in a nice little well-to-do subdivision, or out in the country with a hundred acres and nearest neighbors two miles down the road.

He was going to have to show Tommen the finer points of building a new life. Maybe Micaiah and Kayla could give him a few pointers since they seemed to be really ramping up to their move. Neither of them had said where they were going, though from the sounds of it, no one was going anywhere faster. With humans all but barred from going to the Wheel, that was causing quite a bit of havoc on the normal Time Agents. According to Micaiah, the backlog for the Akarin was something like two years or more. They'd gone with a short form, but even that wait was pretty long, a lot longer than it should have been anyway, or so they said.

Walter was still a little skeptical about the whole thing, but the more Micaiah explained it, the more sense it made, and it wasn't just about the Akari either. At first, he'd dismissed it as something powerful, but amounting to little more than some cultish following, similar to a Holy Grail fan club. Now, though, he understood. Listening to some of the finer points of how it all worked, and reading some of the Authored books in the Archives, he knew exactly where it was going. It was both unsettling and yet comforting.

It was still too early to go to bed, or so his mind told him. He should be getting ready for bed, he knew, so he would be well-rested for the drive up tomorrow and the search, but his mind was still too active, too intent on trying to figure out this puzzle. There was more going on than the search crews understood, but how did he convey that without sounding like a lunatic?

Walter had just sat down in his recliner when there was a knock at the door. Groaning, he got up from his recliner. There was another knock. Then another.

"I'm coming, I'm coming," he growled irritably.

He opened the door. Initially, he saw no one. Then he looked down and saw Becky.

"Where is he?" she demanded.

Walter sighed. "I don't know."

He invited her in, and she was talking the whole time. "I saw the story on the news. He was supposed to be helping rescue some campers from a wildfire in camp when he went missing. Search crews are still out there. They say they think he might be injured and lost, wandering around out there in the mountains somewhere. So where is he?"

"Believe me, Becky, if I knew where he was, he would be home by now, or safe anyway." He appreciated Becky's concern, but he really didn't want to deal with her forceful personality right now. Now he wanted to go to bed. Just perfect.

"I've tried texting him, but all my messages bounce back," she was saying. "And the calls don't go through either. I can't even leave a voicemail."

"I know. Believe me, I know." He elected not to tell her about the strange signal coming from Virginia. "Search crews are out there working as we speak. I'm heading out there again tomorrow morning."

"Can I come with you? I can fit in a lot of places you guys can't."

Walter managed a tired chuckle. "Unfortunately, that would only matter if Tommen were a child. I highly doubt he's going to be hiding under a rock like a frightened six year old."

She sighed. "I know you're right. Still. I wish there was something I could do. I mean, praying is nice and all, but if God doesn't mind, I'd like to see some results for my efforts."

Now he laughed. "Believe me, I am right there with you. I'd like to see some results, too. As it is, though, right now all we can do is pray and search."

Becky nodded slowly. "I know." She looked around. "Well, I guess if you're going all the way to Wellspring in the morning, you're going to be getting up pretty early and need to get some sleep. And if I'm going to be stowing away in the trunk of your car in order to get up there, I'm going to have to be up even earlier, which means I need some sleep, too." She puffed out her cheeks and let out a breath. "All right. Promise me you'll let me know if you find anything? Or better yet, have him call me so I can chew him out for getting me all worried."

Walter smiled and nodded as he opened the door. "I will make absolutely sure to do that." That would be something worth seeing. "Good night, Becky."

She wandered off down the driveway, disappearing down the street in the growing dark. Walter wished he had something to give her, but he didn't even have anything to give himself. After a minute, he closed the door, locked up, and headed for the bathroom, hoping that a little routine might break his mind a little and force him to think about something else. But that was the thing about habits. They were habitual. His body knew exactly what it needed to do, so he could do it and leave his mind free to think and brood.

He didn't like where his thoughts wandered off to, but in his tired grief, he had a hell of a time trying to rein everything in. The only thing that saved him for a potentially torturous night was his phone ringing.

"Hello?" he answered.

"Walt, it's Micaiah."

"Have you found something?"

"Well, if you're asking whether Micah and Kayla found Tommen, sorry to say they didn't. But they did bring me up to speed on everything that happened, including their little adventures with the Trackers. Kind of makes me wish I'd been there."

"Oh, it was an adventure all right. A real trip. So why are you calling?"

"Call it a hunch, but I think that even if you're about to go to bed, your mind isn't going to let you sleep for a while. Am I right?"

"Could be."

"I was going to head to the fortress for a bit to see if I can't do a little research. I was wondering if you wanted to come along. You might feel like you're making some kind of progress in the whole thing. I don't know. It's entirely possible that I'll be called away to deal with other issues while we're there, but, *c'est la vie*, I guess."

Listening to a French idiom with an Irish accent was so comical, Walter almost burst out laughing. It wasn't even that funny; he was just that desperate.

"Would your council or leaders or whoever let me in to do research?" he wondered.

"Sure," Micaiah said. "And anyway, you're my guest. And my friend. If they have nothing to hide, they should have no problem with anyone going through their things. Believe me, politics is politics no matter where you go, but it's nowhere near as bad as the Hands, let me tell you."

"I don't think you can escape politics anywhere, no matter how utopian the society may seem."

"Hm, true. Anyway, those are my plans. Do you want to come with?"

Walter wanted to say yes. It was a course of action that could lead to a way to find his missing son. At the same time, despite understanding the deeper workings and mysteries of the Akarin, he still felt like an outsider. Micaiah had praised him for figuring things out early, but that didn't make him feel better. Why did an outsider see things that much more clearly than an insider? Something didn't feel right about that.

Furthermore, if they did find something in their research, that would mean that, once again, Time and the Akari were the root causes of his son's misfortune. Here they go again on another epic adventure worthy of another novel. Did it never end? Was there no foreseeable conclusion to this tale?

At the same time, what else was he going to do tonight? He'd lie in bed, stare up at the ceiling, watch as his thoughts ran off in a thousand different directions, none of them good. On the off chance that he did get to sleep, it would only be plagued by worries, nightmares, and his own personal demons. He'd wake up feeling useless, rotten, worthless, and not the least bit sleepy still. Or he could go out and watch TV until he fell asleep in his recliner. Wash, rinse, repeat.

"Walt?" Micaiah prompted.

He let out a breath. "Okay. All right, I'll come."

"Don't make me twist your arm or anything."

"No, no, it's fine. I'll come. As long as you're sure they won't mind."

"Well, if they do, they're going to have to deal with Kayla. She'll give them a piece of her mind."

"I have no doubt about that. All right, give me a few minutes to find something presentable and I'll be over."

Chapter Seven
The Physics of the Impossible

The first clue that Julianna was bullshitting him came in the form of uniformed police officers. They did a search of the house and surrounding area, all looking for Tommen. They even said so to the homeowner. A kid named Tommen Forbes from West Virginia had gone missing, and his phone had pinged in or around this house. Homeowner told them to search all they wanted; he had nothing to hide. As was to be expected, the search came up empty. Tommen watched as the leader of the search crew called his dad to relay such information before packing up and heading out.

The second clue that something was amiss came with Micah and Kayla. Tommen could only watch them when they weren't in a Band. What they did while they were moving Faster or Slower than Base Time was anyone's guess. Tommen tried to move into a Band of his own, try to match them and see what they were up to, but every time he felt a Band start to form, it slipped away, like sand through his fingers. So he just waited in Kayla's truck for them to return.

When the two of them did finally return to call Walter, Tommen discovered he'd missed a lot more than he thought. Trackers. Micah and Kayla had brought Trackers to search for him. As in, the same Trackers that Rifun had used to seek and destroy any renegade Time Agents and Akari-bearers after his coup. Anyone who hadn't been trapped and imprisoned in the Wheel had been hunted down by those things.

At the same time, it was kind of genius. If they really could sniff out Time, maybe the Akari, too, then how better to find someone who was trapped in-between dimensions, right? Maybe when he'd used his phone to cross the dimensional boundaries, it had triggered something, a scent marker of some form, which the Trackers had picked up on. Had they done something similar at the campsite? He'd been stuck down in the diner with Laura, so he wasn't entirely sure what they'd done. Would it have made a difference if he had been up there with them?

Too many what ifs and uncertainties. Tommen got out of the truck before Micah and Kayla left, shoving his good hand in his pocket and walking to the end of the block where Julianna waited, picking at some dirt under her fingernails. She began to speak.

"So, I assume—"

"You're bullshitting me," Tommen stated.

She straightened. "I beg your pardon?"

"There's something you're not telling me. I don't know what it is—about this dimension, about Time or Energy or whatever—but I can say that you are a very bad liar. Okay, I was able to get my phone to ping to dispatch and get cops out here looking for me. Now, if I can do that within half a day of landing in this dimension, do you think it will take me long to figure out how to bust out of here?"

Julianna merely raised a brow. "Even prisoners can call out to the outside. That doesn't mean that they are free to leave whenever they wish."

"Even so, there's something you're not telling me. I want to know what it is."

"You wouldn't be interested."

"Why not?"

"As far as you're concerned, it's all magic and hocus pocus."

"I believe what I can see. Tell me what I see."

"Which would you rather learn, the big picture or the details? I was going to show you the individual parts, the details first. You seem to insist that you only need to see the greater machine in order to understand how it works."

"It would be nice to have a map of the maze I'm running around in."

She stared at him for a moment longer, scrutinizing him with a gaze that could make a nun question her purity. Finally she said, "You're in the in-between dimension. Some call it the dream lands, spirit lands, whatever. There is a lot of mythology surrounding it because there are some who understand how to move within it or manipulate it. In the real world, we call them ghosts or phantoms if they make apparitional appearances. Some try to speak through others, and are called demons or bad spirits. Still others go a different route and have learned to walk in people's dreams."

Okay, so she had the right of it at the beginning when she said he would probably dismiss it as magic and hocus pocus. The problem was, it was hard to dismiss the existence of something when it was literally staring him in the face. Spirit lands? Dream lands? A week ago, he would have been like, yeah, sure, prove it. Well, now he appeared to be standing in the dream lands. Hard to doubt the existence of the ocean when he seemed to be adrift at sea.

"Is this Hell, then?" Tommen asked, looking around. "Looks a lot like home."

Julianna shrugged. "If this is Hell, then I should think it ought to be a lot more populous, don't you? No, I don't think this is Hell. I simply believe that this is a dimension between dimensions, where people become trapped and may move about, but die all the same in the end, your lifespan determined only be your exposure to Time."

"See, that's another thing I don't understand. Why doesn't Time work here? I watched my hearing aids and my phone charge. It took five and a half hours, but it certainly hasn't been that long. You call it Condensing, I call it Banding. What's the deal here?"

"The in-between dimension, regardless of all the mortal mythology that has shrouded it, is the land of the Akari. It's the only thing that works here. Time is nothing. It has no power, no jurisdiction. Even in the real world, it is a diluted, poisoned misrepresentation of the Akari." She paused and seemed to remember herself. "You may have noticed a few odd things about Traveling around here."

How Tommen wished he had better use of his left arm. "Ask

and ye shall receive, right?"

"Something like that. The Akari is a living thing, a part of you that must be nurtured and exercised the same as any muscle. Speaking of which, I did take the liberty of researching burns a little more. You should keep your arm and fingers stretched and moving as much as possible, when not elevated. It keeps the muscles from contracting, keeps the blood flowing, prevents cell death, all that."

Tommen nodded absently as he painfully moved each of his fingers. "So is everyone here an Akari-bearer?"

Julianna shook her head. "No. Most aren't, in fact. You can arrive here through a Time portal just as easily as an Akari portal, easier even, I believe. Some learn how to use it and get around. A lot don't. Many people are like you, proclaiming to believe only what they can see. Sometimes, though, it's not about the seeing, but the will to accept it. Even when they stand here, they still reject the Akari, but they have no use of Time. As you've noticed, the population of this dimension is pretty low."

"And that's it. They just...die?"

"Afraid so. Once they're confronted with a reality where everything they've ever known and done and used means nothing, well, change is hard. Not everyone takes it well. Once the initial determination to get out and get back to the way things were wears off, once they realize they're not getting out, the mind breaks long before the body."

"Shit."

"But then there are some, like you, who may be a little more willing to listen and learn. Even if you can't get out, you will find a way to survive with the Akari as your only companion."

"Is that why you're willing to teach me?"

She nodded. "It is. You have a gift, Tommen. You're quick to challenge, true, but you are also very quick to learn. Who knows? Maybe you will be the one to find a way out of this awful place."

"Well, the only way we're going to find that out is if you teach me everything you know. Then maybe my modern, invincible, stupid teenage mind can come up with something."

"Very well, then. Come with me."

He followed her down the street. "Where are we going?"

"The best place to learn anything is in the field, where you can use what you learn immediately. For you, that means going home."

On more than one occasion, Tommen had been told and subsequently learned that it was easiest to learn new Time abilities when under pressure. Predict had come to him during a fight with Tyler Freeman, and External Banding had been a result of holding his dying father in his arms and reaching for anything at all to keep him alive.

Now, however, with that knowledge in mind as well as Julianna's cryptic words about going home, Tommen was less than enthused about learning something new.

"I get it now," he said suddenly as Julianna stopped and turned, preparing to Travel.

She paused and looked at him. "What?"

"I can see it. The Traveling and Predict, I can see where we're going. Or, you know, that general direction, but I can see it. It's not random."

"No. It never was. Come along."

He found that he could also use Predict while Traveling to keep an eye on her and know where she went and where she stopped, that way they didn't end up hundreds of miles apart, waiting for each other or constantly missing each other trying to meet up. It was almost like going through a tunnel, Traveling from one spot to another.

They ended up high on a mountain overlooking the city of Charleston. It was beautiful at night, all lit up. He could see the capitol building and the bridge, the little highways snaking their way here and there around the mountains. At night, the city almost appeared small, just a little dot on the map. During the day, though, when you could see the outlying neighborhoods and all the little houses and farms scattered along the hills, the city grew tenfold.

"I know Rifun already told you some of this, but I'll give you a little better explanation," Julianna said. "The Time industry is concerned with only one aspect of the universe, and that is Time, as you may have guessed. Matter encompasses the observable, physical universe. Solid, liquid, gas, plasma, all those basic things you learned in Chemistry. Atoms and molecules and the things they build. Every civilization out there has their own Matter industry, but most just call it commerce or trade. All those people down there in Charleston? They deal in Matter every day. Iron is turned into steel. Wood is shaped into tools and furniture. People trade the Matter of dollars for the Matter of clothes, food, whatever they want. Sometimes they trade Matter for Energy when they pay for their electricity.

"Energy, as far as the Akari and manipulating said Energy is concerned, is fickle and dangerous, as you have experienced yourself. It is used to open portals between dimensions, but it is also used as a barrier to keep those dimensions separate. The ensuing paradox is how we end up with the in-between dimension, a way to store and regulate the Energy.

"Time is the only thing left which all creatures in the universe crave, which the Hands of Time learned to manipulate, monetize, and monopolize to put themselves in power. They watered it down to make it accessible to anyone and everyone. But in order to keep the masses in line and keep them from discovering the true power which they could wield, they demonized the Akari and made it a hated thing, if it could be acknowledged at all. By now, most Time Agents understand it only as a myth."

Julianna paused and faced Tommen. "That is the big picture. Everything we do with the Akari falls into one of those three categories."

Tommen looked around. "My dad was one of those who thought the Akari was a myth, and he could do some pretty scary shit, or so I was always told. If that's the watered down stuff, then what's the real thing?"

"That is what I am going to teach you. You Traveled well. Really, it's not a difficult thing to do, once you get the hang of it. Do you know what category it falls into?"

"Time. Maybe Energy, too."

"Why?"

"Because we're not manipulating Matter and shrinking the ground between places. Time, because it works like a Double Band, distorting our perception of Time. But it could be Energy, using the Energy of the dimension itself like a pseudo-portal to get us from one spot to another."

"Fascinating theory. I like it."

"Am I right? Is this a quiz or something?"

"Not a quiz, but you are right. Mostly, it is a manipulation of Time. The Energy I'm not so sure of, but definitely the Time. Now, what about the time traveling bit?"

Tommen let out a breath and chuckled dryly. "Fuck if I know. Energy would be my best guess, but it seems like the answer would really be Time, because, you know, 'time' travel and stuff? I don't know."

"Think it through. Is it Time or Energy?"

Tommen shook his head as he stretched his fingers. It was difficult to do with the gauze between them, but he managed to touch his thumb to his forefinger and middle finger. His ring and pinkie fingers he was too afraid of loosening the gauze, to say nothing of how much it fucking hurt. He was pretty sure he had a blister sitting at the base of those two fingers that hadn't lanced, so every time he moved those fingers, he was pressing hard against the blister.

"Tommen?" Julianna prompted.

"I know, I'm thinking," he lied. "It would have to be some combination of Time and Energy. Gravity, like the gravity of a black hole, is said to make time slow down. If Gravity is an Energy, then maybe it's possible to make it work in reverse." He shifted his stance. "But then, it's not really going backwards, we're just seeing it, like watching a movie. Maybe it has something to do with Matter, too? Or the electricity, the Energy in your brain, projecting something that you can see? Some combination of the three?"

This was like quantum physics, man, or maybe something beyond that which hadn't been conceived of by common scientists. And to think he'd once thought he was the coolest kid in town because he got moved to AP Physics class. This was all way over his head.

Julianna grinned. "Honestly, I didn't expect you to get it anyway. It works similarly to the principles of dream-walking, except there you are projecting yourself versus merely watching a projection."

"So what's the answer?"

"Primarily Energy. In the case of the time traveling, there is a bit of Time mixed in. But mostly it's Energy."

"Time is a form of Energy," Tommen stated.

"Is it? Time is simply the increments in which we measure cause and effect. A clock measures Time, but the clock is not Time. Just because the batteries die and the hands stop does not mean Time stops. A fire starts, a fire burns, and a fire goes out, but Time does not stop. Nor is it affected by the fire in any way. Time would be Time regardless if the camp had burned or not. But here's the mind-bender, could the fire have burned if there was no Time?"

"Fire is fire. It's Energy."

"Ah, but think about my previous statement. Fire starts, fire burns, fire goes out. Cause and effect. Before and after. Is Time a form of Energy, or is Energy a form of Time? And think about this one, too: Some say that God is timeless, that there is no Time in heaven, there was no Time before Creation. But God must be, at the very basest level, regardless of your personal beliefs, some form of Energy, right? If He has no beginning and no end, that indicates an existence outside of Time. Energy without Time, but with the power to create Time. Fire burning or not burning, Time without Energy."

Tommen let out a breath and rubbed his eyes. "You're making my brain hurt."

"Good. At the very least, I'm getting you thinking. Are you ready for the practical exam on this one?"

"What do you want me to do, create another universe?"

"No, nothing quite that special. I simply want you to use the time travel a little more, play with it a little, and see how well you can tweak it. I saw that you used it in Wales, though it appeared crude and uncoordinated. I want you to use it deliberately."

"What do you want me to do, prove that the CIA assassinated JFK or something?"

She waved a hand. "Please, I've already done that. No, nothing like that either. As in England and Wales, just go and visit somewhere that is meaningful to you and try to carry it from one room to another as it were without it changing every ten steps. Then come back."

Tommen immediately knew where he wanted to go, but he didn't want to go there with Julianna watching him. Instead, he pretended to take a minute to think it over before heading down into Charleston, Traveling there in the blink of an eye. He headed home, momentarily overwhelmed by emotion and homesickness when he walked in the door — or, more accurately, pushed through the door. He was home, and yet he wasn't.

Laura was over, making dinner while his dad brooded silently in his bedroom, taking a lot longer than necessary just to change his clothes. Tommen might have said that he was trying to get all dressed up to impress his girlfriend, but the expression on his dad's face spoke of desperate worry, of trouble concentrating. Even picking out a shirt appeared to be a chore. His mind was still up on that mountain, in that forest where he knew his son must be. Or could be. Where did Virginia fit into all of this?

For a moment, Tommen considered plugging his phone in and making another 9-1-1 call, tip off dispatch and get another investigation. Then he decided against it. It would get him nowhere, and it probably wouldn't go too well for his dad to have all of his coworkers suddenly showing up on his doorstep saying his son had just called from inside the house. No, he would wait until he had more of an answer as to how to contact him or reach out or just blast his way out of this fucking dimension if he had to.

He followed his dad out to the kitchen where Laura served up the meatloaf, and they headed out to the living room to watch a movie. Tommen looked longingly at the meatloaf. He wasn't normally a fan, but he was hungry and it was looking mighty tasty. With any luck, Julianna would teach him about pulling things into the dimension pretty soon.

The movie was an old one, easily the grandfather of modern romantic comedies. Tommen wasn't particularly interested. He could see his dad had no clue what was going on, and Laura was watching only to be polite.

If he really wanted to be honest, Tommen was kind of hoping to catch his dad — and by default, Laura — in a red-handed, hypocritical lie. That is, he wanted to know whether they were sleeping together. Given his dad's state of mind, it wasn't exactly a surprise that they didn't get it on, but still. Wasn't there something to be said for grief bringing people together? As it was, the only thing that happened was Laura gave him a kiss. On the cheek, at that. Was their relationship moving that slowly, or did they operate on a level of chivalry that he, the Chivalrous Welshman, wasn't even aware of? Was it really possible to date someone and not sleep with them? People actually did that?

Well, it wasn't as though Tommen had been desperate to see two graying, middle-aged, slightly heavyset adults get naked; mostly he'd just been curious. But nothing happened. Laura left, and Walter returned to his recliner. No sooner had he sat down than there was a knock on the door. Then another. And another. The frantic knocking could only mean one thing.

Becky had heard. And she wanted answers. Unfortunately, Walter had no answers for her, none that he could share, anyway. Tommen hated seeing Becky's dejected look almost as much as he laughed at her idea about stowing away in his dad's car so she could go out and help search. He was torn over whether she would actually do it. She might, just because she was worried and wanted to feel like she was doing something to help besides frantic pacing and harried praying. She might not, seeing how she would have a tough time climbing up and down those hills in her bulky orthopedic shoes.

Her departure left Tommen feeling more depressed than he thought it should have. It wasn't just the homesickness or the hunger or the desire to hug and kiss his girlfriend. Maybe he had been hoping for more from her. Maybe he'd been hoping that with her professed connection to God and belief in His power that she might be the one to see him and alert Walter to his presence. Maybe he'd been hoping that her "spiritual eyes" would be open to him. But they weren't. She was as blind to his presence as everyone else.

Becky couldn't see him, despite having both Catholic and Jewish faith to fall back on. Was that the punishment for them planning to go all the way? Would it have mattered if they were a good little couple who hardly dared to look at each other for fear of divine wrath?

Micaiah couldn't see him, despite being a very proficient Akari-bearer and leader within the Akarin community, reluctant though he seemed to be. Did that mean he wasn't the Akari-bearer he thought he was? Was there more than one version? Which version was the one that ran the in-between dimension?

Worst of all, though, was that Walter couldn't see him. There was no way in which Tommen could let him know that he was okay. Even if he did have to resign himself to living in the in-between dimension for the rest of his life, his dad deserved to know that his son hadn't perished up on that mountain.

Or maybe that was how it should be. As far as anyone was concerned, he'd been helping to rescue kids from a burning summer camp. That was pretty heroic, all things considered. His dad would grieve, but he would get over it, and he would have a happy memory of his son, something he could almost brag about instead of hanging his head and sullenly admitting that his kid had gotten in another fight or something really bad had happened.

Walter headed to the bathroom, evidently getting ready for bed. By force of habit, Tommen went to his room. Well, at least his dad hadn't started on the compulsive cleaning yet; everything was exactly where he'd left it. Not that it did him much good seeing how he couldn't do anything with it. He couldn't read, couldn't listen to his music or —

Tommen brought out his phone and the charger. The battery didn't last nearly as long in this dimension, but at least he knew how to charge his electronics now. He didn't have a lot of music on his phone, but something was better than nothing. Before he could make a selection, he heard his dad's phone ring. Curious, he stood and went to listen in.

"Hello?" he answered. Talking. "Have you found something?"

Tommen leaned in to hear as best he could, but his dad kept the volume on his phone low intentionally in case it was business he didn't want anyone to overhear. If he had to take a guess, Micah or Micaiah was on the other end.

"Oh, it was an adventure all right," his dad sighed. "A real trip. So why are you calling?" More talking. "Could be."

Tommen jumped as his dad laughed suddenly. As soon as it came, it was gone, obviously something that wasn't supposed to be funny, but the situation demanded humor. Walter cleared his throat.

"Would your council or leaders or whoever let me in to do research?" he wondered.

More talking and a bored expression from Walter indicating that whatever it was, was old news.

"I don't think you can escape politics anywhere, no matter how utopian the society may seem," he said finally.

There was a little more talking, but Walter was silent for a long time after that. What had been said? Was it important? Did it involve him, Tommen? Had someone planted a body to pass off as his so the search crews would abandon their mission? Sounded crazy, but with Tommen, Time, and the Akari involved, anything was possible.

Finally, Walter let out a breath and said, "Okay. All right, I'll come." Pause. "No, no, it's fine. I'll come. As long as you're sure they won't mind." He smiled at something on the other end. "I have no doubt about that. All right, give me a few minutes to find something presentable and I'll be over."

Where was he going? The bakery most likely. Or, at this time of night, probably the twins' house. Even with only half the conversation, Tommen could deduce that they were heading to the Akarin fortress. He wouldn't be able to follow them. It burned him, and he almost wanted to go with his dad and try anyway, see what would happen.

So that was exactly what he did. He got in the car and patiently waited for his dad to be ready, which he was in record time. The drive across town to the twins' house was quiet, his dad brooding and occasionally drumming his fingers on the steering wheel. Tommen hadn't really gotten a chance to charge his phone, so it sat dormant in his pocket. He'd charge it once they arrived.

Both twins and Kayla were still awake, though Micah appeared to be on his way to bed, citing his opening shift the following morning.

"What exactly did you have in mind for this venture anyway?" Walter asked. "If I recall correctly, time passes normally in your fortress as you call it, which means I'm losing sleep by going."

"You can sleep on the couch and I'll Band you," Micaiah said dismissively. "Besides, think of it as saving twenty minutes tomorrow morning just driving across town, plus I'm sure Kayla will be nice enough to make breakfast."

Kayla raised a brow but said nothing.

"Still doesn't answer the question. What did you have in mind to research?"

"Honestly, I'd like to do some research on Tracker behavior. Why do they behave differently for different things? What does it mean? What are they trained to do? What are their capabilities? If we can find answers to that, it might help us figure out what they saw. If we figure out what they saw, we might be able to figure out exactly what happened, especially if that incident in Virginia was involved in some way."

"I have a feeling that it is." Walter hesitated but nodded. "All right. I have no better ideas. Lead the way."

Micaiah and Kayla shouldered the portal to the Akarin fortress.

These portals did not stay open once someone walked through them, so it was a lot harder to create and maintain one, especially for multiple people. As Walter stepped through, Tommen tried to stay hard on his heels, hoping to follow through and suddenly appear there with the rest of them. Surprise! What he got was nothing of the sort.

Now, Tommen was a science nerd, and he loved science fiction movies, especially the moderately-older ones. Not the old black-and-white garbage where the props, costumes and acting were so bad that it was hard to watch the film or take it seriously. He preferred the ones that, even though they weren't super-CGI, still had good budgets and took themselves seriously enough that the audience took them seriously, too. *Jurassic Park,* for instance. A classic.

There was a scene from that movie that he was reminded of as he hit the portal—and yes, he did run into it the same way he might normally run into a solid brick wall. It was that scene where the ranger was leading the two kids out of the enclosure. The electric fence was down and they had to hurry up and get out. The man and the girl get down, but the boy was having problems and he got caught at the top of the fence when the power came back on. He was thrown off the fence, and the ranger had to do CPR to bring the kid back.

This was about like that, Tommen thought, once the colors sorted themselves and became tangible objects. At first, he thought he'd gotten pretty lucky, a little shock and nothing more. Only once he pulled himself to a sitting position did the pain start coming in. The worst was his arm and chest, already burned and now feeling like a live current was running through it. Again. Everything from his shoulder down was shaking, fingers twitching uncontrollably. The bandages looked wet and heavy. If he had just taken an electric shock, maybe it had lanced whatever blisters he'd had left in tact.

He drunkenly tried to stand, fell back to his knees with a new pain around his ears. He took out his hearing aids. They did not appear damaged too badly, thankfully. When he put two fingers to his ear, he found that he had some kind of wound around his ears, where his hearing aids normally sat. So they'd burned him. Lovely. Well, might as well turn them off and wait for those burns to heal. At least those burns didn't feel much worse than a sunburn, though his arm dwarfed everything else.

He was still dizzy when he finally managed to stand and get to a chair. The living room was empty, and Micah had gone to bed. Tommen wasn't sure what time it had been when he walked in the door, but it was almost midnight now. He rubbed his face. Fuck, that hurt. Cautiously, he removed the bandages from his arm, tossing them in the trash out of habit.

Fucking hell, it looked awful. The blisters were crying rivers, and not a little forest stream, more like the whole Mississippi. Between the ooze, the shredded skin, and the melted coat, his arm looked like an enormous sausage that had been ravaged by a bear. He kept his arm over the sink while he rummaged around in his coat pockets for some of the medical supplies Julianna had packed for him. Grudgingly, he opened the bottle of sterile water, gritting his teeth before actually pouring it over the wounds.

It hurt just as bad as the last time, but with more pus and ooze. At least it looked like some of the infection was coming out; he could hope, right? He had to get out of this fucking dimension and see a doctor.

His head was spinning by the time he was done, and that was just the first part. Now he had to somehow wrap his whole arm. He dumped out the supplies on the counter, grabbing gauze squares and stuffing them between his fingers which were sticky and sore. He tried to move them a little as he did, keep them from getting stiff, but they still hurt like a son of a bitch, and the rest of his arm wasn't much better as he wrapped it.

When all was said and done, he collapsed onto the couch and leaned back. He was exhausted and in some excruciating pain. If he really wanted to be honest, he wanted nothing more than to curl up into a ball on his ma's lap and go to sleep, pretend it was all a bad dream.

Tommen stretched his legs and looked out the window. A

moment later, he was Traveling through the mountains, though he didn't go far. He found his familiar valley. Once he added in a little time travel, he found the familiar cabin, too.

Before he could process what was going on, he found himself on his knees, sobbing uncontrollably. By the time he realized what he was doing, the tears had dried, and it was almost as if it hadn't happened. Still, he stayed on the ground and looked down the slope where his ma was out feeding the chickens.

She was older than he remembered, but maybe it was just him. Her long brown hair was gathered in a loose bun, and heavy muck boots clashed with her modest yet vibrant yellow and gray dress. She'd borne six or seven children in her life, and it showed.

What was even stranger, though, was watching the little boy toddle after her. It took him a minute to realize that was him, when he was about three years old. Strange, he watched it happen in front of him even as he could remember it happening in his mind. He chased after his ma, not wanting to lose sight of her, only to be distracted by the chickens, getting a huge kick out of watching them squawk and fly away, ignoring his ma's words.

His merriment was cut short by Welly, the rooster from Hell. Welly didn't take kindly to anyone messing with his hens, and he let Tommen have it, chasing him, pecking him, finally cornering him. He scratched Tommen with his claws and beat him with his wings. Tommen put his arms over his head and shrieked until his ma finally swatted Welly away with a stick. The rooster squawked and looked like he was going to go after her, too, then appeared to think better of it and wandered away to protect his harem as they scratched at the feed.

"Oh, my love," Tommen's ma said, bending down and scooping him up. "Did Welly scratch you up again?"

"Can we butcher him?!" Tommen wailed.

His ma smiled. "No, we can't."

"Why?!"

"Because he's just doing what he does. He's protecting his

hens. What use would he be if he let anyone touch them? Yes, he can be a handful during the day, but at night, he lets us know if something is trying to break into the henhouse. A coyote, a wolf, a bear. They all want to get in and eat our chickens, but Welly protects them and tells us about it. 'Come! Help! Save us!' he says.

"It's kind of like pa. What kind of man would pa be if he didn't defend us, hm? What if he just let anyone near the house and slept through danger?"

Tommen sniffed. "But he doesn't attack people during the day."

"Well, chickens are a little dumber than humans. But the overall premise is the same. You'll understand one day, my love, when pa teaches you what it means to be a man, when you become a man yourself. Then it will all be clear."

"I wanna be big now so I can attack the rooster like he attacks me."

She smiled gently. "I know. That's not happening today." She shifted him in her arms. "Come on, let's get you cleaned up. Then you can help me with the goats."

By this time, older Tommen was right there with them, fighting the tears for all he was worth. He was seeing and remembering at the same time, and it killed him. He wished he could be that child again. He watched her carry the younger him inside, heart heavy.

When he turned back around, his ma was coming round the corner of the house. Apparently he'd lost his grip on the timeline or something. It was evening now, and some unknown time later than what he'd just witnessed, at least six months if not more. His ma was heavily pregnant and looked worried as she walked, meeting up with his pa and Teo on the tiny porch. Tommen knew where this was going, just as sure as he knew what Teo looked like the last time he'd seen him.

"Did you find him?" she asked frantically.

His pa shook his head slowly. "No. We managed to track him into the woods heading up toward the old salt cave, but we lost the trail in the dark."

Tears began streaming down his ma's face. "He's been begging to go up there. Now he's gone alone. No one's ever come out of that cave!"

His pa tried to hug her, but she pulled away, trying to keep herself together. She sniffed hard. "Teo, you know caves and mines better than anyone. Can you look for him, maybe in the morning?"

"Ma, I don't think he's in the cave. He's been begging to go there, but he knows it's dangerous to go alone. He's a foolish child, true, but he's not reckless or stupid. He's probably lost in the woods somewhere. We'll find him, though."

"But you will check up there, just in case?"

Teo nodded. "We will."

Tommen could take no more. He turned his back on the cabin and stalked off into the woods, letting the past melt away as he climbed the hillside, forging a new path to the cave. It wasn't quite the same as it had been back then. New hiking and skiing trails snaked through the woods. The path to the cave itself had been changed, lowered so that it was a small rock climbing expedition just to get up there to the original path. Well, that was an exaggeration. It was only about six or seven feet, something Tommen might normally climb easily. The first time he'd been hindered by snow and ice. This time he only had one arm. He tried several times to scale the cliff, looked around for an easier path. He found none, but not having to worry about the solidity of trees meant he could forge his own path. He reached the cave entrance and sat on a rock.

He was tired from being up so long and trying to learn and master these new abilities. He was tired from his body being split between doing normal stuff, doing this new phantasmal stuff, and trying to fight off infection, healing itself. He was tired from watching memories of his old life, seeing his ma and pa again, seeing Teo, never mind all that shit from his dad's past life, holy fuck. And he was tired because he was hungry. He hadn't eaten anything since before the fire, and fear and adrenaline could only carry him so far. His high was ending and real life was crashing down around him. He rubbed his face roughly.

When he looked up, he found himself in another time travel scenario; he knew it only because the original path was restored, the trees had changed, and it had gone from a warm summer night to a chilly winter evening.

Without his hearing aids, Tommen saw the men before he heard them. One was his pa. The other was his dad. Looking at them side-by-side, he could see the resemblance, and Walter was definitely the older brother. He was older, bigger, and, although Tommen's pa was hard from an unforgiving frontier life, Walter just looked tougher, hardened by an unforgiving life of crime. Now, though, having been through Beaumaris Gaol and his encounter with the Confederates, he was the subordinate one of the pair. He bowed to his younger brother's word. He wanted to make things right, but his little brother had the final say.

Tommen watched them walk up the trail toward the cave, pausing about fifty feet from the entrance.

"This is the cursed cave," Teo stated. "As you can see, even those who were here before us knew something wasn't right about this place. If I had known it was here, I would have built my house somewhere else. Anywhere else. Even after I learned of it, I thought that surely it was too far away for anyone to want to make the trip. Even if someone did, the warnings ought to be enough, especially for a child. I don't know, maybe I just didn't teach him right."

"I'm sure you taught him fine," Walter said. "But while we're talking about me being a despicable person, let's not forget that you got into trouble sometimes, too."

That got a small smile from Teo. "Yes, I suppose you're right. I just...I wish innocence wasn't punished so forcefully, so...absolutely." He looked at Walter. "You really think you'll be able to find him?"

"I don't know. I've never done anything like this before. But I want to at least try. I want to do something right."

Teo sighed. "I hope you're right. For your sake. Which is why

I'm going to tell you this one thing: if you're serious, if you really intend on going in there and looking for Tommen, either you bring him back alive, or don't come back at all."

"What?"

"I believe you want to change. I really do. I just don't know how far I can trust you, and I have a wife and children to look after. If you can find my boy, then we'll talk. But if not, then don't bother. I don't mind if you want to stay in the community and try to build a life for yourself, make a good life for yourself as a good man. You're just not going to do it with or near me."

"What if I find Tommen...not alive?"

"Maisy and I are still trying to get over it. I thought I was, or near enough. Maybe I never was, clinging to this superstitious hope, whatever you want to call it. The fact of the matter is, our boy is gone. Short of him walking in door alive, nothing is going to change that fact. And again, I don't know how far I can trust you. Stay in the community, fine. But stay away from me."

The hurt on Walter's face was painfully obvious.

"If you want," Teo said, "you can sleep in the barn tonight and come out to start searching at first light."

After a second of hesitation, Walter shook his head. "No. If you don't want me here, then you don't want me. No time like the present to begin my search."

"I want to believe the best in you, Owain. I do. I wish I had the kind of open trust that ma has. But I don't."

"I'm not saying I blame you," Walter said, preparing his lantern. "I probably wouldn't have been so nice if our positions were reversed. I'm grateful for the chance, and I'm going to do my damnedest to bring your boy back to you alive. I guess I just never quite get over how much the stupidity of my youth has really cost me."

Teo's expression was unreadable, but sorrow was definitely in there. "Be safe, brother. Know that no matter what, I wish you the best."

Walter did not reply as he handed Teo the lantern before climbing over the logs and debris to get in the cave. Once his feet were safely on the ground, Teo handed the lantern back over. It took a minute, then the wick sputtered to life.

"I would wish you all the best, too, Teo," he said. "But it looks like you've already got it."

Then he turned and let the lantern take him deeper into the cave.

The only way Tommen knew when the time travel ended was because of the change in the trail, the carved out stone; otherwise everything looked about the same in the darkness. He still sat alone on the boulder. His first instinct when he heard rustling in the bushes was to jump up and go for his pocket knife, the only weapon he had on hand. It was only Julianna.

"How did you find me?" he asked.

"It's not so hard," she told him. "If you're desperate to get out, you won't be visiting Mount Rushmore. You'll be looking for motivation and the method of escape."

He collapsed on the boulder in a heap, rubbing his eyes. "I have to get out of here. I can't take this anymore."

"You've been here for twenty-four hours."

"It feels like forever. I've seen too much. I shouldn't have come. I should have just walked away from that damn fire."

"But you didn't. And now you're here."

"No shit." He stood and ran his hand through his hair. "I have to get out. You're going to help me."

"Yes, we've established that. But it will take time. Running around haphazardly and spearing yourself with painful memories is not going to help you get out of here."

Tommen stopped in his pacing and sighed. "I followed my dad to Micaiah's house—well, it's him, his twin brother Micah, and Kayla— and they went to the Akarin fortress."

"And you tried to go through the portal with them," Julianna stated. "I can tell by the burns and the fresh bandages. Basically, you touched a live wire. Nothing terrible, but it gave you a pretty good shock, didn't it?"

"Yes, it did. I just hope it didn't fry my hearing aids."

"Well, you can test them out later once the burns have healed."

He nodded absently. "Why can't you just walk through a portal again and be okay?"

Julianna sat down on the boulder. "You've obviously figured out how to move through Matter—walls, car doors, all of that. It's a simple manipulation of Matter, given that we're here and yet not here. Energy doesn't work like that. When a portal is opened, that's like holding up a waterfall so you or others can go through. But when you try to go through, you're walking straight into the water. Water is nice, but Energy is a little more forceful. You can't handle it. It just zaps you right back."

"Is there a way to neutralize it?"

"Once again, no one has ever escaped this dimension. I don't know. More people commit suicide than die naturally, if that tells you anything."

Tommen sighed and shook his head. "There's got to be a way out. I mean, Micaiah is a pretty good Akari-bearer from what I've gathered. You talk all about Time and Matter and Energy and a manipulation of the physical universe. I know all this stuff. I'm good at this stuff. There's got to be some way to connect the two, get me talking to him and figuring a way out."

"As I've said, I will teach you what I know. But there is one element you are forgetting, and Rifun mentioned it, too."

"What's that?"

"Faith. The little bit of Something that makes it all go round." She smirked. "I know you're rolling your eyes at me where I can't see, trying to tell yourself that there is a rational, logical, predictable, mathematical explanation for every speck of space dust in the universe. But until you accept that there is one tiny pinprick of light at the center of it all, that one tiny force of Faith-Gravity that keeps the universe spinning the way it should, you will get nowhere."

"Teach me what you know, and then I'll decide."

"No one is guaranteed tomorrow, Tommen. You know that better than some. Sometimes a decision delayed is a decision never made." She stood. "But no manner of pithy sayings or arguments will change your mind here. All I ask is that you have an open mind."

"Said every religious person ever."

"And you never claimed that atheists have the most opened and enlightened minds out there and religious people should have open minds?"

Well, couldn't deny that one. "Fine. We could debate this all day, but we haven't even touched on anything. Teach me, then I'll decide."

She dipped her head. "Fair enough. Come with me."

Chapter Eight
Richard's Journal

Julianna took Tommen to an all-night diner in a seedier part of town, pulling an almost cartoon-like heist as she stole two burgers while the cook's back was turned. The expression on his face when he turned back around and the food was gone was absolutely priceless, and Tommen couldn't help but snicker.

"All right, so is that what I'm learning now?" Tommen asked, picking the lettuce off his burger.

"No," Julianna answered. "For tonight, I am just going to give you a history lesson." She noted his expression. "Don't give me that look. You're exhausted as it is. Akari abilities are a little more potent than Time abilities, so you need to be awake and alert in order to learn them and get used to them. Furthermore, history will provide a little background knowledge of what you're learning so you have a better understanding of it."

"Yeah, well, Rifun tried that. Sounded like New Age bullshit to me. Learning the 'names' of things and being one with nature and whatever."

"Isn't that what it is, though? You yourself advocate for clean water and food that hasn't been 'vandalized' I believe is the word you use. Forty years ago, you would have been called a tree-hugging hippie. Now people are beginning to see and understand. Isn't manipulating the very fabric of the universe kind of like being at one with it? Just because there's a scientific explanation doesn't mean the emotional or what you might call superstitious connection isn't there."

Tommen sighed. "Fine. Hit me." He took a bite of his burger. Before Julianna could begin, he said, "As long as it doesn't involve the

Crusades, the Knights Templar, evil Jews or Jesuits, or some weird, mind-bending, alternate history, mysticism bullshit from Hitler or World War II."

She shrugged. "I make no promises."

He rolled his eyes but motioned for her to continue. Seemingly out of nowhere, she produced a book, an eerily familiar leatherbound journal.

"Is that...?" Tommen asked.

Julianna nodded. "This is the journal my husband wrote, the one Cassius and Rifun killed for, the one you so naively picked up and ran off with."

"What did he write, though? I mean, it was all gibberish."

"Not gibberish. Imprinted text." She opened up the journal to a random page. "He wrote in such a way that different parts of the letters were just slightly out of sync with each other. But, if you know how to Imprint and how to reverse it..." Suddenly it was like invisible ink became visible, and all the writing made sense. " — then you can make sense of this 'gibberish.' "

"Holy shit." Tommen sat back and cleared his throat. "I mean, it makes sense. But then, you would have to know how to Imprint before reading the journal. And Imprint is an Akari ability, isn't it?"

"It is. You learn quick. Frankly, it's no different than your probationary period as a Time Agent. Give them a little something to test their motives, their character, see if they're a good fit. If they are, bring them in all the way."

Tommen nodded. "So then, where did Rifun and Cassius learn?"

"Rifun learned from Cassius. Cassius learned from another Akari-bearer."

"But who would want to teach Cassius? He was a bloodthirsty maniac. Or are you going to tell me he wasn't always that way and he had some sob story?"

Julianna shrugged. "If by 'some sob story' you mean being betrayed by your own people and sold into the white man's slavery, then yes, he had some sob story. In my research, Cassius was often beaten and abused by his slavemaster to the point where he killed said master and went on the run. A man who was a Harvester met him and tried to teach him a better way of life by opening him up to the wider universe. Well, Cassius took the Harvesting and used it to turn himself white, at least long enough to gain access to the upper crust for a short time."

"Where does your husband come in?"

Her expression saddened a little. "My husband was a great Akari-bearer, or he tried to be. At the time, there was one Akari group, called the Akarin. Like the Hands of Time, they held the monopoly on their industry. They were still smaller than the Time industry and less liked, but they were powerful. They were a real force for the Hands to reckon with. At one time, it had been a good thing, a way to keep the Time industry in check. But, as they say, absolute power corrupts absolutely.

"Richard tried to be good and stay faithful, but too many were falling into the power trap. So he did a bold thing. He sought the Author. The Books which you have no doubt seen and have received yourself, they were corrupt and convoluted. Richard wanted to speak directly to the Author and have the Author speak directly back. Write down the absolutes without the narrative that went with it. So he did. I helped him do it, and I sought the help of others who were of a like mind. Perhaps our eagerness was our downfall.

"The Hands of Time thought the Akarin meant to rise against them and overtake the Time industry, effectively controlling everything. The Akarin thought Richard was a troublemaker who was trying to undermine them. It was actually the Akarin who asked Cassius to imprison my husband and take the journal so they could destroy it. Cassius had different ideas; he wanted to use the journal for his own vile means. But I, who had helped him write the journal, and other supporters, decided to split up and hide it away, leaving a copy for the people to read in the meantime."

"Just another day as a missionary, right?" Tommen said.

"But it worked. Many of the Akarin did not appreciate what was going on with their leadership, how corrupt it had become, and they were relieved that someone was finally speaking the truth. Not everyone wanted to read Richard's journal, but we figured that as long as they lived peacefully and didn't cause trouble, what did it matter? The Akari was the Akari and the Author was the Author. That's not to say we didn't have conflicts, and that those conflicts didn't turn violent sometimes. The Akarin themselves saw a significant rift as old met new. Pretty soon, they were divided into a number of different factions. We ourselves had disagreements, and some will claim that there are factions among us, but the only heretical faction we recognize is the Cult."

"So what do you call yourselves, then?"

"Akari-bearers. The true Akari-bearers, to be certain."

"Certain, huh?"

"Of course. What better words to follow than the words of the Author?" She indicated the journal. "This is an instruction manual, not a novel or an anthology. When you were faced with your father's impending death and all the uncertainty over whether there could be a cure, whether or not the Hands would help you, would you have rather had a clear map that said, 'Go here to this place at this time and get this antidote' or a novel that bores with detail that may not even be relevant to the situation?"

"What does this have to do with training?"

"It's a matter of Faith, Tommen. We went over this."

"Yeah, but...this is like giving me a model airplane kit with all the pieces, but telling me that it won't fly unless I sprinkle it with fairy dust."

"Bad analogy." Tommen shrugged. "Think of it as assembling a real airplane with all the parts. You have everything you need to physically build a plane. But until you add Faith, until you add the gas and turn the key, you're grounded."

"Great. Can we please build the airplane before getting into the rest of it?"

Julianna sighed. "Tommen, you've already built the airplane. You've already flown. You opened the portal that brought you here, and you Traveled across the ocean. You've time traveled within this dimension. You know there is an Author, and you've tasted the power of the Akari. You know what I think? I think you're afraid."

Tommen went to fold his arms, but his left arm quickly shut down that idea. Instead, he shifted in his seat and did his best to look bored. "Of what?"

"First, you're afraid that you've been wrong this whole time. You know there's an Author, but you don't want to acknowledge it. Because that means that you aren't the be-all end-all in your own life. Second, you're afraid of commitment. This one I understand. Rifun introduced you to the Akari through the Cult, and a good friend of yours is an Akarin leader. Now here I am with another brand of the Akari. Which one is true? You certainly don't want to get it wrong."

She licked her fingers and wiped them on a napkin before pushing the journal over to Tommen. "Nothing anyone says is going to sway you one way or the other. You have to see it for yourself. You have to read it for yourself. So I'll loan this to you to read. When you're ready, then we'll train."

"Why can't we train first?" He put up his hand before she could say anything. "I know, I know. Faith. The little thing that makes the world go round. Whatever." He picked up the journal for a moment and flipped through the pages. "Fine, fine, I'll read it tonight or something. I'll need something to put me to sleep."

"Just be gentle with it. I realize it is only a hokey book of mysticism to you, but to me, it's one of my last connections to my husband, besides the memories we share. I visit them every so often, but as you can appreciate, it can be hard."

Guilt washed through Tommen then, and he nodded. "I can do that."

"Thank you." She stood and straightened her dress. "I suppose I shall see you at some point tomorrow, then. We can have lunch, and you can ask me whatever questions you have about my husband's writing."

She left then, but not before giving the journal one last, longing glance. Tommen felt another wave of guilt hit him. A century and a half later and she still missed her husband. It probably didn't help living in a dimension where she could time travel at any moment to watch and remember all the good times they had together. After the events of the day, Tommen figured he could relate.

At the same time, being in a dimension where he could time travel at will proved advantageous to him. He picked up the journal, flipping through the pages, occasionally stopping to read a short passage here and there. Directly from the Author, huh? Verified and certified, signed and sealed. Well, he would see about that.

Tommen finished his burger and stood, force of habit telling him he should leave a tip, no matter the fact that they'd stolen their food in the first place and had gotten essentially zero service. Plus the part where his money would probably just sit there forever and never get claimed. He sighed, conflicted and not entirely sure why. After a minute, he shook his head, picked up the journal, and left the diner, turning in the direction he was pretty sure was east.

If there's an Author, and the Author is any kind of powerful and trustworthy, then seeking the truth ought to be the biggest declaration of Faith out there, Tommen reasoned. He nodded to himself. *Okay. Take me to the truth.*

Maybe it was the placebo effect, or maybe there really was an Author out there who was all like, "Finally! He's getting it! Find the truth! And here, have a little push while you're at it." Whatever the cause, Tommen was pretty sure that his first trip across the ocean had been twice as long as this trip. He was almost dizzy. He put a hand to his chest and coughed. His heart was going wild. What was this? Was it like in the Wheel, going through too many portals in a day had some side effects? Well, maybe he ought to take it easy for a while.

Then the dizziness and his racing heart passed, and all was normal and right with the world. He straightened and looked around. He was outside Beaumaris Gaol once more. The differing time zones meant it was early morning here, but that was no matter.

If there was an aha moment to be had as far as mastery of the time travel was concerned, this was probably his aha moment. At a mere thought, he got where he needed to go. All the fresh paint, the new landscaping, and the pretty signs all melted away. The sky didn't go black with a foreboding bolt of lightning, but the general feel of the place was enough to accomplish the same thing, and Tommen felt the hair on the back of his neck stand up in sheer terror. He closed his eyes and effortlessly brought to mind the sights and sounds and especially the smells, tried to prepare himself for them even as he knew there was no sufficient preparation for those things.

He approached the prison feeling like he had lead in his shoes. He would never claim that he approached fearlessly, and every instinct told him to run and get the hell out of there.

He froze as soon as he stepped inside, momentarily overwhelmed by the fear and death that overrode every other sense. There was no higher reasoning here, only the bestial instinct to survive. And to think this had once been considered too humane of a prison. If this was humane, Tommen hated to see what the inhumane prisons looked like around here.

As for Cassius and Julianna, they were in a small room that might have been mistaken for an office with all the paperwork stacked here and there.

"I found the journal," Julianna said, handing over the leatherbound book. "He thought to leave it with one of his friends."

Cassius grunted and took it, opening it up and flipping through the pages. "It appears to be genuine."

"Appears to be? Of course it is. Why wouldn't it be?"

"In case you thought to use it for yourself and try to get out of our bargain."

She glared at him. "I have the support of many of the Akarin. You've seen how fast Richard's word has spread."

"The Author's word," Cassius cut in.

She hesitated but dipped her head. "Of course. The Author's

word. The ubiquity of the Time industry and the power of the Akarin together, we would be unstoppable. No more separation and feuding, but one power with one law, the law of the Author. But it only works as long as you free Richard as we agreed."

"You don't have to remind me."

"He goes free, a goodwill gesture from the Zero Hour. Richard proclaims peace, unites the two of us, and together we crush the Akarin."

"Why are you saying all of this? We both know what the agreement is."

"Because I feel compelled to remind you. You don't have the best track record for honoring agreements."

"Maybe, but I am your best bet. You don't have time to waste waiting for the next elections, waiting for the next Zero Hour to come into power. The Akarin are ready to crush you. You need power, you need arms, and you need it now. Which I can provide."

Tommen took a step back, then another, quietly, quietly, until he was out the door, as if afraid Cassius would look at him through time and space and death to kill him on the spot. He kept backing up until he was twenty feet down the corridor, pressed up against a wall. His heart was racing again and his breath came short. He half-expected one of the other gaolers to appear and cart him off to a cell, but it never happened.

Julianna was no grieving widow desperate to save her husband. She was intent on making a power play, a way to combine the Akarin and the Hands of Time into...what? A theocracy? Intergalactic communism? Something else entirely, and far worse?

Ask and ye shall receive, Tommen thought humorlessly. He'd asked, and he'd gotten much more than he bargained for. He'd stumbled into what amounted to the crux of the last century and a half of Time civil wars and Akari holy wars. Before, there had been Time and the Akarin. Now there was any number of groups out there, all with their own beliefs, systems, and agendas.

Tommen stumbled outside, letting go of the time travel. As the mirage faded, he was left staring at a white rabbit, sitting there in the grass. It sat perfectly still and watched him, nose twitching only slightly, just enough for him to know it was a real animal and not some weird lawn ornament.

"I know why Julianna felt compelled to remind Cassius and exposit everything," he said to the white rabbit, as if it could hear and comprehend his words. "It's because this is going to end up in a future Book by the Author as a way to record events as they actually happened, not as they wanted them to happen."

He shook his head in disbelief. Purple ink. That was the reason for the purple ink, the signature and stamp of the Author. Tommen opened the journal in his hand and looked at the pages. Richard had relied on magic tricks to sign his original copy, but that had all been done in real time under the scrutiny of his wife and others. And if the original was destroyed, there was no one to say whether one or the other was true. But the Author existed outside of Time, moving back and forth at will to ensure that even if some of the Books were tampered with, an original copy would always survive, always with the purple ink. Her words, unmolested.

Tommen headed to a rocky outcrop and sat down, his legs dangling over the cliff. As he looked down at the frothing waters below, he felt a sense almost like Predict, except it wasn't Time, but...air? Energy? Before he knew it, small droplets of water and tiny rocks were floating up toward him. He grinned. Gravity. In his revelation, he'd just learned Gravity all by himself. Well, to be more accurate, he'd stumbled onto it. To say he'd learned it, inasmuch as he controlled it and could call it up at will, well, that would take a little practice, and he didn't plan on going cliff diving anytime soon to test it out.

Still, he had some fun with it. Micaiah and Saul had said that Gravity had to operate along a track, and stepping outside that track meant plummeting to one's death, theoretically. This proved to be true as Tommen experimented a little with some small rocks around him and any insects unfortunate enough to grab his attention. He almost felt like a little boy again, in his giddy excitement. Finally, an ability that he'd learned because of a mind-blowing revelation, not because he was in trouble or fighting or holding his dying father.

After a short time, he stopped and let everything go back to where it was. The sun was rising here, but it would be a few more hours before the east coast saw sunlight. He knew he needed sleep, but that was suddenly the last thing he wanted to do. He was excited. He wanted to go, do, explore, run, whatever. More importantly, he wanted to do a little sleuthing to see if he couldn't figure out the rest of this story. This had to be how his dad felt when he was on a case and everything was starting to come together, that sweet feeling of everything coming to a satisfying close.

Tommen had no illusions that he was some kind of "Chosen One" hand-picked by the Author to fulfill a prophecy and complete his mighty destiny, but the coincidences were starting to add up, and the scene he'd just witnessed smelled of a rotten egg that needed cleaning up. Julianna was hiding something, and as Tommen prepared to Travel back across the ocean, he realized one part of it.

Julianna had been tracking her husband's journal for some time. Given how long she'd been in the in-between dimension, it was logical to think she'd already known where it was by the time the first murders happened. She said that she'd been keeping an eye on the area. Micaiah said that the last person to have Richard's journal was Rifun when he took over the Wheel. Julianna had shown more than enough proficiency with taking things from the real world and bringing them into the in-between dimension. If Cassius had betrayed her, and he and Rifun were as dangerous as she claimed to fear, why had it taken her so long to get the journal back? What had been stopping her? Just as Rifun could have Banded and walked into the evidence room of the precinct to steal it, Julianna could have just stolen it and the whole situation at the warehouse could have been avoided.

Not that he was an expert on such things, but Tommen smelled a juicy conspiracy. At the same time, sticking his neck out too far, he was liable to get his head chopped off. This wasn't Hell. He could very easily die here. He still had to get back to his dad somehow. Tommen ran his tongue over his teeth. He couldn't go to the Wheel to look through the Archives, and he couldn't get into the Akarin Archives either. The only source of information he had on the Akari and the power it possessed was in his hands now, but how far did he want to trust it? At the same time, maybe the only way to beat it was to dive headlong into it and destroy it from the inside. He had to become the student in order to kill the teacher. There was no other way.

It sounded romantic, to be sure, but by the time he set foot in Virginia—or he thought it was Virginia, anyway—most of the heroic feeling had faded, and he was back to being regular old sixteen year old Tommen Forbes. Hey, wasn't his birthday next Tuesday? He counted off the days on his fingers. Yup, he would be seventeen next week. Well, he wasn't much for birthdays, but everybody else was, and he would try to be home by then, if possible, so that it wasn't a shitty day for everyone who knew him and wanted to celebrate but couldn't.

He paused and looked around, momentarily forgetting his entire epic tirade where he single-handedly bested Julianna, destroyed the journal, defeated Rifun, and obliterated the Cult of the Akari from the inside. It certainly sounded nice, for some dumb ass middle school novel. But, as even Tommen's first Book had proven, he was no hero. He wasn't going to be the one to pull Excalibur from its stony hold, slay the dragon, and rescue the fair maiden. He wasn't even going to be the leader of a little band of heroes. If he was any sort of hero in this story, he would probably be the dopey sidekick.

Well, didn't matter anyway, he supposed. That was the end of the road, and he was still stuck at the beginning. If he wanted to bridge the gap between here and there, he was going to have to open the journal and start studying.

It was still dark out, but it didn't take long for him to find a small town with a street lamp bright enough to read under and a bench comfortable enough to stand for more than a few minutes. When he opened the journal, he found that all the words had scrambled again. He stared at them for a minute. Julianna had said that they were Imprinted, different parts of the letters slightly out of sync with the rest of it so that it looked like gibberish. If he knew how to Imprint, that would be a good start. But he needed to know more than that; he had to figure out how to reverse it.

Problem was, the only time he'd really Imprinted had been an experimental accident. He'd seen it done before and had it explained basically how to do it, but never actually done it himself. It was like taking a snapshot and leaving it suspended for a moment or two, just long enough to confuse someone. An illusion. What he needed to do was undo the illusion that Richard had Imprinted in this journal.

He'd seen Julianna do it, and he tried to picture if she'd made any motions, touched it, moved it, said anything about how to actually undo the Imprint. Furthermore, how and why had it gone back to the way it was? Was there some sort of timer on it, so that after a certain amount of time, if it had been undone, it would be redone? It would make sense, given the sensitive nature of the information contained within, or so they said. But then, if it really did contain the words of the Author, and if the Author really was that powerful, why go to such lengths to protect it? Wouldn't the Author protect it herself? In the purple ink books, they would be released no matter what at a set time. This journal, it was one man's word and one man's duty to protect it. And he had died. Even from a logical standpoint, Tommen found something very fishy about that.

Trying to get the letters to un-Imprint and assemble themselves in some sort of logical order was like beating a stone against a heavy duty padlock. He either needed the key, or a pair of bolt cutters.

After a minute or two, he leaned back in his seat. Maybe he'd just learned too much today. He'd learned the Traveling, the time travel thing, a bit of Gravity, plus that whole conspiracy bit. Maybe asking for a little Imprint ability was too much for today. Maybe he should get some sleep and try again in the morning.

Before he left, he made one last valiant attempt at reversing the Imprint on the letters. He almost didn't realize it when he did find a fingerhold, and a few more tiny pieces of letters started to come back. He focused intently on the paper, trying to feel out the Time as he brought a few more bits and pieces together. It was kind of like sticking his hand underwater and bringing up a bunch of silt and seaweed and rocks and shit. Was that a good analogy? He couldn't decide.

When he finally got all the letters to appear, he could feel that there did seem to be a timer on it, like the paper was water and all the letters just floating on top. After a predetermined amount of time, they would sink once again and he would be fishing. Was there a way to solidify everything? Could he bring everything to the surface and keep it there? Had there ever been any regular copies made to distribute to the common peasants? Then again, those copies were only valid as long as this one original remained. Destroy the original, and the copies are void, right?

Not necessarily, he decided. As long as Julianna was still around to proclaim the journal as the original. Well, once again, it didn't matter right now. He just needed to read it, know what was in it, then he could turn it over to someone else who might have a little better understanding of it, like Micaiah. Now that he understood how to unlock the letters and have them make sense, they might be able to get this show on the road.

At the same time, he was going to need something a little more comfortable than a park bench, and something a little brighter than a street lamp. Grudgingly, he stood and looked around, trying to determine which way was home. It wasn't quite dawn yet. Maybe he could find a road sign saying "Charleston, That Way." But, like the Great Lakes not posting "Canada, That Way" signs, he did not find one for Charleston either. He did find a highway, however. Odd numbers meant north to south, and even numbers meant east to west.

It took a couple of tries, but he was back in Charleston before too long. He made a quick stop at the twins' house. His dad's car was still there, and he, Micaiah, and Kayla were still absent. Micah slept soundly, his alarm clock set for only a couple hours from now.

Tommen left the room, left the house, and headed for one of the few places he knew was not only open this late—or early, depending on how one wanted to look at it—but had sufficient light to read by.

Charleston had a large population, but was not actually a huge city. Most of the people who claimed Charleston as a mailing address lived scattered across the mountainside, flung far and wide over hill and dale. So the night crew at the precinct was comparatively smaller than other cities of similar population but with greater population density. Tommen did not know any of the officers on duty now; most of them looked like new hires fresh from the Academy, the guys who were hired to fill the holes left by the deaths from last Christmas.

He went to his dad's cubicle and sat down in the large, comfy chair, putting his feet up on the desk. After a second, he felt guilty about it and sat up normally, even though he knew no one would yell at him for it. Still, habits were a bitch. He was momentarily distracted by his school picture, sitting on the desk next to the computer. It was his school picture from last year. He hated it, as usual, but at least it was better than the one from the year before when he'd had braces.

He had to get another school picture this year.

He opened the journal.

Truthfully, Tommen wasn't sure where to start, and there was something icky about opening up someone else's journal. Yeah, yeah, words from the Author and all that, but he'd always heard it referred to as a journal. Journals were supposed to be personal things. He himself didn't have one—and no, his notebook full of stories didn't count—but if he did, he wouldn't want anyone else to read it, regardless of whatever profound truths he espoused in there. But still, he had to know.

Regardless of how crazy Richard may have been, at least he had a decent system of organization. The first few pages were something like a personal letter, explaining why the journal had to be written, why the Akarin were corrupt, and why the Author was angry with them. Okay, so the guy hadn't been a completely deranged lunatic. At least he had a reason. It may not have been the right reason, but it was a reason, one he believed in. Enough to attempt to form an alliance with the Hands of Time, overthrow the Akarin, and establish a single communist, monarchal, whatever type rule.

The first section he labeled, "The Nature of the Author" in which he detailed how the Author was an infinitely infinite being of great might and power, so on and so forth. Personally, Tommen thought it sounded more like a Catholic preacher giving a grand sermon on the might and power and wrath of God and woe to ye heathens. There was a subsection about misconceptions about the Author that the Akarin routinely taught as truth. For instance, that the Author was not the end-all of end-alls, that she was yet subject to another unknown power. Another apparent misconception stemming from this was something that amounted to multiverse theory, that there were multiple universes existing inside each other. According to Richard, there was one universe and the Author was the end-all power over it. Period. The end.

The second section was titled, "The Novels" referring to the purple ink Books like Tommen had received and were stored in the Akarin Archives. Richard argued that the Author could not have authored those Books because that would involve other people; standard publishing demanded extra readers, editors, printers, any one of whom could alter and embellish at any given moment. The Author needed no other people except to write down things exactly as she said them, someone loyal, without any other interference. Once again, Tommen found himself wondering just how great and powerful and infinitely infinite the Author could be if she wasn't even willing to deal with those who were still publishing in her name.

He'd just gotten to the third section, "The Nature of the Akari" when he put the journal down and rubbed his eyes. This was way too philosophical for his taste. If he wanted to be honest, he really preferred the Time Civil War over this. At least the civil war had been more clear cut. Working for Rifun, bad guy. Working against Rifun, good guy. Even the Borelian declaration of war was pretty simple. Borelians versus humans. Humans were to be killed or taken as slaves.

This...this was a holy war if there ever was one.

Tommen sighed and closed the journal. He looked around the cubicle. His dad was a pretty sparse decorator, but the paperwork and case files more than made up for the empty space.

He wasn't even fucking religious. He'd barely even considered God before this year. He'd never considered the Author until recently. The more he read through the journal, trying to think critically, scientifically, considering everything he'd seen from both Micaiah and Julianna, he was tempted to just throw up his hands and say fuck it all. They're all right, they're all wrong, what did he care? He had Richard's journal, claiming to be the words and teachings directly from the Author. He had a purple ink Book in his bedroom, also supposedly directly from the Author, but with knowledge and details he'd never shared with anyone, had barely even thought about until it showed up.

Both books were supposed to be from the Author. Richard's journal said the novel was false because the Author didn't need anyone to help, and its status as a "novel" versus an "instruction manual" immediately pointed to human interference. The Akarin claimed Richard's journal was false because it negated itself, claiming the Author was infinitely powerful while not even bothering to clean up the mess the Akarin had made. Richard's journal was supposed to be the words of the Author, yet the novels kept appearing. And where did the novels come from, anyway, seeing how the copyrights didn't start for years in the future? Who would suffer a counterfeiter that long?

Groaning, Tommen stood and made a few laps of the office. Couldn't he just escape the in-between dimension without all the bullshit? Give him the power with none of the fluff or philosophy. He smiled grimly to himself as he momentarily wished he could communicate with Becky and get her thoughts on things. He was trying to look at things objectively and getting all sorts of confused. Maybe what he needed was a biased opinion, something he could springboard off of.

At the same time, wasn't Julianna a pretty biased opinion? Why was he stumbling off of that springboard? Was it because he smelled a conspiracy? Was it because he knew somewhere, deep down, that the whole thing was bullshit? He didn't know. But he did know that he was tired. He'd been up too long, been reading too long. His eyes hurt and the burger was starting to wear off. Damn, he wished he knew how to sneak things into the in-between dimension; he could really go for a burrito or something.

He made another lap of the precinct before returning to his dad's cubicle to grab the journal. He paused as he picked it up. Could he just wing it, try to force something back through the dimensional divide and set the journal on the desk? A brief, very vivid memory of the portal to the Akarin fortress made that decision for him. He'd had enough of that, and he really didn't want to test his luck twice in one day.

As he stepped outside, the first indication of dawn colored the horizon, a dim gray as clouds rolled in, promising rain at some point. Great. They could have used this, oh, a week ago. Even a couple days ago would have been pretty sweet. As he thought about it, his arm began aching. Great. Now he was going to end up like an old person who could predict the weather with their joints. Except for him it was going to be his arm and whatever scars formed from the burns.

He stopped at Becky's house on the way home. She was asleep, as was to be expected, her machines shut down and quiet, mounds of fabric reduced to just a few piles as she wrapped up her summer work. She slept with the sheets pulled all the way up to her chin, Mr. Snuffles, the gray, long-haired cat curled up around her pillow on the bed. As Tommen was about to leave, the cat looked up, yellow eyes glowing in the dim light. It stared at him for a long moment, ears pricked forward intently.

Tommen turned around to see if there was a mouse or a dust bunny, but he didn't see anything. When he looked back at the bed, Mr. Snuffles was on the edge, still intent, poised and ready to pounce.

"Can you see me, cat?" Tommen asked, feeling foolish.

The cat did not hiss or do anything except leap off the bed, race across the room, and bolt out the door. Tommen did not miss how the cat's natural projected path would have taken it right through him, but the cat had deliberately avoided him, going around his legs. Looking back, Becky just sighed and rolled over.

Well, that was one horror movie trope he could check off his list, the weird cat who could see ghosts and other apparitions between dimensions. With chills running down his spine, Tommen left the room and wandered back out to the street, heading for home. It was time to go to bed.

He wasn't sure why he headed for his own bed, other than for the familiarity. With his invisibility, he could feasibly sleep anywhere, a swanky hotel, a castle or a palace anywhere in the world, a resort in the Caribbean. If not for the freaky incident with Mr. Snuffles, he even could have laid down next to Becky. Well, on second thought, her bed was not full size. He'd have to scrunch up something awful, and that would just be uncomfortable. Cute girl or not, looks couldn't ward off a kink in the neck come morning.

His dad had returned home at some point while Tommen had been at the precinct, but he wasn't in bed. Rather, he appeared to be just getting up and around, starting the coffee and rummaging around for something quick for breakfast. It was still a couple hours until the bakery opened, so he was going to need something a little more substantial than a bagel with cream cheese. Given that it was past time for him to be heading to the precinct for a shift, Tommen could only conclude that his dad was heading back up to the campsite.

Tommen sighed. "Dad, I'm right here. I don't know how to make you realize that, but I'll find a way to come back home. Well, I mean, I am home, technically speaking, but I'll find a way to make myself visible and get out of here and whatever else I need to do. Just don't give up on me."

Maybe that was really what scared him the most, that he wouldn't find a quick and easy answer, that it was going to take a long time, longer than the search crews were willing to search, longer than his dad was willing to wait before giving up and finally laying his son to rest, at least in his mind.

"Don't give up on me, Dad," Tommen repeated. "I'll find a way out."

He headed for his bedroom, unsure of just how he intended to do that. Carefully, he lay down on his bed, minding his arm. After a minute or two, he managed to shift around and get his arm up on his pillow. That did nothing for his back, however, and soon he was back to lying normally.

If he was technically in the "dream lands" or whatever, did that mean he wouldn't dream while in this dimension? Had that white rabbit he'd seen at Beaumaris Gaol been in the real world or the in-between dimension? Had it seen him? Was it possible for animals to see him but not humans? Why? What was the difference? Cats were weird; everyone knew that. But rabbits?

He thought he remembered reading somewhere that an animal's whiskers were incredibly fine-tuned to atmospheric disturbances, which was how animals knew when bad weather was coming. Could it also be tuned to some kind of electromagnetic field? Maybe it wasn't so much that Mr. Snuffles had seen him, but he'd sensed a disturbance in that field, in the Energy. Was that scientific or New Age-y? He didn't know.

Didn't help him figure a way out anyway, nor did it help him sleep. He lay there in his bed, trying not to think of anything, about the contents of the journal, the conspiracy he'd witnessed, Mr. Snuffles' weird behavior, the screaming pain in his arm. He closed his eyes and tried to breathe, let it all out, drift away, fall asleep. After a short time, he heard his dad leave the house, start the car, and head out. Tommen had a fleeting thought that he should have accompanied him. Even if they couldn't have a conversation, maybe Micaiah would call or something and there would be some other interesting news to be had, something that would shed soe light on the situation, give them hope, give him hope for rescue.

Well, didn't matter. He was exhausted and had to sleep at some point. He rolled over onto his side, minding his arm. He could Travel up there later, once he'd gotten some good sleep and a good lunch. Before he knew it, he was asleep. He didn't know how he knew he was asleep, only that he was. Come morning, he couldn't say that he remembered his dreams, only that they'd been horrifying.

Chapter Nine
Fledgling

Walter hated portal travel no matter where it led to. He stumbled forward into the Akarin fortress, catching himself on a wall, and stopped to breathe. *Just breathe. In and out. In and out. Ignore the feeling of nausea and being sick to your stomach. Just breathe.*

When he finally turned around to look at Micaiah and Kayla, he found Micaiah kneeling on the floor, rubbing and almost clawing at his eyes, groaning in pain. Kayla stood over him with a hand on his back, looking rather uncertain about the whole thing.

"What happened?" Walter asked, trying to sound strong but feeling anything but.

Kayla gave him an incredulous look, and it was a moment before Micaiah spoke, saying, "I saw Tommen."

"What? Where?" Walter looked around.

Micaiah got to his feet, still rubbing his eyes. "I don't know. Behind you? At first I thought it was here. Then he was at home. But when I looked, I couldn't see anyone. It all came in a flash of light and electricity, like a bolt of lightning touched down right beside me. Didn't kill me, didn't strike me at all, but blinding as hell." Finally he put his hands down by his sides, eyes red and rubbed raw. "I don't even know what I saw. But I could have sworn it was Tommen."

Walter glanced at Kayla who shrugged helplessly. "I didn't see anything, but I did feel like there was a surge of energy right after you went through, Walt. I thought it just came from the both of us trying to force the portal to stay open. But like I said, I didn't actually see anything."

"Have you ever seen something going through a portal

before?" Walter wondered.

Micaiah shook his head. "No. And here's the thing, I wasn't going through the portal yet. I was still there trying to hold it open, waiting for you to get through."

Walter grunted, wanting to hope but not wanting to get foolish hope up too high. "What was he doing? What did you see?"

"He was..." Micaiah let out a breath as he thought. "I can't say for sure, I only saw him for a flash, if I saw him at all. But it was like he was trying to follow you through the portal but couldn't. He was right there in the middle of it when I saw the lightning or whatever it was." He shook his head. "I don't know, maybe it's just wishful thinking."

"Don't discount anything yet," Kayla told him, echoing Walter's thoughts. "Between Time, the Akari, and Rifun, anything is possible. Try to remember as much as you can and we'll—"

"It was only for about a billionth of a second; there's only so much I can remem...ber..." He trailed off.

"What?" Walter prompted.

"I was on his left side," Micaiah said.

"Yes, because you were on the left side of the portal."

"No, there was something about it that wasn't right."

"What do you mean?"

"I don't know. I can't think of it now."

"Maybe we should get going to the Archives," Kayla suggested after a quiet moment. "Give it a few seconds and let your mind sort it out a little, like remembering a dream."

"Maybe," Micaiah conceded. "First I want to go down to the kennels. Maybe he left a scent."

Walter had only been to the fortress once, and it wasn't exactly a grand tour. He knew there were eight aboveground levels and three sub-levels, but that was about it. He'd never been to the sub-levels, and something about it unnerved him. Somehow he equated sub-levels with dirty little secrets the Akarin didn't want exposed. Given that one level was said to house a type of prison, and another level housed vicious beasts that had been used to track down and murder those who had gone into hiding after Rifun's coup, his blood pressure wasn't exactly low as they headed down, down, down to the third sub-level where said beasts were housed.

It wasn't as much of a dungeon as Walter had feared. Actually, it reminded him very much of Animal Control. Stone, yes, but well-lit, sterile, echoing with the noise of caged animals. The current tender appeared to recognize Micaiah and Kayla and let them through with no problem. He—or she or it—was more leery of Walter, letting him in only because Micaiah claimed him as a guest.

Maybe it wasn't so much Animal Control as it was a stable, or something similar. A few years ago, he and Tommen had gone to the Braxton County Fair, just for something to do and a little road trip outside of Charleston. Some of the larger Trackers were kept in huge stalls like the draft horses. Other, smaller Trackers were kept in goat-sized pens. Still the smallest of the Trackers fit well in duck-sized pens. Rows upon rows of them, growling, snarling, barking, hissing, bleating, and making other assorted sounds Walter had no name for.

The two Trackers they were looking for were about halfway down the fifth row. Evidently, the beasts had formed some kind of bond with them—with Kayla, anyway. They greeted her like a couple of loyal hounds. Micaiah and Walter stayed back while she released them and bade them sit and wait.

"*Tadaso!*" she commanded.

The two Trackers went to work, sniffing down the row one way, then turning and heading the other direction, almost methodical in their search. Finally, one of them approached Micaiah, giving him a good once-over. It sat about halfway, then stood and sniffed again. It circled him and made a noise almost like a whine. Then it sat. Then stood. The second Tracker walked over and did a similar routine. They abandoned Micaiah for a minute, went to Walter, sniffed him, abandoned him. Then they went to Kayla. They gave her a good once-over, looked uncertain, returned to Micaiah. There was more sniffing, more circling, more sitting, then standing, then circling again.

"Well, they smell something on me," Micaiah said after a

minute. "I just wish they could tell us what."

"But there is something," Kayla said, calling off the dogs and offering them a treat as she put them away. "That's all we really needed to know. Once we do more research, then we might make more sense of it."

Walter felt very much like the outsider as he trailed along behind them. He wasn't sure how he felt about that. On the one hand, he was usually the one in charge of the investigations. At the precinct, he was most often the lead investigator on his murder cases. In Time, he was the Captain in charge of the District. Micaiah had once been his Lieutenant and answered to him. Now the roles were reversed, it seemed. On the other hand, how many times had Walter wished for someone else to take the lead and call the shots? If he ever retired from Time or got ousted as Captain, that would be one very likely possibility, at least on the one side.

They stopped briefly at the front desk.

"Those two seem to like you," the attendant observed, its expression and tone impossible to judge. "Maybe you ought to take them home and free up some space around here."

"As interesting as that would be, I don't think that would go over well with the neighbors," Kayla said, grinning. "Actually, we were wondering how much you understood about Tracker behavior."

"Not a lot."

"Well then, who trains them? If they've been sitting down here for God knows how long, how were they trained to search?"

The attendant made a motion, which Walter interpreted to be a shrug. "Most of the Trackers here came from the Wheel of Time; they'd been kept in the Judgment Wing while Rifun was in power. I imagine he trained them or had someone else train them. Right now, we just try to figure out what to do with them."

It was hardly an encouraging answer, but it was honest at least. Micaiah and Kayla thanked the attendant, and the three of them headed out, past the prison, all the way to the main floor. Walter was exhausted, and it didn't help that they still had research to do. He had little doubt they could and would send him home if he asked, but he had to find something that would help him find his son. He had to find out what all this meant, the Trackers' behavior and now Micaiah's vision or whatever one wanted to call it. He had to hope that there was an answer and Tommen was alive and well out there somewhere.

They went up to the Archives on the fifth floor. It might as well have been the fiftieth floor for as well as Walter's knee took it. Micaiah and Kayla asked after him, but he shrugged them off. If Micaiah could get up to the fifth floor with only one leg, he could manage it well enough with two. Still, he found himself limping into the Archives and he made for the first chair he saw, sitting down gratefully.

"Are you sure you're going to be able to go running around a mountain tomorrow, Walt?" Micaiah asked.

No. "Of course. A good night's sleep is all I need. And we'll be sitting down a good chunk of time here, so I'll be fine."

"All right, if you're sure."

I'm not. "What are we researching exactly?"

"I want to look up Tracker behavior," Kayla answered, heading for an aisle and disappearing.

"I'm going to do a quick search on portals and see if there might be an answer for what I saw," Micaiah said, wandering off down a different aisle.

That left Walter alone in the middle. Honestly, he liked the Akarin Archives better than the Wheel Archives. It was true that the Wheel Archives had about a hundred thousand times more information, but there was something nostalgic about the look and feel of an old library, of ancient books and even older scrolls. Of course, the information contained within those scrolls was far beyond anything humanity could come up with in the twenty-first century. To hear Micaiah tell it, the only reason the Akarin used books and scrolls instead of tablets was for that very reason: nostalgia. And so the information couldn't be hacked and compromised. But mostly nostalgia.

No one offered to get Walter a book to read, which meant he

was going to be limping all over the place to find what he wanted. Problem was, he wasn't sure what he wanted to research. He had no idea where to begin. Kayla was looking up the Trackers, which made sense because of their odd behavior up there in the campsite. That was something tangible that merited investigation. Micaiah wanted to know about the vision in the portal. Again, something potentially relevant to the case that was worth investigating to see if it could lead to more.

But Walter had nothing else. Those were the only two clues they had to go on. Trackers and visions. What else was there that was tangible and not fanciful?

Well, he did have one idea. Even so, though, he didn't understand the layout of these Archives. It wasn't like he could just pick up any book and find a map inside. Could he? Should he ask someone? The Archives were large, but they weren't empty. It was like a library, really. People were everywhere; they just couldn't be seen on account of all the books. On the other hand, maybe it would benefit him a little to do some wandering and get to know the place a little. Besides, some of the greatest discoveries were made on accident.

For example, he discovered very quickly that his knee did not appreciate being used while it was already sore. He also discovered that his addiction to his painkillers might be a little worse than originally anticipated, as he found himself dry-swallowing two of them. He'd never dry-swallowed any pills in his life. He couldn't do it. But apparently he could if his body demanded it. It helped his knee, but did nothing for his fatigue except make it worse.

Whether by chance or providence, he eventually found what he thought would be a resource for his research. *Water, Fire, Air: Elements and the Akari.*

By the time he returned to the table, Kayla and Micaiah were already there, digging into books and scrolls.

"What did you find?" Micaiah wondered quietly as Walter sat down. He nodded when Walter showed him the book. "Could prove useful. I imagine that—"

"What do you imagine?" Walter asked.

Micaiah set down his pen. "That's it. That's what it was."

"What?" Kayla looked up.

"I was on Tommen's left side, like I said, but there was something wrong. It was burned." He closed his eyes. "His jacket had the right arm cut off, his shirt, too. And I could see that he had burns on his left shoulder and ear. And his left arm was wrapped, bandaged all the way from his hand to his shoulder."

Kayla chewed on the end of her pencil. "That's something new. He could have only gotten burns that bad from the wildfire. Question is, what did you see, and where is he?"

"That's what we're going to find out," Walter said, opening his book.

Unfortunately, his book was much less helpful than he'd hoped, at least as far as finding Tommen went. It was very enlightening when it came to the Akari, however. Time could not control fire, but the Akari could, as the Akari encompassed Time, Matter, and Energy. Though the book never failed to mention how volatile Energy could be, especially when it came to things that were "pure" Energy, such as electricity and fire.

Walter leaned back in his chair. "What if...?"

"What if what?" Kayla wondered, placing a marker in her book and looking up.

"This is going to sound crazy."

"We're the masters of crazy," Micaiah told him. "What's on your mind?"

"What if Tommen was trying to control the fire?"

"What do you mean?"

Walter shifted position. "Rifun wants to train Tommen in the Akari. He may have done so in that fire. You want to train Tommen in the Akari. Saul managed to get one lesson in about the Akari. Tommen views the Akari as religion of some form. We all know that he's a little stubborn when it comes to religion. He doesn't want to be taught; he wants to discover for himself, at least to an extent. If the Akari includes

Matter and Energy in its repertoire, what are the odds that Tommen would try to play hero and stop the fire by himself?"

Micaiah nodded slowly. "If Rifun taught Tommen how to feel those boulders and suck them dry, it is very possible that he tried to show him something with the fire, too. Maybe it got out of hand."

"Yes, but Tommen is right-handed," Kayla said. "You said his injuries were to his left arm."

"What difference does that make, really?" Walter asked.

"Typically, when you start out learning about Matter, it's easier to touch the things you're manipulating. It's like an object lesson, a physical representation up until you can do it without touching. If Tommen is right-handed, he's going to naturally reach out to touch something with his right hand."

"Unless Rifun ordered him to use his left for some reason," Micaiah pointed out.

Walter took an even breath. "Would it matter if he was right- or left-handed? Does it make a difference in our quest to find him?"

The couple exchanged a guilty look. It was Micaiah who answered, "No. I guess not." He shifted. "But, it did appear as though it had been tended to, bandaged and whatnot, so he's okay there."

"Yes, but for how long? Emergency medicine is just that, for emergencies. If he's burned, he needs to see a doctor as soon as possible. Which means we have to find him."

They returned to their books and scrolls. Speculation was great, but it wouldn't make Tommen appear out of thin air. They needed clues, facts, evidence. Walter almost hated to admit it, but Kayla had the right of it. The Trackers were their best lead. They had found something. Problem was, they, the humans, didn't understand enough about Tracker behavior and training to make sense of it. It was like the average person asking a drug dog or a cadaver dog to search. The dog would search, and would do its thing when it found its prize, but until the person understood the dog's training and behavior and knew what to do when the search was complete, nothing was really accomplished.

Walter found his book more personally educational than

helpful to the investigation. He could understand why the Hands of Time worked so hard to cover up the Akari and claim it was only a myth. Having control over pretty much all physical aspects of the universe was pretty intimidating, and there they were with only one meager set of abilities. Of course, since Rifun's coup, now everyone knew the Akari was real, or some version of it.

Walter didn't like that he seemed to have a stake in each side of that war. On the one hand, he was a Time Agent, a Captain Timekeeper, with decades of good service and experience. On the other hand, he'd come to understand the Akari and what it represented, and one of his good friends was a leader of the Akarin. He didn't want to be torn between the two. Of course, then he was forced to question what kind of loyalty he held for Time and the Hands. They'd been so corrupt as to sign their own death sentence. They'd left him to die while his teenage son trekked across the universe for him. Then they'd tried to apprehend his son for treason, and Tommen had to be rescued by a bloody terrorist in that respect. And now they were war-happy, going against the very group who had sought to liberate them from Rifun's regime.

So if he wanted to be honest, Walter held no real loyalty to Time. He would continue to do his job, certainly, but if push came to shove, he wasn't going to betray Micah or Micaiah or Kayla or any of them. If Tommen was persuaded to join them, he certainly wasn't going to go against his own son. Did that make him one of the Akarin, or just a sympathizer? An honorary member, perhaps? His intuition had taken him from beginning to end pretty quickly, and he was preparing to retire from Time in a few years. Micaiah made it sound like most of the leaders required all members to be active at all times, though he said that there were some Core members who did retire in the end. They understood what the Akari was, what it meant. So they lived with what Walter might call a quiet faith. They'd run the race and done everything they could to please others and with new souls to the cause. Now they just settled down for a little while to take the last few years to themselves.

Walter rubbed his eyes and yawned. "Oh, shoot. I'm exhausted. Did either of you find anything particularly useful? Kayla, you've been poring through a dozen different books; you must have found something."

"Well, sort of," she said uncertainly. "A lot of this is old stuff, old manuals, old stories. Doesn't mean it's bad, but it's just weeding through what's old-old and what's old that's still being used, if you get what I mean."

"What have you found so far?" Micaiah wondered, stretching in his seat, twisting to crack his back.

"I found that it takes about a year to train a somewhat decent Tracker, and upwards of three years to train a very good Tracker."

"And which kind was our Trackers?"

"I don't know. Sounds like they're on the lower end of the spectrum. The way the really good Trackers are described, they're all business and no play. Ours were still pretty carefree."

"Maybe we should try and see if there are any really good Trackers in the kennels, then," Micaiah suggested. "Did you find anything else?"

"Trackers have different maneuvers to indicate different strengths of Time. If they pick up an old scent, they'll do one thing. If they pick up a really fresh scent or something really strong, they'll do something else."

"Do you know what those somethings are?" Walter wondered.

She shook her head. "No. Usually it's specific to the trainer. Back in the day, it sounds like Tracker breeding was like horse breeding. You have your stables, your trainers, your breeders, your champion stock, the works. But, just based on our experience, I'd say the jumping around means that there's something pretty significant."

"They were jumping around at the site with the boulders, the cabin, and that spot out in the woods," Micaiah stated, then sighed. "But, as you said, he was there for five weeks. We don't know anything about those sites. That could have been where he did all his Time shenanigans, with or without Rifun."

It was like trying to solve a murder with no body and no evidence. Even if they caught the guy, they'd never be able to prove that he had anything to do with it. Walter rubbed his eyes, feeling like he was going round and round in circles in his thinking and getting nowhere. No new evidence was miraculously popping up, and they weren't making any decent progress here. Maybe they were just tired. Maybe they should all go home and get some sleep, start fresh in the morning.

"Did you find anything on your portal vision or whatever?" Kayla asked Micaiah after another minute or two.

Micaiah shook his head as he closed another book. "Nothing but ghost stories."

Kayla tapped her pencil on the table. "What if it was an Imprint? If he Imprinted at the exact location where we opened a portal, it may have caused some kind of reaction."

"But an Imprint is just a momentary flash; they last only a couple seconds, max. He would have had to have already been in the house, and we would have seen him."

"They last a couple seconds, but they can be suspended for a decent amount of time if you know what you're doing."

"Does Tommen strike you as the kind of kid who knows what he's doing?" Micaiah shifted in his seat. "And anyway, why Imprint?"

"Maybe it's the only way he can get a message to us, if Rifun is with him and is watching him," Walter suggested. "Or he could still be injured. If he's concussed, he might have the mental capacity to dress his wounds and know basically where home is, but he can't quite grasp the concept enough to stay in one place or fully know what he's doing. If he's haphazardly Banding, using Time, using the Akari, whatever, it might explain the erratic behavior of the Trackers, the strange jaunt into Virginia, and now this."

"Great. Now how do we catch him? How long did it take his last concussion to clear?" Kayla wondered. At Walter's raised brow, she shrugged and said, "Cai told me all about his skiing accident."

"Last time, it was only a mild to moderate concussion. He

knew who he was, where he was. His biggest thing was that his language skills got mixed up and he couldn't speak English for a short time. This severe of a concussion, I don't know. But if we don't get some kind of signal or message—something coherent anyway—soon, he could be looking at severe concussion, traumatic brain injury. If he doesn't know enough to go home or get to a doctor..." Walter looked away.

"I think we let our horses run away on that line of thought," Micaiah jumped in. "Maybe we should go back to the part where Rifun could be with him, and a two-second message is all he could get to us. If Rifun was using the fire as a lesson in Matter and Energy, splitting those boulders and potentially injuring Tommen in some way, it seems a very likely scenario. Can we all agree? It's a worst-case scenario, so if Rifun isn't with him, it just makes our job easier."

Walter grudgingly agreed. He hated to think that Tommen was running around anywhere near Rifun, and yet, as long as he continued to demonstrate talent with the Akari, Rifun seemed to be inclined to keep him moderately safe. Usually it involved blackmailing Tommen with threats over him, Walter, as well as the twins and anyone he cared about, but as long as Tommen did what Rifun said, he might just be okay for the moment.

"Now then, did Tommen ever mention anything to you, Walter, about what Rifun was telling him to do, what to practice, what to say, any of that?" Micaiah asked seriously.

Walter shook his head. "No. He only told me that Rifun had contacted him and wanted to train, but that was all, aside from the usual threats. He didn't give any specifics."

"He didn't tell me anything either. Just that said Rifun contacted him, threatened him, and wanted to train. 'Just thought you should know' were his exact words, I believe." He grinned and shook his head. "This shit is becoming so commonplace we almost don't know what to do with it anymore. How much do we take seriously, and when do we dismiss it?"

Kayla stood and stretched and gathered some of her books and scrolls. "I'll be back in a minute. I need to stretch my legs, and I have another line of thought I want to look at briefly. Keep talking and see if you can't figure out something before I get back."

That didn't seem too likely given their circular conversations so far, but Walter wanted to remain optimistic.

"What do we know about Rifun's movements since he escaped the Wheel?" Walter began.

Micaiah frowned. "Not much, sorry to say. He was completely invisible up until he contacted Tommen."

"How is that possible? The manhunt for him on all sides was like John Wilkes Booth."

"He's got a hiding spot out there somewhere, Walt. I'd be willing to bet that he's got Tommen with him in that hiding spot, which would account for the Imprint. He's letting us know that he's alive, but that's all."

"Which means the search up there on the mountain is useless."

"We don't know that for sure. Something could still turn up. Tommen's a smart kid."

So they had two situations, neither of them promising. First, Tommen was squirreled away in some hidey-hole with Rifun. Second, Tommen was injured badly enough that he only had half a mind to get home but couldn't think to contact anyone beyond haphazard bursts of Time and the Akari.

"What if we're looking at this backwards?" Walter said suddenly.

"What do you mean?"

"What if our order of events is off? How long can an Imprint be suspended?"

Micaiah let out a breath and thought a second. "Well, the longest I've heard of is a day, but that was a very proficient user. That's, like, black belt level. Tommen is only just beginning."

"Yes, but humor me for a second if you would. What if the Imprint came first? What if Tommen was in your house first, trying to tell us he was home, he was all right? What if that's when Rifun got to him and then they headed for Virginia? Tommen tries to make a 9-1-1 call, and then...poof! Nothing since. But because his Imprint was still suspended, it was a way of him getting a delayed message to us?"

"That...actually sounds interesting. You think we should be looking at Virginia, then?"

"I don't know, but it's a start. Do we know if Virginia holds any special meaning for Rifun?"

"It would do well for us if you stopped talking about that murderer."

The two of them looked up as several people walked toward them. Walter figured it was a safe bet they were part of the Akarin Council in some fashion. Micaiah had once said it wasn't really much of a council, more of a loose confederacy, but after understanding a little more about the hierarchy, yes, it was a council.

Walter recognized one of the aliens as a Qalik, humanoid but with green skin, huge eyes, and vines instead of hair and all around its body, resembling something of a Medusa. The other three he could not speak for. Two were humanoid, one with white skin and black spots, the other with what may have been black scales. The fourth member was quadraped, looking like an unfinished dragon almost with no horns, no discernible ears, and no wings, and its black scales were more like plates, and much larger than one might expect.

Micaiah stood and Walter followed suit, unsure of the protocol in this situation.

"Micaiah," the Qalik greeted stiffly. "We agreed that the Akarin are to stay out of the war between Borelians and humans."

"This isn't about that war," Micaiah informed him. "One of our own is missing, and we believe Rifun Ndolo is behind it. Seeing how humans are...greatly discouraged from visiting the Wheel at this time, the only place we can conduct meaningful research is here."

"Are the resources of your world not enough?"

"Is that a trick question?"

"Why come here?" the black and white humanoid asked.

"Why not come here? Aside from the Wheel, this is the largest

Archives known to us."

"We are on the brink of war ourselves; you shouldn't be wasting time with—"

"My time. I shall spend it how I choose. If you don't like it, you can appoint someone else in my place. You yourselves said that Rifun, a human, caused this mess, so a human should be responsible for cleaning it up. Now he's taken a dear friend of mine. When we find him, this whole mess will be cleaned up, I assure you."

"And your guest here?" the black-scaled one inquired. "We have shut down all recruiting at your own suggestion. Why do you bring him here?"

"Because the one missing is his son. I'm not going to deny him a chance to do research and try to find his son. And when I suggested that we delay or put off recruiting, I didn't mean that we had to go into complete lockdown."

"Your words contradict themselves. First you want us to shut down, and then you don't. First you do not want to be placed as leader, and yet now you seem to enjoy bending the rules as it were. Do you think yourself above the rules you yourself suggested?"

Walter could hear Micaiah grind his teeth in frustration. "We need to get rid of Rifun. That's what I'm trying to accomplish. We get rid of Rifun, maybe we can salvage the war, maybe even prevent it. As for the humans and Borelians, that's not your problem, so I would kindly point out that you would save yourselves a lot of time, worry, and stress by keeping your noses out of our business."

His words were not kindly received, and there was a stare-down, four council members versus Micaiah. Micaiah won. The council members did not concede anything, merely turned as if to leave. The quadraped was the one who paused and looked back, saying, "From what we understand, Micaiah, you are considered the liaison between the human Time Agents and the human Akari-bearers of all factions. Not all factions enjoy being united. Furthermore, your mate is banking on your position of power in order to bring the human colony planets into the war. What would happen if you were suddenly removed from your position, hm?"

Micaiah did not respond, just saw the thing out with a heavy glare. After a moment, he slumped down into his seat and rubbed his eyes. "And I thought politics in the Wheel were nauseating."

"Not quite as utopian as I was led to believe," Walter commented sarcastically.

Micaiah barked a laugh. "Ha! Politics are the same no matter where you go. The grunts on the ground are great, and the Akari works well with them. The farther up you go, well, notoriety and influence speak more than the power does, only because the power is no longer there."

"The Force is no longer strong with them?"

If he got the humor, it fell flat. "Something like that, I guess." He rubbed his eyes. "I think it's about time we call it a night."

"So soon?" Kayla wondered, sitting down with another stack of books. "I was just getting started."

"Well, it's a good thing you missed our little confrontation with the council, or else we'd all be spending the night in jail." Micaiah chuckled humorlessly. "Nah, probably not, but..."

"But you didn't want my big mouth and hot head to get us into any more trouble than we already are?" Kayla guessed.

"You said it, not me."

"Um, excuse me," Walter said. "There's an audience."

"Oh, please, Walter, you're a big boy. And it's not like you and Laura are exactly discreet when you come into the bakery."

"We've been in there twice."

"Three times."

"Why are you watching us, anyway?"

"We don't have to watch you; we can hear you."

Walter folded his arms. "And who is this 'we'?"

Micaiah began counting off on his fingers. "Me, Micah, Jenna, Kyle. If Tommen was still there, he'd probably hear it, too. The laughing and the giggling, and we can practically hear you blushing, Walter. I don't think I ever saw you blush until you started dating her."

Walter looked at Kayla as if searching for reassurance, but the most he found was laughing eyes and a knowing smirk as she flipped a page and pretended to be engrossed in her book.

"She's good for you, Walt," Micaiah said. "That's all I'm really trying to say."

Walter sighed and rubbed his eyes. "Well, sleep would be good for me right now, too."

"What are the plans for tomorrow, then?" Kayla wondered. "Do we want to go back up to the camp if we don't think he's there?"

"I'm going regardless," Walter said. "All of this is information only we know. I have to at least make an appearance, and I will keep searching as long as I have the time off."

Micaiah nodded. "Sounds like a plan. Kayla and I, and probably Micah, too, we'll keep searching and looking on our own time, if you know what I mean."

"I know what you mean."

"Cai," Kayla said, not looking up from her book. "I think I found an answer to one of our other problems we've been discussing."

"Oh?" Micaiah shifted. "Care to share?"

"Well, as Walter said, there is an audience."

Walter grinned. "And as Micaiah said, I'm a big boy."

Her expression turned unreadable. "I would really rather not."

It took half a second for Walter to understand, and he nodded sympathetically. It was no secret that they were trying to get pregnant, but the way that Time and, apparently, the Akari messed up biological clocks made things a little difficult.

"Why don't we go home, think things over a little, and get a good night's sleep?" Micaiah suggested. "Things might look a little better in the morning."

No one objected. Unlike the Wheel Archives where patrons had to return their own tablets—not a difficult thing to do, really, just cumbersome—the Akarin Archives had attending librarians who would return the books and scrolls they left out on the tables. Walter felt a little guilty, but Micaiah simply said that the librarians were sticklers about their organization and would rather do things themselves than have to clean up someone else's mess if things got replaced incorrectly.

They returned to the Durvin household without incident, and without any more Imprints, flashbacks, calls for help, or anything of the sort. Walter took a minute to relax in a recliner while he got his bearings, acutely aware that if he stayed too long, he'd be asleep. After a minute or two, he forced himself to sit up. Kayla handed him a glass of water which he accepted gratefully. Clicking coming from down the hall alerted him to Micaiah's approach as he hopped along on his crutches, prosthetic gone.

"Sore?" Walter wondered.

"Very. Some days are better than others." Micaiah gave an awkward, crutch-inhibited shrug, like, "What can you do?"

"Get you something to eat, Walt?" Kayla offered from the kitchen. "That way you don't have to worry about making something at home?"

Walter shook his head and stood. "No, thank you. That's the last thing I need to do right now, or else I won't stop. I'm thinking I'll just go home and get some sleep."

Micaiah glanced at the clock. "It's almost time for you to be getting up and head to Wellspring. Why don't I follow you and Band you so you can actually sleep?"

Well, there was no getting around that one. Walter gathered his things, including his energy and motivation, and headed out the door. Was this a good idea, to be driving, as fatigued as he was? Maybe he should crash at their house for the night. Sure, he was trained to be awake and alert at a moment's notice, but that usually involved a good dose of adrenaline and even more coffee. Right, now he was getting neither of those. Nothing but the warm summer night and the lull of a running vehicle.

He wasn't sure how he made it home, only that he did. He got out of the driver's seat and stretched. Micaiah hopped up beside him.

"You should not have been driving," he said seriously. "You

fell asleep, I can tell. If I hadn't been behind you, things could have gone very badly for you."

"Then I guess it's a good thing you were behind me," Walter said, yawning. "I know, I know, probably a stupid idea. Equally as stupid was staying so long in the Archives, especially when we have no progress to show for it."

"We don't know that. We found a lot of information and just need to figure out what it means and how to process it. Some sleep should help us with that. Now then, inside."

"Yes, Dad."

Still, he did not argue as he headed inside. A terrifying feeling of déjà vú swept over him. The empty house, an empty bedroom, his son missing. Not just gone, the same way he'd just been off to summer camp, but missing. Disappeared. Maybe kidnapped, maybe not. Maybe injured, maybe not. No clue where he was, how he was, or when he was coming home. Everyone out looking even though it would be totally useless.

"Come on, Walt," Micaiah said behind him. "You need some sleep."

Right. Sleep. That thing that was important that would probably help him calm down and think rationally. He nodded absently. "Yeah. Just give me a minute to get ready."

Micaiah helped himself to Walter's recliner while he went to the bathroom. He'd already done all of this once tonight, so it really shouldn't have taken him as long as it did. Somehow, it felt like he'd managed to stuff two full days into just one day. Well, that was the magic of Time, he supposed. Or maybe just fear and worry and pulling an all-nighter hoping to miraculously find an answer to all their woes. Wishful thinking. Nothing was ever that easy.

"Sleeping out here?" Walter asked, moseying his way out to the living room where Micaiah was leaning back in the recliner, eyes closed, breathing steadily.

"Nope," Micaiah said, opening his eyes and reaching for his crutches. "Just taking a quick cat nap is all."

"I'm sure. Are you sure you should be driving home alone?"

"I'll be fine. Let's get you to bed. I'll give you eight hours, but I won't wake you up after that. It's better if you have a natural wake up. Prevents a Time hangover."

"Time hangover? Is that something you just made up?"

"Pretty much, but I think you know what I mean."

Walter did. It was the splitting headache that came from being Banded in order to get sleep, then having the Band ripped away and being forcefully woken up. The body didn't have time to adjust to the difference in the Banding, the actual time versus how much time the body thought it got, all that stuff.

The only thing Walter needed Micaiah for was crunching eight hours into about ten minutes. He certainly needed no help falling asleep. That was the easy part. Somewhere in the back of his mind, he'd had every intention of waking up and Banding Micaiah as a return favor, at least long enough to see him home safely. But when he woke, Micaiah was nowhere to be seen, and his car was gone. Glancing at the clock, he saw that if the Band had been dissolved after ten minutes, he'd overslept by at least another half hour to forty-five minutes. In a way, it felt kind of pitiful; he'd been fully prepared to get another three to five afterwards. Such was life, he supposed.

He still felt like everything was going in slow motion, or maybe it was just him as he slowly got out of bed, got to the bathroom, got ready, rummaged around for something to eat. Thankfully, with Tommen being away, he'd managed to more or less break his habit of pushing open Tommen's bedroom door to check on him. That didn't make it any easier to walk past said bedroom door, knowing that he was supposed to be in there, sprawled out over his blankets. Or, barring that, he was supposed to be at camp, complaining about being unable to sprawl in his sleeping bag and having to sleep on a lumpy, uncomfortable mattress.

Walter checked his phone just on the off chance the search and rescue commander had contacted him to say they found Tommen. As expected, that hadn't happened. At this point, he would have even taken a call from Rifun demanding some sort of ransom. At least that would be something, some kind of progress, some course of action. As it was, they had nothing. It had barely been two days, but it felt like an eternity.

Normally on his days off, he enjoyed a sit-down breakfast with a cup of coffee, maybe a bowl of oatmeal, and his morning paper. But this time, even on his day off, he was working. Already he felt like he was behind, even as he dragged along. He drank his coffee quickly, heedless of the burning in his mouth, and managed to scarf down a bagel with cream cheese. Then he grabbed his boots, his coats, and headed out the door.

Friday

Chapter Ten
Of Cults and Cadavers

Micaiah groaned as he finished, though he forced himself to keep going anyway as long as he could. Kayla kept a strong grip around him, willing him to do more, but he could not. He was done. He rolled back on his back and closed his eyes, tried to slow his breathing.

"Good morning to you, too," he breathed.

After releasing the Band around Walter, Micaiah had returned home and done the same to his wife who in turn Banded him, then seduced him. Only about an hour or so had passed since they left the Archives.

She kissed him and rested her chin on his chest. "Do you really think it will work?" Referring to something of an old wives' tale she'd found about how to conceive a child by sidestepping the biological fucking that Time and the Akari pulled on them. He wasn't sure of the details since apparently most of the sidestepping had to be done on her end.

"I don't know," Micaiah answered. "I suppose only time will tell."

"So, what are our plans for today?" She shifted position and nuzzled his chin. "I don't have to be anywhere until about lunchtime, and then maybe this afternoon if frickin' Mrs. Bitch ever calls me back about her consult." He could feel her eye roll. "What time are you going into work?"

"Depends on what our plans are otherwise. I definitely owe Micah some time off pretty soon, but it doesn't have to be today."

"Why don't we go back to the Archives and keep researching?"

189

"Researching what? We're at a dead end. The Trackers picked up something, but unless they can tell us what that something is, it's useless. We still don't know whether the call from Virginia was genuine, and if it was, what it means. As for the Imprint or vision or whatever in the portal, it seems to be a unique phenomenon, so unique that there's nothing written about it."

"I know," Kayla sighed. "It's frustrating. But we have to keep trying."

Eventually they got up and around, showering and scrounging up a quick breakfast.

"No prosthetic today?" Kayla asked as he hopped out to the dining room.

Micaiah shook his head. "No, still sore."

"Should you have it looked at?"

"Why? I've been on my leg a lot, been wearing the prosthetic a lot. It was bound to rub and get sore eventually. And it's still healing, so that means it's still changing somewhat. Point is, I'm not worried yet."

She still seemed uncertain. "Okay. If you say so. But I don't want to hear any complaining walking up five flights of stairs."

Oh. Right. That. They still had to do that, didn't they? Maybe he could give Micah the day off today...

Before he knew it, they were in the fortress, no worse for wear and no visions of missing children. Maybe it had been a fluke, a hallucination conjured up by his own stress and fearful imagination. Then Kayla reminded him that he'd been in considerably more stressful situations before, such as going to confront Rifun and launch a revolution, and nothing of the sort had happened. His vision had been relevant to the situation; they just needed to figure out how.

"I think I should have worn my prosthetic," Micaiah said as they passed the second floor.

"I said I didn't want to hear any complaining," Kayla told him, her tone half-serious, half-mocking.

"I'm not complaining. I'm lamenting. There's a difference."

But still, five floors was a long hike with only one leg. Nevertheless, he faithfully click-hopped one step at a time, going ever upward.

"There! There he is!"

Micaiah stopped like a deer in headlights when they reached the fourth floor. A huge crowd had gathered, and for a moment, he could almost envision torches and pitchforks. Not only should he have worn his prosthetic, but he should have made it his running leg. Fuck, this was not going to end well.

Once the worst of the scenarios cleared his mind, he was able to see that the gathered crowd did not have torches or pitchforks, but that did not make them any less angry or confused. All of them were talking at once, each trying to be heard and shouting over the others.

"What's going on here?!" Micaiah shouted, fed up with the noise after about three seconds.

Oddly enough, the crowd quieted and even parted to allow a few council members through. Micaiah recognized them as the same ones who had visited them in the Archives. He might have said that it seemed like so long ago, even though it really hadn't been very long at all. The white humanoid with black spots, known as a Ruib, spoke first.

"We are surprised that you have returned so suddenly. But perhaps you will be able to give a more detailed explanation as to your intent behind this message."

His words were so cold, it could have caused another ice age, and Micaiah was taken aback by them. "What do you mean? What message are you referring to?"

"This one."

Now the crowd parted like the Red Sea to the focal point of their attention. To Micaiah, it almost appeared to be a large black garbage bag lying in the middle of the corridor. With a glance at Kayla, he approached it. Twenty feet from the thing, he smelled blood and death, and he knew exactly what it was, what had happened.

The quadraped council member, a black-scaled thing called a

Kiboz, lay dead on the floor. The kiboz had a spine along its back and along its stomach, but its flanks were completely vulnerable. It had been gutted, both sides split open, entrails torn out. A snarl was still upon its lips as blank eyes stared at something unknown.

"Aw, shit," Micaiah hissed.

"Do you have anything to say for yourself?" the Qalik council member demanded.

"What do you mean? I didn't do this."

The third humanoid, a black-scaled humanoid called an Elif, stepped forward. "Several witnesses in the Archives state that you and Sarlon had an argument yesterday in which he threatened to remove you from power. Everyone knows how volatile humans can be and how they loathe to give up their power once it has been obtained."

"Excuse me?"

"Of course, that's assuming that you are Micaiah," the Ruib went on.

"Of course I'm Micaiah. Who else would I be?"

He barely got the last word out before something reached out and grabbed his left leg, jerking and tossing him flat on his back. His head cracked on the hard stone and stars burst in his vision. His crutches were jammed painfully into his back, and it took him a second to even figure out what position he was in, where all his limbs were. Alien faces and bodies moved over him, as if to devour him on the spot.

"Enough!" Kayla's voice rang out above the din of the crowd. "Get back away from my husband!"

The aliens backed off. Micaiah blindly reached for the hand that was offered to him, getting upright even as his world spun. He wobbled a bit, but Kayla thrust his crutches under his arms to steady him.

"My God, what is all this?" she snarled. "Have you all gone mad?! You judge one man based on the actions of another, and it's even more insane when those two men are mortal enemies! Rifun is responsible for my husband's missing leg! Are you so blind and prejudiced that you would base all your assumptions about humans on one man? What's more, Micaiah has been among you for decades and you know him! Why turn on him now?

"We don't know what happened here. Judging by this little incident, neither do you. I understand. We're all scared because of Cassius' treachery. We wonder if our measures will be enough. We wonder a lot of things. But turning on each other will only ensure our destruction, which is exactly what Cassius and Rifun wanted!"

She looked around at the crowd, glaring. "What would the Author say if she were here right now? What do you think she's saying about us?" Pause. "Well, I know what I'm saying. You're imbeciles. Children! *Qaunaknat!* Paranoid hypocrites who cling so tightly to the way things were that you don't even know about the way things are, and you lash out like a caged beast that doesn't even realize that the snare it's caught in is one of its own making. Well, chew your leg off if you must in order to escape, because once the hunter realizes what's been done, there will be nowhere for you to go."

She walked away with her head held high, Micaiah hobbling meekly after her, head still dizzy. Everyone got out of their way, and even the council members did not try to stop them. No one said a word. Kayla kept up her strut all the way to the fifth floor. Once they were safely hidden by the corridor, she went to a wall, pressed herself against it, and let the tears go. Micaiah set his crutches aside and awkwardly hopped over to hug her tight.

"Oh my God, that was so scary," she whispered.

"Did you plan that speech?" Micaiah asked. "I found it rather inspiring."

She weakly punched his arm. "Cai, I'm scared. This place used to feel safe, almost like a second home. Yeah, there was fighting and everything else you might expect, but this...this is new."

He shook his head. "It's not new, only new to our generation. But it is scary. It's been less than two hours since we left the Archives, which means the perpetrator was already here. Given the circumstances, he could still be around."

Kayla wiped her eyes. "Cai, tell me you're not going to throw yourself into another investigation."

"No, of course not. At this point, it would only look suspicious. We'll let the imbecile, child-like qanakat—"

"*Qaunaknat.*"

"Whatever. We'll let them deal with it. We're not going to hinder them, but I'm not going to roll over as an easy scapegoat."

She nodded. "Good. I would hope not." She sniffed and wiped away a few fresh tears. "Cai, what are we going to do?"

He took her in his arms again. "We're going to go to the Archives, just like we planned. We're going to review what we already know about our investigation into Tommen's disappearance, just like we planned. Then we're going to do some more research into even the smallest details, hoping to find gold in those mines of information. Just like we planned."

"Just like we planned," Kayla echoed. She pulled back and wiped her eyes before handing him his crutches. "God, I feel like a fool now."

"You're not a fool," Micaiah told her. "You're trying to be brave and figure everything out, just like everyone else. I just don't want to see you trying to do it alone. That's why I'm here. All right? Kayla? Aklaq, all right?"

She nodded. "All right."

"Good. Now then, I've had to hobble my way up five flights of stairs, and I took a pretty good blow. I'm ready to sit down. What do you say?"

Kayla grinned. "I say you need to stop complaining. We talked about this."

"I'm not complaining. I'm whining. There's a difference." He sighed when she gave him a look. "Very well then, madam, lead the way."

They headed for the Archives, but before they could get far, Micaiah felt a tap on his shoulder. He didn't recognize the alien except that it looked like a science experiment gone wrong trying to combine a hawk or an eagle with a horse and maybe a dash of elk or moose with some raccoon for good measure and color.

"Go ahead and get started," Micaiah told Kayla before she could speak. "You've done enough rescuing for one day."

She nodded but rolled her eyes, grinning mischievously. "Men and their egos. Always have to save the day."

Once she was gone, Micaiah and the alien got out of the doorway. He spoke first. "What?"

The hawk horse dipped its head. "Micaiah, greetings. I am Zavi. I saw what transpired down there between you and the mob."

"That's a kind way of putting it. Are you here to sweet-talk me before accusing me of killing the council member or conspiring with Rifun or of being Rifun in Disguise?" He was done with the bullshit; he just wanted a straight answer.

"I am not. Actually, I wish to tell you that I believe you. Others do as well. The Akarin already have troubles enough from the Hands of Time that we do not need this conflict among ourselves. You have troubles of your own with the Borelians."

"Well, at least someone recognizes that," Micaiah sighed. "So, what do you want?"

"I ask for nothing; my intent is only to encourage and give heart." Zavi paused as if hesitating. "There is talk once more of splitting up, of abandoning the council and their petty internal wars. I do not wish to see this happen, nor do others. We are hoping that a good leader such as yourself will unite us again before we split. Everyone knows that once a division has been made, we cannot go back."

"I know that very well, too. I don't want to see us divide any more than we already are. We need unity, especially now. Problem is, I don't think I'm the leader you're looking for."

"You led the revolt against Rifun."

"I led one battle, and now everyone wants to promote me to general and crown me king. It's not me. All I want is peace. For me, my wife. We're trying to start a family, settle down, live peacefully. I never even wanted to be a made a leader; they forced me into the position. I admit, I'm using it a little as leverage in the human war against the Borelians, but...I really just kind of want to be left alone after that." He shook his head. "I don't know what the hell I want, I guess. Anyway, thanks for the show of support. Good to know not everyone is wishing for my death."

"Of course." Zavi dipped his head again and made a motion. "Forgive me for interrupting your time with your wife."

The great beast meandered away. Micaiah watched it for a moment before turning and heading into the Archives. Kayla was nowhere to be seen, but she was probably wandering up and down the aisles, looking for her books. He took a minute to sit down and relax. Five flights of stairs really was hard work, to say nothing of the extra jaunt his trip to the floor had done to him. His back was still sore where he'd landed simultaneously on the ground and on his crutches. His dizziness had subsided, but the ensuing headache wasn't much better. He put a hand to the back of his head but did not feel any blood. Probably his first good news all day.

The question now became, what exactly did they research? His mind was distracted already as it replayed the events on the fourth floor over and over again, and he couldn't hold that and the disappearance investigation in his mind at the same time. He'd mix them up, forget details, get confused, and go nowhere.

He closed his eyes, tried to focus, but all he could see was the council member's body, cut open, gutted, and laid out for all to see. It had been an inside job, of that much he was certain. Someone in the fortress was not who they were claiming to be, whether it was one of Rifun's recruit plants or a traitor in the leadership, he didn't know. But there was no invading force involved here; this was straight up internal decay.

He jumped at a hand on his shoulder, but it was only Kayla. She quietly set down a couple books and sat down beside him.

"If you're not going to get involved in the murder investigation, then don't get involved," she told him. "Right now, you look pretty involved."

"I don't know how to not be involved. I'm involved in everything it feels like. Tommen's disappearance, humans and Borelians, Akarin and the Hands, me and you, us and Micah...It's all taking up so much space, all demanding to be the forefront. The only one I really want to focus on is me and you and just getting out of here."

"I know." She stood and went around to rub his neck and shoulders. "Why don't you go home and give Micah the day off? Maybe a day full of useless billing and invoices and cranky customers will help take your mind off all the crap going on here."

"At this point, I think I would rather deal with the politics and the war here." He turned around in the chair. "Besides, what kind of husband would I be if I abandoned my wife to the wolves lurking in the shadows out there?"

She raised a brow. "And who saved whom when he was lying on the floor out there?"

"Mm, so you might have a point."

"Do you at least want to get your leg?"

He shook his head. "No. I'm here now, might as well use the time and get some research done. What did you find interesting?"

"Well, a lot of different things. Fire. Advanced Akari techniques and skills. Akari experiments gone wrong. Those sorts of things. Maybe some sort of theory will form out of this mass of information."

Strictly speaking, that was a pretty big if. Like the information in the tablets in the Wheel Archives, sometimes there was so much information, so exhaustive of a collection, that it was utterly useless. Being thorough was nice and all, but sometimes just a quick Google answer would suffice.

After a minute or two of consideration, Micaiah got up and started hopping around the Archives. He started off, as he always did, very intentional and deliberate in his search. Problem was, that only worked when he knew what he was looking for. As it was, the thing he was looking for probably had a name, but if he didn't know it, it was useless. It was like trying to diagnose a problem in his motorcycle without knowing the first thing about mechanics. He could tinker around a bit and hope to get lucky, or he could take it to a mechanic. Secondary problem, he was the mechanic.

So, tinker he did. More to the point, he hobbled along through the aisles. After a short time, his intentional search turned more passive. He got distracted by books with cool titles or things that randomly popped into his mind as he was looking, picking up this or that as he remembered something he wanted to know.

Eventually, he came to the more fiction side of the Archives. They weren't true fiction, more like fairy tales and mythology and religions from around the universe. Reference was the term he was looking for, he supposed.

He might have passed over the section completely, except for one book that caught his attention. It wasn't huge, but it was the title that caught his eye. *The Space Between Spaces: Quasi-Dimensions and Shadow Worlds.* As he picked it up, the book next to it flopped over, exposing the cover and title. *Ghost in the Mirror: Creatures That Jump Between Our World and the Next.*

"Hardly a time to be reading fairy tales, don't you think?" Kayla asked when he returned, looking over his choice of reading material with a disapproving gaze.

"With all the absurdity going on right now, this seems like an excellent time to read a few fairy tales," he said, thumping down in the chair. "Who knows? Maybe Tommen was kidnapped by witches and trolls?"

Kayla merely raised a brow as she returned to her reading.

Micaiah grinned as he opened the book about dimension-jumping creatures. Well, he'd thought it was about dimension-jumping creatures. Apparently the author was using "the Next World" as a euphemism for the afterlife. It was logical euphemism on Earth or any Unengaged planet, but it might be considered ambiguous in the Archives.

Whoever the author was, they certainly had a well-rounded experience dealing with afterlife mythology. Ninety-nine percent of the stories and references held zero significance to him, but he did find one mention of Anubis, the Ancient Egyptian god of the dead who weighed the hearts of man against a feather. Otherwise, the book seemed pretty useless. He took the pages and flipped quickly through them, hoping a title or subtitle might catch his eye.

Toward the end of the book was a section on servants of the powerful dimension-jumping beasts. Micaiah gave it the same quick perusal as everything else, stopping when a large, beautifully illustrated picture caught his eye.

"Here's something," he said, poking Kayla. She looked over but appeared largely unimpressed until he started reading. " 'Kelinorian are creatures that may take many forms in order to blend in wherever they go. Their job was to accompany their masters to the afterlife, showing them a place in which their souls may rest. Because of their service to—' " Micaiah ran his finger down the page. "Blah, blah, blah, mythology, and so on. 'In more recent times, they were used by the Akari-bearers and called Trackers. They need virtually no training as their very nature is to look for weaknesses and distortions between this world and the next."

Kayla nodded. "Okay, cool. More than what I've been able to really find on them, but how does it help us find Tommen?"

Micaiah let out a breath. "I don't know, but I have a feeling that we're getting closer to the answers we're looking for."

Maybe it was just him getting excited and anxious for any kind of lead. There was every chance he was getting worked up about nothing and his so-called discovery would be nothing more than a pleasant bedtime story for the kids.

He gave the book about the creatures one last perusal before closing it and setting it aside, only at the last moment considering that he might have needed to bookmark that page. Oh well, wasn't like he couldn't go back and look again later if he needed to. So he turned his attention to the next book of fairy tales, this one about quasi-dimensions, shadow worlds, spirit lands, and all the other mythology traditionally associated with inter-dimensional travel.

He glossed over the first bit that explained what a dimension actually was. Then he skipped the disclaimer that all information and stories were for reference and informative use only and not meant to be offensive nor authoritative or any of that. The intergalactic political correctness committee strikes again, Micaiah figured.

A lot of the stories and information actually put Micaiah in mind of Saul, some of the stories he told about his people and their beliefs. There was one particular story that stood out, however, and it was the one where Saul briefly described his people's vision quests to become a man or woman of the people, or the first step of becoming an adult anyway. He couldn't remember the details, but it had something to do with eating a particular fruit which was actually a hallucinogen, but it let one see into what his people called the spirit lands. In actuality, they were peering into another dimension, some quasi-dimension, like the one Micaiah was reading about now.

" 'There are different degrees of quasi-dimensions,' " he read silently. " 'Some may be visible in the dimension in which they primarily reside, but only those within the dimension can manipulate it.' " So that would have been like the warehouse in the shipping yard last winter. Rifun had turned the warehouse into a quasi-dimension that could be seen normally, but could only be manipulated by those inside it. " 'These dimensions are considered very unstable and are always at risk of imminent collapse. Unlike partial dimensions, however, the risk to those inside is minimal, as they will most often simply be returned to the primary dimension.' " So it had been nothing for Rifun to throw up and tear down dimensions as needed because there was no risk to him if something happened.

" 'Other quasi-dimensions are not visible, but they still function within its primary dimension. These are called partial dimensions because they are often situated between two dimensions. Oftentimes, because of the influx of Energy needed to sustain the partial dimension, normal Energy, Matter, and Time-wielding abilities are diminished, if not subdued completely. All known instances of Time Agents and Akari-bearers have resulted in the entrapment of the individual. However, particularly talented individuals, especially Akari-bearers, may be able to make minor adjustments and manipulations in order to commune with the primary dimension. They may be referred to as ghosts, phantoms, or other assorted titles.

" 'While almost no data has been gathered about such partial dimensions, some observations can be made from the primary dimension. First, it is impossible for an individual trapped within the dimension to travel through portals in hopes of escape. As stated before, there is an increased amount of Energy in the partial dimension which suspends it and keeps it stable between dimensions. When a portal is opened between dimensions that passes through this partial dimension, the Energy vacuum of the portal itself, the doorway between the dimensions, acts as a backfeed, with the Energy needed to open the portal acting as the battery. Touching it is about the equivalent of being struck by lightning and can severely injure or kill anyone who comes into contact with it. Many times, the individual doing so will appear momentarily in a great flash of light and possibly something like a thunderclap. These individuals may be mistaken for angels or other heavenly beings.' "

Micaiah sat back in his chair and rubbed his eyes as if to be sure he wasn't making this up as he went along.

" 'While communication is possible in a limited sense, it has been conveyed to the author that while it is possible to live out the extended life that many Time Agents and Akari-bearers enjoy in the primary dimension, the suicide rate in a partial dimension is exorbitantly high. Isolation is believed to be a factor in this.

" 'It is also possible for individuals in the partial dimensions to slip small items from the primary dimension into the partial dimension, but the same is not possible in reverse. All roads into the partial dimensions appear to be one-way.' "

Micaiah sat there for a moment longer, staring at nothing, still perplexed by his find. He turned the page, but only found more stories and mythology about dream lands, spirit lands, and so on. After a minute or two, he got up and headed for another section in the Archives. This time, knowing what he was looking for, finding a book didn't take very long, and soon he was back at the table. After another minute or two of consideration, he went to the front of the large room and politely asked for an Authored book. *Wolf Pack, Book One of The Lone Wolf.*

"What are you looking at?" Kayla wondered, standing, stretching, and yawning, causing Micaiah to yawn in the process.

"I think I found our lead."

She picked up one of the books. *"The Great Migration: How Time and the Akari Shaped Life for the Peoples of Hlohi,"* she read. "This is about Saul's people. I don't get it."

Micaiah went back to the open book about the dimensions and pointed. "Read that while I look for something."

He opened the new book and the Authored Book, comparing them side-by-side. Kiyuga had been Saul's grandfather and one of the leaders of the Migration. He was also considered the most reliable source for information about the transition from Earth to Hlohi.

" 'Many were wary of this new power they had been given,' " Kayla read across the table. " 'To bend the world around them, it was as if each man had become the Creator. Some were frightened and wanted to kill the demons, claiming they had brought blasphemy, witchcraft, an abomination against the natural order of things. Others were frightened of what kind of war would ensue should both sides have this power, a clash of the gods and a roar of the heavens. Still others were eager to learn and use these abilities, to drive back the white demons.

" 'But the white men who brought the power would not teach them to kill with it. It was wrong what the white men did, true, but nothing would be gained by killing them also. Rather, they proposed a compromise, a way to end the slaughter for the peoples that were too small to hope to survive the tide of blood the elders and Anagalisgi had seen on the horizon. There was much debate and much blood spilled as opinions were divided. Eventually, those who wished to leave were permitted to leave, while a small force would stay and fight.

" 'So the white men showed the people how to open portals and where they should go. Then they left the people to save themselves. Some perished as their portals were unable to be opened or sustained. They did not stay on Earth, but neither did they make the crossing. They were simply gone, taken to the spirit lands, dead rather than forced to leave their homes.

" 'Kiyuga remained behind, as did much of Wolf Clan. They fought bravely against the white men, but as predicted, the tide of blood came for them, too, and they were forced to make a decision. They sat around a campfire, praying and dancing and invoking the spirits for guidance. Each man partook of the vision fruit, seeking answers. They saw the faces of the ones who had tried to make the crossing and failed. They told the warriors to flee. Even the spirits were afraid to stay on these cursed grounds any longer. Save the people. Go to a land where there were no white demons, where they could truly live in peace.

" 'The warriors made the crossing that night. It is said that one spirit crossed with each man as well, appearing in a flash of lightning and thunder, sealing the breach between worlds and establishing themselves in the new spirit lands and as protectors of the people.' "

Micaiah leaned back and stretched. Those who had been lost in the portals had ended up in the Land In Between, from which no one had ever returned. Supposedly there was some hallucinogenic fruit out there that allowed a man to somewhat see past the barriers into the dimension which let him commune with those trapped there. To a European, they might be considered ghosts, angels, demons, whatever. To a Native American, they might be beloved ancestors or spirit guides, ready to impart wisdom to a young man or woman seeking to become an adult within the tribe. But they were real people, trapped between dimensions.

"I know where Tommen is," Micaiah stated.

"You think Tommen is in the Land In Between," she said.

He nodded. "I do. Think about it. Tommen is helping to gather up kids and rescue them from a fire. Rifun takes the opportunity to take him aside and teach him a lesson in the Akari, Time, Matter, Energy, the works. He's not passing up the fire. Whether intentional or on accident, I don't know, but somehow, Tommen tries to tap into the Energy of the fire, and it goes wrong. Way wrong. It backfires on him, burning his arm, but also creating enough Energy that he rips open a portal to somewhere. His subconscious tells him to escape, so he tries. But because of his injuries, the force of the explosion, he goes unconscious before he's all the way through. Loses the portal, boom, he's in the Land In Between.

"At some point, he thinks, hey, maybe if I try to go through a portal, I can just walk through and be back home like normal. Bam! Hits him like a bolt of lightning, and I see his flash, his Imprint as we called it."

Kayla nodded. "Okay. I think I follow. But where does Virginia fall into this?"

"Maybe he was injured and got confused. I don't know. But I do know that what I keep seeing is Energy, Energy, Energy. The Land In Between is all about Energy. What is electricity but Energy? He plugs his phone in, he might have been able to tap into a conduit between the dimensions and try to get a message out."

"But if that's true, why can't he call or text?"

"I don't know. I don't have all the answers, only a theory."

She folded her arms. "Well, it's the best one we've had so far. At the same time, if it is true, there's that whole bit of 'from which no one has ever returned.' "

Micaiah shook his head. "I don't buy that. I refuse to believe that in the last five thousand or so years, with all the Time Agents and Akari-bearers, with all the portals that are opened just on a daily basis, all the portals that have closed on someone, that not a single person has escaped. There has to be someone somewhere who knows what the secret is."

"I think you're right. And I think I know where to start."

"You've heard of someone?"

"No. But think of it this way. Europeans would see a ghost or a demon and seek to destroy it and keep it from breaking into our world. Native Americans, my peoples, they seek out their ancestors; they want to commune with the spirits. If Saul's people were doing it two hundred years ago, and he had to do it when he became a man, I'd be willing to bet they've still got some of that trippy fruit lying around somewhere."

"I like how you think."

"Problem is, I can't go today because I'm working. And as much as I know you would love to volunteer, I don't think they would be as accepting of you."

"It's because of the missing leg thing, isn't it?"

She grinned. "Absolutely, dear. And since there isn't much you can do about it, we'll just have to wait until tomorrow when I can get a message to Natalie, get over there, and hopefully get something done."

He pulled her over to sit on his lap. "I don't know. Should you be doing drugs while we're trying to get pregnant?"

"I will remind you that it was only a theory, a test, and it was just this morning. I don't think I'm going to get pregnant that fast. Tomorrow should be fine."

Half of it was a joke, but the other half was serious. They were doing everything they could to conceive, and he didn't want to jeopardize it because of some outlandish theory. Granted, he was the one who came up with the theory, but he might have done more to flesh it out and think it over before proposing it and agreeing to this outrageous plan.

"Wait," he said after a second. "If they've been doing this for over two hundred years, that means they had to be finding the fruit here on Earth. What hallucinogenic fruits do you know of grow in the area?"

"I don't know," Kayla admitted. "But I'm not about to go out and start picking random, strange fruit in an attempt to find out."

"Can't you ask?"

"Once again, I need to contact them. And before you ask, Wolf Clan is the only one that still has real contact with Earth and the outside world. It would be strange to go to another clan and ask them for it, assuming I could in the first place." She shook her head. "No. Easier to stick with the plan we have."

Micaiah sighed. "If I managed to find it in one of the books around here, then—?"

"Cai. Seriously. I'll be fine. Maybe you can start thinking of things you want me to tell Tommen in the event that I am able to actually see and speak to him. I'm sure he would appreciate a plan of escape."

Right. Conjure up a plan of escape from a dimension "from which no one has ever returned." And if she was going to be visiting Wolf Clan tomorrow and tripping with them, that meant he had about twenty-four hours to come up with said plan. Once again, just another thing that was super important, lodging itself with the rest of the things that were super important, and demanding to be attended to as the most important of the super important things.

"Here's the next question," Micaiah said. He noted Kayla's look and her reserved sighed. "Do we want to tell Walter?"

Now she was caught, and she hesitated. Then, "I don't know. I mean, I want to. We have a theory and a plan of action, which are both good things. At the same time, I really don't want to get his hopes up on account of that whole 'from which no one has ever returned' bit. If we don't tell him, and we fail, he's no worse for wear. If we don't tell him, and we somehow succeed at getting Tommen back, he's happy and we can explain things after the fact."

"Yes, but it feels dishonest."

"I know, and that's the part that gets me. Walter isn't stable, but this is his son. He deserves to know. And maybe he can bring some fresh ideas to the table, too. We're bickering with each other half the time, so having someone else around might do some good. Get Micah in on it, and we'll have a regular party."

"Yeah, but—"

"And having more eyes on it means you don't have to focus on it all the time. You can set this one on the back burner to simmer a little. I'm the one who has to approach the Krydik and get this fruit. Okay, you can worry about other things for a short time. Let me worry about this."

"I always worry about you. Especially when your plans involve hallucinogenic fruit."

"Oh, please. How often do my plans involve hallucinogenic fruit? Or drugs at all, for that matter?"

"I don't know. Sometimes I wonder if you don't slip me something when you're in the mood."

"It's irrelevant that I sometimes do. Doesn't have anything to do with this."

"Wait, you slip me drugs?"

She grinned and shook her head. "No, my love, I don't." She kissed him. "I wouldn't do that to you. But the point is, you really need to lighten up and take some of the weight off your shoulders. Let me handle this, at least until I've slept off the shroom fruit. Okay? Can you do that for me?"

Micaiah was still uncertain, both about letting her pursue this plan and whether or not she'd ever slipped him drugs. In the end, he relented. He had every intention of figuring out which fruit the books were referencing that way he could go on this potentially dangerous trip and spare her, but, barring that miraculous discovery, he would leave it up to her. And, true to her point, he had to figure out both what to tell Tommen should she make contact, as well as figure out a way to bust him out of the Land In Between, assuming there even was a way to do that.

Kayla put a hand on his shoulder. "Why don't you go and kick Micah out of the bakery and tell him to do a little work here? Go deal with angry customers for a while."

It was still the last thing he felt like doing, but it would certainly be a change of pace. He spent a few minutes going through the books a little more, seeing if there were any "myths" about people escaping from the spirit lands or the partial dimensions or whatever. He didn't find anything so blatantly obvious, nor helpful in that regard, but he did find a short story which involved someone getting trapped. That someone had six Trackers that he kept. Those Trackers were still able to see or perceive their master, and hear his commands. He became known as the Phantom Tracker as he did his work in secret for the next two hundred years until he died. What that work was, was not detailed in the story.

Eventually, he closed the books and pushed them aside. He really did owe Micah a day off. Maybe he'd give him the rest of today and tomorrow off to make up for it. Then he could spend his dull time in the office coming up with a plan to break Tommen out of the dimension. Or he could send Micah to the Archives and have him do it. No, Micah needed a day off, a real vacation day to do whatever he needed or wanted to do. Problem was, they both worked so much, they had no idea what to do with any time they did get off.

"Leaving, my love?" Kayla asked as he grabbed his crutches and stood.

"Yeah," he sighed. "Guess I do owe Micah some time off."

"Okay. I'll see you later, then." She kissed him.

"Just don't forget your consulting appointments."

She blanched. "I think I'm with you on that one. I'd rather be here or fighting wars or wrestling bears than give any more consults or anything that has to do with work."

"Now who was lecturing whom about stress and taking your mind off things?"

"Yeah, yeah, go to work."

He kissed her. "Love you, too, honey."

She waved him off and he hopped along to the exit, grinning stupidly. The good news was that hopping down the stairs was generally easier, though decidedly more dangerous. Gravity did half the work. At least until he pitched forward on his face; then gravity did all the work, and none of it good. He'd had more than one close call on mornings when he went downstairs on his crutches to work out. He'd never fallen down the stairs, though he had lost his crutches a couple times and had to carefully hop down the rest of the way to grab them. As far as he knew, no one had ever witnessed his mishaps, and he was determined it stay that way.

He'd just rounded the corner and was on his merry way toward the stairs when a voice spoke and someone fell in beside him.

"You're Micaiah Durvin, aren't you?"

Micaiah stopped and turned to face what turned out to be another human, young, female, might have been pretty if she got cleaned up from what looked like a hard shift at the garage.

"I am," he confirmed, suddenly wishing he was at the bakery. He didn't really want to be at the bakery, but he didn't really want to be here, either. Was there no way he could win?

"That's what I thought. Your leg kind of gives you away."

"Good to know I'm the only one-legged human running around here. What can I do for you, Miss...?"

"Trish."

"Trish. How can I help you?"

"Well, you can end the human-Borelian war, for one."

Micaiah barked a laugh. "Believe me, I'm trying. I just wish I knew how."

His laugh faded as Trish brandished a knife. "No. You can end the war."

He really should have gone back to grab his leg when he had the chance. "What's this about, then?"

"The Borelians are willing to call off the attack if a few key figures are delivered over to them. Your name was on that list, right next to Rifun."

"You're not from the Cult, then."

"Does it matter who I'm with? I'll act alone if I have to."

"Maybe." Micaiah shifted his stance. "But other than all the fear that the Borelians instill into their foes, what does this war mean to you? There are plenty who don't want to fight or can't fight, and they're going underground. You must know a few places you can hide."

"I work for the good of humankind."

"And you think the Borelians will honor their agreement? They'll throw you into slavery right alongside me."

"Well, here's the catch. The Hands of Time are in on this gig."

"Oh?" Now Micaiah was intrigued.

Trish nodded excitedly. "Common enemies bring people together. Deliver you and the others to the Borelians. The Borelians call off the war on the humans. The Hands of Time lift their ban on the Akari-bearers. Borelians are allowed back into Time. Everything goes back to the way it was. Everyone wins. Sacrifice a few to save the many."

"Poetic, when it actually works. Unfortunately, the reason we're here is because the way things used to be was deeply flawed. Furthermore, the Borelians will never honor their word to call off the war. By taking in their prizes and spoils first, they dishearten the rest of the troops, make takeover easier. And while the election system of the Hands may be different and possibly even more fair, that doesn't make the Hands themselves any more honest or any less greedy and power-hungry than they were before. They just have less time to accomplish their vile schemes, so their blows are harder, faster, less subtle."

He could see the uncertainty on the girl's face. Chances were, she was working alone or with a small group of naive youngsters who had been approached by an intelligent, opportunistic Borelian looking for a way in, straight to the heart of the human defense system. In the time it took her to mull over his words, he Banded and took the knife.

"I'm just going to be taking this for the time being," he told her calmly. "And we're going to forget this little incident. Go back to your friends or whoever sent you, and tell them what I told you. It's a trap, as much for me as for you. But be warned: I only show mercy once."

Trish backed up a few steps, face burning red. She looked like she wanted to cry, not out of sadness, but embarrassment and spite and frustration. She just wanted the war and the uncertainty and the fear to end, and she was taking any offer that came her way. Micaiah didn't blame her, really. He wanted it all to be over, too. He would even take suddenly waking up to find out it was all a bad dream. But it wasn't. This was real, or as real as it could be.

Finally, the young woman turned and hurriedly walked away, back too straight, head too high, wiping her eyes only once she got to the end of the corridor and turned the corner. Micaiah stared after her a moment longer before turning in the opposite direction to leave.

What he found instead was another man waiting for him, but this one he knew well.

"Mercy," Chandler stated. "An interesting choice."

"Are you saying it was the wrong one?" Micaiah questioned, looking over his shoulder as if the girl might run up behind him and stab him in the back.

"I'm saying only time will tell. She was an easy one. Low man on the totem pole as it were. Easy to manipulate. Easy to spot. Not all will be so simple."

"Lovely, now I have to dodge assassins."

"The attempts on your life will be resolved. But the attempts on the heart of the Akari, those will be much more severe."

Micaiah studied Chandler. "The Akari is the power of the Author. What are you saying?"

"This war transcends what is visible to the eye."

Because anything good ever came from cryptic words like that. Micaiah sighed and rubbed his eyes. "I've had quite enough of this shit for one lifetime, thank you. Once we rescue Tommen, I am taking my wife and moving as far away as possible to a deserted planet where we can live peacefully."

"Sounds like a very nice, very well-thought-out dream."

"I hope to make it a reality." He shifted his stance. "Speaking of invisible to the eye, you don't happen to know where Tommen is?"

Chandler shrugged, his expression almost smug. "I thought you knew."

"So he is in the Land In Between."

"He walks where everyone walks, but where few people see."

Micaiah slapped his forehead. "Why can I never get a straight answer out of you?"

"Tommen asked me the same thing once, except his wording sounded like more of a demand. I don't take demands very well."

"I bet you don't. How do we get him out of the Land In-Between? I refuse to believe that in ten thousand years, no one has escaped ever."

Chandler shifted. "Why is it called the Land In Between?"

"Because...it's a dimension between dimensions?"

"If you opened a portal from your home to somewhere on the other side of the world, are you traveling to a new dimension, or just shortening the trip within a single dimension?"

"Um, the second one, I think."

"So then where is that second dimension?"

Micaiah opened his mouth but no words came out. Chandler continued to speak.

"In the book you were reading, the author described the partial dimension as existing in the primary dimension. Which dimension is primary?" He went on before Micaiah could say anything. "The Land In Between is itself divided, half resting against one dimension, half resting against the other. So you might say that the in-between dimension is itself two dimensions set next to each other. Tommen sits in the one closest to you, the home he knows."

"Great. Straight answer. Next question, how do we get him out? If the Energy barrier is too strong—"

"Tommen must go forward before he can go back. Similarly, he must go back before he can go forward."

Had Micaiah had his leg, he would have walked up to the nearest wall and bashed his head against it a couple times. As it was, it was too much effort to hobble over there on crutches. He still had to get down to the first floor after all. Instead, he took a calming breath and said, "Okay. Fine. You obviously probably know about Kayla's plan to eat some weird hallucinogenic fruit and try to contact Tommen. If she finds him, is there anything she should tell him about how to escape?"

Chandler's expression was unreadable. "This time has been coming, and I warned him of it. I even gave him a way out. All that remains to be seen is whether he will listen to me or the one who speaks to him now."

"Who is that? Is Rifun in there, too?"

Now Chandler's expression turned grave. "Worse. It is the power that spawned Rifun."

Micaiah scoffed. "Oh, wonderful. Because today just couldn't get any worse. Can you tell me the date of the apocalypse, too?"

"If you would tell Tommen anything, tell him not to bring that power back into your world, or it will spell disaster for everyone."

"Nothing ambiguous about that, is there?"

"You wanted the straight answer."

"Happy answers, Chandler. When does the happily ever after come into play?"

Chandler chuckled. "Yours is coming soon, my friend. Have patience. And possibly a gun under your pillow."

Micaiah ground his teeth, grumbling, "I already do."

Then Chandler was gone, faded away and leaving Micaiah alone in the corridor. After a moment, he sighed, rubbed his eyes, and plodded along toward the staircase. Happy answers. He wanted happy answers. Hey, this war is over and the Borelians mysteriously disintegrated. Hey, the Hands of Time came to their senses and lifted their Akari ban. Even better, the Akarin council got the sticks out of their asses and are singing kum-bah-yah in the meeting room. Hell, he'd even take the lottery. Enough doom and gloom.

Micaiah elected to open a portal directly into the bakery, straight into his office. It was still morning, but the breakfast rush had passed. He could hear Micah in the kitchen while Kyle cleaned up the dining room. He took a minute to stretch, sit down, stretch some more, and just try to relax. So far, the only super important thing that he really didn't mind being super important was being with Kayla and trying to start a family, but part of that had to do with the sex. Otherwise, everything else could fuck off for all he cared.

He really should have gone home and grabbed his leg.

Groaning, he pulled himself to a standing position and hobbled out of the office into the kitchen, narrowly avoiding a collision with Micah who was carrying a very large carton of eggs.

"So, how'd it go?" Micah asked. He was busy and harried, but Micaiah didn't miss the frost on his words. Micah liked to go on adventures, too, and do research and be involved, and so far he'd been pushed to the side, charged with holding down the home front.

"We figured out where Tommen is," Micaiah told him and relayed the theory, from the research to his meeting with Chandler. Micah kept working, but he always kept one ear on the story. When Micaiah was done, Micah paused and frowned.

"I'm still not a hundred percent on this Chandler person you keep mentioning," he admitted. "At the same time, if Tommen is trapped in the Land In Between, that's a pretty big deal. But what's with the riddles and prophetic bullshit?"

"Believe me, I wish I knew," Micaiah said. "Anyway, that's the story so far. Take it how you will. And get out of here."

Micah stopped. "What?"

"Get out of here. Take the rest of the day off. Tomorrow, too, if you want."

"What the hell am I supposed to do with myself?"

"I don't know. Whatever you want. Go to Florida. Go to Alaska. Go somewhere else. Go do research and help us figure out the puzzle. I don't care. Take a couple days. You've earned it."

"Are you sure? You want to run home and get your prosthetic first?"

"Nah. I'll send Kyle back to keep working in the kitchen; I'll man the front."

Micah still seemed uncertain, but finally nodded and started untying his apron. "All right. If you insist. Who am I to doubt my big brother, right? But if you need anything, just give me a holler."

"Take a day to yourself, Micah. That's an order."

"You're not a Lieutenant anymore. You don't give orders."

"No, but like you said, I am your big brother."

Micaiah watched him leave, then went up front to send Kyle back. It had been a while since he'd been on front, totally in charge of the display case and the dining room. It was almost surreal. This could end very, very badly.

Chapter Eleven
Waterfalls, Sharp Rocks, and Alligators

Tommen woke, initially confused, but with a deep sense of foreboding and a little lingering fear from whatever terrifying nightmares had plagued his sleep. He sat up and looked around, almost daring to hope that sleep had been the final remedy, that one unlikely thing that would bring him out of the in-between dimension and back to the real world. But when he meandered his way out to the kitchen, it was just as his dad had left it in his haste to make it back up to Wellspring to join in the search. Nothing had changed.

He sat down at the kitchen table, placing the last of the medical supplies on the counter within easy reach. Gingerly, he removed his bandages, almost afraid to see what lay beneath. What if his wounds were grossly infected? Could Julianna pull in some antibiotics and medicine to stave it off? Could she at least bring in some painkillers so he might make it through his day without grinding his teeth down to the gumline? Fucking hell, his arm hurt. Worse, it was starting to itch. That was probably a good thing, a sign of healing, but it hurt like a motherfucker.

The last layer of bandages came off. A few small flakes of burned skin fluttered to the ground. It wasn't much, really, just the outermost layer of skin, but it made his stomach twist. Good news, his arm was healing. But God Almighty, did it have to look so gross? When the dead skin really started sloughing off, he was going to look like a damn leper. He'd have to wrap himself in bandages and roam the streets crying "Unclean!" for a month until it was all over. As it was, some of the broken skin around the blisters was drying out, the skin beneath red and raw, but in the earliest stages of healing.

He discarded the old bandages, wet from fluid and who knew what, replacing them with clean, dry bandages, reflecting how his arm seemed to alternate between having no sensation at all beyond pain — he couldn't feel the bandages, whether they were wet or dry, hot or cold air, nothing — and being so hypersensitive, even the faintest breeze was like scalding water. Half his nerves were dead, the other half were in overdrive, and both seemed to be vying for top spot in his brain.

Cautiously, he stretched his fingers as best he could, trying to relax the cramping and stiffness that had taken hold in the night, but his hand was still terribly swollen. He tried to touch each finger to his thumb, finding it a much more difficult task than he thought necessary. It should have been just one, two, three, four, right? Apparently not. His forefinger was the easiest, only because it was the closest, but it also hurt the most. All the way down the line until he had to force his pinkie with his opposite hand. Shit. This was not good.

He sat at the kitchen table for probably half an hour, pondering his injuries. He was supposed to meet Julianna at some point, but he didn't know exactly when, how, or even how he felt about it. She was lying about a lot of things, covering up a bunch of skeletons. But with exception of the little scene he'd witnessed in the prison, he couldn't say quite how he knew or what evidence he had against her. It was mostly just a gut feeling. But hadn't he always said, it's only paranoia until it's true? He'd seen too much to just dismiss his intuition. At this point, it was like trying to ignore the smell of skunk spray. He couldn't say where it was coming from, but it was most certainly there.

At the same time, what other option did he have for getting out of this dimension, assuming there was a way out? It wasn't like he could just walk up to anyone on the figurative street and ask them to teach him some cool stuff that might help him get through the Energy barrier. Actually, he hadn't seen anyone in this dimension except Julianna. That was another thing that bothered him. He had no reason not to believe the suicide rate was sky-high, or that the population was decidedly less than seven billion, but there had to be someone out there, right? What about all those "ghosts" that were supposedly people trapped in this dimension?

His stomach grumbled irritably. Well, regardless of his doubts and misgivings about Julianna and her honesty, he was going to have to find her if he wanted to eat today. Might as well get out there on the streets; chances were, she would find him before he ever found her. Grabbing his phone off the charger, he headed out the door.

He must have slept later than he thought; it was almost lunchtime already. He hadn't even thought to check the time or anything, not that it mattered, he supposed. His first stop was Becky's house. Her lighter workload meant she actually had time to leave her room. She spent her new free time helping her dad prepare for Sabbath, pre-cooking all the meals needed for the day of rest, saying whatever prayers or blessings had to go with them. Tommen didn't speak a word of Hebrew, wouldn't even pretend to know more than hello or goodbye, but he was fairly certain he heard his name in their conversation several times. Well, why not? He was her boyfriend and he was missing as far as they knew. She was worried and going over a thousand worst-case scenarios over whatever fate had befallen him.

His next stop was the bakery. To his surprise, Micaiah was the one on the counter while Kyle manned the kitchen. Of course, without his prosthetic, Micaiah wasn't exactly going to be carrying huge vats of dough around. Still, it was unusual to see him in the functional part of the store versus the business side. Had something happened to Micah? Was Micah up in Wellspring with Walter? There was no way to know. Even eavesdropping produced no satisfying answers.

Tommen stared longingly at the front case, full of donuts, pastries, cinnamon rolls, fresh bread. If they were on schedule in the back, Kyle would be starting in on the afternoon discourse, the cookies, brownies, cakes, and so on. All baked fresh and delicious. Tommen's stomach grumbled again. Fucking hell, he needed to learn how to bring stuff into this dimension. Maybe he could learn to "steal" flour from the back table in the kitchen, like when the baker dusted it to keep the dough from sticking, and write messages in it. Wouldn't that be something? Ha! Bakery na hÉireann has its very own ghost.

The ghost of a former employee in fact. Double ha!

Tommen left the bakery with an empty stomach. He looked around, wondering what he had to do in order to get Julianna's attention and let her know that he was ready for her. Or maybe this was a test, to see if he could find her. Maybe it was a test of his abilities so far. That was great, except he had no idea where to start. He didn't know her well enough to know if she had any favorite hiding places, or if any place was particularly meaningful.

Well, when it doubt, go where you know, right? She first found him at the campsite, so he might as well start there. He looked around until he got his bearings, then started northeast, Traveling almost as easily as if he were Banding.

When he arrived at the campsite, he was not heartened by what he saw. The search and rescue crews were packing up, tearing down the base they'd erected in the parking lot. They couldn't have given up already; it had only been a day and a half, two days max. Give it at least one more day, maybe two. Or five. Or a month. They put out the notice for a missing child; don't abandon the search now.

His racing heart calmed down when he saw the papers and heard the command team say something about moving to a new search site. So they'd cleared this area and were moving on. Fine. He could deal with that. He just didn't want to think that they'd already given him up for dead, run into the woods injured and afraid only to be torn apart by some wild animal.

As he thought about it, he looked around for his dad. He didn't see him. He didn't even see his car. He didn't see Laura's truck or Kayla's truck or Micah's car or anything familiar. Had they given up? Or had they simply abandoned this futile exercise in search of something substantial, pursuing the more likely Time route? Where would he find them? How did he get a message to them?

"So, you came back."

Tommen turned to see Julianna walking across the lot.

"I wasn't sure where you would be, so I decided to pick a familiar place," he said, only half-lying.

"Fair enough. I had every intention of coming to you, but my business ran late, and when I got to your house, you were already gone. So, like you, I chose a familiar spot. Good thing we chose the same familiar spot, hm?"

He nodded uncertainly. "Listen, I really need to learn how to bring things into this dimension. I'm hungry, I'm thirsty, I'm out of medical supplies and my arm is painful as hell—"

"I know, I know. I understand. Believe me, I do. I've had to do my own doctoring for the last few decades; we're not invincible here, after all. Now, because I know men, the first thing we ought to do is have lunch. What's your fancy?"

They ended up going down to the dinky town of Wellspring to the even dinkier grocery store, if such a place could be called a grocery store. It was tiny, but not too small for a hot rotisserie chicken and half a cheese pizza. Julianna opted for a salad and some fresh fruit.

"I feel like a thief," Tommen said as they sat on a nearby park bench to eat.

"You are a thief," Julianna told him, not missing a beat. "But how did you plan on paying for this food anyway? You can only take; you can't give. Else this wouldn't be referred to as the dimension 'from which no one has ever returned.' "

"I know. But I plan on changing that."

"Of course you do."

"You don't think I can?"

"Honestly, I don't know. But I figure I must have some kind of faith in you or else I wouldn't be here."

Another thought popped into Tommen's mind then, though he dared not say it out loud. Julianna had said that bringing things into the dimension was one of the most difficult talents to master. Did that mean that if she didn't have some faith in him that he would be able to get out, that she would have left him to starve to death? Or was there food to be found elsewhere in the dimension? The implications were stomach-churning to say the least. Still, he finished his chicken and pizza, having a small time of it seeing how he only had one hand.

"All right. Lunch was good. Now what?" he asked, wiping his fingers on a napkin and trying to sound upbeat, enthusiastic, and absolutely determined. "I'm ready."

"Ready for what?" Julianna wondered.

"I'm ready to go home, for one. But, given the present circumstances, I'm ready to learn how to bust out of here so I can go home."

"Good."

"So, what's lesson one?"

"Lesson one is you telling me what you did with my husband's journal, assuming you read it."

Tommen felt his ears burn. "Um...I guess I kind of forgot it. I did read it, though. Well, part of it. I'm really not a huge reader, and reading a lot just kind of puts me to sleep."

"But you did figure out how to reverse the Imprint on it. It has a timer."

"Yeah, I found that out. And I was able to reverse it."

"Excellent. You are a promising student already." She stood. "I suppose the first thing we ought to do is get it and start from there."

Tommen led the way, Traveling back home and heading for his room to grab the journal. Julianna followed him, standing in his doorway and looking around.

"So, this is what teenage boys are into these days," she mused. Her gaze swept around the room and settled on his bookshelf. In two long strides, she crossed the room and pointed to the Book Rifun had given him. "You have one of these?!"

Her sudden fury caught him off-guard and he almost stumbled standing up. "Uh, yeah?"

"Why do you keep it?"

He shrugged. "I don't know. It's interesting. Scary as fuck. I mean, it's not even really scary, like horror movie scary, more like, scary because there are things in there that no one else knows. I don't know how it happened."

"How it happened is not as important as how you read it."

"One word at a time?"

Julianna shifted her stance and folded her arms. "Tell me something, Tommen. Would you rather believe the words of some fictionalized novel, sifting through detail after detail to find a grain of truth, or the words of the Author herself as she spoke directly to someone?"

I didn't realize there was a difference between the two, given that both are books written by mortal people. Tommen did not say this out loud, but he came pretty close to it. Instead he shrugged and said, "You know what, I know what you're asking, and I've got to say, I don't know. At this point, I just know there's an Author out there somewhere. A Great Big Something. Who that is, I don't know. Which book is right, I don't know. Right now, I'll go with whoever can get me the fuck out of here. Then we can sit down and have a little more detailed discussion."

She studied him for a moment. If he had to pick a word for her expression, subdued might be it. Or uncertain, as she said, "So, you would still take me with you?"

He shrugged again. "I don't see why not. You're trapped here just as much as I am with no company and no apparent hobbies."

She sighed and nodded, regaining her normal prim and proper composure. "Very well. As you said, our primary goal is to escape. We can hash out the details later."

"Great. Love that we're on the same page. Where do we begin?"

"Well, preferably someplace that isn't enclosed."

Yes. Because bad things happened in small, enclosed, confined spaces. They needed to be out in a field or on a mountainside far away from people. He let her lead the way this time, meandering here and there over hill and dale until they were about as lost as the search and rescue team thought Tommen still was.

"All right. Lesson one," Julianna began. "It's not about how you're going to break out, but about how you got in."

Made sense. In order to reverse something, it helped to have a knowledge of how it worked before.

"Imagine if you will, two rooms. Any rooms you like, in a house, in a barn, wherever. Two rooms. What connects those two rooms?"

"A...door?" Tommen guessed.

"Yes. Exactly. Not exactly a trick question. A door. Now, keep that thought in mind for just a moment. What separates the two rooms?"

"Walls?"

"Once again, not a trick question. But you're right. Walls. In the average house today, are those walls solid?" She went on before he could answer. "No. In the modern, stick-built homes of today, the walls are actually hollow. Yes, they may be filled with insulation and the like, but the point is, there is a hollow frame. That's why, when you want to hang a picture on a wall, you have to find a wall stud so you don't go through the wall into the next room.

"Now, going back to the doors. Imagine, if you will, that the door separating these two rooms is a pocket door of some form, and it's on a timer. You have to cross within, say, five seconds. Ninety-nine times out of a hundred, you've gone through that door with no problem. This last time, however, something happened, and you got caught in the middle of the door when the timer ran out. Door snaps shut and pushes you into the space between rooms, into the frame of the wall."

Tommen nodded slowly. "Okay, I think I get it. Keep going."

"Portals are similar to that, except the physical dimensions are quite a bit smaller. See, around the portals is a ton of Energy. Remember, you're only ripping a hole in the universe to open it. But the portal itself is an Energy vacuum. When portals close, they dispel the Energy into this dimension. You may have noticed, but this dimension has a higher concentration of Energy specifically for that purpose. When the portal snapped closed on you, it sucked you right into that Energy field and dragged you here like a strong river current. Obviously you only changed dimensions; you didn't actually, physically go anywhere."

"So what you're saying is," Tommen said, "is that we're on one side of the bank, the real world is on the other side, and there's a strong current between us."

"If I said yes, you would most likely make some fresh comment about just building a bridge. Instead, I'll go back to the waterfall analogy. You're in a cave high up on a cliff. The real world is in another cave opposite you. There's an enormous waterfall between the two caves. You have to figure out how to break through that waterfall without getting dragged down to whatever awaits you at the bottom, sharp rocks or alligators or something. In our case, probably death."

"Or, you know, touching a hot wire." He briefly relayed his experiences with touching a portal.

"Hm, yes, such an experience can be quite shocking," Julianna mused. "At any rate, that is the best way I can come up with to explain our current situation. Now do you see the problem?"

"I think so. But where does the stealing things from the real world and bringing them in here come in?"

She rolled her eyes. "It's not a perfect analogy. If there's one thing the Author lacks, it's creative wit when it comes to analogies. I mean, just look at everything she's come up with so far."

Her mouth snapped shut then as if she'd said something terribly wrong, like a kid catching his parents swearing. He didn't get what it was and elected just to play dumb and let it go. Maybe it would come to him later. Now, though, he had a semi-decent analogy to work with, something he could envision instead of vague terms for invisible things like Energy and dimensions and shit.

"Now we're going to take a little field trip," she said finally. "Follow me."

He did so, and they Traveled northwest. Tommen still wasn't too precise on his stopping and he almost went careening into Julianna which would have put them both in the water. As he looked around, he knew exactly where they were. Not because he'd ever been here before, but the sign was very helpful.

"Niagara Falls," he said.

Julianna nodded. "Very perceptive of you. Think of this being the waterfall between us and the real world. The force of this water coming down could crush you."

"Some people have gone over the falls in a barrel," Tommen pointed out.

"Yes, they have. But that was moving with the water. This is going through it, against it. Figure out how to build the better barrel. We'll meet up later."

She left him then, to stare at the thousands of gallons of water sloshing over the falls every second. The more he looked at it and the more he thought about it, the more daunting his task seemed to become. He was going to have to overcome the force of the water. Like she'd said, he wouldn't be moving with it, but against it.

Walter had rented a power washer once so he could clean up the siding on the house and do some general spring cleaning. This had been when Tommen was about ten or eleven, been in the twenty-first century a few years, but still pretty clueless. He didn't realize that the "power" in "power washer" was enough to tear the skin right off his body, and when his dad wasn't looking, he went investigating. It had been weeks before his face finally healed up. His forehead, cheeks, nose, and chin all looked like he'd gotten a pretty severe rugburn. His only saving grace was that his eyes hadn't been injured, a small miracle in itself.

This was like that. The force of the water was bad enough, but now it had the potential to drag him under into sharp rocks and alligators. Were there alligators around Niagara Falls? He thought about it, then concluded there weren't.

Build a better barrel. How the hell was he supposed to do that? That was difficult even in a physical sense, never mind a metaphorical sense.

Tommen found a spot on the scenic overlook and looked out over the water, turning off his hearing aids so the rush of water didn't destroy his hearing any more than it was. And to conserve battery life, seeing how he got about half the time he might normally get.

Build a better barrel. Well, the idea of the barrel was to protect the occupants as they braved the rushing currents that would otherwise kill them. So, here he was, rushing down a current of Energy into the in-between dimension. Only going with the flow had saved him. Going against the flow was a whole different beast. He had to be able to protect himself.

How could he protect himself against Energy? It was tempting to think of Energy as electricity only, but heat was energy, too. Rubber might do well against electricity, but it would absorb heat. The last thing he needed to do was build a barrel of death. So, types of energy. Electricity, heat, light, even sound. All with strengths and weaknesses, and none of them the same. It was like facing off against an army of Borelians when every single one of them was a different color. Even that was a bad analogy because at least all Borelians were physically the same and could be killed the same way.

Could he apply the same logic to Energy? Not necessarily, in the same way an electrical fire, a wood fire, and a grease fire couldn't be extinguished the same way. Bad things happened when water hit a grease fire; he'd learned that one the hard way once when he first started working in the bakery.

Was he overthinking things again? Was he trying to add variables to an already complex problem? Or was he trying to add variables to a problem that needed no variables? How could he tell the difference?

Build a better barrel. Maybe what he needed to do was get away from these waterfalls so he stopped thinking about it so literally. Tommen stood and stretched and looked around. Tourists. Tourists, everywhere. Taking pictures, videos, laughing, pointing, oohing, ahhing, as if they'd never seen a shit ton of water before. Well, not like he could say too much. He was from West Virginia. They had water, but not quite like this.

So maybe he needed to start thinking like that. Maybe he ought to observe how people protected themselves from various forms of energy by shadowing those who interacted with that energy for a living. Yes, yes, there were multiple forms of Energy, but there had to be a common thread somewhere.

Tommen picked a direction and started Traveling, hoping the Akari or the Author or whatever knew what he was up to and could guide him where he needed to be. He wanted to start off small, that way he could get in the groove with whatever lingo the workers might be throwing around out there.

So it was that he ended up on some podunk country road out in the middle of God knew where. A storm had apparently just blown through as everything was soaking wet and there were trees and branches down all over the place. One tree had fallen on a power line and snapped it. If there had been any fire, it was long since out, as wet as everything else.

A work truck pulled up, the logo depicting the local power company. A couple of guys got out, sipping on coffee mugs for a minute as they walked up and down the road, from pole to pole, surveying the situation. After a minute or two, they put the mugs back in the truck, then started dragging out huge yellow blobs that turned out to be gear of some form. Clothes, boots, helmets, gloves, until they might have resembled something out of a 1960's alien B-movie. Tommen knew that only because of the retro posters that had graced the walls of the living room for almost a decade.

From somewhere on the truck, one guy brought out a pole which he started adding to, section after section after section until the thing had to be fifty feet long. He set that aside for a moment as he brought out a pair of what looked like binoculars, surveying the scene at the top of the pole. Then he put the binoculars down, took up the pole, and started poking around. Well, that was a crude term, as Tommen was sure there was an art to it.

A switch was flipped. That was all. The guy didn't burst into flames or get electrocuted. The power pole and its components didn't burst into flames or a shower of sparks. Just flip! and that was that. He grabbed the binoculars and moved down to the next pole. The power only flowed one way, but better to be safe than sorry, right? He examined the top of the pole with the binoculars, then reached up and flip! Somewhere inside the line, somewhere on this circuit, the power had stopped and been rerouted, maybe back through the line. But to the casual observer, nothing of significance had happened.

Still the guys kept their gear on as one climbed into the truck bucket, a five-gallon pail of tools by his side. The men conversed for a moment, pointing and gesturing, then the bucket man was raised.

Tommen did not get to see exactly what the bucket man did, but he didn't really need to, not right now. All he really needed to see was that neither of the guys got energized by the lines they were working on, which they didn't. He didn't stay to watch the whole thing, just enough to gather observations and preliminary data.

He started walking down the road, a little curious as to where he was, but after a mile or two with no town in sight, he gave up. All right, so, preliminary observations complete. What had he learned? Well, when dealing with electricity, it was a safe bet that turning it off first was a smart idea. Was there any way he could do the same to the Energy of the universe? After a moment of pondering, he decided probably not.

Okay, so, where to next? Electricity was informative, if uneventful. He needed something with a little more excitement, though, to make him really pay attention. He needed something with a little more danger, a little more obvious risk of injury. Once again, he picked a direction and started Traveling, hoping he would end up where he needed to be.

When he landed, his eyes started watering and he began coughing involuntarily. Looking around, he saw heavy smoke. He also saw sunlight and flashing lights, and that was the direction he headed. Oddly enough, his first thought was how strange it was that, even though he was invisible, the smoke still affected him. Maybe it was the heat and the air, things not normally affected by Time, but were affected by the Akari. Well, it was a theory.

He'd landed at a house fire, and by house, it wasn't some dinky trailer in a trailer park, but a full-blown mansion, or that's what it looked like. At least three stories, solid brick exterior, Old World in just about every aesthetic way, fully engulfed in flames. Off to one side, people he assumed to be the family looked on. Husband looked pissed, wife looked shaken but trying to stay strong for the two little kids who were crying.

The house was out in the country, and a whole line of fire trucks were strung out along the road like a beaded necklace. Tommen wanted to stay back and watch, but he knew he had to get close if he wanted to observe anything. He went to the front of the line of trucks, needlessly stepping over half a dozen hoses to get to the cab where one man was in charge of a lot of knobs and buttons and things. On the other side of the truck was another group of men all with white and red helmets denoting officers of various ranks from several different stations. They talked to each other and talked in their radios, sometimes talking to each other on the radio despite being two feet apart.

A team of three firefighters was walking up the drive, away from the house. They still wore their air packs, but their helmets and hoods were off, coats open. Had all their gear been off, Tommen might have said they'd gone swimming for as soaked as they were, and it wasn't from the water from the hoses either. They were sweating their asses off. They headed for a truck that looked like a retired ambulance, grabbing food and bottled water while a medical team checked them out.

"Quill, Taylor, and Johnson! You're up!" one of the officers said.

"Got it!" someone shouted back.

Three new individuals began their approach from an unknown location, sliding on suspenders, pulling on coats and hoods, shouldering heavy ass air packs before topping it off with helmets and gloves.

Tommen jumped as a window exploded in a shower of broken

glass and hungry flame. The firefighters below scattered and the officers began squawking on their radios again. A couple minutes later, another team exited the house, one limping with his buddies on either side, practically dragging him to the ambulance.

Tommen followed them, unnecessarily dodging gear as it was stripped from the injured fireman. He honestly expected to find the man burned and wailing, but he was only plastered in sweat and favoring a knee. His boots squelched as they were pulled off and his socks were saturated with water that was black and almost tarry in its consistency. The medic confirmed a busted knee, but otherwise, no worse for wear. The other two firefighters breathed a sigh of relief as they began taking off their gear, grabbing granola bars, chocolate bars, and energy drinks.

He'd meant to stay only a few minutes, just enough to observe the goings-on of the firefighters, but there was something enthralling about a house burning down. It was tragic, to be sure, but it was mesmerizing, too. At first it was the fire, the flames and smoke and the sheer magnitude of destruction. Then it was the smoke and ashes as he waited to see what had become of the mansion.

It kind of reminded him of the wildfire, actually. It was absolutely terrifying because he'd been in the middle of it, but once things had slowed down and he could walk right into it—albeit with Rifun—it was stunning in its beauty. Did that line of thought make him a future serial killer, or at the least a serial arsonist? He thought about it, then decided no. There really was just something awe-inspiring about fire and being able to walk right in the middle of it.

When, you know, it was a natural fire and not a house fire with all the plastics, chemicals, and the fact that it could all come crashing down at any given moment. Safe fire. Safe fire was nice.

Eventually, he pulled himself away from the scene and started walking up the road, turning back every so often to still see smoke billowing into the sky. Okay, so, fire. What had he learned from this little experience? First, fire was scary. Well, that he'd actually already learned, hence his injured arm. Moving on.

Always use the buddy system when dealing with major fires. That was a good start. But yet, even in the midst of the fire, the guy had only injured his knee. Maybe it was related to the window incident, maybe not, but it wasn't an injury from the fire. It wasn't a burn. His knee had twisted, but the gear still kept him safe. And the fact that he'd practically been underwater with how much sweat had been coming off him. All of them, really.

Once, in sixth grade, the fire department had paid a visit to Tommen's middle school. They'd done their fire safety presentation, thankfully a little more than stop, drop, and roll, and don't play with matches. It had been as much a recruiting effort as fire safety, really. But after the event, they'd had the chance to go up and try on the gear. Not that they expected anyone to fit, necessarily, it was for the feeling of it and the goofy pictures. Tommen had tried on the gear, and holy hell, it was heavy, even without the air pack which they'd had a competition to see who could lift it the highest for the longest. All of it together had probably weighed more than he had at the time.

It was all in the name of protection. Everything from what the materials were to the thickness and how heavy they needed to be, it was all about staying safe in the middle of a fire. With or without, they'd be sweating their balls off, but at least with the gear, they had a chance at staying safe from burns, debris, and falling objects. It was the same with the line workers; their gear was specially made to keep them safe from an electric shock. Neither set of gear was completely fool-proof; eventually they would both fail when the fire got too hot or the charge got too much.

There were any number of professions out there to explore yet, but it only took two points to make a straight line, and Tommen figured he'd connected the dots pretty well. Actually, he'd understood the basic concept before, but witnessing it on such a large scale made it more tangible.

It was all about insulation, having a protective barrier that could absorb, dispel, or reflect a particular type of energy with minimal or no harm coming to the wearer. Just like setting insulators on posts intended to hold an electric fence wire, to keep the posts from becoming energized. It was building the better barrel. Even the guys who did go over waterfalls in barrels had a form of insulation; they had a—presumably—water-tight barrel, or something good enough that they would be protected from the fall, from obstacles, keep from sinking, and still be able to breathe.

Tommen found a nice chair in someone's lawn and sat down, momentarily pleased with himself. He basked in his own glory for as long as he could until reality caught up to him. Great. He'd solved for the variable of one problem. Insulation equals protection against Energy. Next he had to figure out how that translated into building the figurative better barrel to break through an Energy barrier that had so far electrocuted him at least once. He had no desire to repeat that, nor burn any more of his body than he already had.

He let out a breath. Well, so much for his grand plans falling into place. And in all reality, even an idiot would have figured out the insulation thing eventually. If this little escapade was going to end up in another novel, there would probably be someone, somewhere, going to read something at the beginning of the chapter and be like, "Oh, that's easy. He just needs to find the right kind of insulation." Then that person would be yelling at him the whole time he was out stalking line workers and firemen, shouting, "Insulation! Insulation, you fool!"

So that was where he was now. *Congratulations, Tommen, you discovered the obvious. You've invented the wheel. Now what are you going to do with it?* Problem was, he had no idea what he was going to do with it because his problem hadn't fucking changed.

Groaning, he reluctantly stood and turned in what he hoped was the direction of home. He really just kind of wanted to flop down on his bed and wallow in self-pity. He gingerly checked his arm. Felt a little wet, but whether that was from the blisters weeping again or sweat from his proximity to the fire, he wasn't sure. He'd have to ask Julianna again for the medical supplies the next time they met. She hadn't exactly said when that would be, though, but he hoped it was relatively soon. He was starting to get hungry again.

His Traveling did indeed take him home, or back to Charleston, anyway. Friday evening and the rush was bigger than ever. During the summer, it was the locals getting out of work and going home or going somewhere for the weekend; it was the tourists out and about to see the sights; it was everyone in between going everywhere else. Tommen passed through it all, silently, invisibly, a phantom in a solid world. Well, not entirely true, seeing how he could sit in a chair or run into a wall just as easily as anyone else. But it was nice and poetic-sounding.

He stopped by the bakery for a moment. He took one look at the line and did a small happy dance that he wasn't the one on counter or in the kitchen. He wasn't having to deal with the grouchy customers or their impossible orders. Micaiah and Kyle were both up front while Jenna worked tirelessly in the back. Micah was still nowhere to be seen.

Fuck, he wished he knew how to pull objects into the in-between dimension because everything in that case was looking mighty tasty. Tommen silently added that to his list of things to ask Julianna about the next time he saw her.

And where was she, anyway? Why did she just appear and disappear at will, as if she had little interest in his attempts to break out of the dimension? Did she really have any faith that he would be able to do it? What business could she have to attend to, anyway? It wasn't like the in-between dimension was a hopping place. Maybe she was talking to some other poor soul who'd gotten himself sucked into the dimension. Was she trying to recruit them or just telling them to give up? Tommen figured he would take all the help he could get.

After a minute or two of watching the craziness at the bakery, Tommen left. He could have Traveled home, he supposed, but he decided just to walk. He knew he could have crossed any street at will, but force of habit bade him stay and wait for the proper lights and the walk sign. Even then it was a dangerous thing on a Friday night, and Tommen was convinced that about sixty percent of drivers were red-green color-blind like him and unable to distinguish between stop and go on the traffic lights.

The suburbs outside the city were also busy with cars, the rushing rapids gradually dividing into smaller rivers as more and more people branched off into their individual neighborhoods, their individual roads, and finally into their own driveways. Tommen considered stopping in at Becky's house again, then decided against it. It would do nothing for him except frustrate him; he hated to see the look of worry on her face and hated to think of her prostrate before God, begging for his safe return.

"I'm right here," he wanted to say. "I can see you. Why can't you see me?"

He returned home, shocked to find his dad inside. Had the search been called off? Had he been sent home? Had he given up? Had the precinct called and asked him to come in? Walter was too anxious to make such a sudden change in behavior, so there had to be a reason. Tommen headed inside, determined to find out what it was.

Well, it wasn't hard to guess, though he was forced to question why. His dad had evidently gone up to the campsite to help search; his wet, muddy boots and pants covered in dirt and leaves were testament to that. And it made sense that he would want to shower upon his return, to get the grime and stink off him. That was all fine and dandy. What Tommen couldn't figure out was why he was getting dressed like he was supposed to meet Laura for dinner. Was he meeting Laura for dinner? Was there some police officer's banquet coming up soon that Tommen had forgotten about? He looked at the calendar, but the next banquet wasn't scheduled until the beginning of September, the Safety in Schools conference or something.

So what was this? It wasn't exactly a black-tie thing, whatever it was, but his dad was not a suit-and-tie kind of guy. Outside of his uniform, it was T-shirt and jeans, business casual at the maximum. And the cologne, holy shit. He was going all out.

Stomach twisting, Tommen felt through all of his dad's pockets, in his pants — totally not weird — in his coats, everywhere. If he found a ring, he was calling Julianna up on some emergency frequency and demanding to know how to pull things into the in-between dimension. He liked Laura well enough, but that was too much, too soon.

He didn't find anything in any of the pockets, so he went out to the car. Sometimes Walter put things in the car in advance if he thought he wouldn't remember them later on. But as he rummaged around in the doors, the center console, the glove box, he found nothing out of the ordinary. No rings, necklaces, or gifts of any kind. But that didn't mean something wasn't up.

After a few minutes, Walter walked into the garage and got in the car, his expression a mix of anxiety and fear. He started the car and opened the garage door. Tommen sat in the passenger seat, along for the ride.

Chapter Twelve
Possibilities

It was strange to think that an hour ago he'd been in the Akarin Archives, looking for any leads on his missing son. Then he'd gone home and gotten eight more hours of sleep, and now he was heading back up to Wellspring to aid in a search that was becoming increasingly futile. The search and rescue teams might still hold out hope, but as the clues from the other side of the physical spectrum started adding up, Walter found that his hope was wavering.

He tried to keep a positive attitude on the drive up. Micaiah and Kayla would still be looking, Micah, too. They would look on the Time-side of things, and Walter would look on the Earth-side. Just because there was a Time-side culprit didn't mean there wasn't Earth-side evidence. He just had to be patient and find it.

That was easier said than done as he arrived at the campsite and found it in a partial state of being torn down. From what he understood, the last search teams in the current zone had been dispatched, and command was preparing to move quickly to their new location if nothing was found. They were hoping that something turned up, but if it didn't, they had to be ready. Now that they were passing forty-eight hours into Tommen's disappearance, time was of the essence, and they had to move quickly. They had already mobilized a few specialized wilderness teams to head into the deep mountains to start looking while their teams stayed around more local, more populated areas.

Walter got a refill on his coffee and permission to join one of the teams, hoping he came across determined and not dreadfully anxious. He couldn't tell if the commander bought it, but he figured it didn't matter as long as he was out there looking.

At this point, he wasn't even sure what he was looking for. Obviously Tommen wasn't just camping somewhere, chilling out until help arrived. Footprints would be washed away. Clothing could be washed away or trampled in the dirt. The only thing they were really going to find that would be helpful was either a neon sign or Tommen himself.

Walter refused to let his mind wander so far, telling himself to focus on something else. The weather was still pretty crummy, rain interrupted by sun interrupted by more rain interrupted by a brief appearance from the sun, sometimes all at the same time. The back and forth stirred up quite a mess of fog in the valley, making it impossible to see roots, sticks, logs, stones, anything and everything that tripped Walter at least every six steps. His boots got muddy and his pants got dirty, but he did not spill his coffee, thank God. It was about the only thing keeping him going out here as his hands got wet and cold.

All this rain, just a few days too late, he thought ruefully. He opened his thermos and took a drink, looking around, peering through the fog. In the movies, this was the part where the hero would find a mysterious cave with a wise old sage huddled around the fire, spouting the wisdom of the ages. Or it was the part where a giant moose would come out of nowhere and go on a rampage, attacking the hero and trampling him into the dirt. Either one. Personally, Walter was betting on the moose. It was just how things seemed to be going lately.

He took another drink of coffee and closed the thermos. When he looked up, he found himself momentarily disoriented. Where was the path? Which way had he come from? Which way was he going? Was it the fog getting him all confused? If his orientation didn't return quickly, how was he going to find his way back and not become their next missing person?

The sun broke through the clouds again, reflecting off all the little water droplets in the air, momentarily blinding Walter. After a minute or two, the fog began burning off, revealing the same deep woods he'd been standing and running around in the last two days. Had it only been two days? Why did it feel like two weeks? Well, he knew why it felt like two weeks, because the last time had been two weeks. Would this time be two weeks? Longer? Was there any foreseeable end to this tragedy?

Cautiously, he continued along the path, his orientation and spatial sense returning. He wasn't sure what had happened, and he wasn't eager to find out. Most likely, it was just his anxiety. He knew he had a good reason to be anxious, but somehow it felt like too much. That didn't make much sense seeing how he'd seen parents in full-blown, raging panic attacks when their child went missing. As it was, he still knew what day it was and which way was up. Plus he was out helping to search.

Maybe it was because he'd told himself that he would never again give in to that anxiety and fear. The warehouse had been evidence enough of what happened when emotions led the charge. He was determined to do better, to think about things with a clear head. Problem was, emotions were not shunned so easily, certainly not ones that had been a rather dominant force for the last century of his life. They were as much of a drug as the narcotics, except he couldn't "get clean" of his emotions. They would always be there, lurking, waiting to pop up and screw up his day. Or his life.

He stopped again, closed his eyes, tried to breathe. He didn't need to get emotional now. He had to keep his head on straight and complete the search. Either be a full man on the team or get off the mountain. Just like he told his guys if they were faced with a dangerous situation. If you can't be there one hundred percent, then don't be there at all. Half a man would kill two people. Too bad he hadn't taken his own advice at the warehouse. Ten men might still be alive today.

Well, if it wasn't the anxiety, the guilt had a way of sneaking up on him, too. He took another drink of coffee and moved on. Maybe it was the coffee getting him all hyped up. The coffee these search and rescued guys brewed seemed to have espresso levels of caffeine, which was not good for Walter who already had high blood pressure. He didn't need to have a heart attack out on this mountain.

It seemed to take forever and a day, but he completed his search, meeting up with the search team about halfway through. Almost as expected, they found nothing. As they trudged back to the command post, Walter could see the guys were getting worried and frustrated. This should not be this hard. There was something they were missing, some obvious clue. Tommen was right under their noses; they could feel it. But they just weren't finding him.

Walter wished he could impart his knowledge. Problem was, even for those who understood, he didn't have much knowledge or insight to give. For those who didn't understand, he was a raving lunatic anyway. *Hey, guys, I know we're all out here in the wet and cold, not having any success, but do you mind if I give a small speech about the quantum physics of the universe? I think it might really help us find my son.*

He scoffed internally. He didn't even understand the quantum physics of the universe. Up until recently, it had just been Time with a little extra stuff that he didn't understand, stuff that kept the Wheel of Time spinning. Now the curtain had been pulled back, and Oz was every bit as powerful as he proclaimed to be. There was Time, Matter, Energy, the very fabric of the universe, there for the taking. He was just one small man.

Yes, retirement was looking better and better every day.

When they reached the command post, a table had been set up for a quick snack break. Granola bars, chips, cookies, a bit of fruit, things to tide the men over. According to one of the women putting it on, the full lunch was being set up in the next zone if they wanted to head over there and get something to eat before the next assignments came down.

That motivated a lot of the guys, especially when they heard that lunch was going to be chili, hot dogs, and hamburgers. It was intended to be a morale-booster as much as lunch, keep their spirits high while they trudged around on the mountainside.

Walter, however, was decidedly less motivated to move on to

the next area. He grabbed a little of everything and found a place to sit and eat and brood. There was something missing; he was sure of it.

"How are you holding up?"

Walter looked up to see Harold, the top commander of the search and rescue. He nodded. "Like Atlas."

"Are you sure?" Harold pulled up a chair and sat down. "It's great that you're out here and helping, but if you need to go home or even just sit back and watch, it's all right. No one holds it against you. We know what we're doing."

"I have no doubt about that, but I have to be out there. I have to know."

"Well, I can respect that, absolutely. And you know a thing or two about looking for guys who are hiding. I'll leave it up to you, then, whether you come or go. But we're packing up to move to the next zone."

"Where is that?"

Harold gave him directions and a grainy map. As the crow flew, it really wasn't too far away, but with mountain roads the way they were, it was a fair distance. Walter did not make for his car immediately, instead opting to finish his small plate of snacks and wait until almost everything was packed up and moving. Only then did he get in his car and start down the road, following a small truck pulling a very large trailer.

It was slow going. They had to go all the way back out to the main road, then turn right as if heading back to Wellspring. The road they were looking for was so small, Walter would have missed it if he hadn't been following the truck and trailer. It was dirt, little better than a two-track. He gave the truck a fair head start, then started creeping along in his car. Half a mile in, he knew his car wasn't going to make it. Between the grade of the road and the sorry condition it was in, it was just better if he did, in fact, sit this one out.

Of course, he pissed off a couple people behind him as he had to back down the road; there was zero room to turn around. His skin flushed with embarrassment as he finally hit pavement and let the trucks through. After a few seconds of calming his nerves, he turned around and headed for Wellspring. If lunch was at the end of that two-track, he obviously wasn't getting any. His options were going to be found either at the diner or the grocery store.

The thought of food spurred him on, but it didn't make him feel any better about having to abandon the search. Maybe Harold had been trying the polite tactic of getting him to back down, but saying, "Hey, man, the road we're going up is rutted and shitty and your car won't make it" would have been helpful, too. At the very least, it would have saved him the embarrassment and the guys behind him some time.

He was about two miles from Wellspring when his phone rang. It was Micaiah.

"Yeah, Cai," Walter answered levelly.

"Walt. So, Kayla and I did some more research in the Archives — among other things — and..."

"Did you find anything?"

"Yes and no. Sadly, we did not find any flashing neon signs. You might say we found the little dirt track leading into unknown territory marked only with hand-painted signs, most of them reading 'Keep Out.'"

"I just came down a road like that. Nothing you're saying is comforting me, Micaiah. Out with it."

Micaiah still hesitated. "Well, we think we have a lead as to where Tommen could be. But I don't think you're going to like it. We weren't even sure if it would be wise to tell you, but it felt dishonest to not tell you."

That certainly explained his odd behavior, given that he was normally a straight to the point kind of guy. "So where is he? Or where could he be?"

"That...might be better discussed in person. Believe me, Walt, I hate doing this to you, but I don't want to get you all worked up for the drive home."

"And being ominous is supposed to help me how?"

"Just trust me, Walter. When do you expect you'll be back?"

"Well, my car can't make it up to the next search command post, so I was going to grab me some lunch in town. I guess I can come back now and get something from you guys."

"Should I plan for two hours or two minutes?"

"Plan for two hours. Maybe if I do things in Base Time, yelling at traffic might help to calm me down."

Micaiah laughed. "Okay, fair enough. I'll see you then."

Walter hung up and tossed his phone in the passenger seat, unsure how to react. Micaiah knew how to play the suspense card, but that wasn't suspense. That was being dodgy and ominous. Nothing good ever came from dodgy and ominous.

He bypassed the grocery store and the diner, heading for the zigzag of roads that would get him to the freeway. He had to constantly remind himself that he was traveling in Base Time and couldn't just put the pedal to the metal to get home in half the time. He was a police officer. He ought to know better. And if word ever got back about such behavior, Steggmann would have him mopping floors and plunging toilets for a week. That was a fate worse than death, depending on the day of the week, who was working, and what food got left in the break room.

So he plodded along with the rest of them, "plodded" being a relative term seeing how traffic was actually moving at a pretty good clip, but he had become accustomed to just Banding and expertly zipping this way and that through the cars.

He tried to keep his mind occupied, whether it was turning up the radio or making plans for the evening. As he thought about it, he grabbed his phone and dialed a number.

"Did they find him?" Laura asked.

"Well, they don't know," Walter answered, willing it to be at least half-true. "They think they have a lead, but after so much rain the last couple days, it's difficult to be sure."

"Oh, stop being such a pessimist, Walt. They've got something at least. And they're professionals; they'll have him found in no time.

It's probably not the first time they've had to go searching in the rain."

"No, I expect not. Unfortunately, I'm too old and can't quite maneuver around the landscape where they're searching, so I'm heading home."

"Oh. Too bad. What else is on your mind?"

"What time do you have to be to work?"

"Seven, why?"

"Are you free for dinner, say, around five-thirty?"

"I think I can squeeze you in. My place or yours?"

"Actually, I was thinking we could go out."

"Where?" He told her the name of the restaurant and she whistled, then sighed. "Dammit, Walter, you're going to make me break out my nice clothes, aren't you?"

"I'm forcing myself to break out my nice clothes; what are you talking about?"

"What's the occasion?"

"Does there have to be one? If you want, we can celebrate the one scrap of evidence they found that could lead to Tommen."

"Works for me. I'll meet you there. Five-thirty, right?"

"Five-thirty."

He hung up and let out a breath. In a way, he felt terrible for going out to a nice dinner while his son was still missing. At the same time, there was nothing more he could do. His car couldn't make it up the two-track. He couldn't keep going up and down the mountain like a spry young man, running only on coffee and granola bars. And if there was more evidence to be had on the Time-side of things, Micah and Micaiah would be the ones to have it, and they were back in Charleston.

Walter still didn't like how strange Micaiah was acting, and the long miles only added to a growing sense of dread that had lodged itself in his gut. What if it was bad news? What if Rifun had made contact? What if this time, there was no way around his terms of hostage release? He took a breath and tried to clear his head. Did paranoia run in the family, or was it just an understandable, expected reaction given the circumstances?

He stopped once to get gas, glancing nervously at his phone, just waiting for someone to call and say they found something. Not that they were moving to a new area or there was a possibility that they might have found something, but that they had something real and concrete, a real clue that they could run with. The call never came, and soon he was back on the road.

It was almost two by the time he got within sight of Charleston. The lunch rush had passed, only to be replaced by the end of first shift and anyone else getting off of work early on a Friday, not to mention the tourists. It was only going to get worse as the day wore on into the standard five o'clock rush. Why had he picked five-thirty as a good time to have dinner? Maybe they could have just met for lunch or something, that way they didn't have to face traffic and she wasn't crunched for time to get to work.

But that was neither here nor there. More and more side roads and on-ramps started filtering into the freeway where he was driving, congesting the roadway. After almost being rear-ended, side-swiped, and rear-ended again, he pulled off onto a main city road. His first instinct was to go home. He probably should have so he could change his shoes and pants, but he would see what Micaiah had to say first, then shower, shave, and change before heading to dinner.

He wondered what Tommen was doing, if he was lost and alone in an unfamiliar forest, injured and confused. Even if he had found a cave and managed to start a small fire to keep warm, Walter would have been good with that. He just hated to think of his headstrong, proudly self-proclaimed homesteader son out there suffering all alone and unable to do anything about it.

He pulled into the parking lot of the bakery feeling miserable and hating himself for it. He was a police officer, dammit. He had to put his personal feelings aside so he could find clues, gather evidence, make decisions, and reach a logical conclusion. In this case, he had to think logically in order to track down his missing son. Getting all worked up and emotional wasn't going to do anyone any good, least of all him. So he had to square his shoulders, perk up, and be ready for anything.

His resolve only lasted about to the front door when Micaiah noticed him and motioned him in. The bakery wasn't busy, but there was plenty of clanging around going on in the kitchen.

"I'll be just a second, Walt," Micaiah told him, grabbing his crutches and going back to yell at the grunts in the kitchen making all the noise. Walter couldn't make out exact words, but judging by the tone, whoever was getting yelled at was now whining about it and complaining it was unfair. Micaiah had some stern words for that. A minute later, Kyle moseyed his way reluctantly to the front.

Micaiah sighed and shook his head, looking at Walter like, "What can you do?"

"Everything okay?" Walter asked.

"Fantastic," Micaiah replied, his tone indicating that everything was not fantastic. Still, he jerked his head toward the office door. "Come on in."

Walter followed Micaiah into the office. As he sat down, he instantly knew it was a bad idea; he might not get up. Micaiah seemed to realize this as he smirked.

"Been out running around a little too hard, eh?"

"It's a young man's game," Walter sighed.

"Please, Walt, you're barely a day over fifty."

"Oh, please."

"No, really. You are as beautiful as a spring flower and just as aromatic."

Walter sighed and rolled his eyes, stifling a yawn. "Is there a point to this patronizing? Are you trying to get me all buttered up for...what? Where's my son?"

Micaiah took a breath and hesitated, evidently being very careful about his words. "Well, that's the thing. We only have a theory. It's a pretty shitty one, but it's the only thing we've found that matches all the evidence so far."

"For goodness' sake, Cai—"

"We think he's in the Land In Between."

Walter stopped and looked at him. He realized he'd raised a brow. "The Land In Between? The dimension between dimensions that eats people if a portal closes on them before they've gone through?"

"The very same. The Land In Between, from which no one has ever returned."

Well, it certainly wasn't the news he was expecting, say it that way. He couldn't even decide how he felt about it. As with most things, it was certainly in evidence when a portal closed and swallowed someone up with no trace, but it was often treated just as a myth or a vague concept. He folded his arms. "Okay. So what evidence do you have for this? What made you come to that particular conclusion?"

Most of the evidence Micaiah presented actually came across as myths and legends, and he admitted as much. Everything he found was in the mythological reference section in the Archives, and the stories weren't always true-to-form. But the major details were there. The Trackers could hunt down distortions in Time and the Akari, and portals were one of the most obvious distortion out there. Plus there was that whole bit about Micaiah seeing some kind of vision of Tommen in his portal. According to him, it hadn't been an Imprint, but Tommen trying to get back to the real world via a standard portal, but, because of the massive Energy build-up, was unsuccessful.

Listening to him explain it, Walter simultaneously did and did not want to believe him. On the one hand, it was a decent theory that fit everything they knew so far, and it might be starting point for a new segment in their investigation. On the other hand, this was the dimension "from which no one has ever returned." Even if Tommen was alive, he could be separated from them forever. Walter didn't know how to feel about that.

When Micaiah finished up, there was silence in the office for a long moment, the men staring at each other.

"All right," Walter said finally. "Let's pretend I believe you. More than that, let's pretend that you're entirely correct and Tommen is trapped in the Land In Between. What do we do now? What's our next step?"

Micaiah squirmed a little. "Well, Kayla's already working on the next step, and it's something that she kind of has to do alone."

"Why? What is it?"

Then came a story that was a little harder to swallow, about the Krydik and their way of communicating with their ancestors via hallucinogenic fruit that was supposed to give them the ability to see into the in-between dimension. Even Micaiah seemed a little dubious on that one, but he was willing to give it a shot.

"Kayla is going to talk to them tomorrow, hopefully get an audience," Micaiah finished. "In that time, I'm supposed to somehow come up with a plan of action to tell Tommen so we can rescue him. Honestly, I've got nothing."

"You're not the only one," Walter grunted. "How did he get there, anyway? He's not strong enough to open a portal."

"Portals are only a manipulation of Energy. Tommen may not have been strong enough on his own, but if he was experimenting and trying to put out that fire, and if he touched the Energy of the fire, it may have caused an explosion that ripped open a portal regardless. It snaps closed on him, boom, Land In Between."

Walter let out a breath. "Okay. So, continuing on this assumption that you're right, what do we know about the Land In-Between?"

"Not much, as you might imagine. Some stories say that if a person is really skilled with their abilities, they are able to 'possess' others in order to communicate. Ghosts, phantoms, things like that. Apparitional appearances. Some stories say that people trapped there are able to function as normally as can be expected, and it's just as if they were invisible and unable to be heard. Other sources say that most of the inhabitants go insane and ultimately kill themselves. I think the isolation would have something to do with that. But the one theme that seems to blanket the whole thing is that they cannot open portals because the amount of Energy in that dimension, used for us to open portals to the Wheel and elsewhere, is potentially lethal. It's the difference between drinking a glass of water and being submerged."

"How are we supposed to get him out, then?"

"Believe me, I wish I knew. I gave Micah the day off, so I figure after the shop is closed, I'll head back and do some more research. Assuming nothing else happens."

"Like what?"

"One of the council members was murdered this morning. And I'm the prime suspect because the last time anyone saw him was when we were arguing."

Walter shook his head. "What is the universe coming to?"

Micaiah grinned. "Oh, that's not even the best part. After I was done in the Archives, ready to return home, I had someone try to kidnap me and deliver me to the Borelians for the bounty."

"How much are you going for these days?"

"I don't know. Apparently a pretty penny or two. Obviously they didn't succeed because I'm here."

"First good news I've had all day." Walter sighed. "Honestly, I don't know what to make of your theory. I want it to be true, because then we have an answer. At the same time, I don't want it to be true because you don't get a title like 'from which no one has ever returned' for nothing."

Micaiah nodded. "I know. Believe me, I understand. I don't like it either. At the same time, if these are the cards we've been dealt, then we have to play them. At least now we know the hand we have."

"Do we?"

"I don't even know. I was trying for the comforting and philosophical angle, but I don't think it worked as well as I had hoped."

"Could have been worse. Does Micah know any of this?"

"No, not yet. I told him to take the day off and do whatever he wanted or needed to do. I'm trying to give him a break. I'll bother him about it later."

"I understand. I could use a day off. Want to fill in for me at work on Sunday?"

"No. You've had the last two days off and you're still working. What are you going to do different on Sunday?"

Walter scoffed. "Maybe I'll go to church and ask God to tear open a hole between the dimensions so I can get my son back."

Micaiah nodded, running his tongue over his teeth. "That's a good plan. I'm still not going to work for you, though. I don't think I could pass as you. It's that whole one-legged business."

"Please. Ernie's got two prosthetics, and he didn't get to keep his knees. You'll blend right in."

"As exciting as it sounds, I think I'll pass."

"Suit yourself."

Micaiah leaned back in his chair. "So, now that that's all out there, are you going to head back to Wellspring?"

Walter shook his head. "I couldn't if I wanted to. My car can't make it up the two-track to the new command post, and the terrain is said to be even more treacherous. I'm thinking I might have to sit back and let the professionals work on this one."

"Fair enough. What are you going to do in the meantime?"

"You mean, if I'm not busy, do I want to come and help you with your research and whatnot?"

"You read my mind."

"Well, as it so happens, I am busy tonight, at least for a little while. Laura and I are going to dinner."

"Ooh, you've graduated from lunch to dinner. Things are getting serious, aren't they?" He laughed when Walter blushed. "Please, you know I'm happy for you. What time is dinner?"

"Five-thirty. She has to be to work at seven."

"Oh. Well, the bakery doesn't close until nine tonight. That gives you plenty of time to go to dinner with Laura, go home and get caught up on whatever you need to do there, and then, if you're feeling ambitious—"

"All right," Walter cut in. "I'll come and help. Believe me, it's not that I don't want to find Tommen, I'm just not sure how I feel about being in the Akarin Archives, especially with things heating up like they are."

"As I said last time, don't worry about them. Let me worry about them. You just do what you need to do, whatever you think will help. Got it?"

"If you say so."

"All right." Micaiah grabbed his crutches and stood. "Well, I have to go get the children out of timeout and make sure they play nice." He rolled his eyes and Walter couldn't help but smile. All this talk of different dimensions and missing people and Energy and the Akari and whatever else, and still they had to deal with life's little woes. For Micaiah, that involved disciplining a couple of employees who despised each other.

Even though he was going to dinner in a couple hours, and the fact that his metabolism was wondering why the hell he was eating so much when he didn't need to, Walter grabbed a pastry on his way out, unwrapping it once he got to the car. So, they had a theory. It was a plausible theory, he supposed, but that didn't mean he had to like it. He couldn't decide how convinced Micaiah was of it, either. On the one hand, he was a good researcher, knew how to track things down, what to look for, what to pursue and what to ignore. On the other hand, when one continues to come up empty on every lead so far, a man could get desperate and start grasping at straws.

Maybe his hesitation hadn't come from the theory, but because he'd been expecting more of a reaction from him, Walter. Maybe he thought Walter was going to go into a flying rage or other emotional outburst. Walter certainly felt like it at times. Right now, he was more hurt that Micaiah considered him so unstable that he couldn't even be approached with a theory. Walter didn't deny that he had problems and probably needed help, but was faith in him really so hard to come by right now?

Apparently it was, as the next thing he knew, he'd taken another painkiller. He hadn't even had time to register the soreness in his back and knees before he'd gotten the bottle out.

Stop doing this, Walter, he told himself. *Get help. Ask Laura for help. If you ask her and make an honest attempt, she probably won't hold it against you. Getting help isn't a sign of weakness.*

But for as much as he told himself this, and as much as he promised himself that this was the last one and he could do it on his own, he had the experience to know that it was all a lie. He wouldn't get help. He was wound up way too tight from his physical injuries as well as the stress he was under. Maybe once it was all over and things were back to normal, then he would get help. Right now, his body was craving the narcotics and he didn't have the time, energy, or willpower to wrestle with himself while he was wrestling with everything else.

It was a dangerous mindset to get into, and he knew it. His conscience warred with his cravings the entire drive home where he collapsed into his recliner. He'd no sooner sat than he realized he should probably get out of his filthy clothes before his got his recliner all dirty. Plus he still had to get ready for dinner with Laura.

He glanced at the clock. Only three o'clock. He had some time yet, he supposed. Grudgingly, before he could get too comfortable in his recliner, he got up and headed into the bathroom to take a shower. It should have been a simple enough deal, except when he got out and looked at himself in the mirror, he was decidedly less pleased with what he saw. He needed to lose weight, and the only way he was going to do that was by cutting back on his already comparatively sparse eating. Problem was, he really did like food. So did Laura. They enjoyed going out to eat or just cooking for each other. This did not bode well for him.

Furthermore, he could probably go for a haircut. If Tommen's hair got this long, he'd be telling him to either get it cut or start trying to pull it back in a decent ponytail. That he couldn't do on his own. Could Laura do decent haircuts? Maybe he'd ask her about it tonight.

About the only thing he did have control over was his mustache, which he spent a little time diligently trimming, trying not to cut his nose or his lip or anything else for that matter. Well, seeing how he seemed to be on a self-improvement binge, why not make an eye appointment, too? He managed to get by well enough for the police department, but he didn't exactly have the eyes of a twenty year old. Following on that train of thought, should he make an appointment with Polski, too?

Walter sighed and put down the scissors, tiny things in his too big fingers. Getting old sucked. Nothing worked like it was supposed to anymore.

By the time he actually left the bathroom, went to his bedroom, and got his clothes out, it was just after four. He grabbed his phone and dialed Laura.

"Hey, are we still good for dinner?" she asked.

"That's what I'm calling to ask you," he told her. "I've got my really nice clothes out and just want to make sure I have an occasion to wear them."

She laughed. "I won't make you, but you're the one who picked the venue. Yeah, I'm good for dinner if you are."

That's what he was afraid of. Not going to dinner necessarily, but that she was still okay with the restaurant he'd picked. It would not have broken his heart if she asked to change the location, go somewhere a little less formal. But it looked like he was stuck. He stared at his clothes, what basically amounted to a full suit with tie. The restaurant wasn't a black-tie event where they had to know proper etiquette and use six different forks, but there was a certain expectation of, well, snobbery. The "if you can afford to eat here, you can afford to look like it" kind of attitude.

He wasn't a hundred percent sure why he'd picked the place. It was the kind of place one would pick either to celebrate an anniversary or pop the question, and he was doing neither. Was he just trying to impress her, show that he wasn't a total cheapskate? What for? Neither of them were rich snobs. His house and vehicle were good, but nowhere near that level of sophistication. Was he only trying to fool himself into thinking he was that rich?

Or was he doing things the way he had done them before, with Paige? She'd been rich, and he'd had to act the part. He'd struggled with it ninety percent of the time and overdid it the other ten percent. First she accused him of being cheap, stingy, and an idiot Welshman who had no idea how to spend money because he clearly never had any. Then she accused him of being wasteful, flagrant, and an idiot Welshman who seemed to think that money grew on trees for the rich folk of the world.

Now he was caught in the same struggle, over a century later. He wanted to show Laura that he wasn't destitute, that he wasn't cheap. But he also wanted to keep an eye on his finances and not go overboard trying to impress her, thus getting himself in an embarrassingly tight situation.

Maybe he should call it off, or at least change the venue. That would be smarter on his end. Or would it make him look cheap, backing out after possibly getting her hopes up for a nice meal? If she asked why he decided to change, what would he say? He didn't want to wear nice clothes? Then he sounded like a slob.

He sighed as he pulled the belt tight and clicked it in. Was this all as difficult as he was thinking, or was he just imagining half of it?

Well, one really nice meal wouldn't kill him. And it would be a nice gesture to her. It would be a nice change of pace, something neither of them really got in their line of work. It might even be a little normal. Normal sounded pretty good right now.

Reality came back to him when he walked out of his room and looked at Tommen's bedroom door. He pushed it open as if expecting to find him there listening to music and doing whatever it was he did. *Hey, kiddo, just letting you know that I'm heading out to have dinner with Laura. Be good, don't get into trouble, and don't burn the house down. I'll be back after a little while, okay?*

Yeah, right.

He returned to the bathroom for a last check in the mirror, grooming his mustache one more time and dabbing on a little cologne for good measure. It was like night and day, the difference between his grungy mountain-trekking clothes and his suit. He might even say he looked a little handsome.

Well, no backing out now. He headed to the kitchen to pull on his good shoes which were still new enough that there weren't even any wear marks on the inserts yet. Even the soles still looked fresh out of the box.

Okay, no more time to dillydally around. Five o'clock rush hour on a Friday night was coming up, and he still had to get across town. He went out to the garage and opened the car door. As he sat down, ten kinds of discomfort pushed, pulled, and poked at him from all angles in his suit and shoes. He shifted and shuffled and readjusted for probably two full minutes before getting comfortable enough that he could stand to even sit in the car, never mind how strange it was driving with his nice shoes.

Definitely only doing this once, he decided, backing out of the garage. Maybe twice. But definitely only once. Maybe he just needed a new suit. Or to lose some weight.

For all the cars flowing out of Charleston, Walter almost felt like he was the only one heading in. Everyone else was trying to escape, and here he was, running straight into the fray. Typical cop, he supposed. Always running into danger. Or was that just him? He thought about it but couldn't decide. Or maybe he just didn't want to admit that it seemed to run in the family.

He sighed and tried to clear his head. He had to focus. Dinner really shouldn't be this difficult. He had to appear at least somewhat optimistic. As far as Laura was concerned, the search efforts to find his son now had a direction, something to run with. She didn't need to know that the search she thought he was talking about and the search he was actually talking about were two different things. All she had to know was that progress was being made.

The Land In Between from which no one had ever returned. He wasn't sure how to take it, or whether he wanted to believe it. The whole bit about "from which no one had ever returned" kind of pointed to a distinct lack of stories about it or any evidence of it. At the same time, those who got swallowed up by the portals had to go somewhere; they didn't just turn into space dust or Energy or something. Did they? And anyway, he had a hard time believing that in even the last thousand years, that no one had ever returned. Someone had to be out there who knew something; it was just a matter of finding them.

Once he got into the city, traffic turned to hell. But did he really expect anything less? This was a Friday evening, after all, in August. Who knew? Maybe the restaurant would be packed and there would be no room. Then they'd have to go somewhere else, somewhere less formal. At the very least, he could take this jacket off and loosen his tie a little.

He pulled into the restaurant parking lot, daring to hope that the place was full. He didn't see Laura's truck anywhere. Well, might as well be the gentleman and go inside to inquire about seating. He looked at himself in the mirror once more, then took a breath and went inside.

It was certainly a nice place. Solid wooden floors, fine tables and seats, expensive decor. Compared to his normal dining choice, this was the ritz. Hard to believe it was on the bottom rung of the fine dining world, as in, true fine dining.

"Can I help you, sir?" the host inquired. He was no sixteen year old high school kid, just looking for a little extra cash over the summer. This was a true restaurant host who probably made more than the cooks in most common restaurants.

"Spontaneous dining choice tonight," Walter told him, hoping he didn't come across as an idiot country Welshman. "Do you have a table for two?"

The host raised a brow. "I see. Well, spontaneity is nice, but we are reservation only during peak seasons. As you can see, we are rather full tonight. Would you care to make a reservation for another night?"

"Sorry, not at this time. My lady is heading out of town, and, quite frankly, so am I. Perhaps another time." He turned as if to leave, then looked back. "For future reference, when do your 'spontaneous nights' begin?"

"That depends on the busyness of the season. My

recommendation would be to call ahead regardless."

Walter dipped his head graciously and walked out the door. He might have said he'd never felt more humiliated in his entire life, but that would not only be a lie, but it wouldn't even come close to some of the humiliation he'd experienced in the past. This was like comparing getting a frowny face on social media for a controversial post versus having the Secret Police break in, make an arrest, then torture and beat someone for having a dissenting opinion. This was nothing. So why did he feel so awful?

Maybe because tonight he'd really tried to do something special, go out on a limb and do something nice. Laura would be here any minute and he would have nothing but bad news for her. The clock was ticking and she still had to get to work.

Even as he thought it, he saw her truck pull in the parking lot. She circled once before finding a spot, and by then, he was already waiting. She looked beautiful in her slacks and blouse; usually she wore jeans and a T-shirt when she wasn't in uniform.

"Here to escort a lady to dinner?" she asked, opening a door.

"Actually..." Walter hesitated. "They're...booked for tonight. Reservation only."

"Oh." She frowned. "I thought...well, never mind."

"I know, I know. I screwed up."

"Yeah, well, the longer you stand there wallowing in self-pity means we have that much less time to get going someplace else. What do you say I choose the restaurant this time?"

He was more than happy to let her take the lead the second time. He wasn't thrilled at the thought, but the last thing he wanted to do was screw up twice in a row with the clock ticking. Let her pick the place. At least then it would be someplace he knew she would like.

By the time they pulled into the parking lot, it was ten to six.

"The good news," Laura said, getting out of her truck, "is that I packed my uniform and brought it with me so I can change at the station if I have to."

Walter nodded. "That's good. You seem to have more

forethought than I do tonight."

She gave him a funny look. "I thought you knew that restaurant was reservation-only. I...thought you had already made reservations."

He flushed red with embarrassment. "No, I didn't. On either account. I just knew that it was a really nice restaurant and I thought it would be nice to take you somewhere...nice."

"Well, it was a nice thought anyway. Thank you. Now then, let's get something to eat. I'm starving, and I have a feeling I'm going to have a long night tonight."

Walter had heard of—had met some women who took every little careless blunder from their husbands as the cruelest form of abuse bordering on attempted murder. They sought revenge for every accidental misstep and spit fire everywhere they went. Laura didn't seem to do that. She listened, reacted internally if at all, then filed things away appropriately. If there was cause for reaction—whether angry or joyful or sad—then she would respond appropriately. But she never seemed to sweat the little things, just tucked them away or let them slide off, like water off a duck's back. There was no way he deserved her, as hotheaded as he could be. And next time, he was determined to do better and give her a nice meal at a nice restaurant.

"Are you coming?" she asked from the door.

He nodded. "Yeah, I'm coming."

And he hurried across the parking lot to meet her.

Chapter Thirteen
Dinner and a Show

Was it wrong for Tommen to want to hear a few dirty secrets while he was invisible and had the chance to eavesdrop like a boss? Sure, his dad had pretty much already cleaned out his closet of skeletons, but to say there was nothing left in there, even a few cobwebs? He was a murderer, got it. Were he and Laura fucking? Was he seeing someone else at the same time? Even flirting with someone in the precinct? Hell, he'd even take bad karaoke in the car. But there was nothing. His dad was about as crisp and shiny as they came. It wasn't fair. There had to be something.

But then, why did he feel the need to go digging? Did he really want to know? Did he want to hurt his dad somehow? His demons tortured him enough without finding an ally in his son. So Tommen decided to let off a little. But still. Even bad karaoke would have been something to tease his dad with once he escaped.

But Tommen would admit that he felt bad for his dad when he got rejected at the restaurant. That was a double-whammy, first to Walter himself and then to his man card as he was really trying to impress his girlfriend. How was he going to explain to her that he hadn't made reservations and had basically been told to leave now and call back later? Even Laura seemed a little confused; she clearly understood that such a nice restaurant demanded reservations, why hadn't he? Well, there's your country Welshman for you. Not only does he not understand the ways of society, but he doesn't understand the whys either.

Walter confessed his little mistake to Laura. She took it in stride and moved on to the next restaurant. Well, why not? She only had so much time before having to go to work; she couldn't afford to waste time with petty words or musings over what to do. She was a paramedic. If something didn't work, try a different thing. If the situation changed or became unexpected, roll with it and try to get back in control.

So they chose a different restaurant. It was a nice place so they wouldn't look completely out of sorts, walking in dressed in nice clothes. The more relaxed formality of the place seemed to put Walter at ease, too. Here he only had to be on his best behavior; he didn't have to pretend to talk money or some shit. Whatever it was that rich people talked about. Fancy vacations and stuff, Tommen figured.

There was no wait, and they even got choice seating by the windows with a view of the river. Walter seated Laura like a proper gentleman, and she blushed.

"So, where'd you learn that one?" she asked, grinning.

"Nineteenth century London," Walter answered, more honestly that she could appreciate.

"I see. So you're a history buff, too?"

"Ah...no. Not quite. That's about all I know."

Liar, Tommen thought, sitting down in a chair, literally partway into the table. It felt strange as fuck, but it didn't seem to mess with him too bad, more mentally than physically.

"Too bad," Laura commented.

Walter raised a brow. "Maybe I'll have to brush up and learn something new so I can impress you a little more the next time. And hopefully make up for that awful blunder earlier."

She laughed and badly tried to cover it up. "No, don't worry about it. It would have been nice, but let's be real. You're a cop. I'm a paramedic. We're the boots on the ground taking the fire and flack, while the people who dine in restaurants like that sit in plush offices making huge but generally non-lethal decisions. They wouldn't want us there any more than we would want them in our office, if you get what I'm saying."

Tommen was shit with subtle body language, but he knew his

dad well enough to see the relief that spread through his limbs. She didn't hate him and she wasn't worried about the mistake. In fact, it sounded like each would have gone only to impress the other when the truth was neither wanted to go there in the first place. How quaint.

The waitress came and took their drink orders. Laura made sure to mention that they were on a bit of a timetable. It was impossible to tell how serious the waitress took them, but it was out there. The drinks were delivered, and the lovebirds were left alone, or as alone as they thought they were.

"So, what's the news?" Laura asked, sipping politely at her iced tea. "What did they find?"

Seeing how Time was invisible to the in-between dimension, it was impossible to tell whether Walter Banded or already had his story worked out.

"Well, they found footprints," Walter said. "Actually, they were found by a civilian maybe ten miles south from the campsite. Fresh, obviously, with all the off-and-on rain they've been having. They're the right shoe size, and stride length puts the walker at Tommen's height. It's not much, but it's the best lead so far. They're following the tracks as long as they can before they get washed away."

"Oh, absolutely," Laura agreed. "Which way were they heading? Wellspring is west of the campsite."

"South is the best they were able to determine, avoiding people as much as possible."

"So he could still be concussed or impaired."

"That's what they're thinking. He's avoiding being seen, but he's still leaving tracks. Eventually they'll find him. If it is him."

"Be optimistic. And as weird as this sounds, do you think he could be heading home? Or thinks he is?"

"Anything is possible."

Laura nodded and took another drink of her tea. "Well, it's good that they found something. And if the tracks are that fresh, with all the rain that's been coming through, it means he can't be moving very fast. Now that they have a lead, it's only a matter of time."

"That's what I'm hoping."

"Are you going back up again tomorrow?"

Walter shook his head guiltily. "No. My car will never make it up that two-track. Tomorrow is my scheduled day off before going back to work on Sunday, and I have a few things I need to get done or else I never will. But like you said, they found something and are running with it. They're professionals and know what they're doing. The last thing I need to do is get in their way. Same way you or I would feel with well-meaning, interfering bystanders on any scene."

"Amen to that."

"How long is your shift?"

Laura sighed and rubbed her eyes. "Eighty-four flippin' hours. Three and a half days. Over a frickin' weekend. But I won't argue with the paycheck."

"Amen, but I thought you said it was forty-eight?"

"Hank called in; he's got pneumonia or something, so he can't come in. We're splitting his shift." She sighed. "We're going to run probably twenty or thirty calls in that time. All these tourists and the usual idiots, plus the people who actually need help. It's ridiculous."

Walter nodded. "All that plus the cherry on top: the joy of the internal politics."

She pointed at him. "Don't even get me started on that. I swear the city council is going for a hostile takeover of the EMS system."

"Oh, you guys, too? I don't think a day goes by at the precinct where I don't hear about this councilman or that councilman is on a rampage or going after this person or that person, bribes, secrecy, things going on under the table, all the cops are dirty, so on and so forth. Honestly, it's a wonder Steggmann hasn't resigned."

Laura shook her head. "Nah. Resignation is never an option. Right now, they're still playing games. Once a hostile takeover begins, it's going to be pink slips everywhere and slander on every news channel and in every newspaper. This is the easy stuff right here."

Walter chuckled. "I think we both need a vacation."

"Or a career change."

"I'm too old for a career change. The next time I change my career, Uncle Sam is going to be paying me. My retirement."

"Come on, you're not that old." *If only you knew.* "You're only, what, fifty-something?"

"Fifty-four. I think. I don't know, I'd have to check my driver's license."

"Very funny. Point is, you're not that old."

"Oh, I feel it some days."

Laura nodded. "I know. So do I. Unfortunately, we paramedics don't get quite the cushy pension you cops do."

"Hey, we cops put up with a lot of shit. I think I've earned my pension, assuming I ever get it."

"I know you put up with a lot. So do we. And before you say anything, yeah, we get shot at, too, now. I haven't been personally, but it's only a matter of time. You see all the crazies on TV? They're coming. And it won't matter what colors you're wearing. If you show up in a truck with flashing lights and wear a uniform, they gonna pop you without a second thought."

Walter laughed. "Emergency personnel dinner conversations."

Laura grinned. "What a pair we make, hm? The other diners here must think we're nuts."

"Of course. Crazy comes with the person; the uniform just amplifies it."

Tommen rolled his eyes, shook his head, and rested his head on his good hand. Really? This is what old people talked about on dinner dates? Work, retirement, and being crazy? Weren't they supposed to talk about politics, religion, and the good old days? Weren't they supposed to be complaining about the young whippersnappers steering society right into the flaming pits of Hell? Or at least complaining that they cut them off at an intersection while texting and driving or something?

The waitress returned to take their food orders. Walter might have been conscious about his weight, but Laura seemed to be a little less so. He got whitefish and a side salad. She got a bacon cheeseburger and fries.

"Got the precinct Olympics coming up you have to get in shape for?" Laura wondered.

"I try to watch my weight," Walter said. "I gain weight quickly if I don't pay attention."

"You're not diabetic, are you?"

"No, not that I know of."

Laura shrugged. "I eat what I like. If it's not good for me, I try to eat less. If it is good for me, well, I usually eat less of it, anyway. Life's too short to worry about being a model, especially at my age."

"What if you were able to live longer?" Walter ventured.

She paused a moment and leaned back in her chair. "A lot of the medical patients we get are old people. Heart attack, stroke, COPD, and so on. A few of them are fully cognizant and strive to do better. Most of them, though, are on the slow road out the door. And it's sad to watch them go over months or even years. In January, you're having a nice conversation about the grandkids. By May, they can't even remember they have grandkids. And it's not necessarily Alzheimer's. Sometimes it's just a slowing down of the mental state, that they can't process information fast enough to be useful in a conversation.

"But, back in Minnesota, we had one guy who was a hundred and fifteen years old. A hundred and fifteen. Can you believe it? And he moved and thought just like a thirty year old. Well, he thought like a thirty year old. He moved like a seventy year old. But he was very intelligent, well-read, well-educated, well-versed in the ways of the world. He lived at home still, did all his own housekeeping and chores, his own grocery shopping and driving. He could knock out a crossword puzzle faster than I could even read through the clues. He was amazing."

"Well, I hate to say it, but EMS doesn't make social calls," Walter said.

Laura nodded. "He was like the cat that's too stubborn to die. You know what finally got him?" He shook his head. "He was hit by a car. Neighbor kids were playing T-ball, hit it into the road. Kids are too young to go into the road. He'd been watching them and got excited for them, their own little fan club right across the street. He sees the ball heading into the road and, with the only thought in his head to keep the kids out of the road, he went to get the ball himself. He wasn't paying attention and got nailed. He was awesome, but he was still old, and his bones weren't very good. Broke both hips, femurs, his back, shoulders, skull, everything. He made it to the hospital, but he died four days later."

"That sounds terrible." Tommen could hear the underlying question, "Where are you going with this?"

She nodded again and looked thoughtful. "I suppose if I knew I was going to age well like he did, I wouldn't have a problem. Problem is, he was one in a million. The other ninety-nine-point-nine percent of us are going to deteriorate into something unrecognizable until everyone wishes the mercy of death upon us."

Walter raised a brow. "You must be fun at parties," he said, echoing Tommen's thoughts.

Laura laughed. "I know, I'm sorry. I get carried away sometimes. But in all honesty, to answer your question, I don't know."

"Okay, so maybe I should rephrase it. If you could live longer by pressing the pause button on aging, stop right here, right now, would you?"

"Well, that's a different question." She folded her arms. "I don't know. I suppose it would be fun for a while, to accomplish a few things I always thought I never had time for or that I really don't have time for as it stands now. But eventually, to stand still while the world spins on, I don't know that I could do that. Even if I had the power to go anywhere else and reinvent myself, I don't think I could do it more than, say, once. Just to try it out and see what I could do as someone else." She shrugged. "But eventually, it's appointed unto each man to die once. A few more years might be interesting to contemplate, you know, screw around a little like I was a teenager again, just for a little while. But I suppose that even as everyone is scared by death, we all long for it eventually, an end to the labor, an end to the suffering, an end to the change. The world changes a lot in a hundred years."

"Yes, it does," Walter murmured in agreement.

Laura put her hands up. "Now, to be clear, I'm saying all of this in a philosophical sense. I'm not suicidal or anything. I'm more homicidal, but you didn't hear that from me."

"Do I look like I have handcuffs on me?"

"No, but your little Taurus TCP looks like it might be a powerful motivator to stay put until backup arrives with the handcuffs."

Walter glanced down in his jacket where he thought his little pistol had been pretty well hidden. Laura chuckled. "Please. Working in a big city, you learn how to tell, what to look for. Same as you."

"I guess so."

Tommen was having a hard time deciding the purpose of that conversation. On the one hand, it could be his dad fishing for answers, whether or not Laura may or may not be interested in being a Timekeeper. It was a long shot, and the risks were huge, but it was one possibility. The other possibility was that he was looking for some external, moral, philosophical justification for his desire to retire from Time. It was no secret that he wanted to, but when everyone around him seemed to be having a grand old time, it could be hard to not think that he was the crazy one in the room.

The waitress returned. In one hand, she carried a grilled whitefish in a white wine and herb sauce with lemon on the side next to a fluffy, leafy salad. In the other hand was a half-pound burger topped with bacon, blue cheese, barbecue sauce, and what looked and smelled like some sort of modified cajun spice rub that had dripped over onto huge steak fries.

Tommen wailed internally as he eyed the food, salivating and hardly bothering to hide it. Oh, it looked so fucking good, he could hardly contain himself. He wanted it so bad. He was so hungry. Next time he saw Julianna, he was demanding to be taught how to pull things into the in-between dimension. Once he learned that, he was going to come back to this restaurant, and he was going to get himself a bacon cheeseburger for breakfast and some whitefish for lunch. For dinner, he was going to go over to that hoity-toity restaurant that only seated per reservation, and he was going to find the nicest, most expensive meal on the menu, and he was going to steal it directly from the kitchen. Oh, he wanted food.

Was it bad that he was contemplating theft only because he knew he could get away with it? How was it any different from Time, really? His dad always made him promise not to use Time to steal candy or clothes or electronics or anything else, and he was true to his word—ninety-five percent of the time, anyway. Why was he okay with it now that he was invisible? Probably for the fact that he would starve if he didn't steal. There were no in-between dimension farms that he saw, nowhere to get food except straight from the real world. That involved stealing. It was justified, even if simultaneously hilarious.

Oh, that cheeseburger was looking mighty tasty.

After a few minutes of being subjected to the cruel and unusual punishment of look-but-don't-touch, he got up and went back to the kitchen. The smells were glorious, and the food looked divine. This wasn't even that fancy of a restaurant. He must have been hungry or something because mentally, he was going up the wall. A memory flashed through his mind of Pam the camp cook making jokes about all the starving teenage boys in camp and how they were impossible to feed. He was starting to understand that a little better now.

One of the cooks was just bringing a fresh fish off the grill, salmon with rosemary and lemon and a touch of orange. Tommen breathed deep the smell and reached for it, hoping that sheer willpower would be enough to break through the dimensional barrier and swipe him some dinner. Even if he only got the sprig of parsley, he just wanted food.

His first and second attempts failed completely, his hand waving cleanly through the fish without even a little sticky lemon juice to show for it. By the time he went for his third attempt, it was being handed off the waitress and taken out into the dining room, Tommen looking longingly after it. Well, he might steal from the kitchen, but he wasn't going to swipe a fish from under someone's nose. No need to start any rumors that the restaurant was haunted. Although, the restaurant had a fifty-fifty shot at star-studded publicity if that rumor spread far enough and was convincing enough for the patrons.

Well, another day, once he'd learned how to take items and get himself some dinner. He meandered around the kitchen, observing the cooks and seeing what was on the menu. Friday meant fish fry, but there was a fair share of pasta and pizzas and burgers going out as well. Given that he wasn't going to get anything custom ordered, he was going to have to pick something that was closest to what he wanted. Although at this point, he wanted anything and everything. The first thing he was able to grab, that's what he was getting.

"Ruby!" one the cooks shouted suddenly. "Ruby, my burner is malfunctioning again!"

Tommen headed around to the cook who manned a gas stove. A second later, a heavyset, middle-aged woman also approached.

"Didn't I tell you not to turn this burner off?" she growled. "If you turn it off, there's only a fifty-fifty shot that it's going to turn back on, and those are the best odds. This burner always stays on, from open to close, use it first, use the other burners after."

"I'm sorry," the cook mumbled. "I got going quick and wasn't thinking—"

"Clearly. Trade spots with Joe while I get this figured out."

Tommen watched the woman Ruby practically tear apart the stovetop and go to town on the burner. Something about the electric ignition wasn't working. Personally, Tommen wondered why they couldn't just match-light it and worry about the electric start later on. But, hey, not his kitchen. Maybe it was a Health Department law. Thou shalt not use matches in the kitchen. Whatever.

"I don't know," Ruby growled as Joe the cook came to help. "I think we've got mice again, chewing through the damn wires. We're in a fucking kitchen, and they go for the wires."

"Means you keep a clean kitchen," Joe said. "You're starving the mice of everything but the wires."

"Yeah, well, these wires are just about toast. There's no way this burner is going to get started now. It's all going to have to be fixed. Fucking overtime hours."

Tommen leaned in to take a closer look. The gas line itself appeared to be fine. When the cooks tried it, gas was flowing where it needed to go. It really was just the ignition. The cooks were dubious as to the state of the wires and didn't want to start a fire if the ignition backfired. As they gave it one last try, Tommen reached for the ignition, the Energy between gas and fire, and tapped it. He wasn't even sure how he did it, but the burner burst into flames. The cooks jumped back. Joe reached forward to turn down the gas to a low simmer.

"Fourteenth time's the charm, I guess," he said.

Ruby just grunted. "Keep an eye on it, and make sure Charlie knows not to turn the damn thing off again. We don't need any more problems in this kitchen!"

She said it loudly, generally, but the young cook, Charlie, kept his head down and blushed. Tommen felt sorry for the kid. Not everyone could have an awesome boss like Micah and Micaiah. Well, Micah, anyway. Micaiah was still scary as fuck when he wanted to be.

Nevertheless, he still hadn't gotten his dinner. He sulked back out to the dining room where the waitress had just delivered two to-go boxes and a dessert menu. Laura had eaten everything but the fries, and Walter still had half a fish. She made an excuse that it would give her something to snack on at work; he made the excuse that it hadn't been very good in the first place. He'd have it for leftovers at some point seeing how his cupboards were so sparse. He said the last part with a smirk which Laura mirrored.

She got a brownie sundae for dessert and he opted for a small slice of chocolate cake, emphasis on small. Considering the prices they were charging, Tommen might have expected at least a quarter if not half a cake. For goodness' sake, they could buy a Betty Crocker cake mix for a dollar. Paying five bucks for a single slice seemed pathetic.

Extortion came to mind.

"Well, it wasn't the evening we planned, but it was good, nonetheless," Laura decided, finishing off her brownie. "Thank you."

"Maybe next time I'll ditch the spontaneous and try to think things through," Walter said, blushing.

She shook her head. "Nah. Spontaneous is always more fun. Well, more exciting. You and I both know the other side of that equation."

"The way you talk, I might think you're not looking forward to thirty or forty 'spontaneous' calls this weekend."

"Not even. But hey, chances are, you'll be there right along with me on a few of them."

They made cute small talk, but Tommen was more fixated on the fish in Walter's box. If Laura was going to be gone to work for the next three days, his dad was unlikely to eat more than a bagel with cream cheese and whatever snacks might be left in the break room at the precinct. That fish was going to go bad long before he ever got around to it. And, damn, it had smelled good. Even if it had gotten cold by now, Tommen wanted that fish.

He reached through the box to the fish. He could feel it there, physically, but he could also press through it with almost no effort at all. How did he grab onto it and take it out of the real world, bring it into the in-between dimension? There had to be some trick to it. Or had all the people who had come before him just starved to death? Was that the real reason the population in this dimension was so low?

Tommen made several lazy passes through the box, feeling himself grow weaker with each swipe, even as he felt himself grow closer to an Emmy award for best dramatic performance. He was hungry. He was so, so, so hungry. Even as his hearing aids and phone seemed to go through energy faster, so, too, did his body it seemed. Three meals a day be damned; he needed to eat constantly, or that's what it felt like. When was the last time he had a meal? He couldn't remember. Noon, maybe. He wasn't actually starving, but it sure felt like it.

Then the box was moving. Walter stood, put on his jacket, and grabbed his leftovers. Laura did the same, snagging a last French fry before grabbing her box and starting for the door. The evening was clear, but distant clouds promised more rain overnight.

"You have everything you need for work?" Walter asked, leaning on Laura's truck as she got in.

"Regretfully, yes," she sighed, rolling her eyes. "But then, I do enjoy making money and being able to do stuff like this. Next one's on me, I guess."

"Next one's on whoever calls first."

"Given how bare your cupboards are, how stressed you are over Tommen, and your everyday, common stress of a stressful job, I'm thinking that's going to be you."

Walter raised a brow. "I'm not sure how to take that."

She laughed. "Means you're going to go broke at that rate, if that was how we did it. I'm off Tuesday morning. Why don't we see where things stand at that point, hm?"

"Works for me. A lot can happen in three and a half days."

"Indeed it can. Keep me posted on Tommen. If they found tracks, it can't be too long before they find him."

He nodded. "Will do. Thank you."

"For what?"

"For caring."

She smiled. "Don't even worry about it." She huffed. "All right, I gotta go. I'll see you...when I see you."

Walter stepped back and watched her leave. Tommen watched her go, then turned his attention back on his dad's fish. He wanted that fish. He was dead-set on it now. He was determined not to leave his dad's side until either the fish went bad or he ate it, whichever came first. Alligators and barrels be damned, he wanted fish.

With nothing left to wait around for, his dad got in his car, and Tommen followed suit. The leftover box sat in the passenger seat. Tommen sat in the passenger seat. Maybe if he somehow became one with the fish, he would have a better chance of getting through and taking it. He tried several times to twist and adjust and grab the whole thing, box and all, bring it all into the in-between dimension. Maybe that was the trick; he couldn't grab what he couldn't see. Except, as he thought about it, that made no sense. Julianna had been able to grab medical supplies out of Laura's bag, and that had been zipped up.

So, physical barriers were not a problem. It was all about the dimensional Energy barrier. But how did he breach that just so he could steal a fish? There was some piece of the puzzle that he was missing; he just wasn't sure what it was.

They arrived home. Walter seemed to have a little spring in his step, Tommen thought, but that didn't help him get his dad's fish. He followed his dad in the house where, as expected, the fish went straight into the fridge to be forgotten about for at least a week or two when only its rancid smell would remind his dad of its existence. Tommen bypassed the fridge for a moment, heading for his room. He needed to sit down and think about this.

He lay back on his bed. His door was closed, which meant he couldn't see any of the goings-on in the house, not that he expected there was much to see. It also made it harder to hear the goings-on, even with his hearing aids. At that thought, he sat up and removed his hearing aids. Almost dead. Checking his phone, he saw that it was completely dead. He plugged both of them in, then lay back with a sigh.

Okay. He'd managed to call 9-1-1 and got the cops out there looking. He got the Trackers excited about something. Somehow, he'd managed to breach the Energy barrier. How? Why?

He rolled over on his side, trying to keep his arm up. His phone hadn't been able to call out normally because there was no signal. In the real world, that was because something was blocking signal to the correct towers or satellites. But, when someone dialed 9-1-1, everything was open instantly. All towers, all satellites, every company regardless of the user's chosen provider. Some might even claim that certain military equipment was tapped into in order to connect the person in distress with help. Furthermore, even if the phone didn't ring, as soon as those three numbers were dialed, dispatch was notified. That was why they got all pissy over accidental calls and hang-ups; people didn't realize that everything pinged instantaneously.

His phone had connected because the signal had been caught and amplified. A thread of Energy had managed to break out through the dimensional barrier. Even if he hadn't actually been able to speak, he'd gotten pinged.

The amount of energy it took to take zero signal and turn it into great signal in order to reach dispatch was great, depending on how close one was to the nearest tower and the available network of towers and satellites, how much it had to draw on before actually connecting. Unfortunately, Tommen had no way to know exactly how much Energy he'd used, though it was a safe bet that it had been a pretty good amount. If he'd had to draw on every available device out there just to connect, even without talking, how much more was he going to have to do in order to bust out? He still hadn't even made contact. Tommen sighed and rubbed his eyes. His phone was still dead, so he had no music there, and he couldn't listen to his stereo...

Suddenly he sat up and looked at his devices and their chargers. Yes, he had made contact. He'd started that burner. He had touched the Energy and ignited the gas. That was a breach of the barrier through Energy. If he could do that, maybe he could recreate the scenario that had landed him in the in-between dimension in the first place.

At that thought, the skin on his arm twisted and tightened, remaining blisters straining, pressing tight against the bandages. He groaned and let out a steady breath. Okay, okay, okay. Bad idea. But, it was still an idea. A back-up idea if everything else he managed to come up with failed. Problem was, he hadn't come up with anything else.

After a minute or two, he headed out to the living room. His dad had changed out of his suit and now sat in his recliner, looking conflicted. Tommen knew what he was thinking. *There has to be something more I can do. There must be something I'm missing. Some clue, some little thread that I just need to pull on, something obvious staring me right in the face.*

Tommen knew how he felt. He'd felt the same way when faced with his dad's impending death from Borelian poison. Well, maybe he ought to treat this like that. Maybe he really should ignore his body's protests and go for the no-holds-barred attempt at breaking free. Maybe this was a matter of go big or go home — or go big and go home, as the situation demanded. If he couldn't go out, he wasn't going anywhere. As Julianna said, the suicide rate was sky-high; it wasn't like he was waiting for anything.

Walter got up and went to his room to grab a book. He wasn't a huge reader for the fact that he just didn't have time. His fiction library consisted of a dozen books he'd probably read six or seven times, plus one or two he got from the public library when he visited there about twice a year. He returned to his recliner, muted the TV, and flipped on the lamp.

Tommen got an idea.

He approached the lamp and knelt by the outlet. He couldn't grab the plug and he couldn't flip the switch, but maybe he could manipulate the electricity, the Energy flowing into the lamp, powering it. He touched the plug, then pushed through just enough that he could feel the wires, feel the electricity running through them. He also felt the hair on the back of his neck stand up. This was still 110 current, and it could still be quite a shock if he wasn't careful.

He quickly learned that cutting off the Energy was a lot harder than letting it go, as in the case of the gas stove. The lamp dimmed several times before he managed to snuff it out, like grabbing the wick on a candle. It hurt, but was soon dismissed.

Walter looked at the lamp, at the dead bulb, and flipped the switch a couple times. He sighed, put a marker in his book, got up, set the book in his seat, and made as if to go find a light bulb somewhere. Before he could get too far, Tommen released the Energy, and the lamp came back on.

His dad stopped and turned, staring at the lamp for a moment. He watched it, as if daring it to go out again. When it didn't, he returned to his recliner, picked up his book, and was just about to go back to reading when the light went out again.

This time he reached over to unplug it and plug it back in the other outlet. Tommen released the Energy and the lamp came back on. It was a logical thing, really, given that the house was old and the electrical not exactly up to code. But he'd had his fun, and now he really had to figure out a way to communicate. Tommen didn't know extensive Morse code, but he knew the basics.

He flicked the lamp off for a count of two, then back on. Flick off for a count of two, and back on. Off for a count of two, and on again. Then off for a count of one, then back on. Repeat twice. Then three more longs. Three long, three short, three long. S-O-S.

At first, his dad was frustrated and went to find a light bulb. Even after he changed the bulb, Tommen kept doing it.

Come on, Dad, pay attention, he prayed silently.

Then his dad tried to unplug the lamp entirely. Tommen felt the Energy from the outlet dissipate as the connection was broken, but he wasn't going to give up yet. He felt his body shake as he tried to pull Energy directly from the in-between dimension and channel it into the lamp. Not too little, but certainly not too much. Then, even with the lamp being unplugged, the bulb lit up.

Walter nearly came out of his skin as well as his recliner as the light came on. Once Tommen was sure he had his dad's attention, he started again. Long, long, long. Short, short, short. Long, long, long. S-O-S. S-O-S. His dad watched, eyes wide, for a full minute. After a moment or two, Tommen saw his lips moving, as if reading off the code and trying to think why the hell it looked familiar. Then he blinked and shook his head, daring to take a step forward into the Twilight Zone.

"S-O-S," he said. "S-O-S. Tommen?"

Tommen hoped he could convey a yes by hurriedly flicking the lamp on and off, fast enough to induce a seizure had his dad been epileptic. Then he let the lamp stay on, waiting.

"How do I know it's Tommen?" Walter wondered, looking like he was wondering whether he'd finally gone insane. And, in all fairness, to an outside audience, he probably would have been thought quite mad.

At the same time, the request for proof was almost annoying. Tommen sighed, let the lamp go, stood, and headed for his room. A minute later, his music was blaring loud. His dad walked in the room, hands over his ears, shouting to turn it off. Tommen obliged, leaning against the wall and patiently waiting while his dad sat down slowly on the bed.

"Okay, so either I'm talking to my son, a ghost or otherworldly apparition, or myself, in which case, I have finally gone insane and need to check myself into a mental hospital," Walter breathed. He nodded. "All right. Here's something only Tommen would know. And, this time, please, just do the light-flicking thing. Music is way too loud. When Tommen was in sixth grade, he kept a tally of all the girls he asked to the harvest dance. How many was that?"

Fucking hell, he had to bring that up? Of all the questions of things "only Tommen would know" he would choose that? Well, it would make sense, he supposed. If he was suspecting Rifun to interfere in some way, such a minor detail might be seen as insignificant and not worth knowing. Reluctantly, Tommen went to the lightswitch and felt around for the Energy.

"1-4-2," he flashed out.

Walter nodded and chuckled. "That's correct." He took a calming breath. "Is it you, Tommen?" He shook his head and sat up straight, all business. "Micaiah was telling me earlier that he and Kayla suspected that you might be trapped in the in-between dimension. To the best of your knowledge, is that true? One flash for yes, two for no."

One flash.

"Are you injured?"

One flash.

"Burns on your left arm?"

Now how in the —? One flash.

His dad nodded again, thoughtfully. He went on to explain that Micaiah had seen him, only briefly, when he tried to go through the portal into the Akarin fortress. He also detailed the search efforts so far, everything from the movements of the professional search and rescue teams, to their more unofficial searches using the Trackers.

"You tried to call 9-1-1, but it pinged from Virginia. Were you in Virginia?"

One flash.

"What were you doing there? Well, never mind that. We can discuss it later." He stood and Tommen went to face him, even if Walter couldn't see him. "Listen, everyone knows that it's called the dimension from which no one has ever returned. We are well aware of that. But Kayla has a plan to at least see if she can, I don't know, walk with you and communicate fully for a short time. I don't understand it, but that's going to happen tomorrow or the next day. No one here believes that in a thousand years, no one has ever returned. We'll find a way, Tommen. Don't give up on your end; we're coming.

"Later on, once the bakery closes, I'm going to meet Micaiah and we're going to go do some more research in the Archives. It's apparent that you can't come with us there, but if you come with me, maybe we can have a short chat with Micaiah and you can show him somehow that you are alive and well. All right?"

One flash.

His dad nodded and took another breath, his composure wavering. "I love you, Tommen. We're going to find a way to get you out of there and bring you home."

Tommen nodded as well, bracing himself for the strange feeling of having his dad walk right through him. At the same time, he also felt a sense of elation. He'd done it. He'd made contact. More than that, they already knew where he was. They'd already figured out that he was trapped in the Land In Between. Now that he knew that they knew, and soon they would know that he knew that they knew, everyone would be on the same page and they could work together from both sides to get him out. Him and, making good on his promise, Julianna, too.

His stomach grumbled. Fuck, he was still super hungry. And he still hadn't gotten that damn fish. Great. Made contact with the outside world. Was going to starve before the week was up.

He made his way out to the kitchen, ducking inside the fridge to find the box of leftover fish. Okay, so, he figured out how to manipulate the Energy barrier and communicate. Now how did he manipulate it enough to get this fish? He thought back to Julianna swiping Laura's medical supplies and the burger in the diner. He couldn't recall anything particularly special about it.

Well, maybe it was as simple as trying to open a portal around the fish and snapping it up in the in-between dimension. Problem was, other than this one huge accident, Tommen had never opened a portal to anywhere. He'd been through them plenty of times, but never opened one for himself. How did this work? Fucking hell.

"Tommen?" his dad questioned cautiously from his recliner.

Abandoning his fish, Tommen went to the lamp and flicked it a couple times. His dad relaxed, but only a little.

"It's going to be a couple hours before I go over to the bakery," Walter told him. "If there's anything you can do, any tricks you know of, to communicate, you better start learning or brushing up on them now. The more information we have, the better."

Well, no shit, Tommen thought. *You think I haven't been trying for the last day and a half to communicate with anyone from the real world? You think it didn't take me all day to figure out this little trick, never mind everything else I know?*

One flash.

His dad leaned back in his recliner, still looking conflicted.

Only after Tommen had returned to the refrigerator did he consider his dad might not have done that for Tommen's sake, but for his own, a way to reassure himself that this was an at-will conversation and not a figment of an insane imagination. It still could be, but best not to take chances.

"Okay," he breathed. "Open a portal. Take the Energy between dimensions and tear it open. Rip it wide open and bring the fish inside. Me in this dimension, fish in the other dimension, now bridge the gap. Open it up and let it roll."

He wasn't sure how close he was to the actual process of opening a portal. It was easier to feel Energy when it had a conductor, like wires and such. It was harder to feel it and manipulate it in midair. He pushed and pulled, tried to squeeze and get it to cooperate, but it always eluded him, like chasing jello around a plate with a spoon.

After an easy fifteen minutes of frustrated chasing, Tommen's frustration won out and he threw everything he had into getting the Energy to do some fucking thing to get him his fucking fish. Open a damn portal, reach through, and grab the fish.

Nothing appeared to physically change that he could see. No literal portal opened, though he was still feeling waves of Energy coming back at him, like making waves in a bathtub or a pond. He looked at the box of leftovers. Silent and mocking as ever. And yet, when he touched it, he touched it. He couldn't pass through it like everything else. Getting excited, he grabbed onto it, foolishly, with both hands. His left hand screamed and he reflexively jerked it away, causing more pain through his arm.

After a minute or two of biting back curses and tears and getting himself under control once more, Tommen picked up the box of fish and got out of the fridge. He opened the box and was never so happy to see half a whitefish. He didn't even care that he didn't have a fork or tartar sauce. He was fucking hungry, man.

Tommen tore into the fish like a starving wolf, or starving teenage boy, whichever was hungrier, devouring it in only a couple bites. His tongue was happy because it tasted good, and his stomach was happy because he'd finally gotten food. When he was done, he wanted nothing more than to lie down and take a nap, but he knew that wasn't an option. His dad was going to talk to Micaiah in a couple hours, which meant he had to get his shit together and figure out how he was going to communicate, more than just playing ghost and flashing lights on and off.

Licking his fingers clean, Tommen headed out of the house.

Chapter Fourteen
The Time in Between

Tommen's attempts at figuring out new, better means of communication quickly devolved into perfecting his craft of taking things from the real world. His main objective was food. The fish had been good, but fish wasn't very filling in the first place, and half a fish was even less. So he went back to the hoity-toity restaurant, as planned, and headed for their kitchen. He surveyed the scene and considered his menu options, electing to swipe a juicy-looking steak with fresh vegetables and warm biscuits. He also helped himself to a nicely wrapped roll of utensils, then sat down to eat.

Holy God, it was succulent. It was so good, it almost justified the outrageous price they were charging for it. The vegetables were pretty standard, but the steak was the real deal. Holy shit. He even went back for a second one, being kind enough to take only the steak and not steal all of the restaurant's dishes. The cooks and waiters were having a time of it. The cooks swore they just set the plate out, but the waiters insisted it hadn't been there. Tommen smirked as he sat down again to start in on his second steak.

He was a little torn on dessert, then decided to go for it. He wasn't really interested in the dainty little cups of ice cream the restaurant offered, instead heading out to an ice cream shop to grab himself a nice, tall milkshake which he sucked down as he walked down the street.

Yes sir, progress was being made. Things were looking up. Problem was, he had an hour before any more progress would be made when his dad went to see Micaiah. Tommen toyed with the idea of going and haunting the bakery for a little bit, then decided against it. He needed seriousness, not games, when it came to them. He didn't need to spend half his time proving he was who he tried to convey he was.

He paused and looked around. At the same time, being in the in-between dimension afforded him a unique opportunity, one he would lose once he was out. It wasn't powerful enough to make him want to stay, but while he had the time, he figured he might as well use it.

Even as he thought it, modern Charleston melted away. He wasn't even in the city yet, but he could see the city limits shrinking, retreating like waves, drawn back to a time when things were simpler, or smaller anyway. Highways gave way to byways. Asphalt turned into dirt. Even the majestic Capitol building shrunk a size or two, then vanished completely. American flags with thirteen stripes and fifty stars changed into old Union flags, then Confederate flags, then no flags at all. The land was reclaimed until only a little town remained. It was still big for its time, a real bustling place, but it was only a fraction of the size it was in modern times.

It was fascinating to watch, really, but it was not Tommen's ultimate goal. Instead, he turned east, toward the hills. It was almost unrecognizable in some spots, as mountains grew out of highways, watching hills that had been leveled and decimated regrow.

And then, all was as it had been. Pure wilderness. Tommen looked out over tiny Charleston, but it could not touch him with its long, modern tentacles. It minded its business, and he went about his own affairs. Then he turned his back on it and started into the forest, high into the mountains.

He got lost on multiple occasions and had to call up ghosts of the past to help guide him, listening to the chatter of people centuries dead and getting directions from them.

After a little while, he found an open square. A little church sat empty during the week, and the little marketplace sat vacant as the harvest was not in yet. A Pony Express station long since abandoned was now used by local residents and passersby. But in spite of the general state of abandon, the square itself was populated with children shirking chores and young couples off on ill-conceived love adventures.

Tommen knew this place well, even though he hadn't been here in a long, long time. And even if his eyes did not understand his surroundings, long-buried childhood memories told him where to go.

Of course, childhood memories clashed with modern reality. He passed through trees that were no longer there and found himself walking across pavement where there ought to have been dirt. But he made his way, nonetheless. Up and down little hills, around corners, over a seasonal river.

And then there was the farm. More to the point, there were the pine trees his pa had left standing so as to shield the farm from harsh winter winds and prying eyes. Instinctively, Tommen slowed upon approach, keeping an eye out for that motherfucking rooster. He heard the little bastard somewhere close by, but couldn't see him. Likely he was hiding in the pine trees, ready to attack.

Then Tommen felt foolish for cowering. Not only was he invisible, but this was only the past. That rooster was long since dead; it couldn't attack him now. Right? He looked around suspiciously just in case. He hadn't forgotten the incident with Mr. Snuffles. Maybe undead roosters had strange ESP powers, too.

But he made it without incident, moving past the pine trees into the open. He spotted Welly, the rooster, a short distance away, pecking and scratching away with the rest of his harem. One of the goats was in the pen, bleating inconsolably, screaming even. Tommen saw that he was the only one in the pen; his friend must have escaped. Elsewhere, a couple sheep grazed contentedly alongside the cow.

Tommen saw his ma inside the cabin, doing something in the main room he couldn't make out. Then she appeared in the doorway.

"Teo! Teo, for goodness' sake, are you ready yet?"

Teo Sr. rounded the corner, followed closely by a very young Teo Jr. Tommen stared at his older brother; he couldn't have been more than seven or eight. So he'd ended up in a time before he was even born. Holy shit.

Teo Jr. carried a length of rope twisted and knotted to make a harness and leash, constantly tripping over it as he ran after his pa. They approached the goat pen, and Tommen followed. Teo Sr. climbed over the fence.

"Hand me the rope," he said, holding his hand out.

Little Teo gave it to him. "Can I come in?"

"No, son. He's craving the company of his friends, which makes him really strong and dangerous. You can come in when you're bigger and stronger."

The goat wasn't as feisty as Teo Sr. would have had his son believe, but Tommen remembered getting the same speech. And, really, some goats could be a handful. It was a mercy that this one wasn't, though it did try to make a break for it as soon as the gate was open. Teo Sr. managed to wrestle it away, ignoring the screaming and choking noises it made as it was dragged to the shed. Little Teo followed, staying well out of reach of the goat's large horns.

"Now then, when we want to butcher an animal, like a goat, we want to do it quickly so the animal doesn't suffer," Teo Sr. was saying as Tommen moved into the shed. "You have to make sure your knife is extra sharp. A dull knife pulls while a sharp knife cuts. You want to make a single, clean cut."

The goat was held fast by the rope attached to a series of hooks and clasps. No matter how much the goat tried to move, buck, or throw its head around, it was not going anywhere.

"Why don't you just shoot it?" Little Teo wondered innocently.

"Because it's unnecessary. If you shoot it in the head, then you have no brains to tan the hide. If you shoot it in the chest, then the blood gets on the meat and could turn it bad. Better to cut the throat."

So that was exactly what he did, straddling the goat and coming from behind. Tommen instinctively leaped back to avoid the blood, even as he knew it was unnecessary. The goat died swiftly, its front legs buckling, back legs sliding out. It twitched a little, but otherwise, it was swift and the animal did not suffer.

Little Teo watched as his pa strung up the goat by its hind legs and went to work on the skinning, explaining every part, from cutting out the butthole to getting as close to the skin as possible without tearing through. Tommen watched just to get a few pointers and see if there wasn't a way he could improve his craft. He'd never actually skinned an animal before making the jump into the twenty-first century, but everything he knew came from this speech right here. It almost made him cry.

The hardest part about the goat was getting around the face and horns, trying to make every cut just so, so as to get a clean look. Then the goat skin came off in a heap. Little Teo ran up to it and tried to lift it, but he could not carry it all at once and just got himself covered in fat and a little bit of meat. Teo Sr. grinned and went to the rescue of his firstborn, saving him from the skin and setting it aside.

"We'll get to that in just a second," he said. "Now we have to take the entrails out and cut up the meat."

"And we use the guts to catch bigger animals out in the woods, right?" Little Teo asked.

"Absolutely."

Teo Sr. was no butcher, but he processed that carcass with the deft skill of a man who knew how to survive and get every last scrap of viable meat off the bone. His job was just to get the meat off the skeleton and get it curing; Tommen's ma would separate the sinew and cut it according to what she wanted to make. Pretty soon, fifty pounds of goat meat were hanging up in various crude cuts and Little Teo was taking a few choice organs in to his ma so she could cook them up for dinner. Among tonight's delicacies were goat liver and goat heart.

By the time he returned, the goat skin had been hung over the fleshing pole, Teo Sr. ready with his rocks and knives. All the fat and meat he cut off went into a bucket with the remaining entrails. Once he got down closer to the dermis where he was in real danger of going through, he took flat but dull rocks and began scraping. Over and over until all that remained was skin and fur, no fat, no meat, nothing.

Then, with Little Teo's help, he took it and fastened it to a stretching board, placing hundreds of tiny hooks through the outermost edge to make the skin almost twice as big as the animal itself had been. Then it was just a matter of using the brains to do the actual tanning work, which both father and son did. Well, Senior more than Junior; Little Teo was too fascinated by the feel of the brains in his hands to be of much help. But it got done. In a couple of days, that would be one huge chunk of fine fur and leather, Tommen was sure.

Tommen did not stick around for the cleanup or even to see what had become of that fine piece of goat skin. Instead he took hold of the timeline and moved ahead a few years.

He couldn't say he remembered the time period well, personally, but he did know that some misfortune had befallen them—the farm, the valley, he didn't know. Teo was fourteen when he first went to work in the mines, mostly just as a grunt. His pay was a pittance, hardly worth the effort to walk to the mine, but the farm couldn't afford for him to stay away and camp with the miners. Tommen was only a little boy and all the rest of the children were girls. They needed hands to run the farm, but they also needed Teo's tiny paycheck, and that paycheck was only good at the store that the mine itself owned. It was a dilemma with no good answers.

Their ma had wept that first morning he left to go up there, an hour and a half walk one way. Tommen had tried to cheer her up, but the best she'd been able to do that day was melancholy, verging on depression. She didn't really come back around until Teo returned, long past dark. She had stayed up for him, waiting, wanting to see his face again and know he was okay. He was sore and filthy, hands shaking as he handed over his meager wages for the day. She begged him not to go out again. They would be fine; the farm would survive. But what would they do if something happened to him in the mines? There would be no one to help on the farm or with wages.

But Teo refused. He got only a couple hours of sleep before dragging himself out of bed to go back the next morning, hardly able to see his hand in front of his face, let alone the trail on which he supposedly walked.

Until now, with his ability to time travel through the centuries, Tommen had never gone with Teo to the mines, even to sneak behind him and see how long he could follow without being spotted. Now he did follow. Up and down the hills, through twists and turns he'd never explored before.

The entrance to the mine itself was very unassuming, made visible only because of all the activity moving around it as large carts of coal were shipped out on rails and hauled out by faithful little ponies. Farther down the way was a copper mine, but Teo's focus was the coal mine. Someone yelled at him for not looking ready and presentable, but otherwise he was given no hassle as he claimed his helmet and lantern and got his assignment for the day.

Tommen did not go down in the mines themselves, as much as he might have wanted to. He knew enough. They were dirty, smelly, and a hundred thousand times more dangerous than modern mines. While he felt a certain sense of pride that Teo was a hard worker and willing to do whatever it took, he found that he just couldn't bring himself to watch his brother do such menial, thankless labor, all for a few pennies for the farm. He turned his back.

He advanced the timeline a few more years. Teo was eighteen or thereabouts. When he was fourteen, he had been like Tommen was now: tall, skinny, blowing over for every puff of wind. After four years in the mines, he was tall still, but tough, arms and chest big with muscle. And yet, he still seemed skinny, malnourished. He didn't get enough to eat because he wasn't home to eat but once a day. He got up in the mornings and went straight to the mines. Their ma would leave him some jerky and a bit of fruit when it was available so he would have something to eat during the day, but his main meal came at night as she left the fire under the kettle going to keep the stew warm for him.

Tommen remembered everything as much as he was watching it. But then the memories stopped. He'd come to a point where his life diverged from theirs. On this night, their ma sat up, waiting for Teo as she hadn't done in years. He was surprised to see her when he walked in the door, but he got his soup and sat down across from her at the table.

"I don't want you going back tomorrow," she said quietly.

Teo sighed. "Ma, I've already told you —"

She slapped her palm on the table. "You're not going back!" In the dim firelight, Tommen could see tears streaking down her cheeks. "I've already lost one son to the caves in these infernal mountains. Must I lose another? How long until your luck runs out, hm? Would you see the preacher walk up this road to tell me my only living son, my firstborn, has perished in a mining accident?" She choked a sob and closed her eyes, fighting for composure. "You're almost twenty years old, Teo. I don't know that you've ever seen a girl who isn't your ma or your sisters. You need to find a woman, settle down. You have to have children to carry on your father's name."

For a long moment, there was silence. Teo absently chased a chunk of potato around his bowl for a minute. Finally he nodded. "All right. But tomorrow I have to go back —" He put up a hand as she looked to protest. "I have to go back to tell them I'm not coming back. It's the right thing to do."

Their ma hesitated but nodded. "Yes. You're right, it is the right thing." She managed a wavering smile. "I can see I taught you well. You do your mama proud. But you don't have to leave first thing, do you?"

Teo smirked. "What are they going to do, fire me?"

So, the next morning, after a full night's sleep and a filling breakfast, Teo returned to the mines. First they screamed at him for being late. When he told them he was quitting and would not be working there anymore, they screamed at him again. He was a filthy, lazy, dirty, useless, Welsh beggar. And other assorted names that were not quite as nice. He weathered them all and waited patiently for their throats to grow raw and their voices hoarse. Then he merely wished them a good day, happy mining, and he left.

Come to find out, there was an accident that day that ended up killing sixty miners. There was every chance Teo would have been with them.

He returned to the farm, but it was not a smooth transition. In four years of working in the mines six days a week, he'd either forgotten some skills and let them lapse, or else never learned others, and he and Teo Sr. were left to play catch-up. Together, the family began to plan for his life beyond their farm, which meant building his own farm.

In order to build a farm, however, Teo needed land. There was plenty of it in the mountains, but in the cloud of war, everyone seemed to think he owned everything he saw. Everyone held on tight to what they had, and sometimes what they didn't have, no one willing to give up anything. It was only made more difficult because everyone wanted Teo to stay close to his childhood home, including Teo himself; he had no desire to travel farther than he had to.

In the end, Teo Sr. decided to simply divide his land. Part of his decision was born of the fact that his newest child—the one born after Tommen disappeared and the last Teo and Maisy would have— was a daughter. Daughters would move in with their husbands in time. With Teo being the only son and with the family so poor, land would be his inheritance. As long as Teo Sr. was alive, the land would be divided, each man having his own plot. Once pa died, it would all go to Teo Jr. and he would be responsible for taking care of his own wife and kids, plus his ma and sisters, whoever was still alive and living on the farm.

But that was a long ways away, or so it seemed. Teo had never been very good at talking to girls, and he was even more awkward about it having spent four years in isolation from them in the mines. If not for his ma and sisters, he probably wouldn't have known what a girl even looked like after all that time.

So, really, it actually comforted Tommen to know that his older brother wasn't the cool, suave jerk that most older brothers seemed to be, at least from his experience in school. Derpy younger brother who can barely say three words to a girl has a suave, charming older brother who can woo right and left and have a line out the door of girls waiting for him to ask them to the dance. Teo was none of that. He was big and buff, yes, but he was wretchedly shy. He could hold a decent conversation with another man or even a married woman, but could hardly introduce himself to a girl. If he even looked at a girl across the room, he blushed. And with all his time spent underground, he didn't get much sun, which meant he was pale as death—much like Tommen, in fact. Being that pale only meant that the blushing was that much more obvious.

A few girls found his strong but shy personality amusing as they dared each other to try and get him to say more than four words without tripping up. It was bad enough when he thought they might be interested. Once he figured out the game, his words became even fewer until he hardly spoke at all outside the home.

His—their sisters naturally tried to help, either giving him suggestions straight to his face, or making roundabout suggestions in their secret circles of girls and gossip.

Teo's first courtship lasted about six months. They both seemed to really like each other, or so Tommen thought, but Teo never really came out of his shell. Even when he got to know the girl, Madeline was her name, he didn't become the endless conversation partner she'd evidently been hoping for. She called him aloof and disinterested, and that was the end of that.

Teo reached his twenty-first birthday a single man with no prospects. Eileigh, the oldest daughter at eighteen years of age, was being courted by a rather upstanding young man—for a country farmer—and they were due to be married in the spring. Irene, the next daughter at sixteen years old, had a young man she fancied, though official details were still being worked out. And still Teo labored away beside their father.

Teo Sr. was only about forty-two years old at this time, but he was starting to think that something wasn't quite right in his health. He couldn't say exactly what it was, but there was something off. Of course, he wasn't about to tell his wife and get her all worried, but he mentioned it to Teo Jr. as the first of many clues to be prepared for some tragedy to befall them.

But tragedy was the furthest thing from anyone's mind as Eileigh was married and Irene's courtship made public. Joy bloomed with the flowers that spring of 1859 and all seemed right with the world.

It wasn't until that fall at the harvest gathering that Teo met the woman who would become his first wife. Her name was Mary. Eighteen years old, and she was about as shy as he was. This never really changed throughout their courtship that lasted almost a year and a half. There was joking up and down the valley that their wedding vows would be the longest conversation they'd ever had. When that got back to the couple, they just blushed and did not say a word.

During that eighteen-month courtship, Teo built his cabin and barn with their pa's help. It was a large cabin, for the time period. It boasted three rooms: the main room, for all the cooking and eating; the bedroom, which he would share with his wife; and the second bedroom which was divided incompletely in half, with room for boys on one side and girls on the other. It took longer and was a lot more labor, but it would save Teo time later on, having to try and build additions. That, and Teo Sr.'s failing health was becoming more and more apparent. It would be the last time he could help his son with his log cabin and barn or any large project. Best to do it right the first time.

Teo and Mary were married in June of 1861. Tommen watched the ceremony, modest as it was. There was no cake, but there was food. She did not wear a white dress that she had to take out a small loan for, but her mother and sisters had done a phenomenal job of dressing her up. The music was old Welsh and the fun was universal.

If asked, Tommen would admit to following the newlyweds home. He would not admit to stalking them a little, even if he did do just that. He couldn't deny his curiosity, but they did. For two full weeks after they were married, Teo and Mary slept beside each other with zero interaction. They didn't have sex, didn't do any kind of fun or foreplay. For fuck's sake, they didn't even cuddle. When they did finally do it, it was on her suggestion. Teo didn't even seem to know what to make of it when she finally spoke up.

Tommen couldn't even fathom it. They'd dated—ahem, courted, for over a year. Even when they were married, they didn't get it on. Fucking hell, he and Becky had only been dating, like, six months or something when she finally let him touch her, and they were going to be having sex before the year was out. He could finally check losing his virginity off his New Year's resolution list. His brother hadn't even gotten any until she suggested it, as if he seemed to have no interest. Was his shyness really that deep-rooted?

At any rate, they must have been doing something right at some point because their first child, a daughter, was born a little over a year later.

The two of them still did not speak much, and they seemed to prefer it that way. He did what he did, she did what she did. He helped her when she asked, and vice versa. It wasn't even so much that they spoke as they communicated with expressions and body language. To watch them go about their daily lives was almost like watching a silent film, except for all the chickens and the goats and such.

Their second child, about sixteen months later, was also a girl. She was a breech birth, and Mary bled out. The child was sickly from the beginning and died a few days later.

Teo and his infant daughter moved back with his parents, as much for the girl as to help around the farm. Teo Sr. was past failing health and facing death, though he vehemently denied it. He did what he could, but he was not the man he had been. He'd lost weight, lost muscle, and lost his sight. Less than two months after Mary's death, Teo Forbes, Sr. also passed away.

Tommen sat at his dead father's bedside, completely numb, his feelings reflected on the blank expressions of his ma, brother, and sisters. They'd all known it was coming, so their grief was muted. He'd lost his pa long ago and so thought the wound calloused over. There was a scab there, true, but to actually see his father die still pierced him.

So it was up to Teo Jr. to keep everything running, but he was soon faced with the task of caring for his ailing mother. A year to the day after Teo Sr.'s death, Maisy also passed away and was buried beside her husband on the mountainside. There, even after Teo had gone, Tommen sat and wept. He missed his ma. He really, really missed her.

When he returned to the cabin, time had advanced again. Teo had remarried. Emily was her name. She wasn't quite as quiet as Mary had been or as Teo was, but she was polite and didn't try to push Teo into conversation. Together they had seven children, three boys and four girls. Their oldest boy was called Teo for his father and grandfather before him. Their second oldest boy was, in fact, named Tommen, in honor of Teo's little brother who had gone missing so many years before. But it was their third boy who was the real surprise. His name was Owain. Tommen didn't recall that their pa had ever spoken about Walter before, nor that Teo had ever been present when he showed up at the cabin years later looked for forgiveness and help. Had their pa told Teo about their Uncle Owain after his visit?

Although, it was just as likely that the name Owain came from his great-grandfather Owain, who was Walter and Teo's pa, Tommen's grandpa. Who knew? But fucking hell, all these same names in the same family could be confusing.

Emily died when their youngest child was four years old, a bout of pneumonia in the middle of winter. Teo also contracted the disease, and while he generally recovered, his voice had gone hoarse and his stamina took a huge hit. If not for the efforts of the boys, the farm would have suffered more than it did; a thirteen year old can only do so much.

Teo did not remarry after that. He did his best to raise his eight children by himself. His oldest daughter from his first marriage helped around the house and did her best with the younger girls, but she was soon married and starting her own family.

The years passed and, one by one, the children grew up and left home. Tommen did his best to remember names and dates, keeping track of everything in his phone. Some of the names he kept only for reference, in the event he came across someone of the same name in the real world in the future. As for the boys, who would carry the Forbes name, he recorded more of that information.

Tommen never expected to make a full family tree and show it off publicly, or if he did, he certainly wouldn't include himself. But there was no way he would ever get the opportunity to see history so unaltered and so up close and take his own notes. This was his family, and he had to know.

But that also meant watching his brother grow old and feeble. Of the eight children, five had left the area to make their fortunes in the north—Ohio, Indiana, Michigan—or the west, becoming less wild with each passing year as territories were turned into states and the United States officially stretched from sea to shining sea.

But Teo cared for little of that. His son Tommen was the only one of the boys who had stayed behind to continue to farm. He and his wife had moved back into the old homestead once Teo's health began to fail. First it was just his stamina. He had the strength and the determination to work, but his body demanded rest. After a while, his breathing started to suffer. He coughed and wheezed. Sometimes he lay awake for half the night hacking away. A month or two later, his vision began to go bad, then failed completely. Less than a week later, his wheezing cough turned wet, then wet with blood.

Tommen sat at the end of his brother's bed as he lay in a fitful sleep, frequently interspersed with violent bouts of bloody coughing. His daughter-in-law managed to give him water on occasion, but it was the only comfort afforded to him now. The following morning, the only two of Teo's daughters who were in the area also came to help and pay respects. Word was sent to the others, scattered far and wide, but it was too late. Within two days, Teo Forbes II was dead and buried.

Sitting there by his brother's grave, Tommen wasn't sure what to think. It was the same cabin, same valley that he had grown up in, but everything around it had changed. Charleston had grown up some and America was prospering, her people spreading out far and wide to every corner of the union.

Were any of them prepared for the coming darkness? World War I, the Great Depression, World War II, the Cold War, to say nothing of the shit that came after that? Would any of that really reach this far into the mountains? Would these humble mountain folk even notice?

The turn of the century came and went. People everywhere celebrated. The year 1900, entering a brand new era of prosperity in the wondrous twentieth century. The United States was a grand powerhouse and all knew her strength.

That strength was quickly turned inward as the glorious human race devoured itself in what was then known as the Great War. Tommen's namesake nephew and his family stayed stubbornly out of the conflict, instead digging their heels into the soft earth and tilling the ground for another year, flying under the radar and weathering the storm.

Meanwhile, although the other brothers were too old to join the army, their children were not. Between Teo and Owain, they had seventeen children, six boys and eleven girls. All six of the boys went off to fight and nine of the girls volunteered to become nurses. Of the other two girls, one was too young and the other was what would be considered autistic in modern times.

It was almost surreal to watch, to think that these were Tommen's great-nephews and great-nieces. Had he not gone into that cave and made the jump, he might have met them personally. Hell, he probably would have had children of his own, going off alongside their cousins to fight and die in a foreign land.

Two of the boys did perish overseas. One was confirmed dead and the other went missing. Tommen knew he could have easily gone and figured out exactly what happened to him, but he decided not to. For one, it no longer mattered, a century later. For two, he wasn't sure he could stomach what he found, assuming he found anything at all. War was chaos, and even if he had all the time in the world to watch his great-nephew's movements, some things just got lost in time and history.

The thing about following a single family, though, is that they almost inevitably turn into multiple families as children have children and those children have children. It was how the population of the earth exploded from a million to a billion and then to seven billion and more. As he continued watching his nephews, he found that he couldn't keep track of everything as he just glossed over most things. If he wanted details, he was going to have to follow one family, then go back and follow another, and so on and so forth. He did not have the time, nor the interest. The further he got from his old home life, the less he cared.

Tommen's namesake nephew turned the homestead over to his oldest boy, David, once he returned from the Great War. But David was not a farmer, nor had he ever completely recovered from the horrors he had seen. Most often, it was his wife and oldest son who ran the farm. When news of World War II broke out, David committed suicide, terrified that he was going to be drafted and sent back over.

His wife and son held onto the farm during the war, but when it was over, they donated the homestead and the land to the city of Charleston as it sprawled along the river and up the surrounding hillsides. It was given on the condition that it would be turned into a historical monument or a park. None of them were particularly adept or interested in farming, but they couldn't bear to see it stripped and turned into cold, stone buildings.

Tommen remembered visiting that park. He'd been there multiple times, actually. Even now, as he let the timeline slide along, he watched as all evidence of the original family vanished. The rooms were emptied, the barn was emptied, the pens silent. Not long after, a number of trees were cut down around the area. Some distance away, more trees were cut so a nice pavilion could be built, and trails began to be forged here and there. Access to Forbes Cave was cut off.

Then the killing blow came. The barn, being of an older style and not cared for in decades, rotted and crumbled, falling over in a great windstorm. It hadn't damaged the cabin, but when crews went to investigate, they determined that the cabin was in little better shape. After some heated debates, it, too, was removed, along with any evidence that a homestead had been there at all except for the foundation of the barn and a little sign in the middle of the clearing, reading, "Original site of the Forbes homestead." A new trail skirted the area, a good distance from the sign, so the only way people even knew what the place was would be if they cared enough to leave the trail and read the sign.

Watching it all happen, Tommen felt as though a piece of him was being destroyed as well. That was his home, his cabin. He remembered sitting by the fire, eating or playing games or listening to stories or whatever. He remembered waiting for Teo to come home from the mines. He remembered following his pa around doing this or that. But it was all gone now, reduced to a small plot of land overseen by Parks and Recreation. He let the time travel slip away and stared at the empty site for a moment longer before turning and walking away.

He was an idiot to have come. He'd told himself that it was for history and genealogy only. He'd told himself that it would help to bring himself some closure, to have a definite answer as to what had happened and how the land got from there to here, and to figure out whether he had any living relatives still in Charleston.

Instead, he'd had to watch his whole family die. His pa had a long, slow death, succumbing to old age and frailty. His ma might have experienced the same thing, but more likely, she'd just lost the will to live and died of a broken heart. His brother suffered for his time in the mines long after telling his foreman to fuck off. He hadn't even followed his sisters to find out how they fared, but it couldn't have been much better.

After a minute, Tommen returned to the hillside where his parents were buried. Trees grew there now. Life had moved on. He did not linger there, simply passed through on his way up the hill toward the pavilions. A group of hikers was just gearing up for the short hike it took to reach the tributary to the Appalachian Trail. They were talking and laughing among themselves, completely oblivious to the invisible man trapped in another dimension who walked among them.

By the time he hit the parking lot, his head was spinning. It was almost as if it had never happened, his whole hike and revelation. He still remembered it, but the emotional connection was fading, as if waking from a dream. Or a nightmare. He really couldn't decide which. And then it was gone. He faced Charleston now, the huge city with tall buildings, street lights, and all the modern amenities expected of a big city. Down there was his school, his workplace, and his home.

His home, where his dad was worried sick about him, waiting impatiently until he could meet up with a mutual friend and figure out a way to rescue him. Tommen glanced back at the park, at everyone he once thought he knew. He sighed, but nodded and straightened his back, squared his shoulders. He knew now. He'd learned what he'd wanted to know. He was glad he'd done it, he supposed. The past was a nice place to visit, but he couldn't live there. He had to get out.

He Traveled home, glad to find he hadn't missed his dad leaving, but also astonished that he'd only been gone a little over an hour. He'd reviewed over a century of history in an hour. How was that even possible? Plus he'd gone to dinner. What sort of freaky Akari Time physics were going on here?

It wasn't quite time to go, so Tommen returned to his room to plug in his phone and hearing aids, just to make sure he was good. He lay back on the bed and put his arm up on the pillow. It wasn't feeling too bad, actually, or maybe he'd just gotten used to the pain. Or maybe he'd just been experiencing a greater pain that drowned out the screams from his burns for a short time.

In a way, Tommen wondered if he hadn't learned a little too much about his family. Some things, people expected to keep private or reveal in their own time, or even take to the grave. His dad had been determined to keep his past hidden and take it to his grave. Now that it was out in the open, he was slowly showing more and more of it, a little at a time. In his time. Now Tommen knew the full story. How would his dad react to that if he found out?

Other things he really hadn't needed to know, like how Teo had waited two weeks to consummate his first marriage. It was amusing and embarrassing, but was it really necessary? There was a certain expectation of privacy around those things, for one. For two, Teo wasn't even around to tease about it.

Guilt gnawed at Tommen. He was an idiot. Well, he couldn't unknow what he knew. He just had to file it away, try to forget it, and move on.

He figured he must have dozed a little bit because the next thing he knew, the light in his room was on and his dad stood in the doorway.

"Tommen?" he asked cautiously. "Are you still here?"

Tommen rolled off the bed and went to the lightswitch. One flash. His dad breathed a sigh of relief and went to sit on the end of the bed.

"Were you sleeping? Do you sleep?"

One flash. Fucking hell, they had to find a better way to communicate than this. Yes or no questions could get really boring really fast, and they weren't that useful anyway.

"Okay. I didn't know ghosts slept." His dad laughed once and let out a breath. "Anyway, I'm going to start getting ready to head over the bakery. Given that you got from the campsite back home in a couple of days, I assume you are able to ride in vehicles or have other means of travel?"

One flash.

"Good. As I said, Micaiah and Kayla already seem to have some sort of plan. It will be helpful if you can be there to somewhat communicate, let them know that we're all on the same page, or trying to be. Do you know of any other way of communicating beyond yes and no?"

Two flashes, as much as Tommen hated to admit it.

His dad grunted. "Well, maybe they will have some insight. Who knows? Anyway..." He stood. "Oh, and in the event you didn't know, I have tomorrow off, but I go back to work on Sunday. I will still be doing all I can—assuming we haven't rescued you by then—but know that I'm not writing you off just yet. You crossed the universe for me, and I expect I might have to do the same for you."

It was a strange sort of irony, Tommen thought, but he didn't dwell on it for too long. Instead he needlessly stepped aside and watched his dad head into his own bedroom, rummaging for a different shirt and a clean pair of socks. Tommen flashed the light to let him know he was there.

"What?" his dad looked up from where he pulled on a sock. "Sorry to say, I'm not to well-versed in Morse code, and yes or no questions take a long time."

One flash.

"Well, at any rate, while we're home and it's just me and you, if you're here, it would be helpful if you could turn your light on or..." He hesitated. "Or your stereo. Just so I know when you're around and I'm not talking to myself."

One flash.

"But don't go pulling any freaky phantom tricks if Laura comes over. I know my house is old. I don't need her to think it's haunted, too."

Tommen flashed the light on and off several times, hoping his dad got the point, which he did.

"Don't laugh at me. I'm serious."

Tommen gave him one more flash, then wandered out to the kitchen. At least he knew how to swipe food now, though it seemed to take a lot more energy than what he thought necessary, and certainly more than what Julianna had used to grab things. Still, it was a start. He wasn't going to starve.

"All right," his dad said, walking out to the kitchen to pull on his shoes. Tommen gave him a flash to let him know he was there. "Off we go. Are you...I don't know, riding in the car, or what's the plan?"

He shook his head. "You know what? You move however you are able. I'm just going to go out to the car and carry on like normal. Sound like a plan?"

One flash.

"Excellent. Off we go, then." He still seemed uncertain. Talking to his invisible son was one thing when it was just the two of them at home. Now he was going to have to take his insanity out in public.

Tommen followed his dad out to the car.

Chapter Fifteen
Passing Notes

The ride to the bakery was uneventful. Walter did not speak, though he did appear to be thinking hard about something. Was he trying to convince himself that everything had really happened, that he really was communicating with his son who was trapped in another dimension? Was he trying to convince himself he wasn't crazy? Tommen chuckled and shook his head. Good luck with that one.

Micaiah was just about to lock the door when Walter pulled in the parking lot. As if to show off, even if no one would see, Tommen elected to go through one of the large bay windows. Just one little party trick he had in his bag while he was in this dimension; might as well use it while he could.

"I was beginning to think you weren't coming," Micaiah said, heading to the office.

Walter nodded. "Well, Tommen distracted me."

"We're all distracted by it a little, but—"

"No, I mean...he distracted me. He himself. He contacted me."

Micaiah stopped, his hand on the door to the office. "What?"

Tommen chose that moment to go to the main switch panel and flip all the lights off. He heard his dad sigh and say, "That would be him. Flair for the dramatics to the last."

Tommen flashed the lights on and off for a second, making spooky ghost "ooooooh" noises, even though he was the only one who could hear. After a few seconds, he turned them back to the way they should have been at close, only the security lights on. Then he went into the office to join them.

"That was Tommen?" Micaiah asked disbelievingly. "How can

you be sure?"

So Walter recounted the events from earlier in the evening, starting with the Morse code S-O-S in the lamp. Then he explained the stereo and the lights in Tommen's bedroom, followed by a series of yes or no questions which basically reaffirmed what they had apparently already found out or had a pretty good guess on. Micaiah listened patiently, but his expression was impossible to read. He looked like he really wanted to believe it, that they had made contact with the person they were searching for, but past experience told him to be extremely cautious. Looking at his stump, it wasn't hard to guess why.

"And then," Walter said, bringing his tale to a close, "before all this, I went to dinner with Laura and had fish. I had leftovers that I took home and put in the fridge. Before I left, I was going to finish it off, but when I went to the fridge, it was gone."

Oh, shit, so he had gone after it? Weird. Oh well.

"Well, shit, that just proved everything right there," Micaiah said sarcastically, leaning back and folding his arms. He sighed and nodded. "I want to believe you. I do. How do we know it isn't Rifun or someone playing games with us?"

Walter frowned. "We don't. Not really. But we're not going to know until we do what we can to rescue Tommen. Until then, we're not going to actually see him, unless he touches another open portal again, I suppose."

"Maybe that's what we ought to do, then. Open a portal to the fortress and see if we can't get another Imprint or something."

Tommen jumped over to the switch and gave two quick flashes.

"That means no," Walter said.

Micaiah hesitated, then got on his computer. A minute later, he printed out a Morse code reference sheet. "All right, then. Yes or no questions aren't going to get us anywhere faster. One flash for yes and two for no is fine, but otherwise, you think you can follow this? Tommen or whoever it is?"

One flash. Yes, that would make things so much easier.

"Good." He leaned back in his seat again. "Now then—and I don't expect or want you to try to flash out entire paragraphs; that'll just give us all seizures—why won't you try to Imprint on a portal again?"

Tommen studied the Morse code sheet as he flashed out P-A-I-N. Micaiah wrote down the sequences and translated.

"It's painful?"

E-N-E-R-G-Y.

"Energy?" Walter wondered.

"There is a significant amount of Energy surrounding a portal; that must be what he runs into. But portals themselves are Energy vacuums."

L-I-B M-O-R-E N-R-G.

Walter studied it. "What's that supposed to mean?"

"Land In Between has more Energy." Micaiah nodded. "It would make sense, given the Energy needed to open portals. If the portals are vacuums, the displaced Energy has to go somewhere, especially if the portal closes prematurely with someone caught inside."

B-A-R-I-E-R.

Walter nodded. "It's Tommen. Barrier has two r's there, kiddo."

Tommen killed the lights for a few seconds to make a point.

"It would also make sense for there to be a pretty good barrier." Micaiah ran his tongue over his teeth. "And being exposed to that much more Energy means he probably has pretty good mastery of it, which would explain the ease with which he can manipulate lights and other electrical things. But I do have one question. Tommen, how did you take Walter's fish? Did you use a portal or what?"

I-D-K.

"You don't know? Well, you're a lot of help. If you're able to take things into the dimension, are you able to send things out again, too?"

I-D-K. N-O-T T-H-N-K S-O.

"Doesn't think so." Micaiah took an even breath. "Well, there goes my note-passing idea."

Walter fiddled with his mustache. "You said he can manipulate electrical things. Tommen, do you think you could type something out using the computer?" He glanced at Micaiah. "If you can pull up a document and if he can manipulate the right switches on the keyboard, maybe we can have a little easier conversation."

Tommen liked the idea, but he wasn't sure how well that would go. Generally when he tore things apart, it was for the sheer fun of it. He understood a little bit about how computers and electronics worked, but nothing quite that sophisticated. Still, he didn't have any better ideas. Micaiah brought up a new document and moved away from the computer.

"Okay, Tommen, do your stuff. If you can."

Cautiously, he approached the computer. At the very least, all he had to do was manipulate the keyboard. Carefully, he touched it, then moved to feel the wires and motherboard.

Holy shit, it was like touching a hot stove. It wasn't physically hot, but this was way more complicated than just a light switch. Switches were basically just circuits. On and off, make the electricity stop and go. Simple. The keyboard, however, was like an information superhighway, or maybe a smaller byway seeing how he didn't even want to touch the computer tower itself. But still, he could feel each individual key and all the things it could do. It could type a letter, one way or the other depending on if shift or caps lock was involved. There were a ton of symbols there, too. All the functions and extra little keys to control web pages, searches, music, the works. The electronic complexity of just the keyboard was astounding.

Taking a breath and steeling himself for the sudden flow of electricity and information, he touched the keyboard again. It was still hot, and as he found all the keys, he wrote several lines of total gibberish before managing a very slow and deliberate, "Hi, my name is Tommen, and I am a caveman when it comes to computers."

He stepped back and absently tried to flex and wiggle his injured fingers and hand. With his mind still focusing on the computer, the shock of pain in his hand and arm took him to his knees. Fuck. He had to get help for this. He had to escape this dimension.

"Okay, maybe we can get something done now," Micaiah said, nodding. "Why don't we start at the beginning? What the hell happened in that fire? We heard that you went looking for a lost camper, then never returned yourself. But you guys were already out of the fire; you went back in for some reason. What was it?"

Tommen nursed his arm for another minute before getting up and touching the keyboard. Unprepared for both pains, he let out a small cry of pain. It was a terrible thing, to be suffering in front of two people who had no clue what was going on. Still, after another line of gibberish, he got out, "Rifun wanted to take me and teach me some lessons about the Akari. He wouldn't let me go until I did."

The last part was actually a lie, but he couldn't very well confess to willingly following Rifun back into that fire. Shamefully, he had to admit that the lure of power had done it. Rifun had offered to teach him, and Tommen was willing to learn. He wanted to learn. His choices for teachers seemed to be limited.

"What did he teach you?" Walter asked.

"He taught me about Matter and had me break boulders," Tommen typed, feeling very much like a toddler, both in nursing his wound and plinking out each letter individually on the keyboard.

"You did that?" Micaiah wondered in disbelief.

"Yes, I did. Then he took me out and showed me Energy. I felt the tipping point of fire, when wood chemically changed into charcoal and ash."

"That's a dangerous thing, Tommen," Micaiah said gravely. "Energy isn't something you just master."

"I know that now."

"Did Rifun have you try to put out any fires?"

"He asked me to, but he just wanted to make a point about how difficult it was. Mostly he wanted to show me all the different chemical processes and the changes in the Matter."

"What about the main building there? That looked like it had been put out before the fire at large was out."

"Rifun did that."

"He did that? You're sure?"

"It was only me and him that I saw."

"Why does that matter?" Walter asked. "Other than it means he has tremendous power."

"Well, that's just it," Micaiah said. "Think about it, Walt. Buildings today aren't just wood and stone. They're plastics and chemicals, too. All the changes in the Matter, like Tommen said. Plastic melting, becoming part of the wood, all the toxic gases from the chemicals, hot metal, all of that combined. Putting out a fire takes one of two things, as far as we're concerned. First, suffocating it, which would mean stopping each and every chemical reaction going on. Second, stopping it cold, which would mean taking the fire itself, that Energy, and completely stopping it." He brooded on this for a second. "Is that what happened, Tommen?"

"Yes," Tommen admitted guiltily. "I couldn't stop the Matter because it was too complex. I thought that the Energy might be simpler."

"Energy has to go somewhere. Problem is, that's like strapping yourself to a defibrillator. Or maybe neglecting a grounding line on a lightning rod. Since you didn't channel the Energy, it exploded into a portal, dispersed through the in-between dimension, and carried you inside."

"I guess so. I honestly don't really know. I remember the explosion, vaguely, and then I wake up on the ground. It's early in the morning, raining, no one's around, and I hurt like a motherfucker."

"Tommen..." Walter sighed, pinching the bridge of his nose.

"How bad are your injuries?" Micaiah asked.

"Burns on my left arm, side, chest. They're not minor sunburns, let me tell you. I wish there was a way..."

"Way what? To show us?"

"Hang on. Open your USB console."

Micaiah did so, sliding open the panel while Tommen fished

out his phone. The battery was fast depleting, but he managed to snap a couple picture of his arm, taking one selfie just for good measure. Then he got out his charger and unsnapped the wall plug, leaving just the USB which he plugged into the computer.

"What are you—?" Micaiah asked. Then, "You're using your phone to get around the Energy barrier. That's how you called 9-1-1. It wasn't strong enough to fully connect the call, but it pinged your phone." He nodded. "Working with the Energy barrier instead of trying to break it."

That didn't make it any easier to try and transfer the pictures. The computer kept reading his phone, then dropping it. Reading and dropping, reading dropping. It was there, but it wasn't. The pictures would start to transfer, then fail. Transfer and fail. It was almost as infuriating as having shitty Internet that connected and failed. He tried to make the images smaller, but it was difficult to determine how successful he was.

After probably half an hour or so, the computer claimed the pictures had transferred. Tommen left his phone plugged in so it could charge, and he stood back to let Micaiah open the files.

Of the five pictures, three were considered corrupted. The other two were of relatively poor quality, but it got the point across. When the second picture came up, which turned out to be his selfie, he heard his dad's intake of breath and uncomfortable shifting in his seat, fighting to maintain composure. Micaiah just shook his head.

"Okay, okay. Fair enough. It's you," he said. He returned to the picture of his arm. "If it's wrapped and healing, good. Keep it that way until we can get you out and get you to a doctor. Looking at what I can see of your fingers, these look like second-degree burns. Bad ones. Does your whole arm look like this?"

He brought the document back up and Tommen typed out, "Yeah, basically."

"Where did you get the supplies? Who wrapped your arm for you?"

So Tommen relayed the story of meeting Julianna, who she

claimed to be, her supposed story, and the first time she stole supplies out of Laura's truck to wrap his arm.

"So that's where it went," Walter mused. "Laura was fuming that someone had helped themselves to her supplies when she wasn't looking."

"Tommen, has Julianna told you anything else?" Micaiah asked. "About herself, her husband, any of that?"

"Well, I have Richard's journal still. She wants me to read it."

"Have you?"

"A little. It's fucking nuts, though. Holy shit."

"If at all possible, keep it and bring it with you when we bust you out of there."

"Well, sure, but, I mean, she wants to come with me."

"No. She cannot be allowed to escape."

"Why?" Tommen typed and Walter asked at the same time.

"She is still in league with Rifun. Has been for a long time. That's all I'm going to say about it. But we can't let her back out into the real world to do more harm than she already has."

"You mean like making deals with Cassius?"

Tommen briefly explained the scene he saw in Beaumaris Gaol. But he didn't say he'd been to the gaol or that he could time travel in the in-between dimension. He made up some other story about it, making the same basic point. He didn't want to have to explain to his dad that he'd been to his hell.

Micaiah grunted. "Well, I'll give you points for seeing it in person, but we, the Akarin, already knew about that. It's in the Authored books."

Well, there went his hopes for a ground-breaking revelation that changed the course of history, broke him out of the in-between dimension and carted him off a hero. But all he asked was, "So why didn't you just tell me that?"

"Because when we busted you out, I was going to have you read some of the Authored books. Giving an abbreviated story doesn't do it justice."

Tommen sighed. "Fine, fine. Whatever. How exactly do you plan on busting me out of here, then?" He explained Julianna's analogy of the waterfall as best he could, followed by his observations of the line crews and firefighters, concluding that if he was going to break through the Energy barrier, then he needed sufficient insulation against that Energy.

"Well, you've got the right idea," Micaiah told him. "Problem is, we haven't quite figured out what that insulation looks like, where to get it, or how to use it. That's why we're going back to the fortress to do more research." He looked like he had more to say but elected not to say it.

"How are things going there?"

"Not as well as I would like, unfortunately."

"What about the Borelians?"

"Still at war." Micaiah shifted. "That reminds me, Kayla has a plan to try and at least communicate with you. Properly. I'm not entirely sure how it works, but it involves some pretty wicked hallucinogenic fruit."

"This sounds interesting."

Micaiah told him of Kayla's plan, about contacting the Krydik, and going and trying out some of the fruit which they suspected let them see the in-between dimension and talk to their ancestors who were trapped there, a visit to the spirit world of sorts, he supposed.

"Like I said, I don't understand it and there is no guarantee that it will work like we're hoping," he finished. "Just know that it's coming."

"If you can somehow warn me ahead of time, if there's a place you want us to meet, let me know."

"We'll do our best."

"And if I somehow bust out of here on my own, first place I'm going is home. I'm going to raid the fridge and then take a nap."

Walter raised a brow. "That's only if I'm not home. Otherwise, you're going straight to the hospital to get your arm looked at."

Tommen waved his good hand dismissively, even though his

dad couldn't see. "Fine, fine."

"Be serious, Tommen," Micaiah said. "Burns to the hand are nothing to take lightly. It looks like you're doing all right for right now, but you don't want to lose feeling or function. That can be devastating. Okay, a leg is one thing. I manage fine without my leg. Losing your hand is a whole different ballgame."

He wanted to brush it off and say he was going to be fine, but there was no guarantee of that. They were talking and communicating. Hooray. That didn't mean that he was going to be walking free by eight a.m. tomorrow morning. There was still research to be done, experiments to be tried. They still had to bust him out of there. No small feat considering the whole byline or slogan of the Land In Between was "from which no one has ever returned." And if he wanted to be honest, hunger and homesickness were only two parts of his motivation to get home. Fear of losing his hand was also a pretty good motivator.

"What can I do for it in the meantime?" he asked. "Is there anything else I can do? Can you ask Laura?"

Walter nodded thoughtfully. "I can ask her, but it looks like it's pretty well cared for right now. If it's stable for now, don't mess with it."

"It hurts. Like, seriously, you cannot even see how much pain I'm in right now. This is not fun."

"No, I don't imagine it is. I'll ask her and see if there are any over-the-counter pain meds I can get for you, assuming you can take them into the dimension."

"I stole your fish, didn't I? And seriously, like, you almost never eat your restaurant leftovers. I thought for sure you were going to just forget about it on this whole weight loss kick you're on."

His dad shrugged. "What can I say? It was good fish."

"Yes, yes, it was."

"Okay," Micaiah said. "Is there anything else you need, Tommen? Something you're missing that might help or something you need?"

Tommen thought a minute, running through the list of things he wanted. Eventually, he concluded that he could make do without them for a little while, as long as he held out hope for rescue.

"I don't think so," he finally answered.

"What about some kind of signal booster?" Micaiah said, thinking out loud. "For your phone? If I can get an antenna — or if you can get an antenna — that would boost power and signal to your phone, when you plug your phone in and start tapping into the Energy barrier, maybe you could have enough to make a call or send a text. That way we can communicate freely instead of having to sit here at a computer. Think you can do that?"

"I'm sure I could try."

"Good. Plus, if that works, maybe it will provide a little better clue as to just how much insulation or power boosting we need to do to get you out of there."

"Without killing me."

"Yes. Without killing you."

"I did have one thought, though I'm not too keen on the idea. What if I tried to recreate the conditions, retry the experiment as it were? You know, try to put out a fire, explosion, portal, boom, there I am."

Micaiah hesitated and glanced at Walter who looked uncertain. "As interesting as it sounds, I'm not too keen on the idea either. You're already injured and we really don't want to make that worse. Why don't we save that idea for later, after we've gotten a better idea and maybe tried some other things?"

Tommen wasn't going to argue, that was for sure.

"Is there anything else I can do from my end while you're doing your research?"

"Honestly, Tommen, I don't know. I don't know what things look or feel like from your end. But use the Energy to your advantage. Try new things and keep coming up with ideas and ways to break out. Short of dying, you really can't make your situation much worse." Walter gave him a look which he pointedly ignored. "And above all, keep the journal, and stay away from Julianna as much as possible. It's bad enough we have to deal with Rifun; we can't have the two of them together. She cannot escape."

"I'll do my best, but she finds me."

"Figure something out." Micaiah grabbed his crutches and stood. "Your dad and I are heading to the fortress to do some more research. We'll let you know, somehow, what we come up with. Get a signal booster if you can. Hopefully that will make communicating easier." He nodded and paused, searching his mind to see if he forgot anything. Then, "We're coming for you, Tommen. It's good to hear from you and see that you're in good spirits. Keep it up. We'll be back eventually."

The next thing Tommen knew, he was staring at the ceiling, feeling like a French fry, emphasis on the fry. Groaning he sat up, flopping back down as a wave of dizziness overcame him and his heart thudded loudly in his chest. Micaiah had opened a portal, and Tommen, in his infinite stupidity, had decided to give them something like an encouraging departure gift, an Imprint of himself in the portal. He wasn't sure why, maybe as a "You can do it" or, more likely, a "Don't forget me" statement. Either way, just like before, he'd been zapped and landed flat on his back.

Gradually, he picked himself up, getting on his hands and knees, almost throwing up, but making it to his feet no worse for wear. Okay, so, no matter how well-intentioned, that was always a very bad idea. Got it. He stood stiffly and stretched, trying to calm his racing heart.

Looking around, the bakery was quiet, just as if everyone had gone home for the night. That sounded pretty nice, actually, going home, taking a hot shower, crawling into bed to sleep for ten hours. That sounded like a good plan. Problem was, he had work to do. Finally, he'd made solid contact and had a real conversation. Now that everyone was up to speed, they had to work double-time to bust him out of the in-between dimension and get him home. They could coordinate their efforts to make it doubly effective, even. First they needed a plan. For his dad and Micaiah, that meant doing research in the Archives they still had access to. For Tommen, it meant figuring out more about the dimension from the practical side of things.

How did he go about doing such a thing, anyway? He was trying to learn, really. But while Micaiah had warned him to stay away from Julianna, she was also his best hope for learning anything in this dimension. Did that mean there could be others around here who could teach him things? How did he find them? What was the protocol here?

He left the bakery and started walking around town, right hand gripping his trashed jacket, left hand flexing as much as he dared. He tried to touch his fingertips to his thumb, but with limited success. Trying to make a fist was a laughable effort. Whether it was natural because of the nature of his injuries or huge red flags that something wrong, there was no good way for him to know. And even if he did know, what good would it do him? What could he do about it here?

Well, his first mission ought to be the one he'd been charged with: find an antenna or some kind of signal booster for his phone. Because of the nature of things, it was going to have to be a direct wire, no wireless or wi-fi or bluetooth or any of that. Problem was, who made direct wires anymore? Everything was about being digital and wireless and slick and smooth, as modern as possible.

At the same time, maybe it wasn't about going with the latest and greatest. Maybe he would have to get creative with some old technology. Maybe he'd have to find a way to blend the two together. But with Radio Shack out of business, where did he go?

His first stop was the local phone store. Everything was closed up for the night, all the lights off. Tommen had no trouble flicking a couple on and giving himself a tour of the place. All the goodies were locked up, but it was no matter for him. He left the show floor alone and started on the rest of the merchandise in the back, bypassing all the new phones and tablets until he came across all the practical accessories. But the more he looked through them, from what he could see, there was very little that he could use. Phone chargers, well, he already had a charger. Docking speakers were nice, but largely imp—well, maybe he'd just take those anyway. Hey, he never said he was perfect.

As for anything even resembling a signal booster, they were all wireless. Everything was all about being wireless these days. And, more to the point, they were wi-fi boosters. Could they be used to help him break through the energy barrier? Maybe, maybe not. Didn't matter because they were all fucking wireless! When did everything in the digital world switch from being useful and practical to being stylish and completely fucking useless? It was infuriating.

He left the phone store completely disappointed and a little frustrated. He didn't expect any other phone store to have anything different, so where did he want to try next?

Eventually he found his way to an old music store that sold everything from refurbished 8-tracks to digital downloads and all the equipment to go with everything. Who knew, maybe they would have something of interest?

Strictly speaking, they did have a lot that was of interest. Had his dad not been such a good cop and only paid half as much attention to his son, Tommen might have thought about swiping a few things here and there just because he could. He felt guilty about it after a minute, but the temptation was great.

His search of the music store took about two or three times as long as his search of the phone store, but the music store had so much cool stuff. He didn't steal anything this time, but that wasn't to say he didn't seriously think about it. At the same time, he also didn't find anything that he thought might help boost his phone signal. It had been a long shot anyway, all things considering. Mostly it had been a distraction that turned into a search, rather than a search he got distracted in. Did that make sense? He thought about it a minute and decided it did.

All right, so, phone store was a bust and music store was also a bust but to no one's surprise. Where did that leave him? On the streets of Charleston at almost eleven o'clock at night, for one. He wandered around a little until he found a pizza shop that was open until midnight. It was fairly busy for this Friday evening, and he slipped into the kitchen. He didn't do anything too nasty like steal an entire pizza, but he did take a few single slices and a couple of breadsticks here and there. The waiter took the orders out, customers complained that they got shorted a breadstick, waiter apologized, went back to retrieve that last coveted stick of bread and garlic. No harm, no foul as far as Tommen was concerned. And if anyone cared to watch the cameras and actually saw the slices or breadsticks mysteriously vanish, well, how were they going to explain it, anyway? The pizza shop is haunted? Ha!

He was getting better at this whole stealing business, he figured, walking down the street once more, finishing off his last slice of stuffed crust meat lovers. He'd gone from starving to stealing in two days. Really, he didn't even need Julianna anymore, at least for that bit. Maybe he didn't need her at all now, with Micaiah and his dad and everyone else on the case. They could figure things out on their own, right?

Problem was, Micaiah had told him to learn things about the dimension from inside it. He could do that, but Julianna knew this dimension better than anyone. If he wanted to learn fast, he needed her help, too. As evil as she might be, if he made nice with her for a little bit, he might be able to learn what he needed and escape the dimension with the journal but without her. Once that Energy barrier was back in place and her sealed up along with it, all was well.

Although, if she and Rifun were somehow in cahoots, word could get back. Rifun didn't play nice when things didn't go his way or when people tried to double-cross him. And it was a little hard to deny double-crossing when the person being betrayed lays out the whole story. Tommen was not a very good liar; there was no way he would be able to talk his way out of that one, and he didn't fancy himself on the receiving end of Rifun's wrath. He would have to find another way. The first step, regardless, would be to find a way out in the first place.

Not far from the pizza shop, Tommen came across a computer

and electronics repair shop. He'd been by it a hundred times going a hundred places, and it always looked seedy as fuck. From what he heard from people who went to the place to get their laptops and whatever fixed, the repair guy was seedy as fuck, too, apparently notorious for fixing the problem, then installing malware on a timer, so in four to six months, you'd be back to see him again. The smart ones figured out the game and went elsewhere. The idiots were the ones who kept him in business.

Curiosity getting the best of him, Tommen went inside. Everything about the place was shady, from the new things to the used things to the things being stripped and cannibalized to fix things. It looked like the guy did more than computers; he fixed old DVD players, VCR's, TV's, CD players, radios. Well, he either fixed them or cannibalized them. The whole place looked like it belonged in some kind of horror movie.

In the back, Tommen found a storage room full of old equipment. On the one side, open racks suggested the man didn't give half a damn if his stuff got stolen because it wasn't worth much. On the other side was a steel cage, heavier than the ones found in the phone store. Flipping on a light, he saw that this was all military-grade stuff, from World War II to present day. Radios of all ages, remote controls, unidentifiable computer equipment, even what looked like the remains of an old drone. What the fuck kind of operation did this guy have going on in his shop? Tommen took a step back and wondered if he shouldn't tell his dad about this, like, some potential terrorist operation or something. This was freaking him out a little.

At the same time, though, military-grade equipment might have the power boost he needed to make it through the energy barrier. He just had to figure out what was what and how to connect it to his phone.

Suffice to say, Tommen wasn't exactly mechanically inclined. He could get around on his phone and most any electronic, and he enjoyed taking things apart just to see what was inside. But he couldn't say he knew how to build a supercomputer from an old toaster or anything like that. He could build a basic circuit for the science fair and that was about it. It was a piss poor admission from a professed science nerd.

So about half an hour into his little breaking-and-entering scheme, he found himself sitting on the floor of the storage room with a dozen different military-grade pieces of equipment ranging from radio pieces to something he couldn't identify but looked like it might prove useful. Of course, everything would be going a lot faster if he had both hands. As it was, he was using his useless left hand as more of a leverage point, which did him no favors when it came to pain management.

As midnight came and went, Tommen had quite a contraption wired together. He was proud of it only in that he'd built it with virtually no tools or experience. He would be more proud of it and himself if the stupid thing actually worked. That was the kicker; it had to work or else he'd just wasted an hour of his time. Not that he had anywhere to be in particular, but he didn't like wasting time on projects that didn't work.

Eventually, he set down his pieces and tools and shifted position, leaning back against the wall as far as he dared. He was exhausted, and the elation of having made contact was wearing off pretty fast. Well, might as well give the thing one test before going home and going to bed. If it worked, he'd use it in the morning to talk to his dad and let him know everything was okay. If it didn't work, a good night's rest might help him figure out a solution to the problem.

Briefly, he entertained a thought that if he could manipulate a keyboard, he ought to be able to manipulate an entire computer. Maybe he could get online at home and do some ghost research on how to build a signal booster. Now there was an idea. Holy shit, what sort of fun could he have with that? Ghosts possessing people's computers. That would be fucking hilarious. Just one more thing he'd have to try before busting out.

He got unsteadily to his feet, shuffling things around in his arms so his coat and its stuff hung over his left arm, and he could carry his contraption in his right hand. Looking at it, it probably shouldn't have been as big as it was. The modern military did everything small but mighty. This thing looked like something from the Korean War, like an old radio he'd once seen on a *M*A*S*H* rerun.

But if it worked, it worked. He only had to use it until he got out and got home. And he certainly wasn't going to try and do it again if he didn't have to.

He left the computer store, dragging his feet a little. By now, the only businesses that were open were bars, convenience stores, and a few gas stations. And the drug runners, but those weren't official businesses. Unlicensed pharmacists and all that. Tommen smiled ruefully to himself.

When he heard the scream, he dropped his stuff and almost jumped out of his skin. Looking around, he found a couple of guys about ready to go to town on a young woman. Judging by the attire, she was looking for company, just not this kind. The alley they were dragging her down was not lit and did not appear to have any security cameras.

Tommen stood, rooted to the ground, completely frozen and unsure what to do. Even under normal circumstances, there was no way he could hope to go up against thugs of that size.

But these weren't normal circumstances, were they? And he didn't have to fight them. They didn't even have to know he was there. But he had to get everyone else to look.

Tommen ran toward one of the buildings. Both of them looked like apartment complexes of some form, affordable housing maybe. Either way, there were a lot of windows, which meant rooms, which meant light. Without thinking, he found the nearest lightswitch and used it as a conduit, feeling all the electricity running through the room, through the floor, through the entire building. He didn't have time to pause and try to differentiate; he flipped everything to the on position, connected every circuit. Every light, every stereo, every waffle maker was suddenly on. Then he ran to the second building and did the same thing. He could feel his heart racing as he became part of the electrical current.

Instantly, the alley was flooded with light and the groans and moans of tired, confused, angry people. The woman kept screaming even as the thugs stopped their assault and looked around, confused and afraid. One person opened a window and shouted at the thugs. Another person opened a window and shouted for someone inside to call 9-1-1. Still a third person opened a window and had a shotgun pointed at the thugs, ordering them not to move.

Tommen could have stayed to see the outcome, watched the ambulance treat the young woman and get her to the hospital, watched the police drag the men off in handcuffs like they deserved. It would have been a happy ending for once. But he didn't stay. He couldn't say why. Maybe it was because no one would ever know it had been him who tripped the alarm. Maybe because he didn't want anyone to know it was him even if they could know. Maybe it was for some subconscious reason he hadn't discovered yet. Maybe he was just tired. Either way, he gathered his stuff and continued home, Traveling there to pass the time and get to his bed faster.

The first thing he did when he got home was flop down on his bed, a decidedly bad idea for two reasons. First, the impact on his arm hurt like a motherfucker. Second, if he stayed there too long, he was going to fall asleep before he got a chance to test his contraption. Reluctantly, he sat up, nursed his wounded arm for a minute, still trembling from the surge of electricity he'd stupidly conducted. Then he reached for his contraption, his homemade signal booster.

Of course, his phone was dead, so he had to plug it in and wait for it to charge enough that he could turn it on. While he was waiting for that, he decided to test his computer theory. Turning it on was nothing; that was like turning on a light bulb. His first hurdle came with the login. It was all asterisks when he typed it in, so he had no good way to know whether it was correct or not. Normally he just did it by feel, by force of habit. Half the time he wasn't even sure what his password was. Now he had to do it blind.

After a dozen unsuccessful tries, he gave up and went back to his phone. Well, at least that was charged enough that he was able to turn it on and try to get things going. Now he had to figure out how to connect his contraption to his phone. It was the same problem he had with every other booster he found, all of those things in the phone store. Why had he even bothered with this military stuff when it had only taken up more of his time to give him the same damn problem?

He rubbed his eyes as he took in one of his spare chargers on top of his dresser. He wasn't going to destroy the one that was already plugged in, and he had a few to spare at least. Looking back and forth at his contraption and then at the plug, he decided his first course of action was probably going to be a direct hotwire. In no situation could he reasonably justify some other sort of roundabout loop method of making everything work. It would either work or not. If the simple things didn't work, the complex things would only yield complex problems.

He had no caps or safeties to put on the wires, so everything was open to the air. He had a thought: if his contraption caught fire in the in-between dimension, would his carpet actually catch fire? Would the house actually burn down? If it did, would he be able to use the Energy of the fire to break out of the in-between dimension? Could that actually work?

Well, best not test that theory if he didn't have to. He didn't need any more fire catastrophes this week; one was enough. Time to flip the switch and see if anything happened.

He flipped the switch, and something indeed happened. A few lights lit up. One flickered uncertainly. One set of lights jumped back and forth between red and green; he had no idea what either meant or which one was good in his scenario. Otherwise, well, he had power at least. Time to see if he'd just created a giant light-up pile of scrap.

His phone was warm, but it didn't burst into flames as he turned it on and got to the main screen. Before he could go poking around and check anything, it suddenly blew up. Not literally, thankfully, but it blew up with texts, missed calls, voicemails, the whole works.

"Yes!" he cried, pumping both fists in the air and instantly regretting half of it, pulling his left arm close and cursing. Fucking hell but he was a glutton for punishment.

It worked. Holy fucking hell, it fucking worked. He had signal. Out of curiosity, he unplugged his phone from the wall. Not only did his phone die in like five seconds because of the power overload, trying to stay on and power the booster, but he lost all signal. Okay, so, in order to boost the signal and get past the Energy barrier, he had to be in contact with said barrier. Duly noted.

He plugged his phone back in and waited for it to charge. While it was doing that, he returned to the computer to try his luck at the password. It took a few more tries, but eventually he got every capital letter, every lowercase, every number and special symbol in the correct order.

When that was done, he sat down on the bed. All he needed now was to be visible. Hadn't Julianna said something about some people were skilled enough to make "apparitional" appearances, like ghosts and stuff? Could he do that, but for an extended period of time? Was it possible to live in both dimensions? He could make calls, send texts. If he mastered the computer, he could use the Internet. He knew how to get food. If he figured out how to make himself seen, he could live life as normal, continue his training in the Akari, plus keep all the abilities of the in-between dimension. It would be absolutely perfect.

At the same time, though, no one would ever see what he saw. In order to manipulate an object, it had to be in his dimension. That meant everything in his room, his school books, everything he ever owned, really. Plus he would never be able to leave Earth because he couldn't go through any portals. That kind of put a damper on things when he still wanted to be a Scout. And wielding either the Akari or Time was meaningless when confined to a world that was Unengaged. Hm...maybe he had to think about this a little more.

Although, if he did break out, maybe he could figure out a way to make a safer bridge between the dimensions. The Traveling and the time travel parts were pretty cool. How better to write a history paper than going back and actually visiting and reliving the history in question? That would be awesome.

He went back and turned his phone on, wondering whether he should go through all his missed messages now or wait until morning. More importantly, did he want to reply to any of them? Yeah, his dad and Micaiah were great because they knew what was up. But what about Becky? Did he want to text her? Maybe he and his dad and everyone else should collaborate and come up with a story first.

Out of two hundred new texts, Becky was a hundred and thirty of them. The length ranged from a single emoji to a whole paragraph, the content ranging from a single emoji to a number of mini-sermons about courage and faith and love. Most of them, however, were questions and rants and other emotional messages saying that she missed him and she hoped he was okay and he better start replying because she was getting nervous and so on.

The remaining texts were divided pretty equally, about three to five per person. Camp counselors asking about his location and if he was okay. Friends and even teachers saying they saw the story on the news and he was in their thoughts and prayers, hope he was okay and would come back soon. Central Dispatch from Northampton County, Virginia, sent a few automated computer texts detailing the notes of his 9-1-1 call, the location and nature of the call, actions taken, and so forth.

The missed calls and voicemails were basically the same story. There was one voice message from his dad. It was a long one, more of a narrative, probably the make himself feel better as his mind was plagued with worry. It detailed the search up until about the middle of the second day, Thursday. His dad talked about how he hoped it was a normal search and everything was normal about it, even as he suspected Time and Rifun involvement. But he wasn't giving up. He was going to see it through to the end, no matter what, no matter how long it took or whatever conclusion it came to.

It was a morbid thought, but understandable. Fire was a very powerful, very destructive force after all. Tommen set his phone down and lay back on his bed, a dangerous thing to do given how tired he was. Maybe he should grab a change of clothes; he was starting to stink. While he was at it, might as well grab a backpack of some form in which to keep all the junk he seemed to be accumulating. Did anything ever actually happen to the things he left behind—like the plates, the utensils, the garbage—or would it stay in the in-between dimension forever, like the landfill of the universe? That was a pretty depressing thought, too. Should he go back and clean that shit up?

He jerked back to wakefulness when he heard the garage door close. What time was it? Way too fucking late, that's what. His dad was just getting home. Well, if he didn't have to be to work, he could stay out a little, Tommen supposed. With his bedroom light on to let his dad know he was home, Tommen grabbed his phone and dialed.

Chapter Sixteen
Real Mythology

The second time going to the fortress, Walter was the one to see the Imprint of his son. The surprise was enough to stun him momentarily, long enough for him to fall flat on his face in the fortress with virtually no resistance. Before he knew what was happening, Micaiah was helping him up.

"You okay, Walter?" he asked.

"I saw him," Walter breathed. "I saw Tommen. In the portal."

Micaiah nodded. "He'll be okay. So will you. Now we just need to figure out how to bring you two back together."

Walter took a calming breath and nodded. "Yes. You're right." He gave Micaiah a once over. "When did you get your leg?"

"Huh? Oh, I opened two portals, one here for you, one home for me. It only took a second. Didn't realize I couldn't leave you alone for that long before you start keeling over on me."

"No, I'm fine. It just surprised me is all. Let's go."

Micaiah nodded and led the way, though Walter figured he was getting pretty good at navigating the compound, hideout, whatever they wanted to call it. He at least knew how to get to the so-called kennels where the Trackers were kept and the Archives which was still a long walk up five flights of stairs. Between his bad knee and Micaiah's fake leg, they made quite a pair. But they made it nonetheless, like a couple of weary mountain climbers.

"Someone might think I'm as old as you are, the way I'm limping," Micaiah chuckled, elbowing Walter in the ribs.

"One day you will be as old as I am," Walter informed him. "We'll see who's laughing then."

"Oh, but that won't be for a long, long time, I'm sure."

"Not if you have kids. Those things age you ten times as fast."

"But I'll still look as good as I do now."

"No, you won't. That's another guarantee."

"Well then, I'll see your bet and raise you looking even better than I am now. Kayla, too."

"We'll see."

They reached the Archives and went inside. Kayla and Micah were already at the table, perusing through books and scrolls. They looked up only when Walter and Micaiah sat down.

"There you are," Micah said. "We were starting to wonder."

"I can tell," Micaiah replied sarcastically. "There's been...a development. You might call it a close encounter of the Tommen kind."

"He contacted us," Walter told them bluntly.

"Contacted you?" Kayla wondered. "How?"

So they spent a fair amount of time going over the progression of communication, from flashing S-O-S in a lamp, to Morse code, to manipulating a keyboard to have a text conversation. Walter also mentioned Tommen using his phone as a line between the dimensions so he was able to send a couple pictures. He was injured, yes, but otherwise in good spirits.

"Oh, that's great news," Kayla said, eyes shining. "At least now we know he's alive, where he is, and that he's at least able to survive and get along for the time being."

"Yes," Micaiah confirmed. "Now then, how do we bring him out? We have him looking for a way to try and boost his phone signal or find another way to make full contact with us. Phone, text, whatever. Something."

"So far, all communication has been through the Energy barrier via Energy," Micah stated. "Phone, electricity, Energy. Calling or texting, wireless signal, Energy. Thinking abstractly, how do we move Matter, that is, Tommen, through that Energy barrier?"

"That's what we need to figure out. We need to know how

much Energy we're talking, what kind, and how to manipulate it so we can get Tommen through."

"Well, Dr. Durvin, where do you suggest we start?"

"That I don't know."

Kayla shifted position. "Everything we've discovered so far, up until now, has been through legends and stories. Maybe we can find something in those. I've got a few and Micah found a few. If you two get a few, then something might start to add up. The same story across cultures usually has pretty good credence behind it. Of some form."

"On it." Micaiah stood.

Walter followed, feeling very much like a probie sitting in on a officer's meeting given an officer's task. Out of place was putting it mildly. He wasn't an Akarin, and yet, knowing what he did about them, he no longer really felt like a Time Agent. Maybe because the Time industry seemed so small and insignificant now. Petty and restricted. At one time it had been the epitome of the expansion of his personal universe. Now he'd moved on even from that.

"So, where do we start?" Walter asked as Micaiah picked an aisle.

Micaiah rubbed his face. "I have no fucking clue. Just another instance where everyone seems to think I have all the answers when I don't. I've decided I don't like being in charge. It sucks."

"You really are as old as I am, aren't you?"

"Hey now, that bet only counts after kids."

"How many are you planning on having?"

"Well, that we haven't come to an agreement on. At least two. I'm good with two, maybe three if there's a twin or an oops in there. She wants four. What she really wants is at least one girl."

"I see. Good news is that if you want at least two, you have to start with one. Then see how you feel about the rest afterwards."

"One at a time, we know."

"Although, I've heard that if one parent is a twin, they're more likely to have twins."

"Please, Walter, stop. You're making me nervous."

He laughed and turned his attention to the books. Somehow, he liked the Akarin Archives better, even if it wasn't quite as extensive as the Wheel Archives. They weren't as technologically advanced either, but maybe that was why he liked them. Sometimes there was just no good substitute for a real book in his hands, the feel, the sight, the smell even. And the scrolls? Well, those were bonus points. He'd never held an authentic scroll in his life before this place. It almost felt like sacrilege.

Although, really, he wasn't sure quite what he was supposed to be looking for, whether in the Akarin Archives or the Wheel Archives. Myths and legends about the Land In Between. That was great, except the in-between dimension wasn't always called the Land In Between from which no one had ever returned. Sometimes it was called the spirit lands or the dream lands or heaven or hell or limbo or some other religious, mythological reference. Hence, the myths and legends portion of it. How did he identify which was which?

Well, that was part of the research, he supposed, reading all the legends, sifting through the junk and finding the gems. Where was the big neon sign when you needed it, the one that said, "This is the book you are looking for!"

Eventually, he picked out a few books and returned to the table to start perusing. The least he could do was pretend like he had found something worthwhile and knew what the hell he was doing. Although, *Great Builders of the Past* probably wasn't his best choice. How would he know?

He picked up his first book, titled, *Myths of the Dead*. It wouldn't have been his first choice on the average day at the library, but circumstances demanded the unusual.

To call the contents strange was a bit of an understatement. Most of it was pretty mundane, various beliefs from around the universe. Some cultures spoke of an afterlife, others reincarnation of one form or another. And there were other beliefs, of course, but Walter couldn't find any reference to any place that sounded even remotely like the in-between dimension. No portals, disappearances, anything like that. There were ghost stories, yes, but apparently most cultures believed the ghosts were still rooted in their dimension, not trapped between them. Hell, he didn't know. He could be missing a huge clue and he'd never know it.

And why were they still looking up old mythology anyway? Surely someone, somewhere in the universe, had done a little bit of research on this place and had some concrete facts to go on. Walter took an even breath. That person probably did exist and had done the research, and his findings were probably sitting somewhere in the Wheel Archives.

He closed the book and leaned back, resting his eyes and waiting until everything was upright again. The others were still poring over their texts, but their expressions suggested they were having about as much luck.

"There just isn't enough here," Walter said. "There's myths and legends and stories of stories, but there's nothing concrete."

"We just have to keep looking," Kayla said sympathetically, looking up. "It's all we've got to go on right now."

"Everything we need is in the Wheel Archives. I'd be willing to bet that there is something there that's scientific and absolute. I'm sorry, but, playing devil's advocate, we need science right now, not fairy tales."

"And what plan did you have in mind to get into the Wheel Archives without being apprehended by the Borelians?" Micaiah wondered. "Or even the Hands, seeing how they're in a pretty disagreeable mood right now toward us?"

Walter let out a breath. "What about a Disguise? You say it's just a minor modification of the DNA, an illusion more than anything."

"Even if we Disguise you, you're still human," Kayla pointed out.

"You can't make me look like some alien species? There are plenty of humanoids out there. It doesn't have to be for long, just long enough."

The three of them glanced at each other uncertainly. Micaiah pushed back from the table and stood. "I might have an idea, but I'll have to send a few messages and see if we can't get some inside help. Keep reading while I'm gone."

"Be careful, my love," Kayla called after him. When he was gone, she looked at Walter. "You're probably wondering why we didn't think of this earlier. I'll save you the suspense and tell you that we did."

"Why decide against it?" Walter asked.

"Safety. If the Borelians find out that we can or are Disguising ourselves as other aliens, what's to keep them from doing the same? The Akari is not the only power in these books, Walt. Furthermore, it could give them an excuse to declare war on other species—not that they necessarily need an excuse—but anyone who is sympathetic to our plight right now might back down if they think that association with us draws unwanted attention their way. Given how much power was taken away from the Borelians after Rifun's overthrow, all that tinderbox needs is a spark."

Walter let out a breath and rubbed his eyes. Why did this all have to be so damn difficult? Whatever happened to the days where two sides met on a battlefield? One side dressed in a red lion sigil, the other in a blue griffin sigil. They'd brandish their swords and spears and arrows, then kick their steeds into full gallop. Everyone knew who the enemy was, everyone knew who the friends were. None of this guessing and planning and tiptoeing around the politics. It would be even worse if both parties could and actually did Disguise themselves as other species, effectively turning it into a war of shape-shifters. There would be no escape for any human or any enemy of the Borelians.

Maybe he never should have brought it up. Maybe if Micaiah was able to scrounge up some help, Walter would refuse and say it was a bad idea. It really was.

He was too old for this shit.

Even as he thought it, Micaiah appeared in the doorway of the

Archives, silently motioning for him to approach. Taking a breath, Walter stood and walked toward him. The whole time, he was mentally preparing himself for the gentle letdown and the rational explanation. Kayla's answer seemed to work. It was too great a risk. There had to be another way. No one need die, not this time. They'd find another way to break Tommen out of the Land In Between.

Once in the corridor, Walter stopped when he saw who was waiting for him. Not only was it a Hand, but it was one whom he'd come to know quite well through the stories Tommen told about her.

"Sifura," he stated dumbly.

She dipped her head. "Captain Walter Forbes. I am glad to see you are well."

"We can't Disguise you as an alien and just let you roam free," Micaiah explained. "Even if there were a way, we don't have the time to learn all the nuances right now. So, I went to someone who I believe we can trust. She's helped us before, as you well know, and she's a sympathetic ear for the Akarin cause among the Hands."

"All right," Walter said, "so what's the plan?"

"The plan is to take you to the Wheel, to the Archives, as you require," Sifura began. "I will accompany you. Rather, you will accompany me as my personal guest. You will be Disguised so the Borelians know you only as a humanoid and not a humanoid of particular interest. You will also be shrouded in hopes of deterring any prying eyes."

"But the shrouds were removed because of the secrecy. At this point, it's more likely to attract attention than deter it. What will you say about it?"

"I will say that you are a prospect turned over to me by a Scout. You are considering bringing your race into Time and do not wish to reveal your identity in order to avoid the barrage of questioning by Merchants, Timekeepers, Harvesters, and others. Scouts are always bringing prospects, so it will not matter which race joins and which race does not."

Walter folded his arms. "Something tells me it is not as easy as it sounds."

Sifura nodded once. "You will be Disguised to a minor extent, so will your time there be disguised as a tour. I will take you to the Archives, but our time there must be brief. You must know what you are looking for and how to access the information quickly. We cannot linger."

"The good news, though," Micaiah cut in, "is that as a tour, you'll be visiting most of the areas of the Wheel, which means you can observe how things are going, what's happening, the general feel of the place."

"You mean other Akari-bearers don't regularly report?" Walter asked.

Micaiah hesitated. "Since the Akari ban was instituted, most Akari-bearers across the factions have 'boycotted' the Wheel as it were. Those who still go there send back mixed reports. Most are generally disgruntled about the whole thing, so the whole place is burning down. The others are more on the level of Whispers and see things as absolutely fantastic since the revolution. Hopefully, you can get us a better picture of things."

"So I'm going as a spy."

"Yes, yes, you are. If you want, I can ask Micah or—"

"No." Walter shook his head. "This was my idea, so it's my risk to take."

"And if the Borelians do catch you, your son becomes an orphan."

"I'm sure you and Kayla will do just fine with him." Walter noted Micaiah's stunned expression. "I asked for another way, and I got it. I'm going. What do we need to do?"

Micaiah paused for a moment longer, then nodded. "Okay. I'm obviously not going to talk you out of it. But first thing's first. The mustache has to go." He laughed. "Just kidding, Walter. Well, sort of. You'll still have it; it'll just be Disguised. Now then, hold still."

Walter wasn't sure what Disguise they gave him, and he wasn't sure he wanted to find out.

"Now then," Micaiah said, standing back. "Disguises tend to stick better to Akari-bearers, but seeing how you already know what's up, I think the Author might make an exception for you. Call it a hunch. Anyway, it'll last as long as you aren't captured, beaten, and tortured. You don't know how to hold onto it, so it'll fall right off."

"How will I get back here to have it removed?"

"You won't. I'll take you back to my house and send you to the Wheel from there. Sifura has the shroud."

"Fair enough. Let's get moving, then."

Once again, another trek down five flights of stairs. Hadn't these people ever heard of an elevator at least? Gravity, fine, there were rules. But an elevator. Even an escalator. Walter wasn't sure how much more his knees could take, especially if he had to tour the Wheel with Sifura. Who knew how long that was going to take?

They arrived in the Durvin house no worse for wear, given the trip. And he had to do this twice more today, if not three or four. That stuff wasn't good for you. Still, he squared his shoulders and waited for the portal to the Wheel to open.

"Do you at least want to know who you're going as?" Micaiah asked.

"No," Walter told him. "Knowing you, it'd be Richard Nixon or Abraham Lincoln."

"No, not quite. It's—"

"I said I don't want to know. Now then, we have places to be."

Micaiah sighed dramatically as Sifura handed him a shroud. It wasn't a true shroud like the old Hands and Grandfathers used to wear, but a traditional cloak and hood. Walter fastened it around himself as the portal was opened. Then he flipped up the hood and stepped through.

The other problem with this plan, Walter thought as he picked himself up off the floor of the portal room, was that if his time in the Archives was going to be that limited, he had to actually have an idea of what he was looking for in the Archives. He had to know what he wanted to know about the Land In Between, which meant going beyond fairy tales into the actual science. So what did he want to know? If he had only ten minutes to look for information, what would he consider most pertinent?

He pondered this as Sifura began the tour, giving him a translator, explaining how the translators worked, talking about the portal room, how portals worked. It wasn't a college-level explanation, but a quick gloss over, enough to get the job done and whet the appetite to learn more. And how did one learn more? By joining the Time industry, of course.

But that also meant that the tour really wouldn't be very long, so he had to hit the ground running once they got to the Archives, not that he expected to get there quickly. As expected, a majority of the tour was centered around Time, the marketplaces and the industry, the impact it had on cultures throughout the universe—all positive, of course—the Time Agents, ranks, and so on.

Walter kept his head on a swivel looking for danger as much as he was trying to read the crowd. In all honesty, it didn't look as though much had changed. The awe of the latest elections still seemed pretty prevalent. He desperately wanted to ask about any number of things, but he dared not. As a supposed guest, he should have absolutely no knowledge of anything that occurred with Rifun or Cassius or the coup or the counter-coup or its aftermath, in theory.

The lower marketplaces were full, but not nearly as packed as they had once been. Still, he made an appropriately ignorant comment about how crowded the marketplaces were. Sifura's expression was unreadable as she passively stated that the industry was always growing and bringing new species into the mix. Walter took that to mean that while recruiting efforts had stalled for the Akarin, they'd been redoubled within the Wheel.

The intermediate marketplaces were also comparatively sparse, but still had the feel of Black Friday at the mall. Walter had been posted at the mall on Black Friday more than once, usually as punishment for something. It was not pleasant. Neither was this. He weathered it for the sake of information.

He also decided at that point that the life of James Bond was not for him. Going undercover, gathering intel, risking his life—especially for a group he had only tenuous ties to—that wasn't his game. Even if it was, it was a young man's game anyway. He was way too old for this.

"Now we come to the Auctions," Sifura said, interrupting his thoughts. "Once Time Capsules reach a certain density, referring to the amount of Time they contain, they go to auction rather than be sold at a set price. Are you aware of the procedure for an auction?"

"I am," Walter confirmed. Although his voice sounded different and he was Disguised, he thought it best to keep his words to a minimum and not attract attention to himself, as if the shroud wasn't doing that enough already.

"Very good. But the Time industry and the Wheel is not without its extras and benefits. Time Agents have access to a wide variety of leisure activities. One of these is food at any time in our Food Court."

Actually, he'd been hoping that she would take him to the Archives first, but maybe the tours had to be done in a certain order. Maybe she was just following her own routine for a tour. Maybe she was buying him time to get his poop in a group and figure out what he wanted to actually look for.

Or, another possibility that he considered as he followed her to the Food Court, maybe she was trying to get him noticed intentionally and establish a pattern. They stopped to eat although he was not particularly hungry. They lingered. She talked more about the Time industry and its workings. She went to every end to make sure everyone around them knew she was giving a tour. He asked a few polite questions, finished his meal, and followed her out of the Food Court.

"Another benefit of being a Time Agent is access to our Archives," Sifura explained. "It contains all information across the entire universe, completely at your disposal."

Now that was an outright lie. Even an idiot could see the

logical flaw in that one. At the same time, he pretended to be incredibly impressed, even as his heart thudded wildly in his chest. Sifura took him to one of the chip dispensers and showed him basically how they worked. Then they headed into the Archives themselves.

Even though Walter had been to the Archives a hundred times, he always found himself stunned at just how big the place was. It was as if every point on the Dewey Decimal system had been multiplied by a thousand, given its own library, multiplied by a thousand again, then multiplied yet again across the entire universe as all data and information ever collected from everywhere was compiled and stored in individual tablets. And he somehow had to narrow it down to one or two in a ten minute visit.

"I am very impressed so far," he began slowly, an idea forming in his mind. "However, as you know, my species is from another dimension. This place, this 'Wheel' seems to be adequate. But I would like to know more about the dimension from which so many of your clients come. If the Wheel proves to be an adequate bridge, my people may be able to open up new trade routes with other races."

"Of course," Sifura said, dipping her head graciously. "Follow me."

The life of James Bond was definitely not for him. She took him to the first section, the first row, explaining a little about how things worked, the chips and the tablets, how to open up a map and so on and so forth. It almost seemed childish, going through all the motions, getting a tour like he was some VIP here to check things out and make a decision before investing in a company, even as he already knew all the inner workings. But he dutifully listened and followed her to a platform which took them up, up, and still farther up. Then it was a small maze and half a marathon to get to the appropriate section.

"As a show of good faith, I will allow you fifteen to twenty Base Minutes of research time, in order to ensure your safety here and throughout your travels here and elsewhere. We wish no ill will upon our clients and want everyone to arrive home safely at the end of the day. However, access is normally reserved for Time Agents only, and we do have a tour to complete."

"I understand. It should only take a moment."

Walter badly wanted to Band, but knew he couldn't if he wanted to keep up the facade of a potential new client getting a tour. At the same time, maybe if he played on his own facade, he might come up with an answer. How would things be different for a species from a different dimension? What would he want to know?

Well, how would the physics be different, if at all? Was Time different there? Was it a different Base Time? Using the methods which Sifura "just showed" him on the tablet, he was able to identify a couple tablets which should have helpful information. As he was reaching for them, a Borelian appeared at the end of the row. Walter tried not to stop and stare and potentially give himself away, but a chill snaked down his spine as he envisioned being beaten, captured, and enslaved. The Borelian merely gave him a hard regard, but went away on its own. Walter breathed a sigh of relief as he got his tablets and looked for a spot to sit and skim over the information.

"Not everyone is friendly here, I see," he commented snootily.

"The Borelians are in the middle of a war," Sifura said coolly. "And this after being severely disciplined by the Hands of Time concerning their conduct as a race within the Time industry. The details are unimportant."

Walter grunted and sat down to turn on the tablet. Fifteen minutes. More than he was expecting, less than what he wanted or needed. He wanted at least six hours, needed probably four or five days. It wasn't just about finding the information; he had to apply it, too.

At the same time, though, he had found what he was looking for. Someone at some point had done a little research on the Land In Between and published their findings for the Time industry. It wasn't myths of fairy tales, but facts, data, and, as Walter discovered to his surprise, an anecdote from someone who claimed to have escaped the inescapable dimension.

As far as hard facts went, Time was useless in the in-between dimension, at least as far as the Time industry was concerned. It was too diluted, or so the author said. Apparently, the power needed to overcome the state of physical flux was fifty times greater than standard Time.

" 'Some claim such power can be found in the mythical power known as the Akari,' " Walter read quietly. " 'It is the opinion of this author that such power may exist, though it is unlikely that it is the Akari itself. However, it is worth more research to know what this power could be, given that the storyteller of the anecdote at the end of this dissertation was only a probationary Time Agent, while Warden Timekeepers and Intervention Harvesters have been known to vanish without the power to break out again.' "

So, the moral of the story was that Tommen was going to need one hell of an explosion in order to break out again. But first they had to know what he was trying to break through. He quickly scanned another tablet of information.

" 'The in-between dimension is, as its name suggests, a dimension between dimensions. As such, it exists in a state of flux, where one dimension must be the bridge between two or even more dimensions, thereby assimilating qualities of all dimensions involved. Because Energy is the barrier between all dimensions, it is constantly being used, though it remains constant within dimensions. This is because the in-between dimension also absorbs and dispels Energy as needed to open portals. Therefore, when one opens a portal, it is in fact being opened from the inside, that is the in-between dimension, not the outside, the dimension in which the opener resides.

" 'It must be noted, however, that such conventional doors, while opened from the in-between dimension, cannot be crossed through in such a way. This is because portals themselves are Energy vacuums and cannot be breached conventionally. It has been theorized that passing through a portal is similar to passing through an hourglass. The starting point and the destination are the bulbs at either end, the portal being the neck. Once one passes the neck of the hourglass, he is safe. However, if a grain of sand falls out through the neck, he cannot go back through the same way.

" ' There have been rumors of some who have in fact returned from the in-between dimension, but it is not known how. More research is required to further explore this phenomenon.' "

Immensely frustrated and quickly running out of time, Walter returned to the first tablet with the anecdote of someone who supposedly escaped. However, to his surprise and yet not-surprise, as well as a good amount of frustration, the storyteller said they could not recall how they escaped, only that they had. They said something about meeting a man called Lightning, and then some credit to the Author, whom the tablet author marked to disclaim that she was the deity of the Akari-bearers. Take it how you will.

"Research can be tiresome, even endless, when your resources are unlimited," Sifura said, cutting in on his thoughts. "If you wish to return, we can discuss the details later."

"Of course," Walter said, fighting to keep his teeth from grinding. He stood. "You have the right of it that proper research takes time, but all appears to be in order so far. Please, continue."

They went through one last puppet show of her showing him how to properly return the tablets before leaving the Archives. No one questioned them or gave them funny looks. They simply left and continued the tour. Sifura gave him a brief tour of the Judgment Wing, noting his great anxiety over being there. Then she showed him the Arena and, last but not least, the Coliseum, ahem, Amphitheater.

"A strange place to house your ruling leaders," Walter observed, sniffing.

"Perhaps," Sifura acknowledged, "but it suits our purposes and has many secrets of its own for any who dare to try trickery. The Hands of Time are always prepared."

He couldn't decide how to take her statement other than as a warning, saying the Hands were ready to move at any time against the Akarin. Well, first part definitely, second part speculatively. Surely the Hands had more things to worry about than the Akarin who were already in the first stages of civil war. There had to still be cleanup from Rifun's mess to deal with, right?

Their time spent in the Amphitheater was brief, but that was to be expected. In a world full of paranoia, even as the Hands feared the Akarin and what they could do, they probably had someone or multiple someones available who would be able to sniff them out in a crowd and could spot a Disguise across the field.

Sifura made some sort of exit speech as they returned to the portal room, but Walter couldn't remember for the life of him what she said. It was probably a nice speech about how the Time industry could greatly improve the lives of his people and if he had any questions, don't hesitate to call, and so on and so forth, the same as any sales gimmick. Walter was forced to wonder just how gullible the first humans had been when they got suckered into the Time industry.

"Are you returning with me?" Walter inquired as they approached the portal which would take them to the Durvin living room.

"I am not," Sifura answered. "I have duties to attend to here."

Her unspoken words were probably something along the lines of, *like coming up with a way to more firmly cement this disguise and alibi so no one comes snooping later on and this escapade doesn't bite us in the ass.* Still, he looked at her and asked, "So tell me honestly, why are you helping us when everyone else seems to want us dead?"

"A discussion for another time. Go."

He didn't need to be told twice, and he stepped through the portal without thinking. It was a terrible experience, and Micaiah had to help him into a recliner so he could rest a minute.

"Well, obviously you made it out alive," Micaiah said, sitting down in another recliner. "Did you find the answers we need?"

"I found something. Whether it's the answer we need remains to be seen." Walter rubbed his eyes and yawned. "A lot of it boiled down to a little data, a lot of speculation, and a whole lot of 'more research needs to be done to explore this phenomenon.'"

Micaiah grunted. "I was afraid you'd say that. Do you feel up to another portal trip?" Before Walter could answer, he stood and was already speaking. "Never mind. You know what, wait here, take a nap, take a load off for a minute. I'll get the others. We'll go back to the bakery, get all the vehicles, and come back here. Then you can tell us what you found before you go home."

Walter just waved him off dismissively. Micaiah could do whatever he wanted right now, as far as he was concerned. He was exhausted and really just wanted to go home and get some sleep. He felt like he hadn't made any real progress except to confirm that things in the Wheel were normal. The Borelians were pissed and at war, but that was nothing new. Everyone still feared them, sure, but without their Grandfather status, they were no more fearful than any other alien species. The Hands were pissed and ready to go to war, but it had to be a silent war. Things were going too well in the industry at large to want to cause a panic. If the Hands were going to move against the Akarin, they would do it quietly.

And as far as the in-between dimension was concerned, he didn't even know what he'd been expecting to find. Maybe a step-by-step instruction manual on how to rescue someone from said dimension? Instead, as he told Micaiah, all he got was a lot of I don't know and I need more research.

He figured he must have dozed off, even slept a little, because the next thing he knew, it was daylight and he was walking through the forest on the mountainside. It was late fall and while his dream self did not recognize the terrain, the present-day subconscious part of him said it looked familiar. It hit him just as he passed through a thick row of pines and the clearing opened up in front of him. The little cabin stood, sort and squat, the chickens scratching and pecking away around it. A little farther down the hill, a couple goats and sheep rummaged for the last greens before snow flew.

Then his brother was walking toward him, speaking. "Did you find my boy?" Walter stared at him dumbly. Teo said again, "Did you find him? Did you find my boy?"

Dream-Walter shook his head, feeling like he was himself in a dream. "Ah, no. No, I didn't find him."

"You were supposed to find my boy," Teo said harshly.

"I know. I tried."

"Teo?" Maisy asked from a short distance away. She approached, moving slowly under the weight of pregnancy. "Did he find him? Is Tommen safe?"

"He didn't find him," Teo said, looking at her. Turning his gaze back to Walter, he said coldly, "You didn't find him. I told you to find him or don't come back. Don't come back."

"I don't...I didn't...I mean..." Dream-Walter searched for words but found none.

"He's mine now, Walter."

Walter whirled to see Rifun standing behind him, blocking the trail through the pines. When he looked back, all people and animals had disappeared, but the cabin and all structures remained, the barn, fencing, all of it.

"He's mine."

Walter turned his attention back to Rifun, but the man hadn't moved.

"Do you have my son?" Walter asked, trying to keep his temper under control. He went on before Rifun could speak, making every word deliberate. "Just tell me if you have him, just so I know that he is...not wandering alone in the forest, sick and wounded."

"Interesting choice of words," Rifun mused, clasping his hands behind his back and starting on a slow walk toward Walter. "Of course, you can't bring yourself to say the word 'safe' seeing how you do not believe that he is safe with me. Personally, I don't blame you. However, it will interest you to know that while I do not physically have Tommen with me, I know exactly where he is. I know his every movement."

"You're not God."

"Perhaps not, but I do have friends. They're keeping an eye on him for me, waiting for him to break through the dimensional barrier. I do hope he can do it."

Walter elected to keep his mouth shut. Rifun had just leaked a very small but very important detail. If Tommen was stuck in the in-between dimension, Rifun had no more power over him than Walter. They were both locked in a waiting game, like horses waiting for the bell. Even if Rifun did have friends who could know where Tommen was at any given moment, it was all on him to get out.

"Nothing to say and yet you can see it in his eyes," Rifun said softly, almost a whisper, moving to stand in front of Walter so as to puff out little citrus breaths. "He's thinking. How much does he know? What power does he have? If Rifun taught my boy the power that got him into the dimension and was there to greet him when he got out, what need does he have for the Akarin, for Time, for any of it? Rifun is giving him everything he wants. In spite of everything this psychopath has done, he's still done more for my son than, well, me."

Something inside Walter snapped, then, like a caged beast breaking its chains and tearing through the bars of its cage. He took a swing at Rifun, getting in a good uppercut followed by a left hook before suddenly having both arms wrenched back and being thrown to the ground. The breath was driven from his lungs, but he hardly had time to process his predicament before being mercilessly tossed over onto his back. Rifun stood over him, spitting blood to the side and wiping a bloody lip. But he did not appear angry. Rather, he grinned. Walter had never felt such dread creep up on him.

"There's the Walter I was looking for. Strong, ferocious, the bestial need to survive. The one who laughs at rules and procedure and protocol and does whatever it takes."

"That Walter is dead," Walter told him, his voice strained as he tried to catch his breath.

Rifun shook his head. "Oh no. Not dead. Only dormant. Like the Hulk of the civilized world. But you can never control the beast within. It's part of you." He squatted down beside Walter. "And before this war is over, I'm going to make sure everyone sees it, especially your beloved little boy."

Walter might have tried to make another go at Rifun, but the next thing he knew, he was flying through the air, as if hit by a train.

He went sailing through trees, then pine boughs, until they grew thick and the darkness closed in.

Suddenly he was coming awake, on the floor before he could stop himself. His whole body jerked as his mind tried to connect everything and tell himself it wasn't real. There was no danger here. Still, when he finally got to a knee, Kayla and the twins were a good four feet from him, staring.

"Are you okay?" Micah wondered.

Walter took a breath and nodded. "Yeah. I'm fine. Just a dream."

"One hell of a dream," Kayla mused. "You need something? Hot tea?"

"No, no, I'm fine." He got back in the recliner. "Thank you, though."

Micaiah moved slowly toward the other recliner. "If you're sure. You think you're all right to—?"

"I'm fine," Walter insisted. "Besides, if my sleep is that bad, you don't need me keeping you up all night when you have to be at the bakery early. Now then, do you want to hear the report or not?"

The trio still seemed uncertain, but got themselves situated here and there. Kayla sat on the couch and Micaiah moved beside her while Micah took his place in the second recliner. Still half-expecting Rifun to walk into the room at any minute, Walter began his report, telling himself to deliver everything police-style, exactly as if he were reporting to Steggmann.

Of course, he never told Steggmann about portals to other dimensions, aliens, intergalactic wars, interdimensional holy wars, or anything like that. As it was, though, his report was pretty bland. While he'd certainly been aware of the bounty on his head, nothing about the Wheel or Time industry at large had seemed off, certainly not like it had been around election time. Everything seemed to operate smoothly and Time Agents went about their daily lives as normal. Grandfathers didn't pop up in random places to bind and gag those suspected of being Akari-bearers, and Borelians didn't roam the marketplaces in packs looking for humans to pick off. Humans were hardly a blip on the Time industry's radar, and their absence wasn't even a ripple in the pond.

"Well, the news is both good and bad," Kayla said when Walter was finished. "On the one hand, if the Time industry really is moving that smoothly, it's one less thing we have to worry about. But on that same note, as a unified force, who knows what they could do when they make their move against the Akarin?"

"What about your research in the Archives?" Micaiah asked. "Were you able to come up with anything at all?"

Walter recounted his findings, slim though they were.

"The hourglass analogy is interesting," Micah mused.

"It is, but describing the problem in basic, three-dimensional terms isn't going to help us solve it in four-dimensional ways," Micaiah said. "We need to add another layer to this. Okay, physics are different where Tommen is. We have to think in those terms."

"How are we supposed to do that?"

Kayla ran her tongue over her teeth. "My love."

Micaiah rubbed his eyes. "Yes?"

"You know that equation you use to convert the Wheel calendar to Earth calendar, and vice versa?"

"Very well, though I wish I didn't. Why?"

"And you remember when you tried to help Walter in the warehouse but you couldn't because Rifun had turned it into a quasi-dimension?"

"Yes, I remember that, too, though I wish I didn't. Why do you ask?"

"What if there was a way to combine them? Modify the equation in order to fit a quasi-dimension?"

Micah shifted in his seat. "Kayla, one is a calendar conversion. The other is, as you said, a quasi-dimension. That's like trying to use a temperature converter to measure speed."

"Okay, fine, but what other equations are there between dimensions? Is there anything we can use?"

Micaiah yawned. "We can look that up the next time we go to the Archives. Right now, frankly, I'm exhausted."

"Agreed," Walter said reluctantly. "Maybe some sleep is just what the doctor ordered. Then we can all think more clearly tomorrow."

He hated admitting it, and he hated saying it even more. He wanted to go, do, search, anything but sit around and go to bed like any ordinary night. But his mind and body demanded rest. He wasn't sure how much sleep he would actually get, seeing how Rifun's nightmare was still lingering there in the dark corners of his mind.

But the others agreed and soon they were meandering their separate ways, preparing for bed. Walter headed home, unsure of what to make of the last three hours, plus his time in the Wheel. Somehow it just felt like they were all spinning their wheels, gathering a ton of useless information like aimless vacuums, but unable to pick up anything of substance that would help them rescue his son. They had tiny morsels of useful stuff wrapped up in a whole bunch of myths, legends, and speculations. Even now, he couldn't decide whether his nightmare had been his own overactive imagination, or if Rifun really had been there. He hated to think of what could happen if that had been real. He refused to think about it.

By the time he arrived home, he really could have just fallen asleep there in the driver's seat. Just leaned the seat back, closed his eyes, and he would have been out. After a minute or two, he got out of the car and moseyed his way into the house. He'd no sooner shut the door than his phone rang, and he instinctively reached for his gun which was not there. Then he calmed down and pulled out his phone. The caller ID said Tommen.

"Hello?" he answered cautiously, heading into the living room.

"Dad?" Tommen said.

"Tommen!" Walter almost went to his knees, but managed to make it to his recliner. "Oh my God, is it you?"

"Yeah, it's me." He could hear the waver in his son's voice.

"Are you—? Did you escape?"

"No, not yet. I'm sitting in my room." He laughed nervously. "I kind of broke into a few stores tonight and stole some military-grade hardware so I could build a signal booster for my phone."

"Well, I won't tell if you won't."

"Deal." Tommen took a level breath. "Did you guys find anything? What have you been doing?"

So Walter once again recounted his adventures of the night, trying to include as much information as possible. It might be useless to them, but Tommen might find some of it useful on his end.

"So you went undercover in the Wheel?" Tommen asked. "That is so cool."

"Yeah, well, undercover work isn't for me, I can tell you that. Also, Sifura sends her greetings."

"Cool. Is she, like, on our side, or what?"

"I don't know. A later discussion, is all she said."

"Well, that would make sense."

There was a long pause. Then, "How are you holding up, Tommen?"

He sighed. "I miss you. I miss Becky. I miss the twins. I miss being seen. But at least I got this far, so we can talk to each other."

Walter nodded unnecessarily. "Yeah, that's a good start. How are you physically? How's your arm?"

"It hurts. Like a lot. I have a headache, and my stomach isn't too happy about all the food I've eaten tonight either. My kidneys hurt. I only notice those three things, though, when I manage to get my arm in a position that it isn't kicking my ass with every movement."

"Make sure you get lots of fluids," Walter told him. "That should help your kidneys. And take it easy on the food. If your body is sending all its resources to heal your arm, the last thing it wants is an overload of food to digest. As for your arm...I don't know. It sounds like you're doing everything you can, but I'm not a doctor and you're not a doctor." He sighed. "We're coming, kiddo. It's taking a lot longer than anyone hoped, but we're coming. And it sounds like you haven't been idle either." He took a calming breath. "It's good to hear your voice."

"You too, Dad. I'm doing what I can from here."

"I bet you are. Listen, tomorrow is probably going to be another trip to the Archives. Kayla had another idea that we'll be looking into while she's getting help from the Krydik if she can. We're going to do everything we can, but it sounds like most of the effort is going to be on your end."

"Okay. Listen, you sound tired, and I'm tired, too," Tommen said. "Um, why don't we both get some sleep? Maybe we can talk again in the morning."

Walter nodded again. "I'd like that. I'll talk to you tomorrow, then, kiddo."

He hung up, then, and might have cried if he wasn't worried about his invisible teenage son seeing him. After a minute or two of staring blankly at the wall, Walter got out of his recliner and headed for bed.

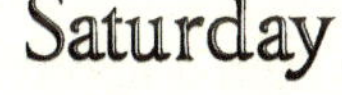

Chapter Seventeen
Breaking Barriers

Micah rolled over in bed, momentarily confused by how good he felt and how not startled he was by an alarm clock. For a moment, then, panic seized him as he leapt out of bed, convinced he was late for work. His frenzy lasted about until he reached the door of his bedroom when it dawned on him that Micaiah had given him the day off. Whole day. Completely to himself. No second shift, no closing, nothing. He would not see the bakery today. A real day off.

Of course, it dawned on him, as he returned to his bed to relax, that he had no idea what he was going to do with his day off. Sleeping in he'd already done, but sleeping any more was clearly out of the question. Was there anything major and pressing he had to get done? Shopping, banking, anything at all? He searched through his brain, but couldn't come up with anything. He tried to think over his last time at work and how often he'd wished he'd been somewhere else doing something else. Oddly enough, nothing came to mind. Well, things did come to mind, but none of them seemed important now that he actually had the time and ability to accomplish them.

He figured he must have gotten a little more sleep, because by the time he finally dragged himself out of bed and into the bathroom, it was a little past ten o'clock. Micaiah was at the shop and Kayla was gone, which meant he had he whole house to himself. He could do whatever he wanted, watch TV, make food, loaf in bed, walk around naked if he really wanted to.

Well, maybe not that last part, he figured, pulling his shirt on and heading out to the kitchen to scrounge up some food. He opened the fridge door and sighed. Kayla's presence was very much in evidence. It wasn't that she'd replaced all the sausage with kale and olive oil. Actually, it was more in the opposite direction. Their store-bought ham and beef and sausage had been replaced with raccoon, bear, and even porcupine. Chicken had turned into wild duck and woodcock, scrawny though they were. Store-bought vegetables, while there were still a few, had been greatly supplemented with wild greens and other foraged goods. Kayla was an interior designer, true, but she'd never lost sight of her roots.

That wasn't to say Micah didn't like the food. Actually, he was quite a fan of the bear sausage as he took that and cooked it up with some eggs and hashbrowns and bacon. He made sure to keep an eye on his food; who knew where Tommen was lurking, ready to swipe food from unsuspecting people? Listening to Walter's fish story was amusing, but now that he sat there with his own plate of delicious food, he found himself on high alert. Invisible enemies were bad. Invisible friends could be worse. An enemy would only kill him. A friend would steal his food and laugh about it.

On the one hand, Micah knew that he should probably go to the Archives to continue researching how to free Tommen from the in-between dimension. On the other hand, he was tired of looking at fairy tales and what ifs, feeling like he was just spinning his wheels and wasting time. It wasn't that he was giving up or didn't want to help Tommen, but there had to be another way. They had to be missing something. Something obvious.

After finishing off his breakfast and washing his dishes, Micah headed downstairs to the basement. Aside from having to do laundry—because Kayla only tended to hers and Micaiah's, not usually his—he did occasionally workout. He said occasionally because for one, he wasn't a health nut. He got up early enough as it was; he didn't need to wake up an hour earlier just so he could go lift fifty pounds on the bar before going to work to lift fifty pounds of flour. And for two, Micaiah could be a bit of a stickler when it came to his gym equipment. Everything had to be just so. Micah could understand putting everything back and leaving it the way he found it, but how Micaiah could know when he'd used the stuff after he'd made sure to clean up was beyond him.

Didn't matter, he supposed, starting out on an easy walk on the treadmill. He was careful not to break anything or hurt himself. He did what he was comfortable with, maybe got a little ambitious on the weights or the runs every so often, but otherwise, it was a comfortable routine rather than an aggressive one. He would leave that to his brother.

But, once he was finished and had cleaned up and taken a shower, he was right back to where he started when he got up. He had a day off and didn't know what to do with himself. Well, it looked like a nice day outside. Might as well enjoy it a little.

His original intent was to go for a nice walk up the road to where the pavement ended and the shady two-track began. That idea got squashed three steps from the front door. He'd just gone for a walk on the treadmill. It wasn't that fresh air wouldn't do him some good every once in a while, but he was no health nut. He didn't need to kill himself on a second walk. The thing about going on walks was that even if he did kill himself getting to the two-track, he still had to walk back home.

So instead he got in his car and headed toward the city, veering off before getting to Charleston proper and arriving a short time later in a scenic overlook park. Being the end of summer, a weekend, and a nice day, there were quite a few cars and trucks and RVs crowding the small lot. Most people were there to stretch their legs and take quick pictures of the view before continuing on their way. A few were families having nice little picnics, trying to keep the kids entertained on a long ride. Only one or two took advantage of the handful of trails that led even higher up to an even better view. Despite his earlier misgivings about going for a walk, Micah elected to take a small hike up one such trail to get to a nicer, quieter view.

He regretted his decision about halfway up, but figured he might as well see it through. But when he got to the top lookout point, he was sorely rewarded with a view of, for the most part, trees. Thirty years ago, the view had probably been spectacular, looking out across Charleston and the river and the valley beyond. Now, though, the forest had grown up and mostly obscured everything. No wonder no one used the trails anymore.

Apparently the group of friends standing on the platform thought the same thing as they griped and complained and carried on. Despite the sign telling people to respect the land and not climb over the fence, a couple of the kids climbed over anyway, pushing their way through the trees for that elusive photo that would make all their internet friends jealous. Few apparently found this elusive creature, as they ultimately returned empty-handed, still complaining about the poor view. Personally, Micah wondered how they had expected to find a spot above the trees by going below them in the first place, but what did he know, anyway?

"How are we supposed to get through that, dude?" one asked as they gathered their things. "I mean there's fucking trees in the way."

"Someone needs to cut that shit down," another agreed.

"I was really hoping for a cool photo for my Instagram," one girl lamented woefully.

Unlike his older brother, Micah was usually a little better about hiding his expressions, at least until the other party wasn't looking. So it was that he kept his expression neutral until the little party of teeny boppers passed by before relaxing his stance and rolling his eyes. Some days he wondered what had become of the world. People said World War II had been Hell, and it certainly had been, for the time. But as time went on, Micah was forced to wonder if World War II had only just been the gateway to something much worse. Jeez, he sounded like Walter now, having philosophical arguments with himself and contemplating shit like that. Maybe he needed to retire from Time, too.

He did his own little disappointed sweep of the blocked view before turning and preparing himself for the hike back down.

"Hey, I know you."

Micah froze and Banded until he could locate the source of his stalker. He couldn't say he recognized the woman, but that didn't mean much. They got a lot of people in at the shop. He released the Band.

"You're one of the brothers from that Irish bakery," she went on.

As far as women went, she wasn't drop-dead gorgeous, but he would do her. Date. Date her. He would date her. Do her. Fuck.

"Ah, yes," he said awkwardly. "Yes, I am."

"Your brother let you off the oar, huh?"

"He offered, so I figured I better take it before he changed his mind. Unfortunately—" He looked back at the trees. "—I think my effort was wasted."

She waved a hand. "Nah. If you've got all day, there are tons of views to be had. I make the rounds to get my exercise. I'm just finishing up, actually. I pick here last because there aren't usually too many people up here."

"Nope. Just us chickens."

"I mean, they really should do something about the trees in the way, but, not my call." She shrugged. "Anyway, I'll see you later at some point, I'm sure."

So she continued her little jog around the top platform and disappeared back down the hill. A moment later, Micah followed. In ten years, one might think he'd gotten used to people picking him out in a crowd. But, given the goings-on in the Wheel and the fortress lately, it just made him a little jumpy.

He returned to his car and got in, unsure what to do next. Maybe he should do a little research, or at least pretend to. If he did that, then he would invariably think of something else he wanted to be doing, which would give him a course of action and a way to spend the rest of his day off. He started the car and looked back up the hill where the higher overlook should have been, mildly wishing the trees really wouldn't have been in the way.

Suddenly, he slammed his brakes, narrowly avoiding one of the young people who had jumped the fence up at the top. He was chasing a Frisbee or something and had jumped right behind Micah's moving car. Micah gave the kid a nasty look. Once the kid had slunk away, Micah continued on his way, slamming his brakes again as some idiot who didn't know how to drive an RV recklessly cut the corner on his way into the little parking lot.

I need to get out of here, Micah thought. *Freedom is dangerous.*

He got about a mile down the road when a new thought occurred to him. He Banded and mulled it over for a minute or two before making quite possibly the worst decision of his day: he made the turn that would take him into the city, that is, to the bakery. He was kicking himself the whole way, but his idea drove him forward as much as he drove the car. Besides, he wasn't really going in to work, he was just going to present an idea that could save a mutual friend. Then, once that friend was saved, he would feel less guilty about loafing around the house.

Well, it sounded good to him, anyway. He sure as hell wasn't going to let Micaiah talk him into working the afternoon. The only way he was going to work was if his brother's other leg spontaneously fell off, and he didn't see that happening. Great, now he just jinxed himself. And screwed his brother.

When he arrived at the bakery, he did not park in back in the employee parking, at least, not right away. It was lunch rush, and he wasn't going to get suckered into working as an extra hand. No, no, he would sit and wait for the dining room to clear out. Looked like Kyle was working the counter while Jenna stayed in the back. It seemed to be the only suitable working arrangement, given that Kyle was Suppressed and the two of them hated each other with passionate loathing normally only found in soap operas and teenage dramas.

So Micah sat in his car and waited. He didn't wait very long before getting out and walking down to a little Chinese restaurant for a bite to eat. When he returned, the line was beginning to noticeably dissipate as people got their orders and left and ten more people did not join the line behind them. Micah had just finished off his chicken when his phone buzzed. It was Micaiah.

"Okay, dumbfuck. Kyle says you've been hiding out there for a while. Crowd's gone so it's safe to come in."

Micah couldn't help but laugh as he put his phone away and went inside the bakery. He gave Kyle a look and the teenager blushed hard.

"Snitch," Micah said.

Kyle just turned an even darker shade of red as Micah headed into the office and shut the door behind him.

"Well, obviously you're not here to volunteer yourself on a day off," Micaiah said, spinning around in his chair. "So why are you here? I thought I told you to get lost."

"You did, but I'm the annoying younger brother who doesn't care what my older brother tells me to do or not do," Micah informed him smartly.

"That much is true, but the point remains. Why are you here? What happened?"

"I had an idea about how to get Tommen out of the in-between dimension. I wanted to run it by you first before wasting a bunch of time in the Archives looking for more."

Micaiah folded his arms. "Sounds like a backwards plan to me, but let's hear your idea."

"So far, we've been trying to find ways to overpower the Energy barrier, right? How much power is in it, how much can he generate, what does that look like, what does that take, all of that. But if the Energy in the surrounding dimensions is fairly constant, and the excess Energy from portals is absorbed into that dimension in order to keep it constant, I think it's safe to say that we are never going to overpower that barrier because that barrier is constantly sucking up Energy like a sponge."

"Okay. I follow. Go on."

"We can't overpower it. But what if we tried to drain it instead? If Energy sucked Tommen into the dimension, what if we did the same thing in reverse? Take a shit ton of Energy out of the dimension, bring it here, dump him out, send the Energy back into the dimension. Like a rubber band. Okay, if portals are Energy vacuums, and the dimension is an Energy sponge, what do you think would happen if we tried to open a portal—or even have Tommen open a portal, or meet him halfway—what if we opened a portal around him? Mark a line in the sand, have him stand there, and open a portal right there. Vacuum meets sponge."

Micaiah was silent for a long moment as he turned the idea over in his mind. Then, "How do we know it wouldn't electrocute him on the spot? If he gets shocked just from touching an open portal—"

"That's because he is still touching it from the outside, the buildup of Energy around the portal. This would be opening a portal directly around him."

Micah found a seat and sat down as his brother shifted position and said, "Essentially, what you are proposing is an EMP. Disable the Energy barrier long enough in a concentrated area and pull Tommen through."

"Exactly."

Micaiah nodded. "I like it. I like your theory. But I don't want to test it on Tommen straight out. If your theory is correct, we should be able to try it on smaller objects first."

"I was thinking the same thing," Micah agreed. "And I was going to head to the Archives to see if I can't find anything else on this. Granted, not on the whole dimensional thing, but on Energy and EMPs in general."

"Do it. Once you find something, let me know. We'll contact Walter and have him communicate the plan to Tommen."

"You got it, boss." Micah stood.

"Oh, and one more thing."

"What's that?"

Micaiah sighed dramatically. "I'm afraid I'm going to have to put an official reprimand on your personnel files."

"For what?"

"Failing to follow directions. Today was supposed to be your day off."

"Oh." Micah shrugged. "If my plan works, you can give me the week off as punishment."

"And two weeks if it doesn't." Micaiah paused and ran his tongue over his teeth. "Maybe switch those two around. Can't have you getting too comfortable."

"Of course not."

"Get back to work."

Micah smirked. "I'm on vacation. You get back to work."

Nevertheless, he opened a portal to the fortress and stepped through. He'd never been completely comfortable going to the fortress alone, especially since one of the council members had been murdered. If rumors were to be believed, Micaiah was the favorite suspect even as more and more council members had either been threatened or else feared for their lives. It was not a good time to be an Akarin, and even worse to be on the council. Micah fared little better as, being a twin, he was sometimes mistaken for Micaiah, despite him having both legs. *Seriously, people, even if you don't understand humans, at least tell me you can spot that difference.*

But he made it to the Archives unmolested. The attendant hardly paid any attention to him as he started up and down the aisles, looking for anything on Energy. Of course, that was a broad term, but he wasn't entirely sure how to narrow it down. How to negate Energy? How to drain Energy? How to break through the Energy barrier that separated dimensions in order to rescue someone from the Land In Between from which no one had ever returned?

The best he could find to start was a very elementary book on using the Akari and the basic properties of the universe. Yeah, because they taught that in grade school.

The book focused on those who had been exposed to Time and the Akari, but had no training; they weren't coming in as a Master Timekeeper convert, but a regular person. Micah might have hoped that a simple explanation of things would shed some light on the more complex matters they were facing, but he would have been wrong in that regard. Everything was just as difficult as it was before, no mind-blowing revelations here.

He leaned back in the chair and rubbed his eyes, tried to think of this objectively. Essentially, they were facing the Red Sea and had to come up with a way to make it part so they could see the dry land and, in this instance, pull Tommen out of the water. Sounded great on paper, but Micah had his doubts that God was going to tear open the dimensions and upset the Energy balance of the universe. Fucking hell, they sounded New Age-y.

So, how did Moses part the Red Sea when God sat back and said, "I'm having no part of this"? At the same time, who said that God wouldn't intervene miraculously? Micah ran his tongue over his teeth. This was getting more philosophical than he wanted. It was only supposed to be an analogy, not an existential crisis.

Okay, fine. So maybe skip the Moses theme and go for something smaller. Part the water in the bathtub in order to retrieve a lost bath toy. Now that just sounded corny.

He ran his hand through his hair and groaned. Three days of this shit and he was going insane. They all were. It wasn't only that they wanted to get Tommen back, but they didn't want to admit defeat. Actually losing Tommen was one thing. Death was tragic and unfortunate, but it was acceptable. Losing him to a parasitic dimension where he would still be very much alive, that was entirely unacceptable. That was prisoner of war level.

With nothing to show for his efforts, Micah stood and reluctantly plodded back to the portal room, still feeling defeated. As he descended the stairs to the main floor, he had a brief thought that someone ought to be documenting everything they were doing so that the next poor soul who got caught in the in-between dimension would have some kind of roadmap to follow to be rescued. If it was true that there was a survivor out there in the universe somewhere, and they didn't have an answer or refused to give it up, well, he or she was an asshole.

"Find anything?" Micaiah asked as Micah returned to the office.

"I didn't even know what I was looking for, so I couldn't say if I found it," Micah confessed.

"Believe me, I understand. What are you going to do now?"

Micah rubbed his eyes. "I'm thinking I might go over to see Walter and tell him the plan anyway, see if he can get a message to Tommen and explain things. If we try it on a small object first and it works, maybe we'll have a better idea of what's going on and how to proceed."

"Go for it. And let me know how it goes. Kayla sent a message to Natalie and they're going to Hlohi tonight to meet with the elders there. If she doesn't have to go, I need to let her know as soon as possible."

"Because you don't want your wife fucked up on hallucinogenic fruit?"

"Exactly. Now then, if you're going to do it, go do it."

"Thought I was on vacation?"

"You're the one who decided to work."

Micaiah made a shooing motion with his hands. Micah grinned, shook his head, but stood and left the bakery after a brief intervention in a brewing argument between Kyle and Jenna. Damn it. If Micaiah weren't leaving and Micah wouldn't need the help, he would fire those two. Maybe he still should.

He didn't leave right away once he got in his car; instead he called up Walter. He wasn't even sure if the man was home or if he was still making a show of it by going back up to Wellspring with the search crews.

"You're late," Walter said right off the bat.

"Late?" Micah wondered.

"I would have expected a call or visit hours ago."

"Um...sorry? I was just calling to make sure you're home."

"Yes, I'm home. We both are, if that's what you're really asking."

"Great. I have an idea I want to try."

"We'll be here."

Micah hung up and started the car. As he pulled into traffic, he mulled over their short conversation. Walter had been excited, but edgy, a taut rubber band ready to fire. No doubt he was as anxious as the rest of them. Micah didn't blame him, but any deviation from his normal, cool demeanor never boded well for others involved.

He made it to Walter's house no worse for wear. From what he could see, everything appeared normal. Nothing was on fire. When he went inside, nothing was on fire, furniture and food wasn't strewn about haphazardly. Walter was clean, not a wild-eyed, unkempt mad hermit wearing only a loincloth and a tin foil hat. But he still appeared anxious, even as he sat in his recliner and spoke on the phone.

"Oh, yes, Micah's here," he was saying. "Hang on."

He stood and looked at his phone, squinting until he found the button he was looking for. Smart phones really weren't designed for people with large fingers and poor eyesight.

"You're on speaker," Walter said.

"Micah? Are you there?"

"Tommen?!" Micah blurted. "Is that you?"

Tommen chuckled. "Yeah, just barely. I'm in lying on my bed right now."

"You don't sound right. Are you sick?"

"I don't know, man. I feel kind of like I did when I first woke up here: sick to my stomach, achy, dizzy. My arm hurts like fuck and peeing is a bitch."

"That's not good. You could have sustained internal damage from the explosion, or it could be a reaction to the burns as your body heals."

"Tell me something I don't know. You have a way out?"

"I have a theory. It might be helped if I knew how the hell I'm talking to you."

Micah sat on the couch and listened patiently as Tommen described a pretty wild night, with the main event being a breaking and entering into an electronics repair shop and the theft of quite a bit of military-grade equipment which was allowing him to talk on the phone. It sounded like it wasn't so much overpowering the Energy barrier as riding with it, finding a frequency and working through it. Well, that was one thought, anyway. No one could be a hundred percent sure of anything at the moment.

"So, what do you think?" Tommen asked as he finished up, sounding like he was fighting a yawn. "Did anything spark an idea or help you out any?"

"Well, no," Micah admitted. "But it's good to know, anyway, in case this idea doesn't work."

"Okay, so what's your idea? How are we going to overpower this barrier?"

"We're not going to overpower it. We're going to drain it."

"What do you mean, drain it?" The poor kid sounded exhausted.

Micah explained his plan as best he could, trying not to sound like the know-it-all kid from the science fair who didn't actually know jack shit, but could toss around a word salad of terms in order to make himself look smart.

"It would certainly be a different approach," Walter commented when he was finished. "What do you think, Tommen?"

"Better than anything I've got."

"Before we try it on you, I want to try it on something else, something small."

"Makes sense," Tommen murmured. "And I've got just the thing to try."

"All right," Walter said. "We're coming in."

They went down to Tommen's room. Just from talking on the phone with him, even knowing the situation, Micah still fully expected to open the door and find the beanpole relaxing on his bed. It was almost a surprise when he wasn't.

"What do you got for us, Tommen?" Micah asked.

"On the corner of the desk—"

"Which corner?" Walter cut in. "If it's going to be a lot of power in a small space, the smaller the space, the more power."

"Front corner nearest the door," Tommen clarified. "It's a book.

Try that first."

"Got it."

Micah wasn't sure how to begin, actually. Was it really just like opening a portal? Did he have to be touching the spot where he believed the book to be? Was there an instruction manual on how to do this?

"Here?" he asked uncertainly, placing his hand on the corner of the desk.

"Yeah," Tommen confirmed.

Micah let out a breath. "Well, here goes nothing."

He opened a portal, intending it to be small and safe, leading to the Akarin fortress. Opening portals on a good day was a monumental task, but this time around, it seemed to sense what he was trying to do, reaching into the in-between dimension to pull something out. It was a bit like watching a front impact test on a new car. Car goes full tilt toward a solid wall and crumples spectacularly. That was about how this was. Or maybe more like running straight into a lance and having it skewer him like a shish kabob.

And yet, for a moment, he could see the book. It was more than a book; it was a very familiar leather-bound journal. Micah made a small motion. Taking the hint, Walter reached for the book and grabbed it. As soon as he did, it was like the portal collapsed and produced a small shockwave, sending both Micah and Walter to the ground on their asses, stunned. After a minute, Micah stood and helped Walter up.

"We got it," Walter said, holding up the journal. He bent to retrieve his phone. "Tommen?"

Apparently the connection had been lost as, a moment later, his phone rang with Tommen on the other end.

"You got it?" Tommen asked.

"We did. How was that on your end?"

"Like a small earthquake."

"Are you all right?"

"No worse than I was before, I guess."

Walter hesitated half a second. "Do you want to try it on yourself next? Obviously we don't know what's going to happen, but it sounds like you seriously need to see a doctor."

"This I know, trust me. And I really don't think that you guys can do me any worse."

"Don't say that," Micah said, only half-joking. "Things can always get worse."

"Well, I'd rather die in the attempt than live out my days in this shitty half-isolation. And if I get much worse, whatever is wrong with me, my days may be shorter rather than longer."

"All right, let's try it out," Walter decidedly quickly. "Where are you exactly?"

"Sitting up on the edge of the bed at the end, facing the door. Is there anything I can do on my end that might make it easier or smoother?"

Micah sighed. "Do you know how to open portals or meet them halfway?"

"Nope. The only portal I've ever opened landed me here and I don't know how."

"That's all right," Walter told him. "Then you just hang tight and let us do all the work. Sometimes the biggest help is not helping."

"Okay. Well, wait a second and I'll get some of my shit together so we're not doing a bunch of small portals trying to get my stuff."

"Will do. And, hey, one last thing before you hang up. Be ready to grab onto me and jump through. No waiting, no hesitating; you see the opening, you take it. Got it?"

"Got it. All right, see you in a second."

He hung up and everything was silent. Micah was almost forced to question his own sanity. Were they really talking to Tommen in this room but not in this dimension, or were they a couple of crazies talking to thin air? Some days it was hard to tell the difference.

"He never did say how long it was going to be or how he was going to indicate when he was ready," Micah said thoughtfully.

A minute later, Walter's phone rang.

"I heard that," Tommen said. "I think I've got everything. When I hang up, I'm going to count to thirty and then I'll be at the end of the bed, same as before. I'm ready."

"All right," Walter said. "We'll hold you to that."

Click.

One, two, three...

Truth be told, Micah was not looking forward to opening up another portal like that. Sponges and vacuums didn't get along; that much he'd learned.

Ten, eleven, twelve...

Maybe it would be a little better this time since Walter was going to be helping to shoulder the burden. Twice the power to try and break Tommen free, twice the stability to shoulder the weight and keep the portal open as long as possible to get him through, and it probably wasn't going to be a pleasant ride for any of them.

Twenty-two, twenty-three, twenty-four...

"Are you ready?" Walter asked.

Micah nodded. "I'll open the main portal; you do what you can to keep it open and pull Tommen through. Just grab and go."

Twenty-nine, thirty.

Standing in front of the spot where he believed Tommen to be, Micah opened a portal. Rather, he attempted to open a portal. The backlash from trying to get the journal was like taking a spear in the gut. This was far worse. It put Micah in mind of old cartoons where the coyote saw the light at the end of the tunnel but was promptly hit by a train and carried off. It was like having CPR involuntarily worked on him, the way his heart and lungs seemed to compress with no hope of restarting. His head was split open with an ax of a migraine, and he nearly dropped the portal right then and there.

Then he felt Walter's strength flowing into the portal, like adding wooden supports to an old mine. Some of the load was lifted. Micah hadn't realized that he'd involuntarily hunched over from the surprise and the weight of the portal. When he looked up, he saw

Tommen. The kid looked haggard, pale and sickly, even more than usual, anyway. His left arm was bandaged but the burns extended up his neck to his ear.

"Walter!" Micah gasped. "Grab him!"

Even as he spoke, Walter took a weary step forward, evidently just as surprised and tired. He reached for Tommen and the father and son clasped wrists. But rather than pulling him out, it was almost as if the dimension itself fought to pull Walter in. Micah felt the pull as well. He could see Tommen's grip tightening on his dad's wrist, but neither of them seemed able to move or do anything.

"Get him out," Micah growled. "I can't hold it."

"Come on, Tommen," Walter huffed, looking strained, like trying to pull a truck with no wheels.

"I'm trying," Tommen said, his voice hardly more than a squeak. "It's like something is holding me back. I can't move."

"Slipping," Micah interrupted.

Walter threw in one last burst of strength and pulled on Tommen for all he was worth, but it was like Walter's hand or Tommen's arm was greased. The grip slipped and both of them stumbled backwards. At that moment, Walter's strength failed and Micah lost control of the portal. It snapped shut with all the comfort of a small bomb, sending a shockwave through the room once more. Trinkets rattled and fell off the bookshelves, and there was some rattling out in the kitchen also.

When Micah finally blinked back to lucidity, he wasn't sure how much time had passed, though he figured it couldn't have been long, given how crummy he was still feeling. He took a quick personal inventory and determined that nothing was broken, though he might have a few bruises here and there. As he sat up, the world began to spin, and it was a moment before he could pull himself to a sitting position there in the doorway of Tommen's bedroom. Three feet away, Walter was already awake, though hunched over on one knee, looking confused and not a little tired.

"You okay?" Walter asked softly, not looking at him.

Micah nodded cautiously. "Yeah. I think I'll be all right. You?"

It was a moment before he answered, sighing and saying, "I lost him. I had him, but I couldn't pull him out."

"Hey now. Don't go talking like that." Micah weakly crawled over beside Walter, pulled his legs under him to get on his knees, and put a hand on his Captain's shoulder. "You saw him. You had him. Now, we don't know what the hell that was that was beating back on us or stopping us or holding him in. We don't know. But now that we know that it is physically there, we can anticipate it."

Walter let out a slow breath. "I can't do that again right away."

Micah chuckled. "I know, neither can I. But like I said, now we know. Maybe if we grab Micaiah and a few others, try it again later, it might be enough to break him free." Grudgingly, he got to his feet. "Come on. Why don't we grab something to eat and relax a few minutes before doing anything else?"

"He hasn't called yet."

"Walt, if Tommen experiences a greater impact on his side from the shockwave or earthquake or whatever, he might still be unconscious. I know you don't want to think about that, but it's the most likely thing, I think, given the circumstances and what we know. I'm sure that when he comes around, he'll probably take a few minutes to rest and recover, like we should be doing. Then he'll call. All right? Come on."

It was a moment or two before Walter was able to get to his feet. Even then he went for his recliner, not the kitchen. Micah found some bread and peanut butter and made up a couple of sandwiches for them.

"I keep trying to lose weight, but between you and Laura, I don't think it's going to happen," Walter grumbled, taking the food.

"Walt. It's a peanut butter sandwich. You're not going to add a pant size from it."

"You might not, but I will."

"I find that highly unlikely."

Walter shook his head. "What the hell was that thing? If I felt it,

I know for sure you felt it."

Micah shrugged. "I don't know. It's the first time I've ever done anything like that."

"And why doesn't it happen more often? Why has it never happened before, in all the hundreds and thousands of portals we've made and gone through?"

"Walt, I wish I knew. Maybe when Tommen calls back, he can tell us. Who knows? Maybe it's not a physical thing, but just a byproduct of us trying to outwit the dimensional differential."

"Did you just make that up?"

"Yes."

"Well, sounds as good as anything I've got."

"Point is, we know about it now. Like I said, next time, we can grab a few others to shoulder the weight and add some extra strength. You had him, Walter. You did. You just...couldn't help me and him at the same time. Next time, we'll open the portal and you will be solely in charge of grabbing him. All right?"

Walter hesitated but nodded. "I don't think that's going to be right away, though."

"I don't either," Micah agreed as he stood. "But now we have a plan. When Tommen calls, you can tell him everything from our end, he can tell you everything from his end. Knowledge is power and all that."

"Where are you going?"

"To let Micaiah know what happened. Maybe one of his fairy tales told him something useful about it."

Walter just grunted. Micah still washed the dishes before he left, never being one for letting dishes sit in the sink for very long. Then he was on his way back to the bakery. It was almost surreal to think that it had been less than an hour since he was there last. With everything that had happened, it might as well have been two days. Still, the place wasn't busy, and Micah walked in unopposed.

"Did you tell him I'm back?" he asked Kyle as he slipped around the counter.

"No, sir," Kyle answered uncertainly. "Did you want me to?"

"Nope."

Micaiah was just getting off the phone when Micah let himself in the office. He turned and raised a brow.

"Forget where they live?" he asked.

"No, found it easily enough," Micah answered. "Even had a nice little chat with Tommen. It was made a lot easier since he figured out how to get a phone call through."

At his brother's surprised expression, Micah took the time to explain Tommen's exploits in stealing military-grade equipment in order to both ride with and override the Energy barrier in order to make a phone call.

"That's excellent," Micaiah said, whistling. "So, you were able to get him out? Or help him, at least?"

"Well, yes and no. We tested out the theory and we were able to get the journal back." He tossed it on the desk next to a stack of papers. "Hopefully it stays completely in our possession this time."

"Or we could burn it."

"I like that idea, too. Anyway, that was hard enough." He explained the process, making sure to emphasize the pushback. "When he finally got it out, it was like a small bomb went off. Walt and I got knocked on our asses."

"Did you try to get Tommen out?"

"Oh yes, we did try. It was a lot harder, though. That was like running into a brick wall repeatedly. Or having one slammed into you. Walter and Tommen were able to grab wrists and hold on, but then something started pulling Walter into that dimension. I don't know how to describe it. Walter managed to resist the pull, but Tommen couldn't move. We did what we could, but I couldn't hold it and we lost him."

Micah hated to admit it. He didn't like to admit failure, but he especially didn't like admitting failure when he hadn't been alone. Micaiah could infiltrate a locked down base, get a message out, warn them of changes, and initiate a revolution. Micah could barely open a portal into another dimension to rescue one kid.

"What did you do after that?" Micaiah asked.

Micah shrugged. "When we finally regained consciousness, we decided to rest a minute and get something to eat, try to recover. I told Walt to sit and wait for Tommen to call back and report what happened on his end, see if there isn't some way we can help him next time. I'm sure that if you and Kayla and maybe a couple others added your strength, then we could better shoulder the weight, hold back whatever force was attacking us, and Walter could focus solely on getting him out."

Micaiah nodded thoughtfully. "Sounds like you guys made some real headway. More than what I've been doing, looking through legends and fairy tales. But judging by your general appearance and how you look ready to fall asleep, you won't be trying again any time soon."

Micah eased himself into a chair. "I was hoping for later today, but the more I think about it, the more I think it won't be until tomorrow at the soonest. I don't know, Cai. It's like that thing just sucked the energy right out of me."

"Maybe that's exactly what it did. Sponge meets vacuum."

"Well, either way, you're up to speed now. If Kayla doesn't find anything tonight in her little drug trip with her pals, maybe we can use her, too."

"I expect so." Micaiah jerked his head toward the door. "In the meantime, go home and get some sleep. You look terrible. And for God's sake, Micah, try to enjoy your day off without causing any calamities or world-ending disasters."

Micah sighed and shook his head as he stood. "Cai, now you've cursed us. You know I can't resist an opportunity to disobey my annoying big brother."

Chapter Eighteen
Sepsis

Because things just weren't bad enough. Tommen had woken up this morning feeling like he'd gone ten rounds with Tyler Freeman and lost at least nine of them. So he'd pretty much just stayed in bed, lamenting his concussion-like migraine as his body roiled in pain. If it wasn't his migraine at large, it was the nausea and his grumbling stomach. If it wasn't the stomach, it was his kidneys and entire lower back. If it wasn't that, it was his arm. Given that his arm already hurt like a bitch and it was now the least of his pains, things were not looking good. He needed to get to a doctor and quick. Even if he had to listen in on half a dozen doctor discussions and steal some kind of antibiotics, he needed to do something or he wouldn't last long here.

He had been more than happy to see Micah and hear that he had a plan, something that sounded off-the-wall crazy and yet so likely to work. Can't go through or over the wall, so go under it. His hopes had really got up when he saw that it had worked on the trial run, getting the journal back out into the real world. Sure, there had been a small earthquake as the portal snapped shut and the Energy tried to right itself, but it had worked. Maybe now they could keep control of the journal for a change. Maybe they ought to burn the damn thing and be rid of the whole problem.

Then came the real test, when they tried to save him. Tommen hadn't realized how accustomed he'd grown to the increased Energy of the in-between dimension until he felt Micah peeling it away from him, like lifting rubble off someone trapped beneath a collapsed building. For a moment, he was able to breathe. For a moment, he was home. Then suddenly, it had been like Energy tendrils had crept over him and latched onto him, holding him in place. It had taken all his strength just to lift a hand and grab his dad's wrist. He tried to hold on, but it was like something, some kind of monster had sunk its teeth into him and dragged him back in. It would not relinquish him, no matter how much he wanted it to. In fact, it had tried to move through him to grab Walter. He could feel his dad and Micah redouble their efforts to keep the portal open and bring him out, but he could offer no assistance. And he certainly couldn't just stand up and go with them.

Finally, their strength gave out and the portal closed. For a moment, it was almost as if Tommen had been electrocuted as the Energy monster seemed to envelop him, draw him in deep as if claiming its prize and making off with him. The next thing he knew, he was lying somewhere he should not have been able to get to normally, except that he could push through solid objects. A few seconds later, he crawled out of his bookcases and lay there on the carpet, just trying to breathe.

If his body had hurt before, that was like a hangnail compared to this agony. Every so often, his body would twitch and seize in a mini-seizure, almost as if he was connected to an electric current that still jolted him from time to time. When he managed to slither up onto his bed once more, his whole body was trembling. His eyes hurt so he could hardly see. His head hurt and he knew he was going to be throwing up here pretty quick. Pretty much all of his organs felt fried, to say nothing of his kidneys. His arm shook and he could see where healing blisters had given way to blood as his body tore itself apart trying to make the jump between dimensions and handle the sudden onslaught of extra Energy. Well, he said he would rather die than be trapped in the dimension. He might just get his wish.

The next few hours felt like a day, wavering in and out of consciousness. He wasn't even sure if it had been a couple hours or a couple days. It didn't matter, really, he supposed. He was exhausted. He was wounded. He needed to take time to recover.

When he finally sat up and looked at his clock, it was a little after five. His first thought was that his dad was going to be worried sick if he didn't call to let him know he was okay. His second thought was that his own sickness didn't feel much better. The only thing that seemed to improve was his general migraine, but that did nothing for his nausea which sent him outside to be sick. The effort it took to throw up only made his back and kidney pain worse which was only exacerbated when he finally managed to stand and try to pee. Things were not looking good for him right now; that much was certain.

He returned to his room and lay back on the bed. As much as he wanted to go to bed and try to sleep it off, he somehow knew that he wasn't going to sleep this off. He needed medicine, and he needed it now. Grudgingly, he forced himself to his feet. Dazed by dizziness, it was a wonder he even made it to the bakery. Maybe it was more of that ask and ye shall receive crap, the Akari somehow reading his mind and taking him where he wanted to go. Still, he stumbled into the office where Micaiah was at the computer, working on something or another.

Grouchily, and with not a little disregard for his own general safety, Tommen reached into the computer—one hand in the tower, the other on the keyboard—and effectively hijacked the whole thing. Startled by the way things suddenly started happening on the screen, Micaiah pushed himself away from the desk, hands halfway up.

"Tommen, I hope that's you," he said.

Tommen opened a new document.

"It's me," he typed.

"Micah said they weren't able to get you out."

"Clearly. Listen, I haven't called my dad, but if you could let him know I'm alive, that would be great."

"Okay..." Micaiah cautiously reached for his phone, as if that, too, was about to be possessed.

Tommen sighed. "I'm not okay, Cai. I'm sick. I don't know, but somehow, I guess I got overtaken by a wave of Energy when they lost me and Micah will tell you, but I'm not okay in general. I've got infection and everything else wrong with me right now."

Micaiah nodded. "He told me something to that effect, yes. If you can hang on until tomorrow—"

"Tomorrow's great, but I need medicine now. Help me find it. If we can search the Internet, I can go to the hospital—"

"Tommen, we don't know what your infection is, and I don't want you to just go around the hospital sticking needles in your arm."

"Then give me something for a migraine so I can think clearly. Give me something for the nausea so I'm not giving up more food and fluids than I'm taking in. I know I need a doctor, but until you guys can get me out of here, I have to be my own doctor."

"I understand. I do." Micaiah took a breath. "Tommen. Go home. Raid your dad's medicine cabinet for some Pepto, Motrin, whatever you need. Get some sleep. Tomorrow, we'll be back to try it again and get you out. All right?"

Tommen hesitated but nodded uselessly and typed, "All right. I'll try."

"I'll still call your dad to let him know you're okay and you've made contact. When you're feeling better, when you wake up later, you need to call him. He needs to hear your voice."

"I know."

"Go home, Tommen. And stop possessing my computer. You're freaking me out."

In another life, had he been feeling better, there were any number of cheeky little mischievous tricks Tommen could pull to accentuate the point. As it stood, he simply took his hands out of the computer, stopped manipulating the motherboard and all the little signals throughout the computer and keyboard, and left the office. Once more, he wasn't sure exactly how he got home, only that he did. His dad was napping in his recliner, his expression still contorted into fitful worry.

Tommen did as Micaiah suggested and went to the bathroom to raid the medicine cabinet. He grabbed anything he thought would help, fully aware that if anything didn't interact well or if he overdosed, there would be no one coming to save his sorry ass.

He read the labels as carefully as he could around the

migraine, then elected to take just under the recommended dosage on each. It might not make him feel completely better, but not dying sounded better than a little headache. Once everything was consumed, he went back to his bed to relax.

"So, how did it go?"

Tommen startled awake to see Julianna standing at the end of his bed, arms folded, expression unreadable.

"Listen, I'm not feeling very good right now, so if we can talk later, that would be great," he murmured.

"Would that be before or after you die? Your wounds are infected, and a little headache medicine isn't going to make it better. I'm no expert, but if I had to hazard a guess, I'd say you're going septic."

Tommen rubbed his eyes, willing himself to sleep. "That doesn't sound pleasant."

"It means you are going to die very quickly if something isn't done."

"Great! So tell me what I have to do!" His frustration and sharpness of tone caused another migraine to spring into his brain.

"Do you think you can come with me to the hospital?"

"Great, so you're a doctor now, too?"

Julianna approached him. "Tommen, I saw what you and your dad tried to do. I saw what you did to try and escape. I think it will work, but it won't work for either of us if you're dead or too weak to go through the portal. I need to keep you alive. You're my best hope of escape. I've been here a long time and I've learned some things. And to your point, yes, I was a nurse once. If you want to try to escape again tomorrow, you're going to need your strength. It may not be a cure, but it will tide you over. Come on."

Reluctantly, Tommen got out of bed and followed Julianna who opened a Travel Band for both of them, carrying them to the hospital in record time. It was busy, as could be expected on a sticky Saturday evening in August. People were out doing stupid things and regular things that unexpectedly did bad things and got people hurt.

The nice thing about being invisible, though, was the ability to go anywhere and do anything without being stopped and detained by security. It was still a little unnerving, but Tommen wasn't in much of a mood to think things through.

"What is septic, anyway?" he mumbled as they ducked into a room and Julianna began looking at shelves upon shelves of books and binders.

"Sepsis is a blood infection that moves very quickly," she answered, feeling all the books as if she could telepathically read them just at a touch. "Your blood vessels dilate and blood starts leaking out of your vessels, causing low blood pressure and low blood volume. It messes with your heart and your entire circulatory system."

"Fuck."

"Yes, well, it's not fun. Give me a minute to find something, but the best thing you can do for yourself right now is stay conscious."

"How did I get it? If it's an infection, why does it affect me in this dimension?"

"You could have touched something while you were running around the fire with Rifun. You could have contracted something while you were out on your little crime spree last night, pulling a bunch of stuff into this dimension. It could be something that developed internally. I don't know. Point is, you've got it and we need to do something about it."

"No argument from me."

"While we're at it, we might as well do something about your arm, too. At the very least, it needs to be rewrapped. How is your hand?"

"Hurts like fuck, like the rest of me."

"Here we are. I think."

Julianna pulled a large book off the shelf and laid it out on the table. Blearily, he looked over her shoulder. Most of it was medical mumbo jumbo he couldn't even pronounce, let alone read and understand. From what he was able to read, it sounded like a bunch of diseases and the medicines to give for them. Personally, assuming that was indeed what the book was, Tommen didn't understand why they couldn't call it as much. Seriously, make it easy for the average person to break in and steal drugs for their life-threatening diseases. What was so difficult about that?

"Okay, doc," Tommen said. "What are you going to give me?"

She scoffed. "I must admit, Tommen, I have to side with you on this. Humanity really needs to stop messing with things nature has already provided for us. Don't get me wrong, modern medicine is incredible. But to have a list half a mile long of when to give a drug and when not to give a drug, what other injuries or infections could be present, changes to make based on other medicines being given...it's like those logic puzzles where you have to figure out where everyone sat and what they ate but you only have three clues to go on."

"Hey, I've done those before. Those are fun."

"You want to come take a guess at this, then?"

"No. Gambling my life isn't fun."

"I didn't think so. But I do think I've found something to start with. Stay here."

"Not going anywhere."

Even just compared to earlier that morning, Tommen felt a thousand times worse. It was hot outside and he was cold. Even his jacket didn't seem to be enough now, though he'd just put that off as hospitals always being too damn cold. What if it wasn't just the hospital, but it really was this sepsis infection? What if he really was losing blood? Fucking hell, but he was just losing all of his bodily fluids, wasn't he? He glanced at his left arm, the bandages still wet and bloody. Fucking hell.

"Okay, I'm back," Julianna said, walking in with a bunch of stuff in one arm, pushing an IV stand.

"Do you even know how to start an IV?" Tommen wondered.

"If idiotic first-year med students can start them while simultaneously texting their boyfriends or girlfriends, I don't think it's too difficult. And it's only gotten easier since World War II. First let's see about your arm and chest."

He didn't want to watch, but he also couldn't look away as she unwrapped the bandages. As she began pouring sterile water over the wounds and blisters, he involuntarily made a fist, then cried out for the pain. She nodded slowly, not looking at him.

"Pain is good," she told him. "Means the flesh is still alive. You ought to keep your hand moving when you can."

"Whatever," he gasped, squeezing his eyes shut. "How does it look otherwise?"

"Like an arm with some pretty bad burns. The good news, though, aside from the pain, is that it looks like it's beginning to heal. That's only my opinion; I can't say for sure seeing how your jacket is still melted into the skin. But some of the smaller blisters have begun to heal."

"Okay. That's good, right?"

"Of course it is. But if you want your body to keep healing, it needs to focus on that and not get distracted by this infection. Hold your other arm out and make a fist."

He did so and she tied a band around his arm in order to find a vein. Actually, given how pale he normally was, to say nothing of how things were going now, finding a vein wasn't usually a problem, and she quickly had a port in his elbow and his hand. But then there was the part where she was pushing drugs she had no training with. World War II was a long time ago, and drugs had changed since then. She could save him or kill him in record time. But if they did nothing, he would almost assuredly die. His odds weren't looking good.

"I don't know," Tommen said when she finally taped down the line, removed the band, and started messing with the IV bag. "Are you sure about this? The whole sepsis thing sounds pretty serious, yeah, but what if it's not that? I mean, you could be giving me drugs for nothing. Or it could make me worse."

"I'm as sure about this as I am about anything else," she told him. She faced him. "I'm not. It's been a while since I've had to do this, but I'm not going to sit by and watch you suffer and die without trying to help. If you really don't want me to do this, I won't. I'll just wait until you go unconscious, then do it against your will anyway."

"Well, at least you're honest." He sighed. "Fine. I got no other option, really."

Given how shitty he was feeling and with the pain still lancing through the left side of his upper body, one might expect that Tommen could hardly feel the IV fluids when they entered his bloodstream. Unfortunately, such was not the case. He most certainly felt it, and it was not a pleasant experience. Well, she told him to exercise his hand a little while it was out of the bandages, and that was exactly what he did. It didn't help, either, when she took his right hand and gave him another injection of some form.

"Couldn't we have gone to a room so I could at least lie down?" he whined.

"We could have, but given how many people are moving here and there and changing beds, I didn't want to be interrupted with some jerk suddenly laying down on top of you, thereby being inside you."

"Don't even use terminology like that. Please."

She nodded and sat down in a chair a short distance away. "Now then, I heard what you did earlier this afternoon."

"How is it that you're never around, but you know what I'm doing all the time?"

"Quite frankly, you never don't advertise yourself. I mean, my goodness, look at what you did to those two apartment buildings. That was a little hard to miss. I saw what you did with your phone and how you made contact. I came back this morning to talk about it, but you were talking to your dad, so I decided to come back later. When I did, you were trying your breakout attempt."

"Oh. Guess that makes sense." Tommen shifted uncomfortably in his seat. "So do you have any insights about it?"

"Well, it looked like it almost worked," Julianna said plainly. "I don't know if your dad and your friend just didn't have enough strength by themselves or whether you were too weak because of your infection or what."

"Problem with that, though," Tommen said, "is that if that's the case, these meds better work. Otherwise, we're only going to get maybe one or two chances a day until I'm dead. The entire Akarin force could be keeping that portal open, but if I can't go through, it's useless."

"I agree, which is why we're here." She nodded and stood. "Stay here. I'm going to do some more snooping around this hospital, see if I can't find anything else that could be of help to you."

"I'll be here."

He watched her go. Only when she was gone did he straighten a little and consider his circumstances. He still felt like like shit and everything still hurt like fuck, but he wasn't quite as passive as he was trying to seem. He had little doubt he had an infection of some form, but he wasn't on his deathbed yet. Well, okay, he wasn't too far from it, or so it felt like. But he had half a mind left to think with.

The biggest question he had right now was why Julianna needed him in order for her to escape the dimension. Sure, he had the best idea so far and it had almost worked, but why him? If she was always away on "business" and left him to figure things out, why couldn't she go to whatever friends she might have on the outside—or even the inside—and ask them for help? He wasn't saying that he wasn't grateful for her help with his wounds and infections, but there was just something off about the whole thing.

Part of him said to stop being so paranoid. She'd been nothing but kind to him, from explaining the situation, to bandaging his wounds in the first place, to getting him to the hospital and looking for medicine for his infections.

But then, if she really did need him in order to escape, and his ideas had worked out so far, it was in her best interest to keep him alive and well.

Or she could be just a nice person who wants to help.

Micaiah said she couldn't be allowed to escape. Her deceitfulness about the journal and her mysterious deal with Cassius only proved that she was hiding something. She could be trying to ingratiate herself.

On the other hand, look at what Cassius did to her. Maybe she had made the deal. Maybe that was all in the past. It's like someone judging Walter based on his actions of over a century ago. He's a completely different man now and shouldn't be judged like that.

Then why not admit to it? Why try to skirt the issue and ignore it?

Maybe she's ashamed of it. Walter didn't admit to his past until he was at death's door. She could still be scared.

She hasn't shown one ounce of shame or fear since you got here. Other than cool indifference to anything, the only time she's shown any raw emotion is when there's the prospect of leaving.

Yeah? Well when you're isolated for a few decades, the thought of escape probably sounds pretty good, especially when it was almost within reach this afternoon.

Tommen wished he could rub his eyes, but his left hand was burned and gross, and his right hand was occupied by IV lines. As it was, the best he could do was shift position. He could argue in circles for a week, pointing out this logic or that evidence or this history or that psychology, and he wouldn't come any closer to making up his mind or actually escaping this dimension. He still didn't think Julianna was being completely honest with him, and Micaiah telling him to be wary only reinforced the point. But just as he might be her only shot at escape, she was his only shot at getting better.

As he sat there, he was acutely aware that he probably should have brought his phone and the monstrosity of a signal booster he had constructed. He ran his tongue over his teeth. If his signal booster let him make calls, could he connect to wifi, too? That might be something to try. Maybe he could make video calls. Well, even if he could, his dad would never be able to figure it out; he'd have to get the twins to help. Still, it might be worth a shot. Although, if he looked as bad as he felt, that might not be such a good idea.

His gaze eventually rested on a landline phone in the corner. What if he pulled that into the in-between dimension? Would it disconnect automatically, or would the phone line itself provide a link to the outside?

He stood and slunk over to the desk, dragging the IV stand with him, until he sat at the desk in front of the phone. It took a little more effort than he thought it should have to bring the phone in, but as near as he could tell, everything was still connected. Carefully, he turned the phone around and physically disconnected and reconnected the phone line. Then he started feeling the line with his good hand, reaching as far as he could, trying to find the exact point where the dimensions met. There was no way he could have pulled the entire line and system into the dimension, so there had to be a breaking point somewhere. After a minute, he picked up the phone. To his relief, there was a dial tone.

"Okay," he said, setting the phone on his shoulder so he could use his good hand to dial. "Usually there's a number to dial out."

Thankfully, the sticky note detailing the instructions for dialing out was not far away.

"Hello?" a familiar voice answered tiredly.

"Dad?" Tommen said.

"Tommen?"

"Yeah, it's me."

"This isn't your phone number."

"No, it's not. I'm at the hospital right now."

"Oh my God, are you all right? Did you make it out? Micaiah called me and said you hadn't."

"No, not yet. Julianna came by and told me I had septic or something."

"Sepsis?" His dad went from tired to worried in exactly 0.8 seconds.

"Yeah. She found some IVs and medicine and stuff. I don't know, but I guess it's working."

Walter let out a breath. "Okay. That's good. Good that you're getting better. How's your arm?"

"Healing, or that's what she says. I mean, my jacket kind of melted into my skin, so it's a little hard to tell. But she said the small blisters are healing."

"That's good. Listen, kiddo, Micaiah said that tomorrow is going to be the earliest we can make another attempt, but it probably won't be until Kayla returns from her other mission."

"It's okay. I understand. And, actually, calling you, I have an idea on how to make it a little easier."

"That would be much appreciated."

"Listen, Dad, I have to go. There's more medicine coming and I don't want to get all loopy on you."

"Fair enough. Stay safe, son."

"I will, Dad. Love you."

"Love you, too. Hang in there."

Tommen hung up a few seconds before Julianna returned with some more syringes and another IV bag.

"Good news," she said. "Someone else in the ER has sepsis, too. Well, it's not good news for him, but it's good for you. I watched them for a little bit and took notes. What I did grab so far was all good, but these might be of some use, too."

"Okay. Listen, I might have an idea of how to make it easier on everyone when we try to bust out tomorrow."

Julianna did not pause in her work as she dumped the supplies out and began sorting them. "I'm listening."

"So, last Christmas, Rifun kidnapped me and lured me and my dad into this warehouse in a shipping yard east of town. Micaiah was supposed to help, but he said he couldn't because the warehouse had been turned into some kind of quasi-dimension. It existed in the same realm as us and could be seen, but he couldn't break into it. I don't know the details.

"My idea is this: What if someone tried that again? Turned someplace into a quasi-dimension or whatever, and got one step closer to us? I brought this phone in here and made a call. Okay, there is no way I brought the entire phone system into this dimension, which means there has to be a cut-off somewhere. If the others step into a quasi-dimension and throw us a life ring as it were, they might be able to pull us out."

Now she stopped and let out an even breath. "Tommen, I like your creativity. But here's the problem with that. There is no guarantee that a quasi-dimension will be a stepping stone to us. It could just as easily be a neighbor to the primary dimension."

"I don't understand."

She brought it a pencil and a piece of paper. She drew a rectangle on it, then drew two vertical lines so there were three equal parts. "Okay, so this left box here is primary dimension one. That's where your dad and everyone else is. This right box is primary dimension two. We don't know what's there; this is just a simple illustration. We're here in the middle. You're talking about making a quasi-dimension here." She drew another vertical line through the left box, dividing it in half. "Assuming that's what happened, we don't know if it would work. And, really, no harm in trying. But, it could just as easy go this way." She drew a horizontal line through the original left box. "Two neighboring dimensions, side-by-side, and no closer to us. In that situation, it puts even more strain on the rescuers because they are trying to hold the dimension and break through it at the same time." She crumbled up the paper and tossed it uselessly in the trash bin. "It wouldn't work."

She went to the table and chose a syringe. As she pushed it into the IV line, Tommen asked, "Is there any way you can think of where it could work?"

Julianna paused and sighed. "The time of the great Builders is gone, when men could construct stable dimensions and bend them to their will, almost as if they were God." She tossed the empty syringe away and went back to her buffet of medicine. "These days, men build quasi-dimensions and call themselves great. There are few in the universe with such mastery of the Akari and the elements of the universe and its dimensions."

Tommen hesitated for half a second before saying, "What about Rifun?" When she stopped, he went on, "I know you don't like him. I'm not too fond of him either. But he's the only one I know of who might have that kind of power and control. He built that quasi-dimension around the warehouse and he completely redecorated the Wheel. He turned *Star Trek* into Shakespeare. I don't know about you, but he might actually be our best bet for help from the outside. In that area of expertise," he added quickly.

It was a long moment before Julianna put down the syringe she was holding and turned to face him. "You would suggest an alliance with the man who took over the Time industry, enslaved millions, almost killed your father, almost killed you, and even now seeks to recruit you as his Apprentice?"

"I'm not happy about it either, believe me. Listen, when I'm done here, I'll go to Micaiah and ask if any Akarin have similar abilities. Whatever infighting they have going on, I'd still rather ask them than Rifun."

She snorted. "I would rather escape by our own means."

"Micah and Micaiah are Akarin and they're our best chance at getting out the way we tried this afternoon! Whatever your beef is with the Akarin, take it outside this dimension. But first, we actually have to get out of this dimension. You might just have to accept their help. In the same way that we might have to accept Rifun's help if he is most qualified. Okay, if I'm sepsis—"

"Septic."

"Whatever. If I'm as sick as you say I am, I can't be picky about who my doctor is." He noted her expression. "We have to get out of here. All other concerns are secondary."

They stared at each other for several seconds. Only when she returned to her syringes did Tommen relax. That had taken a lot out of him, more than it seemed like it should have. Fuck, he really was sick. A minute later, Julianna pushed another syringe into the line.

"How many more of those are there?" he asked.

"Six more, but they're on a regular schedule, assuming you get better."

"How long will it take?"

"Could be days until a noticeable, stable recovery. Weeks for a full recovery. Our concern right now is getting you stable enough to make a jump across dimensions so you can get admitted for real so you can get treated for real. I don't like guessing any more than you do."

"At least we're on the same page with that one." Tommen shifted positions. "So, how long do I have to sit here? Like, here-here? In this chair? When can we go and start planning stuff and see if we can't get something done about quasi-dimensions and shit?"

"You can't go anywhere. You're sounding better, but treatment has only just begun. You walk out that door and in an hour you're dying in bed again. Healing takes time."

"I don't have time. We have an attempt, we have a plan. Let's roll with it, use the momentum to keep going and find a way out. Rolling stones gather no moss, and they hurt a hell of a lot more when they mow you over versus a stationary rock."

"I'm sorry?"

"You know what? Scratch that. Analogies are awful things. Just forget that. But seriously, I can't just sit here for fucking days doing nothing. We're going to attempt a rescue tomorrow, and I want to be there."

"I understand. Really, I do. More than you know, even." She sighed. "Okay. How about this? You stay here until that drip bag is empty. Once it's done, I'll take the line out, but leave the port in. We'll go down to the cafeteria or something and grab dinner. Then we'll wait a little bit. If you don't pass out on me or have adverse effects, then we'll grab the medicine to go, and we'll go and attempt whatever crazy scheme you've concocted in your tiny, teenage brain of yours. Deal?"

Reluctantly, Tommen agreed. Problem was, she had just changed the drip bag so it was almost full. He was getting the fluids he'd been missing, but he wasn't getting them very fast. That was, what? A couple glasses of water? He could drink those just as easily and in a fraction of the time. But he'd made a deal and he would live up to it.

Actually, it kind of repulsed him that he'd even suggested

contacting Rifun and asking for his help. It was like Stockholm Syndrome or something, sympathizing with a captor, being amazed at his power, and wanting to use that power. But if they did end up asking Rifun for his help and they got it, what would they owe him? Rifun did nothing out of the goodness of his heart. He already claimed to own Tommen's loyalty; would he ask for his soul the next time around? A shudder ran through Tommen.

No. They wouldn't ask for Rifun's help until the whole of the Akarin had failed to break them out of the in-between dimension. And if that many Akari-bearers weren't strong enough to get them out, then there was no way Rifun—for all his perceived and boasted might— would have a chance by himself. It just wasn't possible.

Tommen did not voice his fears or concerns to Julianna as they sat there and made small talk. He probed her for information about her family and home life, looking for anything he could use to indict her and fan the flames of his suspicions. He found nothing. If she had once made a malicious deal with Cassius, life in the in-between dimension had smothered any fires of passion and revenge. She just wanted to escape as much as he did and return to a normal life.

Eventually, the drip bag did run out. As promised, Julianna disconnected the line, though the ports remained in the crook of his elbow and the back of his hand. It made movement painful, but it was easier than taking them out, having something happen, and trying to put them right back in again. She also rewrapped his arm, taped new bandages on his chest, side, and neck, but not before giving him another dose of hellfire in a holy water bottle, also known as sterile water. By the time the last pin and strip of tape had been placed, his entire left side from his head down to his hips, and especially his arm, felt numb, as if he'd been lying on ice for a while. Slowly, he stood and followed her out of the room.

They headed down to the cafeteria where patients and employees alike were waiting not-so-patiently for their share of burgers, fries, chicken, pulled pork, salads, and a variety of tasty little desserts. It felt good to be able to jump the line and take as much as they wanted. Tommen had half a mind to gorge on everything, but he knew enough that it was probably a bad idea. He wasn't feeling the best yet, and who knew what would happen when medicine met carbs and calories and sugar? Nothing good, that was for sure.

So he opted for a salad. Not a particularly fluffy salad, mind you, where it was a mixture of greens and leaves. Rather, it was a few leaves topped with egg, cheese, and a bit of ham and bacon, plus his ranch dressing.

"I've always wondered why they even bother calling that a salad," Julianna mused. "Clearly it's only a gluten-free BLT."

"What can I say? I try to watch what I eat." Tommen grinned cheekily as he started in on it.

"Looks like you're feeling better."

"Better is a relative term. I still feel like shit."

"Well, assuming you don't keel over on me before dinner is over, the next dose of medicine is due in four hours. Another at six. Then twelve. Then eighteen, twenty-four, and forty-eight. Assuming we need them and haven't already escaped so you can get real treatment."

Tommen nodded. "Hopefully."

"So what's your plan, then? Where are we going after this?"

"First we're going to the shipping yard. I want to check out the warehouse. Even though it was last Christmas, I want to see if, being in this dimension, we can see anything unusual about it because it was once a quasi-dimension."

She raised a brow. "Like what?"

"I don't know. That's just the sort of smart stuff that someone on *Star Trek* might say. I have no fucking idea what I'm looking for."

"Well, neither do I, but that's not to say that something isn't there. If there is, we can investigate. If there isn't, well, we haven't wasted a lot of time. Walking does wonders."

He nodded and took another bite of salad. "And if I haven't said it lately, thank you for helping me."

"Helping me get out of here is all the thanks I'll need."

"So why is it that—? Oh." Tommen's stomach felt like it flipped over.

"What is it?"

"Um..." He stood slowly. "I'll just, uh..." His stomach growled again, more ferociously this time so that the normal people in the real world might have been able to hear it. "I'll be right back."

He didn't pass out, thankfully, but by the time he was done giving up his salad and a ton of stomach fluids that were not only painfully acidic but precious to his weakened body, he was as pale and shaky as he had been waking up that morning. Julianna patiently waited for him in the doorway while he threw up into the bushes.

"You're not going anywhere," she told him.

"I'm fine," he said, straightening. He certainly didn't feel fine. Just the effort of throwing up had put a strain on his abs, to say nothing of the rest of him. But he kept his head high and tried to be confident.

"You're not fine. You're giving up more fluids than you're taking in."

"Then we better hurry and find a way out."

"Even if I can't keep you in the hospital for days with this medicine, we need to get another bag of fluids in you. At least let me do that."

So, ten minutes later, Tommen was back in the chair with an IV bag drip, drip, dripping into the line and going into his arm. Fucking hell, he was bored. He should have brought his phone or something.

"Can you at least take the one out of my hand so I can use it?" he whined.

Julianna gave him a hard regard, but did as he asked. The needle came out bloodier than others he'd seen, but figured it wasn't too shabby for an amateur.

"So, assuming we don't find anything at this warehouse of yours, where are we going after that?" she asked.

Tommen shrugged as best he could. "I don't know. Home, I guess. I need to get some sleep. Rescue attempt is tomorrow. If we don't have anything to offer, we don't have anything to offer. It's all up to them." He looked up at the drip bag which was almost empty. "But until then, we have to keep trying."

Twenty minutes later, the bag was empty. Julianna removed the line and the needle. Tommen gingerly stretched his arm and hand, both of them. Of course, the right felt infinitely better, but they were both still working.

"All right, we'll go," Julianna said reluctantly. "But sepsis is nothing to fool around with. You've lost blood. You might still be losing blood. If I think that something is going wrong while we're out, we're coming right back here. The Akarin might just have to make their attempt right here in the hospital."

"Fine," Tommen said. "But until then, come on. Clock is ticking and we still have investigating to do."

Eager to be going, Tommen led the way, Julianna hard on his heels. They navigated the twisting, narrow hallways of the hospital until they were back outside. It took a minute for him to get his bearings, but once he figured out where they were, it was a short distance to the shipping yard.

Chapter Nineteen
Battlegrounds and Dream Lands

The shipping yard operated twenty-four hours a day, six days a week. First and second shift were pretty constant, trying to get ships in and out in a timely manner. Third shift was a little more laid back seeing how no boats traveled at night. With the long days beginning to grow short, second shift was scrambling to get work done amid mistakes, mishaps, and an assortment of workplace drama.

"I can see why Rifun chose this place," Julianna observed. "Good cover, lots of activity. Why he needed to run into a quasi-dimension is beyond me."

"Right," Tommen said, swallowed. "So, I guess we'll just walk right in, then."

"No one is going to stop us."

They started in through the main entrance. The maze changed and shifted with each passing day, every ship that came through, so it was easy to get turned around. Tommen stared up at the rows and rows of cargo containers, all bound for parts unknown. At one time, Micah had been up there as the extra, unofficial cover fire for CPD. He'd been one of those to help free Tommen initially, get him out of Rifun's grasp. Of course, that had happened only after Tommen lost his hearing, but it was better than losing his life, he supposed.

"Tommen!"

He jumped and looked at Julianna who stood about ten yards away.

"What?" he wondered dumbly.

She approached. "I asked if you saw something. Then I asked if your hearing aids are still working. Are they dead?"

He took one out and checked the battery. "Almost, but not quite yet."

"All right. Let's keep moving. Warehouse eight, wasn't it?"

Warehouse eight, where the shootout had begun. Where nine had died and three more could never return to the police force, maybe even the workforce at large. Where Tommen had been held by a madman. Where that same madman had tried to kill Lily. Where that madman had lured Walter into his sick mind game, all in the name of a cheap thrill to get him to confess to his bloody past. Where his dad had been shot and Tommen had to hold him in his arms and Band him to keep him from dying there on the spot. Warehouse eight. Also known as Hell.

Tommen's steps were slow and cautious. He told himself he was being necessarily cautious because of the heavy machinery and equipment zipping here and there, moving large containers and smaller crates. It was a lie, of course. Really, he was terrified. He was afraid that at any moment, Rifun would jump out and shoot him. Or come out and have Walter in the same position Tommen had once been in, held tight with a gun to his head. Or maybe Isthim would walk out, pushing all her poisons, fucking with Tommen's mind as much as his body.

"Hey!"

Tommen almost jumped out of his skin at a hand on his shoulder. As it was, he merely stumbled drunkenly to the side, catching himself on a container, breathing hard and fast, heart thumping wildly and yet irregularly. He was shaking all over. He was not all right.

"Whoa, hey, I'm sorry," Julianna said, putting her hands up. She walked slowly toward him until she could gently put a hand on his shoulder again. "I'm sorry. Okay? I didn't mean to frighten you."

"I'm fine," Tommen insisted weakly.

"You're not fine. And that's okay. I know what happened here. I know it's hard. But you've got to pull yourself together if you want to try this idea."

"Isn't there anywhere else that was once a quasi-dimension? There has to be one somewhere in the world."

"I'm sure there are other sites. But how will that help you here? Eventually we all have to face our demons, Tommen. Maybe it's time for you to face yours."

If her words were meant to encourage, they did very little of the sort. He didn't want to face his demons. It might have been different in a time when the term was used metaphorically and he spit on the notion of demons. Problem was, this place was where he'd learned that demons existed and they were much more powerful and cunning than he'd ever imagined. He'd been willing to make a deal with one just an hour ago, ask him for a favor like they were old buddies.

They had to get out of this in-between dimension. And they were going to do it without Rifun's help. Of that much he was sure.

"Take a deep breath," Julianna was saying. "And breathe. Just breathe. In and out."

Tommen nodded as he took one breath at a time. "Yeah. Yeah, okay."

"Just breathe," she coaxed. "Is everything coming back to you now? You know where you are, when you are?"

"I think so." He swallowed and closed his eyes. "Yeah. I'm good now. I'm fine." He opened his eyes. "Okay." Breath. "Yeah, let's go."

It still wasn't an easy thing, trying to get himself to move through the shipping yard, knowing full well where he was going. He almost wished the sepsis would creep back up on him, just to give him an excuse to leave. Maybe they really wouldn't find anything and they could just do a quick in and out.

At the same time, nothing was actually stopping him from leaving, in the same way no one had stopped him from walking in. He could turn around and leave. It wasn't like he actually feared Julianna, as if she might attack him. He could turn around, go home, tell his dad that his idea hadn't worked and nothing had changed. It would be a lie, but they didn't need to know that. If nothing changed, then nothing got worse, right?

"Come on, Tommen, you can do it," Julianna said beside him.

This had been his idea, after all. If he could go over it in his mind and everything without freaking out, he could walk through it without having problems either. Right? He hoped so, because that was what he told himself as he put one foot in front of the other. They were getting closer to warehouse eight. He could feel it. The cargo containers might be arranged differently, but he knew this terrain, this ground. This was all starting to look very familiar.

He stopped as they rounded the last corner and stood facing a large warehouse with a giant 8 bolted on it. He knew that warehouse. He knew the ground around it. It had been covered in slush and ice the last time he stood here, but he knew this ground. He knew the number of steps from here to about the center distance, where Rifun had held him. He knew the number of steps from the cruiser position to the safety of the warehouse. He knew there was a crack in the concrete that was getting worse every year because the owner of the shipping yard wouldn't pay to have it fixed. Tommen had tripped on that crack as he was being dragged inside. Rifun had lost his grip on him because of his newly-injured hand, but Isthim had effortlessly taken both him and Lily inside to hold until Rifun could get situated again.

"Hey!" he barked, instinctively stepping away as Julianna pinched his arm.

"I figured that might be safer than touching or yelling," she told him.

"Oh. Well, it hurt."

"Welcome back."

They looked out over the open area in front of the warehouse. Smaller machines moved around inside, moving pallets and crates from here to there and back again. Just another day at the office, another dollar to put away in hopes of maybe attaining some small goal. Everything completely normal.

"Completely normal," Tommen breathed.

"What?" Julianna looked up at him.

"Huh? Oh, nothing."

"You can do this, Tommen. You've made it this far. And look. Nothing out of the ordinary, just a bunch of guys going about their day."

"Yeah, yeah, I know. I can see that."

"But you can see everything else, can't you?"

Tommen nodded.

"They're not here, Tommen. No one is going to hurt you."

Then, to both of their surprise, he burst out laughing. He couldn't even say why except it was what needed to be done. When he finally reined himself in, he gave Julianna an incredulous look. "You think I'm worried about people hurting me? I've already been hurt. I will continue to be hurt. There is no other way."

"What are you talking about?"

He shook his head. "Come on. Let's go investigate."

He was half-expecting a sudden needle in his neck or his ass, then a nice, long, hallucinogenic sleep while she carted him back to the hospital. It never came, and they crossed the open area unopposed.

As they got closer to the warehouse, Tommen noted that there were large marks on the building, like misdirected sunlight shadowing a dent in the sheet metal. Problem was, they were extremely large and in places where most of the machines couldn't reach, except maybe a crane.

"Looks like someone had a bad day, trying to clean this place up," Tommen said, pointing. "Those dents look new."

"I'm curious to know how you would know whether or not they're new," Julianna mused. "Were you paying much attention to the walls of the warehouse when you were held captive?"

Tommen flushed even as he fought a battle on two fronts. First, he was assaulted by endless images of that day. It hadn't been very late in the afternoon, but on the shortest day of the year, it had already been pretty dark. And if the darkness didn't play enough tricks, well, his wild imagination could fill in the gaps. Second, he was racked by fever and chills and all the aches and pains he'd been experiencing throughout the day, made worse as his skin reddened with embarrassment, pulling blood he didn't have in order to express an emotion he did not wish to convey.

"And anyway," Julianna went on, "those aren't dents." She approached the wall near one of the small man doors. A dent ran straight down the wall to the door. When she touched it, it moved, wiggled, like jelly. "They're scars."

"Scars?" Tommen wondered, moving to stand beside her. "What do you mean?"

"They're the folds where Rifun created his quasi-dimension, the last remnants of it."

"Why aren't they visible to the real world?"

"There are many things visible in the Land In Between that aren't visible in the real world."

"Okay, fine, whatever. What do the scars mean? Is there a way we can exploit them somehow?"

She took a step back and folded her arms. "Scars like this are weak spots between dimensions, with portals being like open wounds. In times past when I have made escape attempts, I've tried to use scars. Unfortunately, they've always been small scars, like these, and the difference in these scars versus any normal 'wall' as it were, was minimal."

"Why do these scars appear? Why don't portals leave scars?"

"Because portals are pure Energy. Creating quasi-dimensions like this involve the manipulation of Matter. In Rifun's case, he pulled this entire warehouse into the dimension and then back out again when he was done. The scars are evidence of the dimensions still trying to right themselves. Of course, the men inside probably wouldn't have noticed anything out of the ordinary, and such a small and unstable quasi-dimension would pose little threat to any accidental touches."

Tommen sat down on the dirty concrete. "I know you said that there's no good way to guarantee where a quasi-dimension will open up relative to other dimensions. Is there a way to figure out where this quasi-dimension opened up in relation to others? If it opened the way we want it to go, do you think we could utilize it as a gateway of some form?"

"I wouldn't know where to begin. And anyway, I don't think it would be quite where we want."

"Why not? We're walking on the same ground as those guys, but we're invisible. When this warehouse was a dimension, it was visible, but only those inside could manipulate it. Then you have the real world. I call that a stepping stone."

"A child's logic."

"Doesn't mean it can't work. How long do those scars take to, I don't know, heal?"

"It's been almost a year and they're still here. They won't be disappearing overnight."

"Awesome. So then we just have to go back, I'll get Micah and Micaiah and my dad and tell them the plan. We can try it tonight or early tomorrow morning before the early shift gets here." He fought his way to his feet once more. "If it works, Kayla may not even need to go to Hlohi. Well, it might be too late now, but whatever. She can still help when she gets back. But then, when we're—Ow!"

He wrenched away from Julianna as she stuck a needle in his shoulder just above the collarbone.

"What the fuck was that?!"

She tossed the empty syringe away. "Antibiotic with a mild sedative. You're running a fever and shouldn't exert yourself too much. If your blood pressure suddenly drops, then so do you."

"Fine, whatever." He put a hand to his shoulder to rub away the pain at the injection site. "Fuck."

He walked up to the scar and touched it. It didn't really feel like anything. At least he didn't get electrocuted. But neither did any of the guys inside suddenly start screaming about a hand coming through the wall.

"There are some old legends that say the Wheel of Time itself is a scar," Julianna said, walking up. "The weakest point between all dimensions. Of course, that's not true. It is merely the hub of a single dimension, like one bubble floating inside another."

"And other dimensions are other bubbles attached to the outside of the larger bubble?"

"Something like that. And when you put all those bubbles in a ring, we make up the center. Of course, we're attached to the bubble of this dimension, moving around and around and around, go nowhere and never breaking back in." She chuckled. "But then, analogies are no one's strong suit it seems."

Tommen raised a brow. "Indeed." He removed his hand from the scar. "Is there a way to recreate a dimension from the scars it leaves behind?"

"Speaking forensically, yes. Literally, I'm not sure."

"Do you know how to build a quasi-dimension? Even a small one?"

"I once heard about it, but it doesn't work from this side of things."

"Why?"

Julianna huffed a sigh. "Tommen, I don't know. I don't understand why some things work and others don't."

Tommen rubbed his eyes. "How is it that you can be the ultimate encyclopedia of this place one moment, and completely clueless the next? I thought you were like the master of this dimension or something?"

"I am the master of this dimension. This dimension. Not all dimensions, and it certainly doesn't help that for all my knowledge, it's not helping us escape. I know that. Maybe you should stop relying on me and keep running with your ideas. They've been brilliant so far; why give up now?"

Because that's exactly what you want. Tommen didn't say it, but he came pretty darn close. He sat down again and leaned back against the wall. Julianna knelt beside him and felt his forehead.

"You're burning up. You've used up whatever time you had to spare; now we need to get you back to the hospital, get you some more fluids and antibiotics."

"I'm fine, just give me a minute. I'm trying to think. There has to be a simple explanation for this."

"Tommen, I already said that the scars aren't going anywhere tonight. You'll be able to think in the hospital, and you'll probably be more productive if your body isn't tearing itself apart between trying to heal and trying to scheme."

"If the scars are a result of the Matter trying to realign itself with the primary dimension, and if we can touch the scars, theoretically, we should be able to move through them into the quasi-dimension. Like you said you tried to do. But it didn't work because there was no dimension there, the same way scar tissue can become thick and calloused, tougher than regular tissue. Just like taking out a door and filling it in with brick. You knew where it was, but you can't pass through. But that part of the wall around it will still be structurally weaker than the rest."

"We have to go," Julianna urged.

But Tommen wasn't hearing her. "In the case of skin, that's all going to be backfilled and shit. But in the case of dimensions, if something were to be opened up behind that brick wall, we might still be able to bust through the door, even if it's been boarded up. And then we can use that quasi-dimension to carry us out into the primary dimension, into the real world." He grinned and looked at her. "I know how we're getting out of here."

"Great. You can tell me all about it once we get back to the hospital."

He put up little resistance as she helped him to his wobbly feet, but as soon as he was standing, walking away from the warehouse door with her arms around him, his knees went out. His chest clenched in uproarious pain, twisting against his heart and lungs. He gasped for breath and went to all fours as dizziness overcame him. Ringing broke out in his ears and everything sounded muffled and far away. Fear coursed through him and he instinctively jerked away when someone put their hands on him.

As fear turned into the bestial instinct to survive, he crawled away a few feet before drunkenly standing and running away, making for anyplace safe. He could feel Rifun's revolver at his back, following him, waiting for the perfect shot that never came. Tommen reached the nearest cargo container and ran straight through it, moving through metal and boxes and crates and emerging on the other side. His heart was racing and his breath came in short, ragged gasps. He dropped to the ground and fought to keep from crying. Too late, that had started somewhere out there in the field. He wiped away the tears and tried to focus, but the fear tore at him like the raven clawing at Prometheus.

A minute later, Julianna knelt in front of him. Gingerly, she reached out and put her hands on his knees which he'd drawn up to his chest. "Tommen. Listen to me very carefully. There is nothing here that is going to hurt you. Whatever happened out there, it's gone now. It's over with. Everyone is safe."

"Nine officers died," Tommen told her.

"But you are safe. Your dad is safe. Nothing going on here today is anything sinister. These guys here are just trying to make a living. Doing their daily jobs. The old nine to five, right? But you are safe. And you have to return to work yourself eventually, right? You can't do that from here. So let's go back to the hospital, get you another round of fluids and antibiotics, and see if we can't make you as strong as possible before trying to cross not one, but two dimensions. That sounds a little tougher than your average trip to the Wheel, doesn't it?" He sniffed but nodded. "Yeah, I thought so. Come on."

He managed to stand on his own power. "Fuck, I'm such an idiot."

"Why?"

"I shouldn't let it get to me."

"It's nothing to be ashamed of. It was a panic attack."

"Yeah. Something that's reserved for people who have actually seen shit, like fucking firefighters or war veterans or —"

"Police officers?"

He shrugged. "I guess."

"You were in a shootout that involved police officers. Many of them died. What you're experiencing is normal."

He scoffed and shook his head. "Nothing about this is normal."

She looked at him, but her expression was difficult to read. Pity was in there, certainly, but the rest seemed to be a mixture of curiosity, uncertainty, and was that irritation in there, too? Or did the little squares on her face throw things off a little?

They returned to the hospital, but when they got inside the lobby, Tommen stopped. He faced Julianna and told her, "I'll do the fluids and medicine and shit, but only if I get an actual room with an actual bed."

She hesitated for half a second. "Is it the machines or the bed you want?"

"Mostly I just want to lie down and take a nap."

"Okay. Well, I'll set you up with the ports and whatnot, but then I think I have an idea."

He followed her back to the room where they'd set up before. While Julianna went off to retrieve supplies, Tommen called his dad.

"Tommen, are you all right?" Walter demanded immediately.

"Getting better all the time," Tommen told him. "Right now I've got more needles in me than a heroin addict."

"And you would know that how?" His dad's tone was teasing.

He sighed. "Whatever, man. Listen, we went and investigated an idea on how to make rescue a little more...likely. It's not easier, but it sounds a little more foolproof. But in order for it to work, we need to reopen the quasi-dimension in the warehouse."

"The warehouse as in...?"

"The one at the shipping yard, yes. I know, I really don't like it either, but it's the only spot I know of where a quasi-dimension has been built recently. Unless you know of another?"

"Sorry to say I don't."

Tommen rubbed his eyes. "I was afraid you'd say that."

"Who do you plan to get to open this quasi-dimension, anyway? I certainly can't do it."

"What about one of the twins or Kayla or any of the Akarin?"

"I'll call and get them asking around."

"No, don't worry about that. I'll call. I have nothing better to do right now anyway." Tommen looked around the room to make sure Julianna hadn't sneaked up on him. "Where's the journal?"

"Micah took it with him. I think he said something about—"

"No. Don't. I don't want to know right now. As long as it's safe."

"As safe as it can be."

"Good. Listen, I'm going to call the twins and start asking around. You just worry about yourself and how the hell you're going to pull me out of here. Okay?"

His dad hesitated for half a second. "All right. You seem to know what you're doing."

"I'd like to think I do. I just hope I can stay one step ahead."

"Ahead of who?"

"I have to go."

Tommen hung up half a second before Julianna returned with fluid bags and more syringes.

"Calling your dad to let him know you're all right?" she asked.

He nodded. "Yeah. He's really worried."

"I can imagine. Okay, so I have all the medicines I think you're going to need. If you can carry a couple, that would be excellent."

He stood. "Carry them? Where are we going?"

His question was answered as soon as she took them in a Travel Band and dropped them off in his bedroom. Tommen was more than happy to be back in his own bed, though the IVs and the medicine put a bit of a damper on things.

"I thought this might be a little better than sitting in a hospital all evening and all night," Julianna said, hanging up the fluid bag and delivering several more antibiotics via syringe. "How's this working for you?"

"Well, it's better than the hospital," Tommen admitted. "Are you going to sit here and play nurse all night, though?"

"No, I don't expect so. I have other business to attend to, and I prefer to sleep in my own bed, same as you. I will be by to check on you, though. Sepsis is nothing to fool around with. If possible, don't go to sleep unless you are honestly feeling better. The biggest thing is not to pass out. If you're asleep when I get back, I will shake you awake just to be sure."

He nodded. "Thank you for the concern. I am feeling better, though."

She dipped her head once. "Good. Let's keep it that way." She turned as if to leave, then looked back. "Oh, and, I was wondering when I might expect to get my husband's journal back?"

"Oh. Um, well, I was going to call my dad first just to let him know I'm back in the house. But if you want me to stay awake, I'm going to need some kind of reading material or something to keep me occupied. Listen, once we get out of this awful dimension, you can have it back."

She studied him for a moment, and Tommen was almost afraid she was going to call his bluff. Finally she nodded. "Of course. I'll be back later, then."

He watched her leave, then waited a few minutes just to make sure she was gone before doing anything. His first order of business was turning on the light to see his dad know he was there. His second order of business was setting his hearing aids to charging seeing how they were just about dead, then plugging his phone in and reconnecting it to the monstrous signal booster so he could make a call.

"Is it safe to talk now?" his dad asked.

"As safe as it can be," Tommen sighed. "I'm back in my room."

The chair out at the kitchen table grated noisily across the floor and a minute later, Walter walked in, looking almost disappointed when he couldn't actually see his son.

"Are you all right? Are you still septic?"

"Like I said, more needles than a heroin junkie. We brought the hospital stuff here just so I could relax in my own bed. I've still got fluids and IVs and medicine and whatever else in me."

"Well, you sound better, anyway."

"Still hurts, though."

"I know. But let's hear this plan of yours."

"I haven't even called the twins yet. Mostly I just wanted to let you know I'm here."

His dad nodded. "Okay. I appreciate it. If you want, I'll dole out some soup in a bowl so you can suck it in and suck it down."

Tommen laughed weakly. "That sounds pretty good. What kind of soup?"

"Just homemade chicken noodle."

"Sounds good."

"All right. I'll bring it in. You call the twins."

His dad left the room, returning with a bowl of soup which Tommen eagerly brought into the dimension to scarf down. It probably wasn't his best idea ever, but he needed to keep his fluid intake up, and his dad could make a mean chicken noodle.

"Hello?" Micaiah answered as Tommen was about halfway through the bowl.

"Micaiah?" Tommen asked around a mouthful of soup.

"Tommen?"

He swallowed. "Yeah, it's me."

"Fucking hell, Tommen. What's this I hear that you're septic?"

"I'm getting better, okay? I've got a shit ton of meds in me right now. Listen, I have an idea on how to break out tomorrow. It's not easier necessarily, but it might have a better chance of working. The only thing I need to know is whether you or someone, anyone, knows how to build a quasi-dimension."

"A quasi-dimension? What for?"

Tommen explained the dimensional scars at the warehouse and his plan to exploit them in order to rebuild the dimension to use as a stepping stone. Micaiah listened patiently and was quiet for several seconds after he finished.

"Cai?" Tommen prompted.

"It's certainly an interesting idea, and I've no reason to think it couldn't work. Except, to answer your question, no, I don't know how to build a quasi-dimension. That kind of Building...even the current Builders would be hard-pressed for that kind of talent."

"It doesn't have to be huge or super stable like the Wheel, just enough that we can get through. What's the worst thing that can happen, we're stuck back here a little longer while we work out another plan?"

"That's great, but I still don't know how to do it."

Tommen sighed. "The art of Building is rare and diminished, but Rifun still managed to build that quasi-dimension in the first place. You have the journal. Maybe it's in there. I know you don't want to, but the answers really could be there."

"I don't know, Tommen. Let me make some inquiries around the Akarin, see if anyone else with more training has some insight or knowledge of these quasi-dimensions. We may get lucky."

"Okay. Guess that's the best we can do right now. Has Kayla left yet for Hlohi?"

"I don't know. She had a pretty full schedule today as it is, so she was planning on going straight from work to Hlohi—or to the fortress to meet Natalie, then to Hlohi, but you get what I mean. I haven't seen her since this morning. Even if she hasn't left, I'm not going to call her back. If your idea doesn't work, we may need whatever insight she brings. And even if it does work, then we can use both testimonies to perhaps help others in the future."

"Makes sense, I guess."

"We'll get you out, Tommen." He paused dramatically. "And only you."

Tommen sighed. "Listen, I know what Julianna did, conspiring with Cassius and all, but, don't you think that maybe she regrets it? Just a little bit? Maybe she's changed in the last century. My dad has, you know that. I mean, she's helped me with my arm and the antibiotics for the infections and everything else. Isolation isn't good for a person. What if she is different?"

"I'm sorry, Tommen, but I can honestly say she isn't."

"How do you know? Is it in one of the Authored Books? Can you send it to me? I'll bring it back with me, I promise."

"Unfortunately, I can't. There are always two initial copies of an Authored book, one in the Archives and one directly to the main person himself—or herself. The Archive copy is not to be removed for any reason. Doesn't matter who you are."

Tommen scoffed and shook his head. "Stupid arbitrary rules."

"Just trust me on this."

"Okay, so I can't read it for myself. Spoil the ending for me; I don't mind."

"Would you really want the power that spawned Rifun walking the Earth beside him?"

Well, that was a pretty loaded question, wasn't it? Still he asked, "But why don't you think she could be sorry and actually want to change?"

"And if Rifun, in a century, decided he was utterly repentant for the crimes he's committed, would you tell him all is well and forgiven and he can walk free? Or would you still punish him for the millions he enslaved? What if Hitler came out and said he was sorry for Auschwitz? Forgiveness is good, but punishment is just." Beat. "No. She's not coming out."

"What did she do?"

"You already know. You've seen this before, albeit from the sidelines."

"No, I don't. You're speaking in riddles. Fucking hell, you're almost as bad as..."

"As...?" Micaiah goaded.

"Almost as bad as Chandler."

"Well, there is that. Anyway, I'm going to make those calls." He paused a moment. "I don't know whether to take that as a compliment or an insult. Maybe I'll ask him next time I see him."

Tommen rolled his eyes and hung up. Fucking hell. Why did

everyone insist on treating him like a child? He propped up a couple pillows and leaned back. As he stared at his computer desk, an idea struck. The Chandler person seemed to communicate via visions and dreams and shit. Rifun did that, too. If that was merely a form of Energy manipulation, maybe he could try it, too, seeing how he was in an Energy-saturated dimension.

But how did one go about initiating this "dream-walking" or whatever New Age bullshit wanted to call it? Was it a matter of ask and ye shall receive? Did he have to hum and go into some sort of weird trance? Did he even have to be asleep? Did the other party have to be asleep? It seemed logical, given that it was called "dream" walking. He lay back as far as he could and closed his eyes, willing himself out of his own mind and into the dreams of others, feeling very foolish for doing so.

After a few minutes or fruitless trancing, he got up and shut the lights off in his room, hoping the dark might help him a little. He returned to his bed, got as comfortable as he could amid the IV lines, then closed his eyes and began again.

He couldn't decide if he'd actually entered someone else's dream or was just having one of his own and it was a lucid dream where he could do whatever he wanted. Either way, it was a pretty bleak place, dark and empty. Maybe he really was in his own mind. But then again, maybe not. There wasn't enough sex for it to be his mind.

"So, I heard you wanted to talk to me."

Tommen whirled to see Rifun walking toward him. He moved slowly, casually, hands behind his back, long hair tied back. He wore his signature gray sweatshirt, jeans, and work boots. His freckles were still out of place on an otherwise handsome face, but it was the eyes and the smile that won the girls, Tommen was sure.

"You've made a lot of progress since getting sucked into the in-between dimension," Rifun said, walking right up to Tommen to stand face-to-face. "Maybe this was just the kick in the ass you needed to start actually learning."

"That dimension you built at the warehouse, can you recreate that?" Tommen asked, willing himself not to get lured in by Rifun's charm, and also very aware that only one person had heard his musings about asking for the man's help.

"Why would I want to do that? More importantly, why would you want me to do that?"

Tommen explained his idea one more time, finishing with, "Micaiah doesn't know how to do it, and he's not sure of anyone who does. But I know you can do it. Obviously, I've seen you do it."

"So you're asking me for help, to get you out of a mess which you put yourself in?"

Rifun's eyes laughed at him as he grudgingly answered, "Yes. Will you help me? Please?"

"He even remembered his manners," Rifun smirked. "Just for that, I will help you. And because I know the circumstances are difficult, I will even let it be its own reward and I won't ask anything for it. This time. Don't go getting any ideas that I'm a charitable person."

Tommen shook his head. "Never cross my mind. But I do wonder what the price of information is."

"Oh, now things are getting interesting. What kind of information?"

"Who is Julianna?"

Rifun raised a brow. "Julianna? Well, I suppose it's not surprising that you've met her given where you are and all."

"Is she as evil as Micaiah seems to think?"

"As the Akarin seems to think, you mean. The Akarin blame her for the rise of the Cult and the dissent within their own ranks. Of course they're going to paint her as an evil sorceress of sorts."

"Were you her Apprentice once? How are you two affiliated?"

"Affiliation is one way to put it, I suppose. She and Cassius were affiliated long before I was involved. The deal was that she would give him the journal and he wouldn't execute her husband. You know how that turned out."

"I know that she tried to make a power play," Tommen cut in. "I saw it. In the time travel. Cassius was the Zero Hour and he was going to release Richard in order to win the loyalty of his followers and overtake the Akarin. Julianna looked like she was a partner in the whole thing."

Rifun sighed. "It wasn't a power play. It was a peace play. It's the same one Micaiah is trying to make by using Kayla to bring in District Nine in the war against the Borelians. Just as he is attempting to unify all the human colonies, so Julianna was trying to unify Akarin and the Time industry. But that wasn't going to happen as long as the Akarin were corrupt and dissolving. Richard wanted to stop the dissent by bringing everyone together under the words of the Author, not some so-called novels full of pithy mistakes and needless errors. Suffice to say, it didn't work. The Akarin were still too powerful. Everything went to hell from there.

"When it failed, Cassius—a power-hungry, blood-thirsty bastard as you well remember—sought to destroy Julianna. He chased her into the old mine the first time where she stashed the journal that you found. When he came out, I picked him up. He told me about the Akarin and the journal, the words of the Author. He was sure Julianna still had the journal. My interest was solely in the journal. His was seek and destroy. I didn't find the journal, but he found Julianna. She escaped death, but not before he'd cut up her face."

"And when you came out, you just started murdering women in your quest for the journal," Tommen stated. "I don't believe you're entirely innocent."

"Did I say I was?"

"Why should I trust anything you just said?"

"Because if you had a better source of information, you wouldn't be asking me in the first place. In the same way you went to Micaiah first to ask about rebuilding that dimension."

Tommen sighed. "If you show up there tomorrow with them, they'll kill you on the spot."

Rifun barked a laugh. "Ha! I'd like to see them try. Honestly,

Tommen, I really wish you would have a little more faith in me."

"Why should I? You're the one who left me to my own devices and now look where I am."

"Perhaps, but as you like to remind everyone, you're not a child who needs to be supervised all the time. You're an adult, capable of making your own decisions and acting on your own. Which you most certainly did."

"I had no fucking clue what I was doing!"

"And whose fault is that?"

Tommen snorted and looked away. He could feel Rifun's mocking gaze and lopsided smirk. He sighed. "Okay, fine. Just get me the fuck out of here. Can you do that?"

"I make no guarantees on anything. The in-between dimension is a fickle beast, or so I hear."

"And one more thing. How did you know I wanted to talk to you?"

"You project your dream-walking intentions as badly as your fistfight moves. Subtlety was never your strong suit."

"Fine. Okay, so, sorry, I lied. One last thing. Can you not kill anyone, if you do show up to help with this?"

Rifun raised a brow. "Your terms are steep. I shall simply say this: I will not initiate a fight, but I will not allow myself to be taken in. I will act only in self-defense."

Tommen ground his teeth. "Fine. You guys can deal with that one. But I'm not going to have a second horror show at that shipping yard."

"I do not wish such a thing either. After all, we are all coming together with the intent of freeing you from your miserable prison."

"Well, don't sing kum-bah-yah too loud or you'll overload my hearing aids."

"Ha! Always such wit. I admire that about you. Was there anything else you'd like to talk about during this therapy session?"

"You said your help was free. What's the price of the information?"

Rifun folded his arms. "See, that's the surprising thing. I don't know. I haven't decided. Every encounter thus far has been me approaching you, and usually only when I want to teach you something and get something in return. This is the first time you have reached out to me." He smiled and looked at Tommen. "Maybe we'll just call that square, then."

Tommen didn't like his tone or his cryptic words. Nothing good came from ominous tones and cryptic words. At the same time, it seemed like a good thing, so he wasn't about to question it. Not having to worry about what he owed Rifun was a good feeling, even when it wasn't.

Rifun chuckled. "Wakey, wakey, Tommen. Mommy's calling you."

For a minute, Tommen wasn't sure quite what he meant. Then, as Rifun began walking away, the darkness began to close in. Suddenly it was like Tommen was being dragged away into lands unknown. He fought and struggled, but quickly found that it was only the air he was fighting. When he finally calmed down, he saw Julianna standing in the corner of the room, syringe in hand.

"What?" he gasped, feeling the tightness in his chest slowly release.

"You were sleeping," Julianna said calmly, taking a tentative step toward him. "I told you that if I found you sleeping, I was going to wake you up, just to make sure you hadn't succumbed to anything."

Tommen lay back on his pillow and closed his eyes. "Right. I remember." He let out a breath. "So, how am I doing?"

Now she approached and gave him the medicine. "From what I can see, you're doing well. You still have a fever, elevated heart rate and respirations. How's your head?"

"Um...I don't feel sick or anything. A little dizzy still, though."

"And you're not as out of it as you were before either, or so it seems. I'd say you're doing better."

"Good. What time is it?"

"Nine-thirty, give or take." She changed the fluid bag and gave him another syringe. "That should do you for the night. I'll come back later and remove the bag and line so you can sleep a little better. You've got enough meds in you right now to kill a horse. If I give you any more tonight, the stuff that's making you well will end up making you sick again."

"Oh. Makes sense, I guess." He rubbed his face. "I didn't even really mean to fall asleep, it just kind of...happened."

"Your body has been through a lot today; it needs rest."

"Yeah, well, now I'm wide awake."

She nodded sympathetically. "Of course. That happens, too. I expect you'll be reading my husband's journal, then. Where is it?"

"Why?"

"I thought that since I'm here, if you had questions, I could answer them."

"Yeah, well..." Tommen fought for an excuse. "I don't do class reading or discussions very well. And besides, if we're escaping tomorrow, then maybe we can all sit down. There's a lot of myth and rumors about the journal, and having you there to answer questions—the next best thing to Richard himself—might be exactly what we need to at least bring the Akarin back together, or keep it from tearing itself apart any more than it already is."

He severely hoped she couldn't tell how he was deflecting, but he knew he was a bad liar. He tried to keep his expression neutral, if not a little hopeful and naive. Whether it worked or she just decided to tolerate his bullshit, he couldn't decide. Either way, she simply nodded and took a step back.

"That would be a good thing," she said calmly. "Division is the last thing we need, that anyone needs. Perhaps it is time to set the record straight about my husband." Her expression turned grave. "I don't know that the Akarin will take well the indictments against them. They did much wrong to my husband, his followers, and others through the years."

"You can't fix a problem you can't see," Tommen said sagely.

"Indeed. And you speak truly. Not all who are Akarin today

are responsible or in any way related to the horrors of the past. Perhaps it is time to move on." She nodded again decisively. "Very well. As I said, I will be back later at some point tonight to check on you. You appear to be doing much better; I don't want to jeopardize that."

"Everyone goes home."

She smiled. "Everyone goes home."

Maybe it was the cuts on her face that made Tommen recoil at her smile. Maybe it was the sudden image of a grinning serpent that came to mind. Either way, it was repulsive and, if his paranoia had anything to say about it, untrustworthy.

Julianna gave him a final once-over before turning and leaving. Tommen released a breath and tried to calm himself down. Regardless of whether she believed him, he'd bought himself a little time at least. In the morning, he just needed to grab some kind of bag, throw all his shit in it, and tell her that everything was together. Her husband's journal was in the bag with the rest of the stuff. With any luck, according to Micaiah, she wouldn't be coming through at all and wouldn't escape. But if she did manage to get out with him, then at least they still had control of the journal.

He rolled over on his bed, grateful that he didn't have the IV lines to impede him. He knew he should probably try to sleep. Problem was, his mind was going through a thousand different scenarios and a thousand different conflicts.

What if Julianna was right? What if this was all, basically, just a huge misunderstanding? What if her husband had been trying to forge the path to peace both for the Akarin internally and between the Akarin and the Time industry? What if Richard had been unfairly treated by the victors of history? It wouldn't be Micaiah's fault for mistrusting her because he came in after the fact, after Richard and Julianna had been condemned. If her story was true and Micaiah and the others could be made to see reason, then there might be a chance for peace. It probably wouldn't help the Akarin against the Hands of Time, and it certainly wouldn't do anything for the human-Borelian war, but it would stop the internal decay of the Akarin and give people a place to call home again.

On the other hand, what if she was playing him? What if she had made a power play and tried to unite the two sides for evil purposes? What if she was coming up with some sort of probable story in order to gain his trust? But why would she need his trust?

He closed his eyes and thought back to the scene in the prison. Julianna delivered the journal and confirmed the agreement with Cassius. The Time industry and Richard's followers would unite and destroy the corrupt Akarin.

Then Tommen had another thought. What if the whole thing was made up? What if Richard had simply been opportunistic? He took the crisis of the Akarin dissent and came up with a way to tip the balance. Assuming the Time industry was fifty percent and the Akarin was fifty percent, if the Akarin faltered, that would mean their destruction by the Time industry. But if Richard started writing in his journal and claimed it to be the words of the Author, he would be able to save a good portion of the Akarin, making himself look like a hero. He and Julianna conspire with Cassius to make his arrest look like some kind of peace agreement in order to bring the sides together. Crush the rebellion, save his friends, and set up a singular government. That way everyone looks like a hero which quells future dissent.

Tommen stared at his ceiling. Maybe he watched too much TV. Not everything had to be a complex, mind-bending, super-twisty, ultra-confusing chess game. Some things really could be as simple as a peacekeeping operation gone wrong. Besides, Julianna had been nothing but good to him. Regardless of her actions or intentions beforehand, she really could be sorry about the whole thing.

And if Hitler said he was sorry, would you let him go?

Fucking hell. Tommen rubbed his eyes. He had the trust of his friends and the actions of this woman. He really didn't know which way he wanted to go on this. Maybe he should help her escape, then let the rest of them decide what to do with her. If they wanted to listen to her and have peace talks, great. If they wanted to make her disappear into another portal and seal her back in the in-between dimension, then that was their call. But he wasn't going to play judge and jury when he had so much conflicting evidence.

He yawned and sat up, telling himself the whole time to roll over and go back to sleep. Leave it alone. Just wait, escape tomorrow, let others decide what to do with her.

Then he paused. Why was he turning this over to the grownups like a child? Was he incapable of looking at evidence and coming to his own conclusions? He was stuck in the in-between dimension with all this time travel shit. He had the best evidence of all: front row seats. So maybe it was time to do some investigating.

Chapter Twenty
Twice Planned

Walter spent much of his afternoon just recovering from the failed attempt at rescuing his son. The shockwave from the collapsed portal had rattled his bones, but that was nothing compared to the shaking and frantic worry in his mind. He was too glad for the call from Micaiah saying Tommen had stopped by and seemed to be relatively okay, but he was forced to wonder why Tommen himself hadn't called. Had his phone been damaged somehow? Well, with that kind of Energy surge, his phone could have fried. Walter forced himself to relax and told himself that Tommen was alive and in relatively good spirits, well enough to be out and about and communicating.

It was a while before his phone rang with an unknown number.

"Hello?" he wondered.

"Dad?" Tommen said.

Walter sat up in his recliner. "Tommen?"

"Yeah, it's me."

"This isn't your phone number."

"No, it's not. I'm at the hospital right now."

"Oh my God, are you all right? Did you make it out? Micaiah called me and said you hadn't."

"No, not yet. Julianna came by and told me I had septic or something."

"Sepsis?"

That was not good. According to Laura, by the time doctors actually diagnosed sepsis, it was usually already too late. Patients who went into septic shock only had about a fifty-fifty chance of survival, and those who did survive usually suffered side effects that could follow them for their entire lives. Tommen was young and healthy, true, but he was also severely injured.

"Yeah. She found some IVs and medicine and stuff," Tommen went on. "I don't know, but I guess it's working."

Walter let out a breath. "Okay. That's good. Good that you're getting better. How's your arm?"

"Healing, or that's what she says. I mean, my jacket kind of melted into my skin, so it's a little hard to tell. But she said the small blisters are healing."

"That's good. Listen, kiddo, Micaiah said that tomorrow is going to be the earliest we can make another attempt, but it probably won't be until Kayla returns from her other mission."

"It's okay. I understand. And, actually, calling you, I have an idea on how to make it a little easier."

"That would be much appreciated."

"Listen, Dad, I have to go. There's more medicine coming and I don't want to get all loopy on you."

Walter grinned even though Tommen couldn't see. "Fair enough. Stay safe, son."

"I will, Dad. Love you."

"Love you, too. Hang in there."

He hung up and leaned back, closing his eyes and trying to calm his racing heart. Sepsis was not a good thing, but if it had been correctly identified and was being treated, then he would probably be all right.

Walter wasn't sure quite where he stood on this Julianna person, or her husband for that matter. He couldn't really condemn him for writing an evil book just because one madman had turned into a fanatic over it. Well, okay, so an entire evil cult had come about because of it, but that wasn't the fault of the author, was it? It could be, if Micaiah could be believed. According to him, the whole thing had been a power play for Richard, a way to capitalize on the internal conflicts of the Akarin, destroy them, and guarantee power for himself. As for Julianna, she was the silent figure in the background, the one who had really made things happen, gathered the troops and distributed the weapons and propaganda.

But the thing about history was that it only happened once, and if you weren't there to see it, well then, you missed it. Even cameras couldn't be trusted anymore. *History is written by the victors,* Walter thought, *and they're all liars.*

Some days, he didn't know what to believe. It was a terrible thing to admit, especially when he worked homicide. He gathered the evidence, examined it, weighed it for relevance and credibility, and he made the best damn guess he could.

Maybe it was because there was no murder here. This wasn't a physical case, but a philosophical one. Who did he believe was correct? He trusted Micaiah as his friend, but he presently had no real reason to discredit Julianna because he'd never met her and she was reportedly doing well to help his son. Which book did he want to believe? A collection of books supposedly written by the Author herself? Or a single book supposedly containing words coming directly from the Author? Could they both be true? If not, which side was right? Both claimed to wield the Akari, and both had demonstrated considerable power, beyond what even the greatest Time Agents were capable of.

Walter rubbed his eyes. He was never very good at holy wars, which was what this was turning out to be. Maybe he was becoming as cynical as Tommen. Ironic, considering how uncynical Tommen was becoming. Was that a word? Uncynical? He thought a moment and decided it was. Didn't matter anyway, he supposed. If someone out there was going to have a tiff over his misuse of grammar, they'd be yelling at the Author about it, not him.

He turned on the evening news, but, being a weekend, things were pretty slow. Nothing major in local politics because the city government only worked the standard business week, and he mentally skipped over the national politics because he was tired of all the bullshit over the 2016 elections which were still over two years away. That left basic local news like car accidents, break-ins, school sports, and the like, and the weather. Early to mid-August, so things were still pretty nice. Warm temperatures, scattered rain showers quickly giving way to sunshine.

After a minute or two, he stood and did another lap around the interior of the house. He didn't like the recharge. They had an idea about how to rescue Tommen and it had almost worked. He knew it had taken a lot out of Micah. It had taken a lot out of him, too. But did they really have to wait a whole day before trying again?

After about the fourth or fifth lap, he headed out to the kitchen. He wasn't really hungry, and he knew that stress-eating wasn't good, especially since he really was trying to lose weight. He told himself that as long as he got real food and avoided the sugar that his body was craving, he could justify it. Still, while the tuna sandwich was good, the chocolate ice cream he knew was still in the freezer was sounding pretty good, too.

The stress cravings were only made worse when he considered that he had to go back to work tomorrow. Damn it. He hadn't even thought of that. They'd either have to try the rescue later tonight, wait until he got off tomorrow, or designate someone else to pull Tommen through the portal. The only one he had a real problem with was the third one simply because he wanted to be there when his son finally came out, came home. He didn't want to get "the call." He wanted to be the one there to pull him through, hug him, and send him off in an ambulance against his will.

He ended up eating the chocolate ice cream. Not a lot, just enough to feel guilty, which didn't take much. When that was finally put away, he sat at the tiny kitchen table, turning his phone over and over in his hand. At last, he hit Dial.

It went to voicemail. He couldn't decide if it was a disappointment or a relief. Either way, he returned to his recliner to relax and watch some evening programming. How bad was it when he was doing better than the *Jeopardy!* contestants? By his personal scoring, he had ten grand. Maybe if he wrote to the studio and could prove his worth, they'd send him that check. Nah, too much of a hassle. And if they didn't send him the money, he'd be out fifty cents for a stamp.

When his phone rang again, he recognized the hospital number.

"Tommen, are you all right?" he demanded.

"Getting better all the time," Tommen told him. "Right now I've got more needles in me than a heroin addict."

Walter raised a brow. "And you would know that how?"

He sighed. "Whatever, man. Listen, we went and investigated an idea on how to make rescue a little more...likely. It's not easier, but it sounds a little more foolproof. But in order for it to work, we need to reopen the quasi-dimension in the warehouse."

"The warehouse as in...?"

"The one at the shipping yard, yes. I know, I really don't like it either, but it's the only spot I know of where a quasi-dimension has been built recently. Unless you know of another?"

He wished he knew of another. Even if he didn't, he wished he could think about that warehouse and not be overcome by sudden fear and loathing. He wished he could think about that warehouse without feeling searing pain in his chest and leg, without tasting phantom blood in his mouth as he drowned. He wished that this plan could be anywhere but there.

"Sorry to say I don't," he said at last.

"I was afraid you'd say that." He could hear the disappointment in his son's voice. No doubt he had some very raw memories of that place, too.

"Who do you plan to get to open this quasi-dimension, anyway? I certainly can't do it."

"What about one of the twins or Kayla or any of the Akarin?"

"I'll call and get them asking around."

"No, don't worry about that. I'll call. I have nothing better to do right now anyway." Tommen lowered his voice. "Where's the journal?"

"Micah took it with him. I think he said something about—"

"No. Don't. I don't want to know right now. As long as it's safe."

"As safe as it can be."

"Good. Listen, I'm going to call the twins and start asking around. You just worry about yourself and how the hell you're going to pull me out of here. Okay?"

Walter hesitated for half a second. "All right. You seem to know what you're doing."

"I'd like to think I do. I just hope I can stay one step ahead."

"Ahead of who?"

"I have to go."

Click.

To say Walter wasn't worried by such a cryptic call would have been a lie, but he tried to focus on the positive. First, Tommen sounded a lot better than he had before, so whatever meds he was getting must be working. Second, he seemed to have a plan. Sure, it might not be easier, but if there was a higher chance of success, Walter was all for it.

The show went to commercial and Walter headed for the bathroom. By the time he emerged, he wasn't concerned about the show being back on so much as his phone that was ringing. He reached it half a second before it went to voicemail.

"Tommen?" he asked.

"No. Laura. Sorry, I saw you called, so I figured I'd call back. Is now a bad time? Did they find him?"

Walter harrumphed back into his recliner and considered his next words very carefully.

"Well, yes. They did find him."

"That's great! Oh my God, how is he? We just got back from a run, but next time out, I'll look for him in the hospital."

Walter shifted uncomfortably. "See, that's the thing. He's not in the hospital."

"Maybe you should start at the beginning."

"So, one of the rescuers did come across a message he'd set out for them. Somewhere along the line, he came back to his senses and pointed them in the right direction where he was hiding. He'd found a cave, got settled in, waited for rescue. At some point, for some unknown reason, there was a rockslide. He's trapped in the cave."

"How bad? Like, can they talk to him or what?"

"They were able to make contact, yes. To a small extent, they can see him, too. They did a few small trials, safe trials, to try and get him out as safely as possible. When those didn't work, they went to slightly more drastic measures. They tried to pull him out, even had a grip on him at one point, but then they lost it and the cave collapsed even further. They are able to talk to him still, which is good. Supposedly, they have a way to slip him food and water, but the cave and surrounding rock is very unstable, so they have to work out how to get to him without causing another collapse."

Laura let out a breath. "Oh my God...But. Hey. They found him. He's alive. Is he hurt bad?"

"Concussive symptoms. His entire left arm and his side is burned; he thinks second- or third-degree. Apparently, it's become infected. Since they can't get a doctor in to see him, they're sending basic antibiotics in so he can self-administer until they get him out. Right now, their main concern for him is sepsis."

"Oh, absolutely. What are they doing? Are they bringing in crews or what?"

"I don't know. I mean, I assume so. Sounds like they're getting geologists, engineers...I don't know the specifics. The really good news, though, is that he was able to make a phone call before the second cave-in."

"Did he call you?"

Walter took a breath. "Yes, he did. It was good to hear his voice."

"I can imagine. Where is he exactly?"

"I don't know the exact location, just that it's south of the camp. I wanted to go up there, but with all the crews up there digging around, I'd just get in the way. Besides, once they get him out, they're just going to airlift him back here anyway."

Laura chuckled. "Makes sense, I guess. Hey, that's some really good news, though. You know where he is and how he's doing and a bunch of professionals who know what the heck they're doing are on the case."

"Yeah. Just a matter of time."

"Listen, I have to go. There's some stuff we have to get done before trying to head off to bed. Notice I said 'trying.' Anyway, I'll call you back after we're done if you want."

"Please, Laura, I'm an old man. I'm going to win my ten thousand in final jeopardy and then I have to get going to bed to get my beauty sleep before work tomorrow."

"Oh, please, Walter." He could imagine her eye roll. "Okay, fine. Just keep me updated, all right? I'm happy for you, Walt. And if he is rescued and gets airlifted before I'm off shift, I'll be sure to meet you here when you come see him."

"Okay. Thank you, Laura."

"Do they have any estimation on time when they might pull him out? I mean, I know rocks are terrible and unstable, but did they give you anything?"

Walter sighed. "They're hoping tomorrow—you know, when it's light out. Maybe Monday. Those are the current hopes."

He heard the smile in her voice. "Okay. I'll talk to you later, then. Bye."

"Bye."

He hung up, but joy, relief, all of those normal emotions were the furthest thing from his mind right now. Instead, he only felt disgusted at himself. He hated lying to her. He wasn't even sure why he'd called her to give her such a made up story. It would only take one call to the search team to debunk the whole thing. And if someone did come sniffing and questioning him, what would he say? He hadn't been out to the search site lately, so he might be accused of being disinterested. His fanciful story might be used as evidence of dissociating from reality. And if he ever tried to pull a story about his son being trapped in an alternate dimension, he would inevitably live out his days in the loony bin. The worst part was, that was the truth. His son really was trapped in another dimension.

The regular evening programming ended and made way for the latest crazy sitcoms on TV. Walter couldn't even say what he watched except only half of it was actually amusing, and of the stuff that was amusing, half of it he felt guilty for because it made him feel like a stupid teenager. A year ago, he might not have laughed at all except now he was dating Laura.

Did he want to sleep with Laura? Well, yes, he wouldn't deny it. She was attractive, intelligent, funny, and a great storyteller. He enjoyed being with her. A century of celibacy apparently hadn't killed him completely as he thought about her bright smile, shining eyes, and great body. She wasn't a perfect model, true, but she was like him, and that was what he liked about her. She had more confidence in herself and was more comfortable with herself than he could ever say about himself.

He sighed and got up. *No use thinking about it now, old timer. She's on shift, for one. And even if she wasn't, you still have to set an example for Tommen. You haven't even solved the Timekeeper business yet, and how shameful would it be if you loved her and dumped her?*

He hated these philosophical conversations with himself. Two in one night, even. Where was Tommen when he needed him for some nice atheistic cynicism? For as much as people, himself included, found Tommen's attitude exasperating and hard to deal with, it could be refreshing at times. Not everyone wanted cake and pithy sayings. Sometimes when a person really wanted a brick to the face, he actually meant he wanted a brick to the face. Philosophically. Not literally.

His phone chirped, signaling a text. It was Laura.

"Hang in there, Walt. He'll be home soon."

"Thanks," he replied. "But just so you know, I'm going to be in bed soon."

"And back to work even sooner."

Damn her quick wit. Came from being a medic, he supposed.

She'd probably heard it all.

Before he got too far, however, his phone rang again. This time it was Micah.

"Tell me you got him, Micah," Walter sighed.

"No, not quite," Micah admitted. "But he did contact Micaiah and offer up a plan."

"Does it have to do with recreating the quasi-dimension that Rifun built and use that as a stepping stone between dimensions?"

"So he called you."

"Yes, he did. What do you think?"

Micah let out a breath. "I don't know. We're in uncharted waters, Walt. Everything we're doing is a brand new experience."

"Any word from Kayla?"

"Just a note letting us know that she left for the fortress, going to meet Natalie. After that, it's all up to her. We probably won't hear back until she returns."

"How's Micaiah taking it?"

Micah laughed nervously. "His wife is going off to an alien world to get high on hallucinogenic fruit. How the hell do you think he's taking it?" Pause. "He's anxious. Personally, I don't think he's going to sleep much tonight. Is there anything you need done around the house? Nervous cleaning, anything like that?"

"Sorry, I got all my stress cleaning done already."

"What about food? Got any food you've been trying to get rid of? Stress does wonders for cleaning out the fridge or the cupboards."

"No, I've done pretty well on that, too, sorry to say."

"How about your car? I know you're not much of a mechanic."

"My car is fine. Why are you trying to pawn your brother off on me anyway?"

"Mostly, I'm trying to give him something to do so I can get some sleep."

"Micah, I'm just about ready to go to bed. I'd like to sleep tonight, too."

Micah sighed dramatically. "Fine, if you won't take him, I

guess I'll have to take him back to the pound."

"Why, because you can't handle that he only has one leg and special needs?"

"I heard that, Walter," Micaiah said in the background.

Walter couldn't help it. He burst out laughing. "Oh, Micaiah. You know we all love you."

"Fuck you, Walter."

After a moment, Micah said, "Okay, he's gone. He's going to go work out for a while."

Walter sighed. "Okay, Micah. So why did you really call me?"

"Well, I called because I want to get all my little ducks in a row about this rescue attempt we're planning. Tommen sounds like he has a good plan, but is that what we want to go with?"

"Was Micaiah able to find someone to build this 'quasi-dimension' in the warehouse?"

"He asked around, but the best he could find was someone who knew what he was talking about and had seen it done. Her name is Urix; she's a Kardovan. She'll be there tomorrow, if we decide to go with that plan."

"A Kardovan on Earth? Openly?"

"Walter, we're opening portals to other dimensions. If anyone sees, well, go big or go home, right?"

He didn't particularly enjoy the idea, but he relented. "Fine. Continue."

"Well, that's the thing. Are we going with that plan?"

"I don't see why not. Yes, it sounds harder, but if it is a safer plan for getting him out, I'm willing to try it."

"Easy for you to say; you're not the one opening the portal."

"Then don't go with that plan!"

"Easy, Walter," Micah coaxed. "Relax. I'm just looking for any reasons why we shouldn't, or if there might be another way we haven't thought of. I come in peace, really.

Walter sighed and rubbed his eyes. "Next question. When do we want to do it? I have to work tomorrow, so either I won't be there or it's going to have to be before or after."

"Your shift starts at five?"

"Yes."

"Well, damn."

"I mean, we could try it in the early morning. It really shouldn't take that long, should it?"

"I don't know. I don't know what dimension-building entails."

Walter paced his bedroom and ran his hand through his hair. "What if we tried this. What if in the early morning, we tried the first way, just straight opening a portal. No quasi-dimensions or anything like that. If it works, it works, great. Everyone goes home happy. If it doesn't work, then we go back to the warehouse late tomorrow night and do this whole dimension stuff. It tries both ideas, and gives everyone time to rest and recover and get back for round two."

He could imagine Micah nodding. "We could certainly try that. Are you able to get a message to Tommen? Is he home?"

"Ah, his light isn't on. Either he isn't home or he's sleeping. Damn it."

Micah huffed. "I don't know, Walter. Early mornings kind of suck because everyone's sleeping and it's hard to plan and get messages to the right people in time, especially when some of them aren't even from our galaxy."

"Why don't you give me a couple minutes? If Tommen is just sleeping, I'll wake him up. Getting everyone together to open the portal is useless if he isn't even around to pull through. I'll call you back in a bit."

Walter hung up, then headed over to Tommen's room. He opened the door and turned on the lights.

"Tommen!" he barked. "Come on, kiddo! If you're here, time to wake up! Call me! Right now! We need to talk!"

He could effortlessly imagine Tommen grumbling and groaning, rolling over and pulling the blankets up over his head. Then he'd flop over on his stomach, mumble some complaints, then start feeling around for his phone to check the time. Gradually, he'd kick the blankets down to the end of the bed and half-roll, half-slide off the bed and head to the bathroom to get ready. Assuming that's the routine he was following now, Walter expected him to call in three...two...one...

"Hello?" Walter answered his phone before the first ring even ended.

"Sorry, I was out doing stuff," Tommen said, sounding unusually awake and alert for the time of night. "What's up?"

"What stuff?"

"A little bit of research, but, whatever. What's up?"

"Micah called and we're trying to coordinate the rescue efforts."

"Cool. What do you have so far?"

Walter explained the two-attempt plan, one in the early morning and another late at night if the first failed.

"So Micaiah was able to find someone who can build a quasi-dimension just based on the scars?" Tommen wondered.

"Well, no. He found someone who had watched someone do something similar once. It's the best we have, kiddo, which is why we're going to do this in two parts, if necessary."

"Oh. Okay. Makes sense. What time, where, give me the details."

"The biggest point is where you're going to be. Do you have any plans or anything early tomorrow morning?"

"Believe me, Dad, getting rescued takes priority."

"Glad to hear it. Now then, since I don't fancy having a sudden party at my house at four in the morning, we're going to open the portal at the twins' house. Their house can't be seen from the road, so it's perfect. You can camp out there or whatever, but that's where we're going to be."

Strictly speaking, he had just arbitrarily volunteered the twins' house as their base of operation. Easier to ask forgiveness than permission, he supposed.

"Sounds good," Tommen said. "I might just camp there, then. If it doesn't work, can I assume we're going to make secondary plans at that time or are we doing that now?"

"At this point, I think we're playing it by ear. One plan at a time."

"Okay."

Walter shifted his stance. "So what are you researching?"

"Doing a little fact-checking on Julianna, or what little I can."

"Seeing if she's the villain Micaiah says she is?"

"Something like that. I mean, she's been nothing but nice and helpful to me, but there's something off about it, Dad. I don't know how to describe it other than a gut feeling that something isn't right."

Walter grunted. "Well, as a cop, let me tell you that my gut has saved me a time or two. I wish I could ask you what you meant, but I get my own gut feeling that you don't think you're quite safe and comfortable with spilling the beans."

"Something like that, yeah."

"I won't push, then, but I would like a detailed explanation of your exploits when we do get you home."

"Oh, I have some stories to tell, believe me."

"Speaking of stories..." He hesitated. "I called Laura earlier."

"Okay...?"

Walter gave him the story he'd told Laura, about leaving a message and finding a cave, hunkering down, getting caught in a rockslide, the whole works. It sounded like such a foolish story now, riddled with holes and flaws. He found himself shocked that Laura hadn't called him out on it immediately upon hearing it. Maybe she was as desperate for good news as he was. Now his paranoia was up, afraid that she would suddenly call or come knocking on his door to know why the search crews had no clue what he was talking about.

When he was finished, Tommen was silent for a long moment. Then, "Wow. That is a very detailed story. And such an obvious lie. You know that one call to the search crews would—"

"I know that," Walter cut in. "I don't know why I did it. Maybe just to have a story that way I could tell someone that essentially I had found you and I am talking to you. I guess I just didn't want people to see me as the man who lost his kid and had no clue where he'd gone. I know where you are, Tommen. And I'm coming to get you."

"I'm ready to come home," Tommen said softly. Then he got serious again. "Listen. I think your secret is safe with Laura. She seems really nice and understands discretion. But whatever you do, don't tell Becky, not until I am actually, literally standing beside you. Okay?"

"No need to tell me twice on that one."

"Good. Otherwise the whole city is going to hear about it. There's no escaping that."

"Indeed not," Walter laughed. "Okay, kiddo. I'll let you go now so I can do some more coordinating with Micah and whoever he's got coming."

"Okay. Good night, Dad."

"Good night."

He turned and went back to his bedroom, figuring Tommen could handle his own lights. He called up Micah again.

"For a minute, I was worried you'd forgotten to call me back and went to bed," the younger twin said.

"Me? Forget? Never. What were we talking about again?"

"Ha ha ha. Did you talk to Tommen?"

"Yes, I did. I volunteered your house to be our ops location tomorrow." He explained his idea and reasoning. When he finished, Micah just sighed.

"I get your logic, Walt, but that doesn't mean I have to like it."

"Will you do it?"

"What are you talking about? Of course I will. I have to be up anyway to get to the shop, and Cai, well, he's not sleeping tonight anyway."

"Good. Thank you."

"Hey, if anyone has any complaints, well, you're the District Captain. We're just your lackeys. And speaking of which, have you been keeping your new Lieutenants up-to-date on this search and rescue?"

Walter let out a breath. "No, I haven't. I've gotten too used to you and Micaiah being my Lieutenants and having you close. But anyway, there's nothing they can do to help."

"Maybe not, but if you don't include them, it could mean that you don't trust them. Being inclusive is important is all I'm saying."

"Hm...maybe you're right. But I'm not going to bother them at this time of night. If the morning rescue attempt doesn't work, I'll call them later in the day and bring them up to speed."

"Sounds like a plan. And we don't know that they're completely useless. If it really is a matter of strength, we could use all the help we can get, I think."

"Indeed." He yawned. "Listen, I'm going to let you go for now. As if tomorrow isn't going to be bad enough going back to work, now I have to be up extra early so I can tear open some dimensions in order to rescue my son."

"Nothing like a lofty goal for the day," Micah laughed.

"Sunday is supposed to be the day of rest, isn't it?"

"I wouldn't know. I'm too busy working."

"Amen to that. All right, Micah, good night."

Walter hung up and set his phone on the charger. He yawned again as he got in bed and pulled the sheet up. Enough to feel like he was under the blankets without smothering himself in the heat.

He was just about on the edge of sleep when sudden, excruciatingly painful fear closed in on him, grabbing his chest and his head and throwing him into a mental brick wall over and over again, sucking him underwater, making him choke. For a moment, he floundered in his blankets and sheets, fighting for air, looking for any way out of the tunnel he was in. Hope was a tiny pinprick of light that eluded him at every step and swipe. He came out of his bed like a wild banshee, running into the wall and groping his way along until he found the switch.

The light came on and everything appeared perfectly normal. There were no monsters here to carry him off or devour him whole. The ghosts and shadows had retreated. Gingerly, keeping the hallway nightlight within sight at all times, he turned the overhead light off again, trying to search out the problem and assess any threats. He identified the problem immediately; his nightlight had gone out.

He flipped the lights back on and went to sit on the bed for a second. God, he felt foolish. Like a frightened child sent screaming for Mommy because the boogeyman in the closet might get him. He rubbed his face, feeling the sweat on his body, feeling disgusting because of it. He was a grown man. There was no way he should still be this afraid. And yet here he was. Any thoughts he'd had about wooing Laura to his bed vanished.

After a minute or two of simple breathing exercises, he made his way to the floor to take the nightlight and inspect it. It appeared in tact and he didn't see any negative signs on the outlet. When he plugged the light into a different outlet, it turned on right away. He let out a breath. Just a bad outlet, then. Nothing new there.

He returned to the switch and turned off the lights, reassuring himself that the nightlight worked and all was as it ought to be. He glanced at Tommen's room to see if his son might have seen that embarrassing and shameful retreat. Tommen's light was off, and Walter breathed a sigh of relief.

Cautiously, he turned out his light and made his way back to his bed. But even as he lay there, for as tired as he had been before, he couldn't find any trace of sleep now. All fatigue had deserted him as adrenaline still pumped through him, as if afraid the light would suddenly go out again. He yawned, closed his eyes, tried to get comfortable and tell himself it was just a normal night, but he still found himself watching the dim red numbers on his alarm clock. He had gone to bed way too early. Just how old was he, anyway? He wasn't even retired yet.

Finally he sat up and turned the lights back on. He rummaged in his nightstand and brought out the pill bottle. He rolled it around in his hands. He wasn't even in any pain, really, but he knew they could help. Opium was a depressant and would slow down his heart and breathing in a way he wasn't consciously capable of right now. Besides, he'd been pretty good about it lately with his knee. He hadn't even gone to get a refill yet.

He closed his eyes. *Don't do it. You're not in pain. You're in shock. You're in fear. But you're not in pain. Keep it that way. No pain, no pills, no addiction. You can do it.*

But one look at his nightlight convinced him otherwise. He justified it by only taking one instead of two. Then it was back to the lights and back to bed. He lay down and stared up at the ceiling, waiting for the pill to kick in, which eventually it did. He felt his heart rate go down, then his blood pressure. After a few minutes, he shivered and had to get under the blankets. His breathing came under control and any aches and pains he'd had from the day relaxed away. His eyelids dropped and he felt himself drifting off.

He snapped awake, or he thought he did, as the fear tore through him again. But this time, he couldn't move. His body was too relaxed so he couldn't fight back. He didn't even have the breath to call for help, and he was powerless against the fear monster which consumed him and dragged him down to Hell for a night of torture.

Chapter Twenty-One
Across the Dimensional Boundary

In ninth grade English, the class had been given a genealogy assignment. It wasn't anything too in-depth, just a quick introduction to genealogy, family histories, and the like. The teacher challenged each student to trace their history as far back as they could. Mini-awards were given out for the longest definitive line; the longest line overall which included guesswork, speculation, and leaps of logic; definitive, provable famous ancestors, and so on. Given the fuckery of Time and how it messed up Tommen's lineage, he was given the award for the smallest family tree.

What he'd turned in had made sense as it applied to him being born in the modern era, plus details he "vaguely" remembered about his real family. When he and his dad had gone back to create a more true-to-form family tree, well, it hadn't been much better. Since Walter's confession, that tree had filled in a little more, but personal recollection only went so far. The Forbes family was not famous; there would be no sudden breakthroughs and a line of ancestors half a mile and a millennium long. They were poor country folk who were born, lived, and died, with no great king ever batting an eye over it.

His search for Julianna and Richard proved to be just as elusive. His original idea had been something along the lines of returning to the prison, then manipulating the time stream to follow their footsteps backwards and trace things back to where everything went wrong. This was easier said than done, and the more he dug and the more they gave him the slip, the more he was convinced that not all was as it should be.

Tommen could easily remember the look and feel and activity

in the Wheel during election season when Grandfathers were everywhere and trust was a more valuable commodity than even the most expensive Time Capsules. It reeked of fear and death and everyone looked over his own shoulder. If the Akarin had been in such disarray, he would have expected to see or feel something similar. Even Rifun's coup and cutting off Earth from Time had produced a noticeable shockwave for those who knew what to look for. But as far as he was concerned, during the time period that Richard was writing in order to unite a crumbling Akarin and wroth Time industry, everything seemed mostly normal.

Eventually, he did find the house that Richard and Julianna called home. It was a small thing just outside of Cardiff with a rather abundant garden, a chicken coop with a dozen or more chickens squawking away, and a cow that seemed to enjoy greeting all passersby.

It was evening as Tommen entered the house. A warm fire heated up a large pot of stew. The man whom Tommen assumed to be Richard sat at a rickety table in an even more rickety chair, candle burning low, ink blots staining everything, feather frayed, eyes bloodshot. Julianna was busy chopping vegetables to put into the stew and working on some sewing project. Without the cuts on her face, she was almost beautiful, but her expression was anything but country kindness.

"I'm trying to set the record straight," Richard was saying, "but I have so little to go on that isn't in the Books."

Had Julianna been a cat, Tommen might have expected her to hiss. As it was, she merely said, "So make something up. That's what they did. What does it matter if the details are fudged? As long as the major points are made."

"But that's dishonest. And it's the same thing as the Books. A bunch of detail surrounding only little bits of truth. We're talking about the words of the Author."

"It is not the same thing as the Books." She rubbed her eyes. "Another one appeared, you know. *Alpha Wolf*, the story of the people of Hlohi, those red-skinned savages over in America who were forced to leave Earth for new lands. Why would the Author want to write about them? What makes them so special? They breathe lies, all of them. They think they have a right to everything. We were right to expand our influence over there, even if we did lose the colonies in the end."

"Please, my dear, not now," Richard sighed.

She didn't appear to have heard, or if she did, didn't care. "Someone in the Akarin is using their power to manipulate the Books, dishonoring and even bastardizing the Beloved characters. We have to set the record straight. The words of the Author herself."

Richard set down his quill and leaned back in his chair, farther than Tommen thought possible. "I ask and consider, but you can't rush her. Even the Books are slow to appear. Such is her wisdom."

"And every day that we don't act is another day that the Akarin dissolve into chaos! If we have any hopes of uniting the Akarin and the Time industry, there needs to be an Akarin left to salvage. The Author gave you a brain for a reason. Use it; you're not an imbecile. At least I hope not. If something turns out to be wrong, you can correct it later. A new interpretation as it were. But we need to gather the remaining followers, and fast."

"We set out to unite the Akarin under the truths of the Author. When did it become—?"

"When the Author began speaking to you. We have an opportunity to end all wars. Yes, it may involve some moving and adjusting, possibly even a little bloodshed. Not all races out there will accept that they've been duped. But once they see, then all will be well among them."

"Bloodshed," Richard echoed somberly, looking toward the fire.

"Not everyone, of course," Julianna said. "Some Akarin are naive, yet peaceful. It's the warriors that I'm worried about, the ones who won't take no for an answer, the ones who won't accept a change of power. Peace will win over the peaceful. But war will speak to the warriors."

"But that does no good now, when the Author is silent."

"As I said, use your brain. Make something up. Something logical. If we need to 'reinterpret' then that's what we'll do."

Reluctantly, Richard returned to his table and picked up the quill. "It still sounds dishonest."

Julianna set down her knife and went to kiss her husband. "The ends are what matter, my love. You have been chosen by the Author to set the record straight and bring peace to the galaxy. What nobler calling could there be? And don't worry. I'll look over everything to make sure it makes sense and we can use it. Once we get it all polished up, it will flow from hand to hand like a fast-moving river."

"But how will we protect it against saboteurs?"

She patted him on the shoulder. "Get everything written down, then we can discuss it later. Right now, you have a few pithy statements written down, hardly worth stealing and sabotaging. Once you have something substantial and worth protecting, let me know."

Tommen stuck around a few more minutes to see if anything else serious might be said, but the household lapsed into relative silence. Richard's quill scratched away and Julianna's knife moved swiftly and surely, slicing, dicing, and chopping into little cubes.

Tommen moved ahead a little bit, maybe a couple months to a year. Richard had amassed quite a stack of papers which Julianna studiously examined, making marks and notes here and there. Looking over their shoulders, Tommen saw what amounted to the first manuscript of what he'd read in the journal only a couple days ago. He saw the dissertation on the nature of the Author, the nature of the Akari, various Akari abilities and how to master them, the whole works. Of course, everything was criss-crossed with punctuation error marks, grammatical mistakes, and plenty of advice on which phrases and "truths" to include and take out.

Then the door opened and Tommen watched as Cassius walked in and helped himself to the Browns' hospitality. He went to Richard's writings and perused them.

"Why are you editing these things? Didn't I make it clear enough? Didn't the Author speak clearly enough?"

"We're only trying to make it flow better," Richard answered, looking a bit cowed by the big man.

"I told you what to write. The Author spoke through me! That is what you are to write!"

"Calm down, Cassius," Julianna said. "We are only correcting our own mistakes."

Cassius did not seem convinced of this, but he said nothing more.

Now what in the world was Cassius doing? What was he saying about the Author speaking through him?

Moving forward again, Tommen watched as Richard finished writing the last few lines in the final leatherbound journal he'd come to know and despise, Imprinting the text and scattering the letters, just a few seconds out of sync in order to disguise the writing from prying eyes. If he had to guess by the man's demeanor, Tommen might have said that any reservations that Richard had once had were now gone. Either he'd had some sort of divine revelation that reassured him this was the right thing to do, or he'd started to believe his own lies. Or were they Julianna's lies?

Tommen was ready to move on and investigate more, but as he turned, sudden dizziness forced him to drop the time travel mirage and find a nearby chair. The city had grown up in the last century and a half, and a new structure had been built over the little thing Richard and Julianna had called home.

Right. Still sick. And what was he going to tell Julianna if she visited and found him gone? He was supposed to be resting and gathering his strength to make the jump tomorrow morning.

As he stood, his stomach growled, and he paused. He was currently stuck in a dimension that allowed him to go anywhere and do anything without worrying about any repercussions. It wasn't enough to make him not want to return, but if he still had the ability, why not use it?

So he spent the next hour traveling the world and trying various foods. Yeah, he saw sights and monuments and such, but his main focus was the food. Real escargot from France—never again— fresh fish and feta in Greece, zebra from Uganda. He took only a few bites of each dish so he could sample as much as possible, but he stopped when he got to India.

His once-best friend Varad had moved back to India with his family almost a year ago. Because of the whole kidnapping and being exposed to Time thing, he'd abandoned and blocked Tommen out of his life, but he was still friends with Tommen's other once-best friend Eric. According to Eric, Varad loved India and was doing very well.

But in a country with a population rivaling China, how did he find a single person? Could he really just ask and receive?

He spent almost fifteen minutes Traveling here and there, asking and going and searching but not finding. He found plenty of farms and Hindu temples where Varad was said to frequent, but as for the man himself, there was no trace. Either he was excellent at playing hide-and-seek, or maybe his appearance had changed so that Tommen wouldn't recognize him anyway.

Maybe it was for the best, Tommen figured as he moved on in his food tour. Varad didn't want to talk to him. Stalking him from another dimension wasn't going to help anything. If he somehow managed to call him and convince him that yes, he was standing right there and could see him from that other dimension, that probably wouldn't be a good thing either. It was probably better to just let that go and move on.

So Tommen continued his food tour through Southeast Asia, Indonesia, and down to Australia before turning and heading back up the coast through China, Japan, and both South and North Korea before skipping across the Bering Strait into Alaska. Seeing how even in the middle of summer it was still pretty damn cold above the Arctic Circle, he didn't stay there very long. Instead, he meandered his way along the west coast down into Central and South America, then did a little island-hopping in the Caribbean before hitting Florida and speeding home.

The whole trip had lasted a little less than two hours. By the time he got home, it was just before midnight. As he looked around the house, nothing appeared to be disturbed. But when he checked to see if his dad was in bed, he not only found his dad in a rather fitful sleep, but Julianna standing beside him, her hand on his head. She was facing away from Tommen, so he couldn't see her face.

"What are you doing?" he asked.

She turned and looked at him, her expression unreadable. "He's having nightmares. I was hoping I could influence them and calm him down."

Tommen had his doubts, but he said nothing more as she got up and followed him into his room.

"And where have you been?" she inquired.

"Got hungry, decided to do one last hurrah to get something to eat before I have to start paying for it again."

"And in the process, expended energy you can't afford to lose." She went to his nightstand and picked up one of the syringes. As he sat down on the bed, she stuck him with it, most ungracefully and without warning. He flinched, but the medicine got in and started to do its work. "You should be resting. Even if you're not sleeping, relaxing is also beneficial."

He smirked. "As people like to remind me, I am a growing teenage boy. I need to eat constantly."

"Well, they're not wrong. But you also need to rest. And that's an order."

"On what authority?"

She got in his face. "On my authority. On the authority that I'm not going to be the one responsible for screwing up this escape attempt because you passed out halfway through. Got it?"

He blinked. "Yes, ma'am."

"Good." She straightened. "I'll be back bright and early, then, and we'll go from there."

Tommen nodded. "Sounds like a plan."

He couldn't really say why he didn't give her the details of the current plan except he just didn't trust her. He didn't feel that she had been completely honest with him. If she really was repentant of things she'd done in the past, why didn't she say so? He didn't want to hear a Confession necessarily, but if she was going to push that journal on him and diss his friends and the Akarin, she could at least give him something. Maybe something along the lines of, "Hey, I know there's a shit ton of conflict surrounding this journal, and I know my past actions weren't the best since they got my dear husband killed, but here's why and how I'm sorry and how we can remedy the situation."

Instead, she seemed to be playing the kill 'em with kindness card. Everything she'd done for him so far had been super nice. Not once had she argued with him, and the one time she had raised her voice, she'd smothered it herself. He might have said it was merely conditional per the time period she was from, but observing her conversations with her husband made him believe she was not the subdued little country wife she was trying to portray.

There was no way he was going to sleep, and tossing and turning held very little appeal. Eventually, he got up and headed out of his room. His original intent was to raid the fridge one last time. His stomach was grumbling a little over all the different, unfamiliar foods he'd just consumed, and he was hoping that something gentle and familiar might ease the discomfort.

But as he passed by his dad's room, he paused and looked in. Easing the nightmares, his ass. Somehow, he had a greater suspicion that she had caused the nightmares, at least the ones his dad was experiencing this night. Cautiously, Tommen pushed open the door.

Walter was less fidgety, but Tommen knew better. He could see the rigidness of his body, how every muscle was taut and ready to fire. Even his chest muscles were contracted, making his breathing shallow and slightly labored. On a normal night, if Tommen tried to wake his dad from such a state, he would literally launch himself out of the bed, gunning for whoever or whatever had touched him, his every instinct to seek and destroy.

Tommen sat on the edge of the bed and closed his eyes, wondering if it was really possible to enter someone's dreams while still awake. He might have danced around the edge of sleep himself, he wasn't sure.

Suddenly, it was as if huge talons had grabbed him and sucked him down into a terrifying nightmare where everything was dark and yet there were voices, screams, whispers, wails, and an enemy that could not be seen but attacked from every angle. Tommen was pushed and pulled, tossed and turned, rolled around and rolled over, like a huge dog tearing into its favorite ragdoll. He tried to breathe, tried to scream, tried to figure out where all his limbs were, but the only thing that mattered was the fear.

In a split-second of clarity, he was forced to wonder why. This wasn't his dream. This wasn't his nightmare. It wasn't him.

As soon as he realized that, his body came back to him and he stepped away from the monsters in the dark. When he turned around, he saw his dad in the same predicament. At first, he couldn't see the monster. Then he realized that the dark was the monster. It was darkness, emptiness, fear and shadows all around. The noises were the sounds of the gaol, but also the emptiness of the black cells within the Wheel.

Tommen's first instinct was to run, leave and never come back, never tell his dad what he saw and felt. He should never have come. His dad's personal hell was a monster only he could tame. Then he felt guilty. He'd come with the intentions of helping. Any other nightmare might have been fine; this hell was more than he could stand.

He stood there, conflicted and rooted to the ground. If Julianna was being honest, and she had been trying to tame the beast, what hope did he have if she couldn't do it? But if she was a liar and had caused this nightmare, he owed it to himself and his dad to at least make an attempt.

Taking a breath, Tommen moved forward into the darkness, heading for his dad. It started out easily enough, but as he got closer, he could feel greater resistance, like walking against a strong current.

Finally he reached a threshold, maybe ten feet from his dad. On the one side, the current was strong, trying to push him away. On the other side was the opposite, and the darkness would suck him in if he breached the invisible wall.

"Dad!" he called. As he did, all the noise around him in the darkness got louder, as if trying to block or drown the sound. He took a breath and called out again, "Dad!"

His dad looked at him briefly, but still did not come. Tommen took in as big a breath as he could, but instead of calling out to his dad, he mustered up the best drill Sargent voice he could and shouted, "Stop!"

There was movement in the darkness, like the ripple in a disturbed pond. If he had to hazard a guess, the darkness was laughing at him. Tommen didn't take too kindly to being laughed at. Rather than yelling again, he bulled his way past the threshold, determined to go in and drag his dad out if he had to.

But the current was stronger than his willpower. He was swept off his feet. He could no longer see his dad as the darkness pulled them both in. Tommen turned and floundered, his only thought now to not let the darkness and the fear overtake him. He had to get out of this dream, this horrifying nightmare.

The darkness obliged, spitting him out like Jonah. Tommen stumbled and slammed into the wall in his dad's bedroom, feeling the impact a second before tumbling through the wall to the outside, landing on his left arm ad crying out in some pretty severe pain. When he finally got rolled onto his back, his face was hot and wet with tears. Blindly, he pulled himself into a sitting position, then a drunken stumble back into the house to the bathroom.

He wasn't dirty, but his arm was smarting something awful. Gingerly, he peeled off the bandages. Any dead skin that had been slowly peeling off had ripped off, taking live skin with it, tearing and rubbing the raw nerves. Tommen tossed the old bandages outside in the neighbor's yard, then went back to commandeer some new bandages he had stashed away. He also took a washcloth and tried to clean up his arm as best he could from the blood, minding the nerves, almost certain that whatever progress they had made with this sepsis deal had just gone to hell.

The parts of his skin where the jacket had melted into him, which was most of his arm, the pain was slightly deadened because of the melted plastic protection. The parts of his skin that were exposed hurt like a motherfucker. He wished he could have applied some kind of ointment, but everything he'd read and heard said no ointments, creams, or gels. Seeing how he was close but still not out of this dimension to get to a real hospital, he was inclined to follow directions.

He returned to his room and lay down, putting his arm up above his head and closing his eyes. His stomach was churning, likely a combination of a whole bunch of foreign foods and the sight of his bloody, burned arm that was sloughing more than it ought to be sloughing. Even the thought of it sent a second wave of nausea through him.

Fucking hell, he needed to get out of here. He opened his eyes. They were trying this at the twins' house first, which meant he had to be over there early. He'd already said he was going to be camping out there in order to be ready. Fucking hell.

Grudgingly, he sat up and started gathering up his stuff in his backpack. Before he could turn off the light, he saw his dad in the doorway of his own bedroom, looking frazzled and yet exhausted.

"Tommen? Are you still here?"

One flash. Tommen grabbed his phone and other accessories and dialed.

"What's up?" he asked, trying to sound curious and not let on that he'd experienced his dad's nightmare with him.

"I thought you were going over to Micah and Micaiah's house," his dad said, sounding a little confused.

"Yeah, I was just making sure I had all my stuff so I didn't leave anything behind."

"Oh, okay. So you are still able to carry out the plan tomorrow morning?"

Tommen nodded uselessly. "Yeah, as long as you guys are ready for me. Did something change?"

"Huh? No, no, nothing changed. Just wanted to be sure before I have to get up extra early before work."

"I'll be there, don't worry."

"Okay. Good to hear." Pause. "Good night, Tommen."

Click.

If Tommen didn't know better, he might have suspected his dad had just been sleepwalking and made a sleep phone call. Was that even possible?

Well, he supposed it didn't really matter. He gathered up his stuff one more time and did a last sweep of his room, trying to identify anything that could be left behind. Well, nothing that couldn't be replaced, he figured. He had his phone and small stash of medical supplies, including the syringes. He'd be all right.

He still made a quick stop in the kitchen for a snack before heading out. Beginning of August, the nights were still warm but not quite so sticky and humid. It helped ease the pain in his arm and clear his head enough that he could walk straight. He knew he should probably cut his time by Traveling to the twins' house, but he didn't.

Instead, he made a quick stop at Becky's, heading up to her room, on the lookout for her ghostbusting cat. Said cat was up on her workbench when Tommen walked in. Mr. Snuffles froze in his position, looked straight at Tommen, then bolted under the bed. A second later, he turned and looked out at him with glowing yellow eyes. As Tommen got closer to the bed, the cat hissed at him and retreated farther underneath.

Christmas was a long ways away. Four months at least. Seeing Becky curled up all small and adorable aroused Tommen and he bent down next to her. He wasn't going to get another opportunity to do this. He felt her soft pajamas, then pushed through to her skin, rubbing her arm, her side, her hip. He was just moving to her belly and below when Mr. Snuffles suddenly bolted out from under the bed, clawing

Tommen's pants and legs, then running screaming out of the room down the stairs.

"Ow! Fucking cat! What the hell?" Tommen growled.

He looked down where Mr. Snuffles had ripped his pants and bloodied his leg in eight long claw marks criss-crossing both legs. It didn't hit him until three seconds later that the cat had actually clawed him. It had touched him and injured him. How in the hell had the cat been able to do that?

His attention was diverted as Becky rolled over and blindly reached for her glasses. She grabbed them and flicked on her lamp.

"Mr. Snuffles?" she wondered sleepily.

"Becky?" Tommen asked. "Becky, can you see me? I'm right here. It's Tommen."

But she looked right through him, around the room. After a minute, upon concluding there was no immediate threat, she took off her glasses and flipped off the light. Tommen growled in frustration and sat down angrily on the bed, his arousal gone. He reached down and carefully rolled up his pant legs to inspect the damage. Minor scratches, nothing serious. The thin lines of blood had already clotted.

He sighed and looked back at Becky who had already gone back to sleep. So, cats really were mystical creatures who could see and touch between dimensions. Fucking hell.

Eventually, he stood and grabbed his bag, trudging outside, half-expecting it to be twenty below and a blizzard. But it was a mild sixty degrees, just humid enough that it didn't feel cold. He walked through Charleston at night. For a big city, it wasn't quite as busy as one might expect once the sun went down. There was a nightlife scene, yes, but most things ended around one or two in the morning.

So while he passed by a number of bars and clubs, those were the only things open besides a couple fast food restaurants off the interstate. Otherwise, the roads were pretty quiet, all the businesses closed up for the night. Some places had just a turnkey lock while others had cages and alarms. At one point, he stopped to observe a robbery in progress. He probably could have done something to intervene, but the cops got there first, whether from a silent alarm or sneaky passerby. The thieves were apprehended and taken away.

Tommen moved on, leaving the city and heading north. He was about three miles out from the twins' road when dizziness overtook him and his knees gave out. He went down, only just able to catch himself, this time on his good arm. He was too confused to throw up, though his stomach certainly felt like it.

"Fuck," he whispered, getting to his feet and stumbling sideways, narrowly avoiding going down a second time. "Fuck, fuck, fuck."

Once he got his head on as straight as it would go, he Traveled the rest of the way to the twins' house, effortlessly moving inside and making for the spare bedroom. He offloaded his pack and flopped down on the bed for a moment, trying to gather himself. Once the room stopped spinning, he dug around in his pack for the syringes and laid them out.

Fucking hell, why did they have to be so confusing and with such shitty names? He couldn't even begin to pretend to pronounce them, never mind know what they were for or under what circumstances to use them. Supposedly, they were all antibiotics, but how did he know which one to use and when? Weren't they supposed to come with instructions? Maybe if they were prescribed, but as long as the doctors were using them, they ought to know what the hell they were doing. That left Tommen high and dry. And he certainly didn't dare to inject all of them. Maybe he should just pick one and hoped it did something. It was all medicine, right? It should all be helpful in some way.

He picked up the first one. Then he put it down. He got out his phone and plugged it in, relieved when his phone picked up the wifi and connected him. Well, it kind of did the back and forth connected, not connected, but it worked well enough that he was able to type in the name of the drugs and look up what they were used for.

Everything he got was either too complex—detailing the chemical compounds, chemical names, reactions, and other super chemistry stuff that went way over his head—or too simple. Yes, he understood that it was an antibiotic for such a bacteria. That didn't tell him how to use it or when to use it or not use it.

Well, only one way to find out. He picked the one he'd been able to find the most information on, removed the cap, attached it to the IV port still in his hand, and depressed the plunger. That was an icy sensation. Between that and the pain in his wrist and hand, he was left lying on the bed, shaking terribly. Why did medicine have to be this difficult?

He closed his eyes and let out a breath, daring to sit up again and contemplate the three remaining syringes. Did he dare try another one? He had no illusions that he was going to start feeling great immediately; these things took time to work, after all. No, he would wait until he got up to try the portal. It was only a few hours away now. And how did he expect to wake up in time for that? There was no guarantee that the twins knew he was staying here, or that his phone would work.

He ended up going down to Micah's room and relaxing in the chair there. The younger Durvin twin had kicked his blankets off and was sleeping on his stomach, almost falling off the edge of the bed. Hopefully his alarm would wake up both of them. As he relaxed and tried to nod off, he remembered feeling guilty about leaving his dad alone. If Julianna had been causing the nightmares, what if she returned and, finding him gone, decided to plague Walter again? Was there anything worse that she could do to him?

Tommen's conscience forced him back awake, but he ultimately decided to stay where he was. His dad had bad nights sometimes, but he always woke to his alarm. He would be over to help with the rescue attempt. As long as Tommen stayed at the Durvins', it might buy him time to escape before Julianna noticed him missing. If he went home, the next time she came by, she might not leave. While she'd been nothing but good to him, the things he'd seen from her past made him not want to let her escape.

At the same time, if the first go round didn't work, how would he explain that to her, that he'd intentionally left her behind? She didn't seem like the forgive and forget type. She would come after him. She would force her way out of the in-between dimension if she had to, climbing over anyone who stood in her way.

Or maybe that was his overactive imagination again. It had a bad habit of sneaking up on him from time to time. Kind of like his paranoia. Eventually, he did manage to drift off to sleep. He wasn't sure how he knew he was sleeping, but he was grateful for it. Even more, he was grateful that he seemed to have escaped the darkness and the fear of his dad's nightmares. And as everything melted away, he could have sworn that he was being watched. Not in a creepy way, like Julianna or some other serial killer was waiting to kill him, but in a comforting way, as if some fierce guardian stood watch over him to make sure Julianna or some other serial killer didn't kill him. The last thing he remembered as he surrendered to the blackness was, "Come to me."

Chapter Twenty-Two
Enlistment

You knew it was a bad day when the frigid cold and blasting wind of the Arctic Circle was more welcoming than the icy words of another satisfied client. You knew it was a bad day when cold starvation and having nothing to taste except seal fat seemed a better option than going grocery shopping on the fat check that was finally turned over. You knew it was a bad day when battling angry walruses and fighting on the front lines of a revolutionary war sounded more appealing than fighting some bullshit claim in court.

But that was exactly how Kayla felt when her workday finally ended. Because some people couldn't be pleased, couldn't be made to own their own mistakes, and couldn't be made to see reason and have mercy on the working class. Oh, to finally get out of Charleston and be anywhere else in the world. That was the magic of building a life however they felt like it, she figured. All she and Cai had to do was just up and leave. Well, assuming the paperwork ever made it their way. The hamsters were running, but the wheel wouldn't turn, or so it felt like.

So it was that she spent the better part of an hour in the recreational area, beating the straw out of dozens of dummies. Some were stationary, some had crude, predictable motions, and others were a little more sophisticated. Of course, the recreation area was kind of like a holodeck from *Star Trek*, except it responded to her mood and mental wishes—up to a point—rather than going through a thousand verbal commands trying to get everything just perfect. And, using the Akari which was timeless and had a life of its own, it could correct certain details as needed.

By about dummy number thirty, Kayla figured most of her frustration had effectively gone out of her system, and she collapsed onto a bench. Other than the frustration of the day, she needed to train for whatever was coming down the pipe. One dead council member was bad enough, but she'd heard whispers and rumors of another one going down, too. Supposedly it was to be kept hush hush in order to avoid a panic, but tell the right person and word inevitably got around. But she wouldn't spread any rumors. Her interest in Akarin politics was waning. It was a dangerous position to take, but maybe if the leaders stopped having followers, they might just have a revelation that something wasn't quite right with their leadership style and skill. Maybe she expected too much out of politicians.

Of course, her husband was one of those politicians now, so she shouldn't say too much. As much as she supported him in his position, though, she secretly hoped that he either left or they kicked him out of the position only weeks after forcing him in. If he didn't have that ton of bullshit on his shoulders, he'd probably be a happier person for it, plus it would be easier to leave and do their own thing for a little while.

Kayla wiped the sweat from her brow and headed up to the common barracks to shower and change. She'd walked in wearing her street clothes, jeans and a dressy top, as could be expected for a professional. But, going to meet another tribe and treat with them, well, when in Rome. Or Hlohi, as the occasion demanded.

Natalie had mentioned that their location on Hlohi was just coming out of winter. The days might be be fair and mildly warm, but nights were pretty cold. Given that she was to meet with the council and elders first, she ought to act as the ambassador of her people. Kayla agreed wholeheartedly, not mentioning that she had already been to Hlohi once recently. So she'd packed some of her finest furs, clothes she hadn't worn since her last trip home probably a quarter century ago.

It started with leather pants and a shirt made from polar bear hide. Over that she donned a dress made from caribou fur. The hat and mittens she pulled out of the bag were also caribou. Then came her finest piece, a shawl, almost large enough and long enough to be another dress, made from seal fur. Actually, it had been her mother's, and her mother's before her, an heirloom piece, one Kayla hoped to pass on to her own daughter, assuming she had one.

Looking at herself in the mirror sent a touch of homesickness through her. Charleston was nice and all, but, call her crazy, she kind of missed the icy tundra and stunted plants, the snowshoe hares and arctic foxes, the polar bears and the whales, and everything in between. It was her heritage, the life of her people. She owed them a visit. Maybe she would call Putu up at some point and see what arrangements they could make.

There were two villages, the last settlements of man, as far north as north could go on solid ground, where all the residents were Time Agents, if not Akari-bearers also. Their sole purpose was to give Inuit Time Agents a place to call home and continue to practice their heritage long after they'd left their own villages due to the slowed aging. From what Kayla understood, it was similar to the situation on Hlohi, except the Inuit camps had little interest in expanding and making themselves known. They were temporary residences, not full villages and whole lives. There were no children, no families, just homesick Inuit looking for familiarity, a reprieve from the craziness of the Wheel and the universe, maybe a little spiritual guidance, too. They shared stories and kept the old traditions alive, reminiscing for a little while before returning to whatever lives they'd constructed for themselves.

Eventually, Kayla returned to the main floor, figuring that if Natalie was looking for her, that would be the place to start. She didn't see Natalie right away, so she headed to the cafeteria to sit and wait and do a little people watching.

The cafeteria was pretty empty, actually. If they weren't scared away by the war from the Time industry or the civil war, then the death of the council member might do it, too. What conversation there was, was hushed and suspicious. Not a few glances were cast her way.

Watch out for the humans, guys, they're violent and unpredictable.

"Kind of depressing, isn't it?"

Kayla looked up as Natalie sat across from her. "Hey, you made it."

Natalie looked exhausted, as if she'd just gotten over a bout of crying.

"What's happened?" Kayla asked.

She shook her head. "Another funeral. He was old, one of those who made the Migration. I might not be so torn up about it, but two deaths so close together, especially with Saul..."

"It's okay. I understand."

Natalia cleared her throat and shifted position. "I got your message this morning. As I understand it, you would like to come and meet with the council because you're searching for someone who once escaped the spirit lands and may be able to help someone who is experiencing the same thing. What exactly is going on?"

So Kayla did her best to explain the situation, starting with a brief history between Tommen and Rifun, then moving on to the wildfire, Tommen's disappearance, and all the adventures thus far. Natalie's interest went from bedtime story to serious consideration. When Kayla finally finished, Natalie leaned back as far as she dared. For a long moment, she didn't speak.

Then, "Well, I commend you for reading up on our history a little."

"The least I can do," Kayla said, dipping her head respectfully. "Do you think you can help?"

Natalie hesitated. "When our people made the Great Migration, we brought over animals that we knew we could hunt. We also brought plants—vegetables and other forage—that we could cultivate. The fruit of which you speak we were able to take with us and grow. But as I said before...we're just coming out of winter. We wouldn't have any of the fruit freshly available, which is the only time the hallucinogen really works. Once they're cooked, dried, whatever, the hallucinogenic properties are diminished or dissolved completely."

"How do your young people become adults, then?"

"They seek their visions in the fall." Natalie shrugged like the answer was obvious. "Once they have had them and tell their families of the message from the spirits, then the family has their harvest to celebrate new adults, new life, and the lives of those now past. The ghost supper season may last two wolf moons, if not longer."

"All right. Is there another way to do this?"

Natalie shifted in her seat. "I know the person of whom you speak, who escaped the in-between dimension. He is very old now. Even if we can't find a way for you to see into the dimension, or the spirit lands, he may be able to shed some light on the situation and help rescue Tommen."

Kayla nodded. "At this point, every little bit helps."

"Well then, I guess we better get going."

Natalie stood and Kayla followed. Three steps in, Natalie turned around. "I love your furs, by the way. What are they?"

So as they headed to the portal room, the women talked Native fashion, the furs, the leathers, the cuts and various style differences between their two peoples. While Kayla dressed in her best, Natalie's attire was decidedly plain, leather pants and shirt covered by a deerskin dress modestly adorned with beads. Her hair was braided all the way down her back, the long black feathers at the end seeming to extend it all the way to her knees. Kayla kept her hair tucked under her shawl, but it, too, was braided, though not adorned.

"If you don't mind," Natalie said, "I would like to stop at Saul's home to pick up a few things, to ensure they're saved before cleaning it out completely."

"Of course." Kayla nodded. "And actually, I do have to confess that I've already been there. Not in the house, but I did make a trip to Hlohi already." She briefly explained her failed trip and attempt to call for help.

She might have expected Natalie to be upset that Kayla had disturbed them during the funeral ceremonies, but she only seemed mildly amused as she said, "Well, you learned, didn't you?"

"I suppose," Kayla said meekly. "I guess I wasn't thinking."

They reached the portal room and Natalie opened the portal. Kayla stepped through first and Natalie followed a moment later. They were in a forest clearing, but the edge of the trees could be seen not far away. Where it had been almost midnight on Earth, here is was about early to midmorning. Kayla let out a breath.

"I'm going to have one serious case of jet lag by the end of the day."

Natalie laughed. "You'll be fine. We'll head up to Saul's house, grab a few things, then go to the village. Once you've met with the elders, if you want, you can rest in my home before going to speak with the old man."

"No, I can't afford to sleep and take any more time than I already am. Tommen is sick, and every minute I waste on folly is another minute he could take a downturn without any of us knowing or being able to do anything about it. It's bad enough I had to work today. And believe me, with the day I had, I would have rathered take on a charging walrus."

Natalie laughed again as she led the way out of the forest and up a small hill to a trail. As they walked, she spoke.

"I can't tell you how many times I walked this way to see Saul. He actually exiled himself as a way to spite the council. They said he could never survive without his clan, and he proved them wrong. Then he sealed his fate when he left to join the Marines."

"Saul wasn't allowed to be part of the clan?" Kayla wondered.

"Oh, he would always be Wolf Clan, whatever the council said. A wolf may abandon the pack, but the pack never abandons a wolf. He was just never suited for clan life, for village life like the rest of us." She let out a breath. "After he came home from the Marines, with his injuries, he would either have to move back into the village with someone or get someone to come out to help him. Everyone said to let him suffer a little and maybe he would come back to the pack. I knew better. Saul would have frozen to death before returning to the village." Natalie shook her head and sighed. "And that was exactly how I found him the first day after bringing him home. It was the middle of winter. He was conked out on painkillers, couldn't move anyway, and his fire had gone out. So I got that going again, warmed him back up, made him some food..." She trailed off.

"At least someone cared for him," Kayla said.

Natalie grinned. "If people didn't know I was his sister, they probably would have mistaken me for his wife, at least for the first year or so."

"So if your people are matrilineal, why didn't Saul marry and leave the village? From what I've heard, his conflict came from the split-lives you guys have."

"That was a major part of it, yes, but it wasn't just that. Saul was always an angry person. He was his best when he was alone or when he was teaching, believe it or not. Want to learn how to string a bow, go hunting, fishing, trapping, tanning? He was your man. Want to have a decent conversation with another human being? Well, fuck off."

They reached the same house Kayla had seen before. The last time, she'd just peeked around without disturbing anything. This time, Natalie moved a couple rocks that served as a doorstop or maybe even a locking mechanism, pushed a large fur aside, and entered the abode.

Aside from a light dusting of snow blown in through the window, everything appeared untouched.

"Saul had a certain way of sealing his house before leaving for summer camp, to keep the weather and larger critters out," Natalie said, brushing the snow aside. "When Logan and Blake came back to look for any more singular possessions to give to him to take to the spirit lands, they evidently neglected to put things back the way they were."

"Did Saul build this house?" Kayla wondered.

"He did, actually. Just enough for him, the way he liked it."

"What will happen to it now?"

Natalie frowned. "I don't know. It's a nice little house; I'd hate to see it go to rot. But life happens in the village. It's a trek from here to the village and back, not something a sane person would want to make every day." She snickered sadly. "I really don't know. There aren't any loners in the village that I know of, at least, not to the extreme that Saul was. Sorry to say, but the council and the elders kind of used him as an object lesson for the kids, to warn them of the dangers of being alone."

"Ouch."

"Yeah. So, I don't know what will happen to it."

Natalie did most of the sorting and gathering, going through her brother's belongings. Seeing how she didn't have any sort of basket with her, she only actually selected a few items to take. The rest went into various piles.

"These are things I'll take," Natalie explained, gesturing to one pile. Looking at another, "Those will go to Blake. A couple things will go to Logan. As for the rest of the stuff, our mother will take anything she wants. The rest will go to any who need it."

"Sounds good," Kayla acknowledged, unsure how she should react. Should she be more somber, that all traces of Saul were being given away? Should she be happy that everything was going to find its proper place and go to good use? In the end, she chose to be the helpful, respectful bystander with little or no emotional attachment.

Natalie gathered her few items and they headed outside once more. By now the frost had burned off the ground, and the sun reflected off millions of tiny dewdrops.

Natalie was right; it was certainly a trek. Kayla remembered making the trip the first time, when she went snooping around, but the second time felt extra long. Maybe it was the chilly wind or the way the fresh spring grass made the landscape look bright and new.

"You ought to feel right at home in the mountains," Natalie was saying. "Granted, we're only in the lower elevations, but mountains are mountains wherever you go."

"Well, it will be familiar," Kayla said, "but you'd have to get a lot colder to make me feel at home. And you'd need a lot more water."

"And some charging walruses?"

"Something like that."

"I don't see how. I mean, walruses look fat and lumbering and slow."

Kayla laughed. "Oh, they're fat and lumbering, but they are anything but slow. And those tusks can be brutal. One of my uncles was killed because he didn't watch out and a walrus gored him."

"Oh. I'm sorry."

"Don't be. It's the peril of the ice."

They walked on in silence along the ridge and down into the valley to the same bowl Kayla had happened upon the first time. If she remembered correctly, it looked like the same two guards. Natalie stepped forward and greeted them. She made only the slightest gesture toward Kayla who followed her through the narrow gap into the bowl. On the north side, the village was partially carved from the rock and partially built.

"I thought all Wolf Clan members could speak English," Kayla observed.

"They can. Those two aren't Wolf Clan, though," Natalie explained. "When a young man wishes to court a woman, he has to prove himself to her. The first trial is through provision, bringing meat and forage to her and her family. The second test is flattery, bringing her gifts to make her smile and adorn herself with to make other girls jealous. The third test is one of battle and loyalty. Those two there are charged with protecting the front entrance of the village, even against their own brothers. I believe they are Deer Clan, but I'm not entirely sure."

"But why? I thought there was peace and only one people? It sounds like you're asking for trouble."

"The Aniyvwiya absorbed a lot of smaller peoples who were facing extinction, and not all peoples were friendly. In the aftermath of tragedy, peace was easier to maintain. But there came divides, along tribal and clan lines. There is still peace, but it's not the same as it was in my grandmother's time."

"How long do they have to stand guard?"

"At least three moons. Once the council and the girl and her family are satisfied of their performance, then the engagement ceremonies take place and the wedding preparations begin. My own fiancé stood guard for five moons before being accepted. To be honest, I think he was trying to impress Saul more than me. But I don't blame him. Logan is with his wife and Bear Clan now, to the south, which made Saul the patriarch. Without him, the responsibility falls to Blake."

"Will that affect your wedding?"

"Not as much as you might think. It's not the first wedding where the father or patriarch has died unexpectedly beforehand."

"Oh."

"Don't worry about it." She grinned as Kayla yawned. "Are you sure you don't want to take a quick nap?"

"I'm sure. I really need to get this done and get home."

"Okay. Well, I'm going to drop this stuff off first, then we can meet the council."

"Where will you live when you get married?"

"In my mother's house, where I live now. She'll move in with Blake. Once he gets married, she'll live by herself as long as she can. When she can't provide for herself anymore, she'll probably move in with me and my husband. But we're talking many decades, even centuries."

"What about remarriage?"

"What about it?" Natalie shrugged. "If she gets remarried, she gets remarried. She'll live with him as long as possible. Then if one or the other dies and the remaining is incapable of providing, they'll move in with us." She grinned. "It's not as complicated as it sounds, I promise."

The village put Kayla in mind of the Pueblo cliff dwellings she'd seen once while on vacation in the Southwest, except with more, well, life. These weren't perfectly preserved historical sites, but real villages with real villagers doing village things. Butchering, cooking, weaving, sewing, beading, yelling at children or spouses.

They headed out of the lower village which were more freestanding buildings and into the higher village which was carved from the mountainside. Natalie's home, or her mother's home, proved to be a simple, two-room abode, much like Saul's house on the ridge. The difference was that the sleeping quarters were more dedicated sleeping quarters and the main room functioned as kitchen, living room, and whatever else the family needed. An animal hide curtain hung in the doorway between the two rooms.

The woman inside was like Natalie in ten common years. Only because Kayla knew Natalie was an only female child did she not mistake her for a sister.

"*Asi,*" the woman greeted cheerfully, mixing something sweet in a bowl. She went over to Natalie to hug and kiss her. "*Etaqui nihsui?*"

"Please, *Tsitsi,* English," Natalie said. "We have a guest."

"Oh." Now the woman took notice of Kayla. "Hello. How are you?"

"No worse for wear," Kayla answered.

"I'm Diane. You may have guessed I'm Natalie's mother."

"You could have told me you were her sister and I would have believed you. My name is Aklaq, but most call me Kayla."

"Where are you from? Earth, obviously. Judging by the furs, I would have to guess...Inuit?"

Kayla nodded. "You would be right."

"Oh, excellent. I must admit, I don't get to Earth often anymore, but when I did, I can't say I ever worked with the Inuit."

"What did you do?"

"Well, you might call it schooling. Mostly I worked with kids who were taken away from their families and sent to the boarding schools. I worked to help reunite them with their families and get them reconnected with the old ways." She shook her head. "I did a lot of work, but it still feels like it wasn't enough. But, I had kids of my own. Logan and Natalie weren't bad; I knew I could leave them for periods of time. Saul, though..." Her expression turned rife with righteous fury. "I swear by all the spirits, if I ever get my hands on the man who did this to him—"

"*Tsitsi,*" Natalie coaxed.

Diane huffed. "Anyway. Saul wanted to be left alone, but his bad attitude, fighting, and general mischief called me home." She shook her head solemnly. "Maybe if I had been home from the start and hadn't left him..."

"*Tsitsi,* we went over this before. Saul was on his own path from the very beginning. No one could have stopped him."

"I know." Diane waved her daughter's comforting hand away. "I know." She took a calming breath. "Anyway, you didn't come here to listen to me. So why are you here?"

So Kayla explained once more the reason for her visit. Diane listened patiently as she added this and mixed that, finally pouring out a lump of dough onto a rock and setting it in the cookfire.

"Well, it certainly sounds like a fascinating adventure," she said once Kayla had finished. "I'm just sorry we have no *nattawodatnu.* It won't be ripe until late summer or early fall."

"Natalie told me as much. But we also heard rumors that someone here may have been trapped in the same way and did manage to escape."

"Such a man does exist. He is very old now, but his mind is still sharp."

"We're going before the council to ask for their help as well," Natalie told her. "The more help they have, the greater the chances that Tommen can be rescued."

"I agree. Now you just need to round up the council."

"Do you know where they are?" Natalie wondered.

"Oh, here and there, I imagine," Diane said. "They have families that need attention, too, so it might take a few minutes to track them down." She gave Kayla a sideways glance. "And before you ask, I don't know if any of them are currently on assignment. Generally, once a person sits on the council, he or she forfeits assignments until they leave or are removed from the council. But that's not to say some don't sneak off once in a while. Politics is politics, wherever you go."

"Amen to that," Kayla muttered.

"I guess we better go find them, then," Natalie mused, sounding a little frustrated herself. She gave her mother a kiss goodbye before heading out of the home, Kayla in tow.

"The good news," she said, once they were a fair distance away, "is that all the council was present at the last funeral. It's possible that they could have up and left in the last day, but unlikely. Preparation for an assignment takes days, even weeks. So it's not a matter of whether they're here, but where they're hiding."

While it certainly didn't look like it from the gateway into the bowl, Wolf Clan was one of the smaller clans, a drastic change from their historical role. From what Kayla could gather, the Paint Clan was the largest, easily four times the size. They lived on the plains about four days southeast of Wolf Clan. But, with Wolf Clan being so small, their council only had five people on it.

Like most Native councils—or councils of the old days, as many often made the distinction—they weren't in a position of absolute authority. They mediated disputes and might organize larger hunts and game drives and raids, but no man ever presumed to tell another man what to do or how to live his life and conduct his affairs. If a man wanted to be lazy and not hunt, no one could force him to hunt, but no one was forced to provide for him either. If a man wanted to be an asshole and separate himself from his clan, no one could force him to stay or go, but no one was forced to go after him and try to bring him back or reason with him. Someone from the council might be asked to mitigate or mediate the situation and bring peace and order, but all was merely suggestion, a talk as a friend rather than a command as a leader.

Council members were often chosen because they were role models within the clan, an example of how to be a good Krydik. So it was that two of the members were currently on a game drive which could last until late afternoon. Another was working out how to fortify an irrigation system that had been damaged over the winter. The fourth was doing some beadwork on new regalia for her daughter, and the fifth was out gathering fresh spring shoots for cooking.

"How did your people do it?" Natalie wondered, seeming to sense Kayla's exasperation.

"The eldest hunter spoke for the family in clan affairs. Of them, one was chosen to represent the clan in tribal affairs. But because of the harsh climate, I mean, this is a lot of people." Kayla looked around. "That's all I'm saying."

"Don't worry. They'll be back. Word will spread. If not that the council members are wanted, but that there's a guest among us."

Kayla was still unsure, but there was little she could do. The last thing she intended on doing was running into the middle of a game drive to kidnap a couple of council members. She would be trampled. No, she would just have to wait a few minutes.

So instead, she followed Natalie around the village, its twisting streets and gorgeous views. There was certainly a difference between the upper and lower villages, not the least of which being the wind. In the upper village, carved into the mountainside, there was virtually no wind. But going down to the lower village, there was a point when it went from no wind to icy bite of death.

"In the summer, the warm south wind bakes the upper village," Natalie said when Kayla commented about it. "Some families will live in the upper village during the winter and the lower village during the summer. Personally, I don't mind the heat."

"Give me a tundra blizzard any day," Kayla said. "Not that I didn't anticipate the thaw in the spring, but I won't deny that I brag about being able to weather the storm."

"Why am I not surprised?"

As predicted, word spread of Kayla's arrival. Upon her entry into the village, she'd had a number of children running up to her in order to feel the strange furs. A few adults greeted her and welcomed her. Now, though, it seemed as though some were seeking her out, eager to see the stranger in the village—they probably didn't get very many of them. Many were courteous, offering greetings and items to trade. Kayla felt guilty about not bringing any trade items, but, really, she had nothing to trade that they couldn't get anyway. This was Wolf

Clan, after all, protectors of the Krydik and liaisons to Earth. At first glance, this was just another humble Native American village. On closer inspection, one could find cotton/polyester jackets, factory-made sandals, store-bought hair ties. Even Saul had had a cast iron cookstove.

That wasn't to say that she escaped without any souvenirs. She counted three beaded necklaces, four bracelets, a few small hair adornments, a clay figurine, and a satchel to carry everything by the time they returned to Diane's home. The older woman looked at her and the gifts and grinned mischievously. "I see we're starting to rub off on you."

"That would be putting it mildly," Kayla said, setting her new bag down. "I'm just sorry I didn't think ahead to bring anything to trade."

"It just gives you an excuse to make a second trip," Natalie told her.

She looked ready to say more when a middle-aged woman approached the home. She greeted Diane and Natalie in their own tongue before switching to English and looking at Kayla.

"So, this is our mysterious stranger," she observed. She stepped forward, extending a hand. "Misty."

"Aklaq," Kayla introduced. "But most call me Kayla."

"Very well, Kayla. I am one of the council members; I was out gathering when you apparently came by my home. I'm sorry I wasn't here to greet you, but I wasn't aware that visitors were coming today."

She cast a look at Natalie that Kayla couldn't quite interpret. Curiosity, certainly. Irritation? Were outsiders not welcome in the village normally? Well, when you have to run for your lives and live in isolation with only a select group of people communicating with the outside world, visitors from said outside world probably weren't too well-received. But if there was politics to be had, they wouldn't be had in front of Kayla; that much she could see. So how did this fare for getting help for Tommen?

"Thomas and Peter should be returning from the game drive

soon," Misty was saying. "Nathan will come down from his project once they're back. Then we can sit and talk about this proposal I've been told about." Again, she looked at Natalie but didn't say anything.

"Of course," Natalie agreed graciously. "Where will we meet?"

Misty told her a place, but Kayla couldn't speak to its location or significance. Then the older woman was gone.

"If you don't mind me saying," Kayla began, "you all have very English names."

Natalie nodded. "We call them our political names, the ones we use when crossing to Earth. It's the same reason you call yourself Kayla instead of Aklaq. It draws less attention and it's easier for others to say. Do you know how disheartening it is when someone can't even pronounce your name? Just that basic piece of your identity, and people get it messed up all the time."

"So what's your name, then?"

"Netami. It means 'the first' as in, the first girl." She grinned and shook her head. "Would you believe Saul was Sabelu? It means, 'shining brightly.' "

"Nature's little ironies?"

"No kidding."

"What about your other brothers?"

"Logan is Galiliga, meaning 'happy' or 'thankful.' Blake is Blaknik, squirrel. Actually, he was named for our grandfather, but in the merging of the languages, 'blaknik' won out over 'kiyuga.' "

"Why not Kiyuga anyway?"

"Kiyuga was Cherokee," Diane explained. "But his wife was Delaware. My generation was the one of transition, where all the old traditions were being merged. Some won out completely, others were blended. There's no rhyme or reason to it; it's just how it is. So I got everything from both sides, but had to put them together in a way that made sense to me in my generation. My father couldn't raise me solely according to his customs, and my mother couldn't raise me solely according to hers. Most of my kin had to find their own way. Even my husband was Choctaw, saved from the Trail of Tears. I suppose that makes us all part of the Stranger Clan."

"Where does the word 'Krydik' come from, then?" Kayla wondered.

Diane waved a hand dismissively. "Oh, everyone wants to claim that, and everyone has a theory. Truth is, no one knows. It's a blend of many words, I expect, until the end result was a word that meant nothing in any language except as a way to unite all of us under one tribal banner as it were." She let out a breath. "Sabelu was perhaps the anti-social epitome of what that meant. He knew everything about everyone, all the tribes, and he lived it all. It was all part of him. Perhaps if he hadn't been so hated by everyone, they might rally to his murder and demand justice. As it is, few people were sorry to see him go, and I don't know that there will ever be justice for it."

"*Tsitsi*, we talked about this, too," Natalie said, sighing as if the fight had already gotten old. "We can't just go over there and start attacking people. Earth has enough on its plate already, and there's still a secret war going on."

"I know, I know. But how do you think that makes me feel, knowing I can't go after the person who murdered my son?"

The women conversed in their own tongue for a short spell before Natalie gave up and turned to Kayla. "Why don't we head off and see if the council is convened? Then we might be able to get something done around here."

Kayla wasn't going to say no, and soon enough, they were on their way.

"She sounds crazy, but she has quite a force behind her," Natalie said. "Saul isn't the first one killed on Earth, but it is rare. Most of the time, it's just talk. Comments, sometimes threats, depending on the job. Occasionally there's a fight. We try to keep a low profile, but everything on Earth these days is about exposure and being in the spotlight as long as possible for the most ridiculous reasons."

"Well, you're not wrong there."

The council building, as Kayla referred to it, was sort of like a large community center. About forty feet wide, a hundred feet long, most of it was dedicated to the young and the old. Elders too old to do much lifting anymore kept warm around a large fire and told stories to children still too young to help with many chores. Other children played games while a group of women sat in a circle, each one working on some kind of sewing project. Another woman had a large skin stretched out which she was fleshing, throwing scraps to a small hoard of cats that had gathered around her.

At one end was another fire with a number of intricately carved stumps serving as seats setting around it. Five of them were filled with what Kayla presumed to be the council members, seeing how she recognized at least two of them.

"Follow my lead," Natalie hissed to Kayla as they approached.

They approached from the east side. Aside from the stump seats, there was a table on which rested a bowl full of some kind of dried herbs. Kayla immediately recognized the smell of tobacco and cedar, though it certainly smelled different than Earth-side tobacco and cedar, but couldn't speak to anything else. She copied Natalie as best she could, touching two fingers into the mixture, then to her forehead. Then she took a small pinch of the stuff and tossed it in the fire before moving to the left, south, and taking a seat.

"So, this is our visitor," one of the men said. "My name is Tali, but you may call me Thomas."

The council introduced themselves in turn, but there was no way Kayla could pronounce or remember their given names.

"My name is Aklaq," Kayla said when it was her turn. "Aklaq White Bear of the Inuit from what is now called Barrow and Kotzebue. You may call me Kayla, if you wish."

"Welcome, Kayla," Peter greeted. "We wish you pleasant days while you are visiting us. But is it not true that you are not coming to us as an Inuit ambassador for Indian Affairs, but some other matter?"

Kayla hoped her embarrassment wasn't too obvious. "It is true. I have come seeking your help for another matter, two in fact. One involves the safety of your peoples and mine. The other is an issue one of your own tribal members has experienced."

There were some silent, stolen glances among the council members. Kayla could feel Natalie's gaze upon her as well. Finally, Misty said, "Begin with the one involving our safety. I am curious to hear about it."

Most likely, the council already knew about the Borelian declaration of war on humans, whether through Natalie or some other Wolf Clan operative. That part likely did not come as a shock. What did get them thinking, Kayla saw, was the defense proposal she and Micaiah had loosely drawn up. Hlohi was not the only colony planet out there, and they were not suggesting that the Krydik return to Earth, but they might have to open up their doors just a little bit to allow for more "visitors" and more defenses.

"Haven't our people suffered enough?" Misty challenged. "We came here because we wish to live in peace with no interference. Has Natalie explained to you how other clans marry into Wolf Clan, how the warriors are vetted? Keeping the secret is of the utmost importance to us."

"And regardless of your relationship to other humans, the Borelians will come," Kayla pointed out. "This has nothing to do with my people versus your people, or your people versus the white man. This is about a greater threat coming against all humans. Earth is also Unengaged, which means Time Agents and Akari-bearers must wage the war in secret. The situation is no different here, except all of your Time Agents are gathered in one spot.

"District Nine has already agreed to help. Attacks on other colony planets have already begun. Do you think the Borelians cared that those people wanted to live in peace with no interference?" Kayla took an even breath. "I do not presume to tell you how to conduct your affairs, I only ask that you consider how you will defend yourselves against a threat we all know and fear. All we ask for is help, and the least we can do is try."

The council spoke among themselves in their own tongue for a minute or two. It was tough to gauge tone and body language, but Kayla tried to remain optimistic. They seemed to seriously consider her offer anyway. Maybe they'd heard the reports from the other colony worlds. Maybe they'd already been considering such a move, but a visitor from another human world was enough of a kick in the ass to get them to make a decision. Or maybe they were lamenting all the things they could be doing instead of listening to her. Who could know?

"Tell us of your second matter," Nathan said finally, once their short conversation had ended. Kayla felt her hopes sink.

Nevertheless, for what felt like the billionth time that day, she explained her mission, starting with Tommen and Rifun in the fire and all the adventures since then.

"I am told that the fruit you use to see into this in-between dimension is not in season," Kayla concluded. "However, if the man who also experienced this is still alive, I would ask to speak with him. If there is any way you know of to help, I would humbly ask for your help in this matter as well."

It was Thomas who spoke first. "Few understand that the *nattawodatnu*, the seeing fruit, allows them to see into this dimension. Even among Wolf Clan, many view it as communing with the spirits and dismiss the in-between dimension entirely. Even Nathan here is a skeptic. But you are correct that it is not in season and will not be in season for many wolf moons."

Kayla hesitated. "Is the seeing fruit you use here also found on Earth? It is summer there. Seeing how Tommen is trapped on Earth, I would have to search there anyway."

Vicky, who had been silent thus far, now spoke. "The *nattawodatnu* used today is derived from a plant found on Earth. It could be the different climate or soil or any number of things on Hlohi changed the plant when we brought it over. We know where it came from, but we cannot speak to its effectiveness or potency. It could be that what we use today is something completely different than what you may still find on Earth."

"I feel obligated to make an attempt anyway."

"Naturally. And are you certainly free to do so."

"And of the survivor?" Kayla questioned.

Now it was Misty's turn. "He was Wolf Clan, long ago, when he was trapped. After he escaped, he forsook all ties to Time and the Akari, terrified of their power. He married and now lives with Eagle Clan."

"Eagle Clan, where do they live?"

"To the east, in the forests near the cliffs overlooking the ocean. Normally, it is a week's journey, but I am confident a portal can transport you there in no time. Just be sure to step out outside of the village. Like all of the clans, those who made the Great Migration from Earth are now very old. Their stories of coming from the stars are intended to delight young children. Eagle Clan especially is charged with rendering new stories, new cultures and traditions for our people, that we may be free of the atrocities of our past."

"And Wolf Clan is charged with holding onto the truth," Kayla finished.

She could see the division in their expressions. The news from Earth was probably rarely good, as far as their people or any Native peoples were concerned, and many probably thought they ought to give it up also. Shut the door, engage the deadbolt, and set the alarm system. At the same time, having one group of people aware of the larger situation might be what saved them now from the Borelians. It almost seemed like a catch-22 for them.

While all the members of the council appeared to be middle-aged but still young and healthy, Thomas was easily the oldest, or oldest-looking of all of them, and he spoke now, slowly and deliberately.

"Surely you can appreciate the struggles we have faced. Ultimately, we wish to coexist and be allowed to live in our own way as our own people. But we cannot fight digital technology with bows and arrows. Even worse when the enemy can strike a fatal blow without ever having to raise an arm. We will deliberate on the best course of action for our people against the Borelian threat. In the meantime, you may seek out the survivor of the in-between dimension."

"Thank you," Kayla said graciously. "By chance, do you know his name?"

"He calls himself Usulagogi, or Lonely Man," Vicky answered. "He is old and some say he is becoming insane, haunted by the spirits he walked with in his youth, meaning the in-between dimension. Or perhaps not, who can know?" She shrugged. "As it has been said, we cannot tell you not to go, but all that happens is on your head."

"I understand."

Kayla understood them well enough. Her actions were her own and she had to own them, simple as that. But surely talking to an old man, no matter how kooky, didn't require such a lengthy preamble and warning statement.

The meeting wrapped up quickly after that. Kayla followed Natalie clockwise out of the meeting circle, greeting and thanking each council member in turn before walking back the way they came. It wasn't until they were back out in the sunshine that either of them spoke.

"Don't let them scare you," Natalie said. "They just like being extra cautious, especially when sending an outsider to the other clans."

"Well, I don't know what to tell them," Kayla sighed, looking out over the valley. "I need answers. I can't return empty-handed."

"Can't return empty-handed, but you also can't go out on an empty stomach. You've been through a multiple portals in a short span already, which is bad enough. You can't go through another without eating first." Natalie went on before Kayla could protest. "Come on. The bread is probably just about done. My mom is a phenomenal cook. It would be insulting if you didn't."

Kayla sighed. "I know. Believe me, I know. I'm just anxious to get going."

"Spoken like someone who's been away from home a little too long."

"You have no idea."

"Let's eat. You can tell us about the magic of your frozen

wasteland over lunch."

Natalie started down the path. After a second of hesitation, Kayla followed. They navigated the narrow, winding streets, sharing greetings and dodging children the whole way. When they did finally return home, Diane was just cutting into a plump loaf of bread. On the table were three settings, each with some smoked meat as well as fruits and nuts Kayla could not identify. Pretty soon, a fluffy chunk of bread was set on each plate to top it all off.

"Sit and eat," Diane said. "Something tells me you have tales to tell and are going to need food before the next leg of your journey."

Kayla didn't have to be told twice. Her stomach growled as she hung up her seal fur shawl and took her place at the table.

The food was unusual, but in a good way, and Kayla devoured everything on her plate, hardly looking up until Diane got her a second helping of everything. After that, she went a bit slower and managed to participate in conversation, which revolved mostly around her people, their home, their traditions, their stories, things she knew by heart even if she rarely thought of them these days it seemed.

"You know," Natalie said, "the only reason we have snow here is because of the elevation. These mountains are actually pretty close to the equator. I don't know that I could live in a place where the most you see of the sun is a small glimpse in the southern sky, and then it's gone."

"If you grow up with it, it's just a fact of life. A depressing one, but it's life."

They chatted a little more about this and that. Before Kayla knew it, she was yawning.

"Well, if you think you can keep your eyes open, wait a second while I grab a few things. Then we can get moving," Natalie said.

Kayla nodded and rubbed her eyes, trying to force herself awake. The last thing she remembered was looking at a nice leather rucksack and thinking that it would look even better with some caribou fur trim and antler adornment.

Chapter Twenty-Three
Forbidden Fruit

"Finally off work. Heading to hideout to wait for Natalie. Hope to be home soon and back in my right mind. See you soon. Love, Kayla."

That had been on the dining table when Micaiah got home from work. While he'd fully expected that Kayla was going to go straight from work to Hlohi, part of him was a little disappointed that he didn't get to see her before she left. It wasn't that he didn't trust the Krydik; in fact, he was more suspicious of the other Akarin right now. It was a terrible thing to admit, but tensions were high and everyone was doing and saying things they wouldn't normally do or say during peacetime. To say they were living in dark times would be a cliche, but it was the only thing he could come up with.

He got something to eat and tried to go about his evening as usual. He gave his car an oil change, watched a little TV, even got ready for bed, telling himself that all was well and there was nothing to worry about. He lay in bed for all of five minutes before deciding that sleep just wasn't going to happen.

When he returned to the living room, Micah was on the phone with Walter. He gave Micaiah a sly look as he said, "Fine, if you won't take him, I guess I'll have to take him back to the pound."

"Why, because you can't handle that he only has one leg and special needs?"

"I heard that, Walter," Micaiah said loudly.

On the other end, Walter burst out laughing. "Oh, Micaiah. You know we all love you."

"Fuck you, Walter."

Grouchily, Micaiah returned to his bedroom to grab his

473

running leg before going downstairs. Maybe a short run would put him a little more at ease. It would do nothing to help him sleep, but an idle mind is a terrible thing, after all.

Since getting more accustomed to his running leg, Micaiah had been able to push himself to about twenty miles. Of course, not having calf muscles to suddenly seize was beneficial, though his thighs could get a little iffy once he started pushing his boundaries. And then there was his slightly awkward gait which put a severe strain on his knees. Never had he considered that he might need knee braces, but here he was, pulling them on before getting on the treadmill and setting up for his "race," picking the speed, incline, and so on.

After a few minutes, he heard Micah go to bed. Though when he checked his watch, it had been decidedly more than a few minutes. Fucking hell, it was almost midnight. Good thing Micah was opening the store tomorrow. Sundays were typically slow, once the church crowd had passed. One rush before service, one after, and it would be dead the rest of the day. They'd toyed with the idea of closing extra early, around two or three, in order to cut their losses and give themselves a little break one day out of the week. But then something big would happen and they would have a Sunday or two where they were just slammed. So the matter remained in limbo.

Micaiah's race ended. According to the computer, he'd placed sixty-second out of three hundred. Well, whoop-de-doo. He didn't see anyone else running around his basement, so as far as he was concerned, he'd come in first.

He sat down and wiped his brow. Well, there would be no sleeping tonight. He got a drink of water and took off his leg. Still a little sore; he'd probably be feeling it in the morning.

He really should get to bed.

After a minute or two, he returned to his bedroom and lay down. Five minutes in, he knew sleep wasn't going to happen. He was still worried about Kayla, to be sure, but then he'd gone and done some pretty good exercise which only made him feel good and want to stay up and do some more. Maybe he should. He could keep working out tonight and give himself a small break tomorrow when he got up. He did that sometimes, and it felt good every once in a while.

Unfortunately, when he did go back down and started adding weights to the bar, his mind was everywhere but on what he was doing. That might be fine, but he wasn't about to monkey around with two hundred and fifty pounds hanging over his head. One wrong move and splat! There he goes.

So he went back upstairs and stood forlornly in the dead space that wasn't quite dining room, wasn't quite living room, wasn't quite kitchen, and wasn't quite hallway. He couldn't focus well enough to work out safely, couldn't sleep, and didn't want to watch TV. So what did that leave him?

Well, he knew his default activity, except he was so tired of going to the fortress. He was tired of researching the in-between dimensions when everything was only myth and fairy tale, and he was tired of dealing with all the politics. When did he get to relax and go to bed without worrying about who could be friends or enemies? Probably when he was dead.

Nevertheless, he took a quick cold shower and swapped out his running leg for his regular leg. It might prove to be a bad idea if the angry mob came after him again, but then, if he was trying to outrun an angry mob, he'd just as soon escape via portal.

Soon enough, Micaiah found himself in the portal room of the Akarin fortress. He hadn't been arrested, drugged, knocked out, or even acknowledged. No one was expecting him to give any kind of press conference. He didn't see any Wanted posters either.

The fortress was looking more and more like a deserted castle with each passing day, Micaiah thought. More and more Akarin were staying home, staying out of the fight, or else just leaving completely, not wanting to get mixed up in yet another civil war and division and just saying, fuck it all, I'm done with you and your bullshit power struggles.

Micaiah didn't blame them. He was sick of the shit, too. In fact, he would probably be in the same boat if not for his sudden, yet unwanted promotion. Yes, it afforded him power and resources he needed to communicate with other human worlds and bring them closer together in the fight against the Borelians, but really, he could have gotten support with or without the position. The Akarin had very little to do with such exclusive affairs. Their primary concern was internal conflict and the ban from the Hands of Time.

According to the gossip, if it could be believed, all known Akari-bearers were being stopped and interrogated, regardless of whether they'd been "spreading propaganda" or just meandering through the marketplaces. So far, no arrests had been made, but there was some definite roughing up going on. As for humans, well, with exception of Walter, few humans who went to the Wheel were seen or heard from again. Those who did return reported swift and decisive moves by the Borelians to capture and enslave.

Fucking hell, but five flights of stairs never got easier. He paused and looked out into the open space in the middle of the spiral stairs. There weren't many people around these days. Maybe he could use Gravity to speed things up a bit, make things easier on himself. He'd just run twenty miles; this climbing thing was killing him more than it normally did.

In the end, he decided against it. The last thing he needed was to have a headstone or obituary that read, "A great leader and commander of many men who died because he thought he could fly." Nah, best to keep walking.

He reached the fifth floor only because he kept telling himself that the struggle had to constitute another six-point-two miles; therefore, he could confidently say that he had, in fact, done a marathon today, and part of it had indeed been all uphill. That wasn't even including all the hopping around he'd done at the bakery. Doing it on one leg had to earn him some bonus points, surely, but did the use of crutches negate those extra points? He thought about it, then decided to give himself the extra points anyway. He'd done a full marathon today, and no one was going to tell him otherwise. Taking a breath, he calmly approached the door to the Archives, forcing himself not to limp too badly.

He wasn't even sure what he wanted to look up. He was sick of researching the in-between dimension. Actually, he was sick of researching period. Research was so boring, and it didn't seem to be getting them anywhere. At least Kayla was out and actually doing something, trying to find an answer. And here he was at the library, reading about stuff.

Micaiah ran his tongue over his teeth. She was out on an adventure, her primary goal to talk to a crazy old man and get high. Maybe he ought to research just exactly what she would be smoking over there. Hey, it couldn't hurt, right? And if it really was something that was also found on Earth, well, maybe she wouldn't have to make such a long trip the next time. Hell, maybe they'd be able to do it together if they were feeling particularly adventurous. Micaiah wasn't a huge fan of weed, certainly nothing stronger than that, but that wasn't to say he hadn't done it. Hey, fifty years of marriage, they had to keep things interesting somehow.

So it was that he found himself wandering the Archives looking for a book on the hallucinogenic plants of Hlohi. He didn't find one exactly like that, but a general book of botany would probably point him in the right direction. He grabbed a couple of those, then sat down to peruse.

Overall, the vegetation on Hlohi wasn't so drastically different. Yes, there were strange plants and species and so forth, but there was nothing super freakishly alien like purple and orange bark with red and yellow leaves bearing fruit that looked like it belonged in a horror film. There were trees that kept their leaves all year round, some that shed leaves, and some that sported fruit as the leaves rather than a byproduct, like an apple tree that had apples at the end of every stem instead of leaves.

There were a few freaky plants, to be sure, but otherwise, there was nothing truly remarkable about anything. Certainly nothing that jumped out and screamed, "Smoke me!"

In one book that proved to be newer than the others, there was mention of the Great Migration, in that seeds and spores from plants found on Earth had taken root on Hlohi, this on top of all the plants they'd taken with them deliberately to cultivate. So in addition to daradigm trees and kalaran bushes—so named by the author of the book, not necessarily Hlohi inhabitants—there were also maple trees, Douglas fir, common ferns, even wild blueberry and raspberry bushes. Along with a fuck ton of Earth molds and fungus, likely small insects, and a variety of microorganisms. Therefore, it was the opinion of the author that the entire ecosystem of Hlohi had been dramatically changed with the introduction of the Native peoples and so modern Hlohi biology was vastly different from what it was hundreds of years ago.

Fascinating, to be sure, but hardly helpful. He flipped around in the book a bit until he got to the section on poisonous plants. There were plenty of them, but none of them made any mention of being hallucinogenic—without being lethal—or used in any sorts of spiritual ritual.

And why would it? This was supposed to be an objective view of the plants of Hlohi. If there was any significance of any plant to the people, it wouldn't be mentioned.

Grudgingly, Micaiah got up again and started perusing the aisles once more, this time on the hunt for religious rituals of the Krydik. He didn't expect there to be much, seeing how they were very careful about the information they shared with outsiders. But as he read about some of the sacred plants, Micaiah was able to recognize at least one of them. He got the name of it and cross-referenced it with a similar plant in one of the botany books.

" 'Nattawodatnu, or "seeing fruit" is used in several rituals in Krydik society,' " Micaiah read from the religious book. " 'The first instance is when a young man or woman seeks to be a full adult member of the tribe. He or she takes the fruit in order to see into the spirit world and commune with his or her ancestors and so receive guidance. Another instance is when a man or woman is dying. He or she may be given the fruit in order to seek help from the spirits, either in healing the disease, or having safe passage into the spirit world.

" 'Nattawodatnu comes into season in late summer to early fall. It is a stone fruit. The skin of the fruit is very sticky, making it useful for bandages; the calming, hallucinogenic properties also lend a natural anesthetic. The stone, if not planted, may be ground into a fine powder used for smudging in certain rituals, or brewed as a tea as a natural painkiller. The flesh of the fruit, when used in rituals, is often mashed into a juice, then poured over hot rocks to create a steam. From this steam, visions come forth. The flesh may also be eaten or mashed and drunk straight if no fire is available, however, the potency of such a concoction may prove dangerous, even fatal.' "

Better hope Kayla doesn't party too hard, Micaiah thought, feeling worry creep back into his system. He turned back to the botany book.

" 'Lophophora krydiksum, locally known as "nattawodatnu" or "seeing fruit" is a hallucinogenic fruit found on the planet Hlohi and is used by the native Krydik people for various religious ceremonies. It is believed to be a carefully and intentionally-fused hybrid plant of the peyote cactus and the peach tree, found on Earth, and two unknown native plants of Hlohi. Speculation and research suggests the other factors may be the "needle tree" (C. splendorum) and "yellow fruit" (R. pintosa) but more research is needed to trace the evolution of the plant.' "

There was very little of interest after that, and Micaiah leaned back in his chair. So, peyote had been mixed with a common peach. Lovely. His wife was going to a distant world to smoke peaches. But if that was true, what in the world had the Krydik been smoking on Earth? Peyote was found in the Southwest. Trade might have brought it this far, but there was no way they could have cultivated it to have it so readily available for their rituals. More than that, how did peyote and peaches get together and have a kid? Even the Authored Books were mum on the details.

Maybe the book was wrong. Maybe it really was a combination of a peach tree and some shrooms. Shroom spores might have been carried over into Hlohi and gotten mixed up with some new peach seedlings. Add in some needle trees and yellow fruit and bam! New seeing fruit. If the hallucinogenic properties could be felt just by eating them straight out, it wouldn't have taken much to figure out how to use it in their rituals.

Problem was, it was all speculation. Worse, it did him no good. At this point, it wasn't going to help his wife, and he certainly wasn't planning on going hunting for magic shrooms. Hell to the no. He might do a little weed if Kayla could talk him into it on a little adventure, but this was way out of his league. And while he could respect his wife's beliefs and traditions, and he certainly wasn't trying to knock any of them, there were some things he wouldn't do, and some things he didn't want her doing either just for her own safety.

But that was neither here nor there. Kayla was gone to smoke peaches and peyote shrooms. Hopefully she would be back in her right mind by the time she got home. Surely Natalie wouldn't send her back half out of her mind, high and hallucinating.

He browsed through the books some more, but found nothing particularly insightful. No one seemed to know just how the seeing fruit had come about except that it was a Frankenstein of several different plants from both worlds. All that was really known was that it was a stone fruit where every part was good for something, it ripened in late summer or early fall, and it could grow just about anywhere, from mountains to desert in climate-adapted variations. In the mountains and fertile lands, it was a tree. In the desert and other otherwise inhospitable climates, it was more of a bush.

This didn't matter all that much to Micaiah except he was really fucking bored and wished he had a course of action that wasn't half-dependent on a waiting game. He would much rather reach straight into the in-between dimension, drag Tommen out by his ears and send him home, that way he could move on to his next big project, whether it was the human-Borelian war or the Akarin division, he didn't care which.

Habit told Micaiah to put the books away; experience told him to not make an enemy of the librarians and let them put the books away. He had too many enemies as it was; he didn't need to add the librarians to that list. So he took a minute to lean back and try to relax, collect his thoughts and tell himself it was time to go home and get some sleep. Of course, when he opened his eyes, he prayed dearly that he had fallen asleep in the chair and was now in a nightmare. It was better than the reality of six council members approaching him. Maybe he should have grabbed his running leg. Or maybe he should just open the portal now and escape before they could bog him down with more politics, drama, and bullshit.

"Micaiah Durvin," one said.

"Depends," he answered. "Who's asking?"

"Come with us."

"Why?"

None of the council members responded immediately. For a second, they just stood there, stunned, as if they couldn't comprehend that he hadn't immediately leapt to his feet to follow like an obedient puppy.

"Follow us," another said finally.

"I don't have to follow you anywhere," Micaiah informed them. "I'm in the middle of doing some research. Either tell me why I'm going, or I won't go."

"There is something you need to see," a third council member replied. "It may have something to do with your 'research.' "

Micaiah's first thought was that something had happened to Kayla. His kneejerk reaction to get to his feet unfortunately cost him his badass leverage. Now that he'd gotten up, he was pretty well obligated to follow. Besides, he still had the option of turning and fleeing, right?

Thankfully, they went downstairs instead of up, stopping on the second floor, the common barracks. Looking around, things were looking pretty bare. On a good day, the barracks might be about sixty percent capacity as people came and went. Some were semi-permanent residents while others just needed a place to crash for a while as they waited for their new life paperwork to get printed up. Now, though, even with the rush of new life paperwork being processed, the danger and division of the Akarin had dropped numbers down to about ten percent or less, with only about two percent present that he saw.

The farther they went, the less Micaiah thought this was about Kayla and the more he thought that this could be another kidnapping or assassination attempt. It could just be his paranoia kicking into gear. Normally he didn't have a problem, but things were not normal. Given that he'd already had one attempt on his life, he wasn't ruling out the possibility of another. But he was becoming less and less convinced that something had happened to Kayla. She had no reason to be here, and if someone wanted to send a message to him, this wasn't the way to do it.

But that wasn't to say it didn't hit home, at least a little bit. He recognized Zavi, the horse hawk beast who had shown him support. He also recognized another one of the council members he'd had an argument with the other day, the Ruib. That made two of the four dead, plus a supporter.

"When were they found?" Micaiah asked.

"Approximately two hours ago," one of the council members answered. "The preliminary evidence has been gathered. We were just getting ready to move the bodies when you were spotted."

"And what does this have to do with my research?"

"It doesn't," another member said honestly. "But it got you to come with us."

"You could have just told me that someone else had turned up dead and you wanted me to take a look. You don't have to play the tiptoe game." He turned to face them and continued before anyone could rebut. "I don't appreciate being treated like the red-headed stepchild. Okay, a month ago you forced me into this leadership position that I didn't want. Now you go around accusing me of abusing power and, apparently, murder."

"We're not accusing you of anything," the lead council member said smugly. "We're charging you."

"Excuse me?"

Even as Micaiah said the words, he knew what came next. There were no Miranda rights for him as he was seized and roughly taken out of the barracks.

"Are you fucking kidding me?" he growled. "Twice in one year? First in the Wheel and now here? Are you out of your fucking minds?!"

He was taken down to sub-level two and locked in a small holding cell. It was comical, really, seeing how he could still technically make a portal and escape. He refrained for the time being as the lead council member remained. He—or she or whatever—was an alien called a Portan. That in itself was a bit of a laugh seeing how portan was Irish for crab, and the face of this thing certainly reminded Micaiah of a crab.

"So you're not even going to try and fight the Hands of Time, are you?" Micaiah said. "Or the Cult. You are going to do exactly as they want you to do. The Akarin are going to turn into a cannibalistic theocracy, where all who do not conform are called heretics and excommunicated, or worse. Tell me, what real evidence do you have against me? The council members argued with me, but Zavi supported me. Why would I kill someone who supported me?"

The Portan was silent for a long moment. Then, "When you were appointed to your position, we as the council had hoped to give humanity a chance at redemption. You led the successful revolt against Rifun and have been a good Akarin for many years. We thought that if anyone could save humanity, it might be you. But you are just like Rifun and Cassius and Doug."

"And how is that?"

"You are selfish. You claim to not want the power, yet you leverage it for your own means. You are volatile, unwilling to accept direction and guidance for others who may be more experienced in leadership—"

"I'm not an ass-kisser is what you really want to say." Micaiah glared at him.

"And you are violent. As evidenced by the dead Akarin."

"Tell me something. How many Akarin fought in the Wheel, hm? How many killed there? How many killed, clawed, tore apart Grandfathers and guards? And of those, how many could also be connected to those who are dead? Why me?"

"Because of your secret allegiance to Rifun and the Cult." At Micaiah's expression, he went on, "Your associate, Tommen Forbes, the one who is trapped in the in-between dimension. You have not only told him to learn under Rifun, but he himself has willingly associated with him, to the point where he not only located the second journal but sent it back into this dimension that Rifun might get his hands on it."

"Tommen not becoming an Akarin is my fault. I admit that. I had my own reservations about it, and there was the turmoil of Rifun's coup and the chaos here. I did tell Tommen to get close to Rifun in order that we might find a weakness or a way to kill him. But I never suggested that he actually believe what that bastard has to say." Micaiah shook his head. "I don't understand what's going on here. I really don't. Like Kayla said, this used to be a safe place where things made sense. We were Akari-bearers, Akarin, chosen by the Author and opposite the Hands of Time. All I see now is shambles, a shadow of what we once were. An impostor borrowing the name of the Akarin."

"Not a shadow," the Portan said. "The real thing. But in order to cleanse ourselves of the treachery of Cassius and fight the evils of the Hands of Time, we must be rid of all our imperfections. There is a saying you may recognize, that a house divided cannot stand. Those who are Akarin and Time Agents are not Akarin at all."

"So that's what this is about? Some sort of ethnic cleansing?"

"The Hands of Time may hold the door closed for a time, but once all the impurities of our cause are stamped out, they cannot hope to withstand our strength. Author permitting, of course. Then, when we have established ourselves again in the face of the Hands, we can purify our name by being rid of the Cult and their infernal journals.

They were manageable when they had only hearsay and legends. One journal spawned the coup. Who knows what two journals will do? Author forbid they find all three."

"Well, I'll agree with you there. But I fail to see what this has to do with me. For one, you can't keep me here. You know I can escape."

"That is the beauty of these cells, though. If you can't escape, it means the Author has left you. If you can, then I would suggest that you take your chance at freedom and not return."

Micaiah raised a brow. "But if I can escape, that means that the Author is still with me. Isn't that kind of what you want in your Akarin, especially your leaders? If the Author isn't with us, then what good does it do us to have power? Then we just have a really cool club that isn't Time."

"You are no longer a leader," the council member informed him. "You no longer have power or influence here. In fact, you are no longer permitted here. As I said, if you have the chance to escape, I suggest you take it."

The Portan started walking away, but only got about ten feet before Micaiah spoke again. "You never did answer my question. What are the Akarin without the Author? What is an Akari-bearer without the Akari?" The Portan paused, shuffled a little bit, but kept going. Micaiah kept talking all the way out the door. "You're going to fail. The Akarin are already leaving in droves, and your ethnic cleansing will do nothing to unify them. The Hands of Time are laughing at you now and they will laugh at you as they crush your foolish attack. The Cult will rise and who will be left to defend the Akarin? The only one who can save you now is the Author herself! What kind of ending do you want?!"

Then the council member was gone.

Well, that certainly hadn't gone the way he planned it. Although, strangely, he did find that he was tired enough that he could probably go to sleep once he got into his own bed. For the moment, though, he just had to sit down and try to process whatever the fuck had just happened.

He'd just been relieved of duty and thrown in jail, told to escape if he could and don't come back. It wasn't that they thought he had killed those council members and Zavi, but they needed an excuse to be rid of him. They could paint him as the scapegoat and use it as an argument against both humans and those who were both Akarin and Time Agents. It seemed as though that in the wake of Rifun's coup, everyone was struggling with not only power, but identity. What group did a person belong to and what did that mean? What made a human Time Agent different from a human Akari-bearer? What separated the various Akarin factions?

Well, the Akarin at large seemed to have their own idea of what an Akari-bearer looked like; they were stooping to scapegoating, blackmail, and exile in order to accomplish their own ends, certain that if they just became pure enough and powerful enough, that they would be able to overturn the Hands of Time and win back all the Akarin currently leaving. Once that was done, it was time to go after the Cult, their mortal enemies who used Richard's journals as their guide instead of the Authored Books. Micaiah was forced to wonder if the Akarin leaders were more concerned with having a grand and exciting story rather than actually following the Author, using the Akari, and doing what they were supposed to, even if that meant being a smidge less than spectacular.

Micaiah rubbed his face. At what point did the Author stop writing? Did she literally write down every little detail, or was some of it really free will? Words couldn't write themselves, surely, but why not write everyone a happy ending? That was the whole point behind their mantra. And if the Author really did write everything and have everything planned and knew everything before they knew it, then why didn't everyone get a happy ending? He sighed and closed his eyes. That was a philosophical argument he didn't have the energy for. Why was this happening, and where did it lead? If the Author wrote everything, what control did he have over it?

Well, at least he didn't have to worry about the Akarin anymore. Didn't have to worry about the politics or the drama or the bullshit. But that also meant he had zero access to Archives from either side, and his ability to jump to other worlds was sorely limited. He also wasn't able to go and check on the status of his new life paperwork, though given the backup, it was either going to be conveniently forgotten, or maybe he would be able to get back into the Akarin in the two years it was supposed to take. Maybe he could get a day pass or something, just for that purpose. Well, he'd have lots of time to think about it.

Something occurred to him then. The council member had mentioned the three journals. One of those was the one Tommen found in the cave. That was definitely in Rifun's possession. But the second one, which Tommen had sent back through the portal, had been taken by Micah. The council member had said that the Cult had two of the journals. So either the Cult had the third journal, or else...

Micaiah tumbled out of the portal before he quite knew what was happening, landing hard on the floor in the hallway, right knee screaming. He groaned and nursed the wound for a second before limping into his bedroom to remove his leg. Once the throbbing had stopped, he grabbed his crutches and went to bang on Micah's door. It took a minute, but his sleepy twin eventually opened up.

"*Cá bhfuil an tine?*" he mumbled. (Where's the fire?)

"*Cá bhfuil an dialann?*" Micaiah demanded. (Where's the journal?)

"*An dialann?*" (The journal?)

"*An ceann a thug Tommen duit.*" (The one Tommen gave you.)

"Oh, from the in-between dimension? Yeah, it's in my safe here." Micah lamely gestured toward the safe in his room. Its contents, Micaiah knew, were about sixty percent guns, forty percent valuables. His own safe was more like eighty percent guns, twenty percent valuables.

"Open it up," Micaiah ordered.

"Why? Cai, it's fine." Micah yawned. "I'll do it in the morning."

"Open it now. I have reason to believe it may have been stolen."

Micah still looked uncertain, maybe ready to protest, but eventually he stepped back and made for the safe. He twisted the knob and unlocked the key lock, then turned the handle and hauled the door open. Six rifles and eleven handguns immediately claimed the attention of anyone looking, while a little black lockbox sat harmlessly on the top shelf. Micah fiddled around with the key for that, but popped the lid on that to show a bunch of important documents—car titles and so on. Underneath all of that was an unassuming leatherbound journal, similar to the one Tommen brought out of Forbes Cave.

"Happy?" Micah growled.

Micaiah nodded absently. "Tomorrow, I want you to take that to the shop and lock it in that safe."

"Why? It's the same safe but smaller."

"Because if someone does come for it, they're not going to ask nicely. Until we figure out what the hell we're going to do with it, I want to keep it safe, and out of harm's way. I don't want them to mow you down to go after it."

"I don't see a real difference. They'll mow me down here, but only at night when I'm asleep. They'll mow you down in the office, but only during the day when you're there. How is one better than the other?"

"Just do it. At least with the shop safe, they're not getting a dozen free guns with their theft, too."

Micah shrugged. "Okay, I'll give you that one." He closed and locked the box, then shut up the safe nice and tight. "Now, if you're quite done, I have some more napping I'd like to do before my alarm goes off in two hours."

Micaiah sighed but nodded. "Yeah. I get it. Okay. Yeah, go back to sleep. I think I should get some sleep, too, with the night I've had."

"I'm sure I'll hear about it in the morning after we rescue Tommen."

"Oh, shit, that's tomorrow, isn't it?"

"Well, technically today, so...I'd kind of like to have some sense of cognition." He made a shooing motion.

"Okay. Well, I don't know that I can get to sleep, so at least let me Band you for a few hours."

That much Micah would do. Seeing how he had about two hours until his alarm, Micaiah Banded him for six hours. It was enough to fulfill eight hours, counting the sleep he had gotten before, but it would let him rest a little longer and gain two extra hours. Once that was done, Micaiah crept back to his room and collapsed on the bed.

This was just not his day. This was not his week, actually. He'd seen several people killed, been accused, been arrested, been demoted, been banned. And if that wasn't bad enough, the same fuckers who did that to him had made his wife cry because of their fuckery. No one made his wife cry and got away with it.

But maybe this was the answer he needed, a way to leave Time and the Akarin, settle down with Kayla so they could live their own lives. He had basically zero responsibilities now with either force. As far as the human-Borelian war went, there were several viable candidates for top dog as it were. He could appoint one of them, then leave to do his own thing. It felt cowardly, no doubt about that, but maybe that was exactly what needed to happen.

Well, he'd give it a day or two before making that kind of decision. Right now, he was going to do his part to rescue Tommen. One thing at a time.

He lay in bed and stared up at the ceiling for a while, wide awake. He'd briefly heard about the two-phase plan to rescue Tommen, the first being sheer power, and, if that didn't work, the second being an attempt at rebuilding the quasi-dimension in the warehouse, the idea being to ease him back through the dimensions so he didn't get electrocuted.

"It's a mystery, isn't it?"

Micaiah just about leapt out of bed at a voice in the room, grabbing his gun and reining himself in only when he saw Chandler in the corner. He lay back and put a hand to his chest.

"Fuck," he breathed, letting the gun slide out of his hand onto his nightstand. "Fucking hell. Don't do that." He closed his eyes and took a calming breath before sitting up. "Is that funny to you?" Chandler was grinning as if trying not to laugh out loud. "You think it's just hilarious to sneak up on someone you know is strung tighter than a fiddle?"

"I will admit, it was a little amusing," Chandler said, shrugging casually.

Micaiah rubbed his face. "Fuck."

"The good news, however, is that the tension on your fiddle will be released. But only once the strings have snapped."

"Oh, God, more riddles. You make random appearances and they're never very helpful, you know that? Why can't we go back to that time you actually, physically helped me out? You know, cauterizing a wound or getting me past the barriers in the Judgment Wing? Or that one time you actually gave a straight answer. That was pretty sweet. So you can either get Tommen out of the in-between dimension or tell me how we can do it. Otherwise, I need to get some sleep."

Chandler raised a brow, his expression suggesting he was thinking a thousand things that would never pass his lips. When he did finally speak, it was with a certain severity.

"They're coming for the journals, Micaiah. The journals and the souls of anyone weak enough to listen to them, including your young protege."

"Tommen is smart enough not to follow Rifun," Micaiah said, though a twinge of honesty deep in his heart questioned whether that was entirely true. It's like the kid who keeps following the gang leader in the neighborhood. Everyone knew it was wrong, but the thrill and the power kept them coming back. One more time, just a little further, push the limits a little more, see how much we can get away with.

"Barring souls," Chandler went on, "they will also take the lives of anyone who stands in their way."

"Yeah, because one war just wasn't bad enough. I'm going to

sleep now, Chandler. Wake me when you want to start making sense and giving me straight answers."

As Micaiah slid back under the blankets, the mystery man still spoke. "You know, I've always wondered how different things would be for you if you understood everything the Author has planned for you. If you had known that you were going to lose your leg, would you have still gone to the Inauguration?"

"Given that the overarching theme is the coup, no, probably not."

"And that is understandable. But if you could understand what the Author has in store for you down the road because of it, would you have gone willingly just because of it?"

"Depends. What is this great mystery thing the Author has planned?"

Chandler chuckled. "You will learn that in time. Until then, good night."

Then he was gone. Micaiah reached for his gun to slide it back under his pillow and found a candle sitting next to it on the nightstand. It was burning very low, would probably be out before morning. For all his mysteries and riddles, Chandler was a lot less subtle than anyone seemed to give him credit for, and Micaiah felt a chill creeping down his neck as he finally rolled over and closed his eyes.

Sunday

Kayla woke with a start and found that she had been moved to a nice bed of furs in the adjoining room. Her seal fur was carefully hung up, her hat resting on top. As she struggled to sit up and get to her feet, a glorious smell wafted to her from the main room. Yawning, she went out to meet Diane and Natalie who were busy cooking something that looked like corn. For all intents and purposes, it probably was corn, brought over during the migration.

"How long have I been asleep?" she asked, trying not to sound harsh.

"Just a few hours," Diane answered pleasantly. "We know you want to keep moving and be back as soon as you can, but jet lag is a bit of a bitch. You needed rest."

Well, she really couldn't argue with the woman because it was painfully true. She was still a little tired, but could hold out for now, long enough to visit Eagle Clan and get the story she needed. Natalie directed her to a wash basin where she freshened up a bit before helping out, what little she could, to make dinner and clean up the little home.

"How will they receive a visitor?" Kayla wondered. "Have any of them even seen someone who isn't Krydik?"

"Oh, yes," Diane said, waving a hand. "We have good relations with District Nine on Earth, and every so often, a couple of them or a group will come over to do a little visiting, trading goods and stories. Not often, of course, but as long as Wolf Clan still exists as the bridge between Hlohi and Earth, there is a door open to good relations, whatever the council may say."

Dinner was a fine thing, Kayla had to admit, and she would be sorry to leave.

"We can always return and feed you again before you go," Natalie told her as she pulled on her shawl and hat.

"I know. On a normal day, I would love to take you up on your offer, but right now, I need to find this Lonely Man and hear what he has to say, then take it back to rescue Tommen."

"Well, I know I can't convince you otherwise, but you will have to visit again."

"Oh, of course. I expect I'm more comfortable visiting here than you would be visiting my home."

"In that you would be right. Our winters are bad enough; I don't need to see the land of eternal snow."

Kayla shook her head and the two of them headed out of the village, past the two guards who still stood watch, oblivious to their foreign conversation. Once they were a fair distance from the village, Natalie opened a portal and they stepped through.

It was like being blasted by hurricane force winds as Kayla stepped through. It hit her, buffeted her face, almost stole her hat, and whistled through mighty trees that swayed like grass on the plains. In the distance, she could hear what sounded like the worst TV static ever, except she knew it was the roar and froth of an angry ocean. Overhead, gray clouds gave way to distant black clouds, lightning streaking through them as they drew ever closer.

"We should hurry," Natalie suggested, her words almost inaudible despite being only a couple feet away.

Keeping a firm grip on her seal fur, Kayla pressed forward behind Natalie, following a path that was felt more than seen. More than once she stumbled, but the violent winds kept her upright. Somewhere close by, a tree or tree branch snapped and went crashing to the ground. Several times, they had to diverge from the path and make their way around a fallen tree. It was freezing out there in the cold and dark, but Kayla found herself almost comforted. It was like being home, but with a few more trees. The freezing rain, violent winds, and biting cold. What's not to love?

If Natalie ever said anything, her words were lost on the wind. Kayla picked up on her cues more from either watching her or running into her accidentally. Neither ever voiced their fears about being lost, though Kayla seriously considered the possibility from time to time, not that she would know, seeing how the terrain was entirely unfamiliar. On a sunny day, this could be a half hour cake walk. But between the weather and their half pace because of the sheer force of the wind, plus all the other minor delays, it was a good two hours before Natalie finally stopped and pointed. Kayla caught about every third word she said, but "village," "shelter," and "warm" stuck out to her.

Despite being named Eagle Clan, this particular group of Krydik actually made their village somewhat underground, in a style reminisce of waffle gardening. Being submerged meant they were protected from the wind, and each one appeared to be angled in such a way that there was even drainage out to the cliffs. This was all a cursory observation of course, as, with the exception of a few spot fires, the entire village was pretty much shrouded in darkness.

The darkness proved advantageous for perimeter guards, as there were suddenly six of them surrounding the two women. Kayla could only watch as they spoke back and forth in their own tongue. Despite being a complete foreigner, in several generations, Kayla could already tell there were some differences in dialect, possibly even total language separation as each group slowly became more and more independent and moved on, those lines between tribes and clans becoming more entrenched. Once again, entirely speculation, but it was bound to happen sooner or later.

"Come on," Natalie said, nudging her in the ribs.

The two of them were surrounded by the six warriors and taken to one of the waffle villages. The sudden drop below the wind current line was a shock and a relief. She could feel the windburn on her face, but she could also hear what was going on around her. It was sloped overall, as Kayla had suspected, professional, permanent trenches and drains keeping the water flowing smoothly out to the cliffs. The buildings themselves appeared to be made of mud bricks, and yet the roofs looked like they were plated in metal of some form, copper if she had to compare it to something.

What she had not expected, however, were the tunnels that connected one waffle village to another. She wasn't sure what she'd expected instead. It made sense after all. But these were not her people, and it was not her place to say, nor would she presume to tell anyone what to do.

A couple of the warriors left the group and went ahead. Kayla and Natalie were escorted to a squat building with three rooms and a cozy fire. They were left alone.

"I don't know about you," Natalie said, "but I like this much better."

"I'll agree to that," Kayla said, pulling off her hat and gloves. Being out of the wind certainly helped, and being out of the mountains meant that things were a little warmer. Kayla did not fancy having to go back out in the cold and wind to open a portal to get back home, but at least home was warm.

The whole building was really about the size of the living room back home, and the room where they sat was a little bigger than the dining room table. With the fire burning hot, the women were quickly warmed up. They waited about twenty minutes before the animal skin over the doorway was pushed aside and four men entered the room. Two of them were middle-aged, one maybe a little older, another about in his late teens or early twenties.

Natalie and the men exchanged customary greetings and light pleasantries and did whatever they needed to do to begin the conversation. Kayla tried to sit quietly and be polite and attentive, but it was hard when the conversation was unintelligible. It was almost like being a child again. First the Russian missionaries came and taught all the children Russian and Old Slavic. Then the Americans and the Canadians and the British all jumped in and squabbled over how to divide a piece of land that was already occupied. English was introduced. And it all went downhill from there.

She came back to the present as Natalie turned to her and spoke. "I'll be the interpreter. Start with your name."

Kayla nodded and tried to discern which one was the leader. Certainly not the young man; likely he was either someone's son or grandson, or else a favorite for future chief and was learning the political ropes. It was tempting to assume the older man, but he could just as easily be a retired chief now imparting wisdom to the younger ones. Of the two middle-aged men, it was impossible to tell without having a better understanding of not only their language, but their culture.

"My name is Aklaq White Bear," Kayla began, giving the same basic introduction she had given the Wolf Clan council.

"We understand you have traveled a great distance to ask the Krydik for help," one of the middle-aged men said through Natalie. "Visitors often go to Wolf Clan first." She didn't miss the slight acid in his tone. "What brings you to Eagle Clan?"

"I have a friend, a young friend, who has been wrongfully trapped in the spirit lands. It was not of his doing." Well, it was, but no need to give them the full story. "No one has been able to free him, but we heard of an old man who has been to the spirit lands and returned. I wish to hear the story he has to tell."

"Usulagogi?" the young man chuckled. "He is insane, a crazy old man."

The other three rebuked him, probably for disrespect of an elder. Natalie did not translate.

"Be that as it may," one of the middle-aged men said, "he is old and not always in his right mind these days. Regardless of whether he walked with the spirits in his youth, he will certainly walk with them before the turn of the moon."

"All the more reason to speak to him now," Kayla pressed. "My friend fears he does not have much time, for he is wounded and sick."

"Ensnared by devils, then. A truly terrible thing."

"Will you help?"

The second middle-aged man shrugged. "It is not our place to say what a man may do or not do. Our intentions here are to merely receive a visitor to our people and hear your intentions. Since you are not here to declare war or call to arms or any other vile thing against our people and village, you are free to act as you see fit. If you wish to seek out the Lonely Man, then by all means, you are free to do it. Whether or not you speak to him is up to him. But know that while he is seen as crazy, he is still an elder, and no man will hesitate to step in if they feel you are harassing him. He is old and sickly, and we wish his journey to the spirit lands to be peaceful."

"Of course." Kayla dipped her head. "I understand."

"If you wish, you may stay the night and have food and drink until the storm dies down."

It was breaking with every tradition and belief she had as she replied, "I thank you kindly, but I fear I haven't the time. Perhaps once my friend is rescued."

If the men were offended, they gave no indication of it as they murmured some sort of assent.

"Where can we find the Lonely Man?"

The men spoke among themselves for a moment. Finally, "Damatoli will take you to him."

With that, the meeting was ended. Kayla pulled her hat and gloves back on and followed Natalie and the young man Damatoli back out into the cold. Overhead, she could still hear the wind whipping, even felt a bit of the residual current, but otherwise, she was grateful for the protection the walls afforded them. The rain had eased, but she had great suspicion that it was merely the calm before the storm as the clouds grew ever darker. Anyone who was out and about doing chores moved quickly, hurriedly finishing projects or gathering them up to be taken inside. Few paid any attention to the visitors.

Damatoli spoke occasionally, always looking back at Natalie, never at Kayla. She replied to him politely, but it was tough to gauge the nature of the conversation.

They passed through a couple tunnels before finding the correct section of the village. Damatoli seemed to know the way well as he never hesitated in his speech or second-guessed his steps. He may as well have been going home for supper the way he moved.

The home they eventually came to reminded Kayla of Natalie and Diane's home. Two small rooms, one for cooking and socializing, the other for sleeping undisturbed. Four adults and three children were crammed into the main room, speaking quietly around a fire. They looked up as the three of them entered. One of the women stood, speaking before anyone else had a chance. Damatoli replied. The woman spoke again. It appeared to be a dismissal as the young man ducked his head, almost as if embarrassed, and left the house.

Now it was Natalie who controlled the flow of conversation, again interpreting for Kayla.

"My father is very sick," the woman, who Natalie introduced as Tama, said, folding her arms. "The wind has given him a chill and a cough. He can barely talk. What is so urgent that you must speak to him?"

Once again, Kayla gave an abbreviated and slightly fudged tale of her young friend being trapped in the spirit lands by devils. Lonely Man was the only one anyone knew of who had gone to the spirit lands and returned, and she wanted to speak with him about it, see what they had to do to rescue Tommen.

Tama hesitated, and her expression turned to one of pity. "My father has always had an active imagination. In his youth, he fell very ill. Perhaps he went to the spirit lands, perhaps not, but he was never the same after that. Everyone who knew him said so." She looked at Natalie. "You may remember from your own tales, as he was Wolf Clan before his marriage." Back at Kayla. "Many from the Old Times suffered some sort of trauma that often made them think fanciful things. They worked hard to contain themselves and keep themselves together in order that their children and grandchildren would live normal, happy, healthy lives apart from their suffering, so that we could move on from the Old Times and their horrors."

Kayla looked at Natalie. "What are the Old Times?"

Natalie looked uncertain. "You might say it's that hazy gray area between creation and now. Creator creates the world and the universe, but he created too many stars; they filled the sky with no room for anything else. So the Creator sends some of the stars down that turn into all living things. The Old Times are like the bridge between that time and modern times."

Kayla nodded and turned back to Tama. "Even so, I have traveled long and far looking for him. If there is even the slightest chance that he can help me save my friend, I would like to take it."

"He is too ill," Tama insisted.

"You're right. He is ill. And he won't get any better. His spirit is departing. Nothing will change that now. But my friend has many years left in him, if we can save him."

Truthfully, Kayla hated pulling that card. Under normal circumstances, she would have been very happy to see Lonely Man die comfortable and happy in his own home with his family, rather than strain to find his voice and struggle to organize his memories, separate fact from fiction, and tell a coherent, useful tale.

She could see the conflict in Tama's eyes. Her father's death was inevitable now. Maybe they had been expecting it for the last season with a particularly harsh winter, maybe the last year or even the last decade as some other illness gradually took its toll. Now they were finally settling down and probably making funeral preparations, and some stranger walks in demanding to hear a story that had originally labeled the man as bonkers. But if his death was so inevitable, was there a chance his wild tale could save the life of someone else, someone they had never met but whose friends were willing to travel an unknown distance to find a way to free? Certainly helping someone in such circumstances was the right thing to do, but what about respect for elders, the dead and dying? Was it less respectful to let them die and not help someone, or more respectful to have them die trying to help someone with a crazy story?

Personally, Kayla couldn't see why there was such a dilemma. At the same time, her own traditions were much colder—no pun intended—and she actually had very little stake in this. Yes, she wanted to help Tommen, but this was like looking for a needle in a haystack. Unless it was the last needle in whole wide world that could be used, it would be nothing to just go out and get more needles. She wasn't actually holding out hope that this story would be the key to unlock that door. She was just looking for anything useful that might point them in the right direction.

Tama turned and conversed with the other adults present, two women and one man. If Kayla was any judge of tone and body language, she might have said that Tama was the only one who was conflicted; the others seemed pretty set on their own opinions. After a minute or two, Tama looked back at them and sighed, relenting.

"Very well. The others seem to think it is a worthwhile idea." Her tone said, "I don't think it's a good idea, but I've been outvoted." She turned and made a motion to one of the other women who nodded, stood, and momentarily left the room, heading into the bedroom. "However, if you wish to speak to him, you must go where he is."

"Is he not here?" Kayla wondered.

"His body is here, but his mind wanders between this world and the next. Trying to speak to him is like trying to catch a slippery fish with your bare hands while still on the bank. At least if you go in the river where the fish are, you have a better chance."

Kayla shook her head and glanced at Natalie. "I don't understand."

Natalie's expression was unreadable as she replied, "I do."

While the one woman returned with a box of something, the other woman gathered the children and took them out of the house entirely. Tama made a motion to join them, and Kayla and Natalie joined the rest of the family around the fire. Tama took the box and opened it to reveal dried pieces of something. Fruit, vegetables, something else entirely, Kayla couldn't be sure. It almost looked like orange peels, but she was no expert.

"The smoke is not as strong now as it would be at a fresh harvest," Tama was saying. "But it should be enough to get you where you're going."

"It's the seeing fruit," Kayla stated, looking at Natalie.

"It is," Natalie answered suspiciously. "Normally, the skins are used as bandages as they contain a natural anesthetic. It is only the flesh that allows us to see. I don't know what burning the dried skins will do."

Kayla took a calm breath and nodded. "No one knows what it would do anyway. The spirits are fickle things. But this is all on my head, and it's what I came here for."

"To get high on a distant planet?"

"Absolutely." Kayla nodded. "All right. Let's do this."

Tama instructed Kayla to remove her hat, gloves, and shawl, lest they be burned. She readily agreed and, once the articles were removed, watched as the older woman laid out three long strips in the fire.

Kayla certainly wouldn't deny that she'd done drugs from time to time. Aside from the rituals of her own people, well, she was a bit of a curious person. Stupid, destructive shit like meth and heroin she'd stayed away from, instead testing out a few rounds of weed, cocaine, LSD, PCP, and ecstasy. She didn't do them anymore, obviously, since she was older, wiser, and trying to have a baby, but she wasn't afraid of what might happen here and now. She didn't have the idiotic excitement of someone taking a hit for the first time, but she wasn't a junkie desperate for another high. She had a vague idea of what could happen and was prepared for it.

That wasn't to say she wasn't a little surprised when she looked up and saw that the small cracks in the wall had twisted into a tundra scene of a couple hunters bringing in a whale. Glancing at the fire, the light blazed a thousand times brighter and it almost felt like she was being burned herself as it got hotter and hotter. A low rumble came from the other room, like a growling bear.

Carefully, Kayla stood and picked her way around the fire, around the people, and made for the other room, pausing only briefly to note how long the fur on her caribou dress had grown. Did hair really keep growing after death, or was that just an old wives' tale? Because it sure looked like the fur on this thing had grown longer.

Walking into Lonely Man's room was like walking into another dimension in itself. A few small candles were burning, but the smoke was dancing in all sorts of shapes and colors. Small birds flew from one smoke stream to another, right up there with the fish that swam to and fro. A light caught Kayla's attention and she turned her head just as a person—if it was a person, perhaps a spirit or other phantom—passed through the wall on the way to somewhere. She took a step as if to go after it, but found she couldn't move.

And suddenly she could. She could move and bend and flex and go any which way she wanted to, like she had no bones at all, nothing to impede or catch or get cranky with movement.

At some point, she did take notice of the Lonely Man, laying there on a bed of furs, bundled up like a small babe. She clumsily knelt beside him.

"Lonely Man," she said, her mouth feeling and tasting like melted wax. "Lonely Man, speak to me. I know you hear me. I know you understand me."

The old man looked up at her with huge dark eyes that appeared almost black in the dim candlelight. They watered like small oceans and the starburst patterns in his irises glimmered like dark suns, totally mesmerizing.

"A tongue," he said faintly.

"What about a tongue?" Kayla asked lamely.

"An ear."

"What about an ear?"

It hit her a second later that he was speaking English.

"An ear that has not heard. A tongue that has not spoken. Such a long time."

"You speak English." Kayla suddenly wished she wasn't high

because then she might be able to have a real conversation with this man. Or was she only hallucinating this conversation? Was there any way to tell? Fucking hell.

"Where are you from?"

"I'm Inuit, from a place way, way north. From Earth. Do you remember Earth?"

"A young man, now many years gone, came from the stars."

"I know. I need to ask about that young man. That young man got trapped in the in-between dimension, the spirit lands. But he got out."

Lonely Man was interrupted by a raucous bout of coughing. When he finally settled down, his words were even fainter than before. "I tried to escape our enemies. They came to kill us. They came with thunder and fire, taking the land and saying it was theirs. White demons from beyond the sea."

"I know. My own people were beset by these demons. What did you do to escape?"

"I ran. A student, first. They brought their sorcery and tried to teach us their ways, their sorceries and connection to the gods. Later they had books of magic as well. They were very powerful."

Kayla frowned, knowing there were discrepancies in the story but not able to say exactly what. Time itself didn't have any magic books, and the only magic books the Akari had were the journals that belonged to the Cult. Unless he was referring to the Books? But they wouldn't have been available at the time he was trapped. Something was missing here, but, damn it all, she was too high to say exactly what.

"Then they turned on us. The white demons tried to kill us with thunder and lightning. We had nothing left. I got some to safety. But the white demons came and found us. We had nowhere to go. Anagalisgi. He was with me. And others. We went into a cave, but demons can see in the dark. Of course they can. Why wouldn't they?

"We were supposed to go together, but Anagalisgi was captured. I tried to help, but I lost control of my magics and the demons dragged me into the spirit world. I stayed there for a long time, wandering in the caves. Then I found my way out. I found Anagalisgi. He had been taken back to the white demons' camp. They were going to kill him. They gave him a last request, and he wished for the seeing fruit, that he may have easier passage to the spirit land.

"He saw me. And we spoke to each other. I helped him escape. We returned to the cave. He helped me escape here, but at the cost of himself, to be dragged into the spirit lands in my place. The spirits do not give up their prizes easily, and it could only be an exchange, not a taking."

Lonely Man coughed again, less violently. "I tried to tell Kiyuga what had happened and explain it, but he loved Anagalisgi and hated me. Soon after, I married, forsook my clan, and became an eagle instead."

"Who was Anagalisgi to Kiyuga?" Kayla inquired.

"His pride and joy, like a father and son, but between brothers. Kiyuga was older, but only by three winters, and that barely. Tsigilili had died because of the plague the white demons brought with them, and Gandoka only had his two sons before he, too, died of their diseases." Lonely Man sighed sadly. "Oh, Kiyuga and Anagalisgi were inseparable, the best children and brothers anyone could have asked for. I am still ashamed I let him be taken. I should have helped him escape and then return to his brother rather than take my place like a coward."

"If he was half the man you say he is, he would have wanted it this way," Kayla said, hoping she sounded a little comforting. When the days before oneself can be counted on the fingers and toes of one's family, the only thing left to consider is the past, and for Lonely Man, it didn't sound like a pretty one he wanted to revisit in his final days.

"Yes," he said finally. "Anagalisgi was always that way. Kiyuga once said that his brother had once told him that his destiny would be to watch over the wandering souls and be a light in their darkness, and Kiyuga would guide them once they had crossed back into the light. He never understood what his little brother meant.

Anagalisgi was always a bit odd. But perhaps now he knows."

"What did you and Anagalisgi do to get you out of the spirit lands?" Kayla asked, tired of beating around the bush. "And I'm not talking about negotiating with demons. I'm talking about the cold facts, about Time and the in-between dimension and the Akari. What did you physically do to escape?"

For a moment, she was afraid he wouldn't answer or didn't understand. Finally he took a labored breath and said, "I don't know."

Kayla took a calm breath. "Please, sir, I know it's painful, and probably the last thing you want to talk about now, but I need to know. My friend is also trapped in the spirit lands and he has to escape. He is very sick."

"The spirits do not give up their prizes easily. If one leaves, one must also be taken."

"The spirits have taken far more than they have ever given up," Kayla said coldly. "Surely there must be a way to get around it." She rubbed her eyes, trying to control the way her fingers wiggled and wobbled like wet spaghetti. "Did any of the white demons follow Anagalisgi into the spirit lands, into the cave?"

"They followed us into the cave, yes. We used the cave to cross over and escape. We did not want the white demons to follow, so he laid a trap. A tunnel, between worlds so close and yet so far away, always in a state of flux from the magic of the spirits."

"What do you mean a tunnel? Is this a place where we might communicate with the spirits without having to go to their land?"

"Only those aware of it may see it, and even then, the spirits will do to trespassers as they wish. It was the only way he could think of to turn the white demons' sorcery against itself and trap them."

This was going nowhere. A traumatic past was clashing with this new reality until the past seemed more like a bad dream he didn't want to revisit and was getting mixed up with the new reality. Eagle Clan was charged with creating a new history for the Krydik, one where the white demons were defeated and all was well. Fairy tales. Now Kayla was asking this old man to go back to the truth behind those stories and relive, essentially, the death of his friend.

"Usulagogi," she began softly, "tell me how to save my friend. Without losing anyone else."

Lonely Man sighed. "You can't. The spirits are fickle, and yet absolute. If you take one from them, they will also take one from you. There can be no other way."

Kayla closed her eyes. Whether or not it was true, Lonely Man believed every word he was saying. If he thought there was no way to rescue Tommen without sacrificing someone else to the spirits, then he would not be convinced otherwise. She thanked him and wished him a restful sleep and safe passage to the spirit lands. The old man did not reply.

When she stood and turned, she nearly jumped out of her skin at the sight of the woman standing behind her. She was in her late thirties and bore a striking resemblance to Tama and the others, yet she passed through Kayla with only a minor regard.

"Who are you?" Kayla asked dumbly.

"Sita," the woman replied surprisingly, causing Kayla's heart to leap. "I was Tama's older sister."

"Was."

"Yes, I was. Lonely Man was my father, also." She looked longingly at the old man as he labored away in a fitful sleep. "He and our mother were from the Old Times, the Great Migration. They had a hard time letting go of the old customs. Rather than having my husband leave his clan to join me, I left my clan to join him. He was Wolf Clan, keepers of the truth and wielders of magic. Also known as Time. My husband tried to teach me Time, but I lost control and was taken into the in-between dimension."

"Can you help me, then? I have a friend—"

"Yes, I know, I heard the whole story. As far as anyone knows, there is no way out. There are some places where the temporal distortions are a little more fluctuated which make it easier to communicate, but the barrier appears to be absolute."

"What about his story about switching places?"

Sita shrugged. "I don't know. Believe me, we tried to free me using everything we knew. Even my father's wild stories. Nothing has worked. It's impossible. I'm sorry."

Kayla shook her head. "I don't believe you."

"Time and experience are terrible teachers, but it's the only way some people learn."

"Well, I'm not giving up just yet. But thanks for the suggestion."

With raw nerves, Kayla left the room. She sat down with the people around the fire. The warmth made her sleepy, and the dancing shadows and smoke toyed with her sense of reality. The others in the room seemed fluid, like the reflections in fun mirrors at carnivals. She blinked several times, fought the urge to yawn, did it anyway. As she lay down to relax, her caribou fur unfurled beneath her to provide a warm blanket. But when she lay down, the fur began stretching out around her. At first, it was nice to cuddle a little, but then the fur started to grab her, hold her down, choke her, smother her.

She sat up with a start and a pounding headache like a hangover from hell. She rubbed her eyes and looked around. One of the men was still sleeping, but everyone else was awake and moving around, doing this and that. One of the women noticed her first and said something to another woman who disappeared. A moment later, she returned with Natalie.

"Good morning," Natalie greeted, her expression a little smug.

"How long have I been out?" Kayla wondered, looking around. She rubbed her face. "Fuck. I feel like I haven't slept at all."

Natalie chuckled. "Well, it's been about eight hours or so since Tama put on the peels. Hard to say how long you were in with Lonely Man, seeing how we were all a little loopy, but I'd estimate maybe three or four hours."

"Three or four hours? Our conversation was hardly ten minutes long."

"Was it?"

Wasn't it? Fucking hell, it was hard to tell because of the drugs.

She sighed and rubbed her eyes. "What about Sita?"

"Who's Sita?"

"Tama's sister. I saw her. She said she was married into Wolf Clan before the whole matrilineal thing took effect. Her husband tried to show her Time, but she got trapped in the in-between dimension, too. Was that all true, or did I imagine it?"

Natalie raised a brow but turned to speak to Tama. The woman's expression turned hostile, then thoughtful, then somber. Natalie looked back at Kayla. "Well, obviously Tama has a little different take on things, but yes, she did have a sister named Sita who was kidnapped by the spirits. Did she have anything useful to say?"

Kayla shook her head. "No. She told me it was impossible to escape and to give up. I have no intention of that right now."

"Good to know."

Grudgingly, she stood and brushed herself off, trying not to let on how bad her hangover was. "So, what's the formality now?"

"Breakfast," Natalie answered. "We'll help clean up, and then we can be on our way."

Kayla would have much rathered shot out the door right then and there and gotten home to tell of her glorious adventures, but she knew that was not only rude to the host, but it was rude to herself. She'd been living in the modern world for far too long. She needed to take a day, take a break, and take a breath. Slow and steady. Better to approach things slowly and calmly with a clear head than rush into action with no clear direction and waste time trying to correct on the fly.

So she managed to enjoy breakfast with Lonely Man's family. It was hardly a formal affair. The kids were back, and there was always the chore of keeping them corralled and focused on eating rather than playing with the food, throwing it at annoying brothers and sisters, or running outside to do other things. Time could be wasted, sure, but food could not, and Tama made sure every child knew it.

Kayla and Natalie also did their part to help Lonely Man eat, sitting him up and feeding him one tiny bite at a time. He ate less than the five year old child and it took twice the time, between his slow movements and persistent cough. When he was done, one of the women ended up eating the rest of the food.

"I hope I never get that bad," Kayla said as she and Natalie helped tidy up.

"Preaching to the choir, babe," Natalie agreed. "Do you ever wonder if the spirits will punish us for cheating death?"

"Cheating death? We might have longer natural lives, but we're hardly indestructible. What if we had gone and wandered off a cliff last night? I wouldn't have survived that fall. I don't know about you."

"True. But do you ever wonder? If we had fallen off a cliff and gone to the spirit lands, do you think they'd hold our long lives against us?"

Kayla shrugged. "I don't know. I wouldn't expect so. If they did pitch a fit, I would ask what the difference would be if a child died or an old man like Lonely Man died. Does he get penalized for living longer than his oldest daughter? I should hope not."

Natalie mulled that over for a minute or two before nodding. "I get your point. Guess it really doesn't matter, anyway."

"Thinking of your brother?"

"Yeah, kind of. Although, knowing him, if the spirits told him no, he'd tell them to fuck off and push past them into the spirit lands, regardless."

"Can't say as I knew him, but from the stories Tommen told, it sounds like something he might do."

Before Natalie could say more, Tama approached them. She held out a closed fist toward Kayla. Kayla stretched out her hand and was rewarded with a leather thong, decorated with tiny bone beads and a claw of some form. As she spoke, Natalie translated.

"The claw of a jalamar. May it bring you strength and fertility. And may we meet again under one roof."

Kayla thanked her kindly and wished her well, making sure to express her condolences over Lonely Man and wishing him an easy journey to the spirit lands. Goodbyes were lengthy and formal, but at least they hadn't been run out of the village and told to never return. So she counted that as a victory as she strung the necklace around her neck, then grabbed her fine furs before following Natalie out of the little house. The wind was still in the village and gray-blue skies were overhead.

"Well, it wasn't as productive as I had hoped," Kayla confessed as they made their way out of the village, "but it wasn't as bad as I had feared either."

"You win some, you lose some," Natalie said. "At least you have not made any enemies."

"No, but I question whether I have made friends either."

Between the hangover from the drugs and the portal jump back to Wolf Clan, Kayla was not feeling the greatest. The thought of returning to the council was less than thrilling. Still, she and Natalie made their way back to the main activity hall and waited patiently for the council members to appear, which they did in their own time.

"I trust your visit to Eagle Clan was fruitful?" Thomas inquired.

"Decidedly less than expected," Kayla answered honestly. "I trust you have reached a decision regarding a certain alliance and defense system?"

"We have decided, yes, but in respect to how large such an operation would be, we wish to garner the full support of the clan before speaking in the stead of everyone involved. We will present your proposal to the clan and let each man decide for himself whether he will help. This may be a special case where a majority rule owns the vote of the clan, even those who wish to have no part, but such are our politics."

"The Borelians are moving quickly. Do you have a day or a timeline when we may expect an answer?"

"Not before we are ready. We may send word through the Akarin or through our Wolf Clan operatives on Earth. Keep an ear out for both channels."

It was not the answer she wanted, but it was the best one she was going to get. Kayla meekly dipped her head. "Of course."

"Then if there is nothing else, we wish you safe travels home."

It was the polite way of telling her to get out and leave them to their business, and she obliged gratefully. Too many things demanded her attention; at least she managed to knock out one of those things, though not quite to her liking. She followed Natalie out of the village once more.

"Why do you always leave the village before opening portals?" Kayla wondered.

"It's an unwritten rule," Natalie explained. "Time and the Akari may be used in the village, certainly, but no portals. It's not expressly forbidden, of course, but it's a common courtesy. And once I take you back, I'm going to get started on cleaning out Saul's house. Sorting, dividing, distributing, that sort of thing. It does no one any good to put it off. And I can just hear him in my head, griping about letting something go for so long."

"So much for Indian time, huh?"

"Well, he was never really idle. If there was something to be done, he'd do it. But anyway, here we are. I'll send you back to the fortress, seeing how you still look a little hungover."

"Fucking hell." Kayla rubbed her eyes. "Either that was the strong stuff, or I'm out of practice."

Natalie grinned and they embraced before the portal was opened and Kayla stepped through. It was another blow to her cognition and she decided to head to the cafeteria to regain her composure before making a third jump back home.

The fortress seemed to be half a ghost town as she found a spot at a table and tried not to look like she'd been out partying all night and getting high. Hardly five minutes after she sat down, another human, one she knew well, sat down across from her.

"Putu!" she exclaimed.

Putu dipped his head in acknowledgment but his expression was grave. "I'd say you have a lot of nerve showing up here, but then, with your little jaunt, I wouldn't expect that you heard."

"Heard what?" Kayla searched his gaze for any indication but found none.

"Two more council members have been murdered and Micaiah was arrested for it. They never charged him because they don't think he did it, but he's been removed from power and banned from the Akarin. All humans have, actually. Word is slow to get around, though. For right now, if they find you here, it's more of a catch and release. That won't last long, though."

"Where is my husband now?"

"Home. He got a message to me explaining what was going on with you, asking if I could intercept you when you returned and give you the rundown. Obviously, he can't come himself." Before Kayla could speak, he stood and said, "Moral of the story, you need to go home right now. You can't stay here."

Kayla stood and grabbed his arm as he moved off. "Putu, what's going on? What's happening here?"

It was a stupid question; Putu was not Akarin. But then, maybe an outsider's perspective was just what she needed. He looked at her, his expression unreadable.

"Do you remember our people's story of the woman who fell in the ice and turned into a narwhal?"

"Yes...?"

"The Akarin have always thought themselves above everyone. But now the storm has set in and their carelessness has caused them to fall and turn into the very things they once hunted. They may be saved by turning into their enemies, but they will never be who they once were."

"Is that what you think of me? What of the others who are Akarin?"

"You've been away from home for far too long, *aakauraq.* Maybe it's time to come home."

Kayla watched him leave, both infuriated by his strategic use of *aakauraq* and yet longing to take him up on his offer and return home.

How nice it would be to not have to worry about the politics and wars and bullshit that had claimed so much of her time lately.

At the same time, however, with being banned from the Akarin, perhaps that was just what she needed. She couldn't worry about something she couldn't worry about. There was nothing more she could do here, so she might as well go home.

She noted a few stares as she crossed the cafeteria and made for the portal room, but she was not assaulted, beaten, or arrested, and soon enough, she was back in the living room, suddenly overwhelmed by how hot it was. Going from cold mountains and cold winds to suddenly August was a huge jump, and she could not get her furs off fast enough.

The closet door squeaked as she opened it.

"Relax, gunslinger, it's just me," she said when she heard Micaiah grab his gun and look for the threat.

"Shit." He set it down on the nightstand and relaxed. "Don't scare me like that. I've had enough of that for one day, thank you." Pause. "Did Putu reach you?"

Kayla stripped off her leathers and changed into her pajamas. "Yes, he told me about your arrest and everything else. What the hell happened?"

As Micaiah recounted his tale with incredible detail, Kayla slipped into bed beside him, still too warm to pull up anything more than the sheets. Another council member plus one supporter had been murdered. He was the favorite scapegoat. As far as the Akarin went, all humans were evil and so banned. As far as Time went, humans were still voluntold to stay home. As for the war with the Borelians, well, there was still skepticism from normal Time Agent humans about their Akarin counterparts, but impending oblivion and slavery worse than death seemed to take precedence over petty fights. Humans already understood they were hostile and violent, so might as well put it to good use.

When Micaiah finished his tale, Kayla recounted her own, from meeting up with Natalie to traveling to Eagle Clan, to getting high and talking to Lonely Man and Sita, to her return to Wolf Clan and their infuriating decision to let each man decide for himself whether he would help with the defenses, to her meeting with Putu and arrival home.

"Sounds like we've both had quite an adventurous twenty-four hours," Micaiah observed. "So you got nothing out of Lonely Man or Sita?"

"Nothing that I've been able to figure out, either explicitly or otherwise," Kayla sighed. "I'm still trying to mull over their cave reference and the tunnel and switching places, but nothing is coming to me."

"Well, get some sleep. It might do you some good. In the meantime, I'm going to get up and get around so I can meet everyone who is coming over to see if brute force isn't enough to rescue Tommen. No offense to Sita, but I don't think they've quite tried everything."

Kayla shrugged. "Whatever. I'm tired. I'm hungover. I need to get some sleep."

He kissed her. "I'll see you when I get back."

Chapter Twenty-Five
A Challenge and a Caution

Tommen woke blearily to the sound of an alarm clock. For a moment, he was completely lost as to where he was and why he was there. It hit him a second later that he was in Micah's room. Gradually it came back to him that he'd come over to see if more strength was all it took to free him from the in-between dimension. As he rubbed his eyes and got his bearings, he could also vaguely recall some kind of conversation between the twins about a safe and more journals. Maybe it was just a bad dream. One journal was bad enough, but more? Sounded like some shitty curveball in a bad novel.

Micah was just as slow to get up and around, but Micaiah seemed bright-eyed and bushy-tailed, beating on the door again and yelling at his brother to hurry up and get around because company would be coming. Groaning, Micah told him to fuck off and sat up in bed.

Strictly speaking, it didn't really sound all that bad, a hot shower and all. After several days of not bathing, Tommen was starting to feel a little on the gross side. Actually, he was feeling a lot on the gross side. But there was no way he was going to get naked in the shower with another dude just so he could get some hot water. Maybe he could call and politely ask the twins to leave the hot water on for him. Would that work? Would he actually get clean, or would the water just pass right through him?

Maybe if this first attempt didn't work, he'd ask them. Otherwise he would just be going straight to the hospital anyway to get drugged up and cleaned up.

Speaking of drugs, he couldn't say he was feeling a whole lot better after giving himself the injection just a few hours ago, but no change was better than a turn for the worse, right? At least he was still thinking somewhat clearly and knew what the hell was going on. Now he just had to actually show up to this shindig and get rescued.

Grudgingly, he dug around for another syringe, uncaring of which one, popped off the cap, and injected it. He gritted his teeth at the pain but told himself it was for his own good. Take it like a man. He had to if he wanted to survive long enough to be rescued. Gradually, the burning in his hand was reduced to a stringing throb.

He stood, wobbled, stretched, flopped back down. His head felt like a lead balloon, and it took a concentrated effort to stand up and just make it out of the room. He stumbled out to the kitchen, plugged in his phone, and dialed. He could hear Micaiah's phone ringing in his bedroom and it was a minute before he picked up.

"Good, you're awake," Micaiah said.

"Yeah," Tommen murmured. "Now come out here and make me some coffee."

"You're very demanding this morning."

"I need the boost, believe me."

"Tommen, you're sick. You probably shouldn't have any caffeine."

"What's to stop me from going down to some cafe or even a gas station and swiping someone else's coffee?"

"Because you're not a coffee drinker and you hate gas station coffee. You just want our coffee because it's really nice and really expensive."

"And really good. Shit, if I could afford this stuff, I'd drink coffee all day long."

"Well, since all the shit in the Wheel, we haven't been able to get any new coffee. We're trying to conserve our resources here. Why are we having this conversation, anyway? No, you're not getting any coffee."

"Fine, whatever. Is Kayla back?"

"Yeah, she just got back. She's sleeping."

"Did she find anything useful?"

"No, but she's...a little hungover still. If this first attempt doesn't work, whatever insights she has about her findings might prove useful."

"Okay."

"How are you holding up?"

"I've got meds in me, but I still feel awful."

"We're coming for you, Tommen. Hang on just a little longer."

"I'm trying, believe me."

He hung up, rubbed his eyes, and looked longingly at the coffeemaker. Micaiah was right; he really wasn't a coffee drinker. But he needed something to give him a little kick and help him focus. He didn't need to chug a whole pot.

It was tempting to just suck in the coffee pot and a bag of coffee and make himself a pot, but he refrained. It was just one more thing he would have to carry around and make sure he brought back with him. Maybe if this first attempt at rescue didn't work, he would swipe something from the gas station or a little cafe. Was it wrong for him to hope the first attempt didn't work so that way he could get coffee before going to the hospital? But why? Once the doctors checked him out and did what they had to do, he could get coffee afterwards, right? And why the hell was he so obsessed with getting a cup of coffee right now, anyway? He didn't drink coffee.

Maybe he was delirious. Maybe his sickness really was getting worse. This first attempt at rescuing him better work because he needed to be seen by a real doctor and quick. If it didn't, he really might not last until the second attempt. What if he went into shock? Would anyone know it? Would Julianna know enough to bring him back around? What if he died?

Tommen went into the living room and collapsed into a recliner. He had to get rescued. That was his number one priority right now. Forget Julianna and whether she was good or evil or whatever. Forget the journals. Forget everything but getting rescued. Once he was back on dry land, then he could worry about other things.

It wasn't easy seeing how everything seemed to be of the utmost importance these days. Wars, assassinations, all of it coming at once, all of it important. And the problem was, it really was important. You couldn't just shove war and slavery into a number two spot on the priority list. But you couldn't put assassinations on a back burner either. Was this what it was like to be president?

That sense of urgency only grew as he found himself scouring the mountainside. He knew he was searching and he knew it was urgent, but he couldn't say what he was looking for, why, or why it was so important. See, just another thing that demanded his attention.

He knew the trails in these hills, but he avoided them as much as possible for fear of being caught. He was following someone, but they were invisible. He'd spoken to them only briefly, and now they were trying to escape together. What was going on? His body felt weak and his vision and senses were both distorted and yet augmented, as if he was tripping hard. He pushed past branches and low-hanging limbs, sometimes going around and sometimes tripping over logs and rocks. Moving up, up, always ever up. Had to go up. There was safety up there somewhere.

Then the cave loomed wide before him. The others had gone in there. They escaped. Now he had to escape, but first he had to save the one who had saved him. It was a daunting task, using the sorceries, but it was all they had.

He ran into the cave as far as he could, letting the darkness consume him. Then he opened a portal. In a flash, he saw the face of his friend. In that moment, he reached out and grabbed him. It was like being struck by lightning, but still he held on. He felt it pulling on him, dragging him in rather than pushing his friend out.

Suddenly, he saw something else there in the flash, in the portal. A vision. Of lightning and fire and candles. He saw an entirely separate world, the spirit world, walking among the living but being not part of them. Seeing through time, the stories of all peoples, from the beginning of time to the end. And he heard the voice of the one called the Author. Not the Creator, but the Author of their world. And suddenly he realized what he must do.

"Anagalisgi," his friend gasped. "I can't hold on."

"I know," he said calmly. "Don't worry. I will come to you."

Then he moved through the lightning, through his friend, into the spirit world. As he did, he took the Energy and tore it open, pushing his friend out into the real world, into the new home where their friends and family waited. Kiyuga would grieve, he knew, but he had found his destiny, to walk the spirit world between spirits and men, to walk through time, to show them the way.

He looked around the cave and could see all. The past, when a tiny trickle of water burrowed its way into the solid face of a mountain. The present, a dark cave where men had hollowed out the earth looking for rocks and minerals. The future, a state of flux that could transport men in but the blink of an eye.

Even now as he looked down the trail, the hunters came racing up, yelling and shouting angrily. They were coming to kill and destroy. But he would not allow such a thing to happen ever again, not from them.

He waited until the men got all the way into the cave, when darkness overtook them. He could still see them clear as day. Once they were consumed by shadows, he took the very fabric of Time, like the fine threads of a woven rug, and began twisting, undoing the normal fabric and recreating something else entirely. He took the entire cave and wove the threads this way and that. Some places were made stronger, others weaker, relative to the normal Time outside the cave. But when the men emerged, they would no longer recognize their world. Indeed, they may think themselves mad.

It was, perhaps, the only purely selfish thing he would do with his newfound power, but he had no regrets. The Author had granted him such a power, and so he would use it. When he was finished, he went out and looked over the valley, seeing it in all time. Virgin land long before any men touched it. Settler development as peaceful farms popped up here and there. Highways snaking here and there, congested with traffic. And even more as the centuries passed.

"See the world through my eyes, Tommen Forbes," he said aloud. "And come to me."

Tommen startled awake, every limb jerking as he blindly reached for something, he didn't know what. Once he got his bearings, he leaned back in the chair and rubbed his face. He knew he'd just had a revelation of some form, but he couldn't say exactly what. The details were fading now. Fucking hell.

He sat up and looked around. He couldn't have slept for too long. There were several new visitors in the house, but his dad was nowhere to be seen.

A few minutes later, he pulled in the driveway and hurried inside. Running a little late, or just anxious to get his son back? Tommen was considering this when he had another thought. After that bullshit story he gave Laura, how was he going to explain his son suddenly turning up safe and sound in the house of one of his friends? Maybe they should do this outside at least? Well, that was their problem. They could fill him in on the details once he was a little more lucid and a little less sick.

Tommen figured he must have dozed off a little because the next thing he knew, Micaiah was barking orders of one form or another, and when Tommen opened his eyes, the number of people in the house had multiplied. There had to be at least thirty people standing around, most of them packed in the living room, some spilling into the dining room and down the hall. Tommen stumbled over to an outlet and called the elder twin.

"How many more are we expecting?" Tommen wondered.

"Just a couple," Micaiah answered. Tommen couldn't find him in the crowd. "Actually, they're just here now. So we're ready when you are. Just tell us where you'll be."

"Once I hang up, I'll be in the beige recliner. Sorry, Cai, but I won't be able to offer any help. I'm just too tired."

"Don't say shit like that. We'll get you to a doctor. All right, you're dad's here. He'll be the one to grab you and run, all right? Don't worry about anything but hanging on to him. Got it?"

"Hey, I'm not arguing, I'm just saying."

"I know you are. Hang on, here's your dad."

"Tommen?" Walter wondered. He sounded every bit as exhausted as Tommen might expect, given his nightmares.

"No, it's your other son, Jake," Tommen answered.

"Very funny, smart aleck. We're ready for you, kiddo. We'll do our best. I'm going to grab onto you, but you need to do the same as best you can. Grab on and don't let go."

"I'll do my best."

"That's all we can ask. Okay, we'll give you a few seconds to get into the recliner, but once the portal's open, it's open. With forty of us here, it ought to do something."

"That's the part that worries me. All right, I'll get off now. See you in a few."

Tommen hung up and unplugged his phone, scrambling to get back to the recliner as Micaiah called for everyone to be ready, explaining what they were doing, how to open up the portal in a specific location and everything from the past attempts. Walter was there only to grab Tommen and get him out. He would not be helping open the portal, and no one helping with the portal should attempt to grab Tommen. Everyone had a job, so they should stick to it.

Personally, Tommen wondered what harm it would do to have twenty people open the portal and the other twenty grab him. But hey, it wasn't his call. If this didn't work, maybe he could suggest that for the next attempt. He didn't particularly enjoy the thought of this attempt not working, seeing how he wasn't doing so hot, but he needed a plan, something to look forward to, a direction of some form. He couldn't sit idly by, waiting for a plan to spring to mind.

He collapsed back into the recliner, willing himself not to fall asleep, wishing he had a cup of coffee. He really should have just come straight here last night and not dillydallied around. He might have gotten a little more sleep that way.

"Is everyone ready?" Micaiah asked, apparently coming to the end of his speech about rules and how-to's and past experiences. The crowd murmured a general assent. "Tommen, are you ready?"

Grudgingly, Tommen reached for the light switch on the wall and flashed once for yes.

"Here goes nothing."

At some point in that one billionth or trillionth of a second as the electricity from the portal hit him, Tommen remembered at least part of his revelation about his dream. He'd been standing in Forbes Cave, years before he ever set foot in it as a child. He'd looked out over the valley long before anyone had ever laid eyes on it. That cave had been a point of escape, but he couldn't say who he had been, who his friend was, or why they were running. Well, pursuit was a pretty good indication, but the reasoning behind it was still lost to him.

Then it was as if he was walking through a beaded curtain, or maybe breaking through the water. The vacuum that opened up around him sucked the air from his lungs and dizziness overcame him. He felt ready to pass out, but then he found himself reaching out for a hand.

As soon as he made contact, he knew it was the wrong thing to do. He knew that no one could help him out, not like this. The in-between dimension was a living thing, and it was a hungry beast, looking only to devour. As soon as his dad grabbed his wrist, Tommen could feel the Energy tendrils dig into both of them, locking him in and working to draw Walter in as well. The more strength the visitors gave to keep the portal open and stabilize it, the stronger the tendrils became.

"Come on, Tommen, you have to come out," Walter said, every vein in his head and neck standing out, every muscle in his arm strained.

The dimension would not let go. This was not quicksand, where rope and sufficient strength would rescue him. This was not a well where they had to bring him up above the water. The in-between dimension was a lion, and he was still trapped in its jaws. Any who tried to pry open its huge mouth would find themselves snapped up with him.

That was the lesson from the dream. This lion would devour anything that got close to it. One man may try to save another, but the only way to hold it open wide enough for the first man to get was to get in and hold it open, like old animated cartoons. But as soon as the first man was out, the jaws would shut on the second man, trapping him. There was no way any one person or any group of people would have enough strength from the outside to hope to pry open the jaws that held them now.

"Tommen, I only have so much strength," Walter gasped.

"I know," Tommen said. He looked at his dad in the eye. "Dad, you have to let go."

"No. Not until you're safe here with me."

"No, you don't understand. We can't do it this way. You have to let go. If you don't, you'll only get sucked in and it will be the same problem all over again."

"Maybe, but at least you can get to a doctor."

For half a second, Tommen almost considered the offer. His dad was healthy and he might be able to devise a way out while Tommen got treatment.

"Come on, Tommen," Walter said, his whole body straining and losing strength quickly.

"Seek me out, Tommen."

Tommen looked around for the voice, but couldn't find it in the sea of bodies. Finally he looked at his dad and shook his head. "No."

He released his grip. His dad, already exhausted, lost his grip as well. Those holding the portal open began to drop their strength one by one until the portal collapsed. Once the ensuing shockwave subsided, Tommen leaned back in the recliner and tried to breathe.

Fuck. Had he made the right choice? Should he have tried harder? Would it have matter if he had been fully healthy and completely rested? Had he just sacrificed his best chance at rescue based on a weird dream, a flimsy revelation, and a disembodied command? What was he, religious? Fucking hell.

Wanting nothing more than to lay back, relax, and get some

more sleep, Tommen dragged himself over to the couch and plugged in his phone.

"Tommen, what happened?" his dad asked. He was in the other recliner, breathing heavily and looking about ready for another eight hours or so.

"It was going to pull you in, too," Tommen said. "That's how it works. It's not just a dimension; it's a living thing. It consumes something, but it never gives up what it's taken. If you tried to pry the door open and get me out, it would only take you in my place."

"I got that part. But why not switch places? You need to get to a hospital. I'm healthy, I can survive a little longer than you. And I'm stronger, so I might be able to do a little more from the inside."

"No, you couldn't. Time doesn't work here, only the Akari."

"Then switch places with Micaiah. Or Micah. Or anyone else."

"No. I can't."

"Why not?"

"It's too dangerous."

"What do you mean, too dangerous?"

"Listen, I don't know about the plan tonight. I mean, we can definitely still try it, but we might have to do something a little different. I don't know what yet, but I'll do a little digging while I'm out and about today."

"Tommen, this isn't a game. If you're septic—"

"I have medicine for it. It's been working."

"And your burns? Tommen, burns to the arm and especially the hand are not something to take lightly."

"I know. Please, Dad, believe me. I know. I'm trying to figure something out, at least something that doesn't take a ton of energy from everyone. We're all exhausted."

"Well, you're not wrong there. But what do you expect to do?"

"I don't know. First I think I'm going to sleep on it some more."

His dad sighed. "I wish I had that luxury, but I have to get to work."

"Okay. Hey, if you get a chance, or maybe you can relay this to the twins, but head up to Forbes Cave at some point today."

"What am I looking for?"

"I don't know. Something weird. Something unusual, beyond what's already weird about it. I'll head up there myself, see if there's a difference between looking at it from this side or that side."

"I make no promises on my part, but maybe Micah or Micaiah can get up there. Anyway, since you're not here as a miraculous rescue, I have to get going."

Tommen let out a breath. "Yeah. Okay."

"Love you, kiddo. We'll keep trying. And if you find anything, please let us know. Preferably before we all exhaust ourselves again."

"I'll try. Love you, Dad."

He hung up and lay back on the couch, willing himself not to fall asleep yet, knowing he really needed to get at least a few hours before doing anything else for the day.

The visitors dispersed one by one, exhausted and a little annoyed by what he'd done. Walter was one of the last to leave, regretfully having to turn his back on his son who was still trapped and go about his normal business of going to work. He spoke with the twins for a few minutes about checking out Forbes Cave, but otherwise, he headed off to the precinct.

Tommen still sat there on the couch for a good hour or so, sort of dozing but not really falling asleep. Micah headed to the shop and Micaiah returned to bed. Then all was quiet, exactly as it had been an hour or so ago. Nothing out of the ordinary.

He couldn't say if he slept any more, but the next time he opened his eyes, he was startled to see Julianna standing in front of him, arms crossed and looking very irritated.

"So, you tried to leave without me," she stated.

Tommen got an image in his mind of a black dress, a wimple, and a very long, very cold ruler about to be slapped across his knuckles. He rubbed his eyes. "It was only an idea. And if it worked, it's not like we couldn't do it again to get you out, too. As it was, it was hard enough just trying to get me out. I don't know that it would have worked to get both of us out at the same time."

"I'm stronger than you, Tommen. I could have loaned some of my strength from this side."

"There were forty people in here. Forty! How much more strength do you want?"

"Ten thousand men may besiege a castle, but if no one lets down the drawbridge, they're going nowhere. I could have done that."

"Great. Maybe you can help tonight when we try again. I might have told you about this last night, but you left before I knew, and I didn't know how to find you."

"All right, fine. Maybe that was my fault."

"Where do you go, anyway? For being a pretty desolate dimension, you sure have a lot of business to take care of."

"It's hard work, getting things to work like they should. I have my own projects I like to tend."

"Like what? Writing more journals to confuse the hell out of people?"

Julianna fixed him in a glare so cold, it reminded Tommen of the time he had been stuck in a cave with Cassius. He'd asked the man how he'd managed to kill his victims without getting caught. Cassius had never yelled or even raised his voice, never made a quick move against Tommen, and yet his calm voice, slow movements, and black gaze had made Tommen wish to die rather than be there at that moment.

Her expression relaxed, then, as she said, "There have always been three journals. The one you found, the one I had, and another which has been lost."

"Bullshit," Tommen cut in. "You could go back to find out what your husband wrote, when, and what happened to it. I followed my family in the same way. And in a couple decades of being stuck here, I'd be willing to bet that you've done that tracking."

"The third journal is gone!" Julianna snapped. "My abilities are limited to this physical world, and we're not exactly going to the moon. We can't open portals to other places. The third journal disappeared through a portal and has never returned, in all my years of searching."

"What about all your copies you were bragging about?"

"Copies are wonderful things, but having the original...there is no substitute. Not really. Forget the Cult and the Akarin and everyone else. I just want something of my husband."

Tommen ran his hand through his hair. "That's it."

"What's it?"

"Purple ink. I get it now."

"I don't. Enlighten me."

"You have copies and copies of copies, but you still search for the original in order to validate your journals. But the Authored Books have purple ink in all of them to show that they're original. Even copies have purple ink so that no matter what, everyone knows that they're approved by the Author."

Julianna raised a brow. "Is that your stunning little revelation?" She sighed. "Take me back to your room. You have one of the Authored Books. I want to show you something."

"Is it going to take long? I mean, I still have to get some kind of sleep. I'm exhausted."

"No, it won't take long. It's not a conversation piece necessarily, more like something to consider while you sleep. Perhaps then you'll come back around."

Grudgingly, Tommen stood and gathered his things. He couldn't tell if his wooziness came from lack of sleep or worsening illness. Better make this quick, then.

They Traveled back to his room. While lay back on the bed, Julianna grabbed his Authored Book, bringing it into the dimension and flipping through the pages.

"So-called 'Authored' Books are nice and certainly fascinating, but they're not authoritative. They don't come from the Author." She paused and considered her words. "The Author needs no one to help her, save for a mouth through which to speak. If she wrote these books, then why are they so riddled with errors? Just as a few examples, 'Alice in Wonderland' ought to be at least italicized. That occurs on multiple occasions. Page 165, it should be 'unfazed.' Page 451, I believe it is Cassius, not Rifun doing the action, but I might be able to suspend the disbelief. Page 472, 'Have no you no'? And those are just a few. To say nothing of awkward sentences, fragments, and for the love of Pete, she does love her semi-colons and dashes."

She closed the book and set it on his bag. "If the Author can't even be trusted with her own writing, how can she be trusted with the greater story? Free will is a wonderful thing and people can do whatever they want, to be sure, and I am certain that this Brooke Shaffer impostor will get her just punishment in due time. But in the meantime, we must search out the real words of the real Author."

Tommen rubbed his eyes, fighting sleep. "How do you know which one is which, though?"

Julianna sighed. "I know it's confusing. I'm trying to help. And, in a way, reading the Authored Books might prove useful as a way to have a more thorough world view, understanding the Akarin platform. But you mustn't lose sight of your goal, of what really matters. The words of the Author and the ending she has planned for each of us."

"Does that ending involve being murdered by psycho terrorists?"

She gave him a look. "I already told you there are three journals. The one you found was the Book of Abilities, the one detailing all the abilities granted to Akari-bearers. Some are available to the Akarin as well in good faith, but only the greatest abilities are given to those who read the journals and seek the words of the Author.

"The journal I had was the Book of Philosophy, detailing the larger questions about the universe, the Author, and all those philosophical things all men ponder at one time or another. Admittedly, it's not the most exciting read, but it can be enlightening."

"And the one that disappeared?"

"The Book of Commands."

Tommen chuckled. "Thou shalt not kill?"

"Among others. How to conduct business both internally and externally, handling disputes, relations with the Akarin and so forth.

It's also called the Book of History as parts of it detail my husband's life and his struggles to write the journals and have them accepted. I added a short chapter on his imprisonment and subsequent execution." Her expression turned distressed. "It was not fun for me to write it, as I was forced to do so on my flight to America. I gave it to a loyal follower upon my arrival in America, but never saw it again. He took it elsewhere and it has not returned. I can only trust that it is safe."

"So why would a book that is supposed to be the words straight from the Author include details about your husband's life?"

"Context."

He shrugged. "So what? Wouldn't commands from the Author be absolute and eternal no matter the circumstances? And why your husband's life? I mean, shit happens. Life changes."

"We could debate this all day, but it does little good if you haven't read the book itself."

"Great. Where is it? I'll even take a copy."

Julianna folded her arms once more. "I don't appreciate your tone."

Had Tommen been in a little better shape, he might have pursued the argument and confrontation. As it was, he had little strength left. So instead he decided to derail the fight and say, "I'm sorry. I'm exhausted. I'm sick and not home yet. I'm tired of being here. I'm tired of having philosophical debates while I'm sick and trapped in a parallel dimension."

Her gaze softened a little. "I know. Believe me, I'm just as tired of being here as you are. More, even. But you do need to rest. Do you have any medicine left?"

He handed her the last syringe which she pushed through the port.

"I'll see if I can't find anything else that might help," she told him. "Get some sleep and get plenty to drink when you wake up. As a matter of fact, you should probably have a glass of water now before you go to bed. Are you hungry?"

She was like a mother hen, the way she fussed over him, making sure he got not one but two full glasses of water, and a quick snack of carrots and ranch. Then she unwrapped his arm to check on that. More dead skin was peeling off, along with melted plastic matter that used to be his jacket. She cleaned it up as best she could before wrapping his arm in fresh bandages. After that, she got him another glass of water and did pretty much everything for him short of tucking him in and reading him a bedtime story.

"Did you ever have kids?" Tommen asked sleepily. "Because you sure act like it."

Julianna frowned and sat down slowly on the end of the bed. "No, but we wanted to. Richard and I knew each other before we became Time Agents, and we were married soon after, though neither of us realized quite how 'for as long as you both shall live' had changed for us."

"And the Time fuckery made it so you couldn't have kids."

"That's right. Of course, we didn't realize how Time messed with us, with me mostly, and because of our lengthened lives, we always figured that we would have time later to have a family. Then we found ourselves in the same predicament that Micaiah and his wife face now."

"I'm sorry."

She looked at him. "It's one of the sacrifices we make when we choose this life, be it Time or Akari. Of course, it wasn't long before we became Akarin, and hardly a year went by before we realized the decay that was happening there. As things grew worse and Richard began writing the journals, we decided that perhaps it was a good thing we'd not had children. Bad enough we had Akarin assassins coming after us, to say nothing of the Trackers."

"The Trackers?"

"The Akarin hounds of war. Like bloodhounds, they are naturally very good at tracking things, hence the name. But they can be trained to do the most savage things. Their use had been greatly reduced up until this time, but when Richard began his writing, the

Akarin began their training once more."

"Oh. I'm sorry."

Julianna got off the bed and brushed out the wrinkles from her dress. "Not all Akarin are evil. I truly believe your friend Micaiah was trying to do his best with what he had in a corrupt system. But they are not the flower-picking, meek and mild, woefully persecuted Akari-bearers they would have you believe they are. After all, if they were, do you really think they could have overthrown Rifun's regime?"

She took a few steps away, then paused and sighed. She looked back at him. "I'm going to find more medicine at the hospital. I expect you're going to sleep for a while yet. If you don't mind, I'd like to read Richard's journal a bit. Where did you put it? Is it in your bag?"

Tommen hesitated. Then, "That was the first test. To see if the portal thing would work. It does work on objects, just not people."

Now her gaze started to burn. "Where is the journal?"

"I gave it to Micah for safekeeping. I don't know what he did with it. Maybe he gave it to Micaiah; that's where I heard something about there being three journals. I don't know. I was half-asleep at the time."

"Well, at least it's easier to bring things into the dimension. I'll just have to go and get it, I suppose." She shook her head. "Teenagers. Good night, Tommen."

She flipped off the light, plunging Tommen into a dusky pre-dawn gray that he knew would only get lighter. He couldn't exactly pull the blankets up over his head, either. Fatigue should have counted for something, except every instinct told him to get up because he was going to be late for work.

Eventually, he rolled over on his right side and closed his eyes. So, the joy of the Cult was now multiplied by three. Was Rifun aware that there were three journals? Probably. Of course, he would have been interested only in the Book of Abilities, reading about all the power he could get. The Book of Philosophy was boring, and he likely wouldn't take too kindly to the Book of Commands telling him what to do or not do.

But how to stack them up and compare them to the Authored Books? Either the journals were true and there was some serious power to be gained as well as a serious flaw in the Akarin, or else the Authored Books were true and the journals were a ticking time bomb. Could both be true? Not likely, if each said the other was false. Could both be false? Absolutely. Except for the part where Tommen had literally read about his own life, including private details which no one should have known. That was the part he couldn't just shake off or explain away.

And why was he having this philosophical debate now, when he was trying to sleep? Already his room was getting brighter as the sun came up. Maybe because it determined whether he was taking Julianna with him.

On the one hand, she really could be the victim, forced to play the tough guy in order to free her husband and confront a corrupt system. If that was the case, he had every obligation to help her, not only escape, but find the third journal and set things to rights. If things were as bad in the Akarin fortress as it seemed, maybe now was the time for some third-party guidance.

On the other hand, what if she was every bit the snake his gut was telling him she was? Terrorists might sincerely believe their ideology, but that didn't make it any less horrific or any more right.

At the same time, what could she possibly do that Rifun and Cassius hadn't already done? Kill a bunch of people? Yup, seen that. Overthrow the government, set up a dictatorship throughout the universe, begin systematic genocide? Been there, done that, too. Both times, the maniac had been deposed. Cassius was dead, and while Rifun was still at large, his power was considerably diminished. What else could Julianna possibly do? Tommen honestly couldn't think of anything.

So he lay there in the slowly growing brightness, crying internally, telling himself to get some sleep. He glanced at his clock once. A little after seven. He closed his eyes and turned toward the door, away from his windows.

"See the world through my eyes."

Once again, Tommen found himself looking out across the valley, through the past and the present and even the future. Before, when he was following his family or doing other things, he had only been able to see the past and present. Where had this future-seeing ability come from? How did he control it? What did he do with it? Could he manipulate it? Change things?

He saw all the people who had ever climbed the rock face to reach the cave. Lost travelers, hoping for shelter. Excavators, hoping to strike it rich. Young lovers, looking for privacy. Young women, hoping to escape murderous pursuit. Little boys, looking for adventure.

He looked back at the cave. His first time seeing it, it had been black, as all caves ought to be. Light did not travel far into the inky shadows, and total cave darkness overtook careless explorers quickly. When he'd looked at it again, after his exploration, he'd seen a tidal wave of awesome color as Time unfurled itself, showing the temporal distortion and just how powerful it was to those who could see.

This time, though, there was even more to behold. If before he had been looking at a woven rug from a distance, now he was up close, inspecting every detail. He saw every string, every thread, every fiber. He saw each weave, under and over, each little knot and handoff to every different color. He saw how every little detail contributed to the woven rug as a whole. He saw how everything could be touched and manipulated, a little tug here or there changing the picture.

Stepping back, the details faded and he was back to observing time as it passed by all at once. He watched as huge groups of Native peoples clamored into the cave. All of them were warriors, but their goal now was not to fight and win, only to flee. But in their urgency, none of the people seemed to take notice of him, instead running headlong through a portal taking them they knew not where. Safety, hopefully. A place where they would not be hunted and pursued.

"See the world through my eyes, Tommen Forbes. And find me."

"Where?"

Now he felt himself again, as though separated from whoever he had been. He could no longer see each weave in the temporal distortion, nor see the future of the valley. Everything looked exactly as it had been.

"Where are you?" Tommen asked aloud. "How do I find you?"

"I am not easily lost. But you must want to find me."

"Well that's a dumb thing to say. Obviously, if I'm looking for you, I want to find you."

"Yes, but for what purpose? Answer that, and perhaps I will be found."

Tommen rubbed his face. Fucking hell, he was going nuts. He really needed to lay off this religion thing. It was going to be the death of him one of these days.

As he turned around, he found himself rolling over in bed, catching himself before he rolled onto his left arm. As it was, he managed to pinch it a little, sending shockwaves of pain through him. Groaning, he adjusted his position. His room was considerably lighter now. Glancing at his clock, he saw it was just before noon. Well, four and some odd hours wasn't horrible, but he was probably going to need another nap before he went to the second rescue attempt.

He sat up and looked around. Nothing looked disturbed, not that he expected it to be. He didn't see any new medicine laid out for him. Either it was sitting elsewhere or else Julianna wasn't back yet.

Tommen thought about waiting for her. His ingrained chivalrous nature told him to be polite to a woman and extend her every courtesy. His gut told him to run and get as far away from her as possible. Fine, let her have the journal. What did he care? But every part of him said not to let her escape this dimension.

He got up and did a quick search of the house, just to be sure she wasn't waiting for him in the kitchen or something. When he confirmed the house was empty, he returned to his room and packed up everything he had with him. His pack was heavy and his head was still not quite right, but he only had to survive the day. He hoped. Otherwise this was going to be a long game of cat-and-mouse.

Chapter Twenty-Six
Graveyard

Walter headed to work in a daze. Tommen had let go. He had basically refused to come out of the in-between dimension. Granted, he'd been sick and tired, and Walter had been at the end of his strength, and neither of them had seemed to make much progress, but still. Tommen had let go. He'd said not to try it that way because it wouldn't work. While Walter had little reason to doubt him, he was still having a hard time just processing the whole thing. Something had happened. Tommen had seen or learned something and he wasn't telling. Maybe it wasn't safe. Maybe he was becoming delirious from infection. Maybe when they tried again tonight, Walter should switch places with him anyway, just so Tommen could get to a hospital and get help, assuming that's what would have happened. Was there any real way to know? Had Kayla found something?

He pulled into the precinct and waited a minute or two before getting out of the car. While a day at work might help calm his mind a little and help get things back on track, it was also the last thing he wanted to do. He wanted to try again. He wanted to head up to Wellspring and help with their useless search. He wanted to do anything but go to work where he would have to deal with so many things he really didn't care about right now. Well, at the very least, he would have to keep up appearances by calling the search team at some point this morning. Hopefully Laura hadn't decided to check up on his story.

Grudgingly, he went inside and punched in. He was just pouring himself a cup of coffee when Jim Standish walked up, red-blond beard as impeccably groomed as ever.

"You look terrible, man," he said.

"Good morning to you, too," Walter grumbled. "How would you feel if you were in my position?"

"Pretty shitty, I should think."

"I'm just trying to have a normal day at work today." He stirred in some cream and sugar.

"Aren't we all?"

"What do you mean?"

Jim nodded toward Steggmann's office. Walter took a drink of his coffee and looked, but saw nothing unusual. Blinds were down, but so what? "I don't get it."

"Steggmann's here. Half the city council is here. A couple guys I don't recognize are here."

"At five in the morning? On a Sunday?"

"Whatever this is, they want to hit at least two shifts, but not make a huge deal about it. None of the night guys have been allowed to leave yet. They're pissed."

"Wouldn't you be?"

This did not bode well for anyone. Before Walter could shape his fears into coherent thoughts, the door opened and more people than could fit in a clown car poured out of the office to the front of the room. He recognized some of the city council members, and not in a neighborly fashion either. Few in the precinct held any love for the city and how they seemed to be trying to run the precinct from the outside.

"Can we have your attention, please?" one of the councilwomen said in a voice that would make an opera singer proud. "Everyone, please, look here. Yes, this way. Thank you."

Incoherent, conspiratorial grumbling gradually died down as everyone turned to face one end of the room where the mass of official-looking people stood. Another officer accompanied them. Walter did not recognize him, but he wasn't liking the looks of the rank on his sleeves. Steggmann spoke first.

"Thank you all for being here this morning, especially those of you having to stay a little later. We wanted to ensure that as many people knew about this as possible so as to avoid rumors and the telephone game." Translation: I want witnesses. "I don't need to remind any of you of the tragedy that happened last Christmas. Some of you may not know that there was an internal investigation conducted afterwards, to see if things could have been done differently, where we fell short.

"The good and the bad of it is that there was nothing we could have done that we could see. No one was directly at fault. That doesn't make it any easier for those of us who knew the men and women who died that day.

"Regardless, it was determined that there was a fatal flaw in our handling of the event, and I take the blame for that." Walter could have sworn that Steggmann looked directly at him when he said it. Then he looked back at the assembled crowd. "Therefore, effective immediately, I hereby resign my position as Chief of Police."

There was an uproar as questions and comments were all voiced at once, each louder than the last, everyone trying to be heard. Judging by the expressions of the council members, they weren't expecting this kind of reaction. Maybe they thought these guys were just going to roll over and take it. Well, that's what they got for never setting foot in a police station while trying to manage it.

"I don't know if I should have called in sick today, or if I'm glad I didn't," Standish commented.

"I wonder whether I should have retired when I had the chance," Walter mused.

Steggmann let the crowd continue their complaining while another council member tried to calm them down. She was ineffective until another councilman gave a shrill whistle.

"We understand this comes as quite a shock," the councilwoman said, every word sounding scripted. "Know that we have nothing but respect for you and the hard work you do to keep us safe. Unfortunately, the events of last Christmas presented, as Greg said, a glaring flaw in structural management. We don't want to see dead cops any more than you do."

A ripple went through the crowd, and Walter almost expected someone to throw a rotten tomato.

"We also understand that many of you would prefer that one of your own be appointed to the position. You work together, train together, and you know each other well. If this were under better circumstances, we would be glad to leave the succession up to you. However, we as the city council feel that a new perspective and management style may be what is needed. Therefore—" She gestured to the new officer who stepped forward next to Steggmann. "—Casey Oldman will be our new Chief of Police."

Charleston was a decent-sized city, but between the main precinct and the west precinct, Walter had never heard of any Casey Oldman, even at the black tie fundraiser events where all higher officers had to attend. The city council was full of idiots, but they wouldn't promote someone who was unqualified. That meant this guy was from out of town. Like, way out of town. CPD had a good relationship with the surrounding rural police, and still the guy's name didn't ring a bell.

If he was from that far out of town, this could be either a good or bad thing. On the one hand, he could be a decent guy who wanted to assimilate in more than he wanted to conform his men. He certainly looked harmless enough. Late thirties, early forties, short blond hair, clean-shaven. Walter might have put him in some branch of the military seeing how he was still in good shape.

On the other hand, the city council was full of foxes who wouldn't hand-pick a replacement for Steggmann without making sure that replacement was in their pocket. So he might be meek and mild, but also spineless against anything the council wanted to do to the precinct. Or he could be fully in cahoots and be an asshole who was going to do some serious house cleaning. And not the kind to fix the toilet that had been broken for the last four months.

The murmur that ran through the crowd was decidedly more muted than the one before, and Casey Oldman had little trouble making himself heard.

"Good morning. My name is Casey Oldman. I understand very well that this comes as a shock to you. I actually come from New York City Police Department." Well, that explained the accent. "The incident last Christmas made national headlines, as most of you know, and there was a lot of talk even at my precinct back home. We train routinely for terror attack response, but you never get used to it when it happens. And to see something like that happen in the least likely of places, it breaks my heart. It really does.

"I'm not here to turn you guys into NYPD or the National Guard. Charleston is a lot different than New York and has its own character, its own needs. I don't understand all of those needs yet. I've only been in the state for three weeks. But I do hope that my experience and training can benefit this department to ensure nothing like that ever happens again.

"There is a lot of work that has to be done, but my door is wide open if anyone has any doubts or concerns or questions about me, my experience, my training, or my intentions here. And if I ask about any of you, know that it's not an interrogation. I haven't worked with you guys, and I want to get to know you, who you are, your background, and so on. There will be changes. I want them to be the right ones. Thank you."

Walter had a hard time deciding the sincerity of his words. His ease of speaking suggested it wasn't his first time addressing a group of people. He knew what to say, what not to say, how to say it. It could be that he was simply defaulting back to this training and going for a pretty standard "hey, I'm your new boss" speech. He could be trying to hide something, whether in spite of or because of the council standing right there. There was no good way to tell after a two minute speech.

Maybe Walter should have called in sick and gone out to "help search" some more. He really didn't need this right now, on top of everything else.

The first councilwoman returned to the speaking position. "If anyone has any questions—"

"Why didn't you promote Harry?" someone asked loudly, garnering murmurs of disgruntled agreement.

Harry Matthews was the other captain in the precinct, Walter's counterpart so to speak. He didn't have as many years as Walter, but he had the youth and the ambition. He also blamed Walter for last year's incident and made no secret of it. As soon as the comment was made, Walter knew there would be civil war in the precinct.

It was a moment before the councilwoman could speak. "As I said before, had this been normal circumstances, we would have happily let you manage your own affairs. But we wanted fresh eyes—"

"And we wanted Harry," the officer retorted.

"Harry? What about Walt?" someone else asked. "He was actually there that day instead of calling in sick like a pussy."

Before the argument could devolve into a full-blown fight, the whistler gave another whistle to grab everyone's attention.

Through it all, Walter watched Casey Oldman's expression, seeing how he might react to this impending fight. It was not comforting. He did not appear startled or surprised or even the least bit interested, in a passerby sense. Rather, his expression was carefully guarded, and he scanned the crowd, picking out people and memorizing faces. He was systematically cataloging the loyalty of each officer present. He was no rookie, and he was no meek and mild replacement for Steggmann.

"Please!" the councilwoman said, exasperated. "We would like to make this change of power as peaceful as possible. We understand it's a shock. We understand that things are going to be different. You may direct your questions and concerns to myself, anyone on the council, Greg, or, most especially, Casey himself. Until then, you may resume work as normal. Those of you who were asked to stay, we thank you, and you are free to go home and get some sleep."

The meeting did not break up quickly, but divided into dozens of smaller meetings as officers grumbled to one another, casting glances this way and that, most often toward the office where the officials had returned. Walter made for the safety of his cubicle and sat down for a minute. Well, this was certainly not how he expected his day to start out.

"So, how bout those Tigers, huh?" Standish said, walking up. "Sounds like South Charleston has a pretty good football team this year."

Walter barked a laugh. "Only because the Jefferson Memorial team got busted for drugs. Otherwise, they would have had it made."

They both sighed.

"One hell of a morning, huh?" Standish mused. "Think he's gonna clean house?"

"Oh, I have no doubt about that. It's just a question of when and how."

"Well, if he was figuring on a hostile takeover, he might have to rework his plans a bit after Mike's little outburst there that he started."

Walter nodded and stood.

"Where are you going?" Standish asked, moving out of his way.

Walter looked at him and shrugged. "I'm going to say hi to the new guy. Introduce myself."

"Good luck, buddy."

The council had cleared out and Steggmann was just leaving as Walter approached. Walter got his attention and they paused in the hallway to speak.

"How long have you known?" Walter asked quietly.

Steggmann grinned and shook his head. "It was always going to be this way. Honestly, it was either me or you. I didn't want to force you out, so I offered you retirement. When you persisted and came back on the force, well, someone had to take the fall." He went on before Walter could speak. "I wasn't going to tell you because then I knew you would leave. The precinct needs good officers. Regardless of what Harry and his supporters think, you are a good officer. And we need good officers more than we need politicians."

Maybe there was some hope to be had. "So, the new guy...?"

"I only said we need good officers more than politicians. I didn't say that was who they hired."

It was the closest thing he ever gave for a warning. Heart sinking, gut twisting, Walter wished Steggmann a happy retirement, then turned and went back to the office that now belonged to Casey Oldman.

Walter stood in the doorway and watched him for a moment, standing, looking, searching, examining, moving, filing, refiling, touching up, and so on.

"Knock knock?" Walter said finally, tapping lightly on the door.

"Yes, come in." He extended a hand. "Casey Oldman. You can call me Casey."

Walter shook his hand. "That's what you said out there; I should hope it didn't change."

"No, of course not. And you are?"

"Walter Forbes."

"Ah. So you're Captain Forbes."

"Please, I'm not here to steal your job. I just wanted to speak to you in person and formally welcome you to Charleston PD."

"I appreciate that. Thank you. Yeah, this is a lot smaller operation than what I'm used to. I might actually remember all your names."

"So what brings you here? Too stuffy in the Big Apple?"

"Ah, well, no. Actually, the wife wanted to downsize a little. She likes the city, but wanted a slightly smaller city and a little better view. Looked around a little bit and here we are."

"Kids?"

"Just sent a couple off to college before we moved. Twin boys, but still got one at home. You?"

Walter Banded for a moment and searched the man, looking for any hint of malice or a trap. When he found none, he said, "Just my son, Tommen. He's turning seventeen in a week. And my girlfriend, Laura. She's a paramedic here in Charleston."

"Very good." Casey folded his arms and shifted his stance. "Tommen Forbes. I heard a thing on the news about a kid up at some summer camp in Wellspring—"

"That would be him, yes."

"Oh, I'm sorry. And you're still here?"

"I took the time off that I needed, and the search teams are getting into territory that my car can't get to. Even if it could, traipsing around the mountains isn't something I can just do on a whim anymore."

"God, don't say things like that. You remind me of what's coming. I've managed to put it off for this long, but it'll catch me eventually."

"Army?"

"Coast Guard. Six years, right out of high school."

"Impressive. Well, I'll let you get back to your work. There's certainly enough of it."

Casey thanked him, but called him back before he walked through the door. "One more thing." Walter turned. "Listen, I know it's the first day and all and everyone's kind of feeling this thing out. Me and you both. All." His expression turned serious. "But there are changes coming. I understand that West Virginia is a little more rugged than most of the country, especially New York, but I do expect a certain level of professionalism from those under me." He pointed. "I like your mustache. It looks well-groomed. It won't be today or tomorrow, but eventually, you and everyone in this precinct with facial hair will be asked to shave."

Walter raised a brow. "If you don't mind my asking, why?"

"As I said, professionalism. We're public servants, and we can't be looking like we just came crawling off the mountain like a bunch of miners. It's lower on the priority list right now, but be ready for the order to come down."

"More than half of the men here have facial hair."

"Then I'll be sure to pick up an extra bag of disposable razors to put in the men's bathroom. Dismissed."

Well, he'd sure made himself right at home, Walter thought as he left the office. On his way out, he passed Standish who stopped him.

"So, how'd it go? Sorry to say, your expression isn't making me feel good."

Walter sighed as he looked at Standish's beard. In the years they'd worked together in Homicide, not once had the man ever come in with a scraggly, unwashed, unkempt beard. It was always neat, trimmed, combed, magazine ready.

"We're in for a roller coaster ride," Walter said diplomatically. "I'm heading out for a few minutes."

Standish nodded uncertainly and moved aside so he could head out to his cruiser, taking a minute or two to let it warm up, or rather, cool down. It didn't hit him until he was actually pulling out of the lot that the whole thing could have been a trap. What if Casey was sending out feelers and testing the rumor mill? If he told a different lie to each higher officer and waited to see which ones circulated, well, that was one way to figure out who was who. It didn't have to be anything big, either. For Walter, it might be the facial hair thing. For Harry, he might say that everyone would have to wear specific shoes rather than whatever was comfortable in black or brown. For Lieutenant O'Hara, a woman, he might say that all women had to cut their hair above the collar. See what came back, root out the weeds.

Walter was suddenly glad he hadn't said anything about the facial hair to Standish. On the other hand, though, what if that order did actually come down? Was he supposed to tell the other men about that impending doom? He would quickly become the most hated person in the precinct, right up there with the man who gave that order. Was it a way to test his loyalty, to see if he would give the order or if he would refuse? Could it be that his overactive imagination was blowing this way out of proportion? Even if Casey did pitch a fit and say that Walter was supposed to notify everyone of the change, Walter could play stupid and say that Casey had not explicitly stated such intentions and they hadn't worked together long enough for him to pick up on verbal and nonverbal cues.

Oh, this was so much more than he wanted to deal with today. How he wished for Tommen to call and tell him that he'd figured a way out of the in-between dimension that was low-risk and super easy. That wasn't going to happen, he knew, but he could hope.

His trip to the bakery was interrupted by a man blowing a red light, then failing to pull over until about six blocks later, all the while weaving nonchalantly through all lanes of traffic. Had it been any other morning than Sunday when it was almost completely dead, there would have been an accident to contend with, too. Walter sympathized with the man and his many problems, but that did not give him an excuse to be drunk at six in the morning, his third time in three years if his record was any indication. He wasn't even supposed to have a license. But he was going to be late for work, assuming he could even remember where he worked.

Truthfully, Walter preferred the drunk guy over the events of the morning, and he was too happy to deliver the man and be on his merry way, out on the roads again. He still had to deliver one traffic ticket before he made it to the bakery, but it was a good way to pass the time, he figured.

"Good morning, Walt," Micah greeted as he walked in.

"Well, it's morning, anyway," Walter sighed.

"That it is." Micah couldn't say too much about the even earlier incident with Tommen, seeing how there were customers in the dining room, but his expression conveyed enough sympathy. If only he knew. He placed a fresh pan of cinnamon rolls in the display case and leaned on the counter. "So, what can I get for you?"

"A pillow, blanket, and a cot in the back."

"Ouch. Well, I know Cai has his little cot in the office, but something tells me that wouldn't actually do any good. So, what's up? Or is it just the usual?"

"The usual." He Banded the two of them. "And a huge new shakeup at the precinct. Steggmann just resigned this morning. City council appointed a new guy from NYPD."

"NYPD? As in, New York? Like New York, New York? Like,

Law & Order New York?"

"The very same. I had a short chat with him this morning, and I don't think he's quite the meek and mild newcomer he's trying to convey. He told me that pretty soon, all the men are going to have to shave. Completely."

Micah gasped, and it was difficult to tell his level of sarcasm. "No more mustache?!"

"But, I can't decide if he might just be trying to play the rumor mill. You know, send out different rumors—"

"And see which one comes back." Micah nodded. "I know the game. And all of this happened just this morning?"

"Just in the last few hours, yes. It's been one hell of a day, and it's not even noon."

"Sounds like a hell of a day."

Walter dropped the Band. "Yeah. Why not give me one of your legendary pastries?"

"Legendary? Ha! You've been away for too long. Time to get back in the swing of things."

Still, Micah got him the pastry and he headed back out to the cruiser where he sat and ate and thought.

All right, so he was sitting here eating his pastry, like normal. He hadn't been fired, and the precinct hadn't burned down. They'd had a bit of a surprise this morning, but otherwise, the world kept turning. He'd nabbed one drunk driver, ticketed a speeder, and he still had a few hours to go. Nothing horrible.

It really wasn't unusual for his mind to be distracted, except now it was torn between distractions. On the one hand, he couldn't get the conversation with Casey out of his head. A sense of doom and gloom seemed to be hovering around the precinct, especially that man. But he was also distracted by the failed rescue effort even earlier this morning.

Well, his options right now seemed to be limited to returning to the precinct and doing paperwork in the cloud of doom and gloom, or doing as his son had suggested and going out to check out Forbes

Cave. Honestly, it wasn't much of a decision.

Technically, Forbes Cave and all the parks and trails surrounding it were not within the jurisdiction of Charleston PD; they belonged to the county mounties. So as Walter cruised along on the highway that marked the edge of city jurisdiction, he picked his exit and Banded to get on the road he wanted to be on. Considering recent events, he couldn't say that he was surprised to find Micaiah's motorcycle in the parking lot.

Being in the Band, everything around Walter was completely still. A couple of squirrels ran around the parking lot, investigating dropped food crumbs and empty wrappers. A flock of birds was just beginning to take off from a tree. A couple of young women were setting up for some kind of party in one of the pavilions.

Walter consulted the trail map before picking a direction and starting off. He figured he must have been on the right track because he ran into Micaiah about a quarter mile in. He brought the elder twin into the Band.

"Nice day for a climb," he observed mildly.

Micaiah startled and looked around a second before realizing what was going on. "You scared me, Walt. Not a good thing to do right now."

"We seem to be in the same boat, then."

"You heading my way?"

"I expect so. So, what's going on with you?"

Walter listened patiently as Micaiah recounted his tale of arrest and intrigue. At the very least, it made his problems at the precinct feel a little smaller. Really, he only had to put up with Casey Oldman for another year or two before finally being able to leave and start his own life elsewhere, where he could grow his mustache freely. Didn't make it any less terrible that his friend had been accused of murder, then banned from a group he once esteemed and even helped lead. Even as he spoke, Micaiah's limp seemed to get more and more noticeable until he finally had to sit down on a rock and take a break.

"Your knee bothering you?" Walter asked, feeling a bit winded himself.

"Just a little," Micaiah admitted. "Really, I need to stay off it for a while, hobble around on my crutches. But it's a lot harder to go rock climbing on crutches."

"If you need to take a rest, go ahead and go back. I can find my way."

"Are you kidding? Not a chance. Besides, we're more than halfway there. I think I can make it the last little bit."

Walter didn't press the matter, and they were on their way soon enough. Their next big challenge was scaling the stone wall where the trail had been deliberately cut out so as to keep curious passersby away from the dangerous cave. Between Walter's age and Micaiah's leg, neither of them were exactly scaling Mount Everest here.

"All right, guess we use Gravity," Micaiah mused, backing up a few steps. "Come here."

"Gravity?" Walter wondered, both curious and afraid as to whatever new Akari trick he was about to pull out of his proverbial bag.

"When I say go, take one, two steps, and jump."

"You're asking a lot of me today, you know that?"

"And the fun is only just getting started. Ready? Go!"

It was a reluctant movement on Walter's part, even more so when he took the jump and found that he was being lifted, high and clear of the stone wall, almost as if jumping on the moon. Panic set in and he landed on the ground in an ungraceful heap. He'd have to come up with a pretty good story for how his uniform got all dusty and wrinkled before returning to the precinct. And to think they still had to get down. Were there no other paths up here?

"You okay?" Micaiah asked. He extended a hand and helped Walter to his feet. "I guess I should have given you a little more warning."

"Maybe next time when we have to get down," Walter told him, brushing himself off as best he could. "So, what else can you do? Breathe underwater?"

"I'm sure something could be rigged to do that, but I haven't cared to try it." Micaiah shrugged. "Anyway, cave's right up there." He turned and moved off up the hill.

"Does Kayla know you're here?" Walter wondered, trudging after him.

"I told her, but I don't know how well she understood me. She's sleeping off a pretty good hangover."

"Little too much peyote, huh?"

"That and making multiple portal jumps. I figured it best to just let her sleep in a little bit."

They picked their way to the entrance of the cave. The boulder was still there, but the trees had long since rotted. The dedication plaque was still there, as was the chain and the warning sign. Personally, Walter thought a boulder was a little more effective deterrent. It was harder to move or sneak under it.

"It's a wonder more people haven't gotten lost in here," Micaiah mused.

"They probably have," Walter said thoughtfully. "Tommen wasn't in there that long. Anyone who had real intentions of exploring this cave could still be in there and may not be seen for another century."

It was a sobering thought, really, to think of how many people could still be in there. Did they ever run into each other? Did anyone think to take a lantern?

But that was not the reason for their trek as the two men pushed past the boulder, stepping just inside the cave, out of the reach of the temporal distortion. Said distortion, even with Walter's Band, moved and writhed like a living thing, a great leviathan with tentacles reaching in all directions throughout the cave system.

"In all your research that you've done, have you found anything on who set this trap?" Walter wondered. "I'll even take a fairy tale."

"A Native man called Anagalisgi," Micaiah answered. "He did it to get revenge on some British soldiers who were hunting him and his people. Problem is, he didn't get too specific on how he set it up."

"And no way to shut it down, either."

"Not that anyone has found. Not from the outside, anyway."

Walter folded his arms and shifted his stance. "Not from the outside. What about the inside?"

"I don't follow."

"Tommen said that Time doesn't work in the in-between dimension. Does that mean that this whole trap is useless?"

Micaiah shrugged. "Even if it was, what are you getting at?"

"Maybe, rather than creating a quasi-dimension at the warehouse and going through that hassle, what if we tried to free him from this spot?"

"The temporal distortions are stronger here than elsewhere, but all the layers on top of one another may provide more loopholes to exploit, which may provide a foot in the door to break into another dimension," Micaiah mused. "Using the Akari, we might be able to funnel the Energy needed to sustain an open portal as well as keep back whatever Energy is trying to pull you in." He sighed. "I don't know. Sounds pretty flimsy, but if we don't have to go through the hassle of breaking into the warehouse and trying to build a quasi-dimension—which no one we know, and trust, has ever done—I'm all for it."

"Agreed. Easiest to hardest."

"Now we just have to let Tommen know."

Walter nodded. "I'll leave him a note to call me when he can."

"Then we just have to devise a way for him to let us know when he's actually here. I don't see any switches or outlets up here."

"We'll think of something. Come on. I have to get back to work."

"That exciting, huh?"

Rather than go through the whole story again, Walter just nodded. "Absolutely. Another day in paradise."

"I'm detecting a hint of sarcasm from you, Walter."

"Sarcastic? Me? Never."

They reached the stone wall where it took another terrifying manipulation of Gravity to see them safely back to the main trail. Walter wasn't sure what to make of such things, being able to manipulate, not only Time, but basically the entire physical universe. It was frightening, it really was.

By the time they returned to the parking lot, Walter was ready for lunch. Problem was, he'd basically just had breakfast. And there was that whole part about him trying to lose weight.

"Guess we just have to wait for Tommen to contact one of us," Micaiah said, unlocking his helmet from his bike.

"Well, with any luck, he got some sleep," Walter agreed. "He looked terrible. He's sick. He needs to see a doctor."

"I'm not disagreeing."

"I should have taken his place when I had the chance, assuming that's what would have happened."

"Maybe he's on to something and has a plan. At least with him, he has a way to communicate." Micaiah sighed. "I'm still not sure about Julianna, though. I mean, I'm sure she's evil and needs to stay in that dimension. But I'm not sure whether Tommen will agree with me."

"She's done nothing but help him so far."

"Devil's greatest trick was convincing people he doesn't exist. His second greatest trick is giving them everything they want. I think she's trying to manipulate him. Either she's trying to win him over completely, or else confuse him long enough to take advantage of his hesitation. She knows he's chivalrous by nature and won't hurt a woman. That's what she's playing on."

You know her well, do you? Walter wanted to ask. He kept his mouth shut, only in that he had places to be and really didn't want to consider any more conspiracy theories than he had to. Once his son was returned to him, then he would consider this, that and the other thing about Julianna. But one thing at a time.

He released Micaiah from the Band as he got in his car. By habit, he did a quick check of the car to ensure nothing had been touched. When all seemed well, he backed out of the lot and returned to his original location before Banding. Then he released the Band completely and maneuvered his way through real-time traffic.

So. Change of plans. They would not be going to the shipping yard later on to build a quasi-dimension. Instead, they would head up to Forbes Cave in hopes of exploiting the Time Trap that was there, using its weakness as a launching point for the portal. There was no guarantee that it would work, but it was the best plan they had so far.

He let out a breath. He didn't like all this uncertainty. He was old, dammit. He liked his routine. He liked having a more or less predictable work day with predictable people. He liked having a fairly predictable home life with his son. He didn't like having such dramatic changes at work and he was really growing tired of losing his son all the time.

After handing out a couple more tickets, Walter headed to a small, secret spot few cops knew of where he could do his paperwork in peace. There weren't a lot of ways to sneak up on him in the car, and with how out of the way it was, he was unlikely to be disturbed at all. He grumbled a little as he got everything organized and dug out a pen. Police work was eighty percent paperwork, ten percent bullshit calls, five percent action, and five percent defending those actions in court.

He got through about four papers before he sat back in his seat, willing himself not to fall asleep. After a minute or two, he dug out his phone and called Laura.

"This is a surprise," Laura said. "Good morning. Did they get him?"

"No, not yet," Walter answered.

"I'm sorry. Hey, so, we were on an accident scene a little earlier this morning, and one of the other officers said something about a huge change over at the precinct. Said Steggmann got ousted? Did I hear that right?"

"Unfortunately, yes."

"Aw, damn."

"If you're free for lunch, I can give you an eyewitness

statement."

"Sounds exciting. Where do you want to meet?"

They made vague plans, but were interrupted as the ambulance got dispatched to a call. Laura wished him a brief goodbye and hung up, intent on her mission.

Walter finished up his paperwork and did another cruise around town before getting up the nerve to return to the precinct. The good news was that it hadn't burned down while he was away and there were no angry lynch mobs outside the door either. The interesting thing, though, was that there seemed to be a record number of cruisers gone, as if everyone had completely abandoned the station. When Walter walked in the building, his suspicions were confirmed. Other than a couple unfortunate souls left behind to answer calls, everyone who could be gone, was gone.

"It's like a ghost town in here," Walter observed as he refilled his coffee mug.

The only other person in the room was Elizabeth, the new college intern helping Cynthia at the reception desk. She nodded and murmured some kind of agreement but otherwise said nothing as she stirred in some creamer in her own coffee before leaving the room.

Normally, Walter was used to jittery new interns. Most often, they were a little intimidated by working in a police station and were a little on the anxious side when it came to general office niceties. But with everything going on, the last thing he wanted was for everyone to be nervous. It made him nervous. Maybe that was why everyone was out and about. It was the same reason he'd slipped out earlier, to get into something that resembled normal.

"Oh, good, you're back."

Walter turned to see Casey enter the room and make a beeline for the coffeemaker.

"Did someone call and I not get the message?" Walter wondered.

Casey grinned and shook his head. "No, no. Didn't take long for everyone to leave, though. I was beginning to think maybe no one liked me."

"We're not used to you. Greg has his way of doing things and everyone knew what it was, how business was to be conducted. Things have changed. No one knows what to expect, or what is expected of them."

"You were the first to leave, if I recall correctly."

How he knew that, Walter was curious to find out. "For those who care to pay attention, it's not difficult to tell when shift change is. Between four-thirty and five-thirty is the time to speed, run red lights, and get into all sorts of trouble. Have to be out as quick as possible."

"Yet you work Homicide."

"Is there a body I don't know about?"

Casey shook his head. "Not that I know of. Really, I'm just trying to get used to a smaller department. New York, everyone has a job and that's the job they do. Homicide does homicide, road patrol does road patrol."

More questions and conspiracies began to formulate in Walter's mind. "Well, as much as the city council wants a fresh pair of eyes and different leadership, don't be afraid to ask us old goats how things have been done in the past. If it ain't broke, don't fix it."

Each man was dancing around the other, and they both knew it. Walter wasn't fooled and he could see Casey understood that. What he couldn't decide was how much of it had to do with testing loyalty and figuring out precinct politics, and how much had to do with the incident last Christmas. And in all seriousness, why couldn't this be a peaceful transition instead of a hostile takeover? Why couldn't Walter take Casey at face value as a new leader who was just a little out of his element right now but would eventually turn out to be a great guy who valued all of his officers and worked to treat them fairly and defend them against the conniving micromanagement of the city council?

Lunch could not come too soon. Walter met Laura at the ambulance barn, bearing sub sandwiches and small bags of chips. Ignoring the stares of the second ambulance crew and the firemen, they went out to one of the picnic tables near Walter's cruiser and sat to eat.

"All right, Mr. Forbes, now that we're both here and settled, why don't you tell me what happened this morning around five a.m.?" Laura asked in her best mock-interrogation voice.

So Walter told her everything that had happened that morning, from the city council being out and about on a Sunday morning to Steggmann's resignation to both conversations he'd had with Casey Oldman, new Chief of Police. He also touched on some of his suspicions, hoping he came off as understandably uneasy and not freakishly paranoid. Laura listened patiently, chewing slowly. When he was finished, it was a moment before she spoke.

"I heard about the incident, too," she said. "I mean, a lot of people did, obviously. My kids tried to talk me out of moving here, but I'd already signed the agreement on the apartment, signed the contract with the ambulance, wheels were turned and they brought me here anyway. When I finally started working after the first of the year, it was still a pretty hot topic. You were mentioned several times, usually because of your miraculous recovery, walking out of ICU like that."

"And the rest of the time?" Walter asked, unsure if he wanted to know the answer.

Laura hesitated. "Are you sure you want to hear this now?"

"If not now, when? Lay it on me. My day can't get a whole lot worse at this point."

"Well, obviously, police and EMS talk. And there were a lot of people there that day. Stories and viewpoints and opinions all kind of mixed together. Opinions were divided over you. A few thought you were secretly behind it, but that got dismissed pretty readily. But a lot of people held you responsible for all the deaths."

Walter thought of Pat, his longtime friend who had taken retirement over the fallout from publicly accusing him of treachery. "You're a brave soul, then, to be seen in public with me."

Laura gave him a look. "I don't think it's your fault. Things happen. You can't control everything. And if that guy is half as nuts as people say he is, you really can't control that. I think people just want a scapegoat, someone they can blame seeing how the guy got away. It's unfair to accuse you, and it's really unfair that Steggmann was ousted for it. But maybe now that the people have their pound of flesh, things can finally move on."

"The people have their pound of flesh, but I have a feeling that more blood is going to be spilled in the precinct."

"I don't doubt it. Just be careful. Do your job. Live above reproach."

"Well, that's great, but we've already seen what's happened."

"You must be fun at parties."

His lunch break over, Walter took the other half of his sandwich, bid Laura farewell, got back in his cruiser, and left. He really didn't feel like doing another road patrol, but he even more didn't feel like returning to the precinct. Plus he still hadn't heard from Tommen yet. Well, he only had a couple more hours on his shift to suffer through. Maybe he'd head out and do some rounds around neighborhoods that didn't get patrolled that often. More likely to catch speeders there.

He fished for his phone and called Micaiah.

"Yeah, Walt," the elder twin said.

"Any word from Tommen yet?" Walter asked.

"Nothing. But it is only noon and he had an early start. He could still be sleeping."

"Maybe. Just checking to make sure before I got involved in anything too exciting."

"Because anything exciting happens around here."

"I detect a hint of sarcasm in your voice, Micaiah."

"Sarcastic? Me? Never."

Walter wished him happy baking as he hung up and made a left turn. Something was wrong. His gut told him so. He had to find a way to rescue his son, and fast. He just didn't know where to start.

Chapter Twenty-Seven
Message in a Bottle

Hiding turned out to be a very difficult thing to do, even with his knowledge of criminal behavior. As Tommen kept his head down and tried to blend in with the crowd—decidedly more difficult on a Sunday—he went through everything he knew and remembered about searches. Most of his knowledge came from his dad who'd pursued dozens of criminals. A few of them had been intelligent, but most were run of the mill idiots.

Rule number one: Don't go home, or to any family member, or to any close friends or girlfriends or what have you. If you feel the need to hide in a home, make sure it belongs to a total stranger or is abandoned.

Rule one-and-a-half: No breaking and entering, and only steal cars that are mechanically sound. Also, drive legally. Most criminals got caught based on their stupidity of trying to get away, whether it was getting pulled over for burned out taillights or breaking into a house, it could have been avoided if they'd been a bit more intelligent on the getaway portion.

Rule two: When blending into a crowd, don't make yourself obvious by looking back, looking around, or wearing the obvious "I'm-trying-to-be-inconspicuous" clothing, such as baseball hats, sunglasses, and so on. There was such a thing as being obviously incognito. Like wearing a fake mustache. Also, learning to look with one's peripheral vision is a beneficial skill.

Rule three: Striking up conversations with strangers could go either way. On the one hand, a criminal on the run is expected to be isolated, and a pursuer will typically pass over anyone who looks to be part of an average group of friends. On the other hand, witnesses are terrible things.

Thing was, though, Tommen couldn't quite strike up conversations with strangers, and it was a little harder to blend in with the crowd when the crowd walked right through him. And when he couldn't open up doors but had to go through them, or through a wall or a car door. It seemed strange to wish for the natural laws of physics to apply to him.

So his attempts at hiding from Julianna were basically limited to being anywhere but a familiar spot. Theoretically, he could go anywhere in the world. For a few hours, he did just that. Similar to his food tour of the world, he decided to do a little landmark tour. He went to the Eiffel Tower, the Leaning Tower of Pisa, the Acropolis, the Sphinx, the Taj Mahal, the Great Wall of China, and a number of smaller sights and landmarks as he found them interesting. He took dozens of pictures with his phone, intent on making his dad jealous when he finally got back. Or when he got back to a power supply and could send them to him.

He was a little hesitant on actually calling anyone, but he knew that was solid, irrational paranoia. He highly doubted that Julianna was sitting in some basement with a pair of headphones tracking his phone and listening in on his conversation. Still, he waited until about three or so before returning to the United States and calling his dad.

"Afternoon, sleepyhead," his dad answered. "You just wake up?"

"No, I've been up for a few hours. Been doing some touring. Hang on, I'll send you pictures." Even as he spoke, Tommen was sending him the pictures from his time at the monuments.

"How did you manage all this, then?"

"I'll explain when I get back. But I can now call myself a globetrotter."

"Sounds like you're feeling better."

"Yeah, I got a little medicine in me."

"That's good. Where are you?"

"Um...honestly, I'd rather not say. I'm kind of hiding out right now."

"Are you all right?"

"I will be once I get home."

"Well, I've been waiting for you to call because that's what I want to talk to you about. There's been a little change of plans on the rescue attempt tonight."

"What do you mean?"

Tommen was feeling better, yes, but his brain was still a little foggy as he tried to make sense of the plan his dad and Micaiah had come up with. It wasn't that the plan was overly difficult, but something about his description of the cave and the Time inside it just wasn't ringing right. What he said about it made sense, but Tommen knew that he had deeper knowledge about that cave, the Time, and everything going on. He knew he'd experienced something at some point, but the pieces weren't fitting together quite right.

"What time are you thinking to try the plan?" Tommen asked when his dad finished up the explanation.

"As soon as Micaiah gets off work, so it'll be about nine-thirty. If you can be at the bakery when they close and call him there, that would be helpful."

"Okay, sounds good, I guess. I suppose I should head up there at some point and see if I can't figure out what to do on my end. Something that doesn't involve getting sucked into a Time Trap for another century and a half."

"That would be preferable."

There was a bit of small talk after that, but Tommen could tell his dad was holding back on something. Something big or very unusual had happened and he wasn't talking about it. It might have been something at work or something with Laura, but he didn't like to speculate. Even just getting the gist of it and knowing that it didn't have to do with him would have been helpful.

When they finally hung up, Tommen poked his head up and looked around. He figured a library was a pretty safe place to hide.

Few people would expect to find him here, and there were plenty of places to hide, like stacks of books, aisles, computer labs, study cubicles, offices and other normally restricted areas.

The whole time he'd been out, he kept telling himself he was just being paranoid. Maybe it was his illness causing some sort of paranoid delirium, maybe he finally had a nervous breakdown. After all, schizophrenia most often presented itself between the ages of eighteen and twenty-four. Seventeen wasn't that improbable. But if he was sane enough to consider that possibility, did that mean it wasn't true? At the same time, didn't he always say that it was only paranoia until it was true?

He didn't know what to believe. He barely trusted himself at the moment. All he knew right now was that he had to get out of this dimension, and he had to keep Julianna from coming out with him. Everything in his gut told him she was bad news. Or was that just his irrational paranoia again?

Didn't matter, he decided. Anything he did to escape, she could very well copy, so it didn't matter if she came out with him or after him. Well, it might matter, actually. If she came out with him, he supposed she was less likely to hurt him for abandoning her. But how did he tell her that he didn't trust her? It was like trying to break up with a girl. The whole, "it's not you, it's me" routine never went over well. In this case, it really was her.

Well, first thing's first. He had to get back to Forbes Cave and see if he couldn't wring some clues out of it, figure out what deeper secrets it was hiding.

Cautiously, he stood and took another look around the room, peeping over the top of the study cubicle. He didn't know what he was expecting, really. A shot to the head, an arrow to the knee, someone to raise the alarm and set the dogs on him. As it was, he didn't even get a second glance from the librarian who was perusing Facebook in between patrons and occasionally looking through the book roster.

Feeling foolish, Tommen stepped out of the cubicle and made his way back through the library to the front door. It was a decent-sized library, really. He could honestly say he was impressed, and he didn't go around complimenting libraries that often. He wasn't about to hack into a computer and write them a nice note about it, but it was a nice place to hide out for a while.

His paranoia told him to take the longest route possible back to Forbes Cave, and he obliged as much as he could, but Traveling was taking its toll on him in his sickness. He was getting better, he thought, but he still wasn't a hundred percent and still had no real access to a doctor if something happened.

He stopped once to check on his arm, at least the fourth time that day. He could tell that it was beginning to heal, but that didn't mean it looked pretty. With the small blisters healing, it made his arm look blotchy, even as the melted plastic of his jacket gave him the appearance of a leper. He'd cut off as much as he dared, but it was still embedded in flesh and couldn't be pulled out. On top of all of this, there was still some lingering infection that was being pushed out, and the blood and pus made everything sticky and gross. He didn't have any sterile water to wash it, and he was too afraid to put alcohol or peroxide on it. Maybe he could just use bottled water? After all, they filtered and chlorinated the shit out of that stuff, so it should be safe for short-term use, right?

He made a quick stop by the hospital instead, grabbing a couple bottles of sterile water and gritting his teeth as he washed his arm. The small blisters were healing, yes, but the rest still hurt like a motherfucker. The nerves were still raw and he had to constantly remind himself to flex his fingers and hand to keep the skin from tightening.

By the time he got his arm washed, rewrapped, and was heading out to the cave, it was easily five o'clock. He made another wide loop before heading toward the park. Even then, he did a thorough check of the area just to be sure he wasn't being watched. He wasn't sure what he would tell Julianna if he did find her and she asked what he was doing, wandering around the forest, but he wanted to be certain anyway.

Finally, Tommen turned and faced the cave. As he neared the entrance, he had an odd sensation, similar to the one when he watched his old life, that sense of both seeing and remembering. The sensation was stronger now, though. He was seeing it now, remembering his first adventure into the cave, remembering his return several months ago. But he also had another memory. No, he was remembering his dream, the one where he — or someone else — was running away. There was the portal, and then a change. He could almost make sense of it, but one final piece eluded him.

He took the timeline and turned it back, looking for the people running away. He backed up and looked all around the valley for some sign. He found himself. He found Julianna and Cassius. Still he kept turning and searching.

Then he found it. A dozen Native American men, warriors from the look of them, running up the hillside while a band of British hunters gave chase. Tommen went with them, but only as far as the mouth of the cave. He peered in and watched as a portal was opened. Those fleeing did not think twice before running through. But the hunters were fast and catching up quickly. They struck one warrior and tried to bind him. The second-to-last warrior stopped, then made a daring charge toward the white men to rescue his companion.

But there was one warrior who did not move. Judging by his expression, one of fatigue and concentration, Tommen guessed he was the one who was opening the portal. He yelled at the other two to move it or lose it. The brave warrior grabbed the one he had rescued and made for the portal. At the last moment, the white men seized the man conjuring the portal, striking him and binding him. Tommen was uncertain about the fate of the other two, but it appeared as though they had gotten through.

Tommen followed the hunters as they took their wounded prize back to their little town. He was held there for a couple days without food or water. But then, watching him, he took out a small fruit from his bag which he managed to procure, and he ate of the fruit. To Tommen's eyes, he appeared to be having a one-sided conversation, and yet appeared completely sane. Was this the seeing fruit?

Eventually, he was brought out to be executed. As he suddenly made a daring escape, Tommen began to put the pieces together. The captured man's friend had become trapped in the in-between dimension. The fruit the captured man ate was probably similar to the one Kayla had gone to find, and it allowed the captured man to see his friend now and make an escape, gaining a lead only by the element of surprise and the mischief they caused.

They returned to the cave, and it was like déjà vú as Tommen both watched and remembered his dream. The two men did exactly as he and his dad had done, trying to open a portal around the one who was trapped and pull them back through. The hunters were catching up and still no progress was being made.

Finally, the captured man made a last-ditch effort to free his friend, trading places with him and being sealed in the in-between dimension while pushing his friend to the safety of Hlohi. The white men arrived at the cave but found nothing. The captured man had rearranged the portal, the Time and Energy of it, and turned it into a Time Trap. It was more than a hundred years before the white men came out of the cave.

Tommen released the timeline, sending everything back to the present moment. He stumbled back a few steps and eventually found a small rock to sit on. His dream made sense suddenly, and he'd learned a few things along with it.

The Time Trap in the cave had been set specifically for the white men attacking the Natives in the area. And that which was man-made could also be unmade, right? Just like an elaborate weaving could be unwoven. Pull the right strings and the whole thing comes undone. There might actually be a way to dismantle the trap and ensure that no one got caught in it ever again.

Second thing he learned, whatever fruit Kayla had gone across the universe to find could be found just as well on Earth. And, if the recent experience said anything, it didn't require any smoking, huffing, or rain dances. Just eating it appeared to be enough. Plus it didn't seem to have inhibited him in any way, not like drugs or alcohol might. So maybe if he could find this plant, he and the others could converse just fine without the need to find outlets and stuff for his phone.

He went back to the cave one last time, just to look and see if he couldn't tell what strings needed to be pulled. But he saw nothing. Only darkness, as a cave ought to be. Just as he remembered it the first time around. He could not see an explosion of colored Bands, nor did he see any strings to pull.

Time doesn't work here, he mused. *It can't be manipulated and it can't be seen. There is only the Akari.*

He did another quick look around before stepping a little farther in the cave, always keeping one eye on the sky outside, just waiting for it to suddenly go wild as he surged forward in time. He was only looking for clues. He didn't need to go another century into the future.

Before total cave darkness engulfed him, he stopped. Taking one last look at the mouth to ensure time wasn't passing wildly by, he faced the darkness and threw up an Akari Band. It wasn't as tight or sophisticated as a Time Band, but he got the job done.

Immediately, the Time Trap burst into color before his eyes. Not just his usual blues and yellows either, but he saw red and green and orange and purple. All the colors leapt to life before his eyes. Here he saw the strings and the threads, where Time had been pulled and twisted and woven to form the trap. But when he went to touch it, it was the same as if he ran into a portal. Shocking, to say the least. It pushed him back a few steps. The colors moved and writhed like a living being, a wild creature circling him, getting ready to strike a second time. Confused and a little afraid, Tommen continued stepping backwards until he hit the entrance to the cave. Then he turned and ducked out.

As he sat down, a wave of dizziness overcame him. He wasn't sure how he made it home, but he did. He plugged in his phone and did a couple of checks just to be sure he hadn't missed a couple months or years or anything. Everything appeared to be normal. It was almost six o'clock, which meant he had about three hours until they would try to help him escape.

What if he did it before then, though? What would happen if he ate the seeing fruit? Better yet, what if he put a concerted effort into using an Akari Band and then trying to pull out the strings on the Time Trap? Even if he wasn't able to escape per se, just getting that thing removed might be an improvement. Then he might be able to go back and explore the cave properly.

First he had to find the seeing fruit. There was no guarantee that it would actually do anything, but if it allowed someone in the real world to see into the in-between dimension, what would it do for someone already in the in-between dimension? Would it have the opposite effect and let him be seen? Highly unlikely, he figured, but it was worth a shot anyway.

He headed outside and turned time backwards once again, past the settlement of Charleston to a time when only trees sprawled over the mountains and game trails were the only roads to be found. He kept turning the time back and forth a little until he found a group of Natives; for the life of him he couldn't say what tribe they were from or what they were saying. He could only hope they led him to the fruit he needed.

After following them around through time fruitlessly for a while—no pun intended—he ended up returning to the stunning escape of the captured warrior. Once he found that, he was able to study the fruit a little better and commit it to memory, then backtrace the timeline to figure out where the fruit had come from.

It looked a bit like a peach, but with the harder, wrinkly skin of an orange. He followed the fruit back to a great battle at a waterfall, where Native and British forces collided in terrible bloodshed. The captured man was not one of the warriors, but appeared to be more of a medicine man.

Backtracing further—this being immensely difficult once he realized the original land and village was now at the bottom of a dammed-up lake—the medicine man had acquired the seeing fruit by means of trade, and it appeared to be a most precious item. And why not? If it could allow them to speak to the spirits, why shouldn't it be valuable? It appeared as though the medicine man had traded everything he owned to acquire it. But it still didn't tell him where to find it.

Frustrated, Tommen backtraced some more. Native tribes from the west traded it to these people, and, following them, Tommen found that it came from yet another tribe west of them. It changed hands probably five or six times before Tommen found the root tribe as it were, a young man of a peoples on the west coast, taking one for himself to see the spirits, then gathering several more for trade.

Tommen released the timeline and found himself standing in the middle of a northwestern forest. In the distance, he could make out a single road, straight and narrow and seeming to go nowhere. There were no cities, no towns, no houses, not even a dilapidated structure or rock monument. A mouse darted from one patch of safety to another while a coyote screamed in the distance.

He found his peyote peach. He had no way of knowing how much he needed, so he figured to start small. It would either work or it wouldn't, and this was in a realm of experimental drugs he wasn't sure he wanted to try again. The humidity was suffocating, but the coolness of the forest helped to relieve some of the pain and burning in his arm. As soon as he had his prize, he retreated to the safety of home in the mountains.

He'd seen the young man and the medicine man both eat the fruit straight up, but he wasn't sure he wanted to try that. He wasn't accustomed to doing these kinds of drugs. Weed, sure, but hallucinogens were in a class all their own. Maybe he should mix it with something.

He decided to mash it up and mix it with ice cream, going to a local kitchen store to "borrow" a mortar and pestle, then sitting down to work. These things didn't give off hallucinogenic powders or fumes, did they? He didn't need to get high before actually getting high. Was he seriously doing this? Was he actually putting stock in hokey Native American rituals? Sure, there was something to be said for homeopathy, but damn. A line had to be drawn somewhere. Was he going to be doing a rain dance next?

Maybe he ought to hold off until he'd proven to himself that simply using the Akari alone, without the need for psychotropic drugs, didn't work. On the other hand, he really was curious to know what it might do to him since he was already in the in-between dimension. Or just in general. After all, this was probably going to be the only time he would get to do drugs without having to worry about repercussions from his dad.

He felt a little guilty about it, as he picked up the mortar and pestle again and kept mashing and mixing, grinding the peach down into a thick paste. Then he visited an ice cream shop and stole a dish of vanilla ice cream. He added the peach paste the same as he might add any ordinary fruit topping. It looked just like a peach sundae.

In all reality, it looked and smelled pretty damn good. Had someone given this to him blindly and dared him to eat it, he totally would have. Knowing that it was made up of probably twenty-five percent hallucinogenic material, well, that gave him pause. He was generally cool with doing a little weed with friends, something to calm down, chill out, whatever. This was a whole new level of drug use. This went beyond weed, beyond bath salts and whatever else wackos could come up with. This was pure, unadulterated, intent to get high, and trip, and hallucinate who knew what kind of shit. This could go very bad, very fast.

He at least had the presence of mind to return to the cave before doing anything. Last thing he needed was to wander off a cliff while frolicking through a field of flowers. He got himself situated, adjusted his backpack, got up the nerve, then started scooping the trippy ice cream into his mouth. The ice cream was nice and sweet, as expected, but the peach was atrociously bitter. Was it not the right season? Was it too young, too old? Did he harvest it right? If he did something wrong, was that going to affect what he saw or didn't see?

Cautiously, he looked into the cave. As before, he didn't see anything. He stepped into the cave, mindful of his actions and trying to stay in control regardless of what he saw or thought he saw. Once he got a few steps in, he put up an Akari Band.

It was more difficult than before, though that wasn't saying too much. Before, it was kind of like trying to get a sheet of cardboard to stand up. Now it was like trying to get regular paper to stand up on an edge. It was more flimsy, and the bigger he tried to make the Band, the harder it got to control. Was that a good analogy? Did it matter?

It didn't make the colors of the Time Trap any less blinding, though. Actually, it might have made it more blinding. The colors were brighter and hotter, and he thought he might have seen shapes in there, too, like being mesmerized by fire. They moved, still, but not as a prowling beast. It almost looked like they were dancing. Swaying back and forth in a nice, gentle motion.

Then the colors leapt, taking on the form of a king cobra and snapping at him. Tommen fell backwards, instinctively throwing out his arms, landing hard on his left side. He cried out in pain as he scrambled to get out of the cave. The boulder suddenly shifted in its long-dead position, making the ground shake as it rolled, threatening to seal him in forever with the rainbow cobra. Tommen smacked hard into the boulder, just long enough to sting his pride before pushing through like normal for this dimension.

He found his little sitting rock and collapsed on it, breathing heavily, crying from the pain in his arm which seemed to intensify a hundredfold. He wasn't even sure how much of that had been real. Had he skipped any time since he seemed to have lost his Akari Band when the cobra attacked? Was there any good way to tell?

Dumbly, he looked behind him, back down the trail. It wiggled and moved and changed directions. With the trees swaying like grass, it was impossible to tell quite where he was or how he was going to safely get back down. There was still that sheer drop in the trail, he knew. He didn't need to fall down and hurt himself even more.

Fucking hell, he didn't even know what time it was. He'd once heard that hallucinogens fucked with one's perception of time, making eight hours feel like an hour or something like that. What if he'd already missed the rescue attempt? Well, it wasn't like he hadn't been in the right place. He didn't hear anyone coming up the trail. He didn't see any portals. Why had he thought this was a good idea? For as fun as it could be to do a little weed with friends, as a general rule, drugs were never a good idea.

He waited a little longer, or maybe a lot longer, before finally standing and carefully picking his way back to the sheer drop in the trail. Oh, this was a bad idea, he just knew it. Maybe if he got on his stomach and kind of wiggled forward, moved one leg over...

With the way everything seemed to move on him, at least in his mind, it came as no surprise that Tommen lost his grip and fell a good eight feet to the hard ground below. Only because he landed on his backpack was he spared anything worse than a bruise, though the injury to his pride was the worst of all. Thankfully, no one could have seen it. Still, he lay on the ground for a moment, reeling from his ordeal and not wanting to continue.

When he finally got up, he realized it was pretty dark out. A few colors lingered on the horizon in astounding clarity, but otherwise, it was late. How long had he lay there? Had it always been this dark? Well, if the others were coming, he would probably run into them on the path.

He did not run into anyone on the trail, but he did make close friends with a number of trees, rocks, a stream, and, of course, the ground itself. It wasn't even that he was drunk or had balance issues, but he was so busy fighting what his mind thought it saw that he could barely remember to put one foot in front of the other. And there was that whole thing about his shoelaces being untied, which he only discovered once he hit the parking lot.

At some point, he had the presence of mind to check his phone, but the numbers kept moving on him, untying and retying and all sorts of weird things. He knew they didn't normally do that, but today they apparently seemed to. Fucking hell, how long did this shit last?

Why was it so bad? Was it just because he had no tolerance for it? How much peyote did you have to smoke, and how often, in order to both hallucinate and pull off a coordinated escape from execution? He couldn't even walk straight.

By the time he hit the road, the white stripe had turned into a snake and the yellow stripes had become spiders. Generally he was okay with both, but not in such huge quantities. He unnecessarily tiptoed by them, hoping they didn't snap at him like the rainbow cobra had. Somewhere, in the back of his mind, he felt silly. He knew he was high. He knew he was tripping. But his mind said it was real. His mind told him what he was seeing even as he knew it wasn't true. The contradiction gave him a headache, made him nauseous. Or maybe that was the peaches. Maybe because he was tripping, his immune system said fuck you and left him to die of whatever infection was still in his body. He hadn't really thought through that aspect of it.

If the sensory overload wasn't bad enough out in the country, it only got worse as he reached the city. Lights in windows took off in cascades of fireworks and giant fireflies the size of small dogs. The traffic lights were like tiny suns in their intensity, and he had to look away. Headlights all seemed to melt into an endless river of candle wax that burned in the melted flame of the taillights.

Tommen's first thought was that he shouldn't have left the cave, just sat down and waited for everyone to come and rescue him, or try to. His second thought was that he never should have taken this hallucinogenic concoction in the first place. He was an idiot. But the problem was, he was still high and just had to ride this thing out. But if he was going to ride it out, then he would need something to help anchor him to reality. He had little desire to call his dad and explain what he'd done. He couldn't even come up with a reason why he'd thought it would work. He couldn't call Becky for the simple fact that she wouldn't understand, probably wouldn't stop talking, and God knew what he would say to her while under the influence. That was completely out of the question. So he only had one real option left, and that was the twins. Well, his dad had told him to be at the bakery, right? Might as well go there.

He moseyed his way to the bakery. They weren't closed yet, but cleanup had definitely begun. Sunday nights were slow and it was Jenna in the kitchen and on front while Micaiah made his way between the office and the supply room, gathering notes to send in the stock order first thing in the morning.

Tommen clumsily sat down in a chair and got out his phone stuff. It took some intense focus to navigate his phone, but he got the right number eventually.

"Oh, Tommen," Micaiah answered. "I was hoping you would call sooner or later. Are you ready to give this thing another try?"

"Cai, can I tell you something without you telling my dad?" Tommen asked.

"Depends on what it is. What happened?"

"Well...I'm a little high."

"You're h—what? I think there's a story behind this."

So Tommen guiltily relayed his idea which, at one time, before he was high, seemed absolutely brilliant. Retelling it, though, he had a hard time finding the genius in it. When he was done, Micaiah sighed.

"Well, at least one of us figured out what that fruit is. You didn't even have to cross the universe to do it." He rubbed his eyes. "In a strange sort of way, I honestly think you believed you were onto something. Maybe, under different circumstances, it can be more extensively and more safely explored. But for right now, I'm going to ask the usual question of, 'What the hell were you thinking?' "

"I don't know. I guess I wasn't."

"That much is right, at least."

"Listen, I know I fucked up. It's not the first time and it won't be the last. But I'm still high and I need something to, like, anchor me and help me ride this out. At least until we have to go up and try this escape attempt."

"You realize we may have to postpone it because of this."

"I was afraid you'd say that."

Micaiah looked at the clock. "It's a little after eight. We don't close until nine, and it might be another half hour until we actually get out of here. Why don't we see where you stand? If you took it two hours ago and didn't actually use that much, the effects might start to wear off by then, enough that you can function."

"What about Kayla?" Tommen wondered. "What was her experience like?"

"Not a good comparison. For one, she's more accustomed to things like that because of her own religious practices from her people. Two, the stuff found on Hlohi isn't like the stuff here. It's adapted to a new climate. I couldn't compare your experience to to hers anymore than someone who took LSD. Similar, but not the same."

"Whatever, dude. Just don't tell my dad, please."

"Oh, I won't. But if we have to postpone this rescue operation, you're going to tell him why."

"Fine, fair enough. I brought this on myself, I guess."

"Indeed you did. Listen, I still have work to do."

"But I need help. I need an anchor or something."

"All right. There's an outlet in the supply room. Plug your phone in there, call me, and you can read off stock numbers to me. How's that?"

"Do I get paid for it?"

"You get my word of secrecy on your drug use."

"Okay."

Tommen hung up, took his phone and monstrous signal booster to the back room, set it up again, then dialed Micaiah.

"All right, if you think you're competent enough to help me, then start helping," Micaiah said, and began listing off stock items.

Tommen did the best he could, sometimes having to go slow or read a number two or three times because the damn things kept moving. He could tell Micaiah was growing impatient, but as long as he was allowed to help, he would help. He could tell that the trip was beginning to settle down, though. It was still very noticeable, as the color pop and the wiggling hallucinations and a few other things were very much in evidence, but he was better able to read numbers and focus on what he needed to do.

"How are you holding up there, Tommen?" Micaiah asked. It was about quarter to nine, or so he thought. The hands on the clock were still pretty noodly.

"I'm okay," he answered. "I think it's kind of starting to wear off."

"Why don't you head back up to the cave and ride it out a little more on your own? I'll finish up here."

"You think that's a good idea?"

"Better than the one where I asked you to help me with stock while you're high."

"Oh." What had he done? "But you're not—?"

"I told you I wouldn't tell and I won't. But right now, just go back to the cave and wait for us to come and get this show on the road."

"Oh. Okay."

"You have everything you need?"

"Yeah, I think so. And I think I gave Julianna the slip, too. At least long enough to get through tonight."

"Good."

"But if I do manage to escape, won't she be able to copy whatever it is we did?"

"Maybe. But I won't be the one to release her. We'll worry about that when it comes. Go up there and wait."

"But—"

"Tommen, I'm not going to tell you again."

Sighing, Tommen hung up and dismantled his cell phone rig, hopefully for the last time. He took one last look around the store, snatched up a leftover brownie, then headed back toward the cave. Was he just hungry, or did hallucinogenic peaches give people the munchies? Did he have time to grab one last free meal before leaving? Probably. But Micaiah had told him to go straight to the cave and wait for them. It would only be about half an hour, and it was a pleasant evening, anyway.

He looked up at the stars, watched them shimmer and shine with brilliant halos and short trails as they moved here and there. To think of his tiny, tiny place in such a vast universe. Or maybe those were just planes, going from one airport to another. To think of his tiny, tiny place on such a huge planet that was so small in such a vast universe.

Initially, he jumped and thought the car horn blaring was for him. Then he remembered he was both invisible and things could pass right through him. Actually, the horn was to try and get a herd of deer to scoot their tails across the road, which they did after much indecision on which way to actually flee. Then, as soon as the car was past, the herd congregated back in the road to decide which way they wanted to go.

Tommen returned to the cave without further incident. Most of the psychotropic effects seemed to be wearing off, but a few still lingered. He sat on his little rock, then set his pack down to go through it one last time, just to be sure he had everything. Phone, yes. Assorted military-grade equipment, yes. Wireless stereo set for his phone that he'd stolen from the phone store, yes. Book, yes. Extra bottle of sterile water, yes. Assorted things he'd pulled into the dimension that he couldn't bring himself to discard haphazardly, yes. Looked like everything was in order.

Sighing, he stood and shouldered the pack, unsure what he was going to accomplish since he still had to wait for everyone.

"So, you thought you were going to just leave without me."

Chapter Twenty-Eight
The Master and the Student

Julianna appeared on the trail and walked toward him. The cuts on her face wiggled like worms. Tommen blinked several times to try and clear his head, but the image wouldn't go away.

"I never knew where to find you, so I figured I could just keep going and expect you to catch up when you were ready," Tommen said. It was partly true, after all. He never knew how to find her, nor did he know how she kept finding him. So if anyone was at fault here for not telling her stuff, it was her.

"That might be believable," she began, "except you gave me the slip at your house. You did some world traveling in hopes that I wouldn't find you, and then you changed the location of the escape on me. The traveling bit I really don't mind. Use it before you lose it, I suppose. But intentionally leaving, changing the escape, and not even leaving me so much as a note on the kitchen table. Now that's just rude."

"There's no guarantee this will work. We could have just as much success tonight as we did this morning. We might be here for another week or another month before we figure something out. And if I did escape, you could always copy me."

"You know, I'm beginning to think you might not trust me." Her tone was eerily reminisce of Rifun saying something he already knew but was sarcastically pretending to just find out. "After all I've done for you. Nursed your wounds, showed you how to move around in this dimension, all of it."

"You set me up and then left me. You only started hanging around at the prospect of escape."

"Wouldn't you do the same thing in my position?"

"Maybe. But what about the others?"

"What others?"

"Exactly. There's no one else here. Okay, I get that the population is pretty low and the suicide rate is pretty high. But I have found no one and nothing to make me think that someone else could be here. I haven't even found any of the ghost people who haunt houses or even other people. You never showed me how to bring things into this dimension, said it was too advanced. I learned that on my own. But what if I hadn't? Were you going to let me starve to death? Did you let others starve to death?"

"Of course I wasn't going to let you starve. I was merely focusing on one thing at a time. Caring for your injuries took precedence over teaching you that. It was just good luck that you learned it on your own."

Every part of Tommen was torn. Every fiber of his being told him she was bad news. And yet, his mind couldn't figure out a logical reason why. Because Micaiah said so? Not good enough. Because she turned over a book to Cassius which he would twist and use as some demented holy book for his vile schemes and terrorist activities? Was that really her fault? Because she refused to talk about the past? Walter had never talked about his past because he was ashamed; why should it be different for her? When was her punishment served?

But he couldn't shake the feeling that something was dreadfully wrong here. She was deceiving him somehow. Why couldn't he see it? Maybe it had something to do with trying to shake this trip. Fuck, he always picked a bad time to do drugs. Maybe he ought to stop.

"I understand that you mistrust me. Micaiah has reservations about me, and you trust him. There is nothing wrong with that. But his opinions of me are based on information he gets from flawed books. He may believe the Authored Books are the end-all, but they're not. That's what my husband was trying to explain when he was imprisoned and executed." She sighed. "Think of the elections coming up. One man watches one news station, another man watches a second news station. Both men have opinions and both stations are biased. What happens when either of those men hear a different opinion? They become offended, take up arms. They're convinced the other man is crazy. Why? Because they don't want to consider that their own world view is flawed and imperfect. For goodness' sake, do I even have to tell you about what's happening in the Middle East right now?"

"Believe me. I get it," Tommen said. "But you're using ideas and abstract thinking in order to pardon yourself. Normally, I would be more than happy to have us both escape and let you and Micaiah duke it out on your own, may the best man or woman win. But there is something about you that I can't explain, something that tells me this isn't right and I shouldn't let you out of here. Please, convince me otherwise."

"I nursed you back to health. Your wounds are healing. Your infection is healing. You're still in danger of sepsis, but you're not dying in your bed."

"Even Hitler had friends. If he said sorry and promised to be dirt-poor and work in a monastery for the rest of his life, would you pardon him?"

Tommen watched as she shifted her stance. Her expression was neutral, but her eyes burned. "Have I murdered millions of people? Have I even touched another person but in self-defense? Or in care?"

He let out a breath. "I don't know that you've killed anyone yourself. But I also think that you haven't stopped anyone from dying, either. Not when their death posed a greater benefit to you. Like your husband. He was certainly a revolutionary. I think you told him what to write. Maybe you actually believe the words came from the Author, I don't know. But when not enough people would buy in, you decided to up the ante.

"When you couldn't find support in the Akarin, you turned to Time. Maybe Cassius was already in power, maybe you helped him get into power. But he was a big enough threat that everyone had to take notice. And he was so heartless and bloodthirsty, that he could and would take the heat for imprisoning your husband. It was enough to get the attention of the more wishy-washy followers, that maybe he had something to say. That triggered a response from the Akarin who feared dissent in their ranks and a rise in power of the Cult, even worse if you formed an alliance with the Time industry.

"But Cassius isn't known for his mercy, and you needed to seal your power. By having your husband killed, it made him a martyr. It guaranteed followers of the cause which would later turn into followers of Rifun and Cassius, ironically. To keep your own name clear, you staged an escape. Poor widow fleeing her husband's murderers, carrying the prize with her wherever she goes. She gives one journal to the Cult as a promise, but takes two with her. When Cassius finally catches up, she won't give up the journals. One is lost in the scuffle—which I find and bring out—and the other goes missing. But then, what's the one that you…?"

Tommen grinned and shook his head. "You're the reason Rifun has been able to play God. You're the reason he knew everything about the murder cases, about the journal, where to move, how to move, where everyone would be, all of it. He's the business you've been attending to in between the times we've been talking. You took the journal that the Cult already had and gave it to me. Once I escaped— or we escaped—then you'd just take it back again. Journal recovered, founder resurrected." Now he nodded. "You really are the power that spawned Rifun, aren't you?

"But then the question becomes, why would you want to escape? You're the power behind the throne, the eye in the sky talking to the boots on the ground, the all-knowing power. And if you've been communicating with Rifun half as much as I suspect, I don't think you're exactly lonely for companionship. I don't know, maybe you are. But if you are, well, we're invisible and you know I'm not exactly a virtuous guy."

"You're barely seventeen," Julianna interrupted. "And anyway, you're not my type."

"Desperation does strange things to people. So obviously, you're not desperate. That means that either the urges are gone, or you're getting it elsewhere. Personally, if you are getting it elsewhere, I'd like to know where before I do finally leave here. But that's not the point I'm making."

"Then what is the point?" She was doing her best to sound bored and annoyed, but he could hear the rage behind her mask.

"The point..." Tommen said. "The point is that the eye in the sky has no power to actually work in the real world. A commander on the radio can't fight his troops' battles for them. But if you're the direction behind Rifun, well, Rifun is already pretty powerful on his own. But he hasn't been able to do anything for you either. And the only reason you took interest in me was because I might help you escape.

"In four days, we've come this close to escape. We're refining ideas and trying new ones that almost seem to work. But in fifty-plus years, you're still stuck here." He pointed at her. "You can't escape on your own. You need someone to open the door for you so you can step through. Why, though? If Time doesn't work here, but the Akari does, that means that either escape truly is impossible, or else you don't actually wield the Akari. Not the true Akari. Between the Authored Books and the journals, some things are similar, enough to gather some Akarin to your cause, but not enough to give yourself real power. That's another reason you needed the Time alliance. You were losing your power and needed something to prop yourself up."

Julianna sneered at him. "If I don't wield the Akari, then how come I can Travel just as easily as you can, and move the timeline here as easily as you can? How can I do anything here?"

"Because the Author says so. She says you can do certain things, so you can. Rain on the just and the unjust as the saying goes But you don't have the power to escape, which is why you needed me or anyone else to help you escape. You are bound here because of her words."

God, that sounded hokey. A more logical explanation might be because she didn't have enough strength or power or wasn't on the same wavelength as the dimension, man. But if all they were was words on a page, then who could argue with the one plinking out the story key by key? Julianna had power, but only because the Author said she did. She still had rules to live by.

Fucking hell, either he was still tripping hard or else he was literally going insane.

"Part of the element of the Akari is Faith," Tommen went on. "You filter through your prospects by telling them how hopeless this dimension is. Only the ones with Faith have the strength to even begin thinking about survival. Otherwise, they kill themselves or else possibly live a dreary life as a ghost. Tell me, have any of the other prospects, throughout the whole time you've been here, ever come this close to escape? Have any of them ever really made contact?"

Julianna's composure was wavering. Or maybe he was still seeing things. Nevertheless, she answered, "Communication has been possible as long as there has been electricity to communicate through, be it light bulbs, landline telephones, or email. But never to the extent that you have accomplished."

"Which is why you've taken extra care to be nice to me, make sure I was healthy and happy, even tucking me into bed like a child. You were hoping I might overlook the things in your past—assuming I ever found them—and consider you reformed. Barring that, maybe the confusion would be enough that I'd throw up my hands and tell you to duke it out with the outside world once we got there. I was just about ready to do that, too."

"What changed your mind?"

"Things started adding up." He chuckled. "You want to know the best part? I didn't even really read the journals or the Authored Books. To me, they're both still pretty weird. I went back and looked at history. Nice thing about this place, I get a front-row seat to anything I want to see."

"You still haven't figured out the mystery of Forbes Cave." Now her expression was that of smug satisfaction.

"The Native Americans used it to escape from white settlers. They went to the colony planet Hlohi and are called the Krydik now."

"Not that mystery. The one who twisted the portal into the Time Trap it is today."

"Maybe. But I have a feeling that mystery is pretty close to being solved, too. Just give me a few minutes to work off the rest of this drug."

"Hallucinogenic peaches?"

"Yeah, something like that."

She nodded. "The seeing fruit. Hallucinogenic. In the real world, it lets you see into this dimension, on top of the hallucinations. In this dimension, it just fucks with you." It was the first time he'd heard her really swear. It made him uneasy. "Now then, that was a pretty speech you gave there. And those were some very interesting deductions. Now let me ask you a few questions and get in my rebuttal, hm? Sound fair?"

Tommen shrugged. "Sure, why not?"

"The Native Americans, from the Inuit to the Aztecs, all worshiped their gods. Whether they were gods of the sky, the earth, the animals, named deities, they had their religions which they followed for thousands of years. When the missionaries came over— and your friend Kayla can attest to this—many of the people converted. Why?"

"Guns are a very persuasive tool. As are burning down temples or other religious houses and monuments."

"I will give you that. But words and persuasions of lifestyle are also very powerful. The Natives who converted for peaceful reasons did it because they believed in the white man's version of the Creator. Many would say it's the same Creator under a different name.

"Why am I much different? I simply brought a better, more simplified, more straightforward version of the Author to the Akarin. Yes, it contradicted some of the things which they'd been teaching for centuries, but it was the Author correcting them. No different than someone writing into a newspaper to correct some misinformation as propagated by the printers of the paper."

He rubbed his eyes. "Once again, you're trying to use an abstract element to defend yourself. You sent your husband to be killed as a martyr. Did he even know that he was going to die? Or did he think that a rescue attempt failed? You staged the whole thing. If it was just that, I might say that you learned your lesson, but you keep working with Rifun."

"You have no proof of that."

"No? I'd be willing to bet that he shows up to this party tonight. I asked him to come to the warehouse to help with the quasi-dimension. You only know of the change of locale, not the change of rescue plans, which means he might still show up."

"So you would punish me for trying to correct a corrupt system? The Akarin have murdered just as many —"

"Do I sound like I'm defending them?" Tommen cut in. "I'm not indicting them yet. It wouldn't matter since you've already done that yourself. I'm here to indict you. Or, in your own words, I'm here to express an opinion and make you consider that you might be wrong." He let that hang there for a second. "Regardless of whose version of the Author is right and which books to believe, you're a lying, murderous, conniving, scheming bitch. And I'm not going to let you escape. I don't know what plans you had once you get out of here, but I'm going to cut them out right now."

She glared at him. "If I'm stuck here, then you will be, too."

"We'll see about that."

Before either could make a move, they heard noise on the trail. A moment later, Micah, Micaiah, Kayla, and Walter all appeared. Tommen really hoped they had some kind of backup or extra firepower because they were going to need everyone they could find. Kayla still appeared tired, but not exactly hungover. Walter looked particularly stressed out. Micaiah seemed about as amiable as he always was at the end of the workday. Only Micah resembled anything close to alert and upbeat.

A quick track of Gravity got the group safely onto the ledge,

Walter still seeming a little unsure and disconcerted about the whole thing. The four of them picked their way up to the cave where they all peered inside, looking a bit like a cartoon where four heads appear on top of one another peering around a doorway.

"All right, everyone ready?" Micaiah wondered.

They stepped back from the mouth of the cave and Walter brought out his phone. He looked around. "Tommen, if you're here, you should have no trouble hijacking my phone and poking out some kind of message."

Keeping one eye on Julianna, Tommen stepped forward and touched his dad's phone. It was decidedly less traumatic than hijacking a computer as he opened up the messaging app and typed out, "Beware. Don't read these texts aloud."

The four adults huddled around the phone, their expressions grim. Tommen kept typing. "Watch out. Julianna here. Raving mad. Don't know what she'll do. Threat to all."

"So what should we do?" Micah asked.

As Tommen went to type out another text, a new voice spoke. "You should turn and welcome the one who is going to save our beloved friend."

Immediately, four concealed weapons were brandished as Rifun walked into view. He appeared only mildly concerned, like a dad facing off against his four young kids in a Nerf gun war. It was all a game to him.

"What are you doing here?" Micaiah demanded.

"Tommen asked me to be here," Rifun answered. "Seeing how I am the most powerful one here, it seemed only logical. And the thing he asked me to do, well, only I can do it."

"We're not building any quasi-dimensions here," Walter told him. "So you can—"

Everyone hit the ground as a shot was fired. Everyone, that is, except Kayla, who fired, and Rifun, who casually stepped forward to face her eye-to-eye. He chuckled. "I admit, that was both unexpected and yet so tragically predictable. Did you think I came unprepared?"

He lifted his shirt to reveal his bulletproof vest. It had blocked not only Kayla's shot, but the ones from the warehouse as well. "See, Tommen also asked me not to kill anyone tonight. To the best of my ability, I intend to uphold that promise as well."

Micaiah took a step forward and put his gun to Rifun's head. "Block this, motherfucker."

Without the ability to use Time and get a feel for what was going on, the only thing Tommen knew was that Rifun suddenly had Micaiah on the ground, his gun knocked to the side, Rifun's own shiny revolver pointed at him. Micah, Kayla, and Walter had their guns trained on Rifun.

"We could do this all night," Rifun said, holstering his weapon. "But it would only produce dead bodies and no Tommen."

Reluctantly, Walter also replaced his gun and bent to pick up his phone which he'd dropped in the frenzy. "Tommen, did you ask him to be here?"

Tommen sighed and poked out, "Yes."

Rifun nodded once. "There you go."

Grudgingly, Micah and Kayla lowered their weapons.

"Fine. You're here," Micah said. "What do you plan to do?"

"If you're not building a quasi-dimension—which I guessed as soon as I heard the locale was moved here, away from the shipping yard—then that means you intend to exploit the dimensional weakness here in the cave. But if a whole troupe of Akarin couldn't sustain the portal to get Tommen out, what makes you think I would make a difference?"

"It's not opening the portal that's the problem," Kayla told him, glaring at him. "It's getting him out. There's some kind of force in the dimension that's holding him back and tried to take Walter in with him."

"I see. And are you hoping that I will be able to overpower this force, or are you hoping to use me as bait to swap places with Tommen, rescuing him and sealing me inside the in-between dimension?"

"*Ní cuma an dara rogha leath-olc,*" Micah hissed to Micaiah. (The second option doesn't sound half-bad.)

"*Chuala mé sin,*" Rifun informed them. (I heard that.)

Beside Tommen, Julianna sighed and folded her arms. "Well, at least they made it past the guns. But we're not making much progress beyond that."

Tommen could only grunt his agreement as the bickering continued. Maybe this was a bad idea. Well, he'd tried to give them the slip, but they'd caught up to him nonetheless. Maybe he should let Julianna escape so they could kill her. But then, he had a sneaking suspicion that they would be about as successful as they were just now trying to kill Rifun, and Micaiah had literally had the gun to Rifun's head. Maybe his mistake had been in announcing the shot with a dramatic, Hollywood-style one-liner. Had he just taken the shot, he might have been successful. Details, details.

"So, how do we go about doing this without jumping a century into the future?" Walter was saying. "Regardless of whether there is or isn't an eye to this storm, we still have to cross the storm in order to get there."

"Not from this side," Tommen texted quickly. "Time doesn't work here. I can walk right into that cave and the Time Trap won't touch me."

"Can you open a portal, though?" Kayla asked.

"Well, no. But you guys can. If I can find a weak spot in the trap, you guys can open the portal. Rifun can separate the dimensions, and Dad should be able to pull me right out."

"It's a nice theory," Micaiah said, "but how is it any different than anything else we've tried?"

"Because this time you have me," Rifun chipped in. "And on the other side, you have Julianna. We can meet halfway and widen the hole in the barrier, enough to get them out."

"No. Julianna is not coming out."

"Why not? She's a human being, too. And she's been trapped in there far longer than Tommen has."

"She will only cause chaos and disorder."

"By that, you mean she will unite the scattered and sometimes misguided followers of the Cult. You're just jealous because the Akarin have no such leader to do the same since he was accused of murder and imprisoned. You just keep dividing."

"I already lived through your reign of terror." Micaiah indicated his leg. "I have no desire to see hers, too."

"You get Tommen, I get Julianna. Those are my terms."

"We don't need your help," Kayla hissed. "We can do this without you."

"Clearly not, else I would not be here. And to think, it was Tommen who asked me. Must be he doesn't have much faith in you either."

"Enough!" Walter barked irritably. "We don't even know if this is going to work. Why don't we head in there as far as we can, open the portal, and let whoever comes out, come out. We deal with everything else later."

"Walt, you don't understand," Micaiah said. "Bringing Julianna here would be like bringing Cassius back from the dead. Worse, even."

"And you will notice that Cassius is dead. Julianna is human, which means she can be killed. Rifun is human, which means he can be killed. Anyone who needs to die can be killed. But why don't we sort that out later and not try to butcher our chickens before they hatch?"

Tommen was less than thrilled with the idea even as Julianna smirked at him.

"Tommen comes out first," Micah said. He went on before Rifun could speak. "We've already tried and failed. If we're able to rescue them now, it's only because Rifun helped, which means he can do whatever he needs to in order to get Julianna out, with or without us. But we're not going to leave Tommen trapped in there. He comes out first."

"I would never abandon my Apprentice," Rifun informed him. "You seem to think I have not been looking for ways to free him also. I am insulted. And to think I felt honored to be asked to be here."

"Well, don't get cocky," Micaiah growled. "They're still trapped in there." The group of five moved just inside the cave, facing the darkness and the Time Trap within. "Ready, Tommen?"

Walter's phone pinged as Tommen typed out, "Getting in position. I'll help as much as I can."

"We'll give them until a count of fifteen to choose their spot," Micaiah said. "After that, we give it everything we got. We'll do as Walter suggested. Whoever comes out, comes out. Tommen first."

Tommen used a weak Akari Band to light up the Time Trap. He was still a little wayward from the drugs, as the colors were still blinding. But he no longer saw the full spectrum of color, nor was he attacked by any rainbow cobras, though the memory of it still made his stomach lurch a little.

He couldn't say that he saw all the threads like he did before, the way Time wove in and out and twisted to create the Trap and sustain itself. Had that just been part of his dream? Was it just a thing from his hallucination? How did he see it again, if it was an actual thing that could be seen? He did his best to strengthen the Band and maybe do a few other things that he thought he could do—hey, if he could do it in Time, why not the Akari, too?—but nothing he tried made the threads visible.

"Pick a spot," Julianna told him irritably. "If Rifun starts working to separate the dimensions, it'll be like a chunk of wood; it'll split along the weakest point. We can use that."

"What makes you think I'm going to let you out of here?" Tommen wondered.

"Because you don't have a choice. You think Rifun is going to let any of them walk away from this if I'm not out there with you? You saw how fast he can dodge a bullet. Want to know how fast he can draw?"

"Who's to say he won't kill them anyway as soon as you do walk out?"

"He's taken a fancy to you. He is especially appreciative of your use of 'please' and 'thank you' at your last meeting. When he says he won't kill someone, he won't kill someone. At least, not without good reason. Pointing a gun at him, I'm surprised he had such restraint."

"So we can all agree that if we both walk out of here, then everyone gets to go home tonight? Is that what I'm understanding?"

"Yes."

"Good. Okay, then, let's at least make it that far." Tommen readied himself. "We can kill each other later."

"Okay, Tommen, we gave you a little longer than a fifteen count," Micaiah said. "Hopefully you've found the best possible spot. Here's what's going to happen. We're going to open a very broad and very weak portal to start, at least until we find your exact location. It is advised that you stand together so we can reach both of you." Tommen could hear the strain in his voice. "Then the portal is going to close. Be ready because once we locate you, we're going to throw everything we have into opening another, stronger portal, just like we've been doing. Once we get the portal open and as stable as it can get, Rifun is going to do his best to separate the dimensions and figure out what it is that's holding you in there. After he's subdued it, destroyed it, whatever, he is going to be the one to come grab you and pull you out."

Tommen did not like the sounds of that. It sounded too much like the hostage negotiations at the airport, where Rifun had grabbed him by his vest—the same one Rifun was wearing now—and kidnapped him. What was to stop him from doing that again? His word? How good was that? Still, it didn't seem like they had much choice.

"I hope you're ready because here we go," Micaiah concluded.

Julianna moved to stand as close to Tommen as possible as the rescue team began opening weak portals. They only lasted a moment and sometimes seemed to move, as if scanning the area. As each one opened, Tommen noted movement in the Time Trap. Sometimes the Bands seemed to get sucked into the portals, other times the Bands broke around the portals. Was either more advantageous to their situation? Should they try and move toward one or the other? Should they just stay put and see what happened? Was there anything they could do to help?

"I found them," Rifun grunted.

Tommen glanced at Julianna who appeared to be in deep concentration. Maybe they'd made some kind of connection through one of the portals. Either way, they stopped opening, and the team took a minute or two to rest and recuperate.

"Okay," Micaiah said, breathing heavily. "Where are they?"

Rifun pointed in the direction of Tommen and Julianna. "That direction, about fifteen feet. I can't see them, but she and I made brief contact to let me know their location."

"Tommen comes out first," Walter repeated, straightening. "We can kill each other when this is over."

"Gladly," Kayla growled, her gaze never leaving Rifun. He merely smirked and winked at her. Tommen was surprised she didn't draw right there and try to kill him. And why not? He'd only tried to imprison her and make her his sex slave after all.

"All right, Tommen, this is the big one," Micah said. "We're going to give it everything we got. If you see an opening, take it."

He was ready. He was more than ready. He wanted to get out of this dimension, get some pizza, and sleep in his own bed for real. More likely he would end up going to the hospital first, but he was even okay with that.

The four welcomed rescuers seemed to gather themselves, ready to throw every last ounce of strength they had into opening the portal. Rifun had lost his lackadaisical posture, but Tommen couldn't decide if his intent posture was any better, like seeing a tiny pebble holding back a huge rockslide and watching as that pebble got moved slowly out of the way.

The opening of the portal brought Tommen to his knees as it sucked the air from his lungs. This was certainly different from previous portals. Unlike the others, which had been as simple as parting curtains or coming out of water, this portal was almost as

Julianna described, a chunk of wood being split down the weakest path. The only difference was, that path felt like a vacuum. He felt his ears pop painfully and his entire upper respiratory tract congest. He shifted his jaw, trying to make everything right, when he felt huge hands grip his shoulders.

"Come on, let's get you out of here."

Tommen looked up to see Rifun standing in front of him, draped in shadow. It was the first time he'd ever seen the man strained, his hair plastered to his face and neck, veins bulging blue against his skin. Weakly, Tommen lifted his arms to grasp Rifun's wrists and hope to make it out.

As he took a step forward, he still felt the awful congestion and pressure in his head and ears. More than that, though, he could feel the Energy that had gripped him in every attempt so far. It felt stronger, but more localized.

Suddenly he was in his dad's arms. Walter pulled him close and hugged him tight. Tommen was still dazed, but he couldn't say exactly why. He hurt, but he still felt the pull. Somewhere in his mind, he knew he shouldn't be feeling it. Something about it was wrong. With a migraine assaulting his brain, Tommen twisted in his dad's grip just in time to see Rifun pulling Julianna through the portal.

She was the source of the Energy that had held him back. He could feel the Energy pulsing off her, like a battery or a live wire. It was always possible to escape, but she had deliberately held him back until she could be freed as well. And now that she was free, she and Rifun would do as they pleased, regardless of any promises they had made.

"No!" Tommen said.

Taking advantage of his dad's divided attention and strength, Tommen broke away from him, his backpack slipping off his shoulders. He made a beeline for Rifun who held Julianna's hand as if escorting her off a carriage for the ball. The pair turned to look at him as he barreled down on them.

At the last second, Rifun put both hands out and cracked

Tommen in the shoulders. The right shoulder felt only bruised, but the left began screaming obscenities at him. He went down on his knees, fighting every urge to put his hands out, too. He waited until Rifun turned his attention back to Julianna before making a move, standing, twisting, and crashing into Rifun at the waist.

In the movies, the villain would be caught by surprise, go down, and the two of them would tussle a bit until the hero won in the end. Good prevails over evil, everyone goes home happy. Such was not the case here. Rifun was taken a bit by surprise, but he knew how to manipulate a situation. Instead of falling over backwards, he folded forwards on top of Tommen's head, effectively smothering him and not in a very pleasant position.

As his breathing began to suffer, Rifun dragged him up by the shoulders, making sure to dig his fingers into Tommen's left arm.

"Maybe a few more days in the dimension will teach you a little lesson in gratitude," Rifun said simply.

He pushed Tommen backwards, then, into the portal. He stumbled and fell, but just before Rifun could fully grasp Julianna and lead her out into the real world, Tommen stood and pulled her back. It was the one and only time Tommen used the cheap trick of pulling someone by the hair, but it worked, both on the element of surprise and the pain that came with it. He dragged her back into the in-between dimension. Before he could throw her down and escape himself, Rifun closed the portal. Tommen hit it at the last second, and the sudden surge of Energy from the two dimensions trying to balance out was just like hitting every other portal, a live wire.

On the bright side, all the pressure and congestion in his sinuses went away. On the down side, this was, what, the third time he'd been electrocuted in as many days? That could not be good for him, and he would probably have to see a doctor about that, too. Never mind *how* he got electrocuted three times, but what did he do about it?

Somewhere in the distance, he could pick out the vague sounds of an argument and shouting. Was he just that dazed, or had his hearing aids been fried? How was he going to explain that one to Dr. Polski? Maybe he could just say they were damaged in the fire.

He groaned and rolled over, trying to take a personal inventory while fighting blurry, muddled thoughts. Even his vision seemed a little fuzzy, but he could still make out the five adults. Rifun versus Walter, Micah, Micaiah, and Kayla. For an ordinary person, the odds would be rather extraordinary, something only an action hero with a scripted victory could dominate. Given Rifun's track record, the match now seemed oddly evenly matched, if not tipped in Rifun's favor. Now how was that any sort of fair? If there was an Author out there, why didn't she just say, "his strength was cut in half" or "suddenly, Rifun lost his ability to manipulate Time and the Akari" or something along those lines?

Tommen felt himself rolling over again, unaware that he himself was doing it until he landed on his left arm. Before he could think twice, he cried out in agony. Every raw nerve activated at once, from the still-healing small blisters, to new blisters broken open, to anything truly exposed, to anything else that could still sense pain and relay it to his brain. He might have blacked out; he wasn't sure.

Gingerly, he pushed himself up on one elbow. His heart was still racing, his mind was still fuzzy, and his stomach felt not a little queasy. He couldn't decide if he actually got sick or maybe just threw up in his mouth a little. The taste was still there, but before he could process much more, his head was suddenly pulled back by the hair and he whimpered at such a comparatively minor pain.

"You cost me my freedom," Julianna hissed. "But at least now we know what it takes to free someone. With that knowledge, it just makes you extra baggage. Rifun may yet hold some fondness for you, but with all the trouble you've been causing, I'm sure I can convince him that your sacrifice was necessary."

Some sense of self-preservation came alive in Tommen's mind before he could consciously register it, and he found himself rearing back, less like a horse and more like a goat with long horns that throws its head back with an intent to gore whatever has a hold on it. He felt

Julianna's weight on his back shift, and he was able to drunkenly slither out from under her and stand up.

He was dizzy and a little nauseous. He almost expected the cave to be on fire or something in some epic climactic showdown between hero and villain. As it was, the color from the Time Trap had disappeared, and the darkness outside made it virtually impossible to see. Rifun and the others had moved outside where it was decidedly safer. Tommen made to follow them, but he no sooner reached the mouth of the cave than a hand grabbed the back of his head and bashed it into the boulder in front of the entrance, solid just long enough to daze him before he fell through.

Tommen went down and blindly put out both hands. Again, his arm exploded in a tsunami of pain, wave after wave coursing through his body and overloading his brain, almost as fresh as when the burn first happened. Rather than try to stand and fight, he limp-crawled out into the open where the rest of the group was still arguing. He couldn't even tell what was being said, between his hearing aids not working and his own adrenaline and fear drowning out everything but his own safety and survival.

He had to get out. Had to escape. Had to make contact. He'd left his backpack and everything in it out in the real world, which meant no phone to call his dad. But he still had the option of manipulating other electronics. The only problem was, he had to reach those electronics. He got within ten feet of his dad when a kick to the ribs sent him sprawling and gasping for breath.

Julianna was on him like a rabid wild banshee. Prim and proper from ye olden times she may have looked, but she was every bit as ferocious as a cornered wildcat, glomping on him to pin him to the ground with the element of surprise, clawing and kicking and scratching, even trying to bite when she had the chance. It was just as well that she didn't have a knife on her, but it was only a matter of time before she got smart and went after someone's gun.

Well then, maybe he ought to get smarter and try something clever. What that was, he wasn't sure, but he couldn't just let himself get clawed to shreds like a Mr. Snuffles plaything.

He quickly learned how to use her proper dress against her, moving out of range where the fabric of her long skirt restricted her movement. A few sly moves later, and he managed to heave her off himself and stumble away ten feet or so.

"I will not be denied my escape," she hissed. "I am getting out of here, with or without you."

"Except you can't," Tommen told her, leaning over with his hands on his knees and panting. "You need me. Sheer outside power isn't enough. You need someone to act as a conduit, someone to want to let you out from the inside. That's why you held onto me."

"You're right. I do need someone. But I don't need you specifically. Rifun may begrudge me, but he'll find a new pet soon enough."

She ran at him again, but her fighting style was more blitz attack, guerrilla warfare versus the battlefield. He fended her off, too tired and weak to do much more than self-defense at this point. He hoped this resolved itself quickly and he was rescued because he wasn't going to last much longer.

"Here's one thing I don't get, though," he said in a moment of pause. "If you're doing the Author's work and spreading her words and all this, why did she imprison you here? Why lock you away in this godforsaken dimension with no good way to escape?"

"Perhaps I am being tested. I know not the ways of the Author. But being here was not without its advantages. The ability to keep an eye on things from afar, coordinate my followers, watch and examine history as it unfolded and not as it has been distorted. But now that time is drawing to a close and I will rejoin the real world once more. With. Or. Without you."

Tommen hadn't realized it until it was too late, but she had backed up close to Micah who had one gun out and was fishing for another. As she reached for it, Tommen mustered his energy and ran at her full steam, knowing this could end very badly. He grabbed her by the shoulders and went down, making sure to twist and land on his right side this time. As soon as they hit the ground, Tommen pinioned both arms behind her and wrapped his legs around her waist, holding her tight to his body and immobilizing her, a little trick his dad showed him once.

Julianna struggled against him as hard as she could, hoping to break him in his injury and weakness. Truthfully, he almost let go several times. But he held his posture, watching and waiting until the rescue team had calmed down a little and agreed to all walk away without firing any more shots. Watching Rifun go one way and the twins, Kayla, and his dad go the other way, it was less like a challenge that had been won or lost, and more like a promise to return later to finish the job.

He still waited a good five minutes after they left before releasing Julianna who had finally become still. She got right up with little issue, but Tommen staggered to his feet, ready for a nap.

"There is nowhere you can go, nowhere you can hide, where I won't find you," Julianna told him, in a manner that was very reminisce of Rifun. "And it's not just you that I'll be watching either. Your dad, your friends, all of them will be under tight observation. If I can't escape this dimension, I'll make sure that you don't either."

Tommen found himself chuckling at that. "Where did you find that threat? James Bond? Jason Bourne? Seriously, that is, like, so fucking cliche it makes my brain hurt. You're spouting hot air, lady. I'll get out of here, and I don't need you or Rifun to help. We're done."

He turned and walked away with every intention of looking like a badass, minus the epic explosion, but he figured that his coolness factor was at about a three or four. Hey, give him some credit for the fight, plus fighting while injured and exhausted. Had to count for something.

His hearing aids were dead or fried, so he heard nothing, but the sudden crack on the head, stars, and blackness were pretty hard to miss.

Chapter Twenty-Nine
Trial and Error

To say that Micaiah was less than thrilled to have Rifun show up was a gross understatement. His disposition wasn't helped any when Tommen admitted to inviting him. Maybe there was a story behind it. Maybe it was duress. After all, with Julianna present, she could be holding him at gunpoint and telling him to say that Rifun was invited. There were too many variables when it came to dealing with an invisible dimension.

Those variables were not limited to invisibility, however, but expanded into all the nuances of breaking into the aforementioned dimension. Such variables included how to not get caught in a Time Trap, how to restrain oneself from pushing someone else into the dimension, how to split or subdue the dimension long enough to pull trapped folks out of said dimension, and a laundry list of other details he didn't want to consciously think about. Maybe if he didn't overanalyze things, it would work out a little better. Reflexes versus active participation.

Truthfully, there was no way to know whether such thinking helped or hurt things. Had everything gone the way it should have, maybe they could have known. But when Tommen decided to play the hero and go after Julianna again to prevent her from escaping, well, things just kind of went to hell. Had it just been Tommen and Julianna, their mission might have been a success. Save him, keep her imprisoned, life goes on. But with Rifun standing right there, well, Tommen was still a hot-headed teenager, after all.

Micaiah greatly disapproved of Tommen's actions, but he disapproved even more of Rifun's subsequent actions, to pick him up

599

and toss him back into the in-between dimension. It was no small feat to open those portals, and he could see it wasn't much easier separating the dimensions enough to get them out. It was going to be at least another day before they could try any of this again.

"What the fuck was that?!" Kayla demanded as the portal closed.

"If Tommen thinks he's going to play the hero," Rifun panted, sweating and weak, "then he's going to learn that...actions have consequences...even for the hero. He can sit in the dimension for a little while longer and...think about his actions."

"He's wounded and sick. He needs help. And how is another day of 'thinking about his actions' going to sway him to your point of view, which is really what you want?"

"Because he will have little choice."

As he spoke, Rifun meandered his way out of the cave, essentially letting the curtain fall back into place and allowing the Time Trap to go back to the way it was. Micah, who was the closest to the exit, led the charge outside, drawing his gun and pointing it at Rifun. Micaiah sighed inwardly.

"You're going to get Tommen back for us," Micah said. "Whatever you need to do to get Julianna out, well, you know the secret now. You don't need us for it."

Rifun grinned and turned to face them. "You think we needed you for any of this? It was never about you. You are the ones who have failed to learn the secret of rescuing someone from the in-between dimension." He put up a hand before anyone could speak. "Don't worry, I'll spare you the suspense. It's about Tommen. But I knew he wouldn't come out for me alone. He would only come out for you. Really, I was just trying to kill two birds with one stone in the most humane way possible by going along with this dog and pony show. But, seeing how this all just turned out, I'm thinking I may need to use more drastic measures."

More guns were drawn, Micaiah's included. He couldn't say why exactly, seeing how the previous show of force turned out, but it made him feel better.

"And what measures would those be?" Walter asked.

"Walter, Walter, Walter. Have you learned nothing from me, in all the time we've known each other? Why should I tell you my plan? Obviously, your guns don't mean much except as a means to comfort yourself that you have them, and your abilities in both Time and the Akari are inferior to my own. Therefore, you have nothing to threaten me with." Rifun shifted his stance and did a dramatic, sweeping bow as best he could with the bulletproof vest. "I have kept my promises tonight so far. I have assisted in the attempted rescue of young Tommen, and you're all still alive. You are free to mark this day on your calendars as the day Rifun Ndolo spared your lives." He straightened and fixed them all in a too-familiar dark stare. "But know that those promises end here. If anyone attempts to follow or stop me in any way, then I make no promises on what may happen next."

With another, stiffer bow, he turned and left, waltzing down the trail without a care in the world despite the hard work and ultimate failure they'd all just gone through. Micaiah shifted his gaze to see Kayla fingering the trigger on her gun, fighting every urge to empty the clip and run at him like a raging polar bear.

She was the first to break with a snarl of frustration, engaging all the safeties and shoving it back into her concealed holster. One-by-one, the rest of them did the same, Walter breaking last. He reluctantly replaced his weapon, grabbed Tommen's bag, then went over to a rock to collapse like a sack of potatoes. Never had the man looked so old and worn out. Micaiah frowned and approached him.

"We'll get him, Walt," he said. "We've gotten him already; we know it can be done. We just have to figure out how to do it without Rifun."

"It's not even that that I'm anxious about," Walter said, sounding almost thoughtful. "Really, I just wish there was a way we could kill the bastard. How many times have we encountered him, and we still can't beat him? What's the secret? What are we missing? Whether it's us four cowboys or a tactical police force or a whole army, what is it going to take?"

"Believe me, you're not the only one asking that question."

"So, what do we do now?" Kayla wondered, walking up, Micah behind her.

Micaiah sighed. "I don't know. We don't know what happened on Tommen's side once the portal closed. His phone is here, but he hasn't hacked into any of ours to let us know he's okay. And we can't do anything without knowing what's going on with him."

"But how would we find out something like that? What if something bad has happened? I can't imagine Julianna is too happy about what happened."

"I'm not worried about them fighting; he does have the advantage there. But that's not to say that something couldn't happen. We just don't know."

"What if there was a way?" Micah said thoughtfully. "I mean, we all know it's called the Land In Between from which no one has returned, but Tommen literally just returned to us. Except for his whole, sacrifice himself to make sure evil doesn't escape thing, he would be here with us now. So we know it can be done."

"What are you getting at, Micah?" Micaiah wondered.

"So far, it's been all of us on the outside doing the work. Regardless of the physics on their side, Tommen isn't especially powerful in anything. What if one of us volunteered to go into the dimension with him? We're powerful enough that we might be able to do something from the inside. Like Rifun and Julianna meeting in the middle for location and strength purposes, maybe we don't need him after all. I'll even volunteer to go. Cai, you and I can touch and open a portal fifty-fifty, like we usually do."

"From the same side, not different dimensions."

"But it could work," Kayla said. "You're both well-trained in Time, and while Micah isn't as strong as you in the Akari, being twins has its advantages. It's easier for you to share strength."

"There are no guarantees it will work, though," Micaiah said. He looked at his brother. "You could end up being trapped there just as much as he is."

Micah smirked. "At least he'll be in good company. Better than her, anyway." He rolled his eyes and shook his head. "We're out of ideas and, from the sounds of it, out of time. Rifun is just as pissed as we are, and he's probably going to try something. We need to get ahead of him."

"Regardless of what we decide," Walter cut in slowly, "we can't do anything until we actually hear from Tommen and can reestablish communication. And even then, we can't try anything again tonight."

He was right; they were all exhausted. Now that the adrenaline was wearing off, fatigue was creeping in. Walter moved over on the rock so Micaiah could sit down and relax his knee. He hoped they rescued Tommen soon so that he could go without his prosthetic for a few days. This thing was killing him, and his knee felt raw. Yeah, the doctors said he should be able to comfortably wear his prosthetic without wearing, rubbing, or pinching, and to call for an appointment if he had any problems, but was this really the kind of stuff they had in mind when they gave that disclaimer?

"Guess we better go home, then," Micah said at last. "Get some sleep. You especially, Walt. You look terrible."

"I'm the first one he'll contact." Walter said it as more of a statement than a protest.

"That's true," Kayla acknowledged, "but, first of all, I'm sure you're going to be awake at every noise that even remotely sounds like your phone. And second of all, until we hear from him, at least for tonight and tomorrow, we should carry on like normal. That means working. Tommen knows where to find us and how to contact us."

"What about Rifun?" Micah asked.

She shrugged. "What about him? We don't know where he went, and we don't have a plan to deal with him even if we did."

"She's right." Micaiah stood, faltering on his knee momentarily. "We can't do anything more for Tommen tonight. He's just going to have to ride it out. Find someplace safe to hide and hope he contacts us. We'll entertain Micah's idea more in the morning."

It sounded like defeat, but there really wasn't anything else they could do. They had no idea where Tommen was or his condition, and none of them were strong enough to attempt something like that again immediately anyway. There was every chance that he was still lying on the floor of the cave, severely injured and calling for help, but there was also zip they could do about it. Micaiah hated turning his back and leaving just as much as the rest of them, but it was what it was. They had to wait.

Despite Micaiah's problems with his knee, Walter was arguably the slowest of the group as they moseyed their way back to the parking lot. Micaiah couldn't decide if it came from physical or emotional fatigue, having to open a portal and sustain it for an extended period of time, or holding his son who had been missing only to lose him when that son decided to play hero. Probably it was a combination of both. Even Micaiah was feeling it. Although, rather than feel sad about losing Tommen—again—there were some days when he wanted to kick his ass for running off and thinking he could be the hero of the novel and save the day. At the same time, though, Micaiah had done some very similar things when he was younger. He could empathize. Didn't mean the kid didn't deserve to be walloped upside the head.

"Who's opening the bakery tomorrow?" Walter asked when they reached their vehicles.

"I am," Micaiah answered.

"I'll stop by and let you know if I hear anything."

"I would expect you to stop by anyway so you can have your pastry. Don't go guilt-fasting on me."

"Of course not. I'm going to need the energy to make Rifun pay for what he's done to my boy."

Micaiah realized then that Walter's quiet demeanor had not been sorrow—or not entirely sorrow—but the quiet brooding of someone who is plotting the murder of someone else in the slowest, most brutal and inhumane way possible. Given the time he spent in

Beaumaris Gaol, Walter probably had a pretty good idea on ways to torture a man and make it last as long as possible. The thought was disquieting.

"Guess I'll see you in the morning, then."

It seemed the only thing he could say as he unlocked the car and got in, Kayla in the passenger seat. Micah and Walter got in their respective cars and headed out.

"So, what do you think?" Kayla wondered as they finally left.

"I think a lot of shit happened tonight, and a lot of shit is going to happen tomorrow," Micaiah answered. "I don't like how it went or where it seems like it's going."

"Where is it going?"

"It's going into a realm where none of us have taught Tommen anything useful in order to defend himself against Rifun and whatever friends he has left. Tommen wants to resist and fight back, but Rifun has not only been his only real teacher in the Akari, he also has a ton of strings to pull to ensure Tommen's obedience, if not his loyalty."

"You think you might be exaggerating a little bit? Tommen's a smart kid."

"He's a hormone-driven teenager who has been let down by every teacher so far except the ones on the Dark Side who have not only promised him instruction and power, but delivered. And seeing how he has basically zero belief in anything, therefore no moral foundation, he's liable to believe anything they tell him if it's packaged correctly. He is incapable of true critical thinking because he has no ruler to measure against."

"There's the innate sense of right and wrong," Kayla said. "For example, holding him hostage and shooting his dad is wrong."

"True, but that doesn't mean that he can't be made to sympathize and see things from their point of view. How often has a 'good kid' or a 'good person' turned to terrorism? No moral foundation, therefore, that moral compass of right and wrong is more of a sliding, situational scale. Stockholm Syndrome."

In his peripheral vision, he could see her frowning, but she said nothing more. In a way, maybe he was exaggerating a little bit. He certainly hoped so. He almost wished he could confidently say that as soon as they got Tommen back, he himself would take him under his wing to mentor him in the Akari. Except that wasn't possible right now. Other than being on the Akarin's Most Wanted list and therefore barred from accessing any of their resources, Tommen was also extremely critical of the Akarin still, and highly mistrustful of their impending civil war. Sometimes, Micaiah wished he could show the Akarin council just how far-reaching the effects of their bickering went. Tommen was a great kid. At one time, his mind had been wide open and ready for tutelage. This shit wasn't helping any, and Julianna certainly wasn't going to be any help. She would only confuse the poor boy.

On top of that, he, Micaiah, and Kayla were getting ready to leave. How would it look if he took Tommen in, taught him some things, then just up and left? They were only going to be staying through Christmas and New Year's, then they were gone. Five months would be enough for a good foundation, but who would take over afterwards? Micah? For how long? Someone else, maybe?

Too many variables and what-ifs, and Micaiah couldn't hold it all in his head at once. Too many things demanding his attention, all of them the highest priority. He'd hoped that the car ride home would cool him down some and help to organize his thoughts. Instead, the opposite had happened. Kayla seemed to sense the conflict. As he pulled in the little carport and turned off the ignition, she put a hand on his shoulder and gave him a brief massage.

His let out a breath and leaned back. "At least wait until we're inside and undressed to do that."

She raised a brow. "Why? Back seat is just as well. Not a common location and nobody can see."

"Maybe, but my knee really needs to soak for a few minutes, and I need to relax."

"Don't relax too much or you'll fall asleep."

"That's half the point."

Nevertheless, they got out of the car and headed inside. Micah was making himself a quick snack before heading into the living room to watch a little TV and just completely veg out for a short time. Micaiah went down to the bedroom to remove his prosthetic, then grabbed a few reusable hot and cold packs, threw them in the freezer for a minute in a Band, and collapsed into a recliner. Carefully, he leaned back in the recliner, wrapping the cold packs in a towel and laying them over his stump and trying to relax.

"Fucking hell," he whispered, closing his eyes.

Eventually, Kayla brought him some hot tea and found her place in the second recliner. For a long while, no one said anything, just watched whatever programming was on TV. Micah fell asleep on the couch; Micaiah knew that by his soft snoring. He felt ready to do the same when he felt the cold packs, long since lukewarm, being removed. Grudgingly, he shifted and sat up, rubbing his eyes and almost pitching forward out of the chair. Kayla took his hand.

"Come to bed, my love. I have an idea I want to try."

He shook his head. "I'll come to bed, but I'm really not in the mood."

"I'm not talking about sex. I'm talking about helping Tommen."

"I don't want to think about that either, honestly. What did you have in mind?"

"Come here and I'll show you."

He didn't really want to do that either, but if he had any hope of sleeping next to his wife, he had to get to bed somehow. While she took his empty cup to the kitchen, he reached over to the coffee table to grab the remote and turn off the TV. Micah didn't stir in the slightest. Kayla returned and handed him his crutches, and he slowly gimped after her, down the hall to the bedroom.

"So, what's this idea of yours?" he asked, sitting on the bed and wanting nothing more than to fall asleep.

She rummaged around in a dresser drawer for a moment before bringing out a couple incense burners. Then she untied a small leather pouch and removed several strips of what Micaiah initially mistook for jerky, then realized they were dried strips of skin from some sort of fruit.

"Is that what I think it is?" he asked.

"You mean some dried hallucinogenic fruit which will allow us to see into the in-between dimension?" She grinned mischievously. "It could be."

"Do I want to know how you got that?"

"Best not."

"What do you expect to do with this dried hallucinogenic fruit?"

"Burn it. Being dried and burned means it will be far less potent than it would be if we were eating it fresh, but it will still allow us to see Tommen and know where he is at least." She ground up the strips, along with some other herbs, until she had a fine powder. "It won't last as long as it did on Hlohi, but we don't need to be high for eight or ten hours."

"Take all the fun out of it, why don't you?" He was still skeptical about the whole thing, really, but hadn't he once wished it was him doing this instead of her? Doing it together seemed like a logical compromise. Maybe the smoke was already getting to him. His eyes felt watery and his throat burned.

Kayla took the little incense burner and placed it on his nightstand. While he remained seated on the bed, she knelt on the other side and closed her eyes, almost as if some spiritual trance where she was really trying to contact her Inuit spirits.

"Is it safe to drive while on this?" Micaiah asked. His words sounded fuzzy and distant to his ears even as the light got brighter and the colors began to intensify. As he stared at the smoke, he began to see patterns, animals and shapes and people and things he had no name for. When he looked at Kayla, she had an aura around her, like one might expect to see around an angel. Well, she was an angel, so that was no surprise.

"We're not going to drive," she answered finally. How long had it been since he asked the question? At least ten minutes. Right?

"We're simply going to use portals."

That was most definitely on Micaiah's list of things he didn't want to do. Even when he was high, he knew he didn't want to do it, and he visibly recoiled. For one, they'd already spent themselves when they opened the portal in the cave. For two, if they weren't careful, seeing how they were high, and they lost a portal, they could end up in the same predicament as Tommen. *Thanks for the offer, Micah, to share Tommen's fate, but we kind of beat you to it.*

Still, Micaiah put up very little resistance as Kayla handed him his crutches. Mostly he was just fascinated by the sharper color, the contrasts, the auras around most lights, and the slo-mo trails that followed some objects. It was astounding, but he couldn't say why. Fucking hell, but he was high. He was no stranger to alcohol, true, and it had been years since he last did any sort of weed or low-level drug. This hallucinogenic thing, though, this was completely new and it wasn't going well for him. He didn't like feeling so out of it. He had full control of himself, but in a delayed, relaxed, lazy sort of way, and his mind was warring with itself over whether that was okay or not okay.

Kayla seemed to be handling it much better, and he couldn't decide how he felt about that. It could be that she simply had a higher tolerance for it because of her upbringing and religious practices, on top of some of the shit she did back in the sixties and seventies. Or at least, that's what he told himself.

They did a quick sweep of the house, just to be sure Tommen wasn't hiding out in the guest bedroom or sleeping on the couch or anything. Micaiah hoped that was the case, anyway, that they really could see into the in-between dimension and Tommen was simply absent at this time. He hated to think that he'd just gotten super high for nothing. And this was the diluted stuff?

Next thing he knew, they were back at Forbes Cave. He was slow to take in his surroundings, and he cursed his sloth as he saw Kayla on the ground, arm over her eyes. In what felt like the world's slowest reflexes, he hobbled over to her, dropped his crutches, and sat beside her. When he touched her, she waved him off.

"I'm fine," she said slowly, her words coming out as blue and red. "Just opening portals while avoiding the Wheel and the Akarin hideout, only the two largest consumers of Energy and directors of portals in the universe. No big deal."

"After what we did earlier, this is not good for you," Micaiah told her.

"Don't worry. Only three more to go."

"Three? That's not good for either of us."

She counted them off. "Walter's house, the bakery, and back home. Those are the most logical places for Tommen to go."

"And if we use portals for all of them, going against the Wheel and the hideout, not to mention just the number of portals we've opened tonight, we'll be in the hospital right alongside him. Or worse, we'll be in the in-between dimension with him."

"I wonder what happens if we're still high and that happens. If this lets you see into the in-between dimension, what if you use it when you're in the in-between dimension?"

"Then you just get high. Tommen tried the same experiment."

"Oh."

They sat there for Micaiah didn't know how long before Kayla finally sat up. After getting her bearings the best she could, she stood. Micaiah followed, and they drunkenly began looking around the area for any sign of Tommen. Maybe he dropped something or made some other sort of sign to let them know where he'd gone. Problem was, everything he'd had with him was either still on him or in his pack which Walter now had. Either that, or else the diluted fruit was useless to see into the dimension, and they were tripping out for no good reason.

But, no matter the case, Tommen was nowhere to be seen, and there was no way to really tell how long they'd been traipsing around in the bushes. Neither of them had a watch, and when Micaiah checked his phone, the numbers went all haywire on him and he couldn't get his mind to settle down long enough to actually read what they said.

"Just so you know," Micaiah said when he and Kayla got back together, "I am never doing this shit again. It's just too fucking weird."

"Well, as long as no one goes and gets trapped in the in-between dimension ever again, I think we'll be okay," Kayla told him.

"We're only doing this to locate him, not because it's going to help get him out."

"Oh, absolutely."

That's what he told himself as another portal was opened and they stepped through. Well, Kayla stepped through. He hobbled through drunkenly and subsequently collapsed into Walter's recliner. If he was high before, now it felt like being high with a hangover. Holy shit. His good trip had turned bad real fast, but that was assuming the trip had been any good before.

The Forbes household was dark and quiet. They did a quiet search of the home, which was easier than one might assume, but Micaiah figured it had to do with every noise, even the tiniest pindrop, being amplified, like, a thousand times, which made it a little easier to stifle those small movements and noises. Or maybe it had something to do with how fitfully Walter was sleeping, tossing and turning and shifting and twitching. Micaiah pitied the man his nightmares, but knew there was nothing he could do about it. He couldn't take them away, and he certainly didn't try to wake him up. That would definitely hurt in the morning.

Tommen's room was empty of it normal occupant, though Micaiah could tell that the trippy fruit was doing its job; he was pretty sure Tommen didn't normally have an IV stand and bags in his room. When he went to touch the things, his hand passed right through them. Good news, the fruit worked and they could see into the in-between dimension. Bad news, if this stuff wasn't picked up and brought back through, it was likely to just sit there forever as the landfill of the universe. How sad. Did getting high automatically make him a hippie?

"No sign of Tommen," Kayla said. "Not even a ransom note, a threat, or a 'help me' sign. He's just...gone."

"Well then I suggest we get out of here before Walter wakes up and mistakes us for intruders," Micaiah replied.

Kayla readily agreed with him, but he did not so readily agree with another portal trip. The only reason he knew such a trip happened was because he woke up in the kitchen of the bakery. The only reason he knew they were still in the real world was because when he tried to get up, he knocked his head on a cabinet doorknob. He groaned and rubbed his head. By now, the fascination and excitement of the drug trip had long gone, replaced by a hangover from hell. He couldn't even be sure if his light and sound sensitivity came from the drug or going through so many portals in such a short period, direct portals at that.

Only one more, and that's going home, he told himself, struggling to get up and situated on his crutches. When he finally got all the way up, Kayla came around the corner out of the office. She didn't look much better than she felt. Even just her shaking her head looked painful and tiring.

"Not here?" Micaiah asked dumbly.

"Not here." She made a motion then, using every ounce of strength she had just to get her shoulders up far enough that they could slump and pass as a shrug.

"Kayla, we can't go through another portal tonight," he told her, trying to put an edge on his otherwise serious tone.

"Just one more, and then we can sleep in. Micah can Band us, too, so we'll feel fine."

"It's too dangerous. You're exhausted, I'm exhausted, we can barely stand up. Even with both of us doing it, we may not be able to get through."

"Then we'll join Tommen in the in-between dimension and get rescued together. But I'm not sleeping here."

Micaiah didn't want to sleep at the bakery either, mostly because he knew he'd never wake up in time to open without someone Banding him. As it was, both he and his wife were ready to pass out given half a second of even mild relaxation. Better to suck it up and just go through the portal.

He figured they must have done something right, because the next thing he knew, he was waking up in bed next to Kayla. It was still dark out, but when he looked around the room, he saw Micah standing in the doorway, arms folded.

"What the—?" Micaiah began.

"I found you passed out on the floor of the bathroom about an hour ago," Micah explained. "I used Gravity to get you in bed, and then I Banded you for a bit to help you sleep. Seeing how I don't think you two were getting it on, want to tell me what you were doing?"

Micaiah glanced once at Kayla who was still sleeping before sitting up and rubbing his face. His head was pounding like a motherfucking hangover from hell and his whole body ached. And don't even get him started on his knee. Anything he experienced from the hallucinogenic fruit and the trip was long gone. Colors were normal, and light and sound in general were about what he would expect from a heavy hangover. Otherwise, everything was back to normal.

"We went looking for Tommen," he said finally.

"Not the traditional search and rescue methods, I presume?" Micah asked.

So Micaiah gave the condensed version of their exploits, from the incense burner—which still sat on the nightstand, though its contents no longer smoked—to the portals, to all the places they went and the things they tried. Long story short, no, they had found neither hide nor hair of Tommen, nor any notes or letters as to where he may have gone.

"You think there might be some kind of in-between in-between dimension?" he finished, sounding stupid even to his own ears. "Maybe he got knocked into that when he tried to escape?"

"I don't think there's an in-between dimension between us and the in-between dimension, no," Micah said. "But I do think you're both idiots. What would we have done if you guys got trapped there, too?"

"Probably the same thing we would have done with you

volunteering to get trapped there. I don't really see a difference."

"One of me. Two of you. You guys are the pillars of power in our little amateur task force."

"All the easier it should be to break out from the inside."

Micah waved a hand. "Whatever. Listen, you guys got a good six hours of sleep. It's two in the morning. I'm going to bed. You can stay up, go back to bed, I don't care, but you said you're opening tomorrow. Or today. Whatever. So I'll see you sometime in the afternoon."

"Sounds good, brother."

Micah left, closing the door behind him. Micaiah saw the faint glow of light from his bedroom under the door, and then it was gone. Beside him, Kayla sighed and rolled over, snuggling closer as he lay back down. He kissed her head and she murmured something incomprehensible.

His head was pounding, his eyes hurt, and even with six hours of Banded sleep, he still felt like he hadn't slept at all. And somehow he had to get up in two hours and go to work. Well, he could probably make it three and push his luck a little. It was only Monday. Just the start of the work week, when those who catered to the business class would be knocking at the door at five a.m., and the business class themselves would be in a couple hours later.

On second thought, it might not be such a good idea to Band that much and push his luck with this hangover. But fucking hell, he felt like shit. Two more hours of sleep was not going to make him feel any better. In fact, it might make him feel worse. Did he chance a crappy sleep and worse day, or risk getting up now, going to work, forsaking all Bands, working like normal, and hope he didn't keel over in a pan of cookie dough because he was exhausted? Maybe he could get the work in, wait until Jenna came in, then have her Band him while he slept in the office. That could work.

Sighing, he sat up again, shifting around and noting how his stump felt better at least. He didn't want to wear the prosthetic, but just a couple hours while he worked in the kitchen wouldn't kill him.

Once Jenna came in, and Micah, he could go back to his office and take it off.

"Cai?" Kayla murmured behind him.

And there went his resolve. He swung his legs back around until he was under the sheets beside her once more. He pulled her close and kissed her. She still seemed pretty sleepy herself.

"Yes, my dear?" he asked softly.

"Where are we?"

"In bed."

"Oh." She blinked and got up on one elbow to look around. "What time is it?"

"About two."

"Are you working today?"

"Yeah. I was just about to get up and go in a little early. I don't think I'll be doing much Banding, the way my head is pounding."

"I feel your pain." She buried her face in a pillow for a moment. "Why did I think that was a good idea?"

"Because you are willing to go to the ends of the earth, and the ends of other worlds, to help a friend in need. Which is one of the reasons I love you."

She kissed him and snuggled even closer, if such a thing were possible. For a long moment, he thought she'd fallen back asleep, and his mind warred over whether he wanted to get up as was his original plan, or hunker back down for another hour and a half or so. Then Kayla shifted and looked at him again.

"Is the incense burner still burning?" she asked.

"No, it's not," he told her.

"Are you sure? Touch it, see if it's still warm."

He did so. As his finger disturbed the ash, a thin tendril of smoke drifted into the air. "Damn. Want me to dump it?"

"No, that's all right. I don't think it's doing much anyway."

"Then why ask about it?"

"I was curious."

Micaiah wiped his fingers and rolled onto his side. Fuck it all;

he was going to get him another hour of sleep.

"You know," Kayla went on, "the hallucinogenic fruit is responsible for a lot of fucked up shit that we experienced, including heightened sensation. Light, color, sound, all that."

"Believe me, I noticed."

"I wonder what it might do elsewise."

"What do you mean? And is that even a word?"

Whether it was a word or not didn't matter, and she showed him what she meant clearly enough. Neither of them felt too great, which was what made it almost hilarious. And yes, it did feel pretty damn good. It might have even helped to mitigate the worst of Micaiah's migraine. Maybe it was just him.

"So, is that a good start to your day?" Kayla murmured, stretching out beside him.

"I expect so," he answered. "But I think I might just lay here and relax a short while until the alarm goes off."

"What about not Banding today?"

"I think I'll make it a few hours, at least until Jenna or Micah gets in."

"That's going to be a long morning."

"I'll survive."

She kissed him again and he relaxed, stretching out as much as possible before letting himself sink into the bed, into his pillow. He might have dozed off a little, he wasn't sure. But he knew that when he woke up to his alarm, the incense burner had been replaced by a candle. That candle was burned low and melted everywhere. Then Micaiah blinked, and the flame went out.

Monday

Somewhere in Tommen's mind, he found himself transported back to earlier in the year, standing at the top of Evolution Park at Snowshoe Ski Resort. It was his third run out of three where he was being filmed for local ski talent. It wasn't anything official, like getting on the news, but the couple who was putting it on had their stuff used by tourism bureaus and they were pretty well-known talent as far as ski photography and videography went. Having them approach him and want to showcase him was like a dream come true, and he'd readily accepted their proposal.

In his blurry recollection, he started off down the hill, hitting the first rail and making for the second, sliding over both with the deft ease of a pro. Then he went for the jumps. With each deck, the jumps got a little bigger. He would never claim to be totally fearless, but he was confident in his abilities.

Once the main decks were behind him, he started down the right side, making for the quarterpipe. His goal was not the quarterpipe itself, but the ramp that went up the side and the rail at the top. He had a signature trick that he liked to do, and he usually invoked Time and Bands to make it look cooler. He would do a backflip with a twist and land on the rail, ride that to the end, then hop off down the quarterpipe and through the rest of the park.

It had taken years to perfect this trick, and there had been plenty of injuries in the process. His dad got after him, but he was never truly angry. Well, okay, yes, he was usually pissed, but it was the loving sort of anger. At least, that's what Tommen told himself. But in recent years, he'd been able to do his trick without incident. He'd done it on the second run, and the video people had been amazed at such talent in a sixteen year old. When they asked if he could do it again, well, hell yeah. Get it in a couple different angles, who knew, maybe there were talent scouts watching their channel. What if he got invited to Olympic tryouts?

Okay, so that was his Narcissism and his overactive imagination again. He wouldn't be approached by Olympic talent scouts. But he would be the envy of a lot of people on the Internet. Of that he was sure.

So it was that he approached the jump, tucking in and going full speed. And suddenly, he was airborne. He was free. He was like a bird. Except birds didn't do backflips or twists. Nor did they Band so the whole world had time to stop and stare. But he did.

And then, everything changed. As he hit the peak of his flip and began the twist so he could land on the rail, he felt something pushing against his Band. It wasn't a gentle push either, more like a forceful slam. And then a yank. Then his Band was shredded. The surprise put him off balance and he found himself staring at the top of the rail as it came speeding toward him.

He jolted awake in the same way he woke up for his alarm, suddenly, but with zero clue what was going on. Somewhere in his mind, Tommen knew that it was unlikely he was dreaming about or remembering the real event. He'd blacked out after getting on the lift after the first run, and came to with Ski Patrol hovering over him asking if he was okay. More likely, his mind was constructing what it thought happened using memories from a thousand other runs in that terrain park. The jumps, the rails, they might get rearranged and shifted here and there, but they were still the same old things. Add in his time spent talking to the couple doing the taping, and he could get a reasonable enough depiction of what the third run might have looked like. Combine his memories of doing his signature trick a dozen times or more, plus his imagination concocting what it thought his wipeout must have been like, and then he dreams up what could have happened that day.

It all sounded very logical, but a secondary thought lurked in the dark corners of his mind, and that was that he didn't want to consider the possibility that his mind did remember what had happened that day and his dream had been a real memory. He couldn't say why that scared him. Maybe because it had been an attack by Rifun's minions, not just a normal wipeout. Maybe because he thought he'd put that whole incident behind him. Maybe any number of a thousand different reasons he didn't want to think about right now, because the more awake he became, the more foolish it seemed to be considering an accident that had happened seven months ago.

That wasn't to say he didn't feel like shit. Literally every part of him hurt in some way. His head throbbed where he'd been clubbed over the head with something. His shoulders hurt where Rifun had picked him up. His left arm hurt for obvious reasons. The rest of him ached from fighting and running into an electric fence for a third time this week. Seriously, this was getting ridiculous, and it couldn't be doing him any favors. Overall, he felt like crap, and it was probably the sepsis making a comeback. Could it come back that quickly? He tried to think back to the last time he'd had any medicine for it. He supposed it was possible; it wasn't like he'd been making leaps and bounds in healing progress, more like shuffling steps. Any infections that lingered in his body had a chance to fester while it dealt with the electrocution and being knocked out.

Eventually, his surroundings started to come back to him, and he could feel beyond his physical body. First of all, the restraints. Those were most certainly a problem, and not of his doing. He might have hoped that Julianna would hold out a little mercy for him by being gentle with his left arm, hand, and wrist by using some kind of soft or padded restraints, but any affections she'd had for him had vanished after the incident at the cave. His left wrist was held in the same cold manacles as his right wrist, as well as both ankles.

Looking around, it was kind of like being held prisoner in some medieval dungeon. The manacles were like solid iron, the cell was made of stone, the door was wooden with a tiny window. It was like the whole thing had been taken out of some castle in England. *Or Wales,* he thought ruefully.

He was able to get his hand up around to the back of his head where he felt blood and matted hair. Great. Because he really needed that right now. Well, it couldn't be too bad if he wasn't sitting here, drooling like an idiot and couldn't remember his own name. Still, head wounds were nothing to take lightly; that much he'd already learned. Didn't make the headache go away, though.

There was no way to judge how much time had passed since he was knocked out, and trying to tell time afterwards was no easy feat either. He couldn't hear anything outside the cell, not the screams of other prisoners, no changing of the guard, nothing. Everything was eerily quiet. Trying to count off the seconds on his own got boring quickly, so he merely waited. If Julianna had brought him here, there had to be a reason for it. He just had to be patient and wait for the villain to come and deliver her evil monologue. Yeah, because anything like that had happened in the past.

Eventually he got an idea that he should just be able to pass right through these walls. The manacles were real enough, but the walls…

But when he stood, he found the walls perfectly solid. Had they escaped the in-between dimension, then? Whatever this place was, Julianna couldn't have brought an *entire place* into the dimension...could she?

So he sat. And sat. And waited. The chains were at least long enough that he could shift position a little so his limbs didn't fall asleep, but the skin on his wrists and ankles began to chafe. His stomach grumbled irritably. His mouth went dry. Someone had to come by eventually, right? Julianna to scream at him. Rifun to taunt him. They wouldn't have just locked him up and thrown away the key. Right?

What if they had? What if they were tired of his disloyalty, disobedience, and crazy antics? What if they really had just brought him here so no one could find him, locked him up so he couldn't escape, and then just left? What if they really had given up on him as some sort of special person? But he'd been crazy enough and smart enough to outwit them, so why leave him? Rifun always said he enjoyed a game. Wasn't this just a game to him? Or was it more?

Tommen forced himself not to panic, just relax and think rationally. That did not come naturally to him, and he was fairly certain his heart rate never went below a hundred for at least a few hours. If it had been a few hours. There was no way to know.

At some point, he found himself wondering if this was what it was like for his dad. Was this how he'd spent his time in prison? Sitting, wondering? No, this was too easy. Tommen knew he was pretty comfortable. The chains allowed him to change position. The cell was clean. He didn't even hear any rats. Here there was no screaming, no pleading, no death, none of the things he'd seen in Beaumaris Gaol. To even consider them remotely similar was an insult.

He jumped as the lock on the door clicked noisily. A moment later, the heavy door opened with a loud groan and Julianna walked in. She bore no food or water, nothing but the key to the door. Her expression was now stone cold and resolute. She was done playing Mr. Nice Guy, done playing games and pretending to be his friend in order to escape.

"I am not happy," she stated. "I am very displeased."

Tommen shifted a little. "I am very hungry and thirsty."

"I tried to help you. I did everything I could to ensure you got medical care to the best of my abilities, to contact your friends and family—"

"Actually, I'm the one who did that. You just up and left me—for, like, the third or fourth time—and expected me to figure something out on my own. Because you already knew the answers, but you couldn't tell me because you weren't willing to give the reasons why."

"Without me, you would be dead," she said shortly. "You would have gone into septic shock and been dead in less than twenty-four hours."

He shook his head. "Without the Author, I would be dead. She wrote you to help me. You are as much her pawn as I am."

In two strides, Julianna crossed the cell and kicked him in the arm. His burned arm. He cried out in pain and did his best to cradle the wounds. With the skin so thin as to be almost nonexistent, he began to bleed freely.

"I am a servant of the Author, yes," Julianna said, returning to her original position. "But do not presume to tell me her intentions. You know nothing of her, except what the Akarin would have you believe."

"Sorry to say, lady, but you're not making a great first impression yourself."

He braced himself for another blow, but none came.

"Your time is up, Tommen Forbes. Now that we know how to get me out of here, that is exactly what we will do, regardless of your cooperation."

"And how is that?" Tommen fought to keep his voice from breaking as pain still shot through his arm and blood seeped out between his fingers as he continued to hold the wound.

"If I told you that, it would only give you information to toy with to try and escape. So I won't be telling you anything." She made as if to leave, but when he started laughing, she paused. "What's so funny?"

"I can see it now," he said.

"See what?"

"You sound so much like Rifun. It's uncanny. I mean, fine, so you've been mentoring him from the shadows for a while, but that kind of, I don't know, alignment, similarity, familiarity, chemistry, whatever. Like, you can't just make that shit up. So, what is it? Are you like his lover, his mother, someone else? Please, there has to be an 'I am your father' moment in there somewhere."

"You will be greatly disappointed then when I say that, no, there isn't." She opened the door. "I suggest you get as much sleep as you can. In a couple hours, we will have a long journey ahead of us."

She probably meant it as a cryptic warning, but how long could the journey be when they had the ability to Travel and couldn't leave Earth? For fuck's sake, he'd toured the world twice and it had only taken him a couple hours. So if there was any sort of spooky or cryptic or fearful meaning there, it was sadly lost in the fog of logic.

Or maybe she was talking about it metaphorically, like the jump between dimensions was long. That was entirely possible, too. It was also very true, when speaking metaphorically. It didn't matter what kind of portal it was, going to the Wheel, the fortress, straight somewhere else, or into a supposedly unreachable dimension, portal travel was a life-sucking parasite.

But, regardless of how she'd intended her parting words, it did nothing to unlock the manacles on Tommen's wrists or ankles. Nor did it open the door or provide any other means of escape. Therefore, he was just going to have to sit and wait and hope she came back in a timely manner. After all, with no clocks to watch, six hours was as good as two. He could have just Slow Banded, he supposed, if he could use an Akari Band, but then he wouldn't have time to consider his options and means of escape once he did finally get out of this prison. In all reality, though, he probably wouldn't have too many options until Julianna was actually attempting her escape. The war for Forbes Cave, round two. Ding!

The humor only lasted so long, and not very long at that. His head still pounded, and his arm still bled. When he moved his hand and tried to examine the wound, he found that it was clotting, just very slowly. He was still losing significant amounts of blood, and that could very well hurt him.

Well, give credit to Rifun for one thing, he did teach Tommen how to Pinpoint Band. His Akari Bands were far less sophisticated than his Time Bands, but it got the job done, healing the wound enough that it at least stopped bleeding. He might have done more and tried to heal his entire arm, but he didn't want to risk fucking it up. Pinpoint Banding would heal his arm as it currently sat. If his arm had been broken and twisted out of place, a Pinpoint Band would heal it exactly as it was; it wouldn't magically twist his arm back and set the bone like a cast would. Burns, he reasoned, were far more complex, especially when it involved the hand and fingers.

Gingerly he brought his left hand up so it could be examined. He managed to touch his thumb to his pinkie and ring finger, though bending those fingers was a chore. As for his index and middle fingers, he could wiggle them only at the first joint, but he couldn't bend them. Well, he could, and he did, but only with significant effort and force which caused the frail, healing skin to split and bleed. The small muscles in those fingers felt like they'd been pulled or torn or some other bad thing. Either way, it wasn't good.

It might have been a couple hours later that Julianna returned; he really couldn't be sure. But he wouldn't say he wasn't grateful for the small bowl of rice and cup of water she brought with her. It hardly touched his hunger and thirst, but it would do. And it took the awful taste out of his mouth, too.

"I forgot to ask," he said, handing her back the dishes, "where am I? This looks like something out of a medieval dungeon."

"Not quite," Julianna told him, expression and voice still icy. "It's an old bunker in Pakistan that the Taliban and other terrorist groups liked to use in order to hold prisoners of war and train their recruits to resist CIA interrogation techniques. This was a pretty active place until the United States blew the hell out of the surrounding landscape and caused a cave-in. But it's amazing the places you can go when Matter...is no matter."

Well if that wasn't a dose of psychological warfare, Tommen didn't know what was. As she moved forward to unlock the chains from the walls—but not his wrists—he asked, "So what are you planning to do?"

Her expression was unreadable when she looked at him. After a moment of consideration, she answered, "Rifun has gone to gather some friends. Your troupe of heroes has exhausted themselves, but they are not as important as the strength they provided. Those who we are joining are just as powerful, if not more so. They will open a portal, just as we did in the cave, and you and I will go through. More to the point, I will go through. You can stay here for all I care, but I suppose it depends on how Rifun feels about it. At this point, I care not. You're no threat to us."

"Then why lock me up like this?"

She gave him another hateful look, but did not answer.

Soon he was standing, shackled like any of the dozens of prisoners he'd ever seen on TV and in movies. Ankles chained together, wrists chained together. He didn't have anything around his neck or waist, but he figured he didn't need to. His movement was limited enough as it was, and his headache wasn't making things any easier.

They did not Travel right away. Instead, Julianna took him on the roundabout tour of the old terrorist bunker. In all reality, it wasn't much. Most of the tunnels and rooms were buried in ten tons of rock, so any weapons or plans or other damning information was gone. He didn't see any bodies or parts of bodies either. Guess no one was home when the bombs hit. The parts that were open were empty, so it was just rock tunnels going nowhere.

Passing through the rocks was a funky feeling, and it dazed him a little until they got aboveground in the sunlight. It was high noon in the Pakistani countryside, and he felt every degree of it as the sun beat down on them. He did his best to keep his arm shaded either by himself or some other thing, but the heat still got him. That wasn't to say Pakistan wasn't a beautiful country with its own character, but something about being held captive by his own terrorist certainly cast a shadow over things.

"So if we're Traveling, where are we going?" Tommen wondered.

Julianna did not answer, simply grabbed his chains and started moving. They walked normally for a minute or two, through unfamiliar hills and mountains. Then they began Traveling. Comparatively speaking, it wasn't a very long Travel, but the landscape changed enough that Tommen could hazard a guess on their location. Between the huge river, the limited green expanses on either side, and the desert beyond, he'd place a bet they were in Egypt.

They were in a city of some form, maybe even Cairo. Streets were narrow and overcrowded, buildings and architecture ranged from ancient to modern, sometimes side by side. Julianna took him on a more direct route this time, through buildings and marketplaces, crossing dangerous streets and slipping down even more dangerous alleys. Finally they came to a building. There was nothing particularly remarkable about it except it was the only one standing in the middle of a desecrated block. Everything but this one building was rubble. Cleanup efforts were barely begun.

"Where are we?" Tommen wondered as they went inside.

"It's a church, not that I would expect you to know that." The voice belonged to Rifun. He waited inside with six men Tommen did not know. Rifun went on. "Next door to this church was a mosque. A couple weeks ago, American intelligence determined that a terrorist cell was in the area and using the mosque next door as a training ground or radicalization center, whatever you want to call it. A drone strike was ordered. Foolishly, it happened on a Sunday, not a Friday. But then, what do you expect from American intelligence, anyway?

"One of the Copts here is a Timekeeper. He pulled the church into a quasi-dimension in order to save the people inside. The Energy from the blast rocked the building and there is some minor damage as the Energy was absorbed and expelled, balancing out as it always does, but no one inside the church died. Some called it a miracle from God. I'm sure there were mass conversions around the world because of it. But for us, it provides enough scar tissue to use as a gateway, like we did in West Virginia."

Tommen stared at Rifun for a second before asking, "How the hell do you know we're here? Or where I am? Or what I'm saying?"

Julianna chuckled and pulled a wire out of the front of her dress, followed by a cell phone and some small hardware. "It's the Middle East. There is no shortage of military equipment lying around. Rifun was able to take your huge, clunky design and reduce it down into what amounts to a wire tap."

One of the six unfamiliar men, all of Arab origin, said something. Rifun responded to him in his casual manner, but stood and said, "But at any rate, we have business to take care of. Now then, if you would kindly take your place at the altar."

The church certainly wasn't like the ones back home with enormous crucifixes, long pews, Bibles by the dozen, and innumerable candles. By all accounts, this was very plain-looking, probably to attract as little attention as possible in order to avoid looting and burning. Did anyone know it was a church just by looking at it? Was this more like walking up to the door and instead of greeters, you had to give the secret code? While it sounded almost Romantic, like a cool spy movie, it was also terrifying. Give the wrong person the password and everyone dies. Simple as that.

Poetically, the altar—which was little more than a standard dinner table—had the most scar tissue of the whole building. Maybe the Coptic Timekeeper had been the preacher. Who knew? Still, Julianna dragged Tommen up there and positioned them both just so.

"Don't try anything funny," she warned him.

"Can I try something sad? Or joyful? Or smart? Or any of that?"

Irritably, she punched him in the arm, in the same spot she'd kicked earlier. As he sucked in a breath and fought the urge to scream, she said, "We're ready."

Tommen went to his knees as the portal opened around them. It was as bad or worse as the first time. Difference was, now he had no friends to rescue him. These people were just going to use him long enough to get Julianna out, then toss his sorry ass back in. But if she needed him in the first place, that meant that he controlled whether she got out here and now, right? She could have done this decades ago, but she needed a conduit. She had to ride someone's coattails in order to escape.

Well, that was a lovely revelation, one he'd learned the last time. How did it help him now, though? He could feel the dimensions separating, could see that for as tough as Rifun professed to be, he was not back at full strength yet, and he was wavering. Then he saw something else.

One of the Arab men was not who he claimed to be. Tommen wasn't sure how to describe it, but he could see that the man was wearing a Disguise. He wasn't even sure if it was a Disguise or just a regular old disguise. But he was only half-assing his part of the strength, instead keeping one eye on Tommen and one on Julianna, whereas the other five were giving it their all and focusing either on Rifun or on Julianna. Tommen meant nothing to them. So then who was the one?

The one man caught his gaze. Was that a nod? If it was, it was the most subtle nod ever. Was that a code? Could Tommen have been imagining things? Was he so afraid and desperate, he was grasping at straws? Could it be that—?

It almost felt like a balloon had inflated and popped in Tommen's chest as he finally landed back in the real world. The second trip was easily ten times worse than the first. But he was out. He was free. Okay. Now, on to figure out how to either keep Julianna in the dimension or else kill her once she got out. But then, he was hardly in a position to do anything, even stand up, much less fight. He felt Julianna's hand on his shoulder and he knew he was being pulled back into the dimension just a little, just enough that she could use him to get out. With Rifun weakened, his efficiency was...inefficient, and this had to be done the hard way.

Time was running out and he had to think of something quick. He could feel the edge of the barrier, feel the balloon inflating in his chest once more. Tommen watched Rifun take a shaky breath. As he looked to put one last push of strength into the separation and retrieval, and Julianna prepared to make her return, the mystery man gave a shout and lunged.

The five other men lost concentration. The portal wavered. Rifun turned, confusion and fury muted and mixed on his face. Julianna grabbed Tommen and pulled him close as if to use him as a shield, but the man did not appear to care. He barreled into Tommen, driving the three of them to the floor. Tommen felt huge hands drag him away from Julianna, and he rolled away without being asked.

"Run, Tommen Forbes!" the mystery man shouted.

At his voice, Tommen knew who it was. Assim Foyez, Captain of District One and a former student of Rifun's, albeit an unwilling one. It was no wonder that it might be him. Though he was Iranian by birth, he would still have enough knowledge of the culture and possibly passable language skills, enough to get by for this one mission, likely his last.

In his moment of revelation, Tommen missed the portal. Rifun actually went down first, but the five other men weren't far behind. The portal snapped shut.

Behind him, Foyez and Julianna were engaged not only in a physical battle, but one of the Akari. It was like watching Walter and Isthim all over again, each trying to use his abilities to gain an upper hand on the other.

Tommen hurried forward, bringing his chains up as if he might be able to choke Julianna. At the last moment, she turned and grabbed his chains, jerked him forward, pushed him back. Before she could do much more, Foyez had thrown himself on her. She released Tommen and slithered away from Foyez's grasp. The Persian man stood and jumped back, tossing something to Tommen. He clumsily caught the thing which turned out to be the keys to his chains.

While he fiddled with the locks and chains, he kept an eye on the fight, trying to determine what, if anything, he could do to help. Two against one shouldn't be this difficult. Tommen had the physical prowess to subdue her; he'd done it once already. Foyez had the physical prowess and some Akari prowess, or so it seemed. Maybe he was being naive.

The manacle on his left wrist popped open. Cold air hit the tender flesh, and his arm flopped to his side. Taking a breath, he put the key in his wounded hand. His wrist didn't want to get his hand in position, and his fingers could barely hold the key. Even when he managed to get the key in the lock, he could only get the basic position to turn the key with his thumb and pinkie, but he didn't have the physical strength.

Bringing his wrist up and praying he didn't get sick, Tommen took the key in his teeth and twisted. The lock clicked, the chains fell to the ground, and he bent over to start working on his ankles. In his peripheral vision, he could see Julianna had the upper hand against Foyez. He had only been a student of Rifun's for a short time and hadn't learned much. Julianna was the one who trained Rifun, which meant she knew all the secrets, all the dirty tricks.

The ankle chains came off, and Tommen had to fight to stay standing. He almost felt like he could float away. He took one drunken step toward the fight and went to a knee. Not only were the chains messing with him, but his hunger and thirst seemed to have caught back up as well.

Taking a breath, Tommen mustered his strength and threw himself into the fray, crashing into the back of Julianna and driving her to the ground. Now, though, with the gloves off, she was no amateur. While the initial blow had taken her by surprise, she managed to catch the landing and move in such a way that she unbalanced Tommen, keeping his weight off her long enough that she could twist around and deliver a most solid right hook. Even Tyler Freeman would have been impressed.

Tommen stumbled off to the side and she took the opportunity to kick his legs out from under him as well. Fucking hell, but this had been easier in the woods. What happened?

He didn't get much of a chance to ponder before she was on him, trying to use his own move against him, wrapping herself around him from behind. But instead of just pinning his arms, she was going for a full sleeper hold, and she probably wouldn't just stop at sleeping. Instinctively—because Tyler had tried the same thing on him many a time—Tommen drove his elbows back as hard as he could, cracking into her ribs. The force of the impact pushed her back a couple inches, as the reflex to curl up and cradle the wound released the choke hold.

Tommen scrambled away even as Foyez came up behind Julianna and grabbed her in a full bear hug, pinning her arms to her sides and robbing her of pretty much every advantage she had. He wasn't a big guy, but big enough and that was all that mattered.

"Great," Tommen panted. "We got her. Now what do we do with her?"

"There is only one thing we can do," Foyez said. "We must kill her."

"Ki—what? Why? Okay, scratch that. I get it. But...I mean, heat of battle is one thing. It just feels like cold blood now."

Foyez gave him an incredulous look. "It's only been fifteen seconds since she was trying to choke you."

"I know, I know. But I'm not called the Chivalrous Welshman for nothing."

"Little fucker," Julianna growled.

"Nope. Sorry. Still a virgin."

"What would you do, then?" Foyez asked. "She knows how to escape. It would only take one more person to accidentally fall in here and she has another conduit. She will not stop. Rifun will not stop. We must end this now."

"You want to end this?" Julianna said, grinning. "Fine. Let's end it. Forward and to your left a step."

Foyez's expression was puzzled until he looked in the reflection on the window and saw Rifun standing behind him. Julianna slipped the gun into the in-between dimension and started firing. First it was Foyez's knee, which made him instantly release her. Then she whipped around and shot him point blank between the eyes. The back of his head exploded and he dropped to the floor. She looked at Tommen.

"Now it's your turn."

"No," Rifun said.

Julianna paused and gave Rifun an incredulous look he couldn't see. "Excuse me? No? He has caused nothing but trouble. He is worthless."

"He is my Apprentice. I am training him. How do you think he got here?"

Tommen briefly entertained the idea of making a move, stealing the gun, then turning it on her. Looking at Foyez on the floor, as well as considering past experience, he quickly rejected that idea. His best move, then, would be to run and escape. But where did he run? How did he escape? Where could he possibly go where she wouldn't find him? Regardless of Rifun's words now, if she found him in some dark alley late at night, he had little doubt that she would just point and shoot. He wanted to go home, but how could he with her still running around?

"Do you have the strength for one more attempt at opening a portal and separating the dimensions?" Julianna was saying. She sounded irritated, like she wanted to kill Rifun right now.

"I do," Rifun answered.

"And your men. Are the rest of them really who they claim to be? No more surprises today."

"Give me two minutes to make sure."

Julianna merely grunted and looked back at Tommen. "We're going to do this again. If I'm not walking free within the hour, I don't care what Rifun says about you. You are going to die. Is that understood?"

Tommen swallowed. "In my defense, I had no idea about Foyez."

She pointed the gun at him again. "Do you understand?"

He nodded vigorously. "Yes, ma'am."

"Good."

Time had run out and he was out of ideas. His only help, which had been one-in-a-million anyway, was dead. His body would probably never be recovered. Now what did he do? He was free of his chains, but he had no more ideas than he had before.

Tommen watched as Rifun conducted brief but rather unorthodox interviews on the remaining men. In the end, he must have determined that they were who they said they were and they were loyal to the cause. Whatever. None of his business if any more of them turned out to be traitors. Except apparently it was still his fault and he would be punished for it. How did that make sense? Well, such was the mind of a psychopath, he supposed.

"Are we ready?" Julianna demanded.

Rifun looked about as exhausted as the rest of them, or maybe that was just the heat getting to him. He'd forsaken his usual sweatshirt for a regular T-shirt, and it was soaked with sweat. His hair was stuck to his forehead and the back of his neck. Perhaps the most intriguing thing about him, however, was that he was also burned and riddled with scar tissue. From his neck, normally hidden by a hoodie, all the way down both arms, was all twisted, sliced, branded, burned, scar tissue. Tommen glanced at his own fresh wounds, then back at Rifun's much older healed wounds. With all the rigorous dimension-bending and whatnot, Rifun's scars looked quite dreadful. Still, he put on a strong face, straightened his back, squared his shoulders, and prepared to try again.

Tommen had little desire to try again. He was tired of being stuck here in this dimension. He was tired of being in Julianna's company. He wasn't too thrilled about being in Rifun's company either. He was sick of being invisible, sick of being away from home, and for fuck's sake, he was sick of the heat. Egypt was not the place to vacation in the middle of summer. Looking around at everyone gathered, considering their intentions and abilities and the things that had happened thus far, Tommen did the only thing he had left to do. He ran.

More specifically, he Traveled. He just picked a direction, asked to be anywhere, and he most certainly received. Apparently, he had picked some variation of north because he found himself in the heart of London.

Not eager to be tracked down so easily, he made several trips to Cairo, then another place, back to Cairo, a third place, and so on, hoping to confuse anyone who was looking for him. By the time he was done, he was somewhere in the Chinese countryside. Tibet. Or maybe Nepal. There was no way to know, and reading signs certainly didn't help seeing how he couldn't actually read the signs.

He had to get out of here and he had to do it now. The only way that he knew of to create that much Energy in one shot, that he couldn't do himself and a whole army of Akarin apparently couldn't do, was a bona fide explosion. He didn't feel like getting too close to a wildfire, though California had no shortage of them, but he had other options. He was in China, after all.

His paranoia still making most of his decisions for him, he did several more decoy trips before actually going after what he figured he needed. It was probably overkill, really, but he was going to take no chances. He took a few smaller items, just in case he didn't need anything big, but when in doubt, or if he had to make a quick exit, go big or go home.

Next he had to pick his location. The obvious choice was at least somewhere in North America, preferably the United States. The plausible story would have him return to the camp or somewhere near where the search and rescue teams were looking. Really, he couldn't see any reason not to. It wasn't like Julianna and Rifun didn't know where he lived. He wasn't exactly a master of disguise and being in cognito and living secret lives. There was no advantage to not returning home in his home territory when he would just be returned to his dad anyway. He really wasn't into the whole, faking his death so he could spare his loved ones emotional distress. Seriously. Julianna and Rifun knew where he lived. That pretty much negated everything.

Well, he might as well go back to Forbes Cave. They'd had good success there, so he knew it could be done. But he was going to have to get moving quick, because Julianna and the others could already be there. Well, maybe not Rifun, but she could be.

So Tommen hopped the Pacific into California and headed east. When he got home, it was about three in the morning or so. His dad was still asleep. After doing a quick check of the house, he went up to Forbes Cave and slipped inside.

He'd just taken the first batch of small fireworks out of the bag when he heard a voice behind him.

"You are so predictable."

He turned and found himself staring down the business end of a pistol, Julianna's slender hand on the grip, long finger on the trigger.

"I've had enough of this. I don't care what Rifun says. He answers to me anyway. Goodbye, Tommen."

"Stop," a new voice commanded.

Tommen looked past Julianna to see a man standing in the mouth of the cave, though it was too dark to make out any features.

"Stay out of this!" Julianna hissed. "He's mine!"

"He broke that bond. He is useless to you as a conduit. And I will not let you harm him."

"Yeah? Try and stop me."

In that millionth or billionth of a second, several things happened. First, Tommen Akari Banded and dodged to one side. Second, Julianna pulled the trigger, sending a bullet speeding toward him at a thousand feet per second. Third, the mystery man moved forward with lightning speed to grab Julianna and the gun. He picked her up, twisted her around, and seemed to throw her out of the cave like a baseball. Then he went outside after her.

As Tommen crept forward, he saw that they were fighting. Julianna was throwing everything she had at the mystery man, still impossible to make out in the dim moonlight, but he was ready for her. He dodged blows, bullets, and a range of Akari attacks. Then, in one impossible move, he blocked one blow, then came around and hit her square in the chest. Had she been lying down, it would have been the perfect CPR compression. She went skidding back across the ground in a manner only seen in fake Hollywood action movies.

She straightened and tried to catch her breath, her expression stunned. In that moment, she also seemed to realize her gun had been taken from her as well. She looked at the man, completely bewildered. She was the master of this dimension after all. How did this happen? Finally, when he took several menacing steps toward her, she turned and fled down the trail.

The man did not pursue. As Tommen crept out of his hiding

spot, the man turned and could be seen.

"You are safe now, Tommen. Please allow me to introduce myself. I'm—"

"Chandler."

Chapter Thirty-One
Chandler

I t's really you," Tommen said. "You actually exist."

"Of course I do," Chandler replied. "The same as you."

"No way, dude. You're like, talking to people in their dreams, appearing and disappearing, handing out stupid ass riddles left and right. You're like a fucking ghost prophet."

"Something similar could be said about you, the way you walk through walls and hijack electronics. Imagine all the mayhem you could cause."

Tommen grinned. "I don't have to imagine."

"Precisely. Now then, about your escape."

"Yeah!" Tommen glanced at the fireworks he'd set up. "Am I about to blow myself up?"

"Let's just say it wouldn't work out very well for you."

"Then what do I do? I've been freed before. I've escaped fucking twice already, but I can't hold onto it."

Chandler chuckled. "You could have, actually, but you chose selflessness over selfishness, trying to rid the world of evil. But you are not strong enough for that yet."

"Cool. So are you going to, like, show me the ways of the Force, or the Akari, or whatever?"

"Why should I?"

Tommen blinked. "Why...shouldn't you?"

"Do I look like Yoda?"

"Um, no. Actually you still kind of look like Saul."

"Well, fortunately for you, I'm not Saul."

They stood there for a minute, staring at each other, Chandler smirking, Tommen trying to determine his intentions. Finally he said, "So then why are you here?"

"Once you broke the bond with Julianna, I was able to step in and rescue you."

"Is she more powerful than you?"

"No, but it was a matter of will on your part. As long as you were willing to work with her and permit her escape, I could do nothing. As soon as you decided you wanted nothing more to do with her and did not want her to escape, then I stepped in."

"Kind of dramatic timing, wasn't it? I mean, what if she'd pulled the trigger half a second before you showed up?"

"I knew what she was up to, and I knew what was going to happen. No worries."

"Then why not help me in the prison? Believe me, I didn't want anything to do with her then. And Foyez might still be alive."

"The will to escape was the final key, that final act of selflessness, overcoming your own fear, to step out in faith to prevent her from leaving the dimension, even though she could have killed you easily. After that, well, as she said, you are pretty predictable."

"Okay, fine, whatever. Can you help me get home or not?"

Chandler dipped his head. "That I can do, but first, we need to do something about your wounds."

Tommen looked at his arm. "Can you heal it, reverse the burns and make it like it never happened?"

"No. But infection is still ravaging your body, and it will not go over well when you do escape. Furthermore, Julianna has gone to get help. If they find you here, they will kill you."

Chandler made as if to leave, but Tommen hung back for just a moment. "So even if I do escape by myself without her, all of this would have been for nothing, basically. She'll still get out, now that she knows how to do it. All it will take is deliberately sending someone into this dimension, then repeating what we did here or in the church. Foyez died for nothing."

"Tell me something, Tommen. Why did you try harder to escape the second time versus the first? Nothing had changed except his death."

"Yeah, and my chains were gone."

Chandler grinned. "Precisely."

That was sort of vague, mystical, riddle bullshit that made any relationship with Chandler love-hate at best. Reluctantly, Tommen followed him down the trail, away from the cave.

"Can I ask you something?" Tommen inquired.

Chandler did not stop or look at him. "I believe you just did, but go ahead."

"You don't seem to be...I mean you're not...Well, what I mean..."

"Yes?"

"You're not...crazy. Okay, you seriously piss me off with all the fuckery you've been dragging me through—and I'm sure Micaiah might have a few words for you—but you're here, right? Like, you are in this dimension physically, same as I am?"

He found out a moment later as the man stopped short and Tommen ran into his back. Then he continued on, saying, "Was that proof enough?"

"I guess. But why aren't you—?"

"Going mad from isolation, desperate to escape by any means necessary? What makes me different from Julianna?"

"Something like that."

"When one is on a quest for power, the thirst can never be satisfied. She has mastered this dimension and so seeks more power, more authority. But, as you can see, the population is lacking, and she can't rule over those who can't even see her and marvel at her power.

"As for me, this is my calling. This is my home. I have been placed here for a purpose. Few know of my existence, fewer still show me any sort of gratitude or respect. But as long as my first duty is to the Author and her work and appreciation, I need nothing more. I seek no power, no fame or glory. I simply do my job and the rest is taken care of."

"Hell of a workplace. Must be nice to have no coworkers to fuck it up. Do you get benefits, too?"

"The benefits are endless."

Sorry I asked, Tommen mused silently, not wanting to hear another success story from some particular religion, as if comparing it to a twelve step program or new gym fad. Maybe things were working out for him and he was happy, that was great. But so far, in the real world, Rifun had launched a coup, Micaiah had lost his leg and led a revolution to counter that coup, only to have his thanks come in the form of being banned and silenced, plus the whole Akarin civil war. Tommen hadn't seen much of that, but civil war never sounded good, and it certainly wasn't a huge boost for tourism.

They made their way down the trail once more. On a normal day, Tommen could have made the trek with little issue. Now, though, he was exhausted already from the events of the morning, and then to factor in the infection only made things worse. His body was being torn in a thousand different directions, trying to fight the infection, keep up with the hike, and carry on other normal functions. He just couldn't do it all. When they finally got back to the main pavilion, he took a minute to sit and rest.

"Why don't we Travel to wherever we're going?" he asked, breathing heavily.

"It will leave a wake that Julianna can follow," Chandler replied gravely, "Better to make her believe you already escaped with my help."

"We are doing that, right?"

"Of course, but you must be tended to first. It will not take long."

With that, he set off once more, Tommen reluctantly following. It wasn't a long walk, really, and going down into the valley was certainly easier than trying to climb mountains. But before they crossed the highway into the actual city, they turned a different direction, heading back into the hills.

"Wait, shouldn't we be going that way, to the hospital?" Tommen asked.

"What for? I have the medicine you need already prepared. We'll go up to my safe house, tend your wounds, get something to eat, and then send you home."

It sounded so simple, like it might actually happen. Did Tommen dare to hope? How did he know Chandler wasn't just another Julianna, preying on the situation, like rival gangs fighting for new blood? At the same time, even if that were true, what could he do about it? He wasn't strong enough to fight back.

In an odd twist of fate, Tommen found himself wishing for a fight with Tyler Freeman. At least that was comfortable, familiar. It was a fight and an adversary he knew. Sure, he was pretty much guaranteed to get his ass kicked, but there was a beginning and an end and everything was clearly defined. Everyone knew who was fighting, who the sides were. There was none of this guessing and double-crossing and complex plots and plans and schemes. People didn't die.

Well, at least he had that going for him, that when he returned to school, Tyler wouldn't be there. His younger brother would, but the old, familiar grudge match was done and over with. Maybe the next two years of school would be halfway decent. Did he dare hope so?

Tommen was willing to bet that they Traveled just a little bit up the mountains, or else he'd sleepwalked part of the way. The next thing he knew, Chandler was telling him to pay attention because they were almost to his safe house and the last part of the climb was a little more physically grueling.

If he had been expecting a quaint little cabin in the woods, he was sorely disappointed. The safe house was part house, part cave. Actually, it was more of a log cabin built out and around a cave. There was a door and a window, a single room which more resembled an enclosed balcony, a place to look out and observe one's surroundings. But then it led directly into a cave which served as the main living area. While cooler than the outside, it was by no means cold. A short distance into the cave, a fire burned low, hot coals and a small chunk of wood glowing red.

Chandler took a moment to stoke the fire and bring flames back to life. Warmth and light brought the dank cave to life, and Tommen saw it was a little more homey than he'd originally given it credit for.

There was a single rocking chair of the highest quality, fine wood, smooth curves and contours, and professional assembly. Along one wall of the cave, cabinets of similar quality made something like a kitchen, complete with a finely cut stone wash basin. On the other side, holes bored, cut, or chiseled out of the rock made shelves for goods and personal belongings, most of which seemed to be candles or candle related. Woven rugs and mats carpeted the floor with a noticeable four foot ring around the fire pit. Large animal hides adorned the walls to keep the chill of the bare rock at bay.

Chandler continued moving about the room, gathering a pot and a pan and various cooking items. He glanced at Tommen, still at the threshold between log cabin and cave.

"Come in. There is no need to be shy. Sit by the fire where it's warm."

Tommen took a tentative step into the cave. He wasn't sure what he was expecting, but his paranoia told him to be on guard always. He did as the man suggested and found a spot by the fire where he hoped he would be out of the way. He'd never realized until now how jumpy the fire made him, and he instinctively turned his left side away from it as the heat touched the raw nerves.

"Nice place you got," Tommen began conversationally. "Did you build it yourself?"

"Some of it. The cave was already here, but the timber came from an abandoned cabin just down the valley. I moved it up here and worked to build it around the cave and seal it off. It does well to keep me cool in the summer and warm in the winter."

"Hey, that's all that matters, right? And it's not very smoky in here, either."

"Well, this cave is but one outlet in a whole network down

here. Every so often, I go exploring, and I've yet to map the whole thing. But these are breathing caves; an air current runs through them. Since I effectively plugged the hole here—" He indicated the cabin. "—the current blows by through the tunnel located about five hundred feet that way and sucks the smoke out with it."

"Cool."

Chandler knelt beside the fire and poked around a bit until he got a spot cleared to lay out a couple pans of food. Eggs, meat, and some kinds of fresh fruit or vegetable, cut into cubes. It looked like carrots, celery, and something else he couldn't readily identify. Possibly beets.

"That smells wonderful," Tommen said. "Seriously. Where do you get the food?"

"I grow it. I took the seeds and planted them. The Energy from the nutrition in the soil and water leaks across the dimensional boundary in a form of interdimensional drip irrigation." Why did that sound like an oxymoron? Because it combined old world farming with modern technology and Time and dimensions and shit?

"What about the meat and eggs? I didn't see any animal pens."

"No, I don't keep animals. But when needed, I will pull in a deer or other game that I may hunt. I take no more than I require, as the Author requests. As long as I do it her way, as you can see, I want for nothing."

"And the eggs?"

Chandler shrugged. "What can I say? Some people don't keep an eye on their chickens. The hens wander up here, scratching and carrying on in search of food, and sometimes they lay eggs where I can find them."

So eggs were a delicacy. Strange to consider seeing how a dozen at the store was only about a dollar.

"Here you are," he said a minute later. "Eat up. You'll need your strength."

Tommen was given one pan of food and a fork. He didn't need to be told twice as he dug into the food. The meat was venison sausage;

that much he could tell. It was fantastic. The eggs might have been just plain chicken eggs, but combined with the beets, celery, and carrots, it was absolutely wonderful. Everything mixed together was something he knew he'd have to try and recreate himself at some point.

"So, you like the food," Chandler stated.

Tommen could only nod around another bite of food. He ended up having two more plates.

"You know what would have been really good with this? Not that I'm complaining, just as a suggestion. Sweet potatoes and brown sugar. That would have been just succulent."

"Perhaps if I get the chance, I'll have to try it," Chandler said graciously. He took Tommen's plate and set everything in the wash basin before returning. "Now then, let's see your arm and side."

With some grunting, groaning, a lot of effort, and a little help, Tommen got his arm unwrapped and shirt off. It didn't take a genius to figure out the infection was making a comeback. It certainly wasn't as bad as it had been when it was first discovered, but it was going to get that way quick if something wasn't done.

"Why did it get this bad again?" Tommen asked. "And why is it going to make such a difference going home? I mean, getting out earlier today and last night, it didn't seem like there was a problem."

"Part of the problem comes from the phase shift of Matter through the dimensions."

"Like the way my ears pop and everything?"

"Something like that. That may be what you feel physically, but the effects are more prominent at the molecular level. If you were completely healthy, as the rest of your body is, the problems would be minimal. Headaches, dizziness, nausea, all of it temporary. With your wound, with the antibodies and immune system going down completely for even a few minutes, the infection spreads and does a lot of damage.

"The second part of the problem is that before, you had help to escape, a lot of help. They did the work and you just had to get rescued, actually make the move through the dimensions. This time around, you are going to be doing a lot more of the work to get out. I will help, but much of it is on you. If you're too weak to hold the portal and escape, well, you just end up back here, but it doesn't help you any."

Tommen sighed as Chandler stood. "So you can't, like, Band it and make it better? Is it impossible, or are you just choosing not to?"

"The medical care you need now, I cannot provide. I can only clear the infection." He went on before Tommen could say more. "My job right now is simply to return you to your own dimension. That's all."

While he rummaged around in jars and pots, gathering this and that, Tommen inspected himself. Five days since the initial accident. All of the blisters had been lanced at some point, which was how he'd contracted the infection. The smaller blisters had healed or were healing, much like any blister he got on his hands. It was a good sign in that they were healing. It was a bad sign because then the infection was held underneath the skin. The larger blisters were still open and weeping blood and pus at just about any given moment. All of that on top of the melted polyester from his jacket beginning to slough off like a leper. Who knew how long that was going to take to fully expel? And for as much as he told himself to keep moving his arm and hand and fingers, he could feel the skin and muscles tightening until now he could hardly move his index and middle finger.

As for his shoulder and side, what blisters had bubbled up were now healing, and the outer reddened skin was almost back to normal. It was murder to move his arm, and moving his shoulder simply hurt.

Chandler returned with several small pots and a couple rolls of clean gauze. He opened up one pot which had some sort of sticky paste in it, and two more pots which looked like herbs or something.

"Who needs antibiotics when you have homeopathy, right?" Tommen said.

"And how have those antibiotics been working for you?" Chandler retorted. "You've barely been staying ahead of this infection, or else it might not be such an issue." He dug out a few leaves of each of the dried herbs. "Chew these. It'll help with the pain and the nausea."

Tommen did so hesitantly. On the one hand, he really had nothing against homeopathy as a first resort. Rather than taking a dozen pills a day for a dozen different ailments, adjust one's lifestyle accordingly and figure out what the people of old already knew. When that failed, then move on to modern medicine. This all seemed very backwards. If the stuff from the hospital was only barely staying ahead of the infections, why was a couple of dried herbs going to make a difference now?

At the same time, the herbs did as Chandler said. The nausea went away and the pain was lessened, even if it didn't go away completely. Once he'd done that, Chandler washed away the blood and pus, wrapped Tommen's arm in one layer of gauze, then set the rest of the rolls aside. He took large gauze pads and stuck them on his side, chest, and neck. He then took the sticky paste and brushed it over the gauze, almost like creating an old plaster cast. He then wrapped the rest of the gauze around Tommen's arm and another layer of pads on the rest. Another layer of sticky paste, and then a leaf wrap. They almost looked like rhubarb leaves.

No sooner had he secured the last leaf than the pain hit. It probably would have been ten times worse if Tommen hadn't chewed the leaves, but it still elicited a rather vocal response.

"The leaves will protect your body against further infection," Chandler explained. "The gauze acts as a slow release for the medication while simultaneously absorbing the infection into it. The leaves will take it from there and breathe it back out into the air. In normal time, the infection would be gone in a few days, maybe a week. Seeing how you will no doubt be going straight to a hospital once you escape, well, it will still do its job while you have it."

Tommen lay on his back, wrapped arm kept away from his chest which was also smarting, right arm over his face, trying to think about anything else in the world but what he'd just endured. Finally he sat up on one elbow.

"Where did you learn that?" he asked hoarsely.

Chandler shrugged. "It is not so hard to learn things when you are in this dimension. Surely you know that."

"Especially when it's knowledge you learned from your own people, am I right, Anagalisgi?"

Now the man gave him a look that was impossible to determine. It was a mixture of sorrow and sarcasm, of longing and quick wit. Finally he said, "So you did get my message."

"I don't understand. You sent me dreams or visions. Why?"

"Because there is much you have yet to learn. You could learn it outside of here, true, but the best source of information is to be there. I know you have wondered about Forbes Cave, even as a child. Why is it so strange? Who put the trap there? Can it be undone? What's the story here?"

"You were there," Tommen stated. "You were one of them. You opened the original portal."

Chandler nodded slowly. "I was. You are correct. I am Anagalisgi. Kiyuga was my older brother. You knew his grandson."

"Saul? So you're his great-uncle."

"That is correct. Or I would be, had he been alive at the time or had we been together. But that is neither here nor there. Yes, Saul would be my nephew."

"Well, that explains the family resemblance. But what about the cave? I don't understand what I saw. I mean, I do, but..."

"When the white men came, they did not come and go or migrate as we did. They came and they settled. They tamed the land. But the land was already occupied. When we moved from a spot, they assumed we had abandoned it, so they took over. And they just kept spreading. Soon, they demanded warriors to fight in their wars. They wouldn't take no for an answer. They attacked. We retaliated. It got to a point where we no longer had to be provoked into a fight; we would take the fight to them. The bloodshed continued.

"I was only an infant when my parents died of smallpox. My

brother and I were raised by our grandmother. She had seen many terrible things come from the Europeans' wars. Her ultimate desire was neutrality, but she really preferred the French over the British.

"One day, the leaders decided to go and offer peace to the British, attempt to find solidarity while some of the younger warriors attacked British convoys. But we were captured and imprisoned, many killed.

"I was approached by a couple of sorcerers, Akari-bearers though they were not called such. They brought Time and the Akari to my people, to try and help us fight off the invaders. As you can imagine, it didn't go well. Some wanted to slaughter every white-skinned person in the land. Others accused me of consorting with demons. But no one could deny the power of the sorceries.

"A decision was made to leave and find a place where we could live in peace with no white demons to chase us. We were introduced to the planet now called Hlohi. Kiyuga and I were chosen to escort the vulnerable to Hlohi, the first city called Aktiya Waya. Later, as the Aniyvwiya made their final stand, we were to save the wounded warriors so they might train and fight another day.

"I loved my brother, and I looked up to him. He wanted me to go with the rest of them, and it would have been terribly easy." Chandler sighed sadly. "I could not accept. From an early age, I had known that my path was different than anyone else's. While I had been to Hlohi and understood the plan, I knew I would not make the journey with them. Naturally, my brother didn't believe me and did everything he could to try to rectify the situation, combine his vision and my destiny.

"We rescued about eighty warriors. Because of the conjuring I had to do to save them from the battlefield, I did not have the strength to open a portal to Hlohi. And many were too weak to make the journey anyway. We fled into the forest, hunters in pursuit. Perhaps our only saving grace was that they were rather lazy hunters, enabling us to get a good lead on them.

"As I recovered strength, I would open portals so that the

weakest of the wounded could escape to Hlohi to get treatment. As we did this, we were able to move faster.

"Finally we reached a place where we could camp safely. There were only about twenty of us now, few with major wounds to speak of. I needed only a few days to rest, and then we could all cross, or that was the plan.

"Then the hunters came. I was not yet fully recovered, but we had no choice. We ran to the cave, and I opened a portal. Most made it, but Adahi was trapped in this dimension and I was captured."

"I saw that," Tommen cut in. "You were kept in prison and sentenced to die."

"I was," Chandler confirmed. "They charged me with assault on a British officer, aiding the enemy, and a bunch of other war crimes.

"They confiscated my pack, which had many of my medicines and religious icons, as well as the seeing fruit. The Reverend was supposed to destroy my pack, but I got a hold of it. I hid it until the day of my execution when I ate of the seeing fruit.

"I saw Adahi and we immediately launched an escape. We fled from the town and headed back toward the cave, using the Akari to give us a head start. When we got there, we did just as you saw. We switched places. He did not understand it, but in that moment, I knew what my destiny was. I understood that the path I had taken had always led me to that moment. I would not be joining my brother on Hlohi.

"In order to protect my people and get revenge on the hunters, once Adahi was safely through, I took the portal and rearranged it into the Time Trap, capturing the murderous hunters and not releasing them for a century. It is perhaps the only truly selfish thing I have done with my power here. The Author punished me for it by making it so I was unable to undo my actions and was forced to watch innocents get trapped in it. But she always had a plan for each one who went through. Including you. And she made a way for it to be undone.

"Anyway, Adahi made the journey to Hlohi. While others were glad to know he made it, I was informed that Kiyuga never forgave him, even blamed him for me not making it. I am told that he changed his name to Usulagogi—Lonely Man—and married into Eagle Clan."

"That's the man Kayla went to see to ask about how to escape from this dimension," Tommen said.

"I would imagine so," Chandler acknowledged. "I am afraid he would be of little help, but I commend her determination." He shifted position. "When I arrived in this dimension, the Author told me that she had chosen me to be the messenger. The head messenger, in fact. She explained this dimension, how it worked, what power I had over it. As long as I worked to serve her, I would never want."

"Sounds like duress to me."

"And Micah and Micaiah allow you a great deal of leeway in the bakery, but only as long as you are doing your job and serving them. Is that duress?"

Tommen opened his mouth but could find no words to rebut his point. Finally he asked, "So if you were trapped here and your brother was on Hlohi, would told you about the things that happened about your brother and him blaming Adahi for your demise?"

Chandler nodded. "A fair question. While those who escaped to Hlohi certainly enjoyed their new freedom, some still retained a desire to seek their ancestors in the old home. Once a year, a certain group of young people questing to be adults were permitted to return to Earth to seek guidance and become adults. I often visited them, and that is how I got news."

"Then why not have your brother return so you two could talk?"

"He did return. I had learned of a way to cultivate the seeing fruit, to grow more. When that tree bore its fruit, my brother returned and we spoke at length. He understood what had happened, but he was yet a mortal being. He was a human with emotions. He did not wish to blame me or be angry with me. Neither did he wish to be angry at Adahi, but Adahi was the only one he saw, and seeing him reminded him of me. Personally, I believe Adahi left Aktiya Waya just to keep the peace.

"Kiyuga sought me out whenever he returned to Earth, but opening portals was much more difficult back then, something only a skilled master could well achieve. And as things got more dangerous on Earth, and as he became more caught up in his new life on Hlohi—his role as skiagvsta, husband, and father—he visited less and less. After the Aniyvwiya were removed, few had a reason to return at all."

"So you've had no contact at all with your people in, like, two hundred years?"

"No, of course not." Chandler shook his head. "Wolf Clan still sought me when they made the trip from Hlohi, when they entered into their secret lives here. Often, it was one of the first things they did upon arrival, eat the seeing fruit and speak to me. Some believed me to be dead and one of the spirits. Others understand that I am simply in another dimension."

"But haven't you visited Micaiah before in other places? The Wheel, the fortress?"

"Special trips as requested and permitted by the Author alone, not by my will. Else I would have visited my people centuries ago."

"I thought the Krydik were well-versed in Time and the Akari. How do they not understand this?"

"Their use of Time and the Akari is extremely limited, to the point where it is simply, well, sorcery. They don't go to the Wheel, they don't train to become Masters, they don't get involved in politics. They are no more skilled than you were six months ago. It is simply a basic tool that they had learned from their parents who learned from their parents and so on. Very few understand the extent of the power they wield. Perhaps it is for the best. I was even told that some clans have begun to dissolve the use of Time and have gone back to a truly natural lifestyle, the ones they lived before the white men came."

"So, they finally got what they wanted. Peace."

Chandler nodded somberly. "Most did, yes. Some in Wolf Clan still wrestle with it. Some had a harder time with it than others."

"Like Saul?"

The man let out a breath. "Sabelu was the first one in almost a century to seek the faces of his ancestors in the old home, rather than on Hlohi. I met him. We spoke." Chandler shook his head. "He was such an angry young man, full of hate and fear and a lot of confusion. He never felt like part of the people, part of the pack as the clan saying goes. Always he felt drawn away from them, a separate path that he didn't understand and so he couldn't make others understand. He knew all the rituals and traditions, knew everything there was to know, but he was still so unhappy.

"Sometimes, a man or woman is chosen to leave the pack and forge his own path, as I was. We don't know where that path leads or what it will do to us and others. But he was so conflicted, with the use of Time, the Akari, the old home, the new home, the Migration and all the wrongs that preceded it. It tore him apart. I wish I could have helped him more."

"And now he's dead," Tommen stated. "Dead on the side of a mountain."

"And now he's dead," Chandler echoed softly.

"Where does Yawi come from?"

"Yawi is simply a messenger from the Author. Messengers come in all shapes and sizes, always in a manner which the intended recipient will understand. Oftentimes, however, a person mistakes the messenger as being the Author or the Creator or whomever. The messenger has no power unto himself that the Author has not given him. The Author is the one to look to. But you can't fix stupid." He shrugged.

Tommen shifted position, minding his arm which was still throbbing. "Is that what happened to Richard? People mistook the messenger for the Author?"

Chandler's gaze grew stony. "The tale of Richard, Julianna, and the journals, is in part caused by the Akarin. The Akarin grew too large, too powerful. They mistook themselves—the messengers—as being their own authors. Then they began to think of themselves as the authors of other people. Their own pride created their worst enemy.

"Richard was young and naive, but when the faith of a child is backed up only by the wisdom of a child, such knowledge is easily corrupted. He wanted so badly to take things back to the way they were that he was willing to listen to any voice he thought would get them there. His real downfall came when he began to not only believe the lies, but live them."

"So he willingly went to Beaumaris Gaol to become a martyr," Tommen stated.

"No. He led a number of propaganda campaigns against the Akarin. Sometimes they were little more than peaceful protests, other times there was bloodshed. This was spurred on by the words of his darling wife."

"Julianna."

Chandler nodded gravely. "Only when she sent him to Beaumaris Gaol did he understand the price of his loyalty to her. He may have thought her the support, but only in that she was the one holding the strings and making him dance. He thought his actions were enough, but greed and power always demand more. Finally, when there was nothing left he would willingly give, she sucked out of him what little she could, only his life."

"Staging it to look like martyrdom in order to win converts."

"Exactly."

"Where do Cassius and Rifun come in?"

"Julianna left one journal with Richard's followers and fled with the other two. At the time, the Author had begun writing again, and not mere fragments, but full novels. It was a very exciting time. The idea was to imitate the style of the Authored Books by releasing them slowly, at regular intervals in order to make them seem more valid. Use something the Akarin were already familiar with.

"By this time, everyone in Time knew about the Time Trap I had laid. She and Cassius sought to use this trap to advance themselves a short time. She would release another journal, maybe perpetuate some story of a widow fleeing her husband's executioner, drum up a little support, and so on. Cassius would still have his DNA in as the Zero Hour and so retain his power, enough of it in order to declare some alliance between the Hands of Time and the Akarin. She gave a second journal to someone she believed was a follower, keeping her eggs in separate baskets with the intent to return for it later.

"While they were in the cave, Cassius turned on her, tried to kill her. She dropped another journal in the cave, in the bones, which you found. She fled and managed to get herself lost in World War II, where she picked up Lily. Meanwhile, when the Dispersal came about, Cassius recruited Rifun and those two began their domination schemes."

"Scheming, backstabbing, double-crossing, crumbling economies," Tommen mused. "Does the Wheel ever have just a normal day?"

Chandler chuckled. "I don't know. I don't believe so."

"So if Cassius tried to kill Julianna, and he also recruited Rifun, where does Rifun get off trying to help her?"

"Perhaps that was poor choice of words on my part. Julianna recruited Rifun to be recruited by Cassius in order to kill him."

"More double-crossing. Got it."

"Exactly. Rifun works for Julianna. Always has. Before he and Cassius returned to the cave to find the dropped journal, he sent her to the in-between dimension and faked her death, much the same way he faked his own death. She would do the leg work to track down each of the journals. When they came out, she could point them directly to the journals. She would be freed and would hand-deliver the journals to the Cult of the Akari as some sort of Jesus, Patron Saint, Mother Theresa figure. Rifun and Cassius would seal the alliance between the Cult and the Hands of Time, crush the Akarin, and all would come under one law as defined in the journals.

"What they weren't counting on was a little intervention. First you took the journal. Then you fought for the journal to keep it away from them. By the words of the Author, Julianna has been kept imprisoned here so she could not escape just at a whim. Rifun and Cassius lost their power in the Wheel, and Cassius is dead."

"But what happens if she does escape?"

Chandler stretched his legs out in front of him. "Many bad things. But you mustn't blame yourself. If not you, then someone else. This has always been coming, as in the Author's timing."

"Can't you stop her?"

"That is not my job here. At this moment, I am only the messenger."

Tommen shook his head. "Whatever, man. But there's one thing I still don't get. If Lily was Julianna's student, and Julianna knew where all the journals were — presumably — why did Rifun and Cassius try to kill her? More to the point, why didn't they get it right the first time?"

"Julianna and Lily did have some contact before the appearance of Cassius and Rifun. Lily was, as you know, exceptionally influential in the Wheel. Julianna was hoping to use that influence to get Rifun and Cassius back into power and make the takeover as smooth as possible. But Lily was also very greedy, and if she lost money and power, she said no. So Julianna told her men to kill her, too.

"The first time, Lily and the woman switched shifts after Julianna gave Rifun and Cassius the day and time. The second time, well, they got the right venue and right time, but the wrong girl. You know from experience that Julianna has a bad habit of appearing and disappearing with very little to go on. She probably told them the day and time, then vanished and waited for them to report the mission complete. After two strikes, well, it was time to up the ante. You know what happened after that."

"Yeah, my friends get kidnapped, then I get kidnapped, then I lose my fucking hearing. Now I'm probably going to lose my fucking arm, too. Micaiah lost his leg..." Tommen scoffed. "And there's nothing that can be done to fix any of this?"

Chandler shrugged. "It would be nothing for the Author to simply write, 'And all the wounds sustained thus far were miraculously healed.' But I think she has more in store for you than you realize. Sometimes, the wounded can go places where the whole cannot, and a broken bone heals twice as strong."

"Very philosophical of you. What doesn't kill you makes you stronger, right?"

"Indeed."

"Yeah. Tell that to my dad."

"At what point? When he ran into a dark warehouse to rescue you? When he endured a year of torture in only a day? Now, as he waits in terrified anticipation for you to return? Do you think that a day goes by when he doesn't worry about you? Do you never consider that you are the reason he still battles the darkness instead of giving in?"

Tommen felt his cheeks and ears burn hot and tried to tell himself it was only the fire. Chandler stared at him a moment longer before getting up to add another log, saying, "When the darkness closes in and there is nowhere left to turn, sometimes the only thing left to do is become the light yourself."

"Have you ever walked in his nightmares? I did that once. It was horrifying. How am I or is he supposed to be a light in that?"

Chandler arranged the fresh logs and poked at the coals a bit. "Coals may provide warmth, but without fuel and oxygen, there will be no light. And soon enough, they will grow cold."

"Are you saying my dad is about to go out?" Tommen was wary and uncertain how he wanted to interpret the man's words.

"I am simply saying that as long as man is fighting the darkness, there is still a distinction and something to be saved and salvaged. As soon as he gives in, there is nothing that can be done until he starts fighting it again. It was the same way with you and Julianna. As long as you were giving in to her and considering her escape, you were one, bound together. If one goes, you both go. Once you separated yourself from her and began fighting, then there was something to save."

"What does that have to do with my dad? After all the shit Rifun has put him through, he's not forming an alliance with him any time soon."

"Succumbing to the darkness is not limited to one single definition."

Tommen swallowed and tried not to let the fear make it to his face. "Has it been long enough? Can we leave now? Or, you know, can I go back and try to escape and stuff?"

"I expect so. But we may need a few things."

Chandler's idea of a few things, and Tommen's idea of a few things, as it related to going out on a short hike, turned out to be two different things. Tommen generally expected a small backpack with snacks, an extra coat, an extra pair of socks, a water bottle, a couple good knives, and whatever other interesting things he might think of. A book of edible plants, wild birds of North America, whatever. Chandler, however, apparently thought that a couple knives and a water bottle for each of them was sufficient. Not that Tommen was expecting anything more, really. They weren't camping, and he definitely couldn't return to civilization with more than he'd left with. It was probably just as well that he'd left his backpack full of stuff with his dad during the first successful escape attempt.

"Do you think Julianna has already escaped?" Tommen wondered as Chandler strapped his knives onto a leather belt which he cinched around one shoulder.

"I would imagine so. If not, then it will not be long."

"Do you think they could be waiting for us?"

"I find it highly unlikely. Julianna hates you, but she has bigger plans than waiting around for you to show up so she can kill you."

Was that supposed to be comforting? Because it really wasn't very comforting. Julianna was out to kill him. That was not a good thing, especially since she had Rifun for a minion. And if Rifun was anyone's minion, it was only because his boss was powerful enough to keep him in line. Anyone powerful enough to subdue Rifun was not someone he wanted to mess with.

Or could this be another case of Rifun pretending to be the minion in order to get the upper hand? It had happened before, so it wasn't impossible. But how did the man play people so easily? Was it just something he did? Was it a case where he didn't know how to do anything else? What was the story behind all this? Micaiah said there was an Authored Book about it, so he might have to check that out when he was able.

"How does your arm feel?" Chandler asked.

"Um..." Tommen looked at his arm, still wrapped in gauze and leaves and hardened with burning paste. "It's still there. It hurts. Like, it really hurts."

"How does your head feel?"

"I don't know. Dizzy, light-headed, nothing terrible. Kind of like a bad cold, I guess."

"Come with me."

Rather than going back down the mountain toward the road, Chandler took him out of the cabin and up a narrow trail to a stream. In the middle of August, the water was down to barely noticeable levels. Tommen could see the different water levels on the banks where it would be at the height of the season, and then at overflow levels. At the height of summer, however, only a small dam kept it high enough that he was able to fill a couple of flasks. He handed one to Tommen and kept one for himself which he drank from.

"The doctors at the hospital will tell you this, but I will tell you now so you know. While you are septic, and even once you have healed, keep your fluid intake high. It will help with the sepsis, the infection, the dehydration, and the painful urination."

Tommen simply nodded and handed the empty flask back to him for a refill. He downed that a little more slowly, then got a third refill which he kept on his person.

"And another thing," Chandler said, standing. "Your little food adventure around the world? Not smart. It upset your system. Your body had to fight to quell the discomfort and figure out how to digest the unfamiliar foods, which meant it wasn't fighting the infection. You lost more nutrients than you took in because of that."

"Oh, come on," Tommen whined, throwing his hands up. "It was the only time I was going to be able to do something like that.

Besides, I'm feeling fine now."

"You're feeling better. You're compensating. You're not 'fine.' Now let's get you to the cave and get you home before you stop compensating and start crashing." He started off down the trail, down the mountain.

Tommen stared after him. "Breakfast was good."

"Let's go, Tommen. Time to go home."

Tommen let out a breath and moved off after him.

Chapter Thirty-Two
Free At Last

"Can I ask you something?"

Tommen could almost imagine Chandler rolling his eyes in a manner reminisce of Saul as he said, "What is it?"

"If I remember right, you have the power to see into the future through this dimension. Julianna doesn't. I certainly don't. Why is that?"

"The in-between dimension is itself split. One half rests on this primary dimension, where you will be returning, and the other half rests on another primary dimension where the Author resides. But because they coincide, few can see the difference. Long story short, the other half of this in-between dimension is where myself, Yawi, and the other messengers normally reside. In that half of the dimension, because it is under total control of the Author, we are allowed certain abilities which those like Julianna are not. This includes the ability to see a limited distance into the future."

" 'Those like Julianna' ?" Tommen echoed.

"She's not the first madman to use this place to hatch a plot, only the latest iteration."

"So if the in-between dimension is split, how do you cross paths or, I don't know, do battle?"

"They only coincide for the time. One day, when the story is over, they will be split and we may cross over no more."

"Okay...so then, how does one get to be a resident of this special dimension?"

"The Author must choose you, but you must also choose the

Author."

"Yeah, because that's not confusing. You make an excellent prophet, you know that? Better prophet than messenger is all I'm saying."

Chandler did not reply.

"So, wait, your name is Anagalisgi, right? I've been calling you Chandler this whole time. Do you want me to stop? Or do you not want me to use your real name?"

"It makes little difference to me. You know me as Chandler, and so you call me Chandler. The Krydik know me as Anagalisgi—or sometimes Agidoda or Aginisi—so that is how they will call me. And I am known by other names to other people."

"Well, you're a whole lot of help."

"Micaiah once called me a sarcastic prison chaplain."

"Sounds like him, and I can see why." Had he been able to, Tommen might have folded his arms. "Okay, so, you're preaching the whole, 'everything happens for a reason' schtick. What purpose did Micaiah losing his leg serve? Humility? Well, that's a pretty shitty reason, if that is the case. So what is it?"

Chandler glanced back at him just before stepping through a fallen log. "Is it really important for you to know?"

"Okay, okay, fine. He's moving off on his own life with Kayla, whatever. Maybe it's none of my business. So why did I lose my hearing? I get that we have to consider the laws of physics that loud sounds are bad for your hearing, but the Author could have just said that, you know, it gradually healed and came back in its own time and everything was well again. Believe me, I would not easily forget what it's like to wear hearing aids and have everything all jacked up. But why doesn't she do that?"

"You might as well just get it all out there instead of this back and forth deal," Chandler told him, his tone difficult to read.

"Why have my dad get shot? Doesn't he have enough psychological problems as it is? And even if that did have to happen—for whatever reason—why did I have to see it? Why did I have to hold him in my arms as he died? Why did any of that have to happen? What about the coup? Like I said, Micaiah lost his leg, his friend Doug is dead, and because of that, it sounds like the Akarin are steadily imploding. What the hell? If the Akarin are the Author's 'chosen people' or whatever—assuming that's what they are—then why doesn't she stop it? Or at least make them pick some better leaders."

Tommen caught Chandler grinning momentarily as he answered, "Why does a farmer harvest his wheat? Why does he kill what is clearly still alive? Because it can be used for other, better things, when combined with other things. Bread, cake, cereal, to name a few. And he can take a hundred seeds off one head and plant a hundred new wheat plants."

"Yeah, well, this field of wheat is turning out to be a field of weeds, from what I hear."

"All the more reason to harvest. Discard that which is bad and attempt to save what you can. True, there won't be as many seeds for the next planting, but better to have a small field that is all good, than a large field that is mostly bad."

"So the Author is intentionally destroying her own people. Wonderful."

"People are not wheat, at the mercy of the elements. They have free will. They are merely destroying themselves, reaping the consequences of their actions."

"But the Author is literally writing down every word. She knows what's going on, what will happen before it does. Why doesn't she stop it, or alter the story, or do anything?"

"She has altered the story, many times. Sometimes on the fly. But some things must happen. It is all for good. You'll see it in the end."

Tommen rubbed his eyes and let out a breath. "You make a better preacher than a messenger, you know that? How many sermons do you sit in on, on Sundays? Or even between Sundays, you know, going back in time to listen to all the greats. Billy Graham and Martin Luther and whoever else you like."

Chandler kept grinning that familiar Wolf Clan grin, half amusement, half sarcasm, but all smirk. Tommen was seeing more and more family resemblance with every word that came out of his mouth.

"Did you and Saul talk a lot?"

Now the man stopped grinning and paused in his steps, looking thoughtful. Finally he shrugged, resumed walking, and answered, "Whenever he came to Earth, the first thing he did was seek me out. Whenever he was returning to Hlohi, the last thing he did before going was seek me out. I went to him several times when he was in the Marines, and especially when he was laid up in the hospital with his back injury."

"I'll bet he was just a ball of sunshine then, too."

"More than you can imagine." His tone dripped sarcasm. Then, more seriously, "Sabelu never could let go of his anger. His injury only exacerbated the problem, I think."

"What made him so angry, though? I mean, like, was there a traumatic event or something?"

"Some would say that he is the culmination of cultural anger, that all the anger and the hate over past wrongs fell on his shoulders, and his death was a way for that to finally be laid to rest. Whether or not it's true, I don't know. If there was some event that happened that took root in his mind, he never told what it was, assuming he even knew and understood what was happening."

Chandler heaved a heavy sigh. "I was there, when he died. I saw him going off alone to hunt, and I sent Yawi to follow him. Yawi's first howl alerted me to foul play. When I arrived, Yawi had gotten into a fight with Rifun and been wounded. As for Saul, there was nothing I could do, save send him into unconsciousness in order to escape the pain. But it was his time."

"So it is possible for you and Yawi and the others to jump between dimensions?" Tommen questioned. "Like, I physically saw Yawi there. He came up to me several times."

"It is possible, by the words of the Author. In the same way that the words of the Author have kept Julianna imprisoned here."

"Guess those words lose their potency after a while, huh?"

"As I said. Some things must happen. But never assume that the Author is powerless against Julianna or any of those like her. All she has to do is write a few words and call evil to heel."

"Yeah, yeah, everything happens for a reason. Whatever."

Chandler chuckled, but it sounded forced. "I would be interested in hearing your thoughts on the matter once you have read more Authored Books, particularly those concerning yourself. You might have a new perspective on things."

"I think I've had my perspective adjusted enough for the time being, thanks. I really just kind of want to go home and sleep in my own bed tonight. Or at least see my dad again. For real."

"Ask and ye shall receive, right?" And there was the smirk.

Tommen rolled his eyes. Then, "Wait a second. If you can jump between dimensions and shit, why can't you do that and take me with you?"

"Because there is one thing that must happen, and it can only be accomplished by you going home the way you will."

"Fixed points in time, right?"

Chandler did not answer.

By this time they had reached the highway and were now walking along the busy road like a couple of hitchhikers. It was early in the morning yet, but the earliest of the working class was out and about on their way to work. These weren't the nine-to-fivers on their way to the office, but the people who served those nine-to-fivers. These were the gas station attendants, the food service workers, the gym attendants, the bus drivers, and so on. One twin or the other would be on his way to the bakery about now, Tommen knew, getting the prep work done and starting on all the tasty breakfast items that had to be in the display case by five when they opened.

"Will I ever see you again, once I'm home and this is all over?" Tommen wondered.

"I expect so," Chandler answered. "It is certainly a possibility at this point. And for the record, this isn't over. Not by a long shot.

Even once you get home, you're just getting started."

"Oh, wonderful. Because that's what I wanted to hear."

"What did you want to hear?"

" 'Sure, Tommen, we'll see each other again. Maybe I'll send a "Thinking of You" card or something before I drop by. We can chat and catch up on old times. Your arm is going to be fine, the upcoming school year is going to be great, and you and Becky are going to be having some pretty great sex once you start sleeping together. Julianna won't escape, Rifun is going to be thrown in prison to rot, and life will go back to normal, the way it was this time last year.' " Tommen nodded. "That's a little closer to what I had in mind."

"Well, I have to admit, I admire your lofty goals. But that's not quite what's going to happen."

"Mind telling me what is going to happen?"

"Actually, I do. And I'm not going to."

"Why not?"

"Come now, Tommen, you're a smart kid. What would someone on *Star Trek* say?"

Tommen sighed. "Because in knowing the future, it alters the timeline, making that future invalid. Or, if you want to analyze it from Righting's point of view, I would try so hard to avoid anything bad that I end up running right into it. So either I'm validating free will or I'm not. Either way, I can't win."

"As I said, you're smart."

They walked in silence for a few minutes.

"Can I at least get a hint?" Tommen asked.

Chandler looked back at him, brow raised. "Now you want one of my confusing riddles?"

"It'll give me something to chew on while we're walking."

"After all the times you've berated me for said riddles, including all the mean names you've called me, why should I give you one of those riddles now?"

"Because I'm asking nicely?"

"Are you?"

"Can I please have one of your stupid ass riddles?"

"See, there you go, berating me. No, you can't have a riddle."

"Please? Okay, fine. May I please have one of your mysterious riddles?"

"No. No riddle for you."

Tommen felt like an embarrassed ten year old as they continued along the highway. Yes, he still thought Chandler could be infuriating, and if his riddles could be compiled into a book, he probably would have burned the book. But knowing that the man knew a little something about the future, and it wasn't as rosy as Tommen was hoping, kind of made him want at least a little peek inside that brain of his. He should have tried using that future-vision a little more practically when he had the chance, assuming he could have anyway.

"Can you see alternative futures?" Tommen asked. "Like, if I hadn't touched the fire with the Energy and blown myself here, what would I be doing right now?"

"No, I don't see things like that," Chandler answered levelly. "There are far too many variations. When you have seven billion people making choices at every second of the day, the possibilities are endless."

"Oh. Too bad." Pause. "Do you see the future all the time, or just when you want to, like the history thing?"

"Only when I need to, when the Author shows me something I need to see. Reduces the risk of me interfering based on something I sought out and saw, or just happened upon. The same reason I won't tell you anything I see."

Darn science fiction logic anyway, Tommen mused as he plodded along after Chandler. They still did not Travel anywhere, and the road seemed to get longer and longer the farther they went. Maybe it was just him. Could the hallucinogenic peaches still be messing with him? How long did that shit last?

"Hold on, Tommen. There you go."

The next thing he knew, Chandler was easing him to the

ground, leaning him against the guardrail on the highway. He wasn't even sure what happened, just that he felt weak and light-headed and was going down. Absently, he took the water flask and drank the whole thing.

"Shit," he said, taking a breath when he was done. "What was that?"

"The infection is starting to leave your body," Chandler told him, "but it is taking some of your good health as well. This medicine is good, but when the infection is severe, it works indiscriminately."

"Oh." Tommen rubbed his face. "Fuck. We have to keep moving."

"Agreed. Can you walk?"

Chandler helped him to his feet and put him in front this time. They continued walking along the highway, past the cars and trucks all heading into the city, to their fabulous, bread-winning careers. Ha ha ha. After a few minutes, Tommen dropped back a few steps to walk beside Chandler. What's the worst that could happen? Not like they would be hit by a car or anything.

"So, in the event that something bad does happen while we're up there, like Julianna waiting for us, why don't you explain to me now how I'm going to escape?" Tommen suggested.

"You would abandon me in a fight just so you could save your own skin?" Chandler questioned.

Tommen felt his face and neck turn bright red. Chandler laughed. "Ah, only kidding. She is of little consequence at this moment, and she will not bother us in your escape. That much I will say."

"All the same, why not tell me?"

"You see? If I told you the things I see, you would no doubt believe me and rush to change the things you don't like. If I tell you what is going to happen, or not going to happen in the next twenty minutes, you don't believe me anyway. Is there no way to win?"

"Please, Chandler? I'm not feeling the best and I kind of just want to go home without any more incidents. No more failed attempts and side quests. Just...an easy out."

Chandler nodded somberly. "I understand. And I will tell you now that it will not be an easy out. Comparatively speaking, yes, it could be much worse. But still difficult for you. It will require every ounce of what little strength you have left and then some. You must break through the dimensional barrier. That involves both a separation of the dimensions as well as opening a portal. Everything the five of them did last night, all by yourself."

"What about you? Can't you help?"

"I can, and I will. I will be there making sure you don't fall back into the Time Trap. As a matter of fact, I will be there to make sure no one falls into the Time Trap ever again."

That sounded pretty nice, actually, Tommen thought. It was a little late to go back and change what happened to him, but if he could keep anyone else from repeating his mistakes, well, that might be worth a little extra elbow grease.

"So, assuming I can do all of that, do I just, like, step through? Ta-da, here I am, I'm safe and well a couple hundred miles south of where you're all searching for me. Should I Band and go back up to Wellspring? Did I tell you about the story my dad made up? It's a pretty good whopper, if I do say so myself."

Chandler grinned and shook his head. "That will not be necessary. And yes, I do know the story your dad told. Actually, I was impressed by his creativity. Not to say I condone lying, but creativity is always a good thing."

"You don't condone lying, but you've been hiding the truth for a while, haven't you? About who you are?"

The man shrugged. "Did it matter? Telling you that my name is Anagalisgi would hold no more significance to you than tell you it is Chandler, or any other name. The only ones who understand the history and significance behind it are the Krydik. Not telling you who I am is of little consequence. Even now, since you know about it, how is that going to change your life in any way?"

"I don't know. But if it's not that important, why tell me in the first place and give your whole life story?"

"Because you needed to know. It wasn't about me, but the cave. You have always wondered about that cave. Why is it here? Who set the Trap? Why? What's the story? Can I undo it somehow? Simply telling you that I did it wasn't enough; you needed the context of why I did it, and why I have been unable to undo it."

"And now, because of me, it can be undone. The Time Trap can be dissolved."

"Yes."

"Are there still people inside it? What happens to them? Do they come out?"

"Tommen, I don't know. The Author hasn't shown me anything regarding what happens when the Trap is released. All I know is that it will be done. That's good enough for me."

Truthfully, it should have been good enough for Tommen, too, but he found himself unsatisfied with the answer. At least if there were still people in there now, they were still alive and could come out. If the Trap was released, would they just get tossed out into present day? How would they handle it? What if something bad happened, like everyone died? How would that go over? Was there a chance, if they managed to catch everything at the moment of temporal flux, that they could somehow return people to their normal time periods? Was that possible?

"I know you're going over it in your mind," Chandler said, interrupting his thoughts. "Do not preoccupy yourself. Let me worry about the Time Trap. You get back to your dimension and see a doctor. For just a few minutes, try to relax and enjoy yourself. It will only get harder from here."

Was that supposed to be comforting? Because it really wasn't all that comforting.

Soon enough, they got off the highway and onto a secondary road, heading higher into the mountains. The road took them up and around to a familiar park. Even at this time of morning, a few cars were in the lot and some ambitious joggers were suiting up for an early morning run. These were the nine-to-fivers who didn't go to the gym with everyone else. Most of them were women, between twenty and forty, slender, long hair tied back in a cute ponytail. Many of them had music players on their armbands and were surfing for their favorite tunes. Because who needed to listen to nature? They just came out here to see it, right?

"I'm surprised," Chandler said as they approached the main pavilion. "You haven't asked the one question I thought you would."

"And what's that?" Tommen wondered half a second before he knew what it was. He shifted his stance. "Did you know all along that I was going to go into that cave?"

Chandler nodded. "I did know. I often roam these hills, as you might imagine, and it was the same two hundred and fifty years ago as it is now. I kept an eye on things, the land, the people. I did as the Author bade me.

"I saw you, too, Tommen. As a child. I watched you take your first steps and get trampled by a goat and attacked by that damn rooster." Tommen couldn't help but smile. "One day, as I was watching, I saw your path. I saw you going up the trail to the cave, so eager to explore. You were hoping to find treasure or just make up some story that you could take home with you to show how brave and fearless you were, in hopes that your pa wouldn't switch you. Yes, I knew what would happen."

"You couldn't do anything?" Tommen asked uselessly.

"No. Believe me, it pained me to see the repercussions of my selfishness, that my revenge would echo through time until a curious eight year old boy would be swallowed up by it. I even asked the Author to spare you. I learned my lesson, and I haven't done anything of the sort since. But she had plans for you, and that was the way it had to be. So that's the way it was."

"Well, hopefully today is the day your revenge comes to a close."

"I would like that very much."

As they turned to start up the trail, the group of joggers got their stuff together and started out. It was less like the proper formation for military runs and more like what Tommen saw in gym class. Everyone had their friends they wanted to jog beside and chit chat with. A few were the actual, determined runners who outpaced them all and kept a good lead on them. But, seeing how he and Chandler were leisurely walking, the joggers were soon out of sight.

"I know you said you talked to Saul a lot. Do you ever talk to his siblings?" Tommen wondered.

"Sometimes. I saw Logan for the first time in years when he came to retrieve Saul's body, but he did not seek me. Natalie stops by from time to time. Blake, I think, prefers life on Hlohi and wishes to get married so he can move to be with another clan and not worry about this anymore."

"What would you do if they ever did decide to seal themselves off? No more of this Wolf Clan liaison secret life business, just cut all ties and go back to Hlohi to live, completely separate."

"As terrible as that would be, I don't expect that a lot would change. I serve the Author, regardless of the status of my people. Am I proud of them? Do I want to help them and guide them? Of course. But unlike Saul, my identity is not dependent on them. The Author makes me who I am, and I am who she needs and wants me to be."

Tommen scoffed. "Must be nice to be that secure."

"I've had a couple centuries to think it over."

They stopped at a mountain stream so Tommen could get something to drink and take a rest. Hopefully, this would be the last time he had to make this climb for a while. Traveling would have been much easier, but if Chandler wanted to be safety-conscious, well, they were playing by his rules right now.

Tommen finished off his flask and refilled while Chandler gave him another once-over, just to be sure he had the strength to carry on and actually make the jump. He was feeling pretty okay, though his stomach was getting a little crabby from having only water. The food had worn off a few miles back, and he craved protein and sugar. Lots of sugar.

"Every unnecessary stop we make is just eating up time until you get home," Chandler told him. "You are strong enough. You can do this. And I'm sure that once you're safe and sound and have been treated for your wounds, you can get anything you want to eat."

"I don't know," Tommen said. "The whole, no salt, no fat, heart healthy menu at the hospital leaves a lot to be desired. And if my burns and infection are as bad as you say they are, who knows what kind of diet they're going to put me on?"

"If you have to go into surgery, I shouldn't even be giving you water on account of the anesthesia, so count yourself lucky there."

"There's no way to win this, is there?"

Chandler helped him to his feet once more. "How about this? We're not stopping again until we get there and get you home."

Going home sounded pretty damn good right now, actually, Tommen thought. His stomach full of water and head a little swimmy, he took the lead on the trail. He knew very well where Forbes Cave was; he'd certainly been there enough times in the last year. Still, the trail felt steeper than it had been.

"Come on, Tommen, you can do this," Chandler said behind him.

He grunted and pushed himself, getting off the main artery onto a secondary trail, telling himself to just keep moving, yet stopping when faced with the sheer rock face that separated the trail from the path to the cave itself.

"Tell me you can use Gravity to get us up there," Tommen said, not relishing having to climb up there.

"I think I can manage that," Chandler told him. "Hold on and don't freak out."

Tommen was too tired to freak out, but manipulating Gravity and essentially making him fly up eight or ten feet to the next level was still a little unnerving. He remembered the time Saul had jumped off a staircase into midair and fallen up. He'd bounced around a bit, then returned, always with that damn smirk. His had been tainted a little by his natural fury and the pain wracking his body, but the same smirk nonetheless. Oddly enough, Tommen kind of missed the cranky son of a bitch. He was a pain to deal with, but he really probably would have been an exceptional teacher.

"And you're sure Julianna isn't hiding in the bushes waiting to ambush us and slit our throats, right?" Tommen wondered as they approached the cave.

"Trust me, Tommen," Chandler said. "She's not here. Now let's go."

Chandler was probably right, but Tommen's paranoia still told him to be cautious. He approached the cave skittishly and made sure to look all around him before knowingly entering an enclosed area where an ambush would be most advantageous. If he had to hazard a guess, Chandler looked a little annoyed by it. Well, he was Mr. All Powerful Master of the Dimension and Future Vision Seer. Tommen was still just a seventeen year old kid whose abilities ranged from hardly better than a probationary Timekeeper, to manipulating Matter in order to put out fires and exploding himself into dimensions that were supposed to be impossible to get out of.

"One more question," Tommen said, pausing in the cave opening and turning to face Chandler. "How is it that in thousands of years, I may be the only one or one of a handful to ever escape this dimension? Surely someone has had the willpower and greater Time or Akari power than I do who has escaped."

"It's not just about willpower, Tommen," Chandler told him. "Willpower is what drove you to discover the truth about Julianna and make the decision to leave her behind. But it's not enough. You lacked that one thing, that one tiny thing that causes Time to be useless and the Akari supreme."

"Let me guess. Faith?"

"Precisely. That selfless Faith that everything would turn out okay, even when Foyez died in front of you and you had little hope of escape. The Faith that even when Julianna betrayed you and tried to kill you, that the Author would send someone you could trust to get you home. The Faith that you can escape this prison today. Willpower will open the portal and separate the dimensions, but the Faith will set you free."

Honestly, Tommen thought that sounded more like something Billy Graham or some other huge televangelist might say to his TV masses. At the same time, there was every chance that it was true. When thousands before him who were more learned and more powerful than he had failed, there had to be some element they were missing that didn't require brains or brawn. Simple Faith.

Still sounded hokey, but he was getting a little more comfortable with it. He wasn't sure that he wanted to completely own it yet, but he could dabble a little here and there. If it got him out of this dimension, he might be willing to consider it.

He stepped into the cave and used an Akari Band to light up the Time Trap.

"How did you make this in the first place?" he wondered.

"I took Time Threads and pulled them out of Base Time, like pulling a loose string on a sweater. Then I rearranged them and tied them together here and there, using Time Tendrils to anchor them so they couldn't decay, or decay quickly. I did that probably dozens of times, all throughout this section of the cave until there was no way to go in or out without going through the trap."

"Holy shit. Why can't you undo them?"

"So the Author has said, and because they have to be taken out from the inside. The only way to get inside them is by doing exactly what you are about to do now."

"Oh. So are you coming with me?"

"You just do what you have to do to get home and let me worry about undoing my mistake."

Tommen nodded and studied him for a moment, looking for anything else. A joke, a punchline, a threat. But the man was absolutely serious. He meant to send Tommen home and be rid of the Time Trap.

"What are you waiting for?" Chandler wondered.

"Um...last words of advice?"

"We're going to see each other again. Maybe then I'll give you a riddle to chew on, as you put it."

"Oh." Tommen flushed red for probably the tenth time that day. "Well then, how about some instructions for how to actually open a portal and separate dimensions and shit? I kind of missed that day of class and went straight for the blowing myself into the Land In Between from which no one has ever returned."

Chandler gave him a look, and for a moment, it was just like looking at Saul. Finally he nodded. "Okay, fine. Come over here." He took him to what might be considered the approximate center of the Time Trap. "This is probably the best place to start; then I can work in any direction. But, like I said, don't worry about what I'm doing. Focus on what you're going to be doing."

"And what am I doing?"

"If you tried to open a portal now, you would be sucked into the trap and sit here for another hundred years before actually getting out. What you want to try to do is separate the dimensions first. It doesn't have to be anything dramatic, just a little foot in the door. Like using a crowbar. Make sense so far?"

"Sure, but I don't know how to do any of that. I mean, I know how to use a crowbar, but I don't know how to separate dimensions either. Okay, Micaiah didn't know how to do that."

"Well, now you're going to have a one-up on him. Actually, seeing how you've already been back and forth between this dimension and the primary dimension a couple of times, you have a better idea of how they both feel. You said it was like having your ears pop and everything else. What you're going to do is reach for that feeling. You want to keep one focus on this dimension, where you're standing now. Keep another focus on the primary dimension, where you want to go and have spent a majority of your life. But you also want to keep a focus on the Time Trap itself, the Threads and Tendrils, and push those out of the way. That's the most important thing. You understand? Good.

"You should feel that pressure in your head like you did

before. You want to feel that tension. Then, once your ears pop, that's the fracture in the dimensions you want. It's a mini explosion in the dimensions, like the one you did in camp, but with less fire. As soon as you feel it, take the exit. Break through the dimensions and just keep running. Out of the cave, out of this park. Get help.

"Just remember that the most important thing is keeping the Time Trap away from you. I'll work as fast as I can to undo it and get the Time Threads away from you and create a little bigger opening, but it won't be much bigger. You still have to run. Do you understand me? Is anything I've said unclear? Once you start, you probably only get one chance before your body weakens too much."

Tommen nodded. "I understand. Let's do this."

He positioned himself where Chandler showed him and readied himself. Step one, separate the dimensions. Well, that was only something Rifun had barely managed to do. Neither Micaiah nor Walter had any idea how to do it, so it wasn't like this would be difficult or anything. And he'd never opened a portal before, so he wasn't even sure about step two. But somehow, Chandler thought he had enough talent or experience to do both at roughly the same time. Should he have asked for more clarification? He still had time.

But already, he was starting to feel things. He felt the air around him, the ground beneath his feet, all the little discrepancies between what was there and what was supposed to be there. He could move through the rock if he wanted to, but that was only a property of the in-between dimension, not the primary dimension. He could tell the difference. He could feel it.

Remembering Chandler's words, he switched his focus to the Time Trap, the Band and Threads and Tendrils all swirling around him. He stood in the mouth of the lion and had to dodge its teeth as he escaped. But he could feel it, all the Time Tendril anchors, the weaves of the Threads. He felt them as a separate entity from the in-between dimension. At the same time, he could follow along its edge back into Base Time, into the primary dimension where it originated. Like playing with fire, he had to find the balance, the fulcrum where all dimensions intersected, and follow the fault line back to the primary dimension he wanted.

With the three of them all present in his mind, Tommen began feeling the pressure in his head, just like a bad cold when he couldn't blow his nose or shift his jaw or swallow enough to get his ears to pop and equalize. He felt it in his ears, his sinuses, even his eyes. He felt pressure in his chest, too. Was that normal? Well, he could either stop and ask and waste his effort, or he could keep going and finally fucking escape.

The pressure continued to build, but so also did his awareness of the dimensions of the trap. Where once they all just melted together, now they were as different as the different varieties of things on a cold cut platter. One was meat, one was cheese, and one was a cracker. Each of them distinct, and yet combined making for a delicious little snack. Was that a good analogy?

No. He couldn't let himself get so distracted. He had to stay focused. By now the pressure was getting past the level of just a bad cold and more into fear of having a brain tumor or maybe a heart attack. His head felt like Tyler Freeman and all of his friends were sitting on top of him. His eyes were watering and his vision was blurry. His ears felt like tiny bombs about ready to go off. His chest was tight, heart racing, fighting against the pressure. His sinuses felt swollen, but he couldn't take in air anyway because his lungs could hardly expand.

How much longer did he have to do this? He turned his head, looking for Chandler. But even if he was in the vicinity, Tommen probably wouldn't have been able to make him out, nor hear anything he had to say.

If this was this difficult from the inside, what had Rifun gone through doing it from the outside? Did it ever get easier? Was there some trick to do this without killing himself? He could feel the sweat on his neck running down his back, under his arms, down his forehead. He could feel the pain and pressure in his left arm, almost as if the fire had returned and was now pressurized under the dressings.

When the pressure finally released, Tommen found himself reeling and wondering if he hadn't internally combusted. Where before there was intense pressure, it was all gone and he almost felt like he was walking on air. He could fly. He could manipulate Gravity. Then his sinuses began to drain and his eyes watered like Niagara Falls and his body produced another gallon of sweat to plaster his body and his ears began to ring.

"Go, Tommen!" Chandler told him, his voice a distant echo in the cave. "Run while you have the chance!"

Right. Run. He had to get out of here before the dimension closed in on him again or the Time Trap snapped him up, not to spit him out for another century or two.

Still, even his own movements felt like they were not his own. His whole body moved and not in the way he wanted it to. First it took him into a wall before dropping him on the floor of the cave. Somewhere far away, someone told him to get up and keep moving. Get out of the cave at least.

Out of the cave. Through the blurriness of his unwanted tears, Tommen found the light, the first streaks of dawn in the sky. Or, more likely, anything lighter than the darkness of the cave.

Drunkenly, Tommen got his feet under him and he half-stumbled, half-crawled toward the huge boulder that still poorly blocked the entrance to the cave. He hit the boulder with his face but hardly noticed as he grappled his way along until he reached open air. The coolness of the morning hit him and managed to wake him up a little bit, enough that he could wipe his eyes to see a little more clearly.

He was out. He was outside anyway. Had he made it? Did it work? Was there any way to know?

He hit the ground as a small earthquake shook the area. The sound of a small explosion hit him next. His ears rang louder. His vision was clouded with dust and debris. His head throbbed and he could hardly form a coherent thought. Every instinct told him to get up and get moving. Had to get out, had to get away. Can't stay here.

Ignoring the pain in his left side, he got to his feet. Memory more than conscious thought got him down the path. But the last thing he could acutely remember was another explosion, another earthquake, and the realization that he could not, in fact, manipulate Gravity.

Chapter Thirty-Three
The Call

Walter jumped awake at his alarm, his whole body shaking so bad he could hardly punch it off. He couldn't remember his dream, but then, maybe he didn't want to. He lay back and closed his eyes for a minute, trying to calm down and get his head together. Every part of his body demanded a painkiller. The better part of him said not to indulge, that he could overpower the urges and break this addiction before it became a problem. Thing was, it was already a problem. He just didn't know how to deal with it without potentially losing everything—his job, his girlfriend, his son. Even if CPS didn't step in, he couldn't bear the thought of facing Tommen and telling him he had an opioid problem.

So he quietly got out of bed and headed to the bathroom, ignoring every ache and pain and fabricated injury his body was using to force him to get a pill, or maybe two. Just enough to get going in the morning, a little pick me up, because coffee just wasn't doing it. He splashed cold water in his face, told himself no. As he turned on the hot water in the shower, he felt his knee and thigh and chest all tighten in pain. All fabricated, he told himself. Those wounds were healed and he was done with them. He was moving on.

But the urge plagued him the whole time he was getting dressed and making breakfast. Just one. Just enough to make it through the morning. A depressant to keep his temper in check in case the new guy did try to pull anything today, having the full Monday crews to deal with. Or, barring the new guy, just something to keep his temper in check in general, seeing how he wasn't the most friendly guy to work with when his son was missing.

He'd thought about little else since the previous night. As far as he could tell, nothing had actually gone wrong except Tommen picked that moment to play hero and try to make things right. Walter had physically held his son, and then Tommen decided he was going to try and keep Julianna from escaping. It might have worked if Rifun hadn't been there to ensure his failure.

The ensuing standoff had done little to help his mood either. He so badly wanted to put a couple slugs through Rifun's head, but no one there who had tried had been successful. Kayla had perhaps come the closest to finally murdering the bastard, but even then, she had failed. What was it going to take to kill him?

More to the point, since they could no longer count on Rifun to provide even temporary assistance in rescuing Tommen, how did they go about replicating his actions so they could do it themselves? Could they go back and ask Micaiah's friend who had seen something like a quasi-dimension once upon a time? Should they try the warehouse idea anyway?

Walter elected to forgo breakfast and head straight to work, telling himself that he really ought to do a better job about trying to lose weight, when he knew very well that it was just stress. He wasn't even sure he wanted to grab a cup of coffee, but he forced himself to go along on that one, just so he had a taste in his mouth, something other than peppermint toothpaste.

He also tried to convince himself that only coffee and no food might do well to make him seem punctual. Now that it was Monday morning, and no doubt word had gotten around to some of the guys about the new chief, everyone would be on edge and on their best behavior as they tried to feel this guy out. Who was he, what were his intentions, whose side would he be on?

Just walking in the door, Walter could feel the tension, like watching the spark on the dynamite fuse get closer and closer to the stick. Looking around the office, it wasn't hard to tell who was on whose team as they lingered around one person's desk or another. Some still thought Harry should have gotten the promotion.

Truthfully, Walter might have thrown his support behind the man if he didn't know it would guarantee his forced resignation. Others were on Walter's side, though his fanbase was considerably smaller. Still a few others made comments about jumping up a qualified Lieutenant, one who could be a Captain if only a position opened up and allowed them the rank. That was a whole can of worms Walter hardly even wanted to consider.

Still, he made it to his cubicle unmolested and was pleasantly surprised that nothing had been ransacked, vandalized, or spray painted with death threats. Everything was exactly as he had left it the day before. When he made his way to the break room for a refill on his coffee, he was intercepted by Standish.

"So, we made it through the first twenty-four hours with the new guy," he began conversationally.

"Maybe," Walter acknowledged, "but that was Sunday. That was the preliminary trial. Today is when it really begins."

"Well, there goes my optimistic mood for the day. Still no word on your boy?"

"Nothing."

He figured that was a safe answer. If Laura had told Standish's wife the story and then it got back to Standish, "nothing" might simply reference that nothing new had surfaced and nothing had changed. If Laura kept the story close to the vest, then "nothing" was simply nothing. No word whatsoever.

"Guess it's a good thing Greg gave you the time off when he did," Standish was saying. "I don't think this new guy is going to be quite as generous."

"I don't know." Walter stirred in a creamer. "The new guy might be a little tougher than Greg, but to deny leave based on extenuating circumstances, especially when it involves someone's kid, I mean, that's just cold. But you are right; I'm glad I got the time off that I did. I just wish I could have done more or that it had been a little more productive."

"He's out there somewhere, Walt, and he's a lot smarter than most of the guys here give him credit for. He'll turn up."

Knowing what he did, Walter wished he could have been so optimistic as he returned to his cubicle to figure out what to do with his day. No midnight murder assignments were waiting for him, and there was no mysterious note or phone call from Casey saying, "See me." So other than a few routine chores, he was basically left to his own devices. After listening to a little more grumbling and office gossip through the thin walls of his cubicle, he elected to head out and see what trouble he could rustle up around town.

The bakery wasn't open yet, but he figured the twins might be running a little behind, having to recuperate a little after the night's escapades. So he bypassed them for the time being, instead managing to catch himself a speeder who turned out to be transporting quite the haul of cocaine. That sent the drug unit on a feeding frenzy, and Walter took a minute to just stand back and watch them rip into the guy, his truck, and start calling around for warrants to search his apartment. The day went from zero to sixty in the blink of an eye.

Of course, opinions back at the office were divided. He was either a hero for catching the guy or else it had somehow been staged so he could ingratiate himself to the new chief and keep his job. As Walter reflected on some of the not-so-subtle comments, he found it remarkable how most of them would not have been given a voice except that the ghosts of Christmas past were coming back to life and making everything miserable. Of the new Chief of Police himself, there was little sign. He'd conversed briefly with the head of the drug unit, then vanished into thin air.

"Asshole or not, he better step up and make sure everyone knows who's boss," Standish remarked. "Otherwise some of these guys are going to go lone cowboy on us and take their followers with them."

"Agreed," Walter murmured. "But if you don't mind, I'm going to go lone cowboy for a minute and make a few phone calls."

A few of the calls were inconsequential, calling this judge or that judge to confirm the status of a warrant, doing special welfare checks on a few elderly folk and another family with a rather violent special needs child, and so on.

He managed to burn about thirty minutes before he was left staring at his cell phone. There was no telling how Casey was going to react to doing a little personal business while on the clock, but there was only one way to find out. Forgiveness and permission and all that.

"Hello?" a sleepy voice answered.

"Did I wake you?" Walter wondered.

"Mm, not really. Just got up and am in the process of pouring my first cup of coffee. Give me about five minutes and I'll be a little more receptive to conversation."

"Late night, huh?"

Laura let out a breath. "You have no idea. First it's this guy who calls for his friend's broken leg. Get there and surprise! It's an overdose. Then we have this other guy who's had chest pain, difficulty breathing, and generalized weakness for the last two days, but decides two in the morning is the best time to call for help."

"Well, of course it is. The roads are clear with minimal traffic and you guys are all rested up in your cushy beds at the station."

"Yeah, tell that to my chiropractor. Cushy beds, my ass. And I mean that literally."

"I wouldn't know."

She snickered a little and he could hear her spoon clinking in the mug as she stirred in her own cream and sugar. "Any news on Tommen?"

"No, not yet." There was no conceivable way he could explain to her how his son had completely escaped the cave he was trapped in, then decided to run back inside for unknown reasons, only to be trapped again. Best to play it off as though it never happened. It didn't make him feel any better. "They're hoping to try something today, but they have to be careful about the surrounding rock."

"Of course. Safety is paramount. And it's good that they are able to get food, water, and medicine to him. He should be able to last a little longer. Have you spoken to him at all?"

"No. I thought I might call the crews in a minute or maybe a little later and ask for an update. If it's still going to be a while, I'll get up there tonight. Or I'll try to. Where they're searching is not an easily accessible area."

"Oh, naturally. Listen, my pager senses are tingling, so I think I'm going to have to hurry up and get breakfast before the tones drop."

"All right. You're off tomorrow, right?"

"Seven o'clock sharp. Ha ha ha."

"I understand, believe me."

"Maybe when you get off tomorrow, we can go up to the cave together and talk to Tommen. Or try to."

"Or try to," Walter echoed, feeling his heart sink. "That might be something worth trying. Listen, I'll let you get back to breakfast while you have the chance."

In the background, he heard tones go off. Laura sighed. "Too late on that one. I'll talk to you later. Bye."

Click.

Walter set his phone down and rubbed his face. Damn. The woman was way out of his league, that much was for certain. But how in the world was he going to pull off that kind of a stunt? There was no cave and search crews hadn't found anything. As of last night, Tommen was completely AWOL, so they couldn't even fake anything.

Maybe he could look at a map and find the most twisty, windy, unnavigable two-track he could. They'd get up there and, whoops, guess we're not going to make it. Of course, he'd have to pick something that even her truck couldn't manage. But there were trails like that, he was sure.

Maybe he could rope the twins into an elaborate set-up where they got some volunteers who would be Disguised as the search team. They could find a plausible cave and send someone inside who could be Disguised as Tommen and imitate him long enough for the charade to work and they could go home. Sounded nice, but it would be way too much coordination in a short amount of time. They'd had enough trouble just trying to get everyone together for the secret rescue attempts that no one else would see.

Or he could sidestep it and claim he was busy or something else had come up. He was needed for an extra shift at work — well, no, that was too easy to corroborate or disprove. Had to be something relatively unprovable. Maybe one of the twins could have some sort of crisis. Maybe Micaiah could say that Kayla was finally pregnant and all the guys had to go out for drinks. That was plausible, and seeing how they would be moving before the birth, well, no one would be the wiser.

If he did that, though, was Laura liable to ask for the location and go up there herself? Walter didn't think so, but he had to plan for every possible contingency. He had to root out every possible way that his lie could be exposed. His first problem came when he considered why the hell he'd started this lie in the first place.

He was not okay. He wanted to be normal. He wanted to not have to worry about Time and psychomaniacs and civil war — or war of any kind — and whether his son was running around in the correct dimension. Problem was, the more he wanted to retire, the more stuff got thrown at him that he couldn't just walk away from. He could walk away from the garbage in the Wheel and the Akarin civil war, but he couldn't just ignore an impending Borelian invasion, or whatever plans those toxic bastards had in mind. Whatever they were up to, humanity was going to need every available hand to help fight, which included him.

Finally, Walter just stood and headed out again. Maybe he would get lucky a second time and bring in some other wanted criminal. Maybe he would get even luckier and not have anything for the rest of the day. That sounded pretty good, too.

He found a quiet spot to sit with his radar gun. As he brought out a bit of paperwork, his phone buzzed.

"All quiet on the western front," Laura texted. "Maybe now I'll get something to eat."

"I'm no medic, but I'm pretty sure you just swore twice in that last text," he replied.

"Quiet quiet quiet. Eat eat eat."

"Do you use that language with your kids?"

"I use the first one, but they insist on using the second one. Thankfully, they're all grown up and can fend for themselves."

Walter let out a breath and did not reply. Instead, he turned his attention back to his paperwork. It was incredibly tedious, but in a court of law, incredibly useful. A moment later, his phone buzzed again.

"Sorry."

"It's all right," Walter answered. "I'm holding out hope."

"That's good. I'll talk to you later."

"Okay."

He returned to his paperwork. He'd hardly gotten through half a sheet when his phone began ringing. Looking at the number, he knew it was local, but couldn't quite say why it was familiar.

"Walter Forbes," he answered formally.

"Walt, it's Lisa from the ER."

This was unexpected. "Morning, Lisa, to what do I owe the pleasure? You know I'm not on Missing Persons anymore, right?"

"Oh, trust me, I am well aware. But I think this is one you might be interested in. A little over six foot, pale as death, hair in need of a trim, about seventeen years old—"

"They found him?!" Walter sat up in his seat.

"Well, more to the point, he found us. Sort of. Anyway, listen to me, Walter. They're taking him in for an evaluation, X-rays, the whole works. It's going to be a few minutes before you can see him. Finish up whatever you're doing, calm yourself down, and then come over."

"You're asking the world, Lisa."

"It's for your own good, Walt. Yours and his. Oh, and if possible, he could use a change of clothes. We're debating whether we should send his to laundry or just burn them."

"That bad, huh?"

"Well, traipsing around in the wilderness for a week hasn't

done him any favors. I'll leave that up to you."

"All right. Thank you, Lisa. You just made my day."

He could hear her smile over the phone. "I try. We'll see you in a bit."

Walter hung up and sat there in stunned silence for a full minute. They got him. He was out. He escaped. He was at the hospital and finally getting the treatment he needed. He rubbed his face, still unable to comprehend it. Maybe last night had been more effective than they'd originally thought. Maybe Tommen had come up with a way to escape on his own. Whatever the case, he was alive and well.

Taking a calming breath and telling himself that there was no need to panic, Walter put away his paperwork and eased the cruiser back into the road. It only took a minute or two make it back to the precinct, but it might as well have been an eternity. He filed away the paperwork he had completed, sorted the stuff he hadn't, grabbed his coat and mentally prepared himself for the inevitable conversation with his new boss.

"Good morning," Casey greeted. "Good to know I haven't scared everyone off."

"They'll come around, I'm sure," Walter said wistfully. "Sir, I need to take a few hours off, possibly the rest of the day."

"Oh?"

"They found my son. He's at the hospital right now getting checked out."

"Excellent! Wonderful news! I'm happy for you, really." Casey nodded. "By all means, go and see him."

Walter raised a brow. "I sense a 'but' coming."

The chief's expression wavered just a twitch, but he waved his hand dismissively. "We'll talk about it later. Right now, you need to be with your son. Did they tell you at all how he is?"

"No, they didn't. But I intend to find out."

"Absolutely. All right, I've taken up enough of your time. Get out of here."

Walter nodded, thanked him, and turned to leave. He got two

steps out of the doorway before Banding and turning around to judge Casey's expression. There was surprise and a certain level of glee; it was always a good day when a missing child was found, especially when it was an officer's child. But there was also that element of scrutiny that Walter had seen the day before when the news broke that Steggmann was leaving and this was his replacement.

Walter was accustomed to scrutiny, of course, but there was certainly a difference between Steggmann's scrutiny and Casey's scrutiny. Steggmann was quiet and thoughtful, and he gave the impression that he was concerned with the well-being of the men under his command. Casey was quiet but penetrating, and he gave the impression that anything substandard was going to be met with a writeup on top of fifty pushups. He was looking for dissent as much as loyalty.

Walter dropped the Band and continued on his way. He couldn't be overly concerned with his boss right now. He should be focusing entirely on Tommen and making sure he was safe and sound.

He paused once to top off his coffee before heading outside, momentarily conflicted on which vehicle to take. Well, if he was taking a few hours off, that meant he was off-duty and should probably take his personal vehicle. At least it wasn't as embarrassing as the Cadillac.

As he started up the vehicle, he called Laura back.

"Morning, Walt." She sounded a little more awake now.

"Laura, they got him. They got Tommen. He's actually already at the hospital. I'm on my way there now."

"That's great! Yeah, that's wonderful news. I'm so happy." She laughed. "Yeah, that's great. Listen, I can't just drop everything here and rush over there, but the next time we transport and head out there, I'll definitely take a few minutes and see if I can't stop in and say hi, see how he's doing." Pause. "How is he doing?"

"They didn't say, just that he was going in for a full evaluation and workup and it would be a few minutes anyway."

"Okay. Hey, that is still awesome news. I'm so happy for you. Yeah, like I said, I'll see if I can stop in on our next run, okay? You go be with your son."

"Heading that way now. I'll text you what room he's in and all that."

"Sounds good. See you soon, then."

Walter hung up and couldn't even think of where to start on finally processing all of this new information. His son was back. Missing for five days and now he's finally returned to civilization and getting treatment.

He slowed down a bit when he considered Lisa's other words. He should probably run home first to grab a change of clothes for Tommen. Running around without a shower for a week was not a pleasant thing. Grudgingly, Walter turned around and headed home. As he drove, he dialed Micaiah who answered after the third ring.

"Yeah, Walt."

"Cai, they got him. Tommen's home. He's back, I mean. He's at the hospital."

"What? How? When?"

"I just got the call about twenty minutes ago. I'm heading home first to get him some new clothes, then I'll be going over there."

"Did they tell you how he's doing?"

"No, nothing. But I'll find out soon enough."

"Keep me posted, Walt. I'll get over there as soon as I can. I want to know what the hell happened."

"You and me both. I'll keep you posted and text you his room number."

"Roger."

As soon as he hung up, Walter Banded the rest of the way home, too excited to see his son and not wanting to waste another second. He pulled in the garage and barged inside, almost as if in pursuit of some criminal. As it was, he barely remembered to take his shoes off so he didn't track dirt through the house.

He half-expected to find Tommen lounging on the bed with a smirk and some smart-ass remark, but the room was empty. Walter grabbed a full set of clothes and stuffed them in a bag. He was almost on his way out the door when he reconsidered and went back for a hairbrush, toothbrush, toothpaste, and other hygienic necessities. Then he was out the door and on his way to the hospital.

The morning rush of Monday traffic had ebbed, but it was still too thick for Walter's liking, and he didn't have the lights and sirens to get him through any faster. Even Time was limited in its usefulness when there was nowhere to go. By the time he made it to the hospital, found a parking spot, and was heading inside, he felt like he'd wasted half the day.

"Well, that was quick," Lisa observed, meeting him at the emergency room desk.

"Feels like it wasn't quick enough," Walter murmured.

"You're still going to have to wait a few minutes."

"Come on, Lisa, stop with the suspense. Tell me how he is. What happened?"

She nodded and took him aside, away from the prying ears of other ER patrons. "He was actually found near Forbes Cave. It got called in to the ambulance as a wounded hiker. A jogging group was making their rounds and said he fell off the sheer drop there that separates the trails from the cave. No broken bones or anything, but when fire crews got to him to get him down the trail to the ambulance, he was in and out of consciousness, muttering in Welsh—well, they said not in English, but you and I know better. There is the possibility of a concussion.

"Anyway, medics stated he started to come around a little in the ambulance, knew his name and address, where he went to school, who his dad is. That tipped them off to the situation. So I called you, and another doctor called the search team to call off the search. Amber alert has been taken down for him, too. Everything is all cleaned up there."

"How is he physically?" Walter asked.

Lisa grinned. "Your boy is certainly a wilderness survival expert. His left side, from his neck to his ribs and all the way down his arm to his hand, was severely burned, mostly second-degree. But when he came in, he had it wrapped in gauze dipped in an old Native American burn ointment and wrapped in leaves. The only reason I know that is because that's what he said. It's probably what saved his life because he's got infection out the wazoo and he's septic. But if he'd left his arm exposed, he would certainly be in a lot worse shape.

"Otherwise, he's reasonably healthy. No other major injuries. Cuts, scrapes, things you would expect from being lost in the wilderness. He stayed well-hydrated, too, which is another thing that kept his infection and sepsis from getting worse than it is."

"When can I see him?"

"Last I knew, he was taken up to ICU on account of his burns. He was also much more awake and complaining how his arm hurt like a mother—you know what."

Walter sighed but couldn't stop from smiling. "I know. All right, guess I'll head up there, then. Thanks, Lisa."

"No problem, Walt. You know I love that boy as much as you, ever since he first dropped in. From Forbes Cave, no less."

He did not reply, seeing how he was already halfway to the elevator. After several stops and one misstep, Walter got off on the Intensive Care floor, making a beeline for the reception desk.

"Can I help you?" the receptionist wondered, eyeing his badge.

"My son just came up here from ER. Tommen Forbes."

The receptionist checked her computer, but informed him that there was no patient by that name in ICU currently. They had a little back and forth about it, including three calls down to the ER and a couple conversations with a few ICU nurses and doctors until Tommen's transfer papers made it up and his name popped up on the computer patient roster.

"So, which room is he in?" Walter asked irritably.

"He hasn't been assigned to a room just yet," the receptionist answered. "At this time, he has been taken in for surgery."

"Surgery for what?"

"For his burns." All that was needed was the unspoken, "Duh" written across the woman's face. Instead, she finished with, "It shouldn't take long, if you want to wait out here."

No, Walter did not want to wait out here. At the same time, waiting out here or in an empty room, it was still waiting. He wouldn't be any less anxious in any environment. Grudgingly, he agreed and went to find a seat.

What kind of surgery would they be doing? Maybe it had something to do with his jacket being melted into his skin, but wouldn't that come off naturally as the old skin died and new skin came to the surface? Maybe it was just a way to expedite the process. He found it amusing to think about Tommen wrapping his arm in gauze and leaves, but where had the Native American medicine come from? Kayla, maybe? Seemed plausible.

Too many maybes to entertain, and he continued to wait impatiently, his mind going off on all sorts of trails and two-tracks. He people-watched as much as he could; ICU had no shortage of activity as it pertained to nurses and other staff, but the real fun came form watching the patients and trying to figure out what had happened, make up a backstory. Hard to believe he'd been in here at the start of the year.

"Walter Forbes?"

He looked up to see a doctor approaching, and he stood to meet him.

"How's Tommen?" Walter demanded.

"Dr. Paul Farrow," the doctor introduced, extending a hand which Walter clasped briefly. "I'm happy to report that Tommen is on the way to a recovery."

Before either said more, Dr. Farrow motioned for Walter to follow, and the two of them started down one of the hallways.

"What surgery did you have to perform?" Walter wondered.

"Well, let me start at the beginning. His left arm is completely burned, along with some tissue around the shoulder, chest, neck, and down his side to his hip. The shoulder, neck, chest, and side are what we call superficial partial-thickness, what you might remember as second-degree burns. They're worse than first-degree, but not all that terrible. From the upper arm to the wrist are superficial partial-thickness and deep partial-thickness. The wrist, hand and fingers are all deep partial-thickness burns with a few spots touching into the full thickness or third-degree burns. It is infected, and he is septic, but it is all being managed and treated, and even since he was first brought in, he has improved drastically.

"Furthermore, the fabric of his jacket and shirt melted into the skin. One of the goals of the surgery was to safely remove as much of that as possible in order to facilitate healing. Anything that could safely be removed was taken, but there are a few pieces that will just have to fall off on their own.

"Another portion of the surgery is what we call an escharotomy. Eschar is the tough, leathery skin found in full-thickness burns, where everything has been burned and is dead. It's a way of relieving the pressure of any swelling and edema. However, because Tommen has been in the wilderness with no proper care—though I will commend his wilderness medical skills—the muscle and fat and any living tissue under the burns is still a little swollen and has begun to contract and tighten. We had to make some incisions on the hand and partway up his arm in order to release that pressure."

They stopped outside one of the rooms and Walter asked, "So, what's the prognosis? Is he going to be able to use his hand and arm again?"

"I expect so," Farrow said, nodding. "He'll need to keep it splinted for at least two weeks. After that, it might just be something he wears at night, but it depends on how well his hand heals."

"Do you think he'll need grafts?"

"At this time, I don't believe it to be necessary. I want to see how things progress with the steps we've already taken and not do more than we have to in order to minimize the possibility of any further damage. They're highly sensitive areas and trying to repair such small spots could result in greater damage to a larger area. There will be scarring, however. That much I can guarantee and really can't do anything about."

"Oh, I'm sure he'll enjoy showing off," Walter said, grinning.

"He's a teenager; of course he will. Especially when it comes to the story that goes along with it, saving campers from that fire up there. Anyway, this is his room. Normally, the procedures described can be done just by numbing, and the patient is free to watch. However, because of his mental state when he was brought in, as well as other factors, we decided it best to fully sedate him. Well, when I say 'fully' it's more like getting your wisdom teeth out. He should be coming around shortly. Do you know how he normally reacts to anesthesia?"

"Well, he did get his wisdom teeth out a few years ago, and if this is anything like that, he's probably going to be sick and extremely uncoordinated for a few hours."

"Very good. Well then, I'll get out of your way for a few minutes."

Farrow stepped aside and moved on to some other task, leaving Walter to enter the room alone.

Never had he been so happy to see his son lounging in bed, though "lounging" was a pretty strong term. Tommen lay in the hospital bed, his left arm splinted and wrapped to kingdom come, propped up on a stand. His head lolled to one side as he slept soundly, an oxygen tube under his nose. He had one IV port in his right arm and another in his hand, the former leading to a bag of clear fluid, the other waiting for a syringe.

Walter let out a breath as he collapsed into a chair, the bag of clothes thumping on the floor. His son was here. He was alive. He could see him. For a few minutes, Walter just sat there, taking it all in, trying to process it. And suddenly, it was almost as if the last five days hadn't happened at all. He could almost believe his own lie, that Tommen had been trapped in a cave and rescue crews had gotten him out. If not for the incident last night with Rifun, he would have been content to let the past lie.

Eventually, he got his phone out and started sending out the messages. Tommen had been found, he would be all right. He's in the burn unit at ICU, and this is his room number, but don't come right away because he's still a little kooky.

Last but not least, he called the precinct to let them—Casey Oldman—know he would be out the rest of the day. His son had been found, he would be all right. He's in the burn unit at ICU and things are looking up. Casey congratulated him and said he hoped things went well. Cynthia the receptionist congratulated him and wished Tommen a full and speedy recovery.

"Dad?"

Walter jumped at Tommen's soft, slightly slurred mumble. He stood and went to his son who slowly and most ungracefully—and unsuccessfully—tried to shift position in bed. If not for his arm, he might have made a little progress, but between that and his drug-induced stupor, he barely got a decent wiggle.

"Hey, kiddo, how are you feeling?"

"Like shit." Tommen let out a breath. "How did I get here?"

"You came by ambulance. A group of joggers found you in the park near Forbes Cave."

"Oh."

And he lapsed back into sleep, or something like it.

Walter returned to his seat, but he had no sooner sat down than the door opened and Laura poked her head in.

"Hey," he said lamely, standing.

"So I did get the right room," she mused as she stepped in. "I only have a couple minutes. How is he?"

Walter nodded. "He'll make a recovery. The doctor said they had to remove a lot of the jacket fabric that had melted into his arm and chest, and then they had to make incisions in his hand and arm to relieve the pressure." He repeated as much as he could remember from the discussion.

"At least he'll be able to use his hand. He is very lucky."

"It's his homesteading blood. Came in handy when he needed wild medicine."

She grinned. "I guess so. I take it he's going to be here a while."

"Probably a couple days at least, just for the infections and everything else. They don't want to send him home just yet."

"That makes sense." Laura glanced at her watch. "Well, my time's up here. I'll probably be back up the next time I'm here. Less than twenty-four hours to go, but you know something is going to happen."

"Take your time, no need to rush," Walter said, then surprised her with a kiss on the cheek. "I'll see you later today or tomorrow morning, I'm sure."

She blushed and excused herself, walking quickly down the hall to the elevator and glancing back only once to give him a shy smile.

Once she was gone, Walter resumed his wait, picking up a few magazines and absently perusing.

"Dad?"

He looked up and returned to Tommen's bedside. This time he was able to better manage a small adjustment, though he did spit up some stomach fluids which mysteriously included bits of egg and some kind of meat. Walter wasn't completely certain as he did not dwell on it for very long past a casual observation. He was just grateful a sick bag had been nearby so it could be easily disposed of and he wouldn't have to smell it all afternoon.

"How are you feeling?" he dared ask.

"Like shit. How did I get here?"

"You came in by ambulance. A—"

"Why, so I could get a haircut? That seems a little extreme."

"What? A haircut? No. You were brought in because you're injured. Your arm is burned and you fell off a small cliff."

"Did anyone see? Were the judges impressed?"

Walter sighed. Anesthesia worked wonders. "Unfortunately, no. They weren't. In fact, they sent you to the hospital to get fixed up."

"Did they have the right bit? Because you're always looking for that one bit that you don't have."

"There's a lot of bits that I don't have. You seem to enjoy

reminding me of that."

"Well, I don't need to be reminded to take a shower and put on deodorant. I'm not twelve. I'm a man. I know how to do things."

"Like what?"

"I can drive and eat a whole pizza by myself."

"And how does that make you a man?"

But Tommen's words had been getting slower and more slurred. Actually, Walter had found the whole conversation very amusing, mostly because he knew Tommen wouldn't remember it anyway. He had half a mind to get a video of it just to tease him about it later.

"I am a man because I have balls," Tommen said at last.

"Oh really?" Walter raised a brow. "So what separates the men from the boys?"

"Boys play junior varsity and men are in varsity."

"Tommen, you don't play sports."

"Nope, but I am a world-class actor. Men can be actors, too."

"Yes, they can, but you're not an actor either, however dramatic you may be at times. You are the backstage manager."

Tommen shook his head and got sick again before answering. "No, not backstage. I'm really not into the anal thing."

Walter sighed. "Well, at least you have that going for you."

He looked like he wanted to say more, but fatigue won out at the last moment and he dropped out again. Walter chuckled to himself as he went back to his chair to sit and wait for the next round of drug-induced conversation. He only had all day, after all. What's the worst that could happen?

Chapter Thirty-Four
The Collapse of Forbes Cave

After stumbling out of the cave and what he was pretty sure amounted to falling off a cliff, Tommen only had blurry, conceptual images of the events immediately following. He couldn't decide whether part of it was a memory of carrying Saul off the mountain, or if he had been carried out of the park. Could have been either, he supposed. He had vague recollections of talking to doctors, and then it all went black as they put a mask over his face and told him to count backwards from one hundred. He thought he might have gotten to eighty-four, but he couldn't be sure.

The first thing he noticed was that his left side felt better, but it was propped up and his shoulder ached something fierce. The second thing he noticed was that his right arm hurt like a bitch from a couple of IVs. Once he got that filed away, all the other aches and pains started making themselves known, including his sour stomach. He did everything he could to push that to the side as he blindly shifted position and cautiously opened his eyes.

"Dad?" he wondered, his throat scratchy.

His dad was sitting in a chair, reading a magazine. He looked up, set the magazine in the second chair, stood and approached the bed.

"How are you feeling, kiddo?" he asked.

Tommen sighed. "How long have I been out?"

"You've been in and out of consciousness since you were found about seven o'clock this morning, barring the time you were in surgery. It's two o'clock now, so it's been a little while."

"What was the surgery for? I don't know, I think they might

703

have told me, but I don't remember."

"That's all right. They removed as much of the melted fabric and dead skin as they could. The doctor also said they had to make incisions on your hand and arm to relieve pressure on the muscles."

"Oh. Makes sense, I think. Definitely feels better, but that could just be painkillers or something."

He closed his eyes and took an even breath as his stomach rumbled and roiled. His dad handed him a sick bag, but he declined after a minute of fighting mind over matter.

"So when can I go home?" he asked.

"In a few days. You're still septic and have infections that need to be managed."

"Fuck. Spend all that time and energy to get home only to get told I can't go home."

"In a few days," his dad repeated. "And stop swearing. I mean it now. You're lucid enough to control yourself."

Tommen lazily found his right hand and managed to lift it enough to wave it dismissively. "Whatever, man."

Before either could say more, the door opened and a doctor walked in. His nametag read Farrow, Paul, M.D., Intensive Care Unit.

"Awake again, hm?" he wondered. "Still giving your dad a hard time?"

"Actually, I think he's coming around," Walter told him. "We're finally able to have a conversation that doesn't change topic every other sentence."

Tommen looked at his dad but said nothing. Great. He probably embarrassed himself in his drug-induced stupor and his dad was never going to let him live it down. He hoped he hadn't voiced any fantasies or revealed his Christmas plans with Becky. That would not end well.

Farrow pulled up a chair to his bedside. "How are you feeling, Tommen?"

"Better than before, I guess. My arm feels better."

"That's good. Now, I'm just curious, what happened out there for you to get these burns?"

"I don't even remember, man. Ask me in a couple days when I can think straight."

"Okay. Fair enough. Do you think you're 'here' enough for me to explain what happened here, what we did?"

"My dad said you had to do surgery."

"Yes, we did. Maybe in a couple days we can talk about what sort of field medicine you did on yourself, but whatever it was, you did well. It made things a lot easier on us. Your skin had begun to heal and slough off some of the jacket fabric; we removed as much of it as we safely could. We also had to make some incisions here—" He pointed to a couple spots on his own hand and then up his arm. " —and here to relieve the pressure and keep your skin and muscles from tightening."

He went into a semi-technical explanation of the procedure, including what to expect over the next couple weeks with healing. Basically, what Tommen got out of it was that there would be scarring, no getting around that, and he was going to have to wear a splint for a while so his hand could heal. Then, when he could take the splint off, he would have to exercise his hand like mad to ensure everything healed properly and he didn't fuck up the small muscles and sensitive nerves.

"So when can I get all this off?" Tommen asked, indicating the layers of gauze that had all but immobilized his arm.

"In a day or two," Farrow promised. "This is mostly post-op stuff, to keep everything exactly as it was at the conclusion of the surgery. It will still have to be wrapped to keep it dry and protected, but you will be able to move your arm and hand."

"Oh. Okay."

"Unlike most surgeries where you have to stay completely immobile for a certain length of time, with something like this, we want you to move as much as possible."

"Okay." Tommen stifled a yawn and turned it into a sigh. "When can I get something to eat?"

"Is your stomach still sick?" his dad cut in.

"A little."

"Give it a couple more hours," Farrow told him. "The dinner menu starts at five, and I would highly recommend the fish."

They had a short chat after that about starvation in the wilderness, which Tommen generally denied, though he knew he had to go along with a little bit. He couldn't just rush into a five-course meal. He had to build up to it with lighter fare. Salads, juice, fish if he really had to go with meat, but nothing fried or greasy.

Then he left, and Tommen and Walter were alone in the room once more.

"Well, now that you seem to be a little more with it, do you want me to release the hounds?" Walter asked.

"What?"

"Do you want visitors? So far I've been telling everyone to stay away for a bit until you started coming around."

Not really. He still felt like shit and didn't want to be seen as a sick, blathering idiot. At the same time, it would be nice to have a conversation with someone not over the phone. It was nice to be visible again.

"Maybe wait until after dinner," he suggested. "That way I'm not eating in front of people and I'm not getting sick in front of them either."

"Fair enough," his dad conceded, pulling up his own chair. "Are you in much of a talking mood right now, or do you want to sleep some more?"

Sleep. "What are we talking about?"

"How about the full story of what happened up there in camp?"

They were interrupted briefly by a visit from a nurse who checked the IV bag and gave him a shot of something through the hand port. She asked him a few questions, entered something on her tablet as he answered, then handed him a menu and left the room.

Tommen fumbled with the menu for a minute. With his left hand immobilized and his right hindered by a port, it was a wonder he got where he needed to be. His dad shifted so he could read the menu also.

"You're going to eat better than I am tonight, that's for sure," he commented.

"What are you talking about?" Tommen wondered. "I can't have half of this."

"Oh, please. You haven't been starving this last week. You had eggs for breakfast, am I right?"

Tommen felt his ears burn red. "Possibly. And maybe some venison sausage, too."

"That's what I thought. Your only limitation right now is your stomach, and I think that's been settling down in the last half hour or so. What are you actually getting for dinner?"

"I don't know. Last time I was here, I had a salad. Not bad, but a salad's a salad. But I also just had venison for breakfast. I don't know, maybe I will go with the fish."

Walter sighed and shook his head. "My child is rich and spoiled. Can't decide between the steak and the fish because he's already had both."

Tommen scoffed and grinned. "What kid are you talking about?"

He set the menu aside.

"So," his dad began, more seriously. "What happened out there? The whole story."

Maybe he should have claimed fatigue. It wasn't that he didn't want to tell the story, but it was such a long one. Maybe this would end up as an Authored Book and he could tell his dad to just read that. But who knew how long it would take for this little adventure to appear on his bookshelf?

He let out a breath. "When we did camper checks, when we were evacuating and stuff, Nathan turned up missing. I found him and brought him back, but then everything stopped. It was encased in a Band, you know? Rifun was the one responsible. He took me back into the fire and showed me things. How to touch Matter and put out fire by actually stopping the burning process at the chemical level. It was pretty sweet, really. Then he had me try it the other way, using Energy, grabbing the fire and forcing it out. It didn't work, and he said that was the point. He...told me to go back to be evacuated and he would be back later to teach me some more.

"I didn't want him to get the credit for me learning stuff, so I decided to try it out on my own, see if I could master it myself. I touched the fire, touched the Energy, and the next thing I know, I'm a hundred feet from the cabin, on my back, hurting like a mo...seriously. The fire was out, so I knew it had been a while. I got up, and, once I got reoriented, made it down to the garage where the search team was. I saw you and tried to get your attention, but then you walked right through me. It was the weirdest thing ever. That's kind of when I figured out that something wasn't right."

His dad nodded slowly and gestured for him to continue. So Tommen told him about all the trips back and forth between the camp and the town, including a short, one-sided lunch with Laura. His dad provided the other half of the story which included the use of Trackers, trying to figure out if there had been any temporal activity in the area, which there had been.

Tommen continued the story which involved his first introduction to Julianna and subsequent theft of some of Laura's supplies. His dad seemed amused by that still.

"How did you end up in Virginia, though?" his dad asked. "And all your traveling, how did you do it?"

"It's just something you can do in the in-between dimension. It's called Traveling. I mean, you kind of just think of a place you want to go, turn in the right direction, start walking, and the next thing you know, you're there. Doesn't matter if there are oceans or mountains in the middle; you get there. It's pretty cool, actually. I mean, I didn't understand it at first, and my first attempt put me somewhere in the Atlantic. I panicked, and when I finally got back to solid ground, I was in Virginia. That's where I had the idea to try and make a call. Normal towers wouldn't work, so I decided to open them all up."

"I guess you do listen to me sometimes."

"Only enough to get me in trouble," Tommen replied smartly.

"Right. Keep going."

So he continued his story, including his time stalking linemen and firemen and what he'd hoped to accomplish, which wasn't much. When he explained his exploits as it pertained to the time traveling and checking up on the family and his brother in particular, his dad's expression grew distant.

"Dad?" he prompted.

"I never knew what happened to them. Any of them," Walter murmured.

"I'm sorry. I didn't mean to—"

"It's not your fault. And I'm not mad. Actually, just the opposite. You might say I'm relieved, now that I know. What else did you learn about them?"

So they spent another hour just on Tommen's time following the family, mentioning that all the family tree stuff was saved on his phone.

"Did you bring my phone with you? It was in my backpack." Tommen looked around the room.

Walter shook his head. "No, I didn't. In my hurry, I'm sure I forgot a few things. Which reminds me, I did bring a change of clothes for you."

Tommen managed to get the boxers and sweatpants on, but that was the extent of it, given his one-handedness.

"You managed to make contact soon after, I think," his dad said thoughtfully. "So I know basically some of the things that happened, but what really did happen with you and Julianna?"

Tommen let out a breath. "The worst part was that she was never not nice to me until I figured out her plans. All of them, not just using me to escape. She got me in the hospital, gave me medicine, watched over me like...like a mom, really." He shook his head and looked away. "I feel like a fool."

"You could only use the information you had at the time."

"She played me, Dad. She played me perfectly. She'd been spying on me, so she knew my...chivalrous code of conduct." He scoffed. "Seems like it's become more trouble than it's worth. I would have taken a hundred fights with Tyler Freeman if I could undo that humiliation."

"Don't go talking like that. You're a good kid and a better man than most men could hope to be. You have your faults, but your chivalry isn't one of them. It's one of the best things about you."

Tommen was still uncertain, so he moved on to his discovery of Julianna's real plans and her role in Richard's journal, which turned out to be three journals in reality. Then there was the failed attempt where they'd almost switched places, his attempts at hiding from Julianna, and the moment she went from trying to be nice to not giving a fuck anymore.

"Last night, at Forbes Cave," his dad began, "what happened? Actually, let me back up. Why did you ask Rifun to help?"

"I only asked him when the plan was to build the quasi-dimension at the warehouse. He was the only one I knew of—or anyone knew of, apparently—who had ever done such a thing. I never told him about the change in plans. Julianna had to have done that. It was a stupid thing to do, but I was kind of banking on his obsession with me in order to escape."

"It was a dangerous gamble in the first place, even if we had stuck with the original plan. But we all lived, so I count that as being a good thing. What about the rest? Tommen, why in the world did you go back? I get that your intent was to push her back in, then escape before the portal closed, but what was going through your head?"

"I had to stop her. I couldn't let her get out. I don't know, I guess I thought I could use the element of surprise, get in and out fast enough that no one would notice. Afterwards, we got into a fight. Technically, I won, but she hit me over the head with something and knocked me out. Next thing I know, I'm sitting in an abandoned terrorist bunker in Pakistan."

"Pakistan?"

He shrugged weakly with his right arm. "Hey, that's what it was and where it was. She took me to Egypt where there was another weak spot between the dimensions. Rifun was there with some other guys to help. One of them turned out to be Assim Foyez. He tried to attack her and get the upper hand, similar to what I did. But Julianna murdered him." His dad rubbed his eyes. "After that, I just figured now or never. I had to do something. So I ran."

"Sorry to say, Tommen, but you're very predictable. How did she not catch you?"

"Because Chandler helped me. He said that because I had fully separated myself from her, that he could now intervene. He told her to get away and she left. I don't know the details, but that's basically what happened."

"Chandler, as in, the spooky ghost man Micaiah has previously mentioned?"

Tommen nodded. "Yeah. He took me to his little cabin, got my arm bandaged up, made breakfast. Dad, he's the one who set the Time Trap in Forbes Cave."

"What do you mean?"

Thus came the story of the young man named Anagalisgi who "died" defending his people from the British and now walked with them in their visions. Or hallucinations. He concluded with their journey back to the cave and a somewhat hazy telling of the events that followed when he finally managed to escape. When he finished, his dad folded his arms and leaned back in the chair.

"It sounds crazy, but it makes total sense," Tommen said.

"That's not what I'm thinking about. You said you were originally going to use fireworks to try and recreate the circumstances in which you got sucked into the dimension, right? Well, in between your bouts of drugged up wakefulness and sleep, I got a little more information on how you were found and brought here. Just before the joggers found you, there were reports of either a small explosion or gunshots in your vicinity. When crews when looking, there had been a rockslide in Forbes Cave, sealing it off."

"You think Chandler lit the fireworks and collapsed the cave?" Oddly enough, Tommen was more offended that Chandler had stolen his fireworks. Escape or not, those things could come in handy for all sorts of mischief.

"If what you're saying is true, it would seem so."

"But why? I mean, I saw him trying to undo the Time Threads."

"Maybe they couldn't be undone. Who knows? Regardless, no one is going to fall into that trap ever again."

Tommen heaved a sigh of relief. It was an odd sensation, really, and it took him a moment to identify it. That cave had fucked up his life, but it would not do the same to anyone else. Its reign of terror was now over.

"So, in the in-between dimension, you could Travel anywhere and even time travel," his dad said. "How much did you see?"

"My primary focus was figuring out a way to escape. I looked back on my brother just because I had to know. And I did extensive research on Julianna and Richard. That's all."

It was a lie, and Tommen desperately hoped that any indications he was giving about it, his dad might pass off as drugs or some shit. Whether he did or did not suspect anything was equally a mystery as his dad appeared to file it away and move on.

"The important thing now, though, is that you are here and you are safe."

"Yeah, but for how long? Julianna knows what it takes to escape, and I'm sure there are any number of Cult lackeys who will be happy to be her vessel for escape."

"That is true. But however evil she is, she is still just as mortal as Cassius and Rifun and any other human being. She can be killed. Eventually, she'll make a mistake, just like Cassius. Rifun, too. They will slip up somewhere. We just have to be vigilant and not waste a shot if we have one. But for now, you need to rest and let your body heal."

"Well, if I'm going to do that, I am going to need some pretty serious chow."

"I see. Care for some company?"

Tommen smirked at him. "Sure. You're going to have to call Becky, though, since I don't have a phone."

His dad rolled his eyes. "My son is rich and spoiled."

"Chop, chop, slave."

"If you're not careful, I'll go down to the cafeteria and tell them you're on a sugar-free liquid diet."

"Would you like to join us for dinner?"

"I do seem to recall that you once suggested a couple's dinner." His dad stood, and Tommen did not like the look on his face. "Maybe I'll see if Laura is in the area. Go ahead and place your dinner order while I'm gathering the other guests."

This was not going the way he'd planned it, and Tommen could only watch helplessly as his dad left the room, cruising through his phone as he did so. Reluctantly, Tommen managed to reach the room phone and dial down to the cafeteria. He ordered his fish, relieved his dad hadn't actually gone down and told them he was on a sugar-free liquid diet. They informed him that it would be about forty minutes for the sheer fact that it was the dinner rush.

It certainly didn't take Becky that long to show up. She made her presence known from the minute she walked in the door. Heedless of his arm prop or any IVs and other lines, she grabbed a chair, moved it as close to the bed as she could, then climbed up so she could sit on his knees.

"Why didn't you tell me you'd gotten back?!" she demanded.

"Because I've been conked out on drugs all day and don't have my phone?"

"I suppose that might be a good reason." He was entirely unprepared for her to throw herself on his chest in as big a hug as her little body could muster. "Oh my God, I missed you so much. I was so afraid for you."

He gritted his teeth against the pain and moved her off to the side that wasn't burned. "Why? I know how to survive."

"Well, duh. Obviously. That doesn't make it any less scary to me or anyone else who doesn't know what's going on or how to help. Just think of everything you've put your dad through."

He didn't want to think about that, even though that was a slightly different story. Instead he settled for, "Well, the good news is, I'm okay, and I'm home. Almost. They still want to keep me a couple days because of the infections and everything."

"Oh, I totally get it. And I agree. You should stay until you are totally healthy again. So what are your injuries, anyway? I mean, I see your arm, so what's the story?"

Tommen explained his injuries as best he could, but he was pretty sure he was getting some things wrong. Seeing how Becky's mom was a nurse, they probably talked medical every so often, so if he got anything mixed up, he was sure Becky would correct him.

"What happened, though?" she asked once he'd finished up with the injury report. "I mean, the news only said that you'd gone back into the fire to rescue a missing camper."

Well, shit. That was the catch, wasn't it? He couldn't use his dad's story because he had been found near Forbes Cave—hell, his dad was going to be in a heap of trouble if Laura found that one out. But he also didn't have any other story made up. He was saved, thankfully, by the arrival of his dad, followed closely by his fish dinner.

"Laura's not around?" Tommen wondered.

His dad did not look at him as he doled out a couple of cafeteria sandwiches to himself and Becky. "No, she's still at the station. Says she would join us if she could, and she'll be by later if they have another transport. If that's all right with you."

Tommen shrugged. "Sure, why not? I'm not exactly tied up in business right now."

As he took the lid off his dinner tray, both Becky and his dad stopped and stared.

"Holy cow, I hope they don't charge my insurance for that," his dad said.

Indeed, the fish dinner looked like something one might expect to find in the hoity-toity restaurant that was "reservations only during the busy season." Potato-crusted and fried to a perfect golden brown, topped with herbs and lemon and a small cup of tartar sauce on the side just in case. Green beans and carrots had been cooked in butter beautifully, but for the rest of America, there was also a side of fries, and even those looked mighty expensive.

"I could get used to this," Tommen said, picking up the fork and starting right in.

It looked amazing, and it was certainly delicious, but it was still just frozen fish that came in on a big gray truck along with the rest of the week's frozen food orders. At least the fries tasted like they might have actually been cut from real potatoes.

The meal was interrupted only once by a nurse coming to push more drugs and give him the usual interview. She left and everyone finished their food, Walter lamenting how he never got such awesome food when he was in ICU; he'd been restricted to the liquid diet plus easier, lighter fare. Like salads.

A food service worker came by to retrieve the tray. She had no sooner left than the door opened again and Dr. Polski walked in.

"So, Tommen, how are you feeling this evening?" he asked conversationally.

"Better than this morning, that's for sure," Tommen answered, casting a knowing look at his dad.

"I would expect as much." Dr. Polski glanced at Becky. "Do I have to pry your fingers off the bed rail, or are you going to come quietly?" His tone was joking.

"No, no, that won't be necessary," she told him. "As long as you bring me back tomorrow when you come in."

"Don't you normally have a ton of work to do?" Walter inquired.

"Normally, yes. But with school coming up, I'm cutting way back on all my projects, especially with all the AP classes I'm taking. There's only so many hours in a day and I can't do it all."

"Makes sense, I guess."

She looked back at her dad who finally relented, not that he seemed to have much conflict over it. According to her siblings, she could get away with murder.

"All right," Dr. Polski sighed. "If you really want to get up that early."

"Of course I don't. But I need to grill him for details about his outdoor adventures and saving kittens from burning buildings."

Tommen chuckled but sobered up as the doctor questioned him. "Did your hearing aids survive all right?"

Tommen's hand went to his ear, but the hearing aids had been removed. "Uh, yeah. I mean, they died, obviously, but they're good. I mean, the doctors took them off and put them on a charger when they brought me in, but I haven't had any problems."

Dr. Polski nodded. "Well, I'm in a bit of a rush tonight, but maybe tomorrow I can take them down and get a good look at them, just to be sure."

"Yeah, that'd be great, thanks."

Becky reluctantly climbed off the bed and followed her dad out of the room. After a minute or two of silence, Tommen asked, "So, any more surprise visitors tonight?"

His dad shrugged. "Well, Micah and Micaiah said they'd be over once they got off. I don't know about anyone else."

Well, it gave him time to relax a little, anyway, and consider his situation. It was almost as if the last five days had never happened. Here he sat, in a hospital, his burns treated and resting comfortably, and everything going well otherwise. The infections were being managed as well, and life was looking up. He was back home with his dad and girlfriend, even if he wouldn't actually be going home for a couple of days.

He stared at his arm, vanished in a sea of gauze, trying to see if he couldn't feel his way around his hand and arm and actually figure out where they'd cut off dead skin and melted sleeve and made the incisions. It wasn't hard to do, really. Every minute muscle movement alerted him to the presence of either stitches or intentionally split skin.

Stitches he was used to, and he understood what they felt like. The escatology, or whatever the hell the procedure was called, that was an entirely new feeling. They'd made incisions the same way a kindergartener might trace his hand to make the palm turkeys for Thanksgiving. Right between the fingers, following them up and down and around, all five of them. Then there were more incisions over his first knuckles. As for the arm, one cut went part way up on the outside, to his elbow, while the other went all the way up on the inside, into the crook of his elbow, over his biceps, all the way to his armpit. There was another incision over his shoulder.

Tommen could not adequately describe the sensation except maybe like cutting into a loaf of bread fresh out of the oven. Not even cutting into it, but pulling it apart and feeling the outer crust give way to a fluffy inside. That sounded good. Maybe he was still hungry. Did the hospital cafeteria do seconds, or was he on a strict feeding schedule? His stomach felt pretty good, all things considering. Was there dessert, at least?

"I think you're going to get a little too comfortable here," his dad said when he returned from the bathroom.

"Do you blame me? Someone else cooks and cleans. The food is great. Not only do I get to choose whether or not I want visitors, who they are, and when I want them, but I get all the sympathy I can stand."

"Well, if that's the case, then you get no more sympathy from me. And I'll make sure the twins put you back to work just as soon as you're discharged. You won't even be able to go home to change, just straight to work."

"That sounds terrible. Speaking of which, when does Steggmann want you back at the precinct? Or are you just off for the rest of the week?"

His dad sat down slowly. "No, no, just for today. And actually, Steggmann isn't Chief of Police anymore."

"What?!"

"He got ousted and replaced Sunday morning when no one

was looking."

"Ouch. How's the new guy?"

"Well, I don't trust him, let me say it that way. And it might be a little harder to keep doing things like I have. I don't know yet, but that's the way I'm thinking things are about to go."

There was more he wanted to say; it was written all over his face. But whatever his fears or concerns were, he was not voicing them to Tommen. But then, would it have mattered if he had? His dad had very little say in who got promoted, as far as the chief went, and even less say if the city council got involved which was almost a given. And if Walter had little say, well, Tommen's opinion would count for even less. Still, he didn't like the idea of change. Steggmann had been a good guy and was always very understanding of Walter and his situation. How was that going to change now?

Tommen's next visitor came around seven o'clock. To no one's surprise, it was Kayla. She grinned hugely when she saw Tommen.

"Hey, there he is," she greeted. "How are you doing?"

"Better than this morning," Tommen answered. He shifted position. "So how was your adventure to Hlohi really?"

She squirmed a little. "A little more interesting than I was expecting, and a little more than I think your dad wants me to share with you while he's present."

"But you'll tell me later when I'm back to work, right?" Tommen smirked and looked at his dad.

"Absolutely."

"So, where's Micaiah?" Walter wondered. "I thought he was opening today; he should be off by now."

Kayla shrugged. "He would be. He planned on it, but then Kyle called in sick and he decided to stay after a little longer. Well, a little longer turned into 'until closing' and here we are." She sat in the chair next to Walter. "So, really, how are you doing? I'm sure you'll give us all the details later, but how did you escape?"

"Chandler helped me," Tommen answered, figuring that was about as simple as it would get. "I don't know how to explain it."

"Sounds like an interesting story. I look forward to hearing it. And the rest of you?"

"My left side is burned, but that's getting better. I have a ton of infection, but that's getting better, too. And judging by the nurses' and doctors' reactions, I'm guessing my sepsis is clearing up also. I'll be out of here in a couple days."

"Excellent. Good to hear."

They made small talk for a bit, until about quarter to nine when the door opened and Micah walked in.

"So, the rumors were true," he said.

"The ones about my demise were greatly exaggerated," Tommen told him. "The ones about my escape, however, those are true."

"Is Cai with you?" Kayla wondered.

Micah waved a hand dismissively. "Yeah, yeah. He just had to turn off the lights, lock the doors, and make a bank drop. He's probably pulling in the parking lot right now."

"Visiting hours end at nine, you know."

"You know, I saw the sign, and it was really intimidating, but I got past it. I don't know how I did it, but I conquered my fear of laminated paper and made it down here."

"Smart ass."

"Good to know I'm the smart ass, but that just means you married the dumb ass."

Kayla punched Micah in the shoulder.

"You see what I have to put up with?" he whined to Walter.

Walter merely raised a brow. "I see what she has to put up with. She gets more sympathy."

"That's cold, Walter. That's really cold."

Kayla glanced at her phone and sighed. "All right, I better go check on him, make sure he didn't find some dusty paperwork he just had to finish before coming out. At any rate, I should be getting home and figuring out what the hell to do about my client tomorrow. But, that's not you guys' concern."

She wished them all well and Tommen a speedy recovery as she departed. When she was gone, Micah turned to face Tommen. "I'm sure you've already been asked a dozen times about your injuries, so I think I'll get the details from your dad. Apparently you and him were having some pretty interesting conversations earlier when you were still a little loopy."

"I don't even want to think about that," Tommen said. "I just kind of want to forget that ever happened. Problem is, I don't even remember it to be able to forget it."

Well, they got a kick out of it, but Tommen just felt embarrassed. He really didn't want to think about any of the things he could have said while still under the influence and having no better judgment or filter. At the same time, his dad hadn't confronted him about anything during the numerous times they were alone. If he had revealed any little details about his Christmas plans, his dad didn't seem to think now was a good time to discuss them, which would be very uncharacteristic.

He was jerked from his thoughts as Micah's cell phone rang. He checked it, sighed, but took it out of the room to answer it.

"Well, kiddo," Walter said, standing. "I have to be going, too. I only got the day off, and seeing how you're on the mend, I see no reason why I need to hover over your bedside. Especially since you have other visitors at your beck and call to bring you sympathy."

Tommen felt his ears turn red. If he wanted to be honest, though, he was pretty tired himself, had been for the last couple hours. Probably a combination of the drugs and the excitement of the day, but he was ready to catch some z's without worrying about an alarm clock.

"Is there anything you want from home?" his dad was saying. "I can make a quick stop on my way to work tomorrow, but otherwise, you'll have to wait until I get off."

"My phone would be nice, so I have something to do besides watch TV all day."

"Because blinding yourself on the Internet is much better. All right, I'll try to remember."

As he was making his way out, the door opened and Micah stumbled in. All color had drained from his skin and he was shaking something fierce. Walter caught him before he fell and eased him into a chair.

"Hold on there, Micah, there you go." He got down on a knee in front of him. "What the hell happened, Micah? What's wrong?"

Micah squeezed his eyes shut and tears began streaming down his cheeks. His body still shook with silent sobs. Finally he took a breath and looked at Walter with absolute fear and panic. "Micaiah's dead."

Epilogue

He waited patiently for the confrontation he knew would come. The sun beat down, but there was no heat, for this was a dream, and dreams couldn't hurt you, or so some liked to believe. He glanced down at himself, shirtless, twisted skin mocking him. He hated it, had hidden it for many years, but it was necessary. He heard footsteps behind him.

"Rifun."

He turned to face Tommen. They stood on the same hillside where he'd murdered Saul. This time, though, there was no wolf to come to anyone's aid, and Chandler was far away from here.

"So, you found me," he said.

"You weren't exactly hiding, which can only mean you wanted to be found," Tommen told him, approaching. "Which means you know exactly what I'm going to ask."

"Did I kill Micaiah?"

"Did you?"

"You would never believe me if I told you; you've already made up your mind to hate me for it."

Tommen looked him over, his posture saying he wanted to be discreet, his expression saying otherwise.

"Are you mocking me?" the teenager finally asked. He gestured to his arm, though in the dream, it remained as he wished it to be, undamaged, and not as it was now. He hadn't fully accepted that reality yet.

"This is me," Rifun told him. "This is who and what I am."

"That's why you always wore a hoodie, then, to cover it up."

Now Tommen openly studied him. "What happened?"

"This is the result of my pride and ego and believing that I could do anything because I could do magic, and that my will alone dictated my life and could save me from evil. I was not as lucky as you, to have a mentor who cared—"

"A mentor who cared?! I—"

Annoyed, Rifun slapped him. Tommen's mouth opened in stunned silence as he put a hand to his face, as if he couldn't comprehend what had just happened.

"I told you to go back to the rescue crews and get yourself evacuated. I told you to appreciate what I taught you and that I would teach you more in time. And what did you do? You ran off and tried to play the hero. Again. Impulsivity and pride have consequences." He gestured to the burned flesh that covered him from neck to waist and down both arms. "Ego has consequences. I'm trying to help you, trying to teach you, but I can't save you from yourself when you decide to take matters into your own hands. No one can. Not Micaiah. Not your dad. No one."

"Then what am I supposed to do with this? The Akari? Am I just supposed to roll over for you?"

"You seem to be running out of other options. The Hands of Time don't like you very much. The Borelians still have their declaration of war out on humanity. And you just blew yourself into another dimension. What else has to go wrong?"

He could see Tommen mentally searching for something, anything. And coming up with nothing.

Rifun grinned. "Tell me the words I want to hear."

There was a moment of tense silence as Tommen glowered at him. Finally, the boy relented as his shoulders dropped and he said, "Teach me everything you know."

Author's Note

Leap Second is kind of the book where a lot of the *Timekeeper Chronicles* series collide and overlap, and let me say that it was a tedious royal pain having to go back, cross-reference, rewrite, and ensure that all those series jived with each other. But it had to be done. There is too much critical information for it to be out-of-sync.

How did Julianna come to be trapped in the Land In Between, and why can't she escape? Why doesn't Time work in that dimension? Where do Rifun and Cassius come in? What are the journals? Where are they? Who is Chandler and what is his role? What is his relationship to Julianna? Some of these questions have been answered, and others are set to be answered as *The Chivalrous Welshman* opens up to a new chapter.

Up until now, Tommen has usually had the ability to call for help, even when he's been separated by both distance and dimension. Going forward, his options become severely limited, and he's going to have to get creative and start thinking through some tough choices. It's no longer just about him and his little world.

The Borelians are mobilizing, even if it's not terribly obvious just yet. The Akarin have going full paranoid recluse. Only Rifun and the Cult are any kind of stable. With the rescue of Julianna, who knows what sort of mischief is going to come about?

As we find ourselves in the later half of The Chivalrous Welshman, even questions will be answered. Who killed Micaiah? Where is the Cult hiding? What happened to Rifun? What will Julianna do now? Will the Krydik join the fight against the Borelians? What other human worlds are out there? What will the Hands do?

Will any unlikely allies step in to aid the heroes?

For right now, I can only tell you two things with any certainty: first, *Imminence* is going to bring even more exciting developments to the story; second, it will be the least of the excitement as we march toward the end of the series.

Stay strong and hold the line. The ride's about to get bumpy.